BOXERS

BOXERS

GENE LUEN YANG

COLOR BY LARK PIEN

:01

First Second

NEW YORK

:01 First Second

Published by First Second
First Second is an imprint of Roaring Brook Press,
a division of Holtzbrinck Publishing Holdings Limited Partnership
120 Broadway, New York, NY 10271

Cataloging-in-Publication Data is on file at the Library of Congress.

ISBN 978-1-59643-359-5

First Second books may be purchased for business or promotional use. For information on bulk purchases please contact Macmillan Corporate and Premium Sales Department at (800) 221-7945 x5442 or by email at specialmarkets@macmillan.com.

FIRST EDITION

First edition 2013
Book design by Rob Steen
Color by Lark Pien

Printed in China
20 19 18

BY ART WE LIVE

Dedicated to the Original Art Night Crew

第一章

Northern Shan-tung Province, China
1894

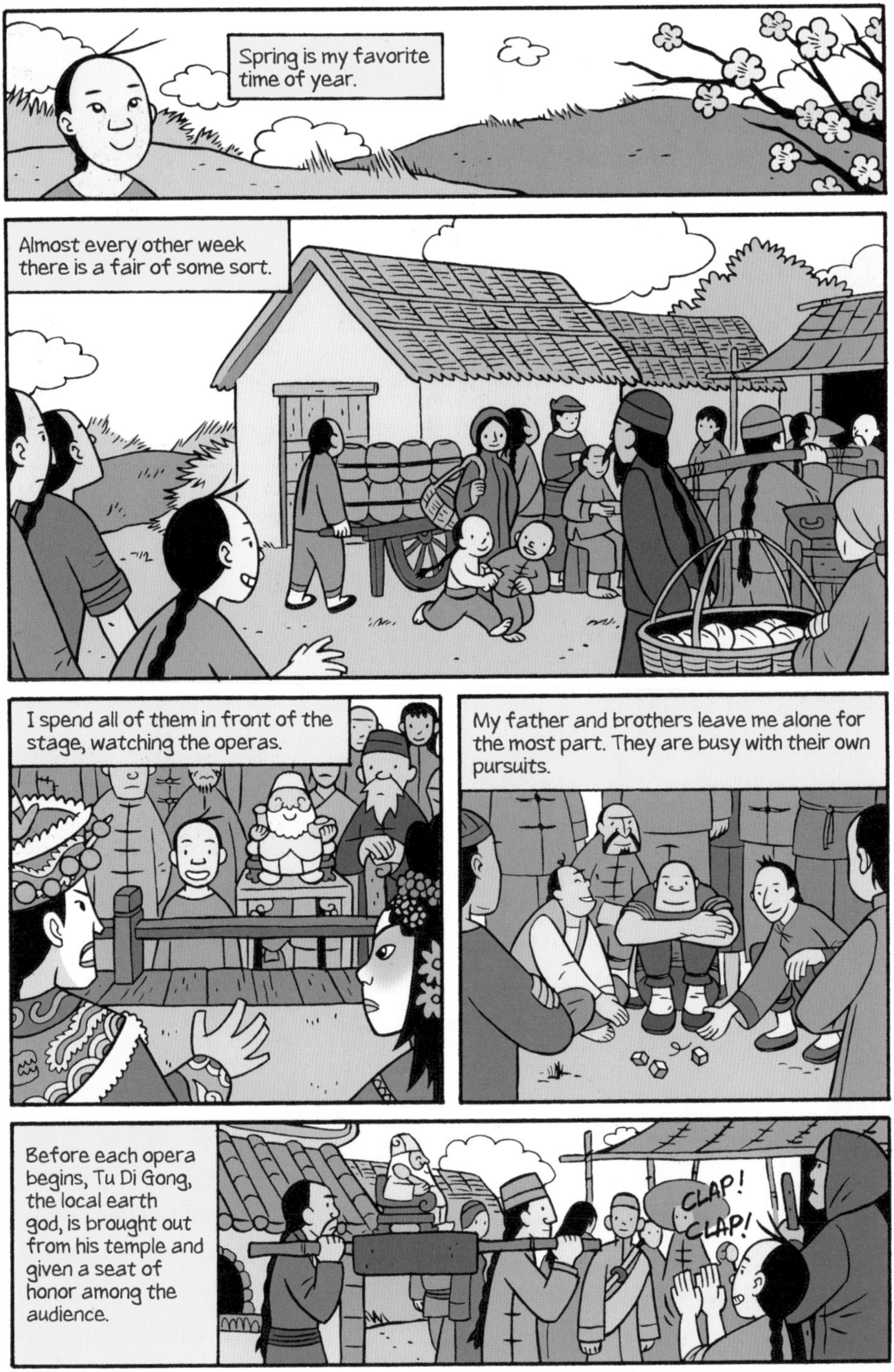
Spring is my favorite time of year.
Almost every other week there is a fair of some sort.
I spend all of them in front of the stage, watching the operas.
My father and brothers leave me alone for the most part. They are busy with their own pursuits.
Before each opera begins, Tu Di Gong, the local earth god, is brought out from his temple and given a seat of honor among the audience.
CLAP! CLAP!

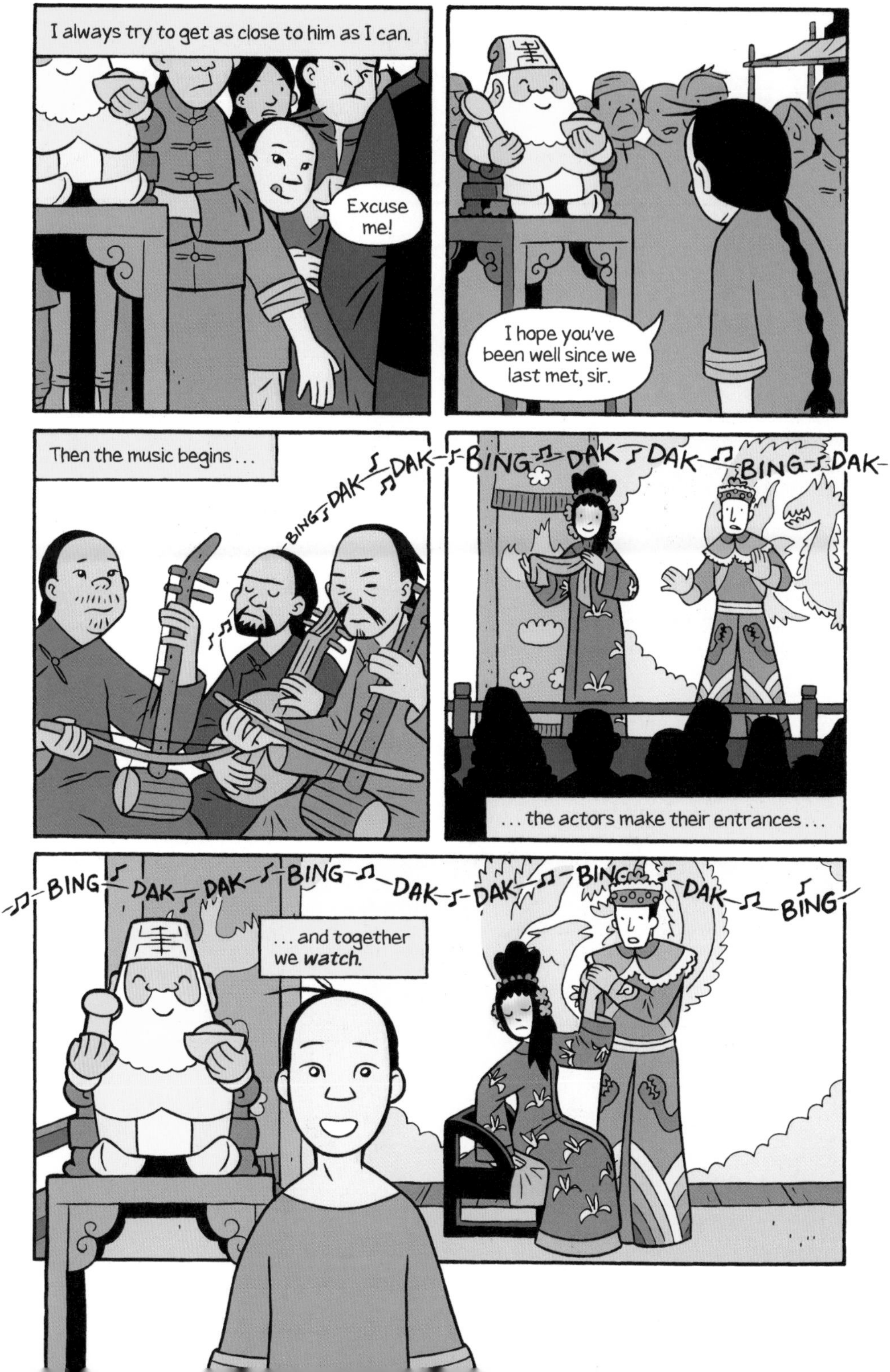
I always try to get as close to him as I can.
Excuse me!
I hope you've been well since we last met, sir.
Then the music begins . . .
BING DAK DAK BING DAK DAK BING DAK
. . . the actors make their entrances . . .
BING DAK DAK BING DAK DAK BING DAK BING
. . . and together we *watch.*

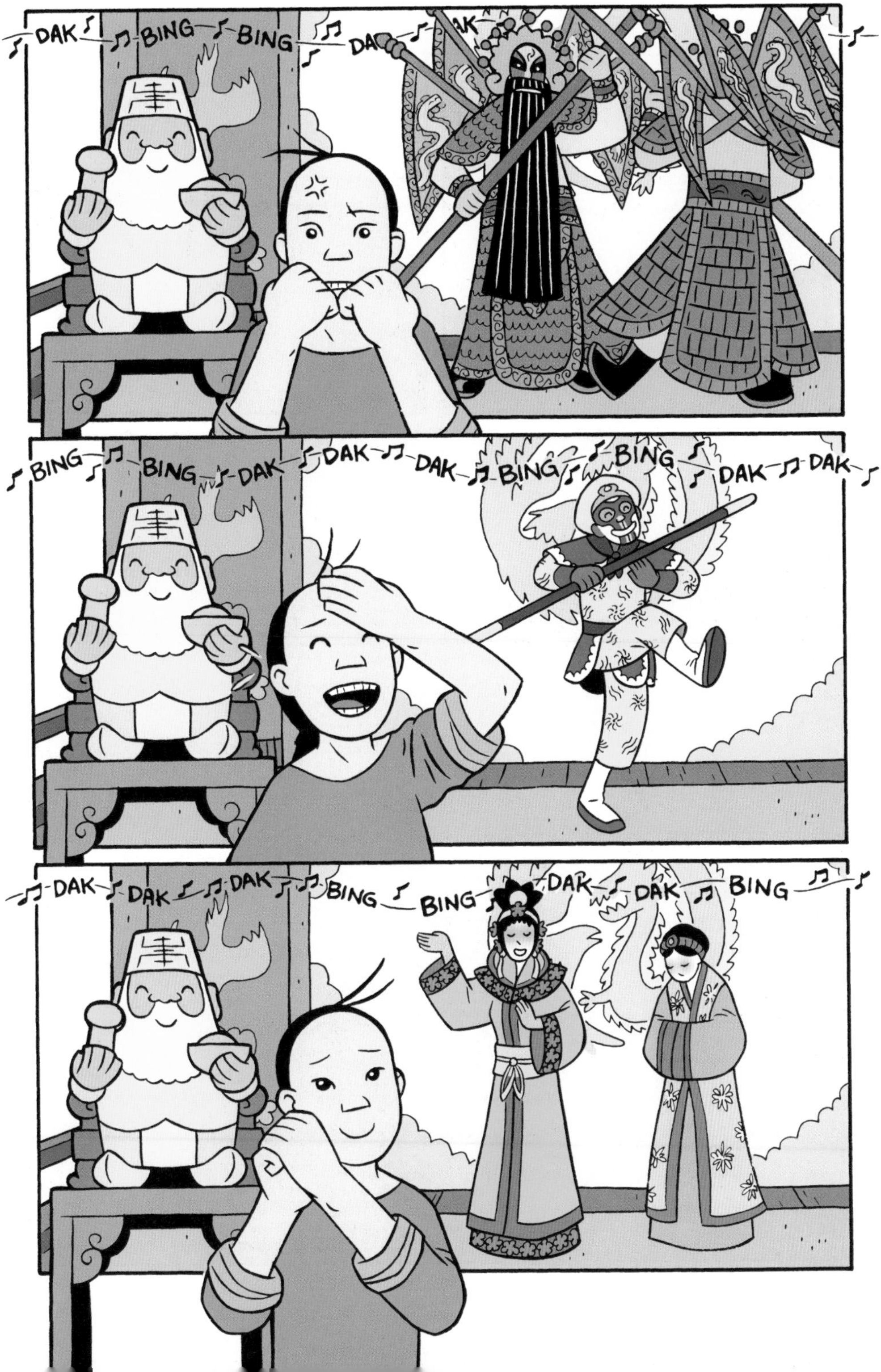
DAK BING BING DAK
BING BING DAK DAK DAK BING BING DAK DAK
DAK DAK DAK BING BING DAK DAK BING

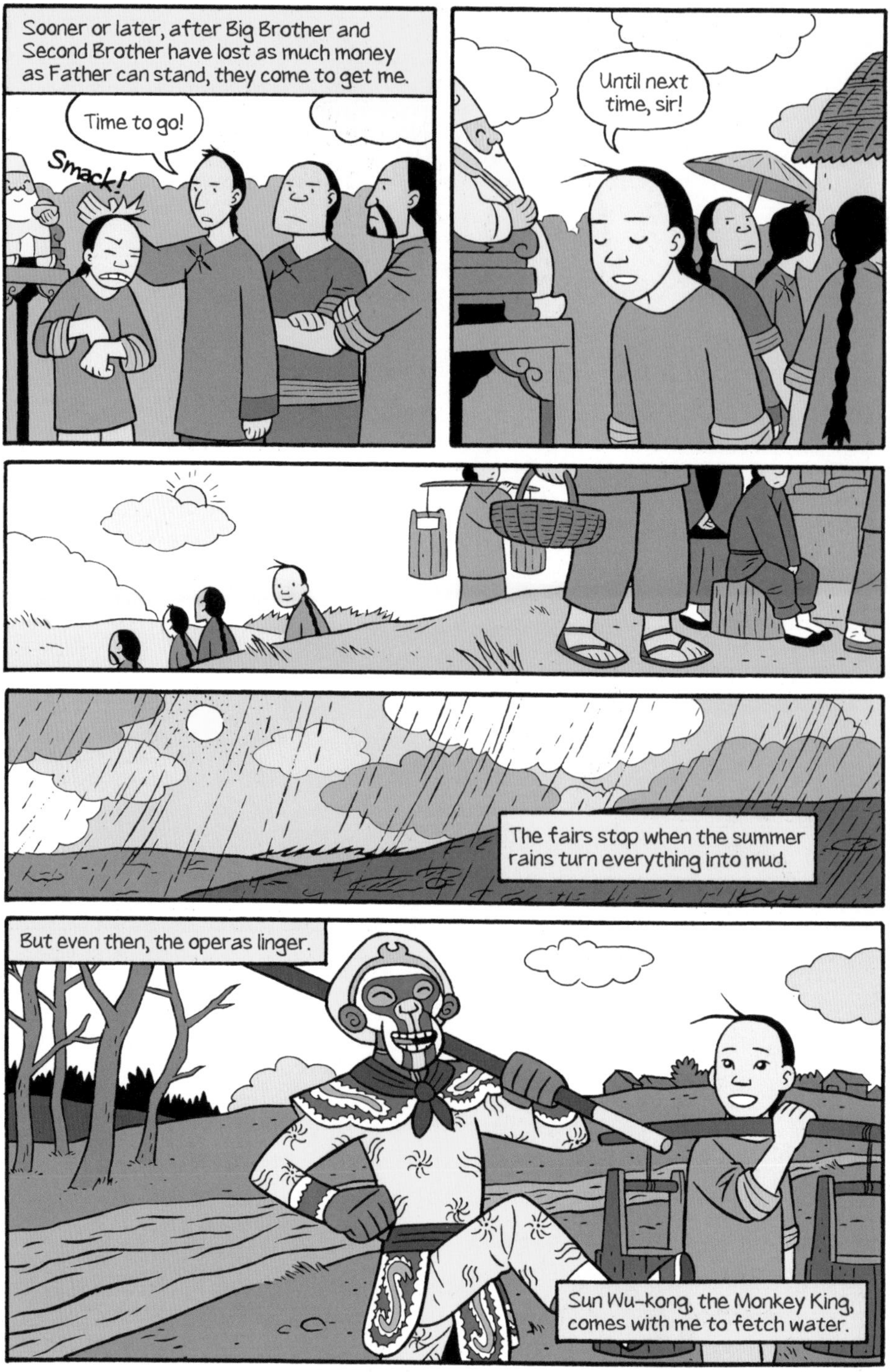
Sooner or later, after Big Brother and Second Brother have lost as much money as Father can stand, they come to get me.
Time to go!
Smack!
Until next time, sir!
The fairs stop when the summer rains turn everything into mud.
But even then, the operas linger.
Sun Wu-kong, the Monkey King, comes with me to fetch water.

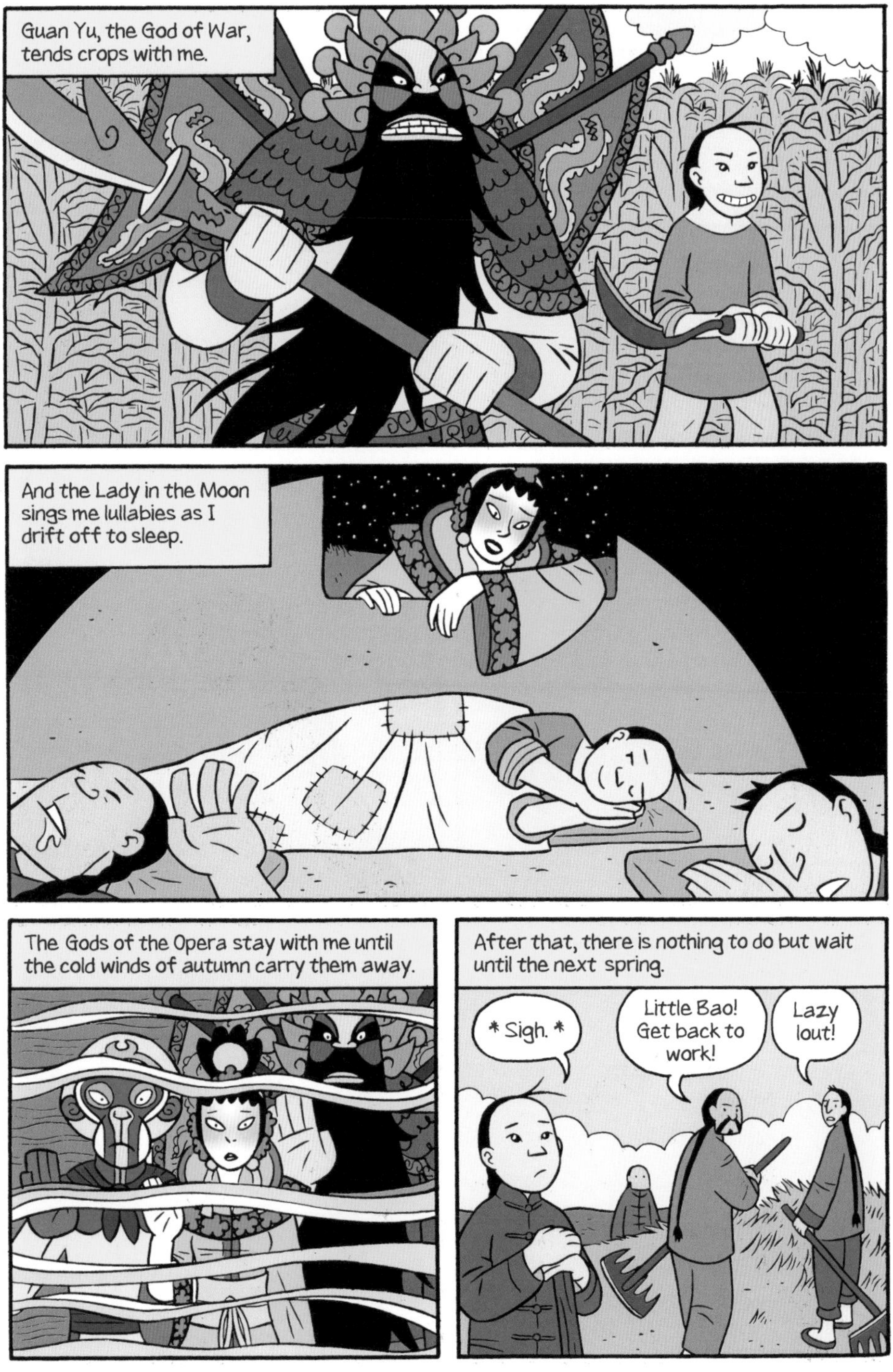
Guan Yu, the God of War, tends crops with me.
And the Lady in the Moon sings me lullabies as I drift off to sleep.
The Gods of the Opera stay with me until the cold winds of autumn carry them away.
After that, there is nothing to do but wait until the next spring.
* Sigh. *
Little Bao! Get back to work!
Lazy lout!

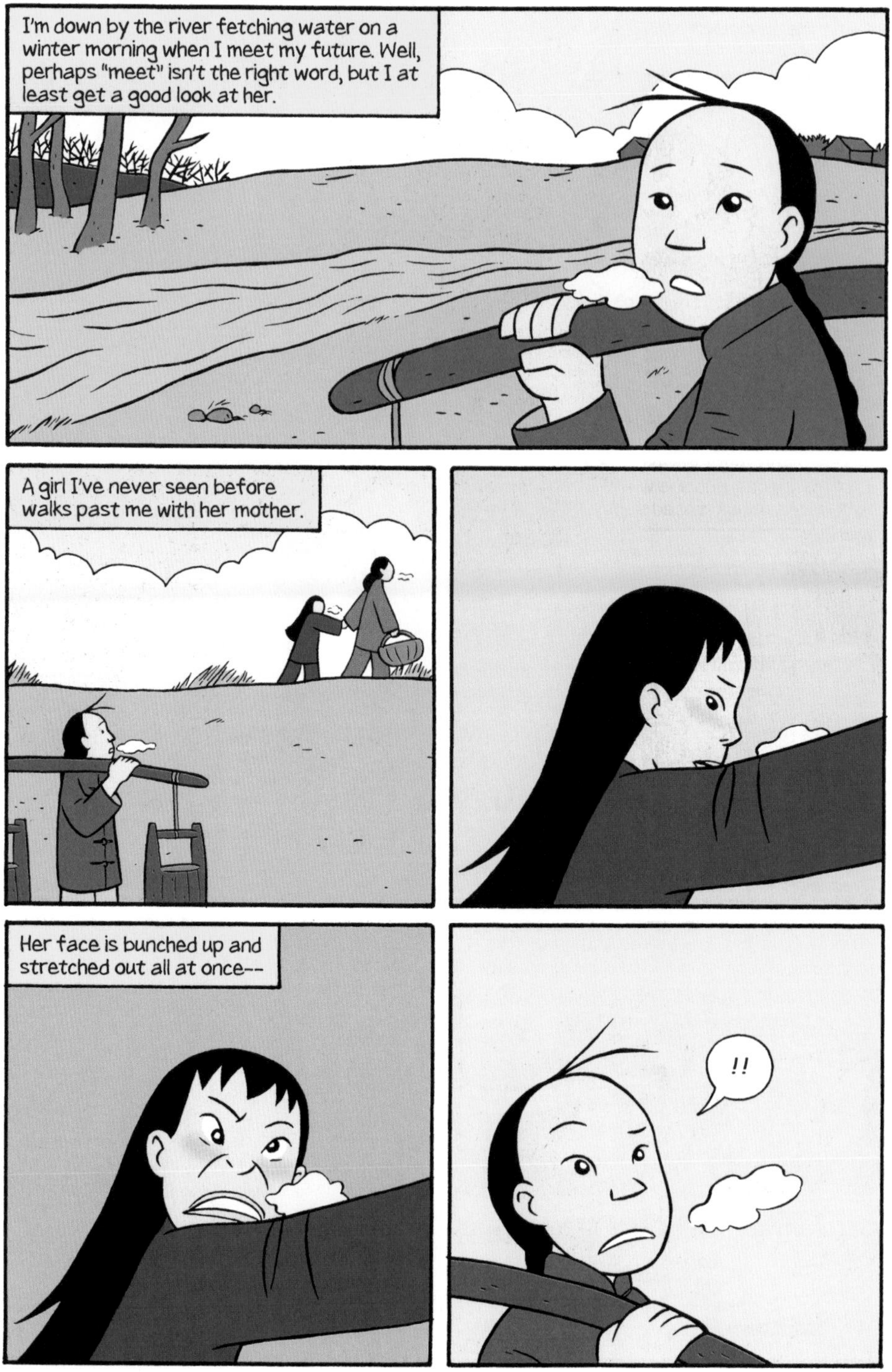
I'm down by the river fetching water on a winter morning when I meet my future. Well, perhaps "meet" isn't the right word, but I at least get a good look at her.
A girl I've never seen before walks past me with her mother.
Her face is bunched up and stretched out all at once--
!!

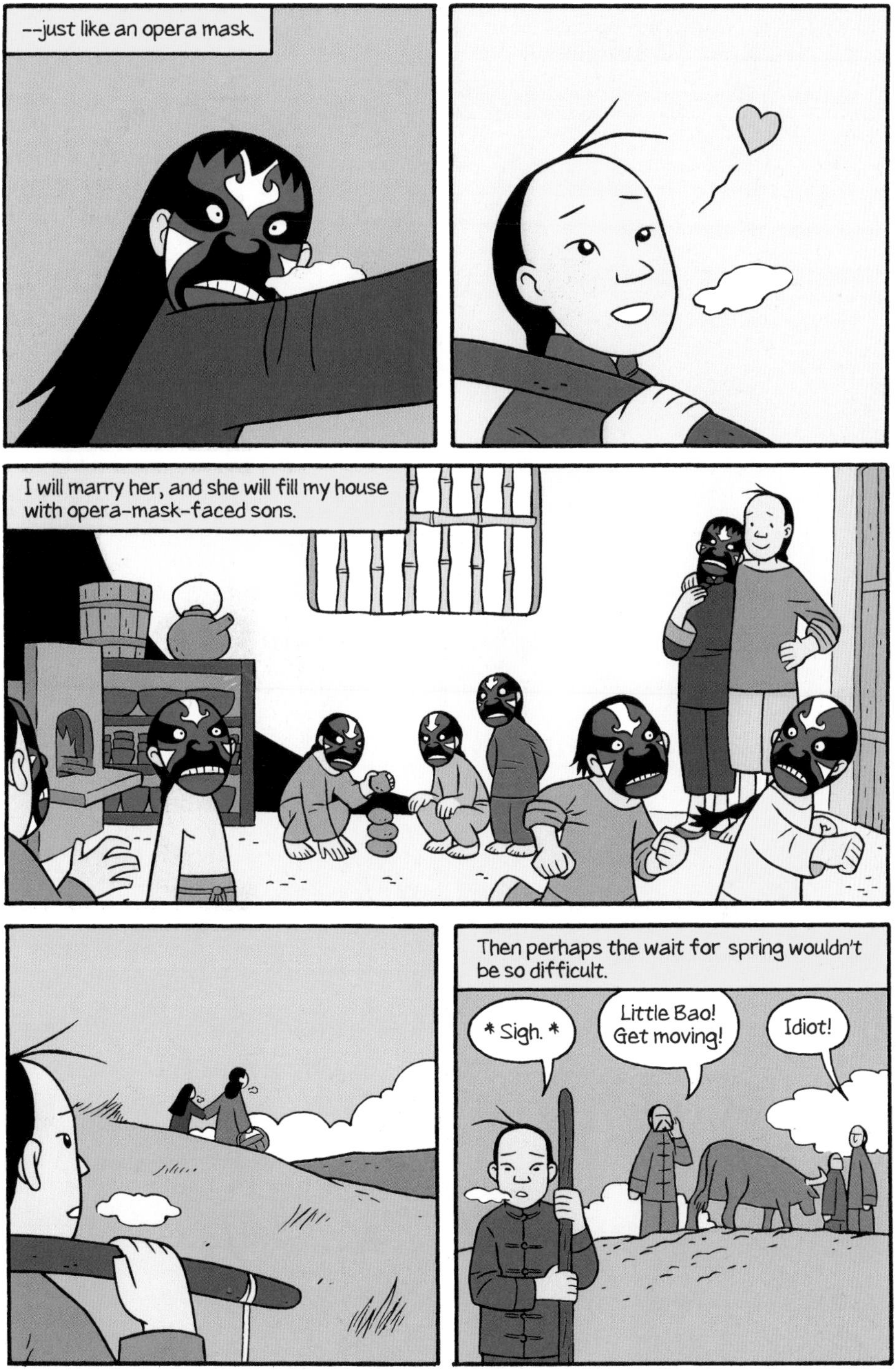
--just like an opera mask.
I will marry her, and she will fill my house with opera-mask-faced sons.
Then perhaps the wait for spring wouldn't be so difficult.
* Sigh. *
Little Bao! Get moving!
Idiot!

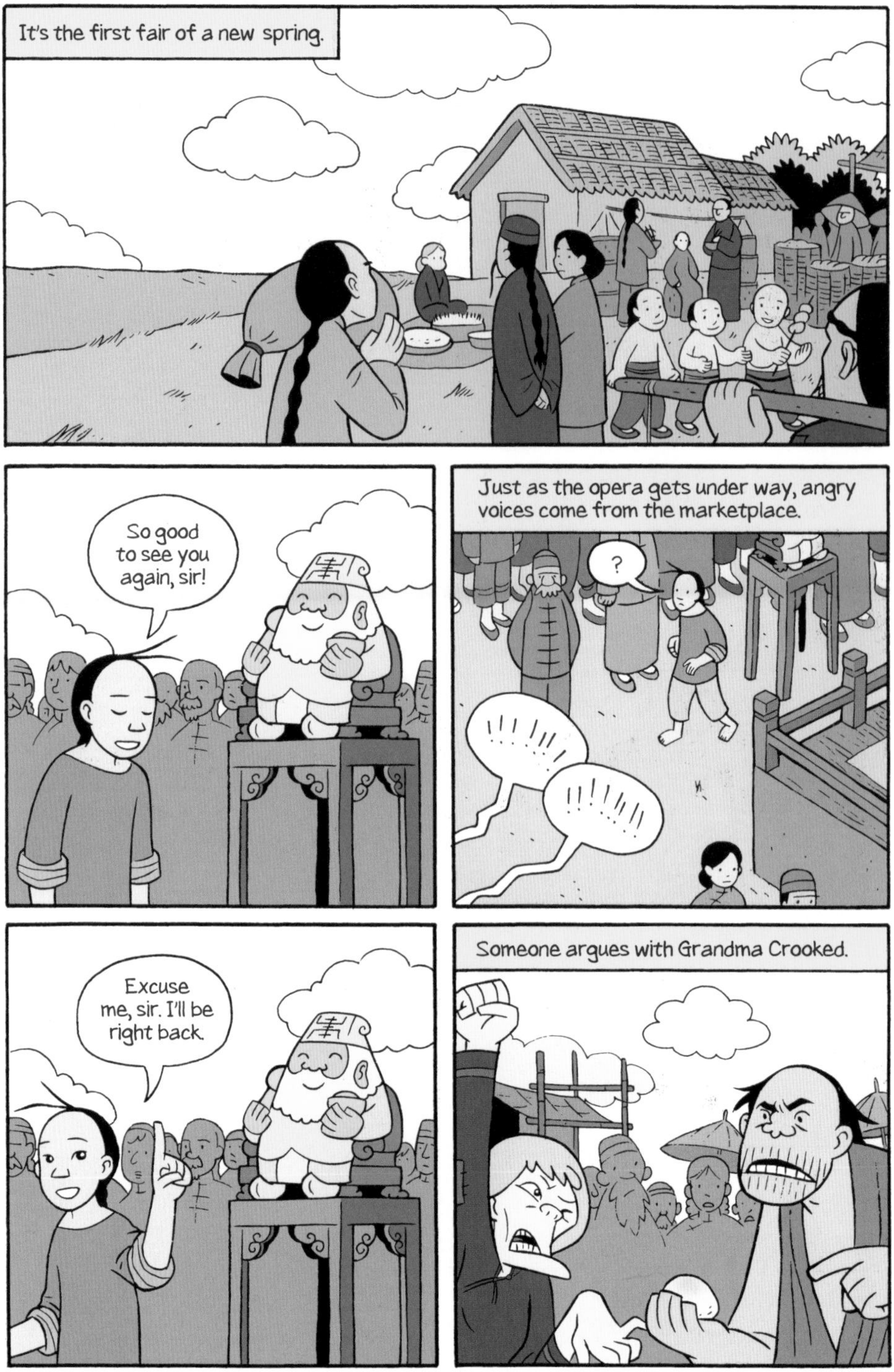
It's the first fair of a new spring.
So good to see you again, sir!
Just as the opera gets under way, angry voices come from the marketplace.
?
!!!!!!
!!!!!!
Excuse me, sir. I'll be right back.
Someone argues with Grandma Crooked.

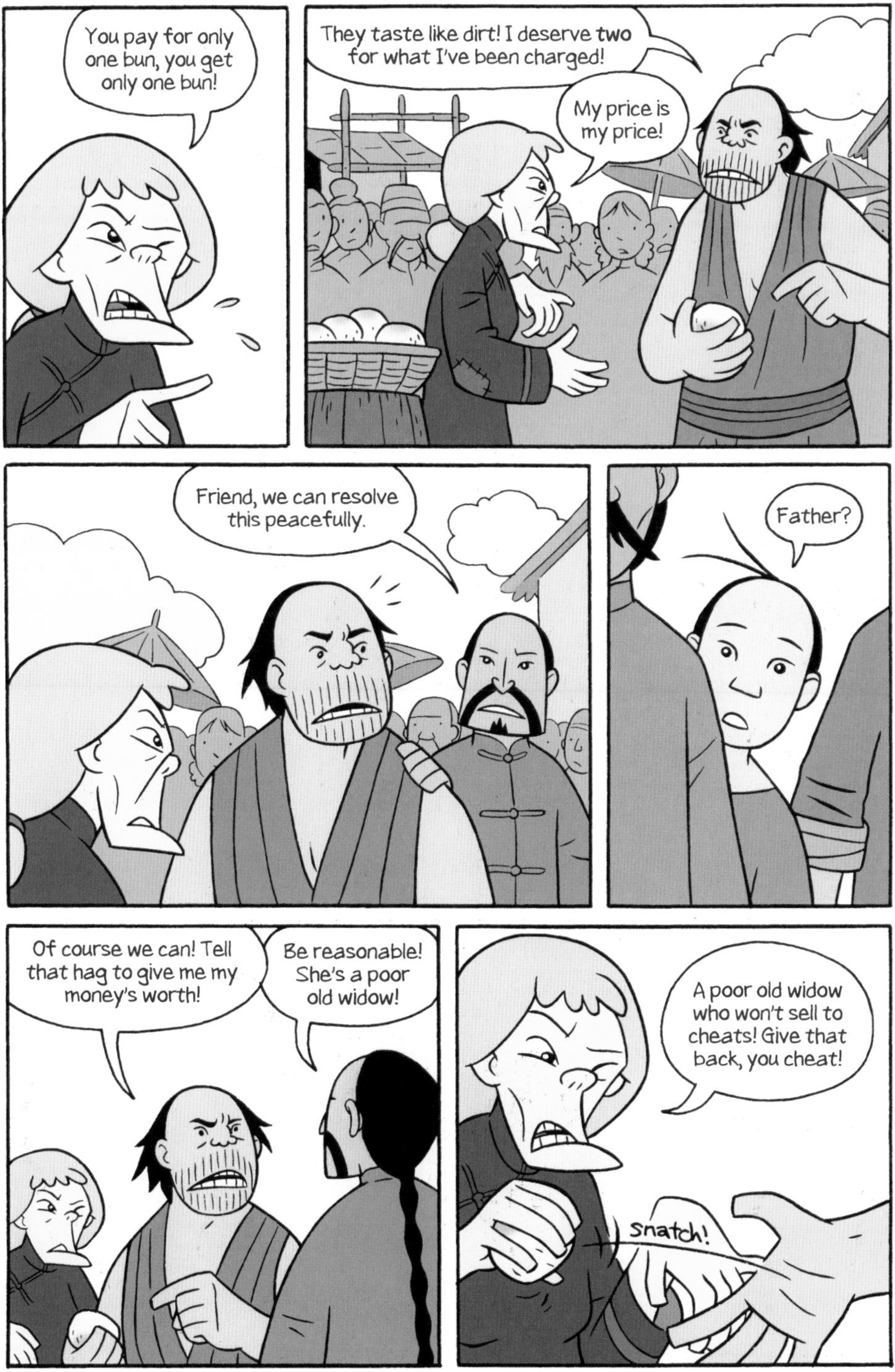
You pay for only one bun, you get only one bun!
They taste like dirt! I deserve **two** for what I've been charged!
My price is my price!
Friend, we can resolve this peacefully.
Father?
Of course we can! Tell that hag to give me my money's worth!
Be reasonable! She's a poor old widow!
A poor old widow who won't sell to cheats! Give that back, you cheat!
Snatch!

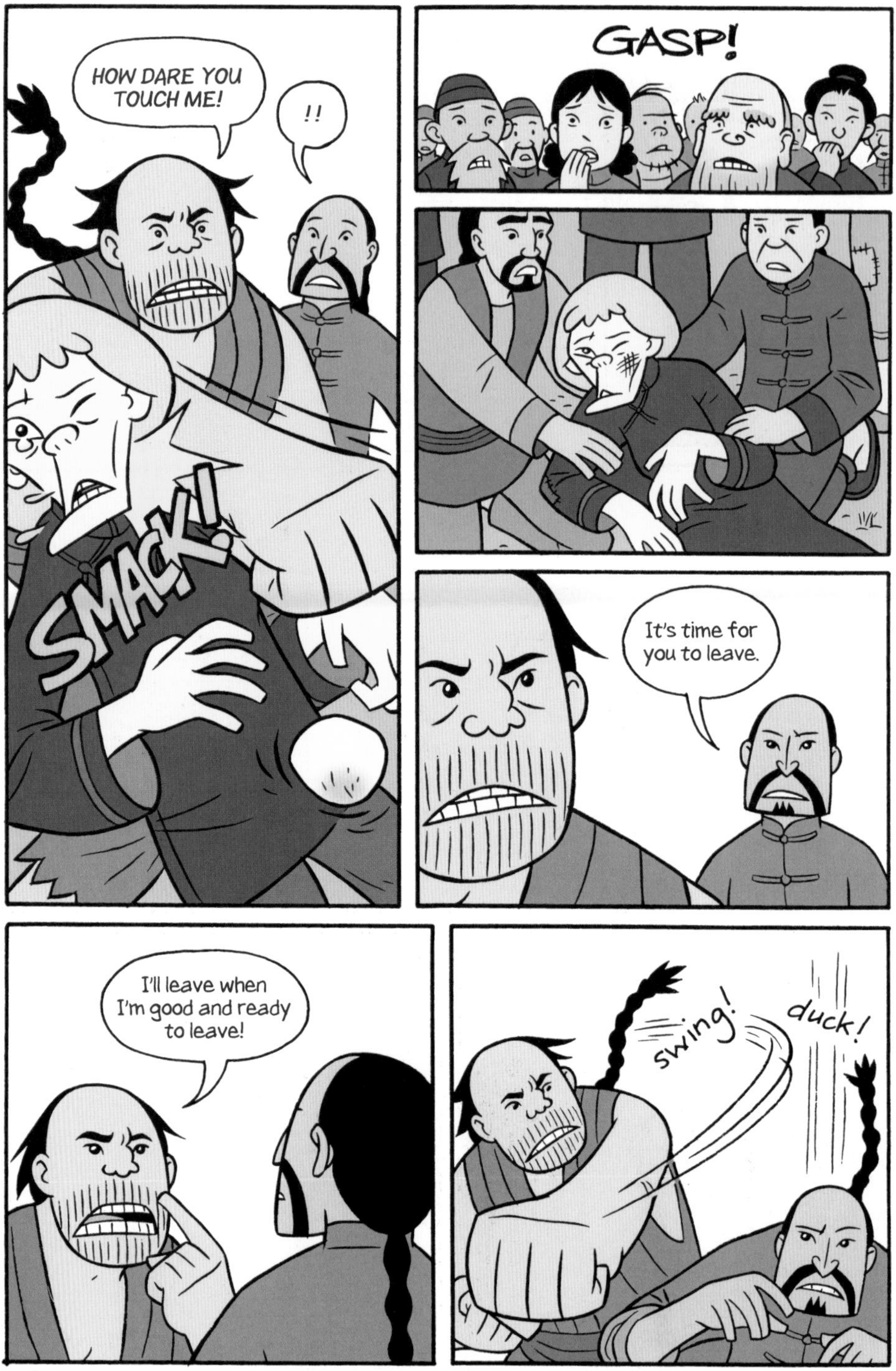
HOW DARE YOU TOUCH ME!
!!
SMACK!
GASP!
It's time for you to leave.
I'll leave when I'm good and ready to leave!
swing!
duck!

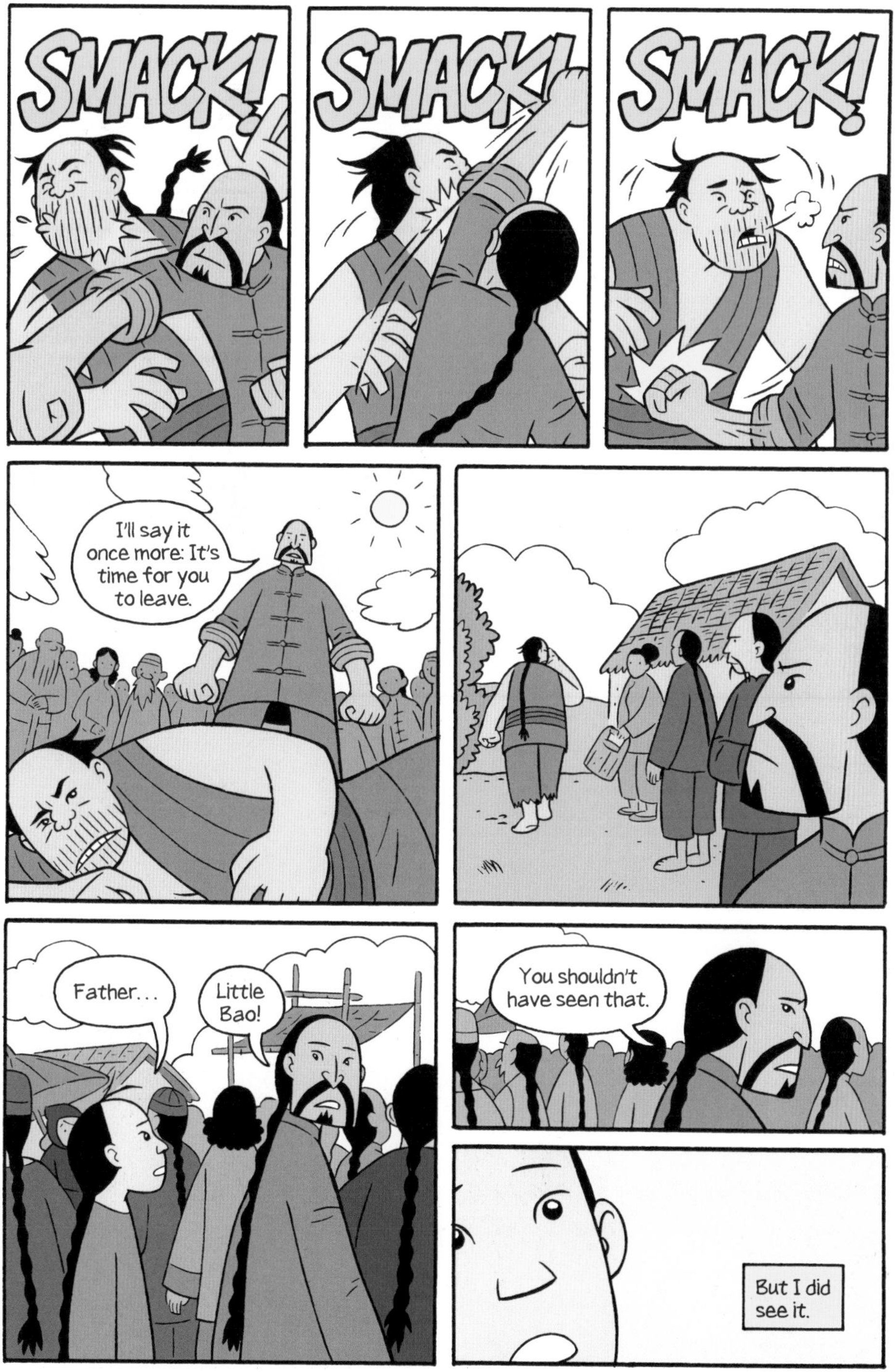
SMACK!
SMACK!
SMACK!
I'll say it once more: It's time for you to leave.
Father...
Little Bao!
You shouldn't have seen that.
But I did see it.

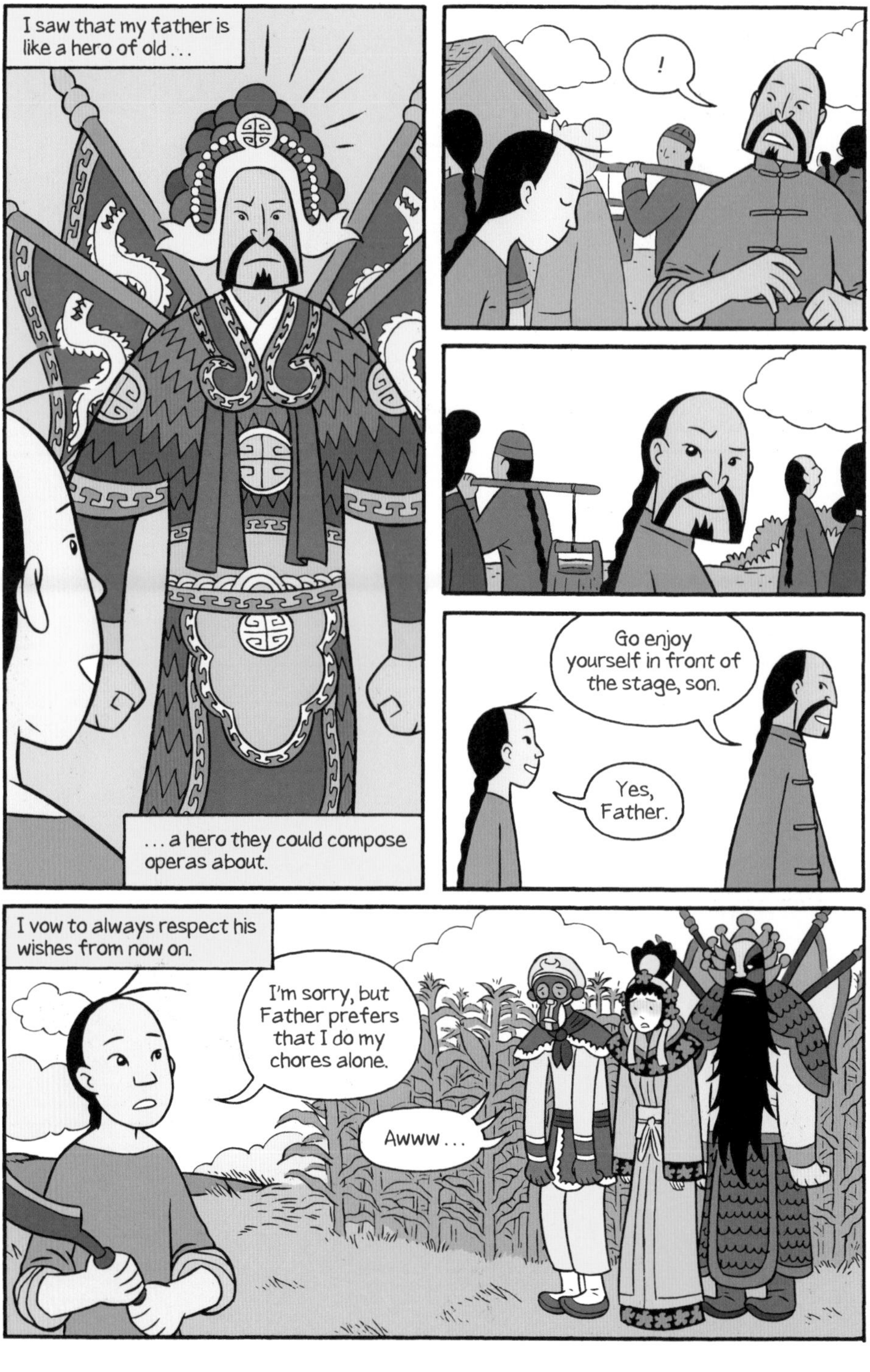
I saw that my father is like a hero of old . . .
. . . a hero they could compose operas about.
!
Go enjoy yourself in front of the stage, son.
Yes, Father.
I vow to always respect his wishes from now on.
I'm sorry, but Father prefers that I do my chores alone.
Awww . . .

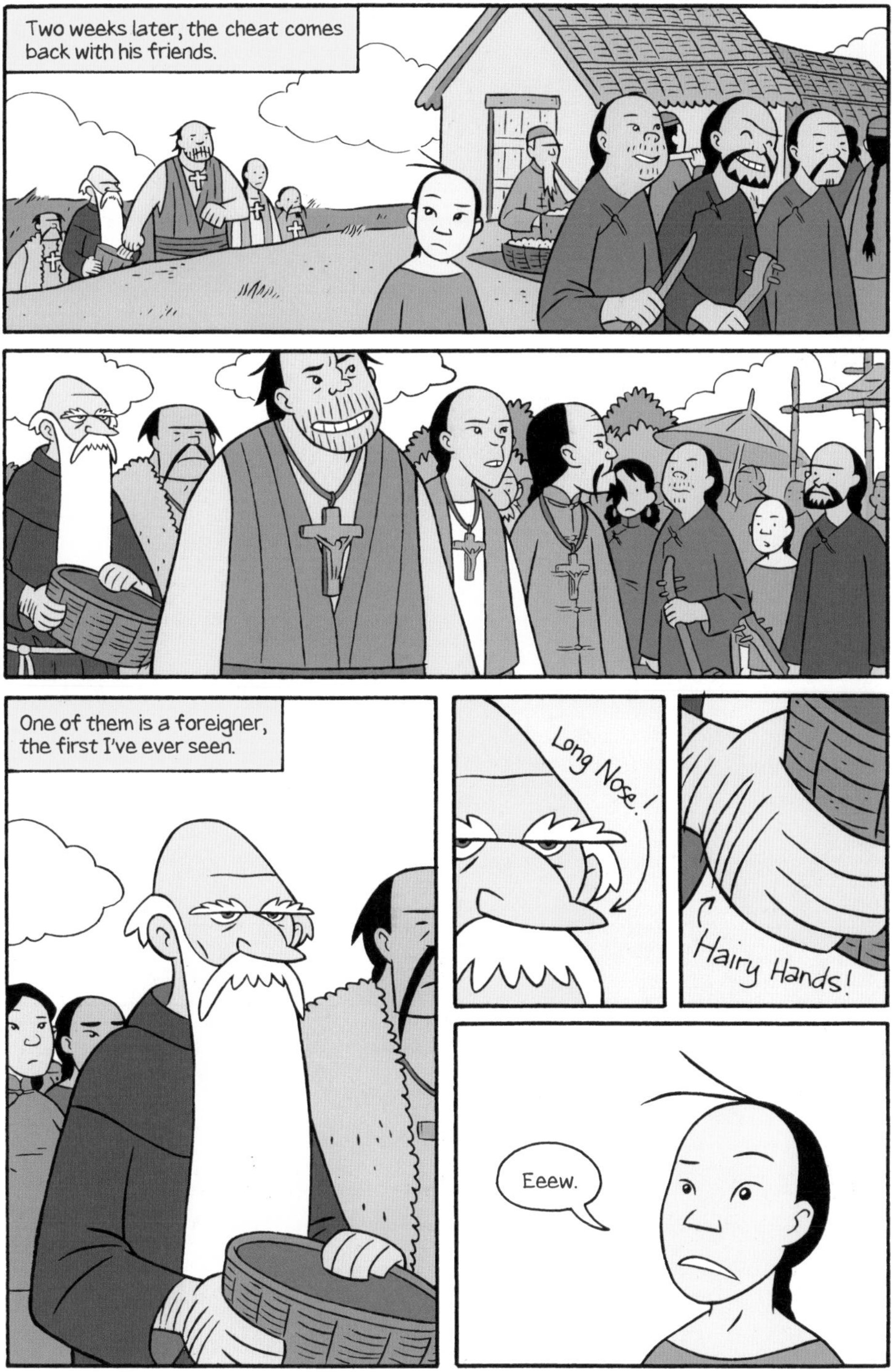
Two weeks later, the cheat comes back with his friends.
One of them is a foreigner, the first I've ever seen.
Long Nose!
Hairy Hands!
Eeew.

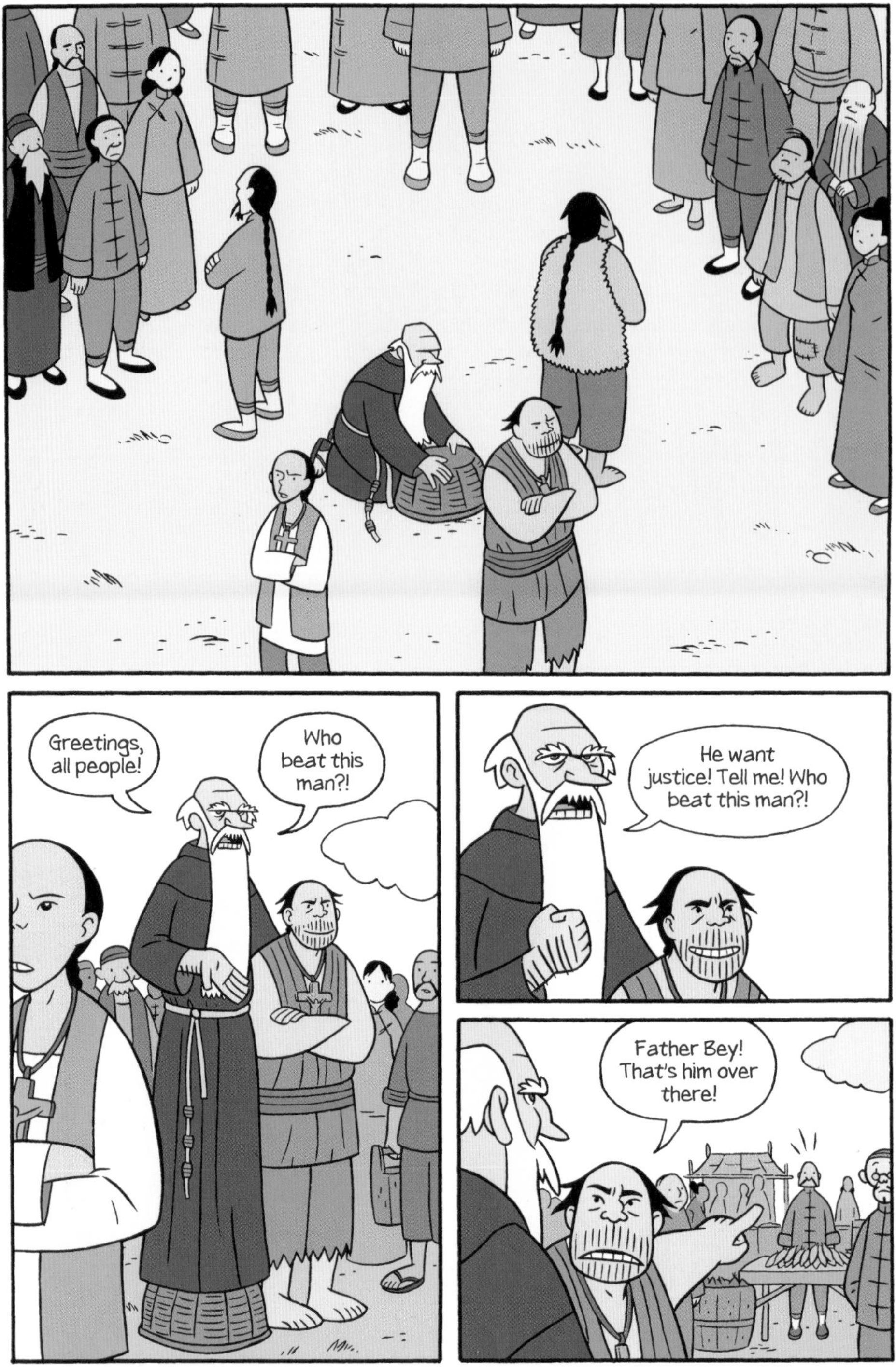
Greetings, all people!
Who beat this man?!
He want justice! Tell me! Who beat this man?!
Father Bey! That's him over there!

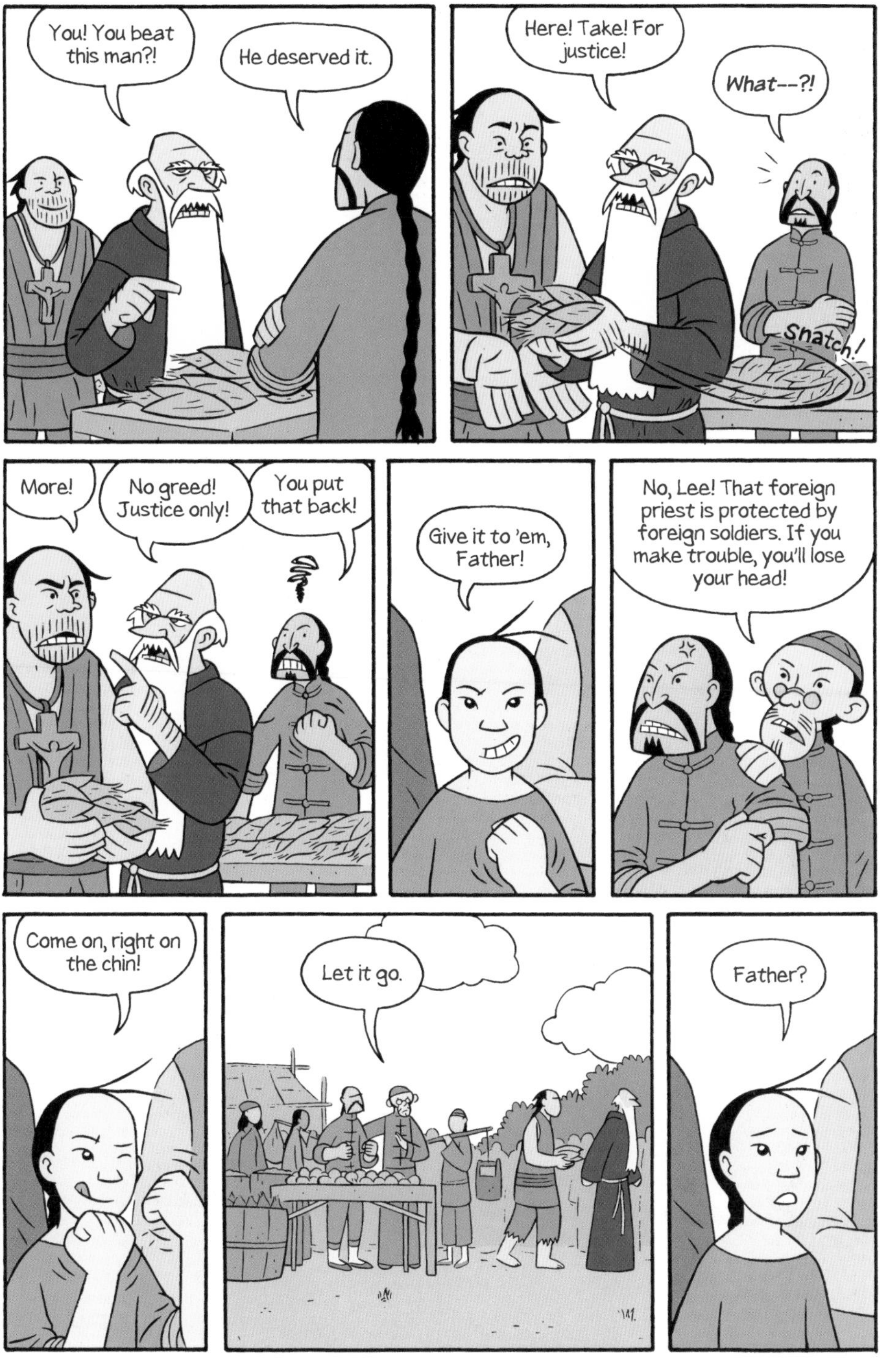
You! You beat this man?!
He deserved it.
Here! Take! For justice!
What--?!
Snatch!
More!
No greed! Justice only!
You put that back!
Give it to 'em, Father!
No, Lee! That foreign priest is protected by foreign soldiers. If you make trouble, you'll lose your head!
Come on, right on the chin!
Let it go.
Father?

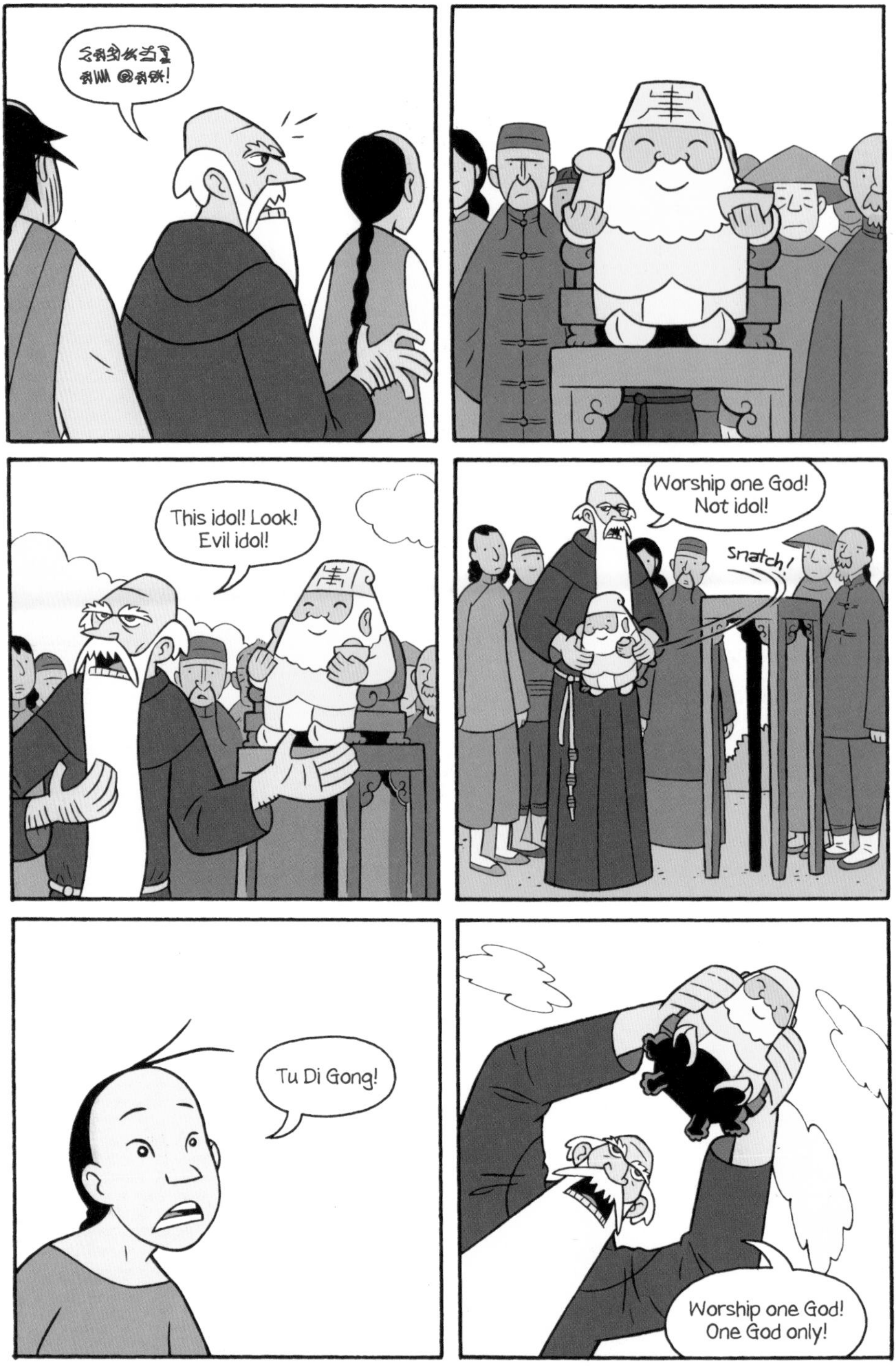
This idol! Look! Evil idol!
Worship one God! Not idol!
Snatch!
Tu Di Gong!
Worship one God! One God only!

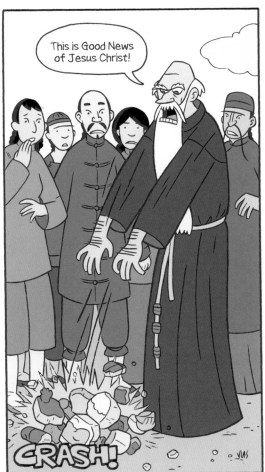

This is Good News of Jesus Christ!

CRASH!

NO!!!

What the--?!

I can't believe--!

Who does he think he is?!

Somebody grab that man!

Out of the way, Constable!

Stop! Please!

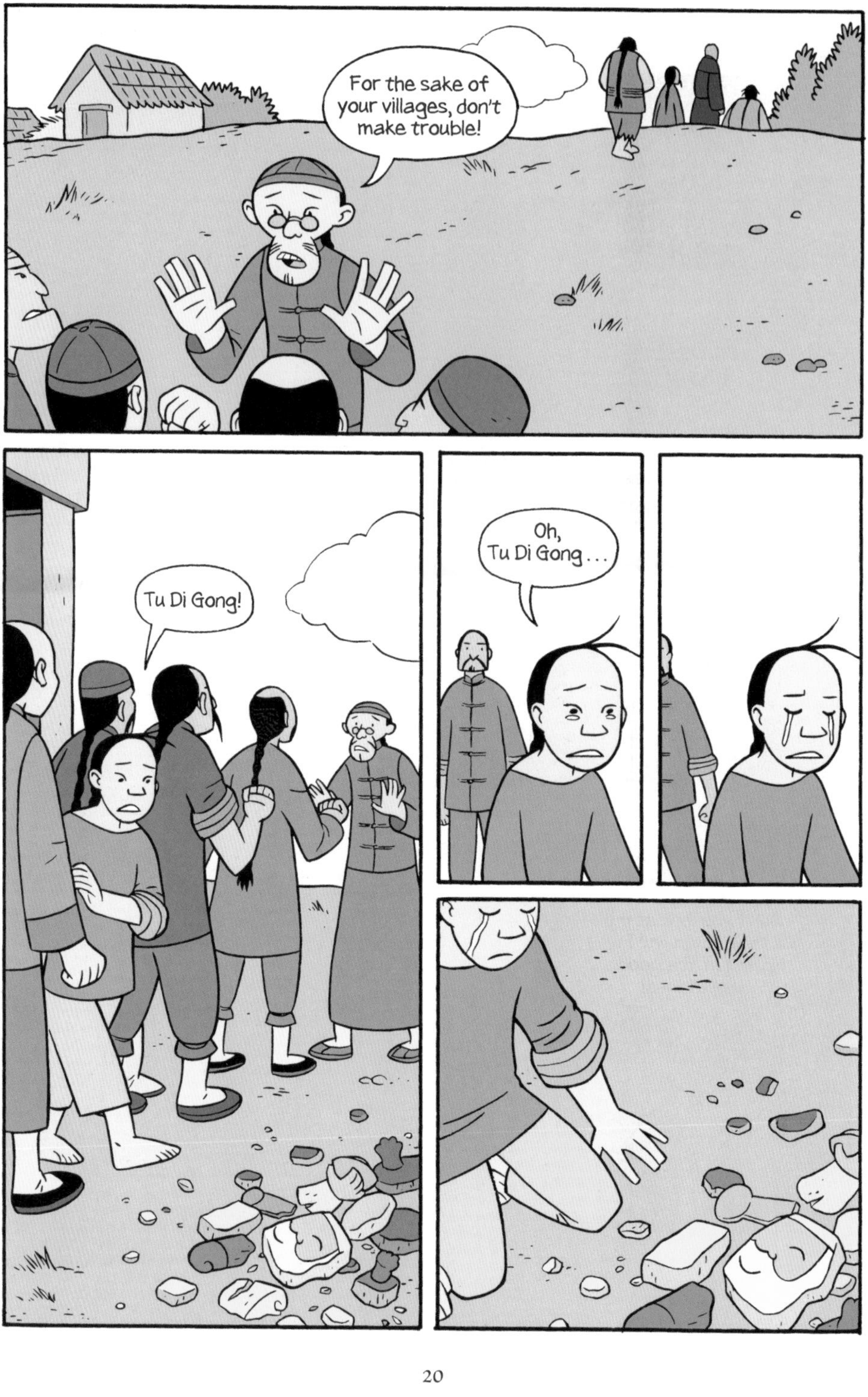
For the sake of your villages, don't make trouble!
Tu Di Gong!
Oh, Tu Di Gong . . .

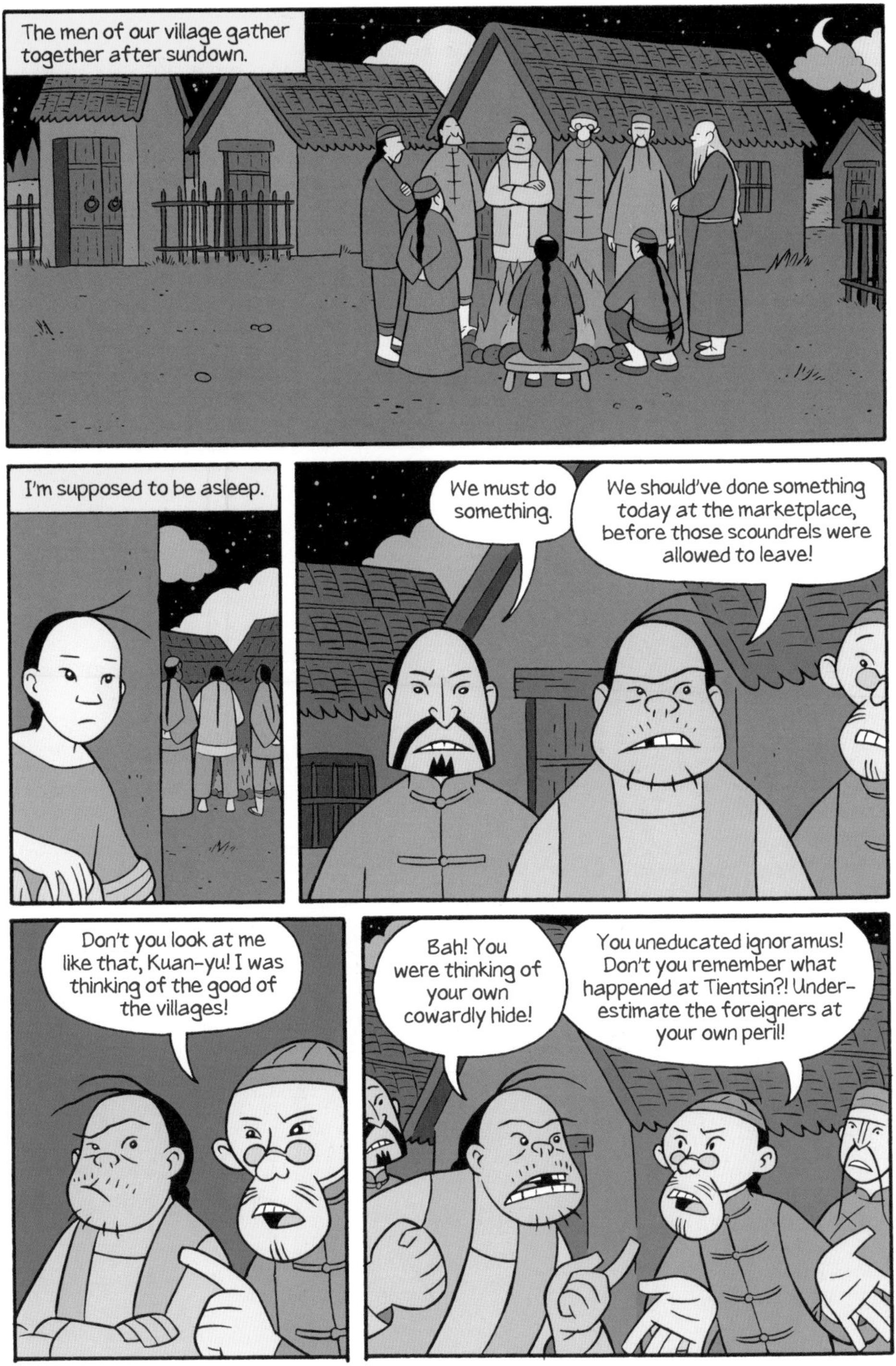

The men of our village gather together after sundown.
I'm supposed to be asleep.
We must do something.
We should've done something today at the marketplace, before those scoundrels were allowed to leave!
Don't you look at me like that, Kuan-yu! I was thinking of the good of the villages!
Bah! You were thinking of your own cowardly hide!
You uneducated ignoramus! Don't you remember what happened at Tientsin?! Under-estimate the foreigners at your own peril!

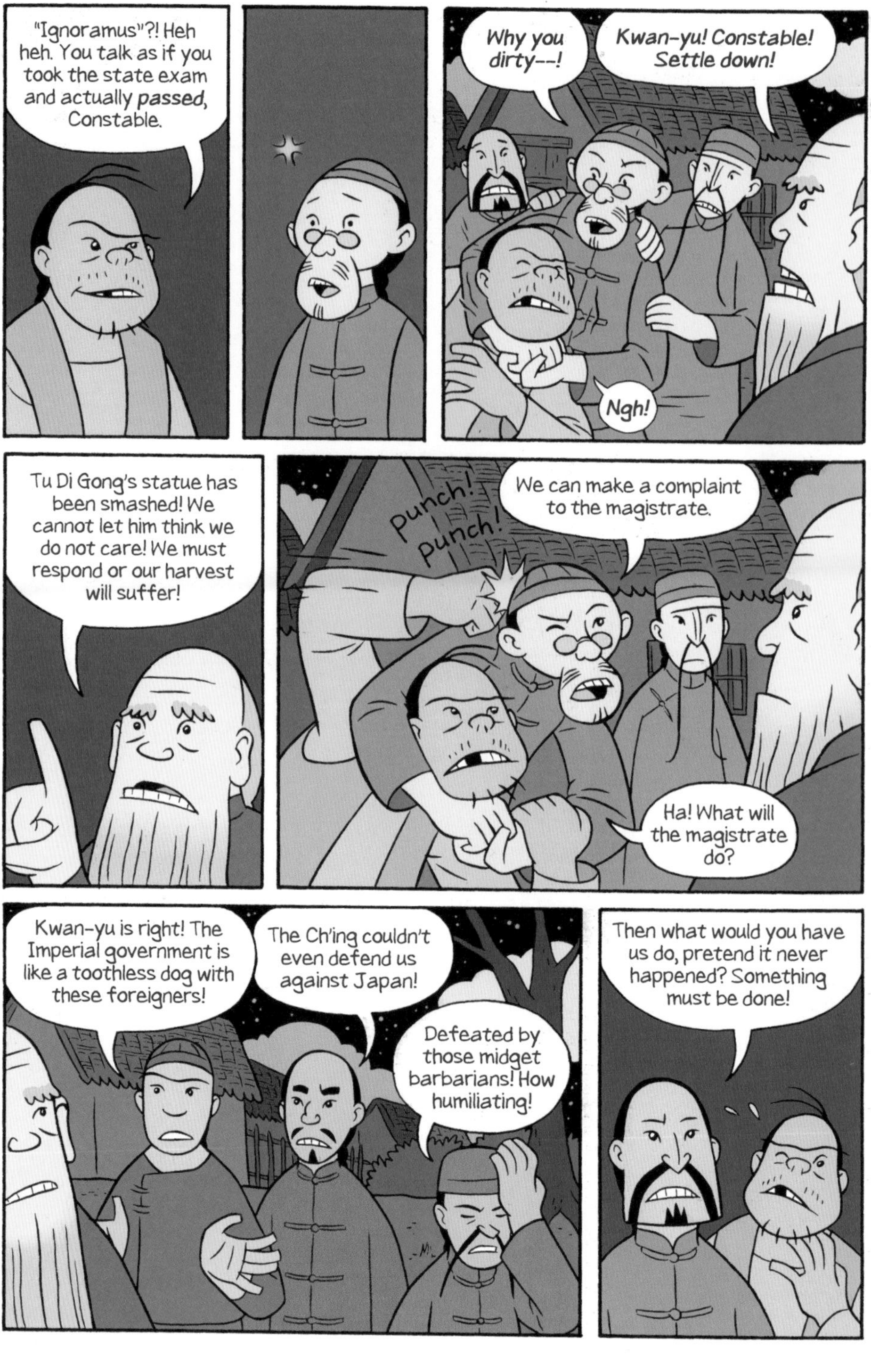
"Ignoramus"?! Heh heh. You talk as if you took the state exam and actually **passed**, Constable.
Why you dirty--!
Kwan-yu! Constable! Settle down!
Ngh!
Tu Di Gong's statue has been smashed! We cannot let him think we do not care! We must respond or our harvest will suffer!
punch! punch!
We can make a complaint to the magistrate.
Ha! What will the magistrate do?
Kwan-yu is right! The Imperial government is like a toothless dog with these foreigners!
The Ch'ing couldn't even defend us against Japan!
Defeated by those midget barbarians! How humiliating!
Then what would you have us do, pretend it never happened? Something must be done!

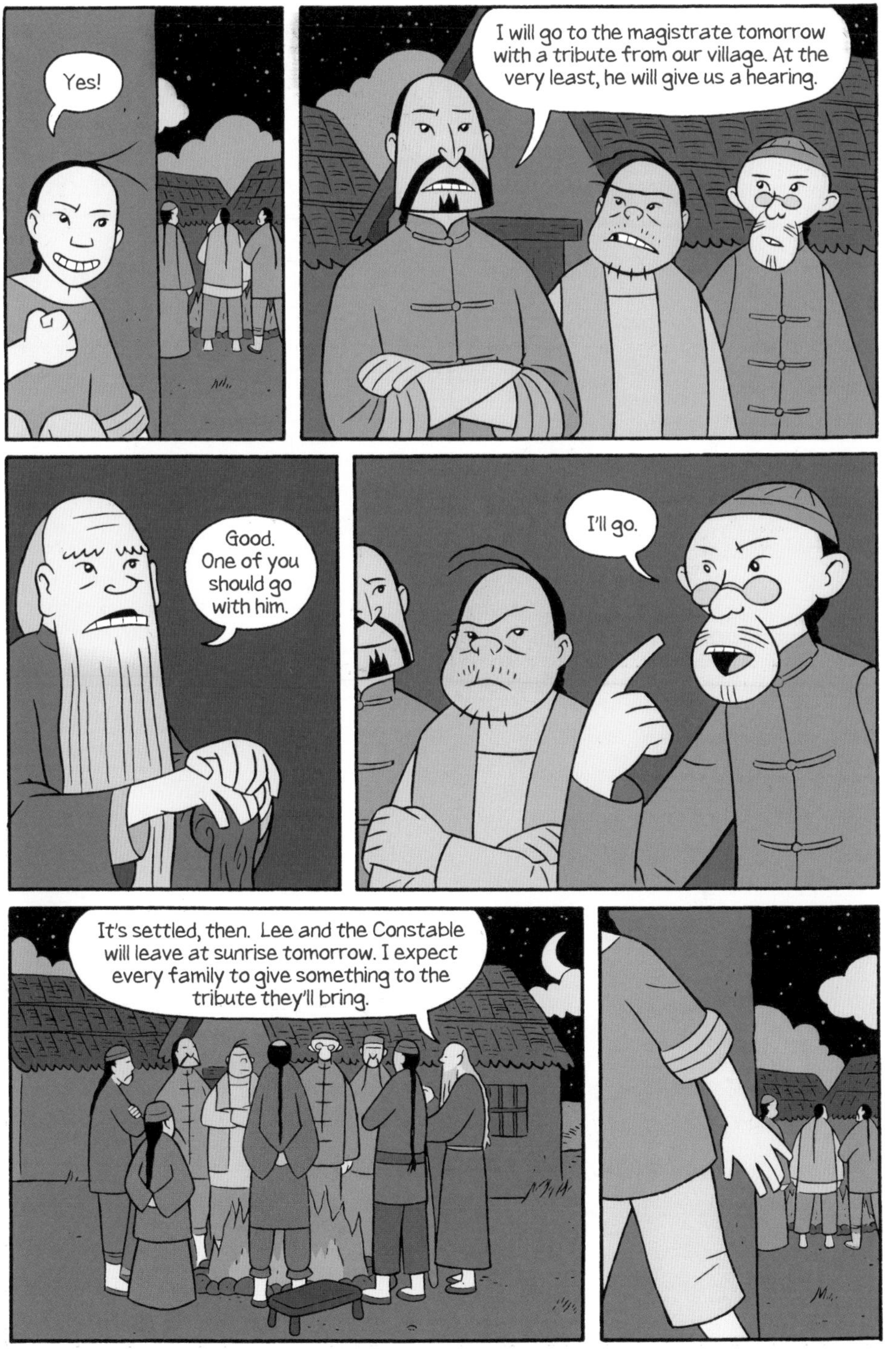
Yes!
I will go to the magistrate tomorrow with a tribute from our village. At the very least, he will give us a hearing.
Good. One of you should go with him.
I'll go.
It's settled, then. Lee and the Constable will leave at sunrise tomorrow. I expect every family to give something to the tribute they'll bring.

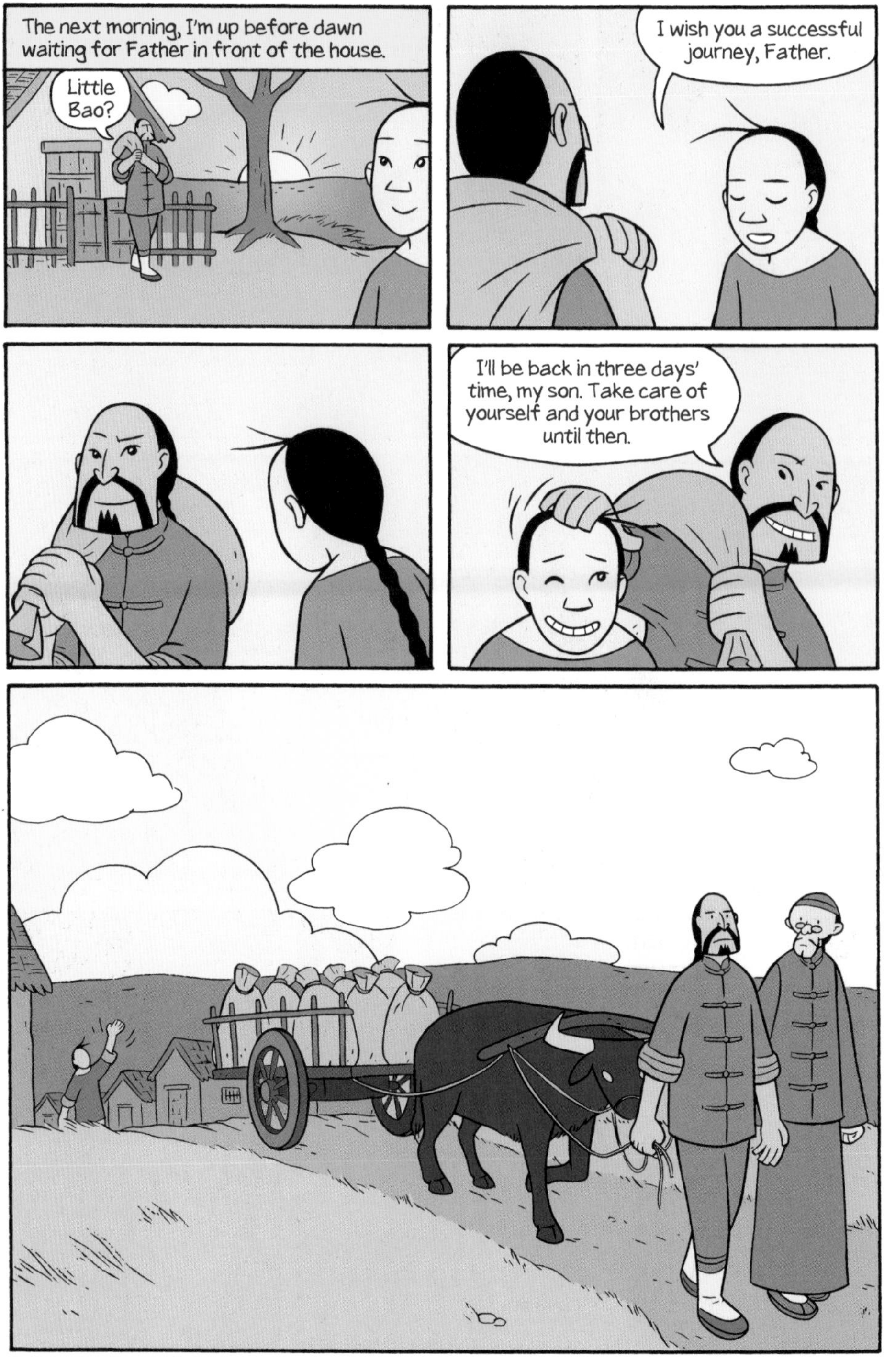
The next morning, I'm up before dawn waiting for Father in front of the house.
Little Bao?
I wish you a successful journey, Father.
I'll be back in three days' time, my son. Take care of yourself and your brothers until then.

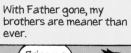
With Father gone, my brothers are meaner than ever.

Bring me water!

Bring me firewood!

Smack!

Smack!

Bring me food!

At night, I comfort myself with dreams of Father's meeting with the magistrate.

I think you'd better listen to him!

Anything you ask! Anything!

Father returns a day earlier than expected.

Smack!

Come on! He's back!

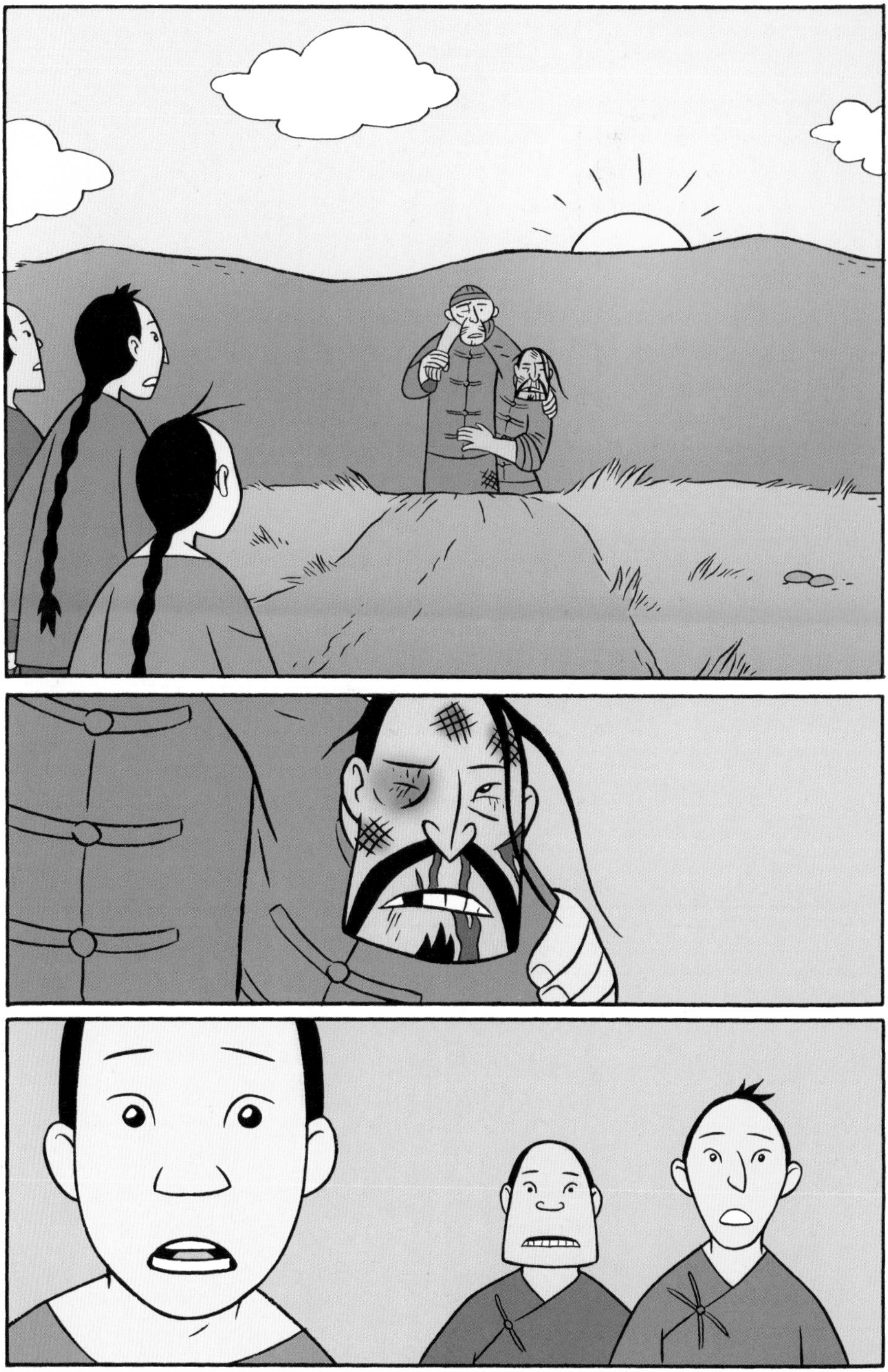

I piece the story together from the whispers of the village.

About a day's journey from the magistrate's residence, Father and the Constable came across a small band of foreign soldiers.

There was a dispute about the right of way.

!!

ㅂㅈㅈㅊ ㅂㅂㅈㅊ!

Have you people no manners? We're the ones with the heavier burden!

ㅂㅈㅈㅊ ㅂㅂㅈㅊ, ㅂㄹㅊ ㅂㅂㅈㅂ ㅂㅈㅂㅈㅊ ㅂㅊㅈㅂㅊㅂ!

All right, all right! Please, no trouble!

27

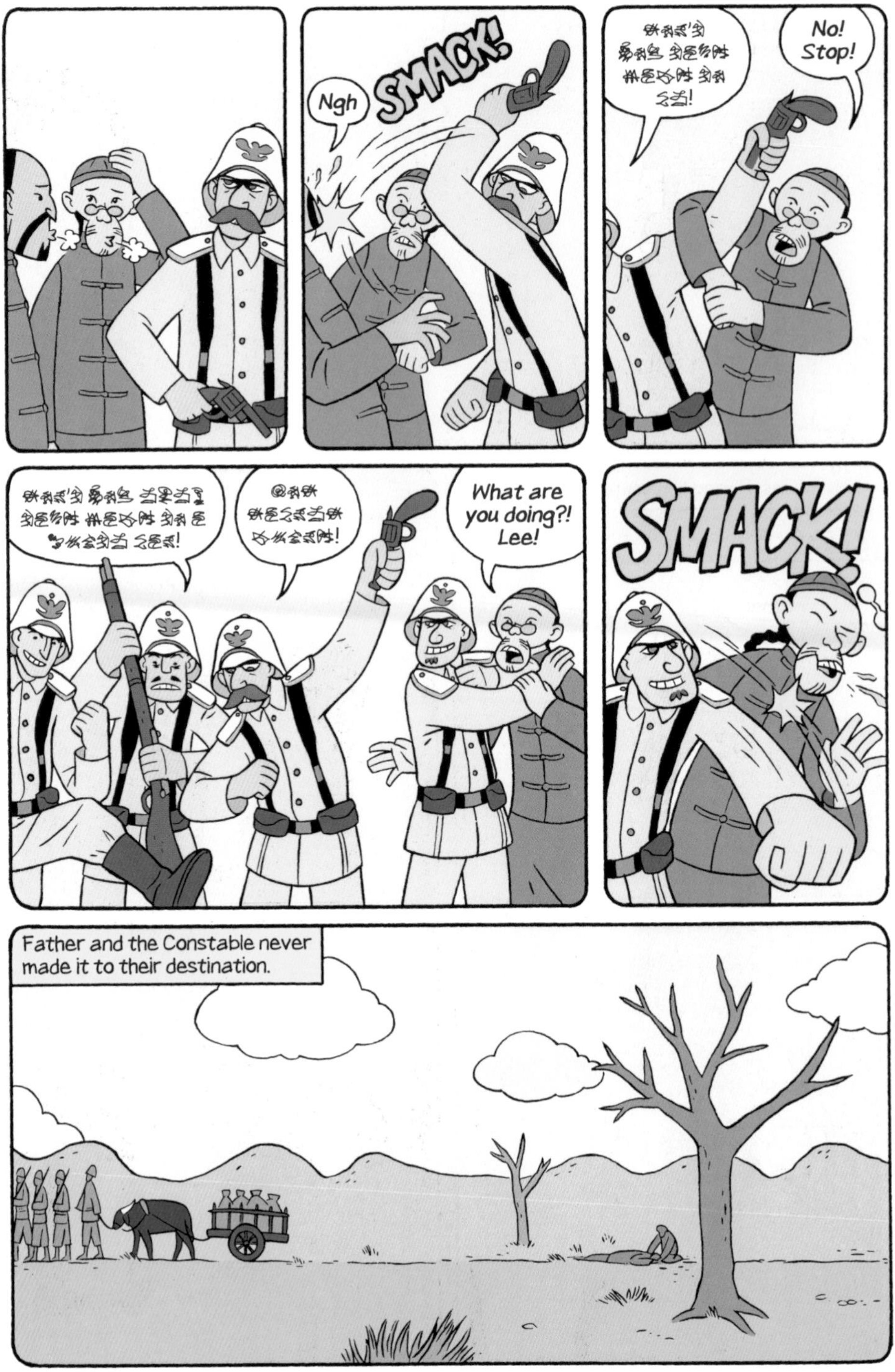
Ngh
SMACK!
No! Stop!
What are you doing?! Lee!
SMACK!
Father and the Constable never made it to their destination.

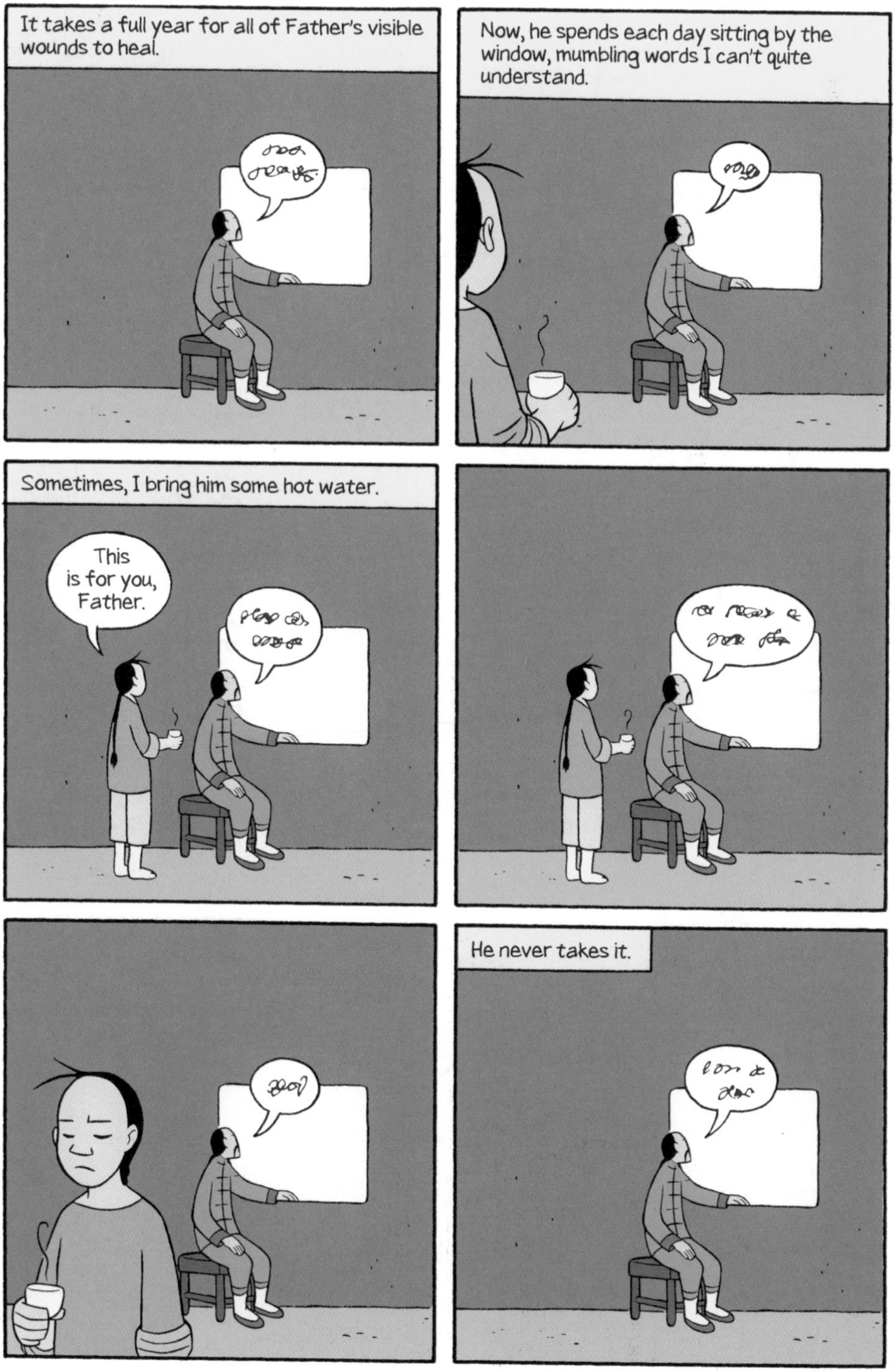
It takes a full year for all of Father's visible wounds to heal.
Now, he spends each day sitting by the window, mumbling words I can't quite understand.
Sometimes, I bring him some hot water.
This is for you, Father.
He never takes it.

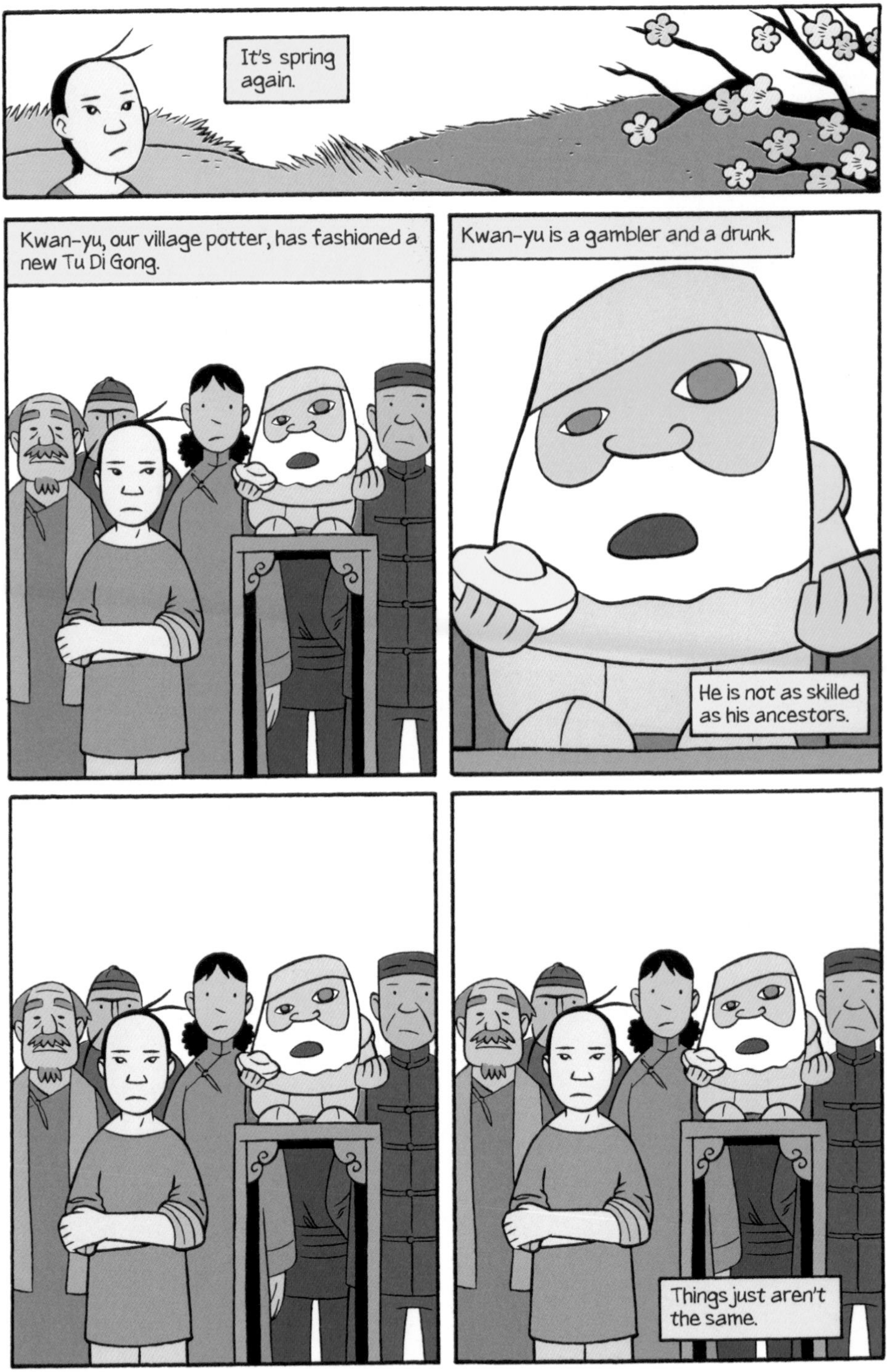
It's spring again.
Kwan-yu, our village potter, has fashioned a new Tu Di Gong.
Kwan-yu is a gambler and a drunk.
He is not as skilled as his ancestors.
Things just aren't the same.

第二章

Northern Shan-tung Province, China
1898

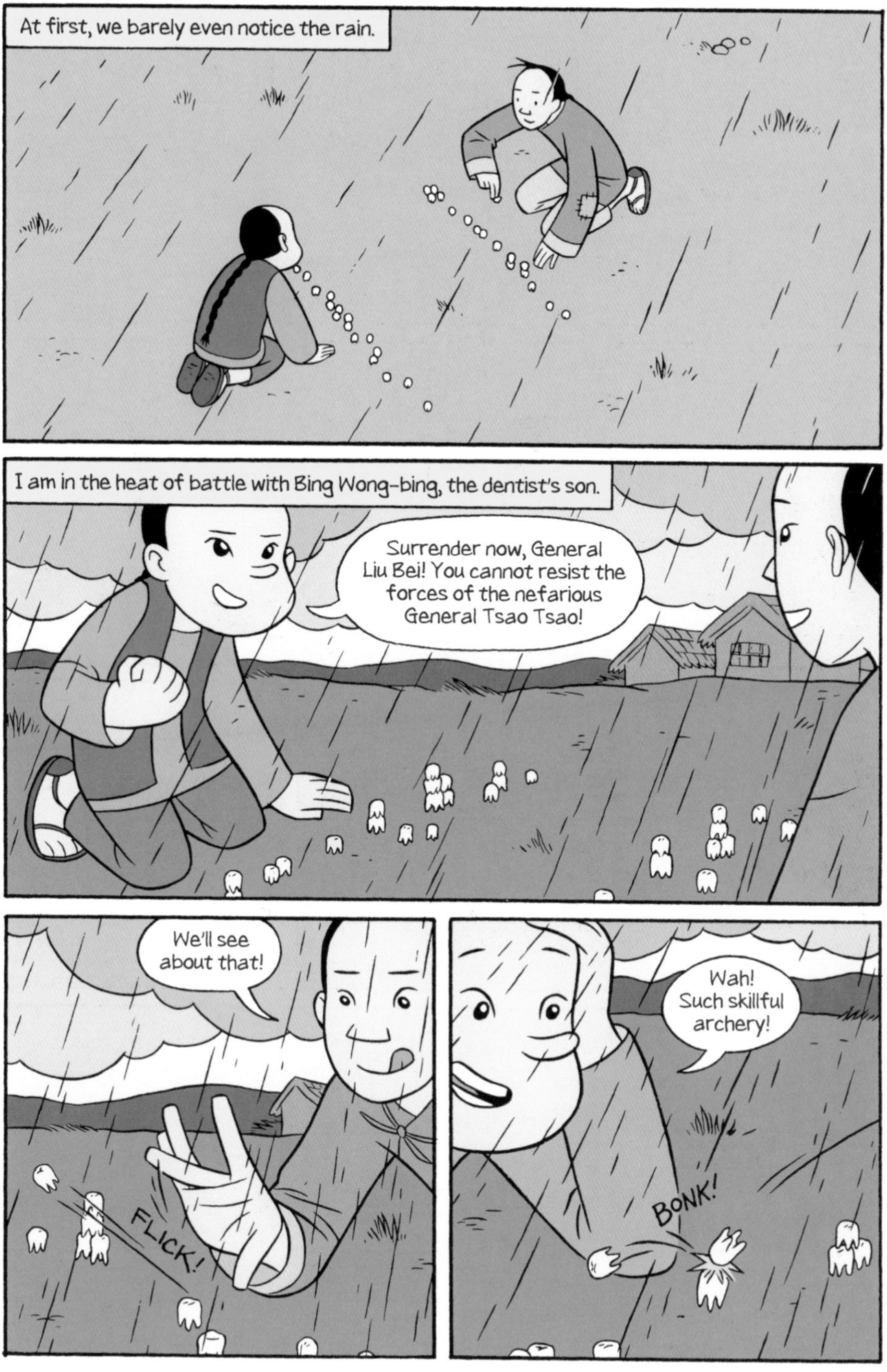
At first, we barely even notice the rain.
I am in the heat of battle with Bing Wong-bing, the dentist's son.
Surrender now, General Liu Bei! You cannot resist the forces of the nefarious General Tsao Tsao!
We'll see about that!
FLICK!
Wah! Such skillful archery!
BONK!

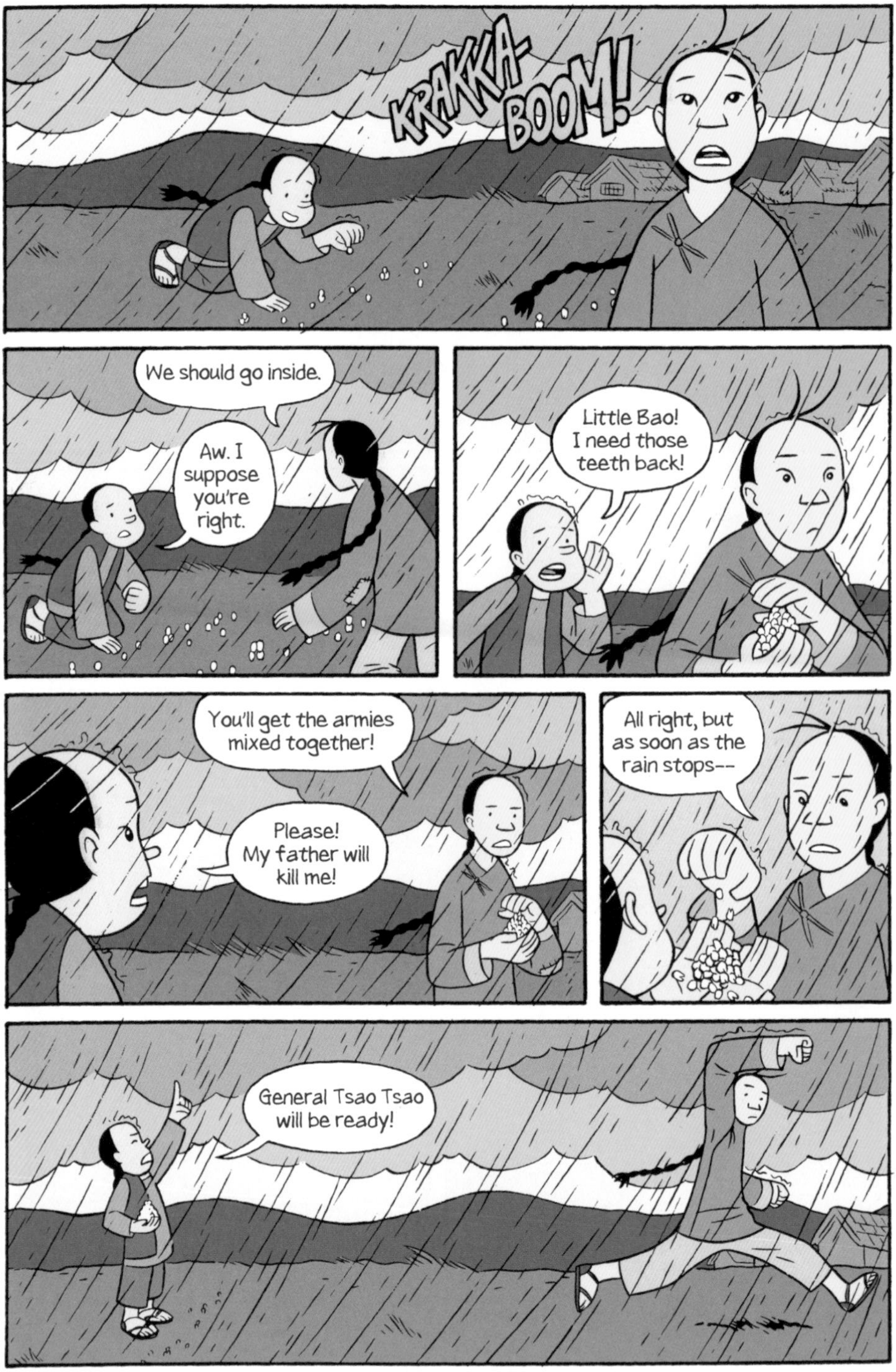
KRAKKA-BOOM!
We should go inside.
Aw. I suppose you're right.
Little Bao! I need those teeth back!
You'll get the armies mixed together!
Please! My father will kill me!
All right, but as soon as the rain stops--
General Tsao Tsao will be ready!

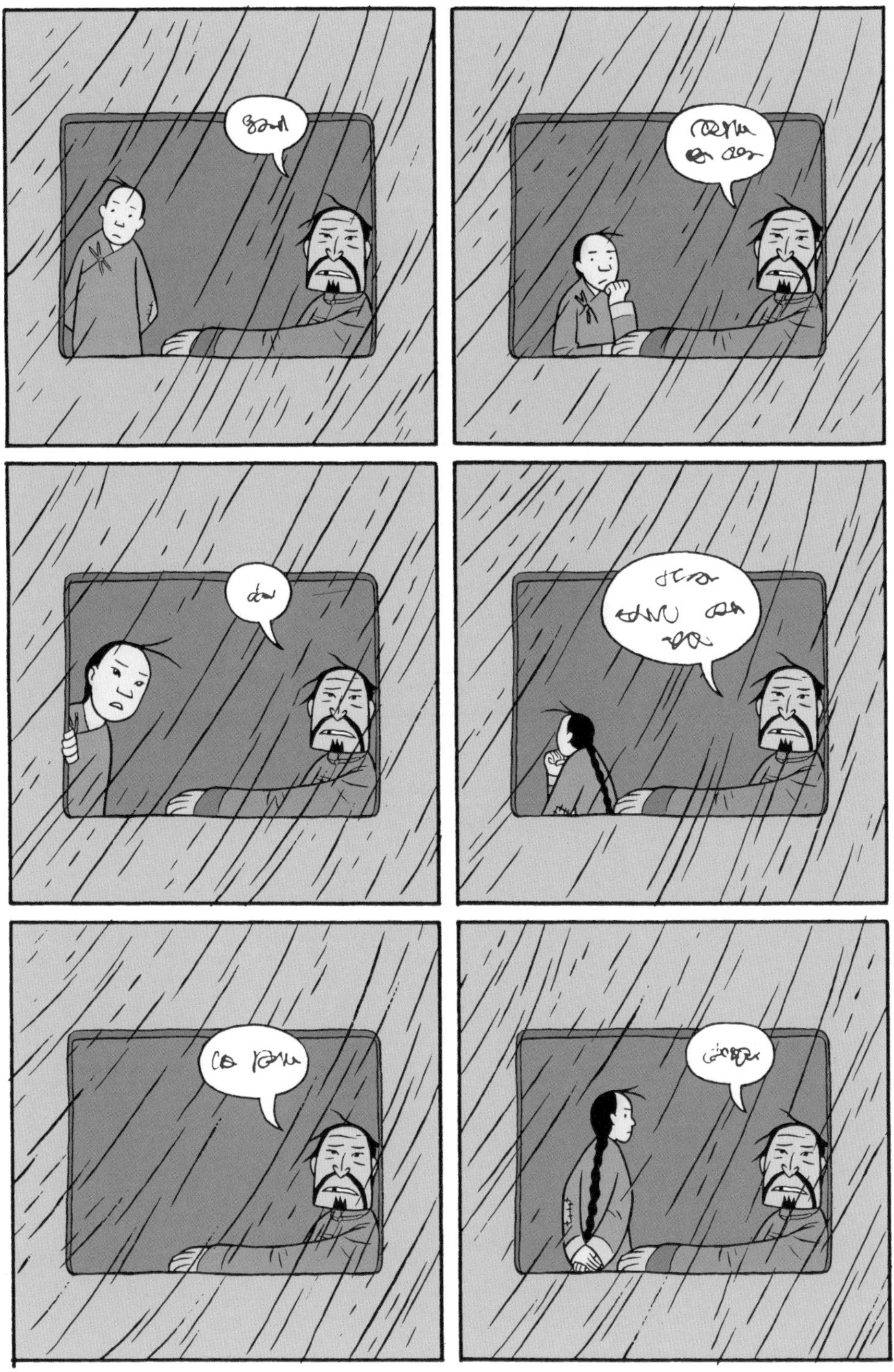

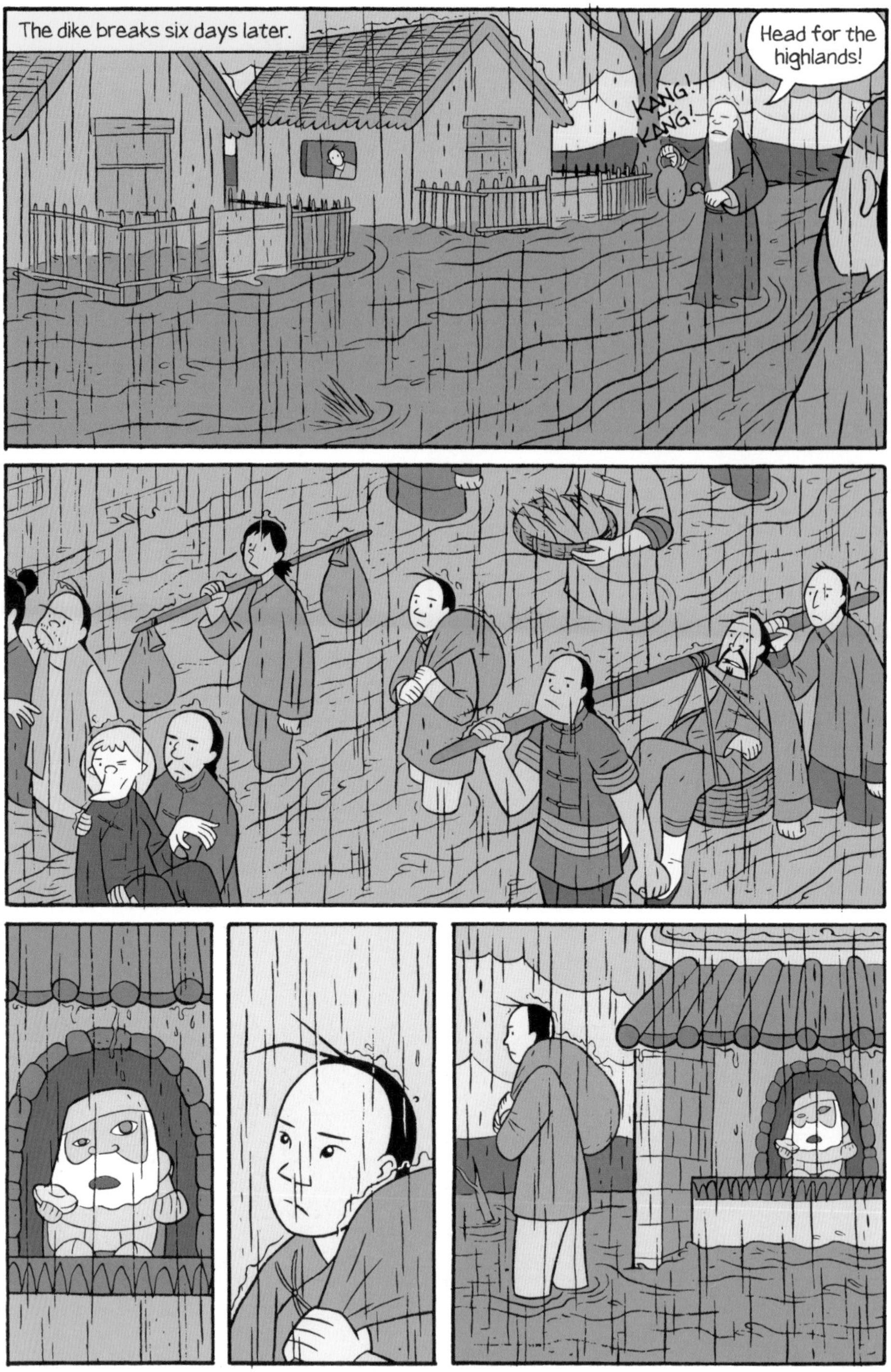
The dike breaks six days later.
KANG! KANG!
Head for the highlands!

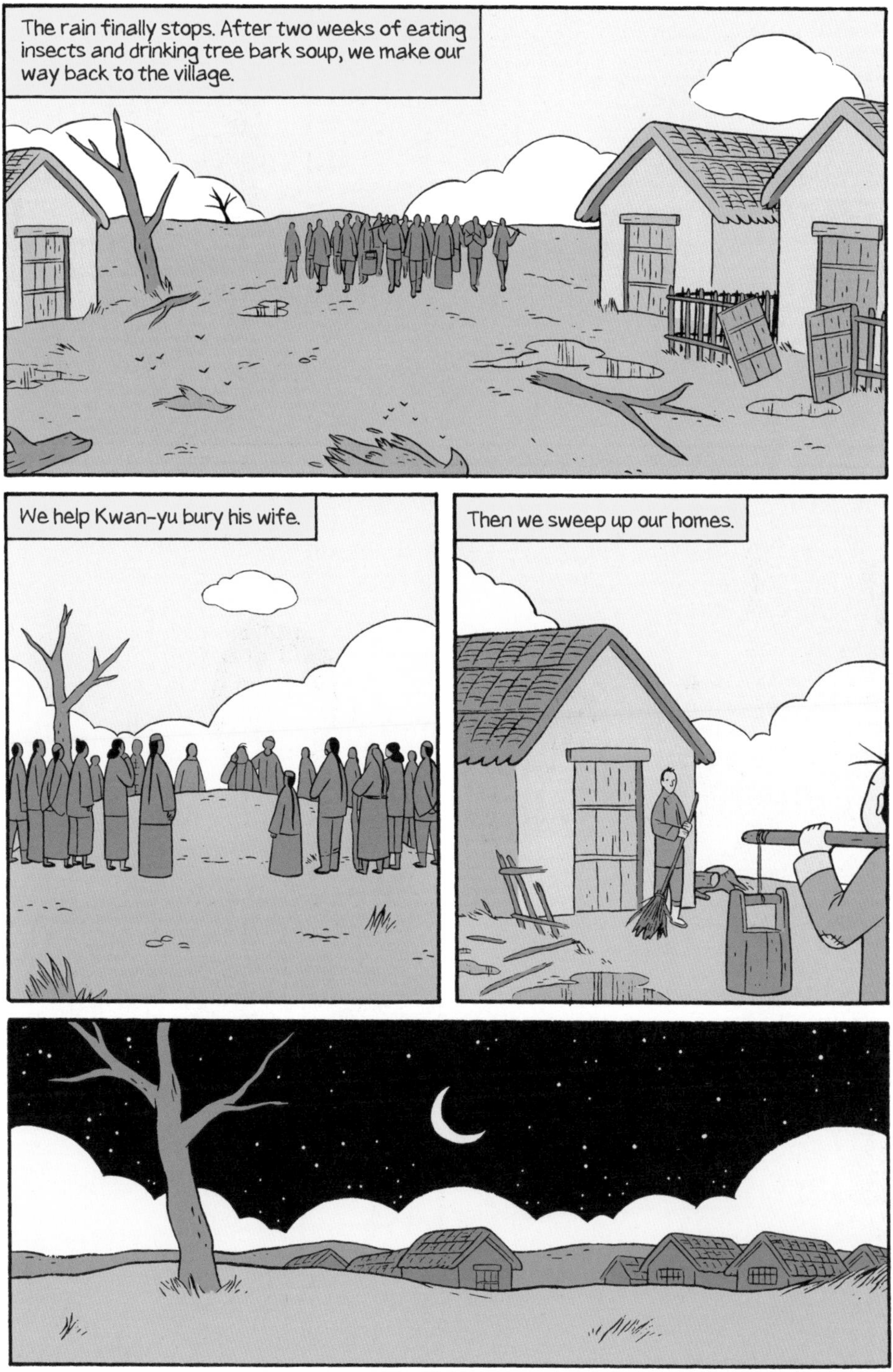

The rain finally stops. After two weeks of eating insects and drinking tree bark soup, we make our way back to the village.
We help Kwan-yu bury his wife.
Then we sweep up our homes.

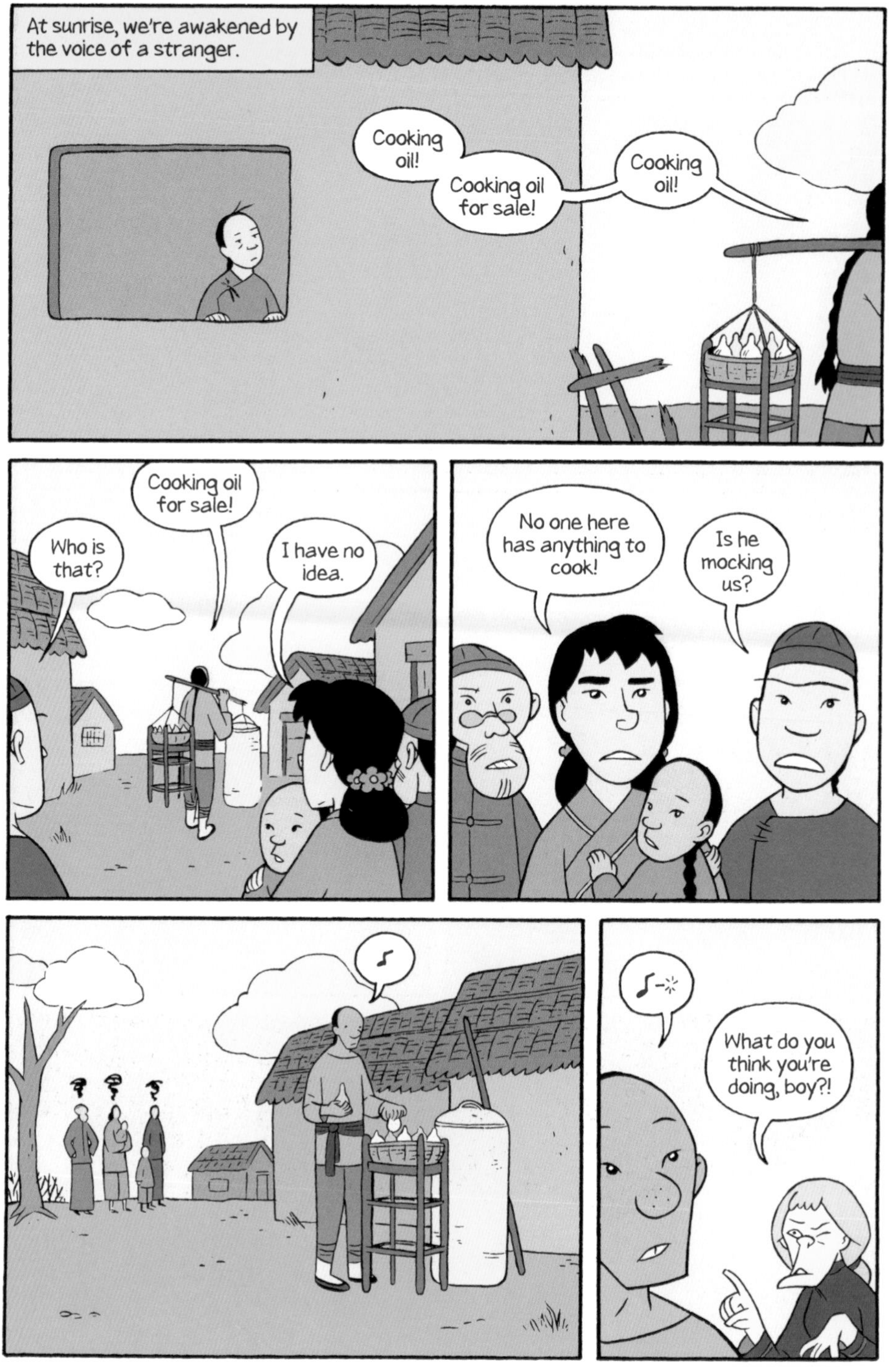
At sunrise, we're awakened by the voice of a stranger.
Cooking oil!
Cooking oil for sale!
Cooking oil!
Cooking oil for sale!
Who is that?
I have no idea.
No one here has anything to cook!
Is he mocking us?
What do you think you're doing, boy?!

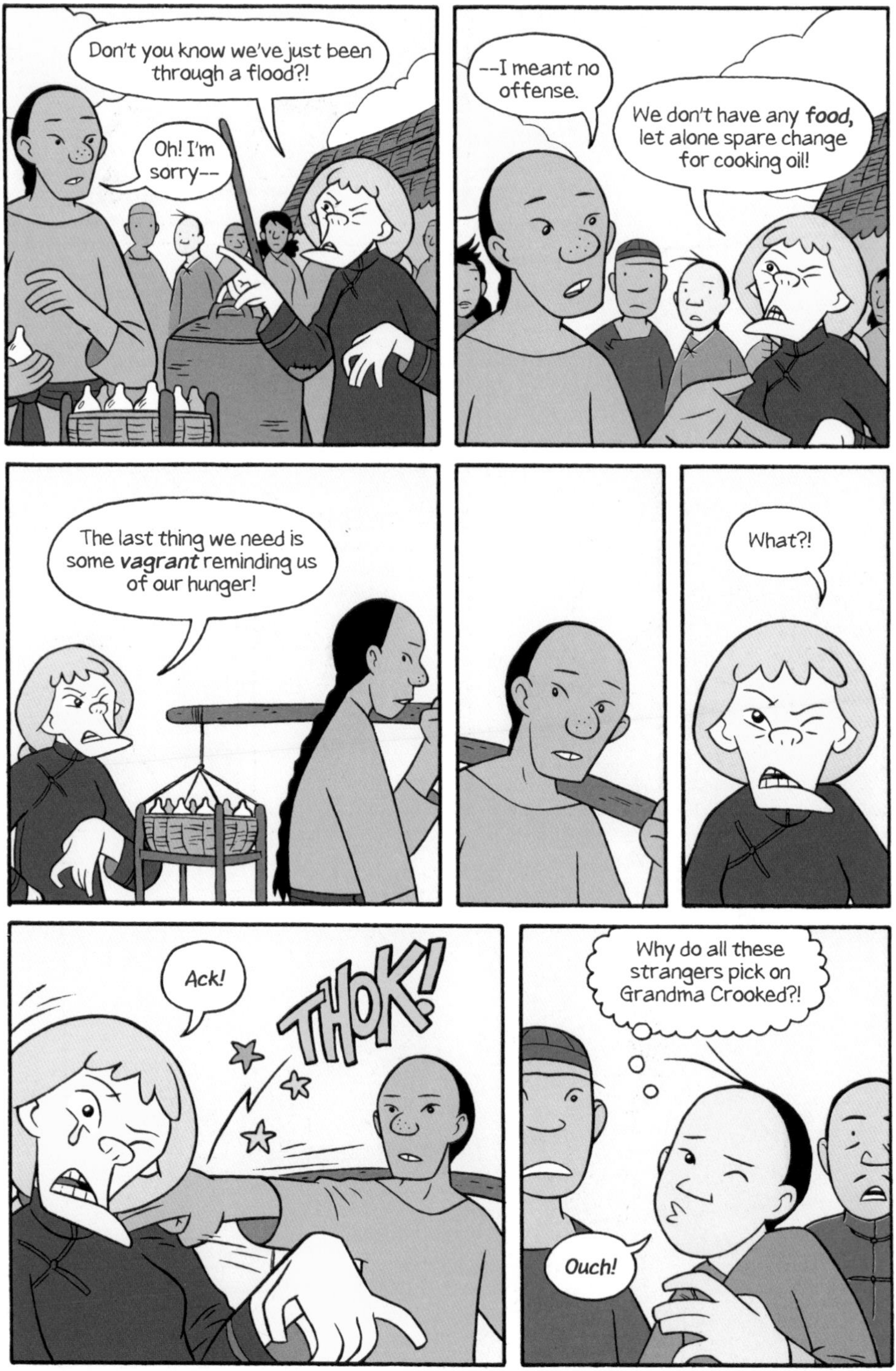
Don't you know we've just been through a flood?!
Oh! I'm sorry--
--I meant no offense.
We don't have any **food,** let alone spare change for cooking oil!
The last thing we need is some ***vagrant*** reminding us of our hunger!
What?!
Ack!
THOK!
Why do all these strangers pick on Grandma Crooked?!
Ouch!

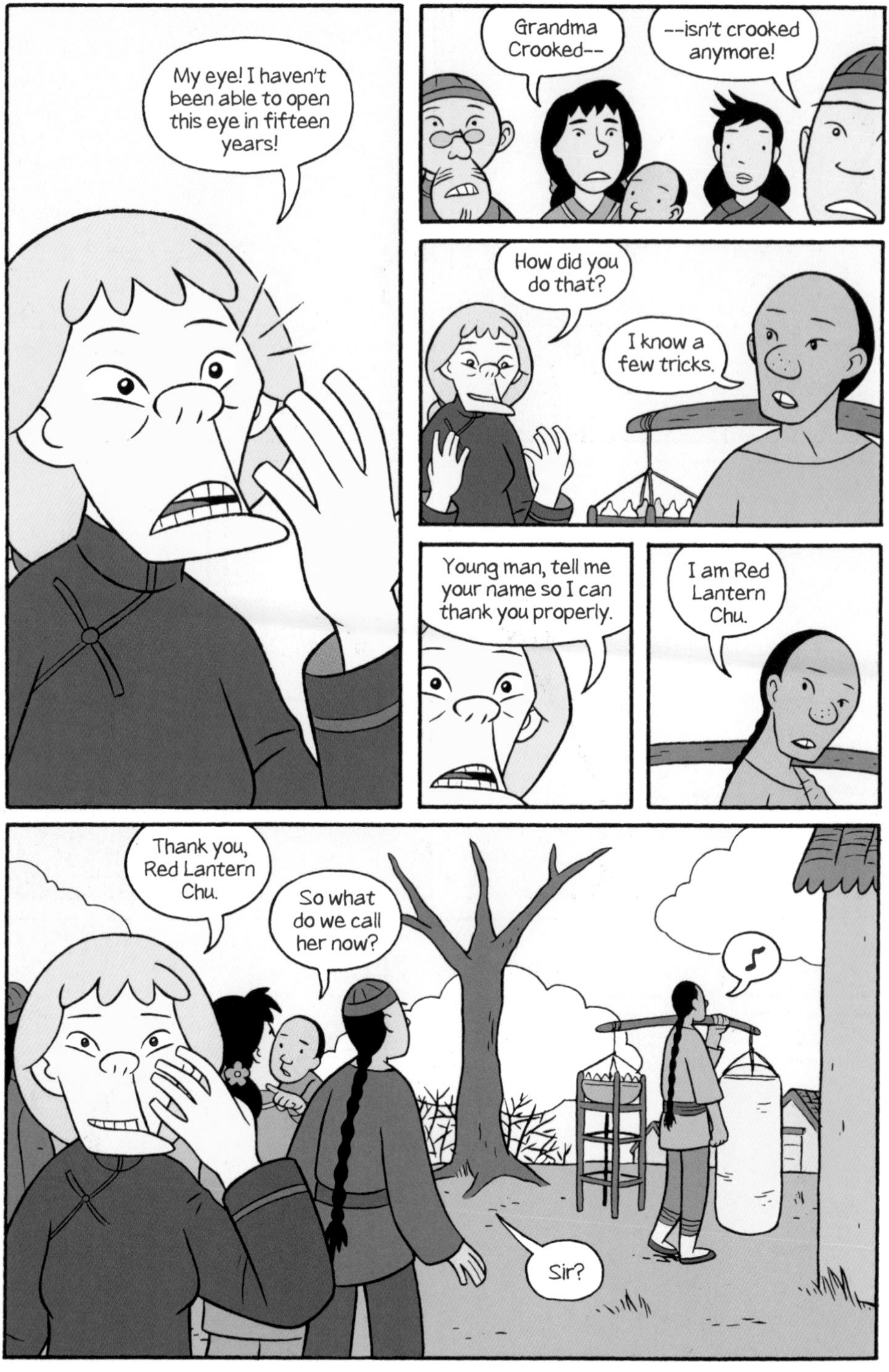
My eye! I haven't been able to open this eye in fifteen years!
Grandma Crooked--
--isn't crooked anymore!
How did you do that?
I know a few tricks.
Young man, tell me your name so I can thank you properly.
I am Red Lantern Chu.
Thank you, Red Lantern Chu.
So what do we call her now?
Sir?

Yes?

I–I...

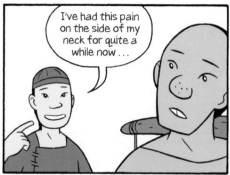

I've had this pain on the side of my neck for quite a while now...

Red Lantern Chu spends the rest of the day tending to the villagers, one after the other.

He never complains or asks for any money.

In the evening, the Village Headman trades him a bowl of bean soup for a few drops of cooking oil. I'm pretty sure that's the Headman's last handful of beans.

41

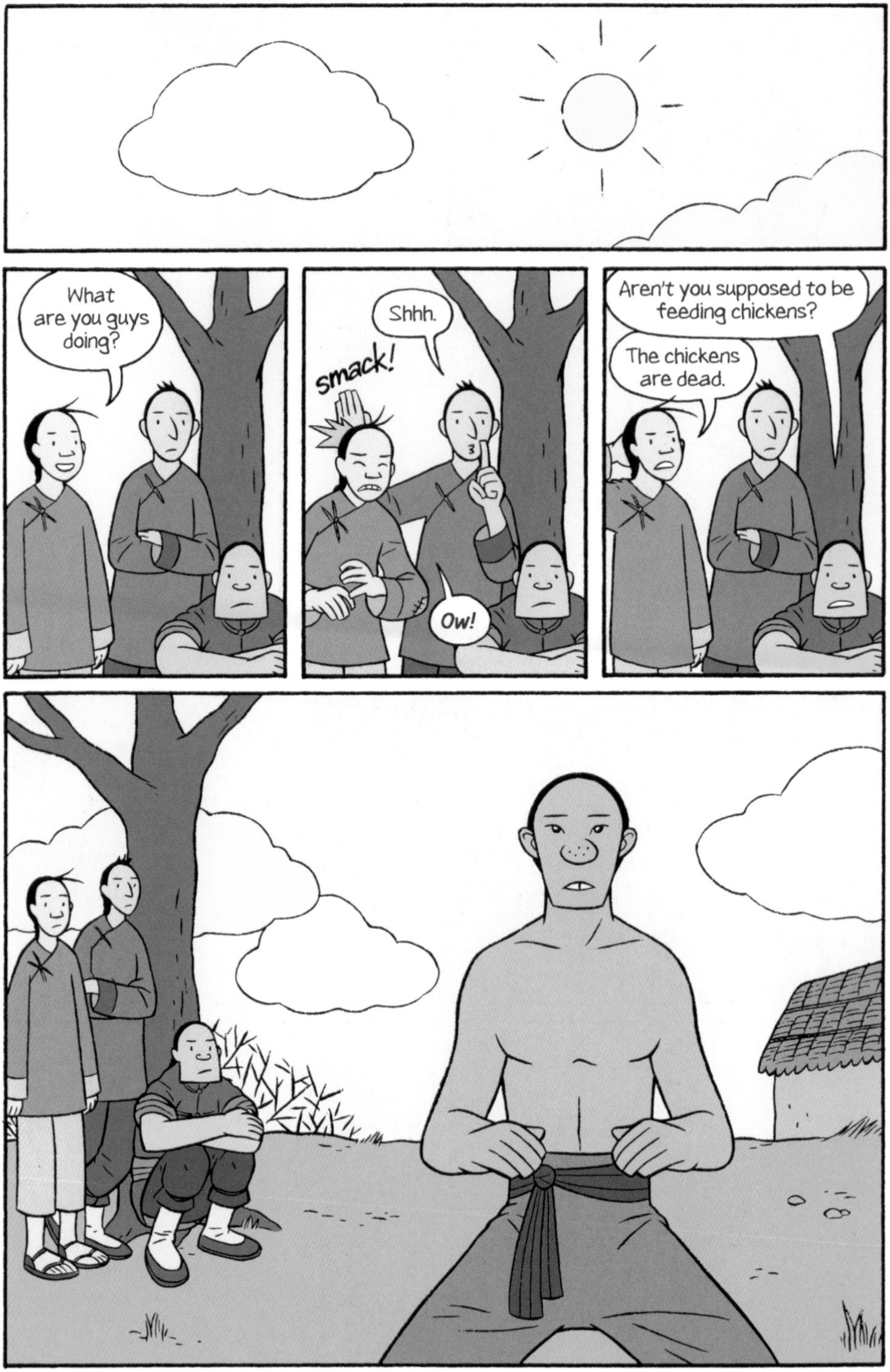
What are you guys doing?
Shhh.
smack!
Ow!
Aren't you supposed to be feeding chickens?
The chickens are dead.

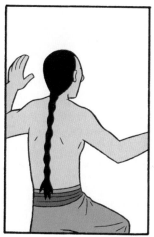
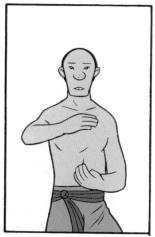
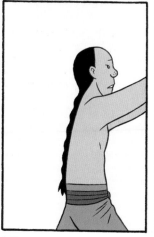
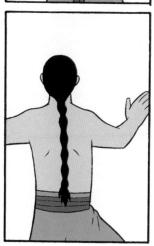

He knows
kung fu.

Yeah.

Maybe we
should ask
him to
teach us.

Sure. Nothing
else to do. All
the crops are
ruined.

Ha! You two? Learn
kung fu?! Like teaching
a pair of boars to sing
opera!

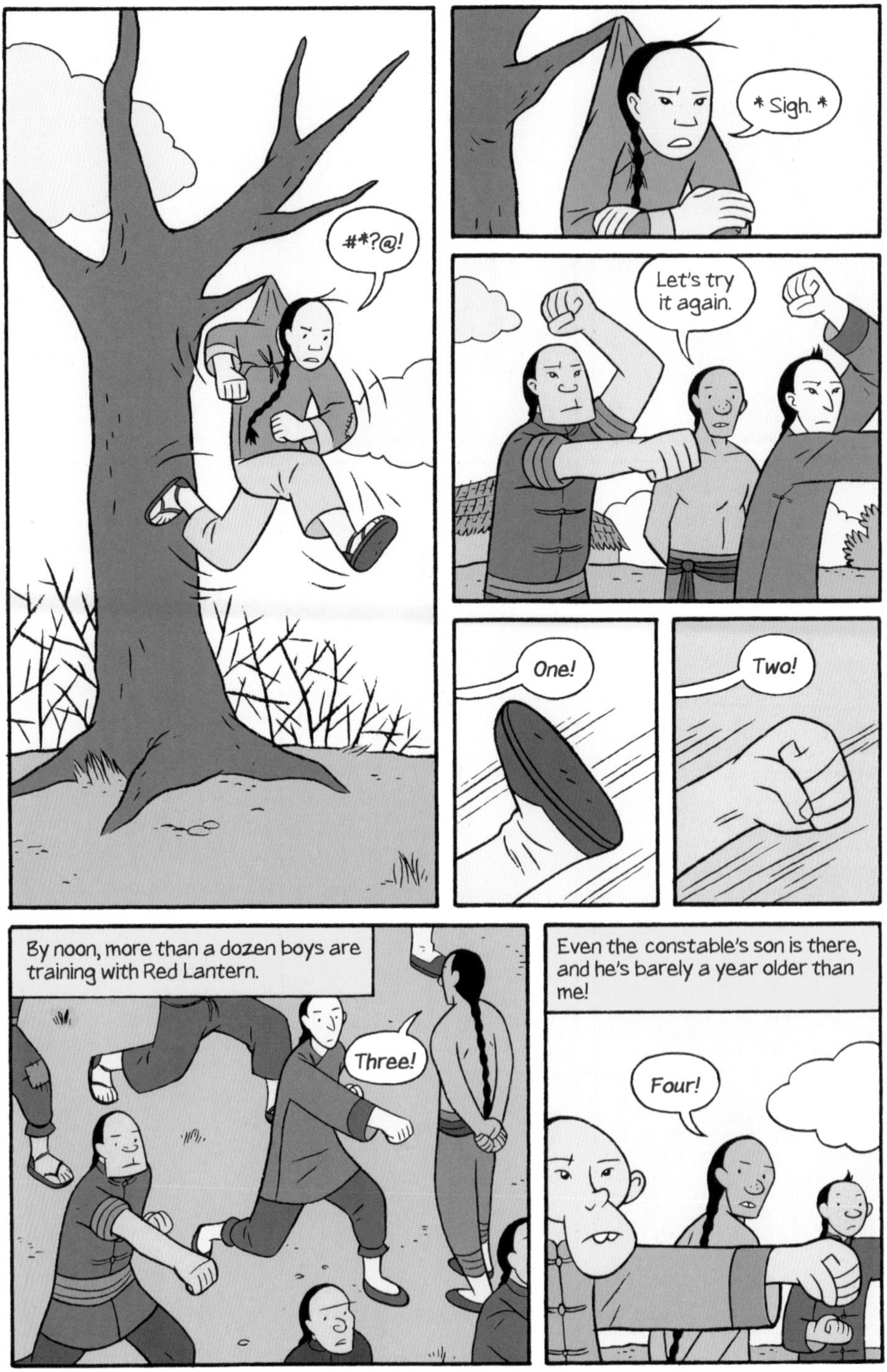
#*?@!
* Sigh. *
Let's try it again.
One!
Two!
By noon, more than a dozen boys are training with Red Lantern.
Three!
Even the constable's son is there, and he's barely a year older than me!
Four!

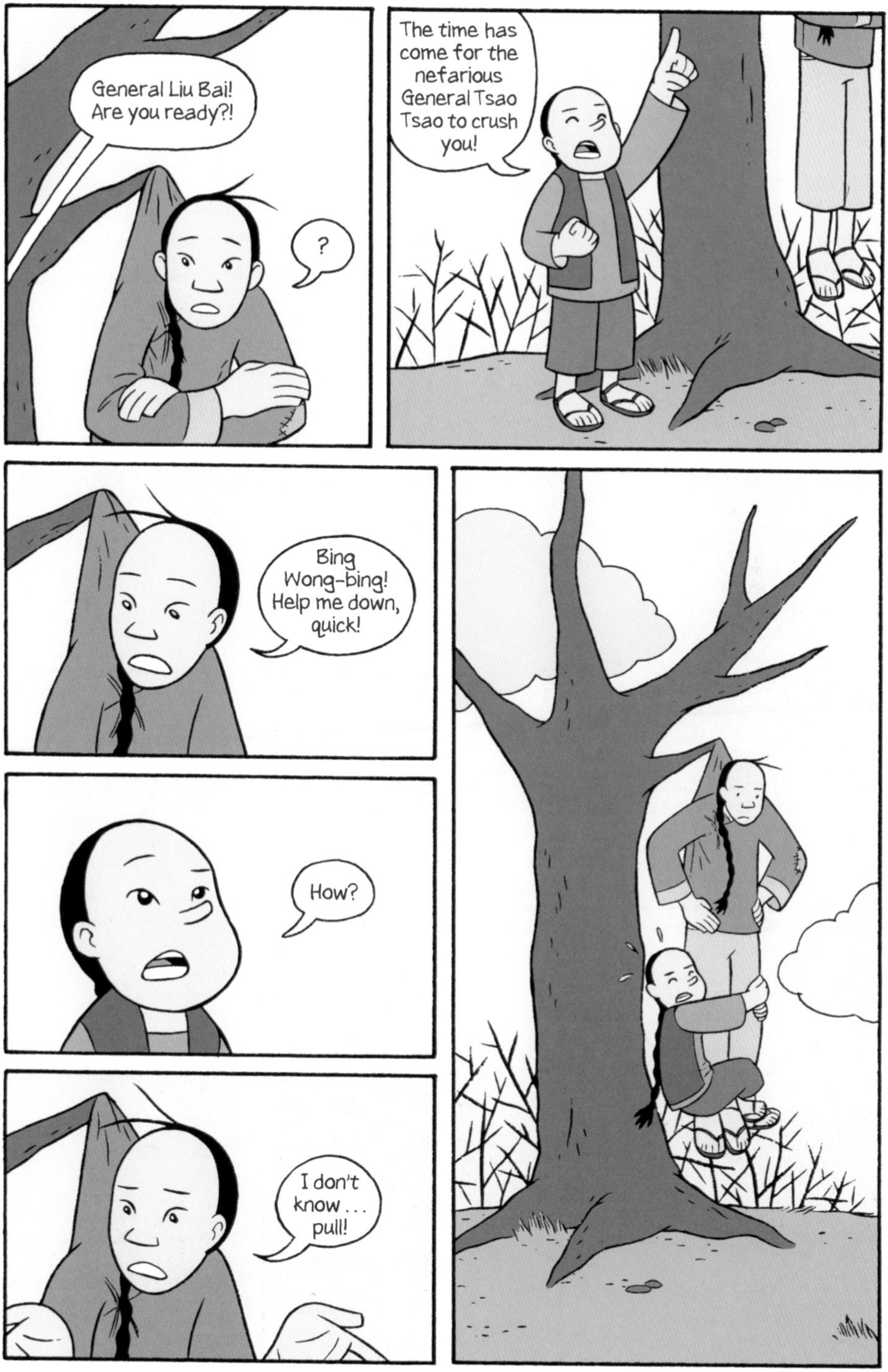
General Liu Bai! Are you ready?!
?
The time has come for the nefarious General Tsao Tsao to crush you!
Bing Wong-bing! Help me down, quick!
How?
I don't know... pull!

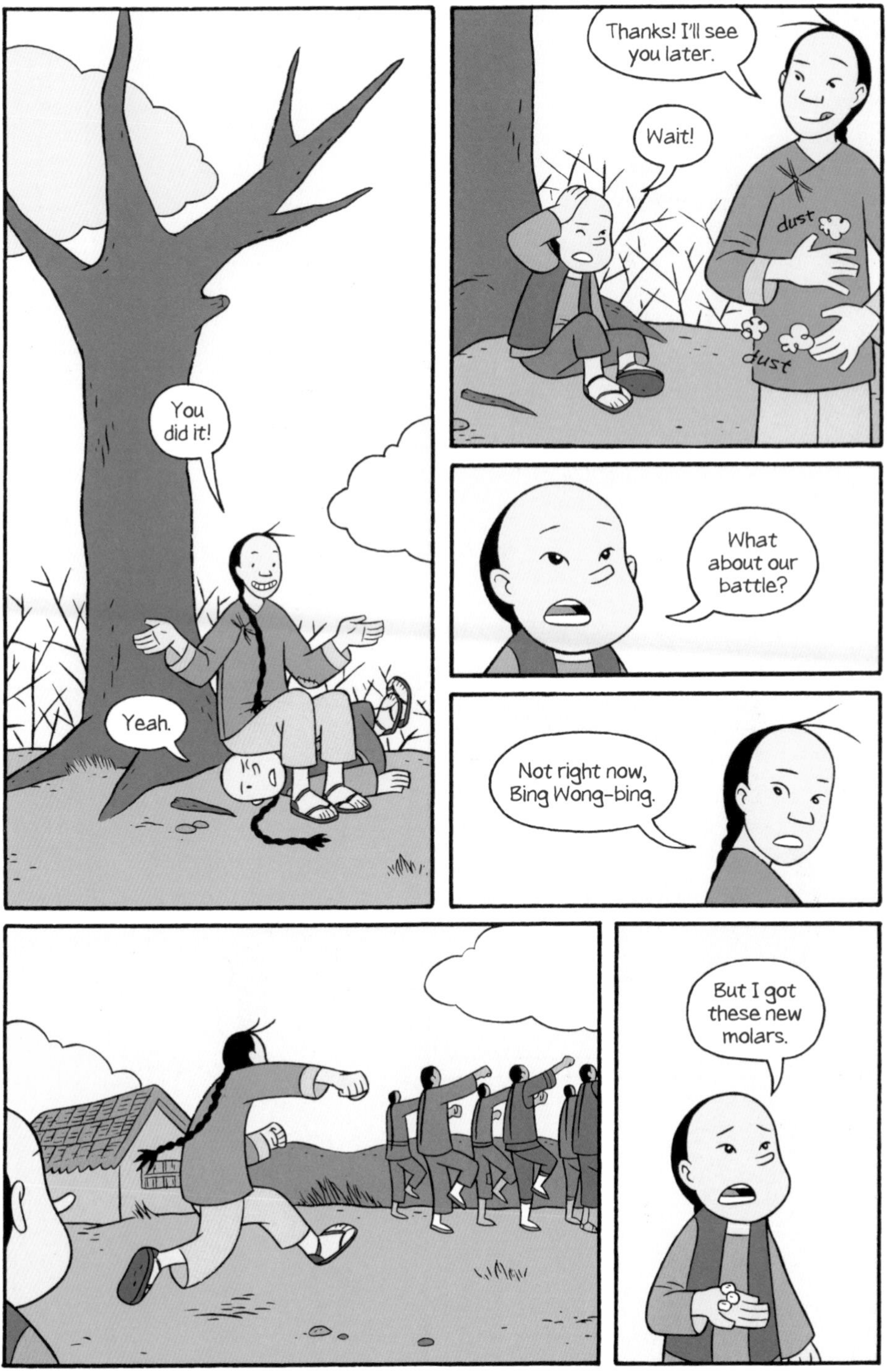
You did it!
Yeah.
Thanks! I'll see you later.
Wait!
dust
dust
What about our battle?
Not right now, Bing Wong-bing.
But I got these new molars.

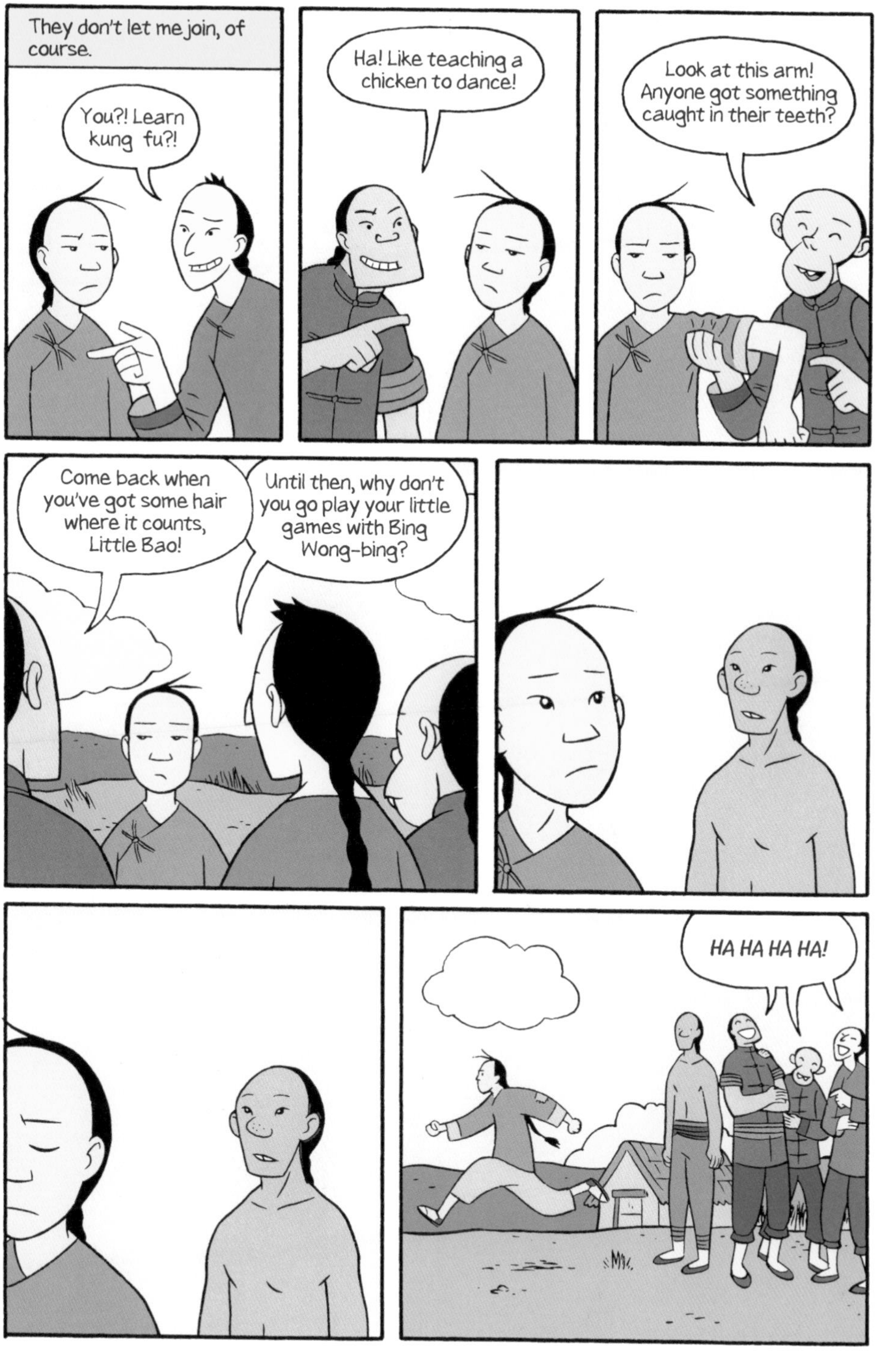
They don't let me join, of course.
You?! Learn kung fu?!
Ha! Like teaching a chicken to dance!
Look at this arm! Anyone got something caught in their teeth?
Come back when you've got some hair where it counts, Little Bao!
Until then, why don't you go play your little games with Bing Wong-bing?
HA HA HA HA!

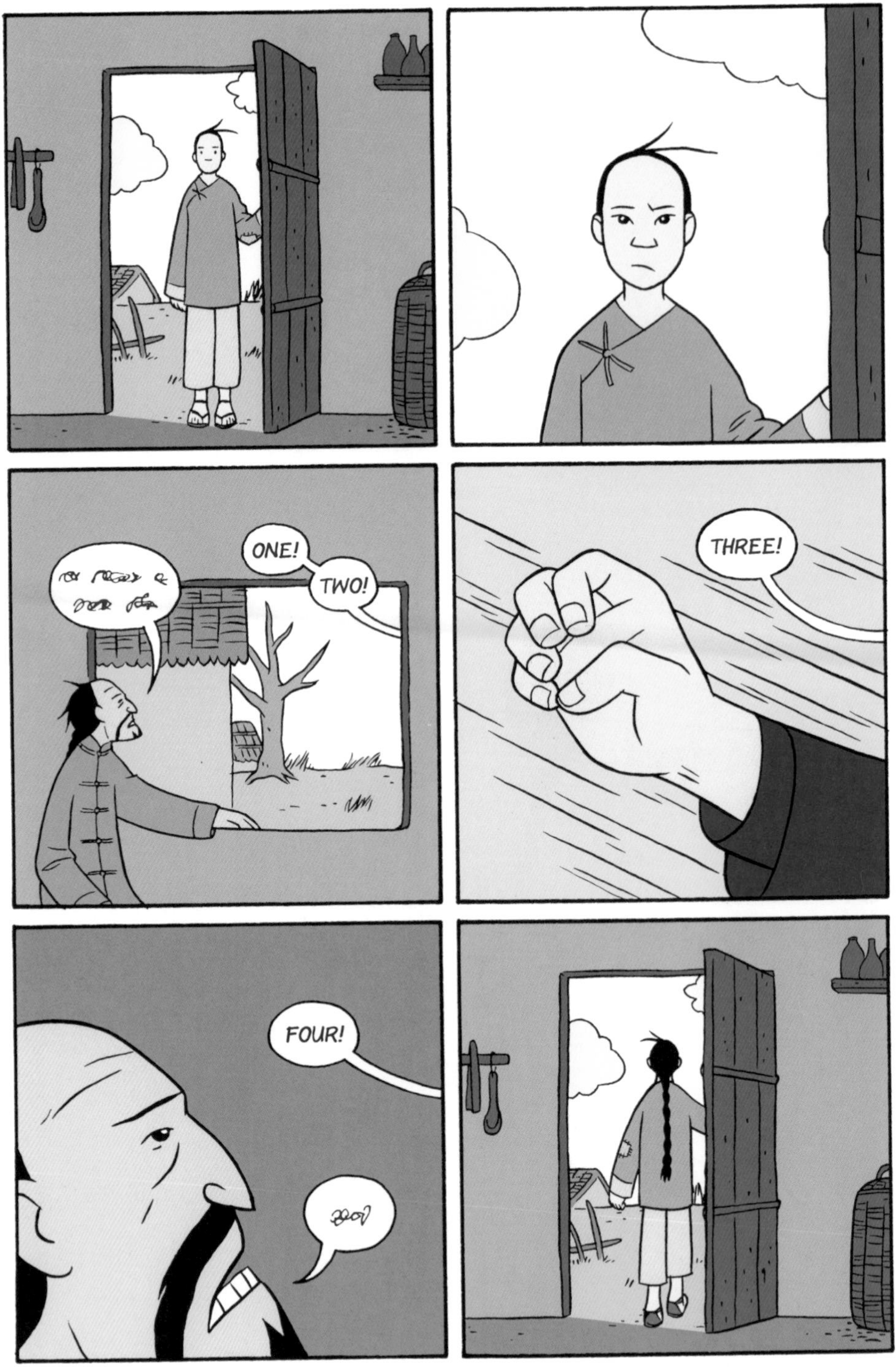
ONE!
TWO!
THREE!
FOUR!

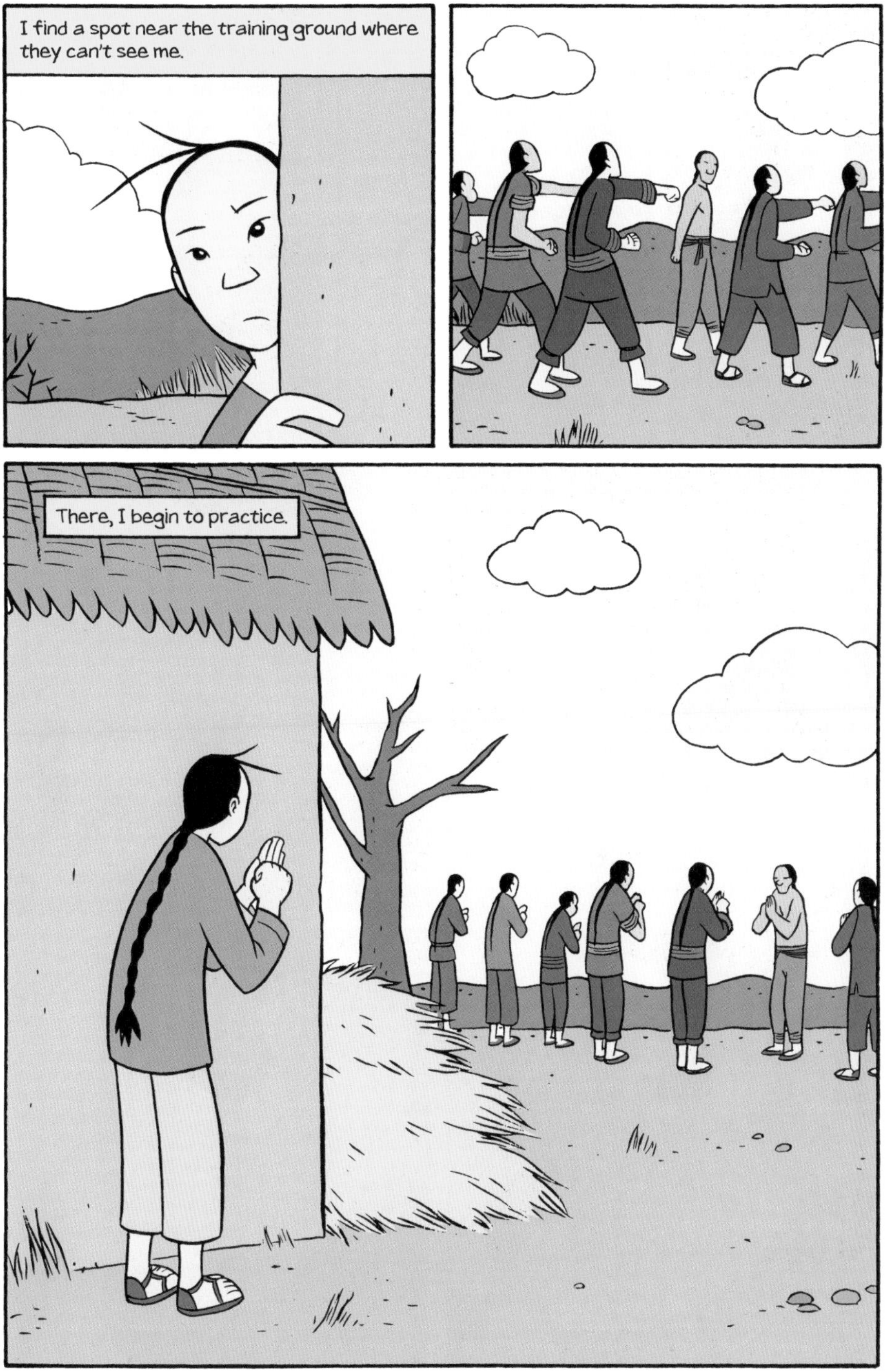
I find a spot near the training ground where they can't see me.
There, I begin to practice.

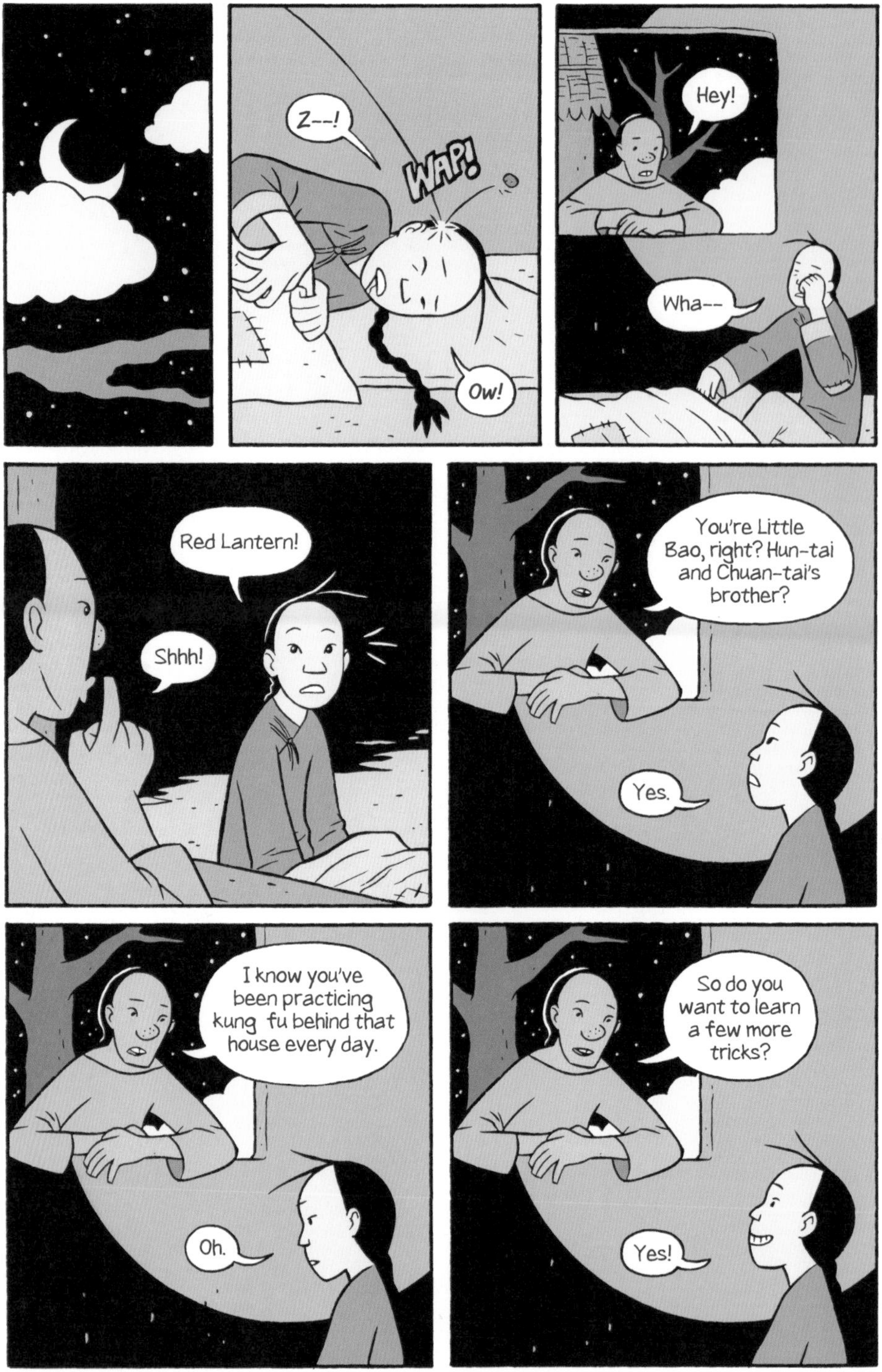
Z--!
WAP!
Ow!
Hey!
Wha--
Red Lantern!
Shhh!
You're Little Bao, right? Hun-tai and Chuan-tai's brother?
Yes.
I know you've been practicing kung fu behind that house every day.
Oh.
So do you want to learn a few more tricks?
Yes!

...I gather my Chi into my right hand so it becomes like a foreign devil's gun.

See that one leaf over there?

Yeah?

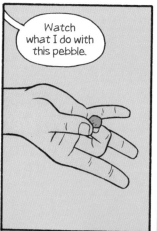

Watch what I do with this pebble.

FLICK!

TWAP!

Ha ha! See? So amazing!

Now you try!

FLICK!

!!

TWAP!

You're as amazing as me! You must've done this before!

Something like it...

--only with **human teeth.**

Hm.

Maybe I should show you some more kung fu combos instead.

Sure!

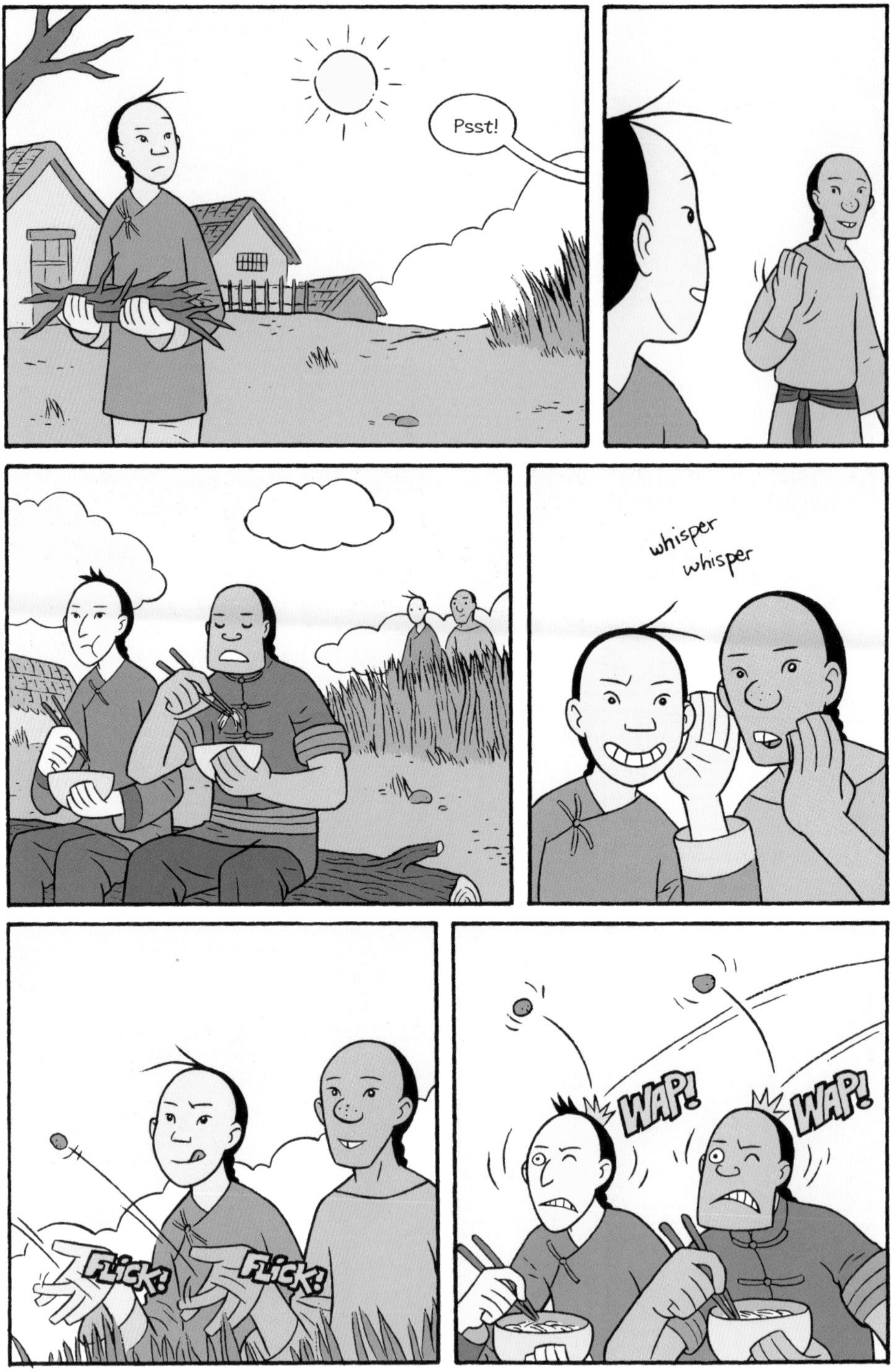
Psst!
whisper
whisper
FLICK!
FLICK!
WAP!
WAP!

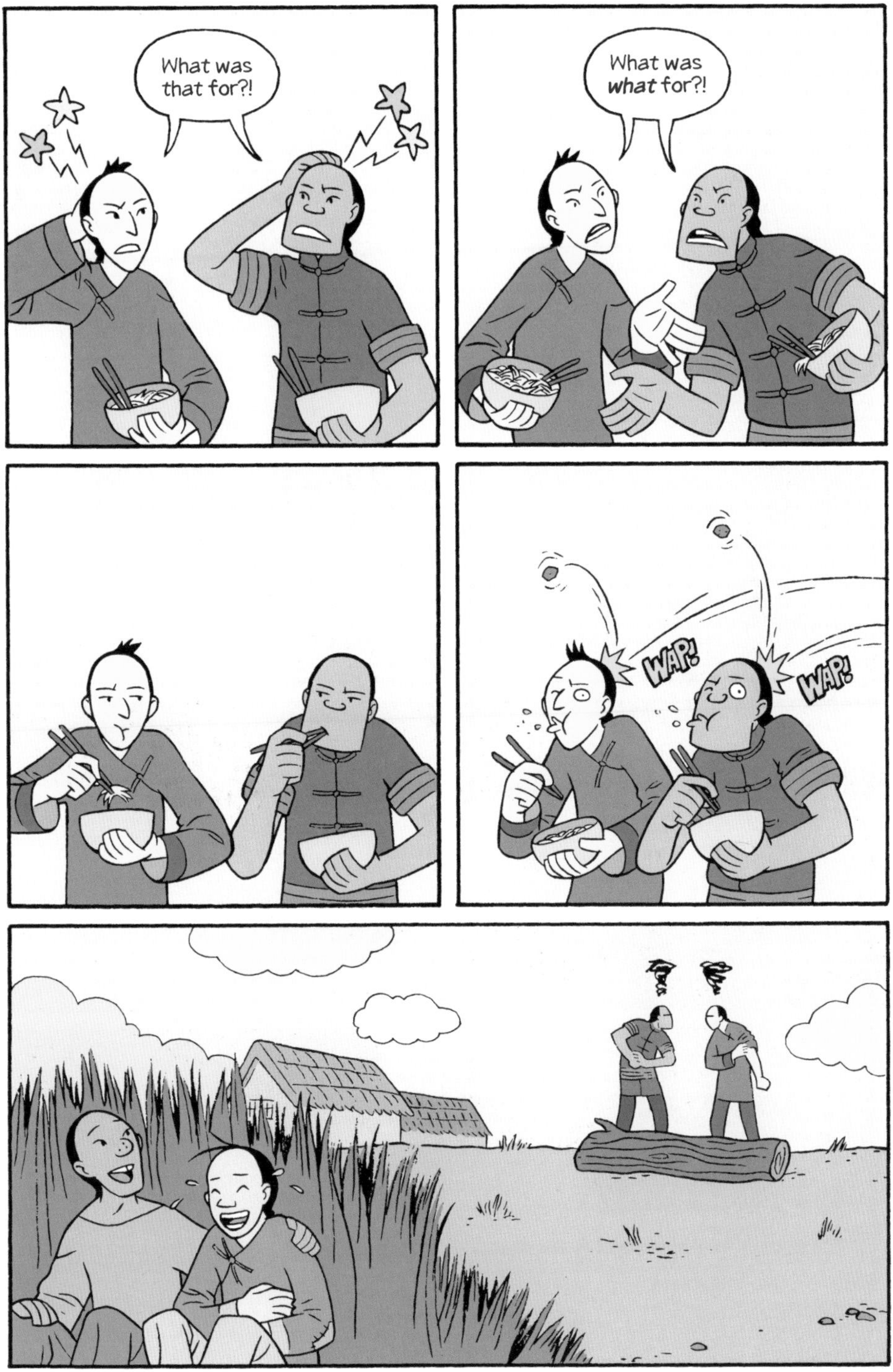
What was that for?!
What was *what* for?!
WAP!
WAP!

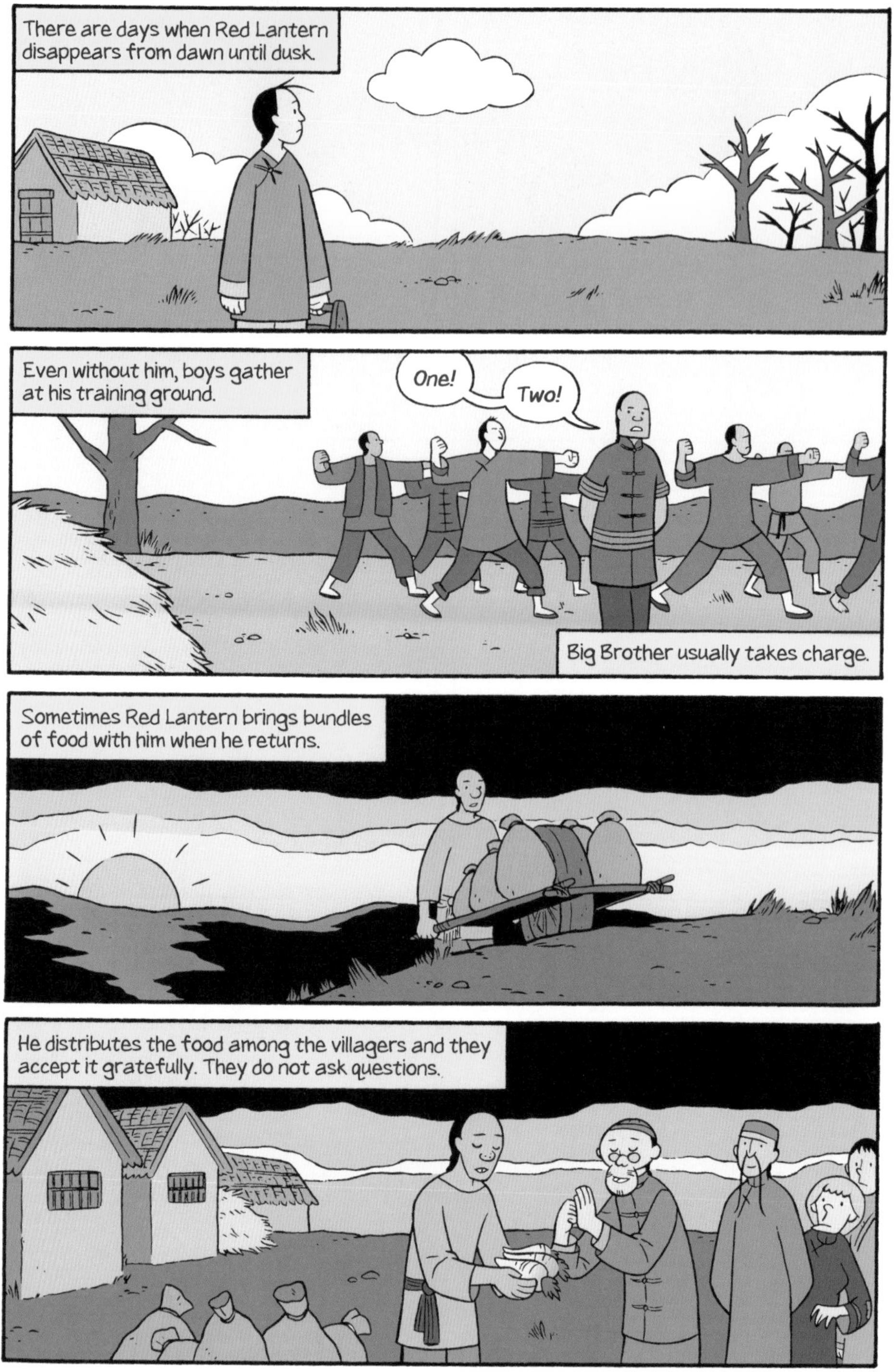
There are days when Red Lantern disappears from dawn until dusk.
Even without him, boys gather at his training ground.
One!
Two!
Big Brother usually takes charge.
Sometimes Red Lantern brings bundles of food with him when he returns.
He distributes the food among the villagers and they accept it gratefully. They do not ask questions.

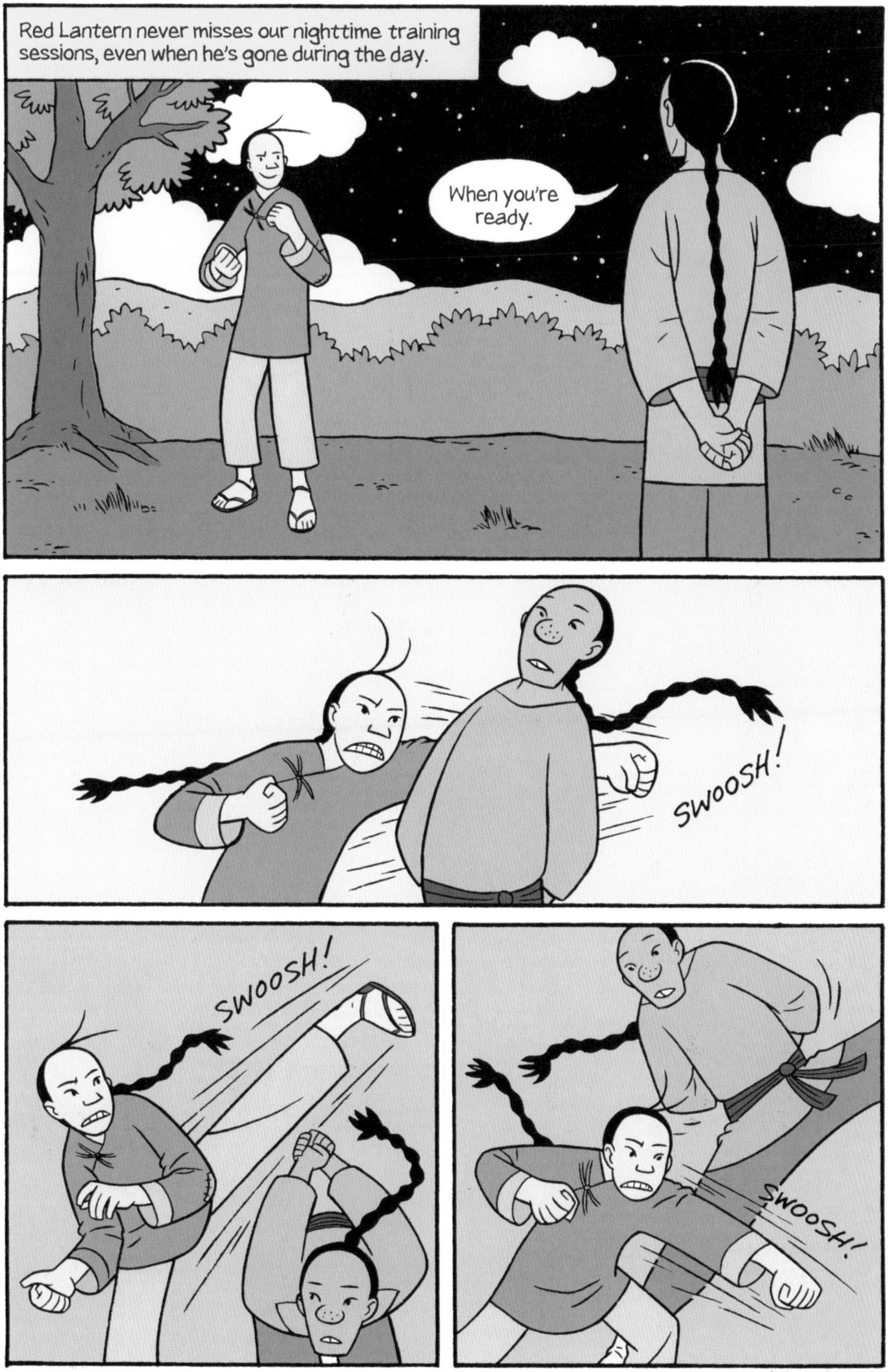
Red Lantern never misses our nighttime training sessions, even when he's gone during the day.
When you're ready.
SWOOSH!
SWOOSH!
SWOOSH!

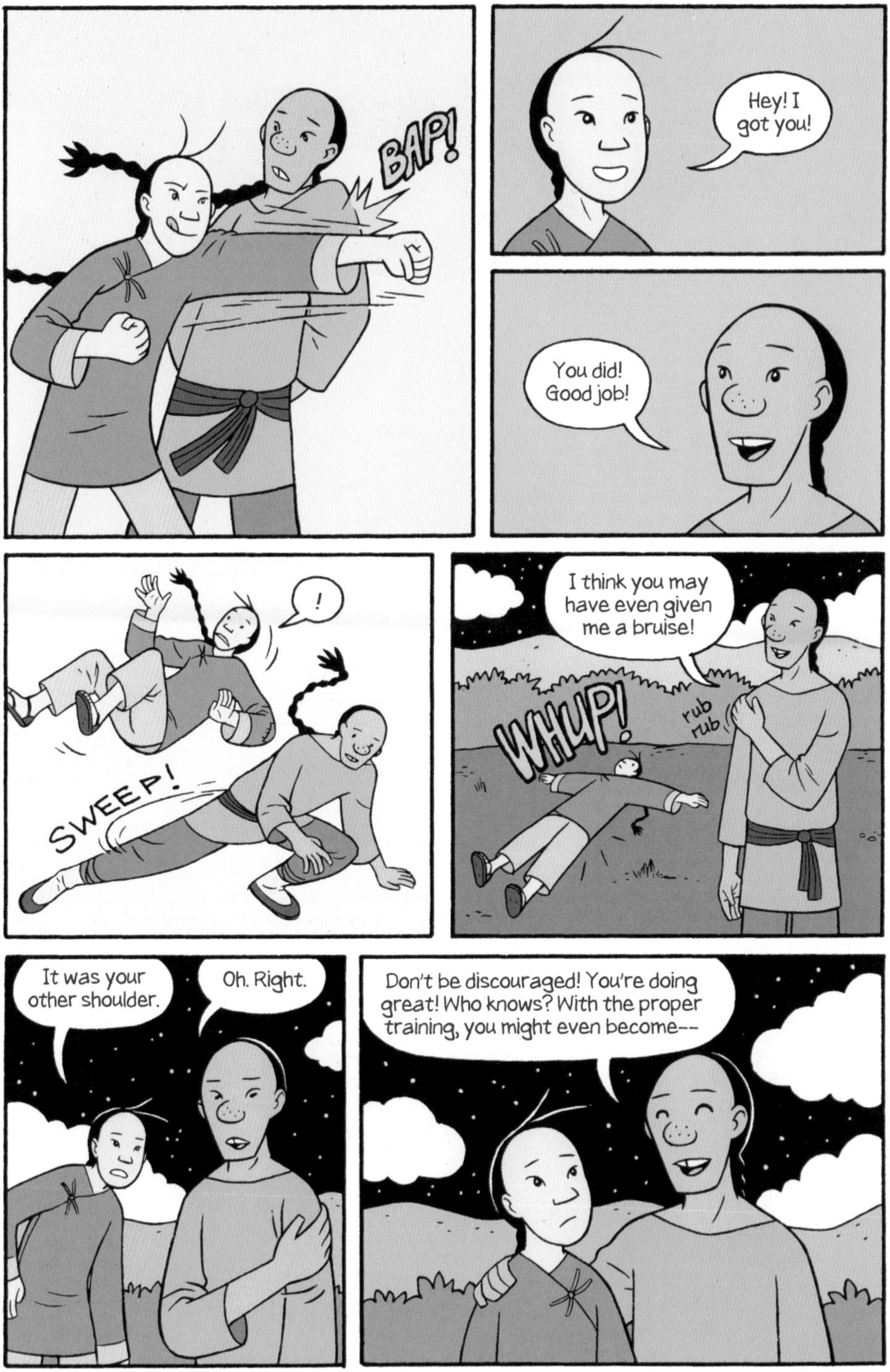
BAP!
Hey! I got you!
You did! Good job!
!
SWEEP!
I think you may have even given me a bruise!
WHUP!
rub rub
It was your other shoulder.
Oh. Right.
Don't be discouraged! You're doing great! Who knows? With the proper training, you might even become--

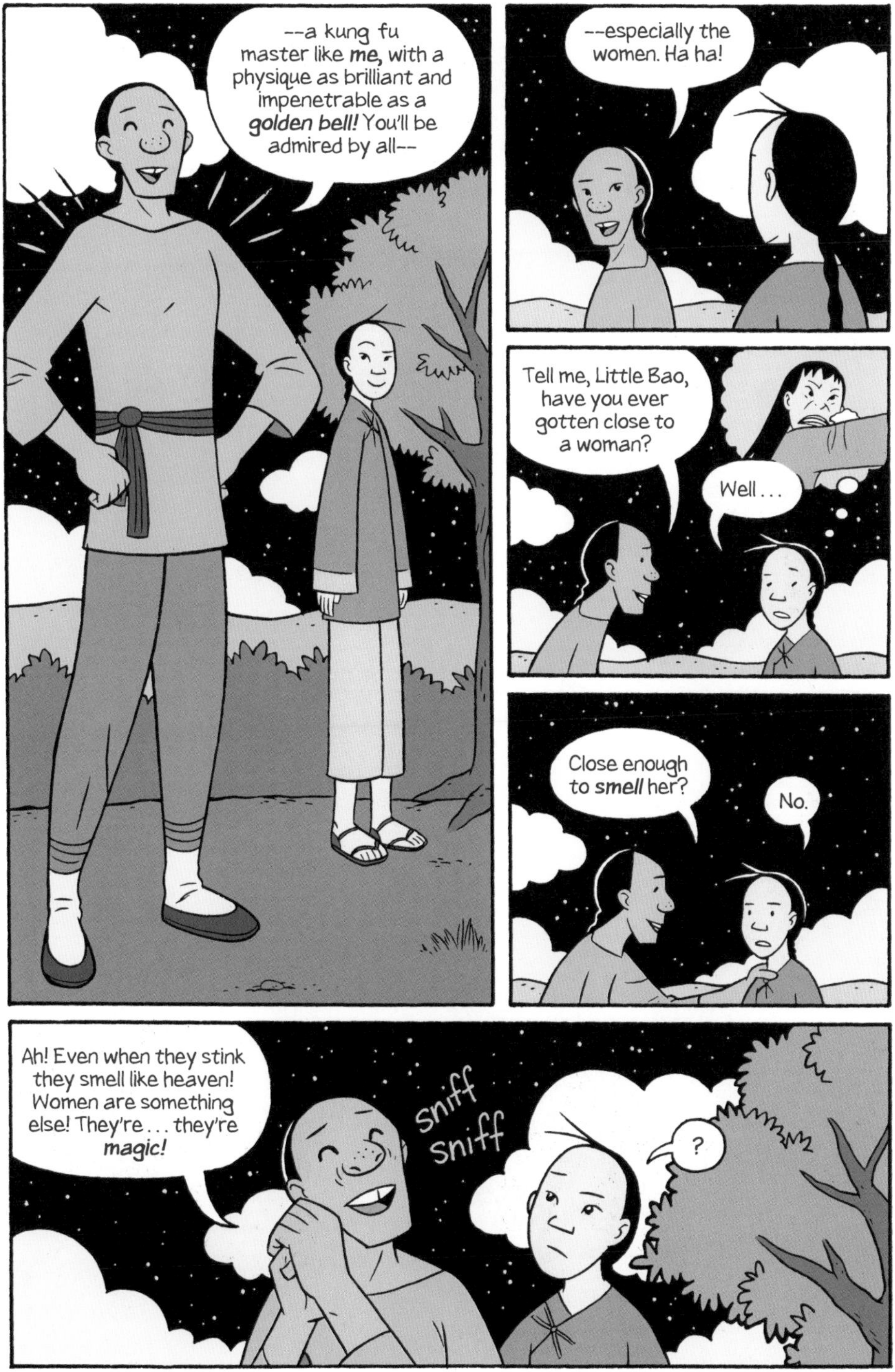
--a kung fu master like **me,** with a physique as brilliant and impenetrable as a ***golden bell!*** You'll be admired by all--
--especially the women. Ha ha!
Tell me, Little Bao, have you ever gotten close to a woman?
Well . . .
Close enough to ***smell*** her?
No.
Ah! Even when they stink they smell like heaven! Women are something else! They're . . . they're ***magic!***
sniff sniff
?

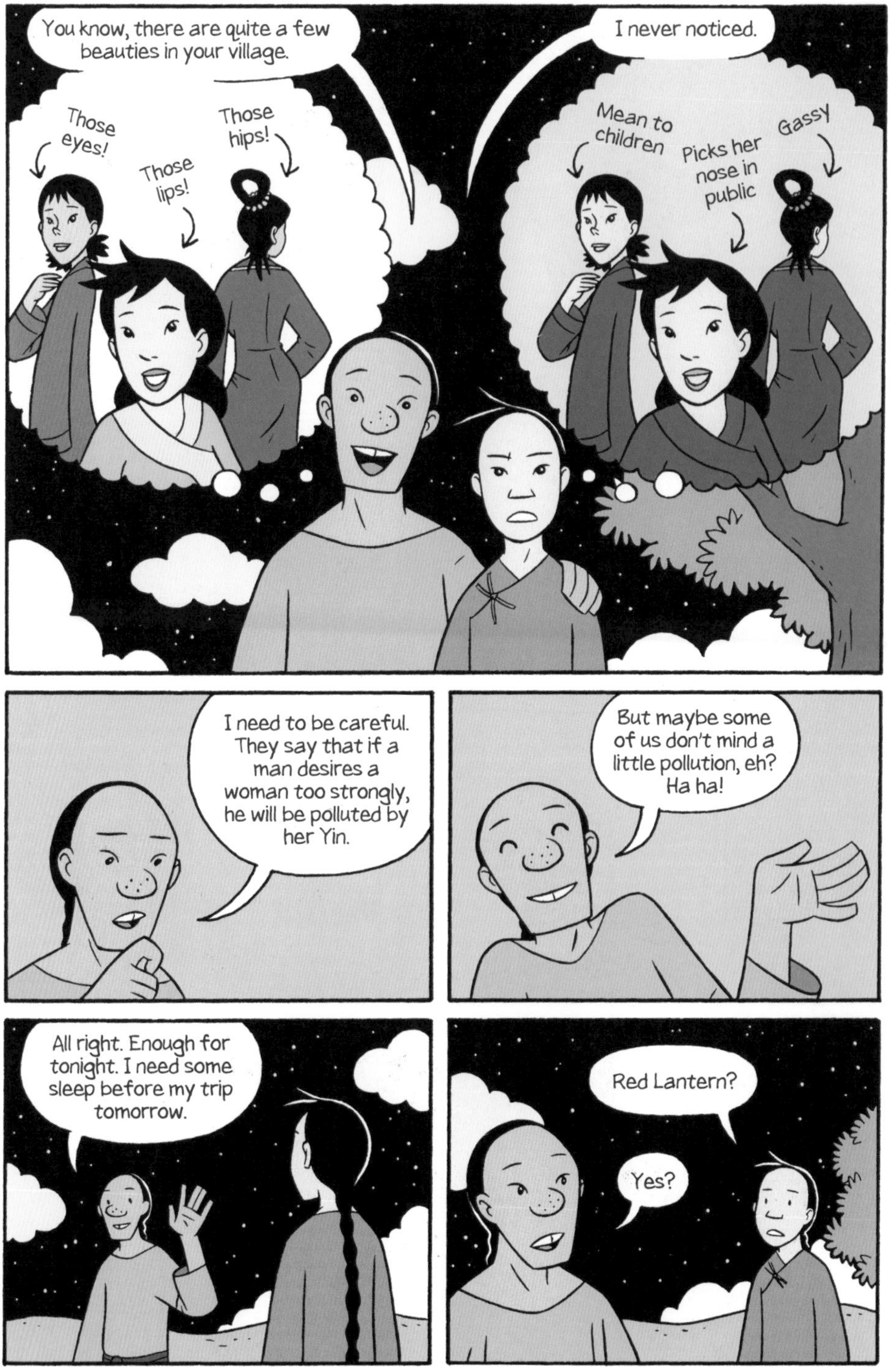
You know, there are quite a few beauties in your village.
Those eyes!
Those lips!
Those hips!
I never noticed.
Mean to children
Picks her nose in public
Gassy
I need to be careful. They say that if a man desires a woman too strongly, he will be polluted by her Yin.
But maybe some of us don't mind a little pollution, eh? Ha ha!
All right. Enough for tonight. I need some sleep before my trip tomorrow.
Red Lantern?
Yes?

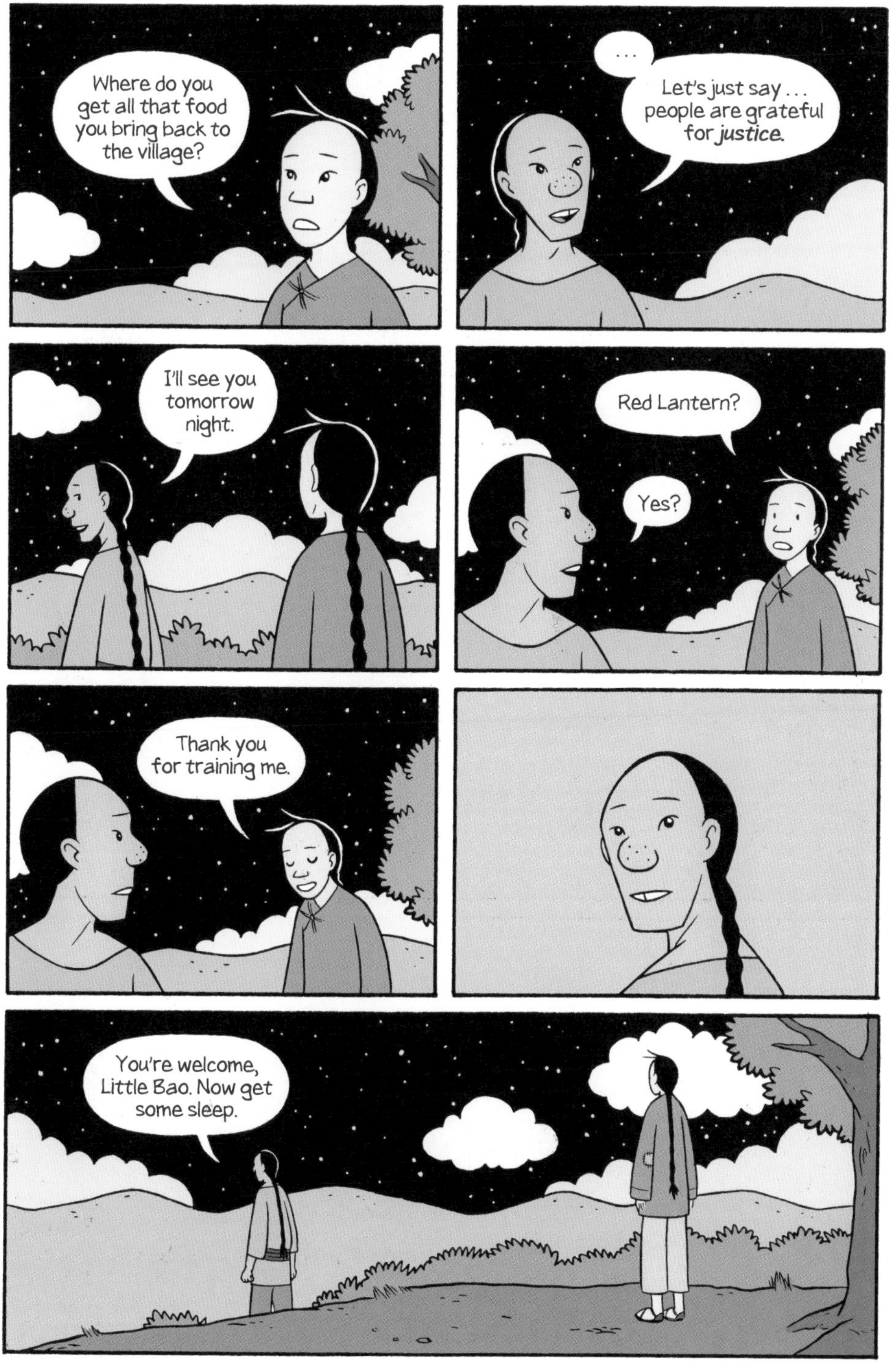
Where do you get all that food you bring back to the village?
. . .
Let's just say . . . people are grateful for *justice*.
I'll see you tomorrow night.
Red Lantern?
Yes?
Thank you for training me.
You're welcome, Little Bao. Now get some sleep.

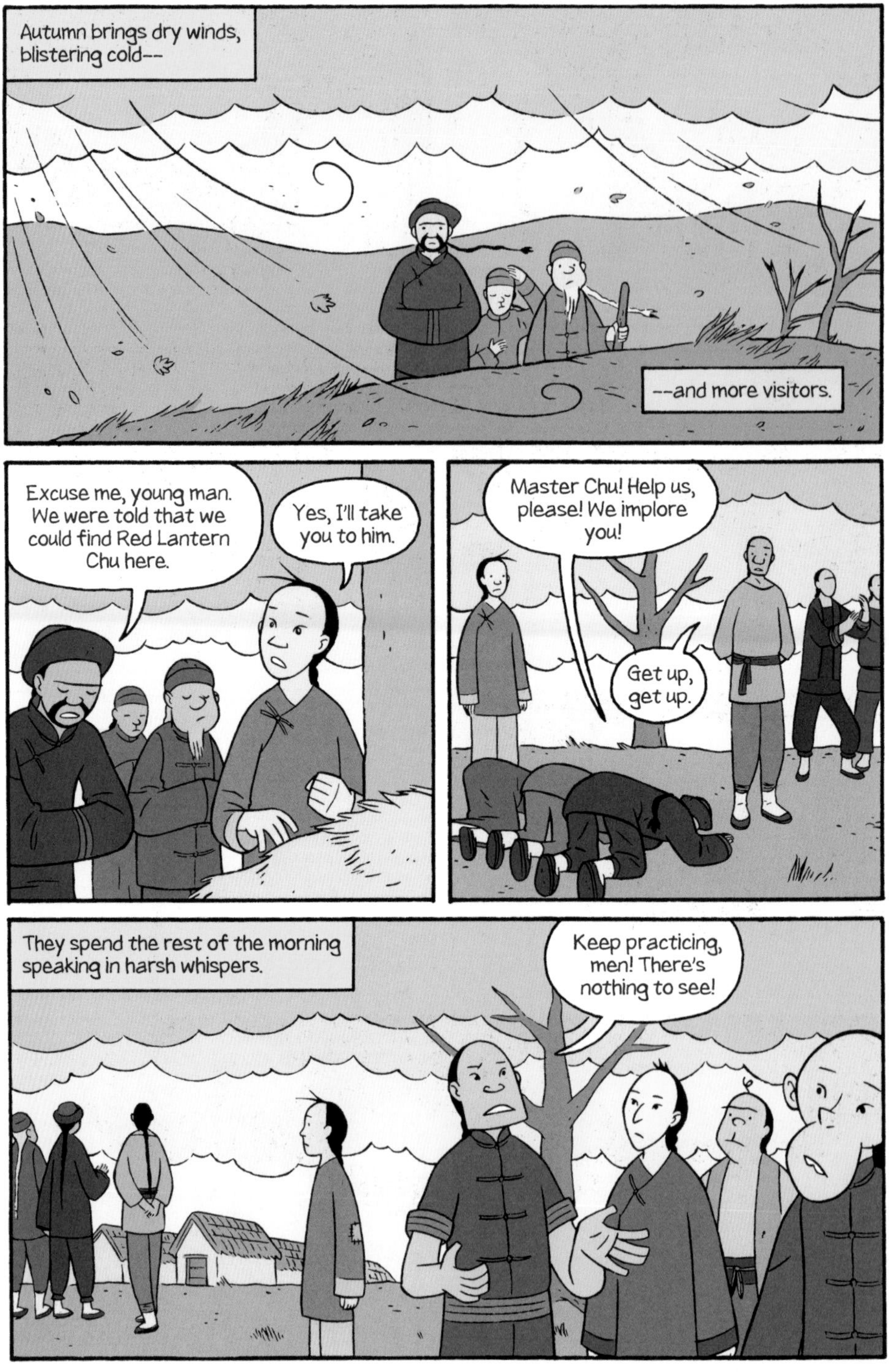
Autumn brings dry winds, blistering cold--
--and more visitors.
Excuse me, young man. We were told that we could find Red Lantern Chu here.
Yes, I'll take you to him.
Master Chu! Help us, please! We implore you!
Get up, get up.
They spend the rest of the morning speaking in harsh whispers.
Keep practicing, men! There's nothing to see!

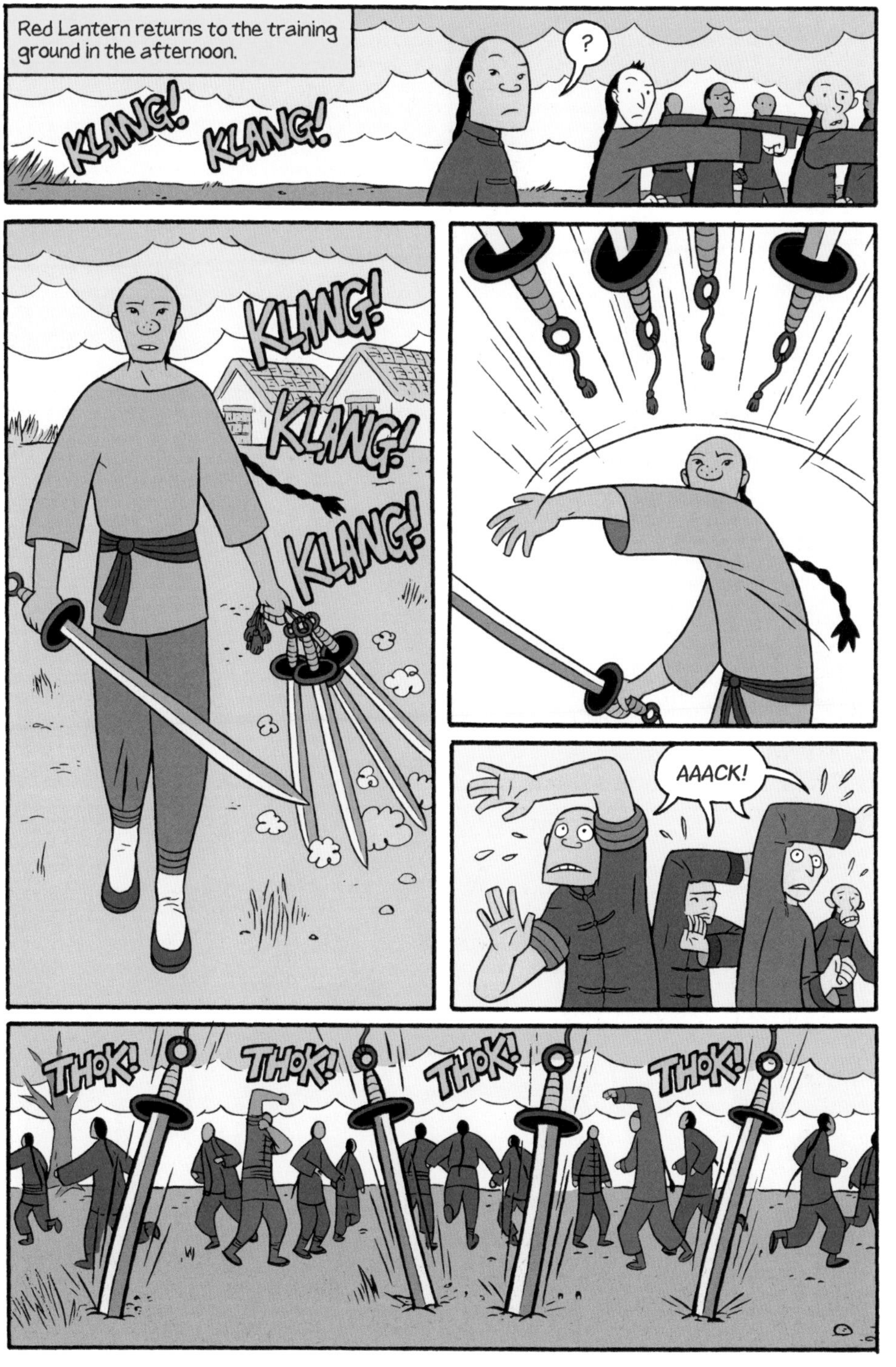
Red Lantern returns to the training ground in the afternoon.
?
KLANG! KLANG!
KLANG!
KLANG!
KLANG!
AAACK!
THOK! THOK! THOK! THOK!

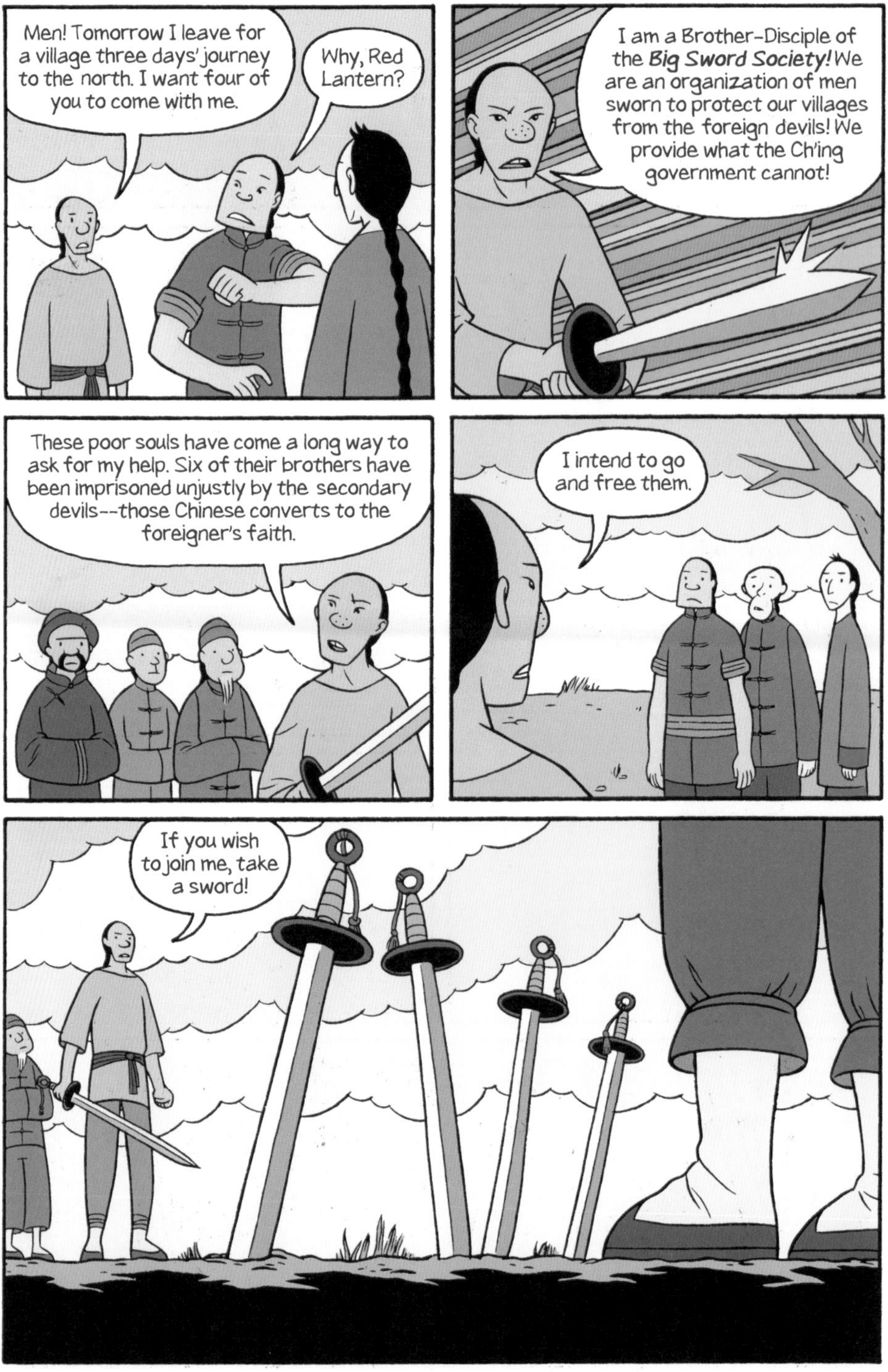
Men! Tomorrow I leave for a village three days' journey to the north. I want four of you to come with me.
Why, Red Lantern?
I am a Brother-Disciple of the Big Sword Society! We are an organization of men sworn to protect our villages from the foreign devils! We provide what the Ch'ing government cannot!
These poor souls have come a long way to ask for my help. Six of their brothers have been imprisoned unjustly by the secondary devils--those Chinese converts to the foreigner's faith.
I intend to go and free them.
If you wish to join me, take a sword!

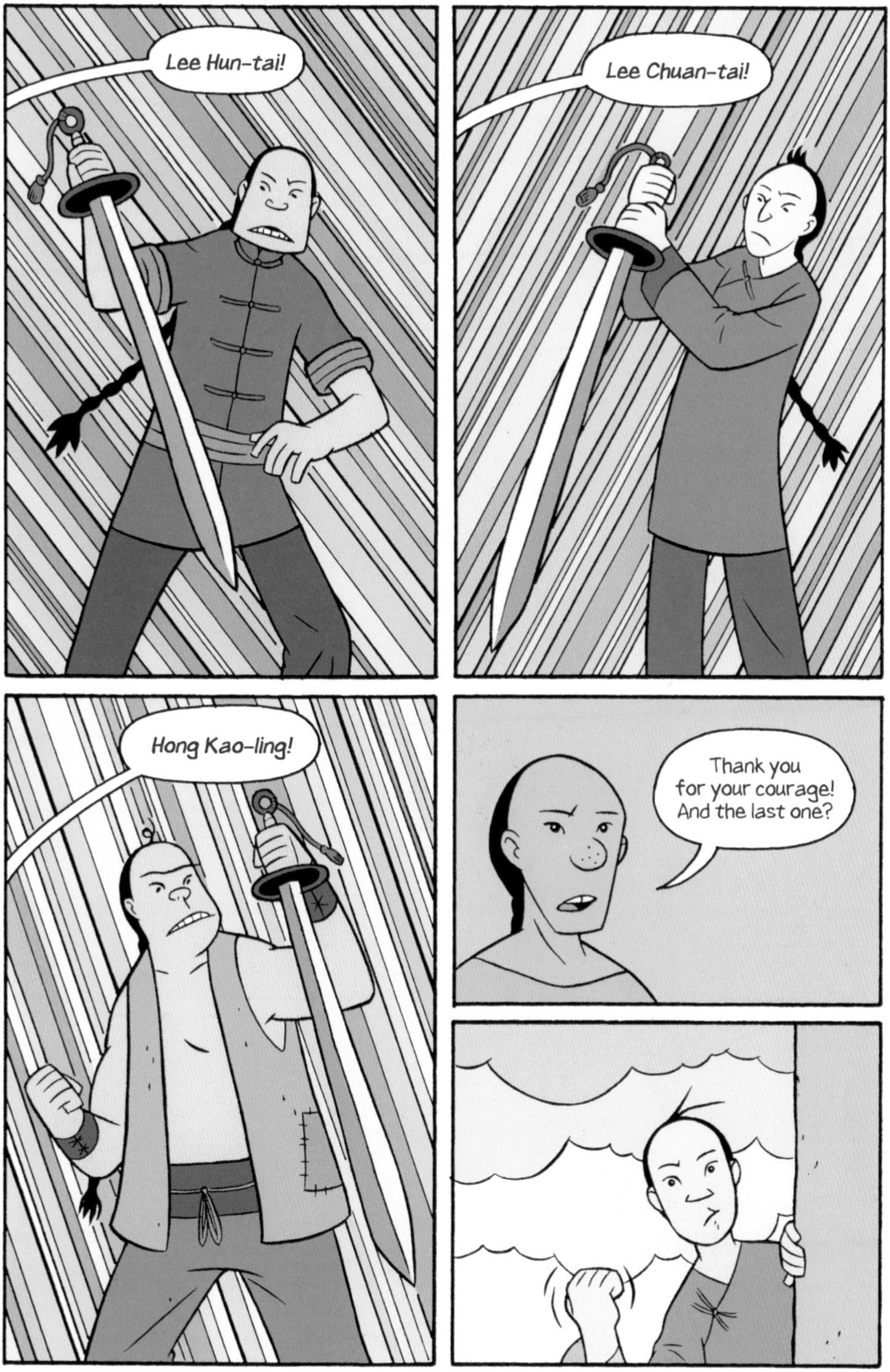

Lee Hun-tai!
Lee Chuan-tai!
Hong Kao-ling!
Thank you for your courage! And the last one?

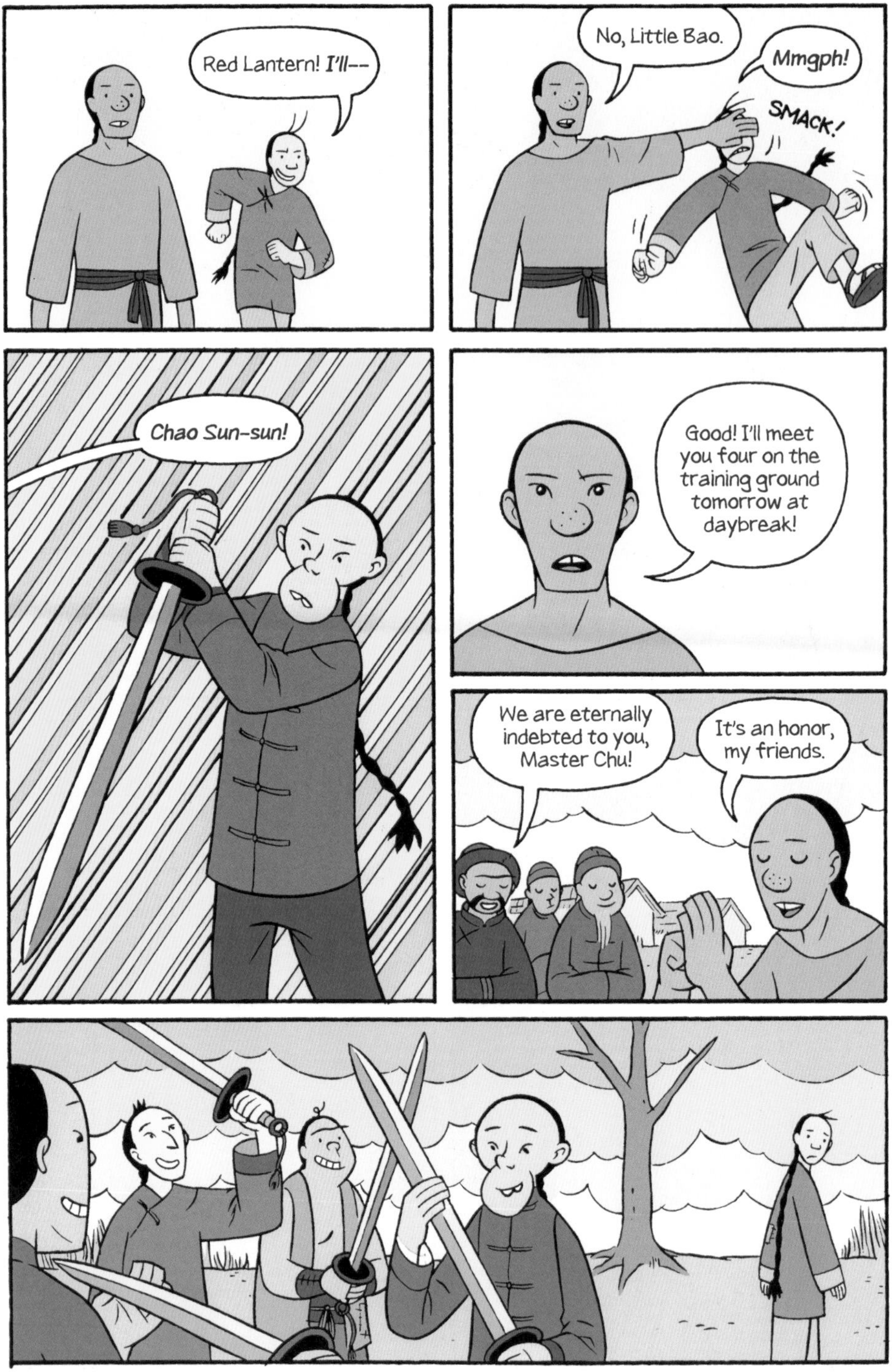
Red Lantern! I'll--
No, Little Bao.
Mmgph!
SMACK!
Chao Sun-sun!
Good! I'll meet you four on the training ground tomorrow at daybreak!
We are eternally indebted to you, Master Chu!
It's an honor, my friends.

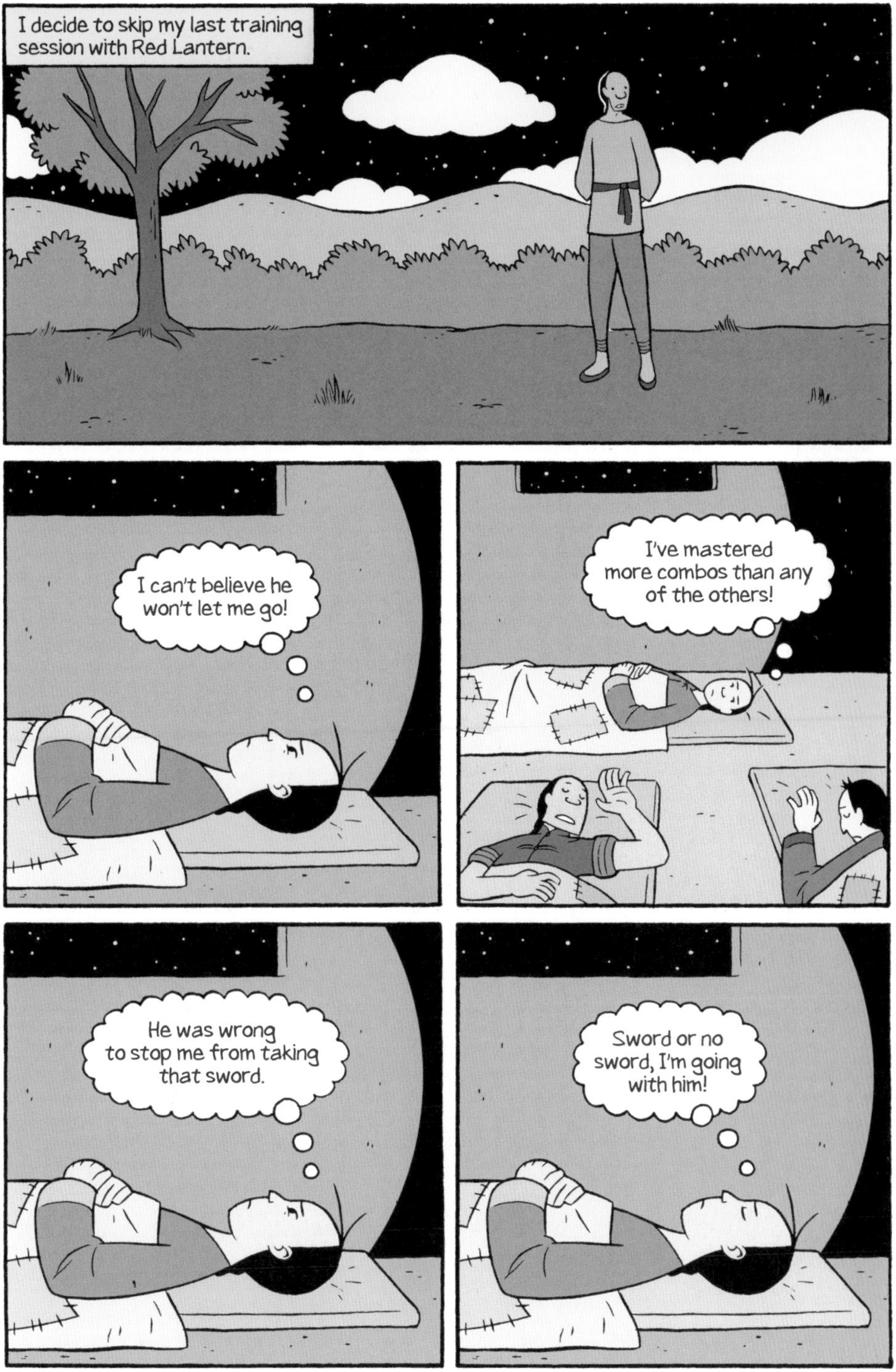
I decide to skip my last training session with Red Lantern.
I can't believe he won't let me go!
I've mastered more combos than any of the others!
He was wrong to stop me from taking that sword.
Sword or no sword, I'm going with him!

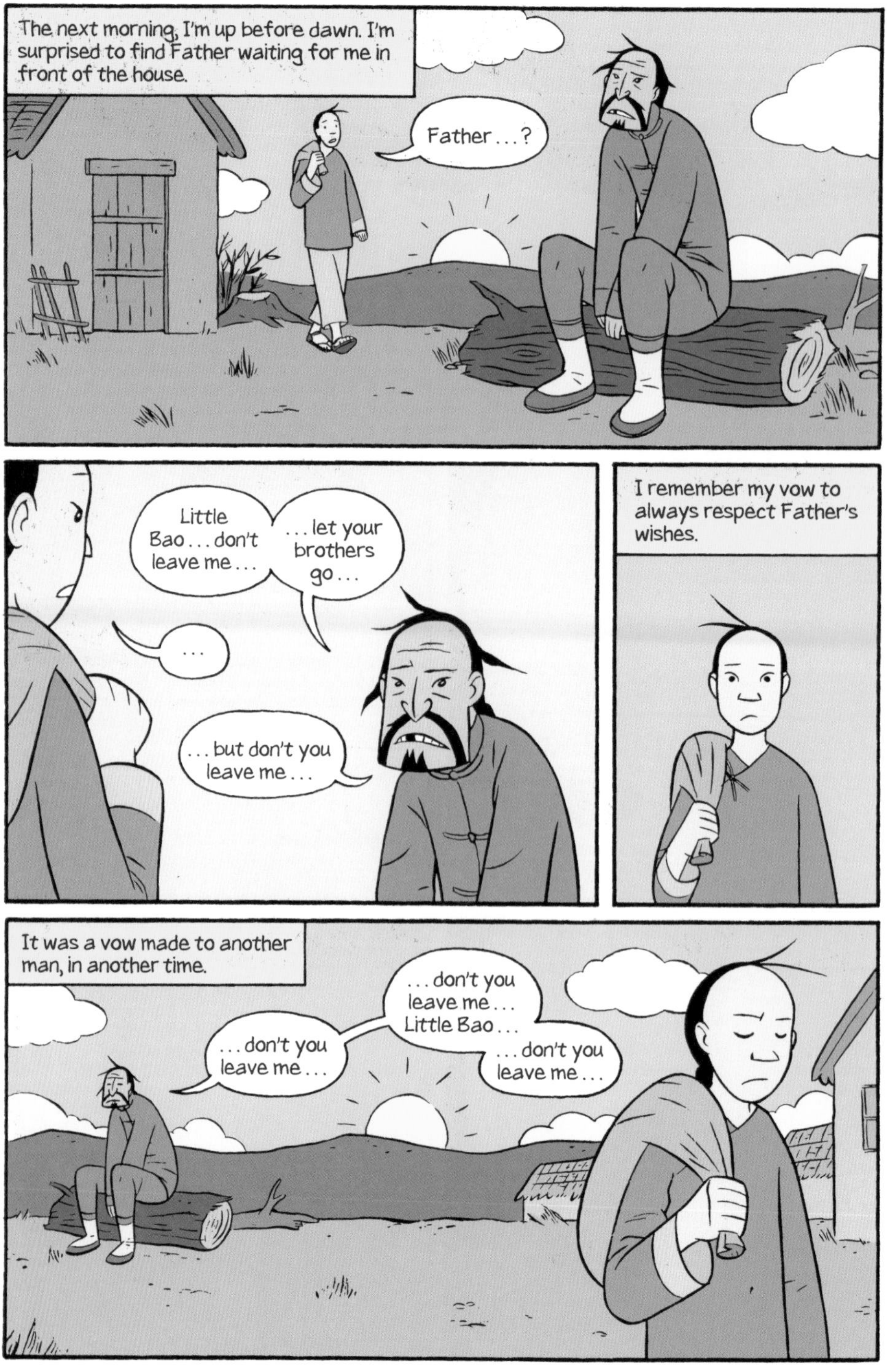

The next morning, I'm up before dawn. I'm surprised to find Father waiting for me in front of the house.
Father . . . ?
Little Bao . . . don't leave me . . .
. . . let your brothers go . . .
. . .
. . . but don't you leave me . . .
I remember my vow to always respect Father's wishes.
It was a vow made to another man, in another time.
. . . don't you leave me . . .
. . . don't you leave me . . . Little Bao . . .
. . . don't you leave me . . .

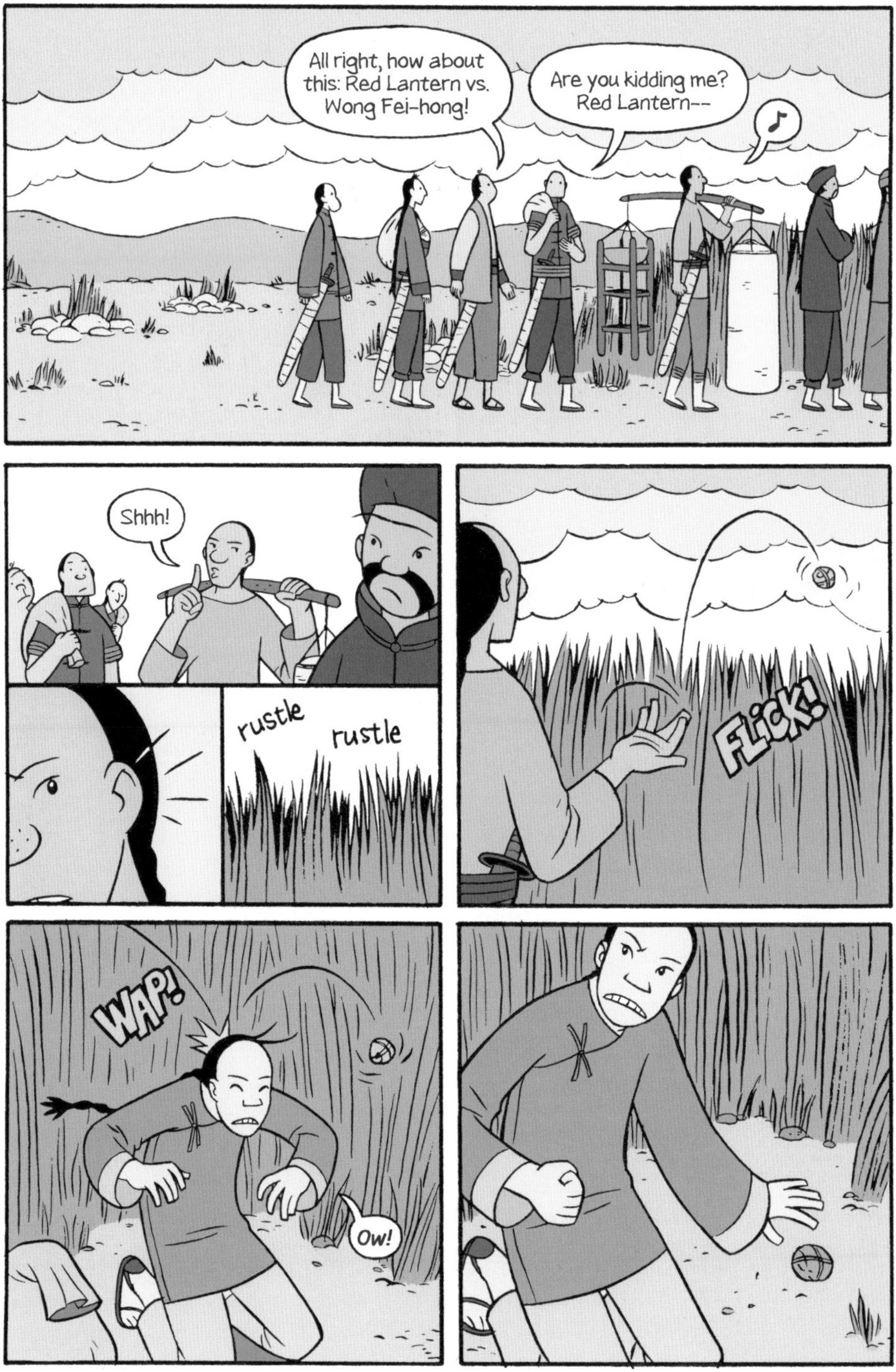
All right, how about this: Red Lantern vs. Wong Fei-hong!
Are you kidding me? Red Lantern--
♪
Shhh!
rustle
rustle
FLICK!
WAP!
Ow!

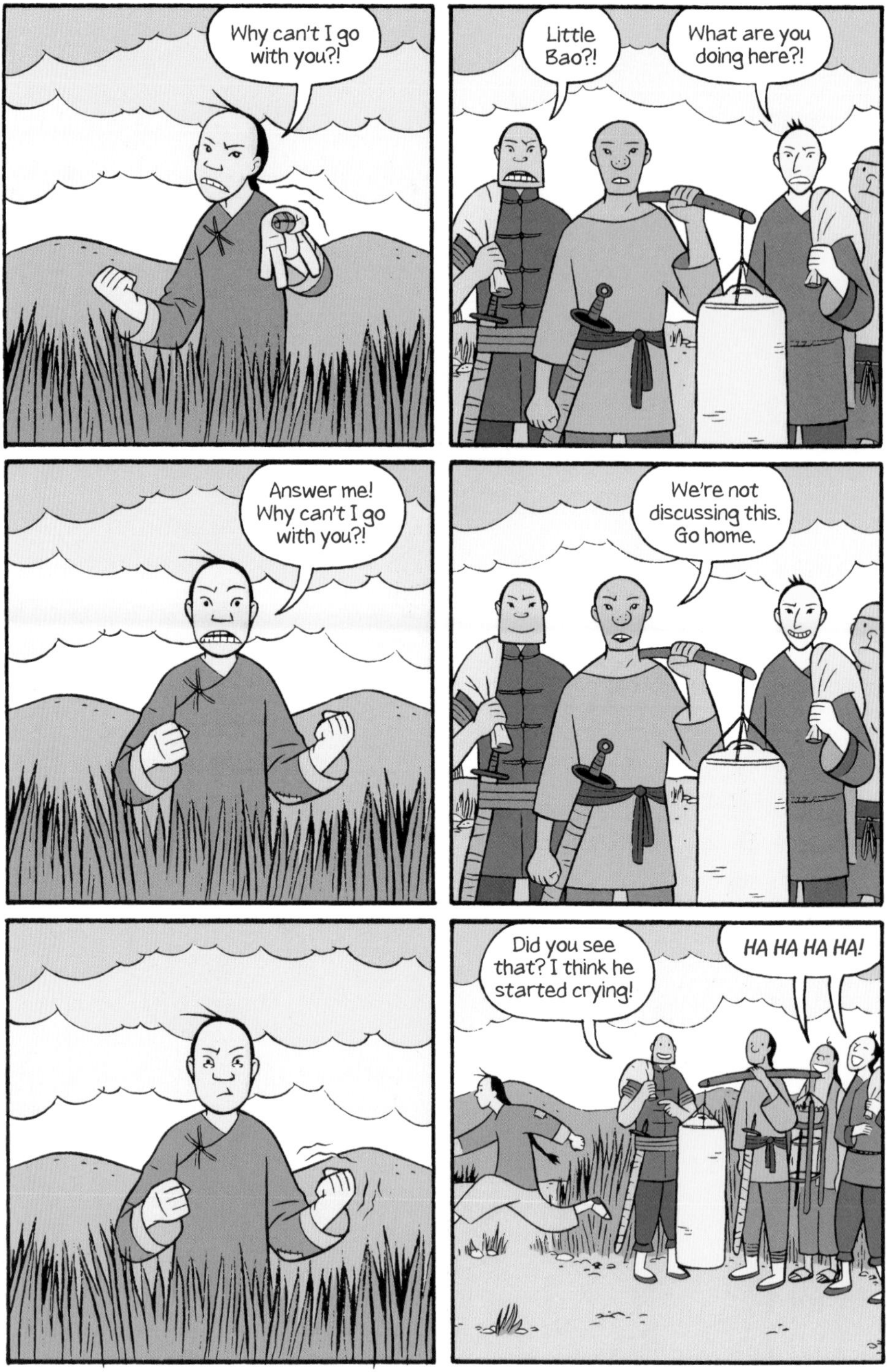
Why can't I go with you?!
Little Bao?!
What are you doing here?!
Answer me! Why can't I go with you?!
We're not discussing this. Go home.
Did you see that? I think he started crying!
HA HA HA HA!

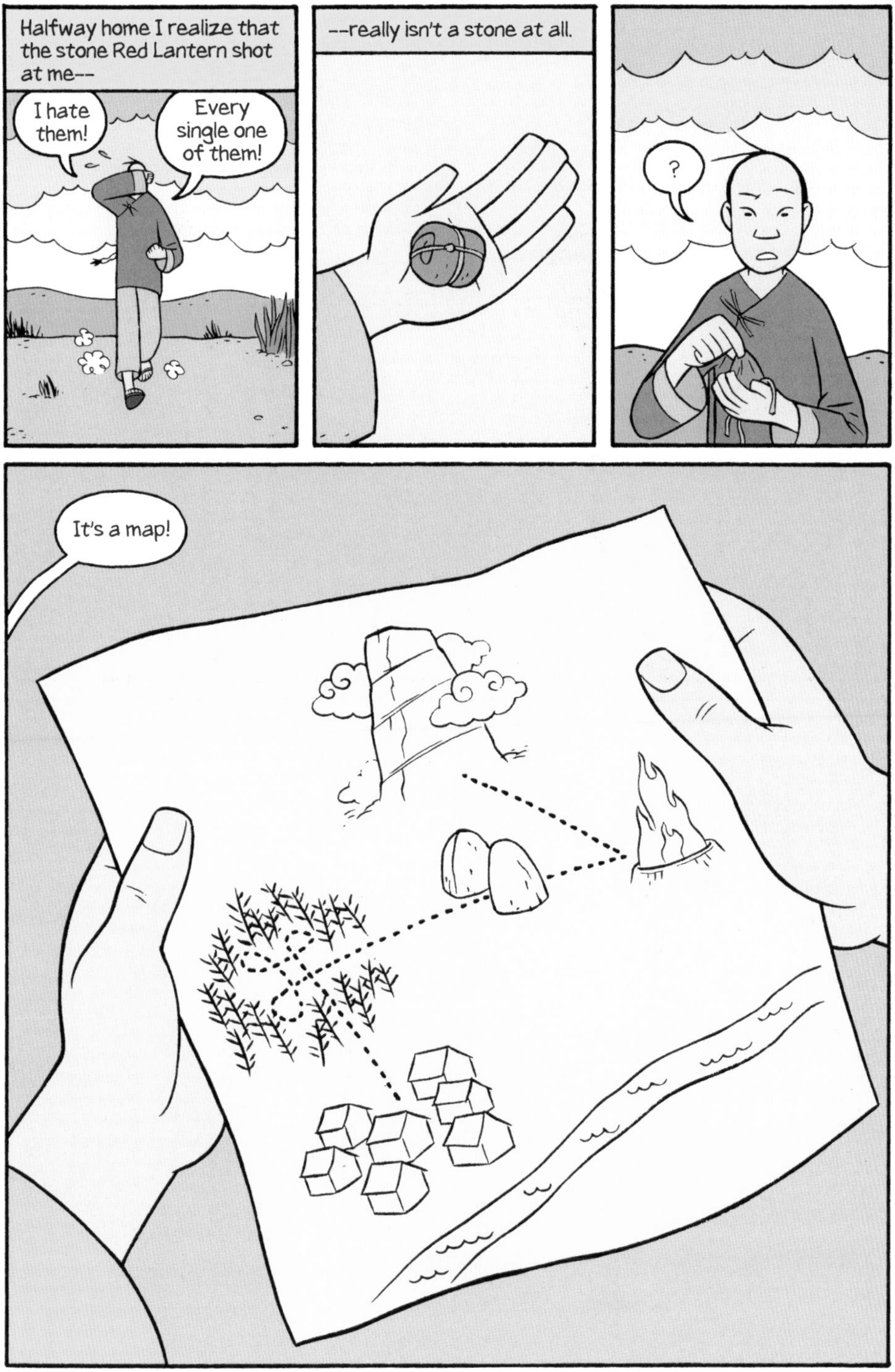
Halfway home I realize that the stone Red Lantern shot at me--
I hate them!
Every single one of them!
--really isn't a stone at all.
?
It's a map!

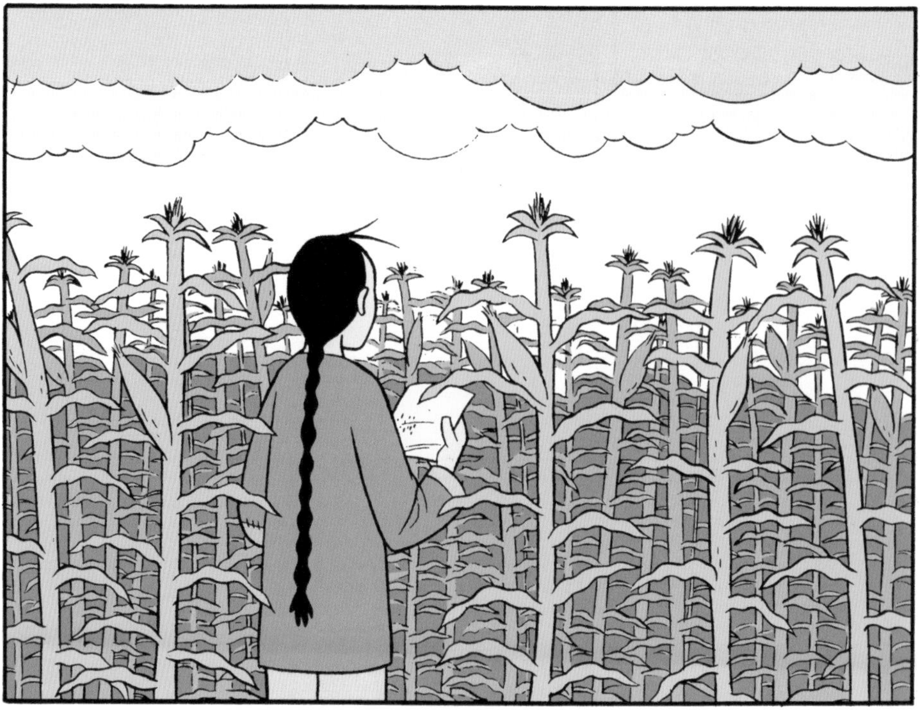

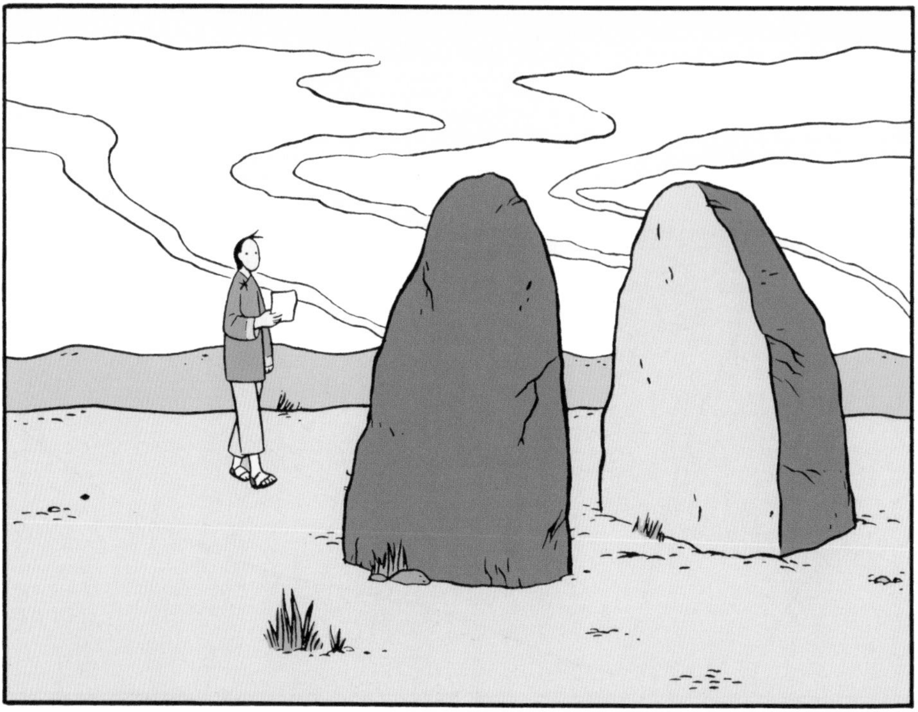

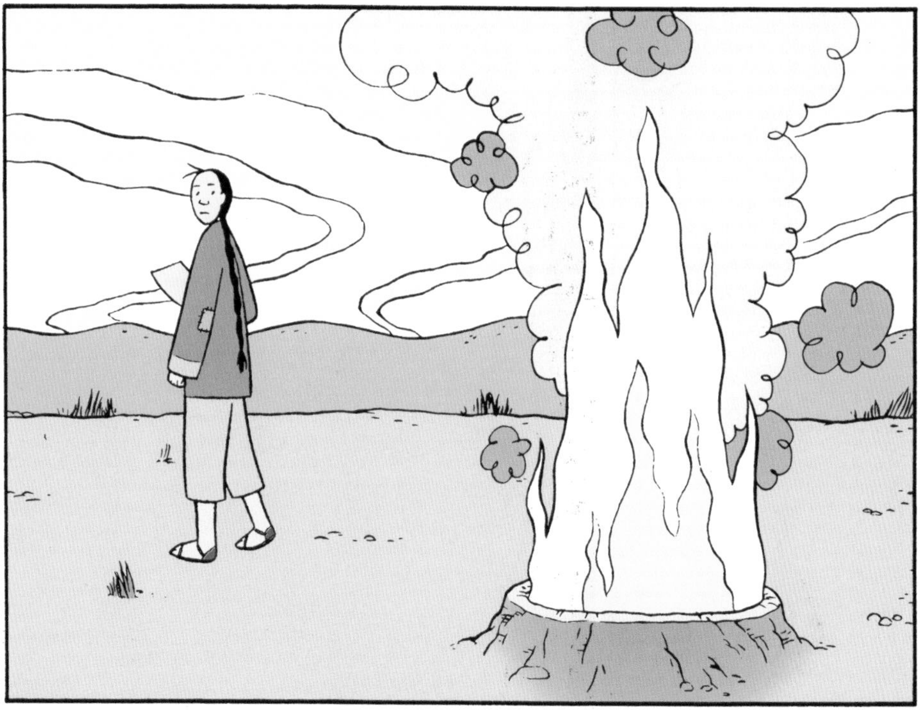

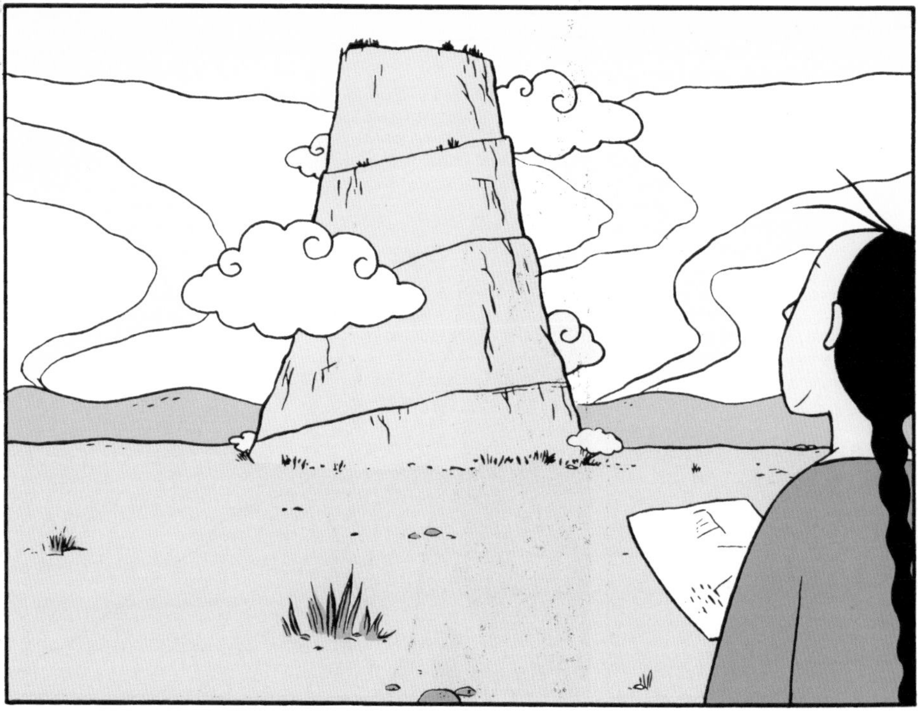

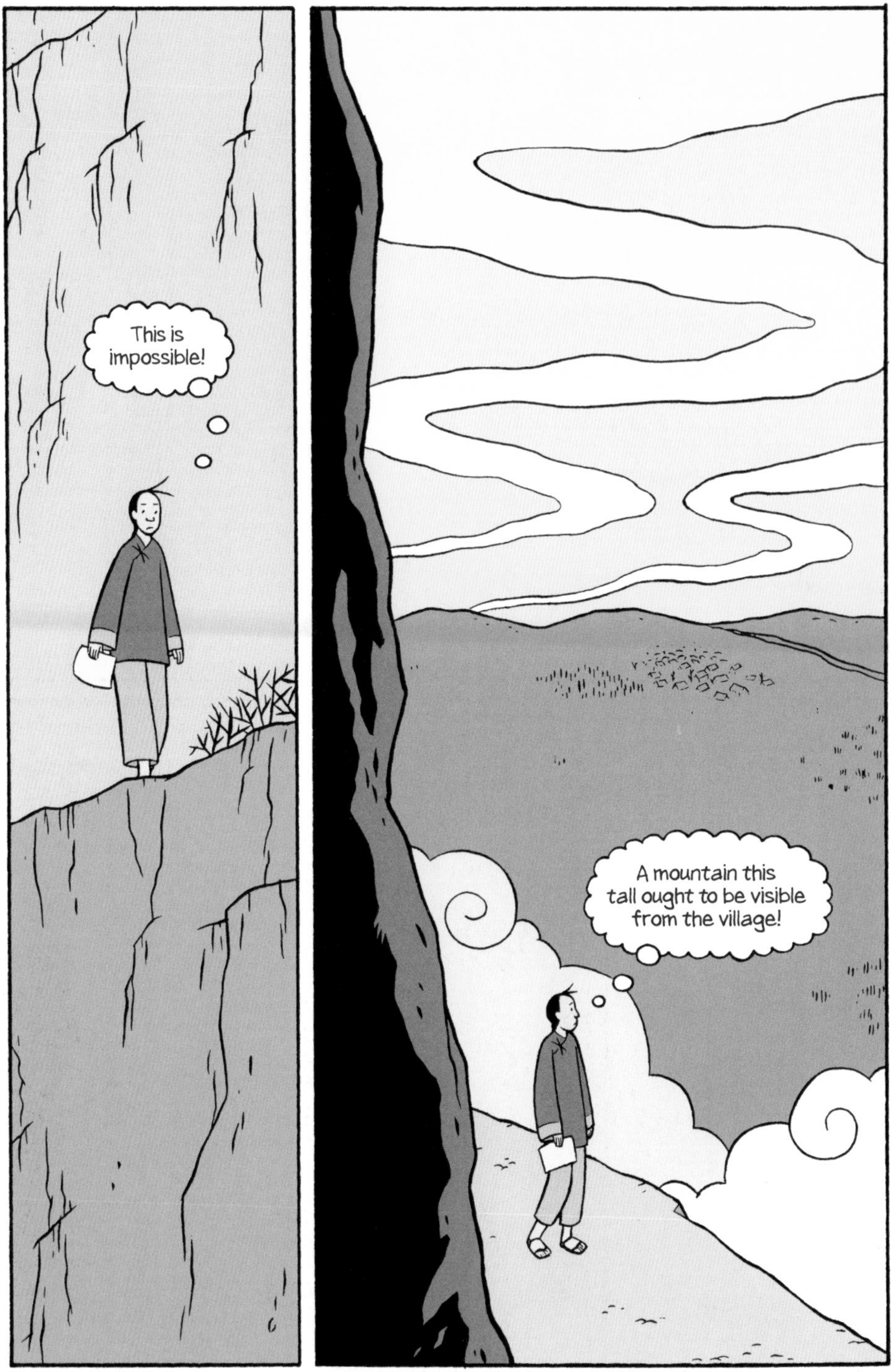
This is impossible!
A mountain this tall ought to be visible from the village!

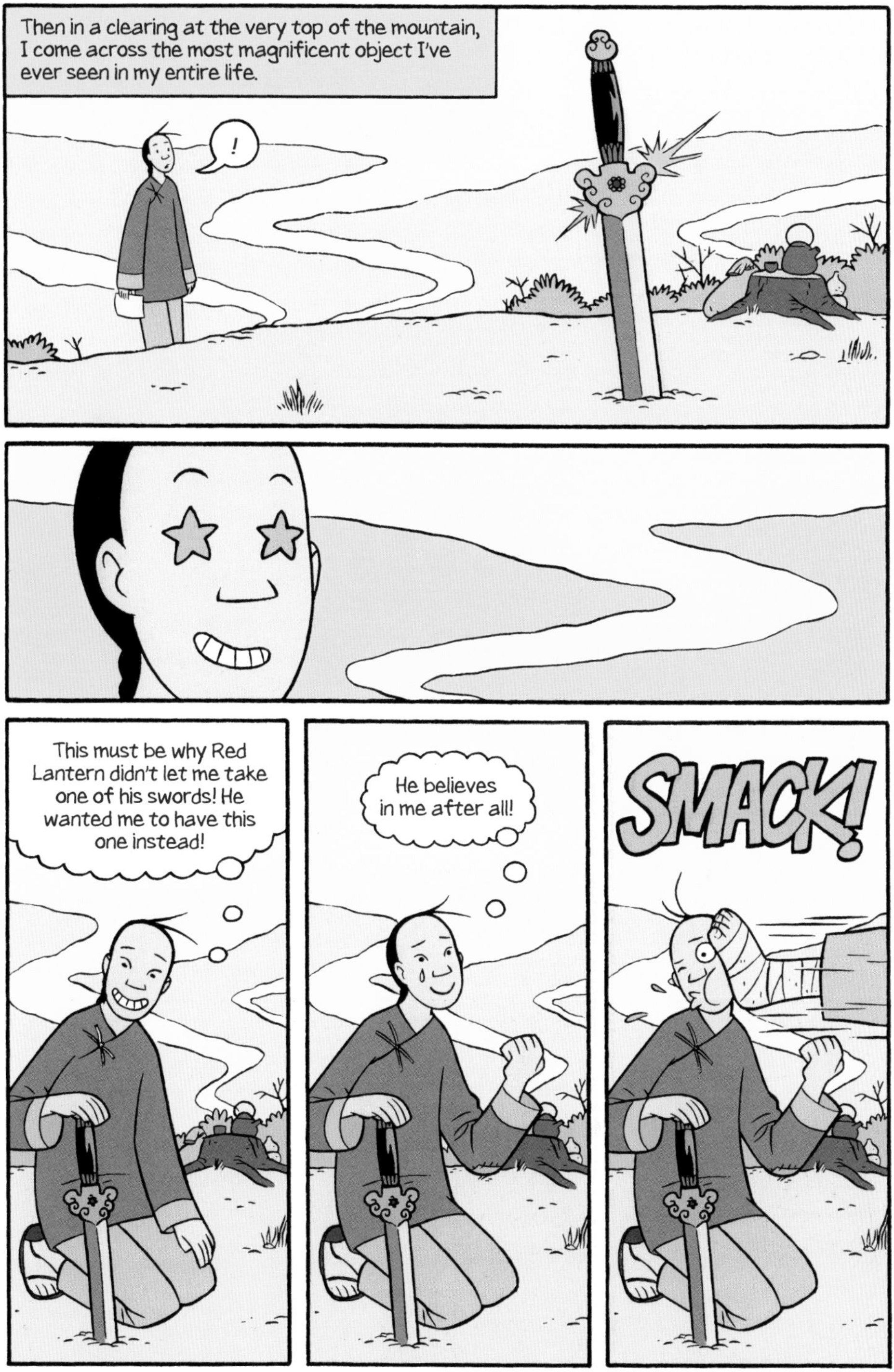
Then in a clearing at the very top of the mountain, I come across the most magnificent object I've ever seen in my entire life.
!
This must be why Red Lantern didn't let me take one of his swords! He wanted me to have this one instead!
He believes in me after all!
SMACK!

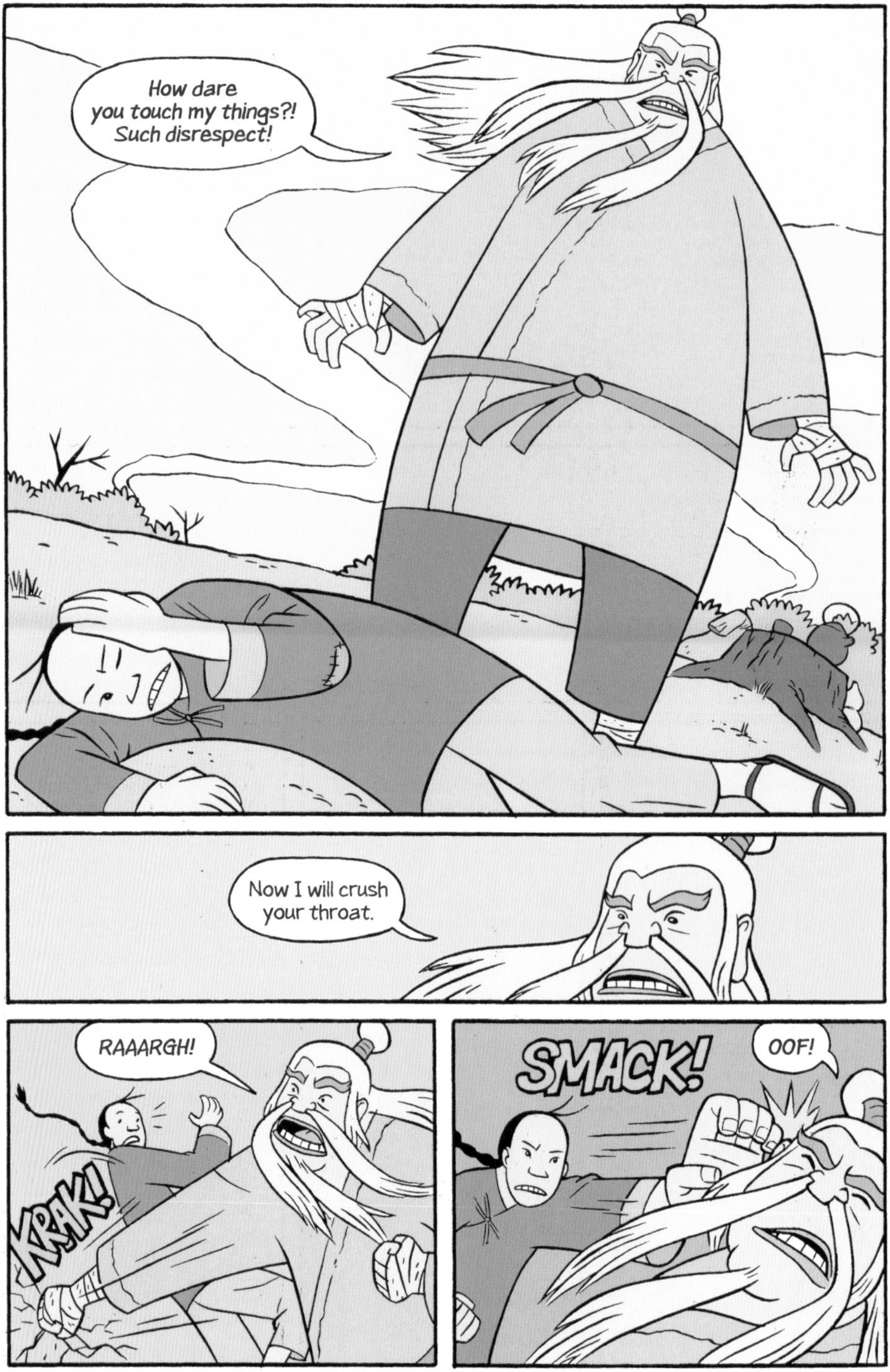
How dare you touch my things?! Such disrespect!
Now I will crush your throat.
RAAARGH!
KRAK!
SMACK!
OOF!

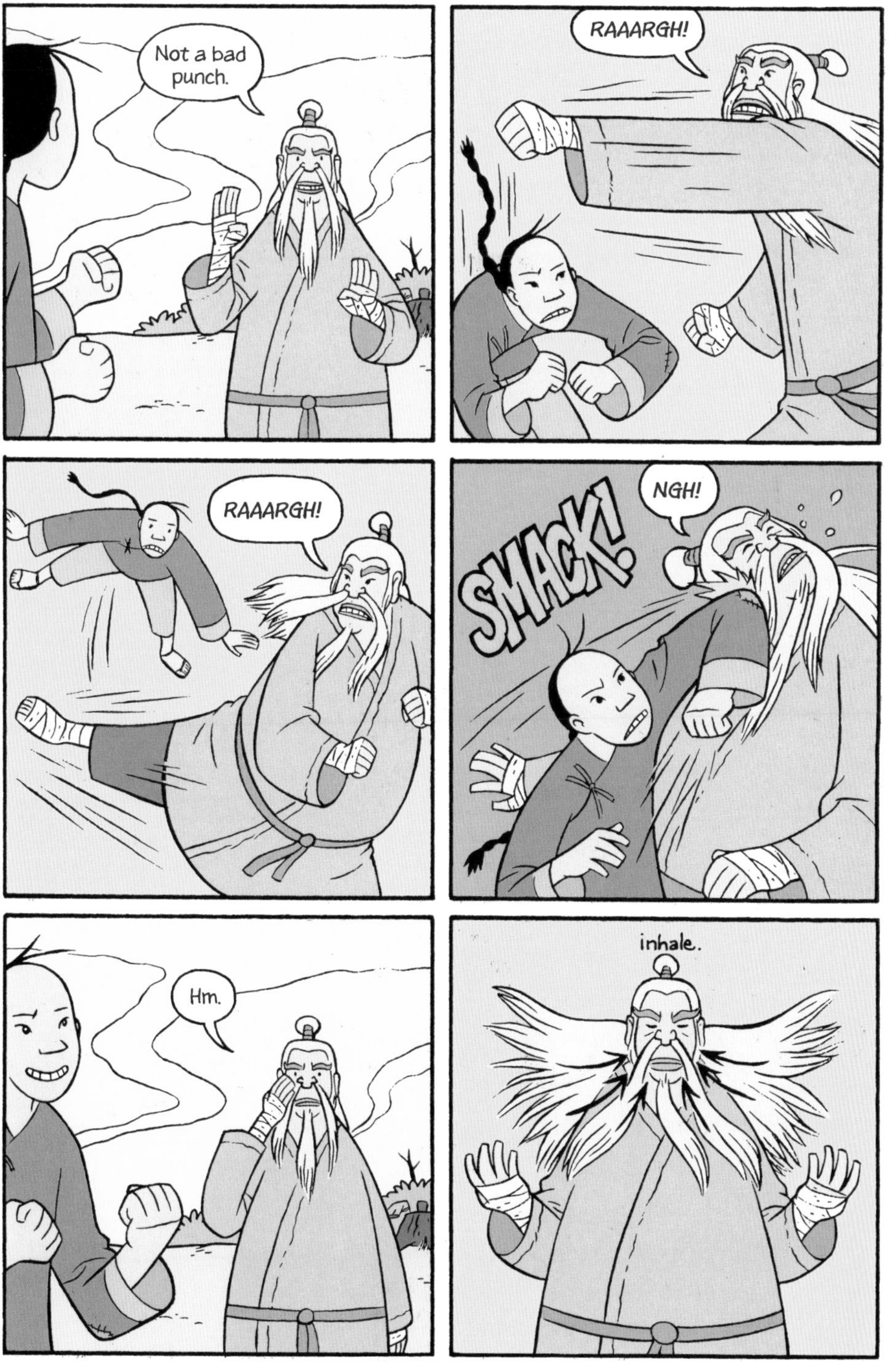
Not a bad punch.
RAAARGH!
RAAARGH!
NGH!
SMACK!
Hm.
inhale.

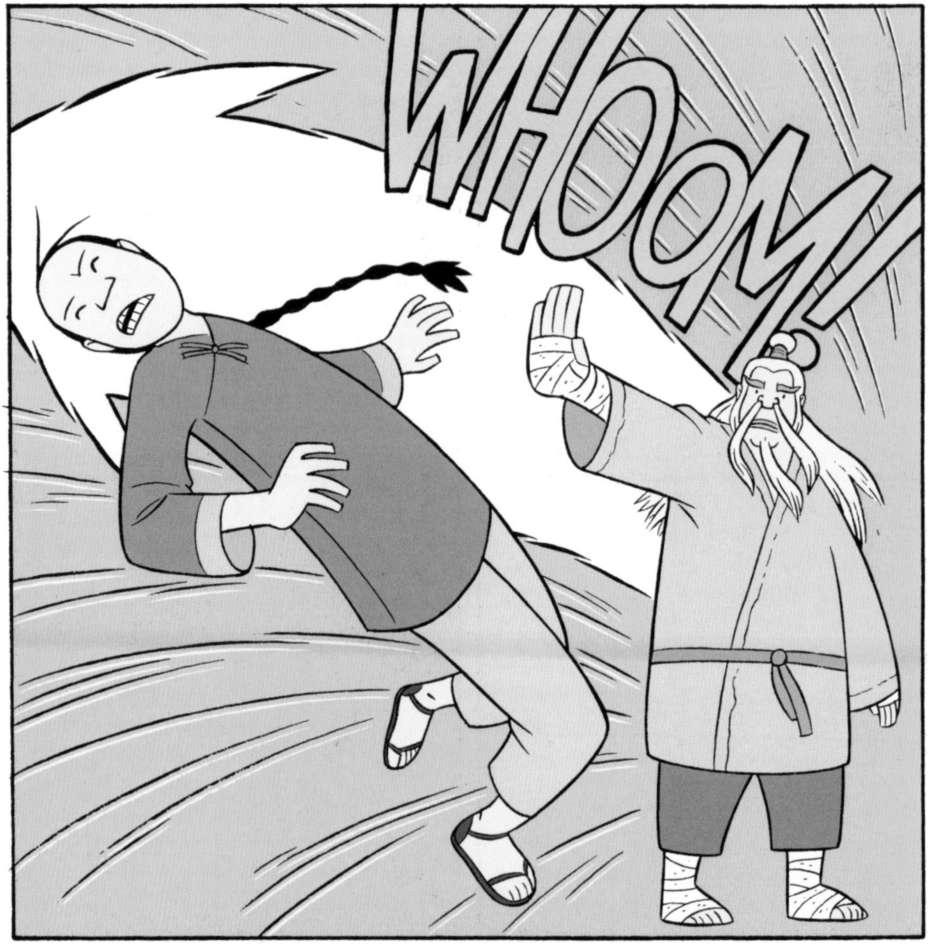
WHOOM!

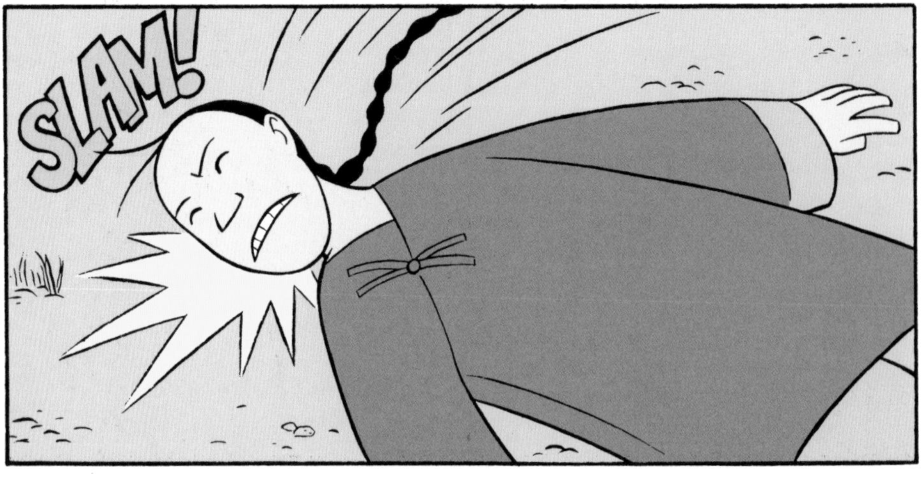
SLAM!

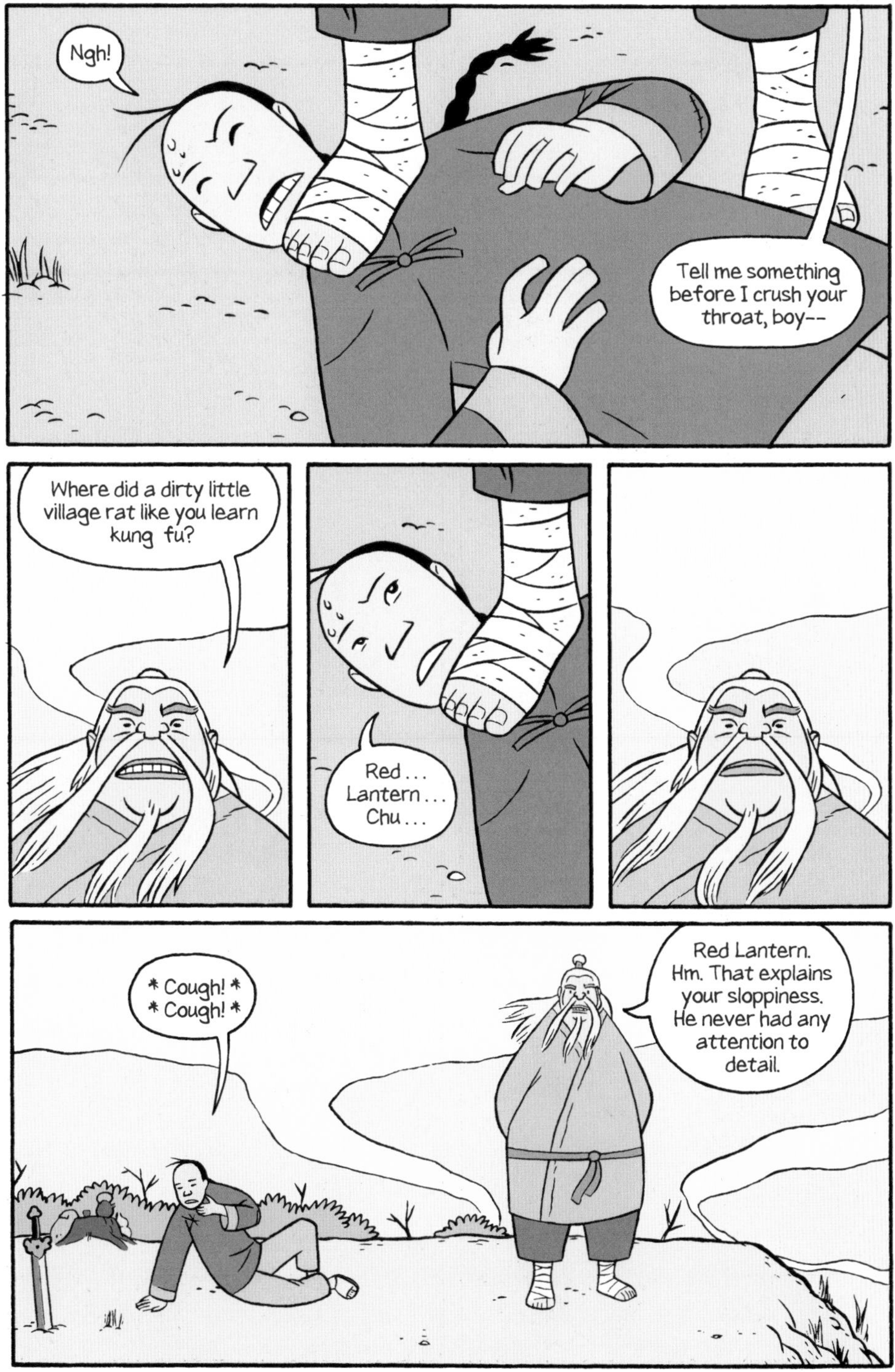
Ngh!
Tell me something before I crush your throat, boy--
Where did a dirty little village rat like you learn kung fu?
Red... Lantern... Chu...
* Cough! *
* Cough! *
Red Lantern. Hm. That explains your sloppiness. He never had any attention to detail.

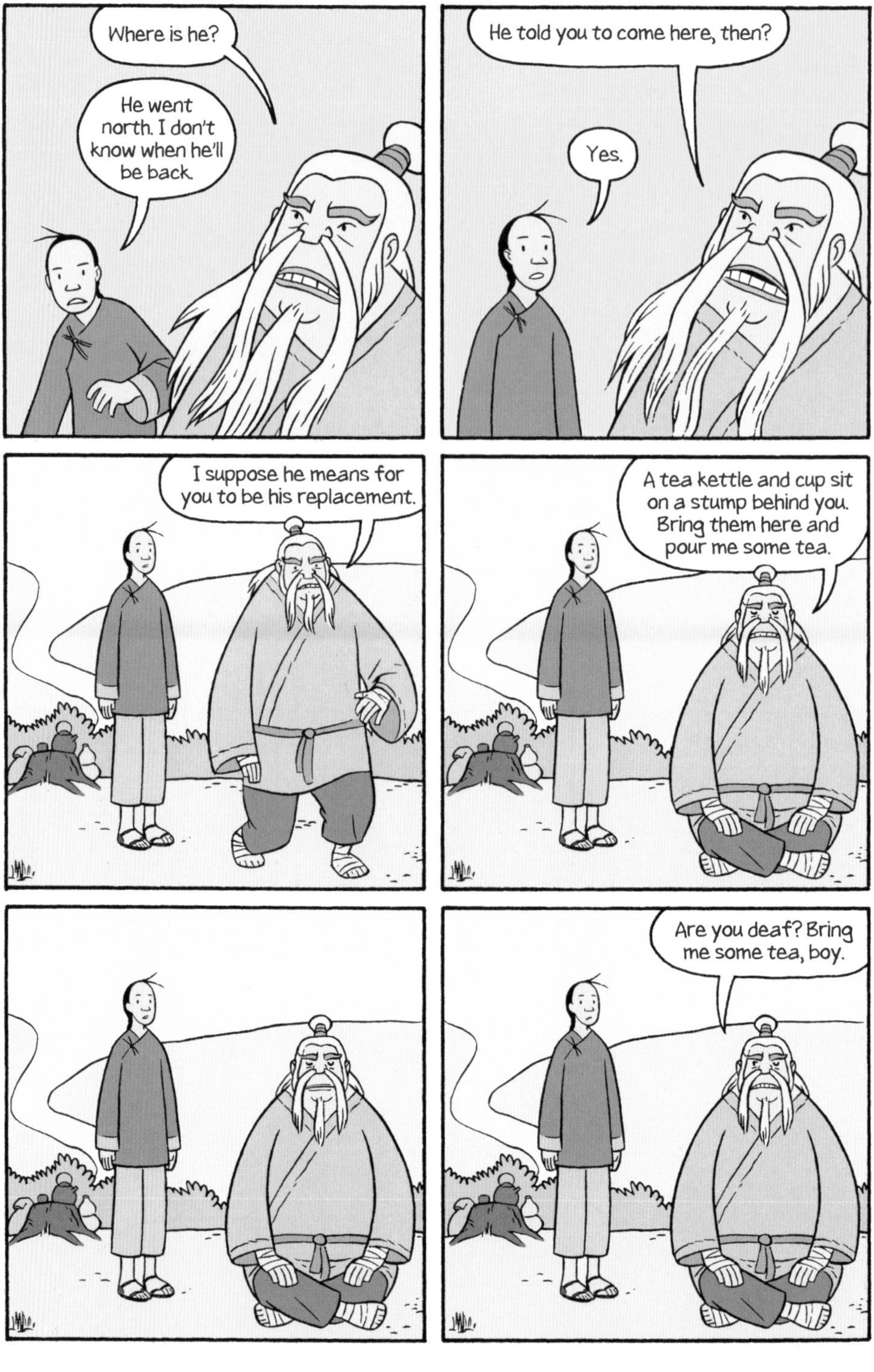
Where is he?
He went north. I don't know when he'll be back.
He told you to come here, then?
Yes.
I suppose he means for you to be his replacement.
A tea kettle and cup sit on a stump behind you. Bring them here and pour me some tea.
Are you deaf? Bring me some tea, boy.

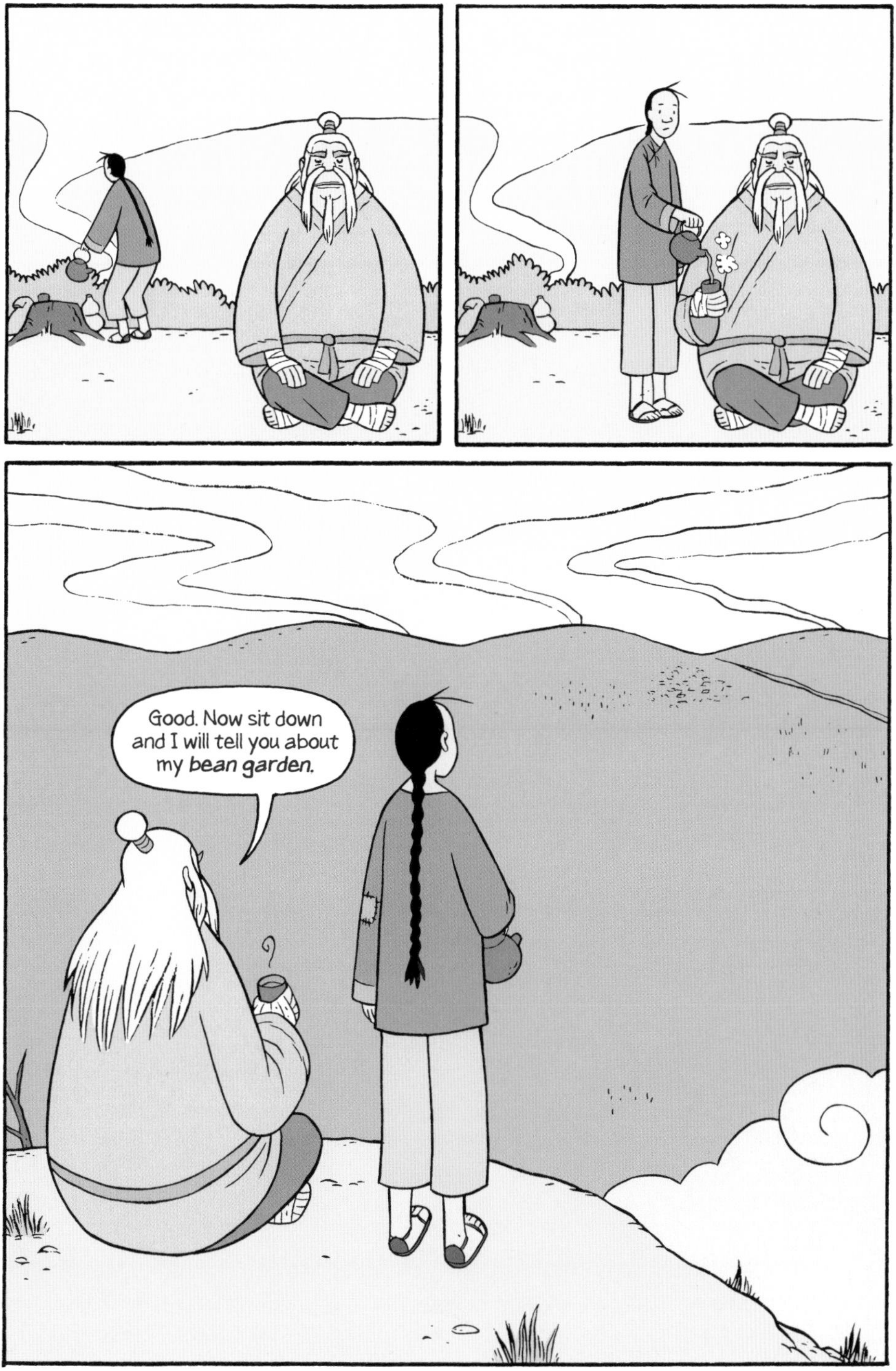
Good. Now sit down and I will tell you about my *bean garden.*

第三章

Northern Shan-tung Province, China

Late Summer 1899

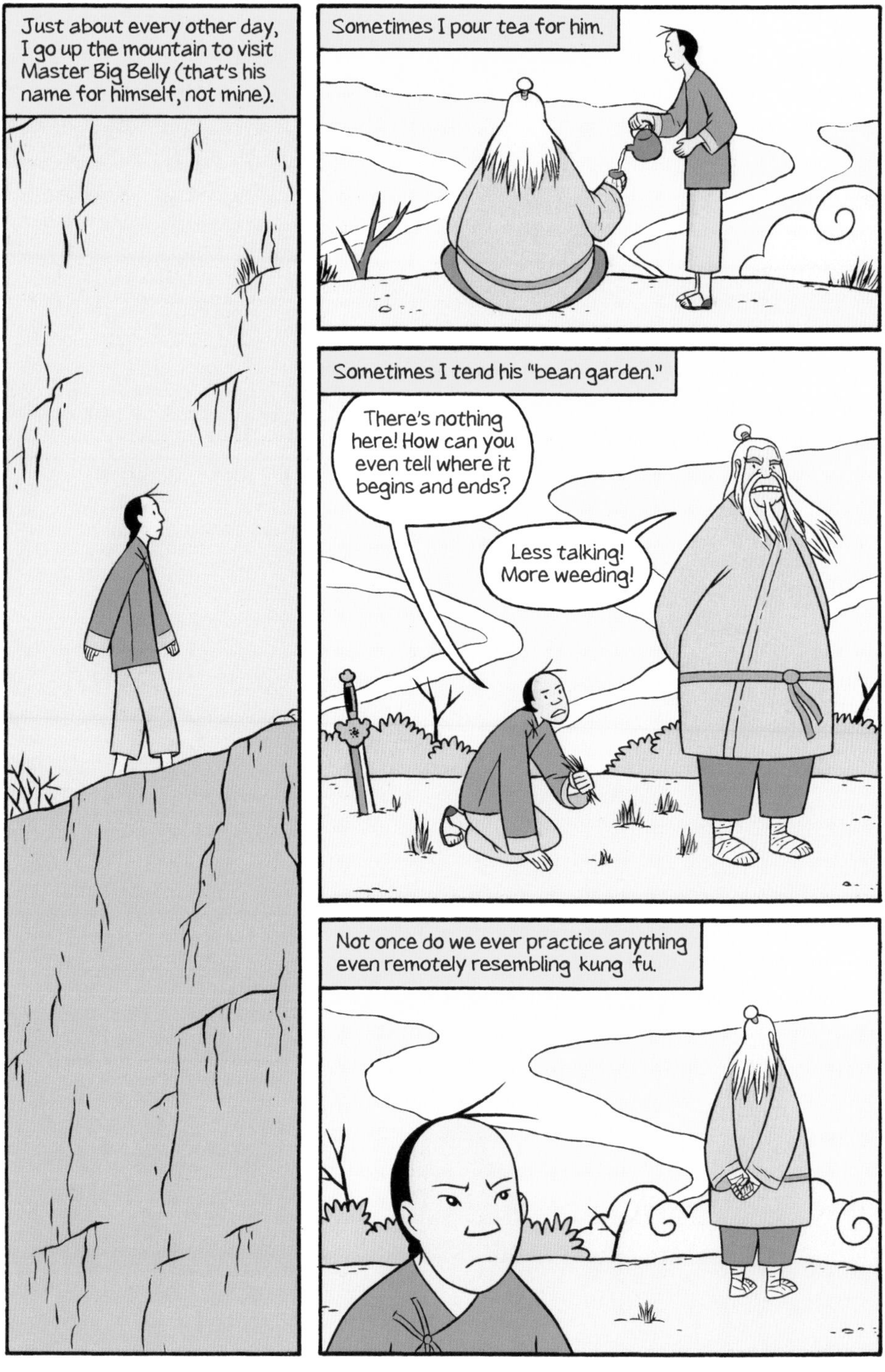
Just about every other day, I go up the mountain to visit Master Big Belly (that's his name for himself, not mine).
Sometimes I pour tea for him.
Sometimes I tend his "bean garden."
There's nothing here! How can you even tell where it begins and ends?
Less talking! More weeding!
Not once do we ever practice anything even remotely resembling kung fu.

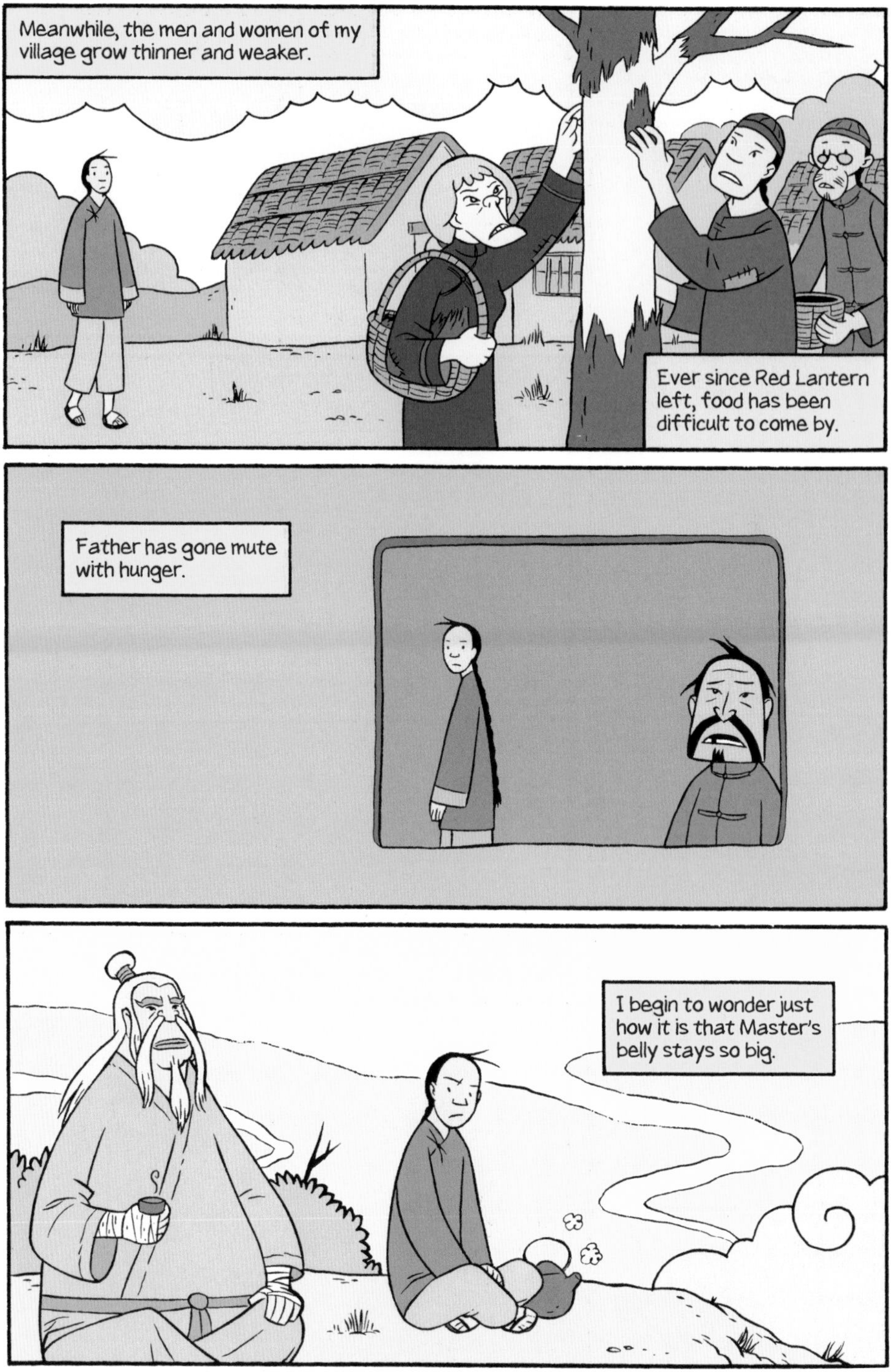

Meanwhile, the men and women of my village grow thinner and weaker.
Ever since Red Lantern left, food has been difficult to come by.
Father has gone mute with hunger.
I begin to wonder just how it is that Master's belly stays so big.

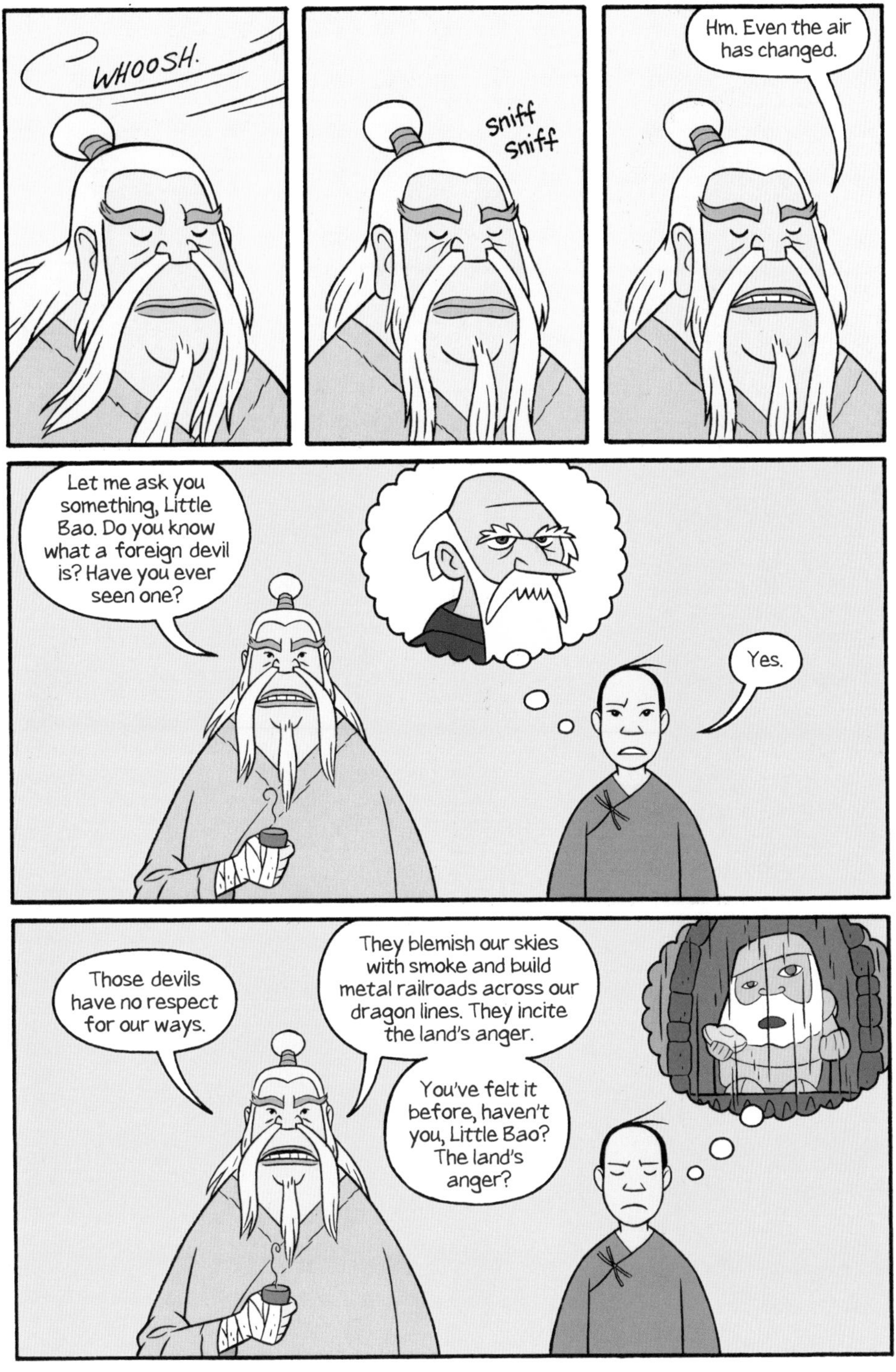
WHOOSH.
sniff sniff
Hm. Even the air has changed.
Let me ask you something, Little Bao. Do you know what a foreign devil is? Have you ever seen one?
Yes.
Those devils have no respect for our ways.
They blemish our skies with smoke and build metal railroads across our dragon lines. They incite the land's anger.
You've felt it before, haven't you, Little Bao? The land's anger?

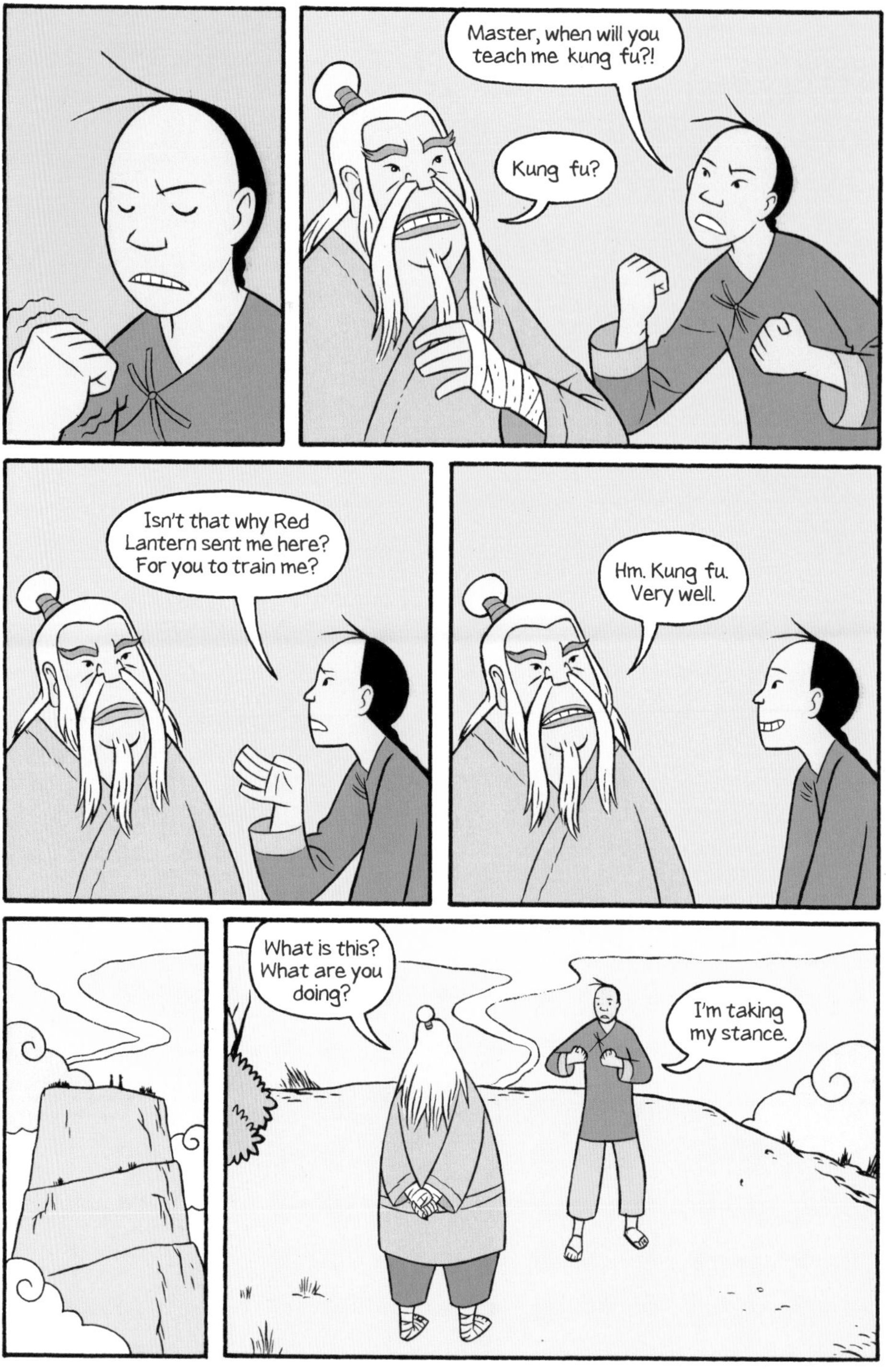
Master, when will you teach me kung fu?!
Kung fu?
Isn't that why Red Lantern sent me here? For you to train me?
Hm. Kung fu. Very well.
What is this? What are you doing?
I'm taking my stance.

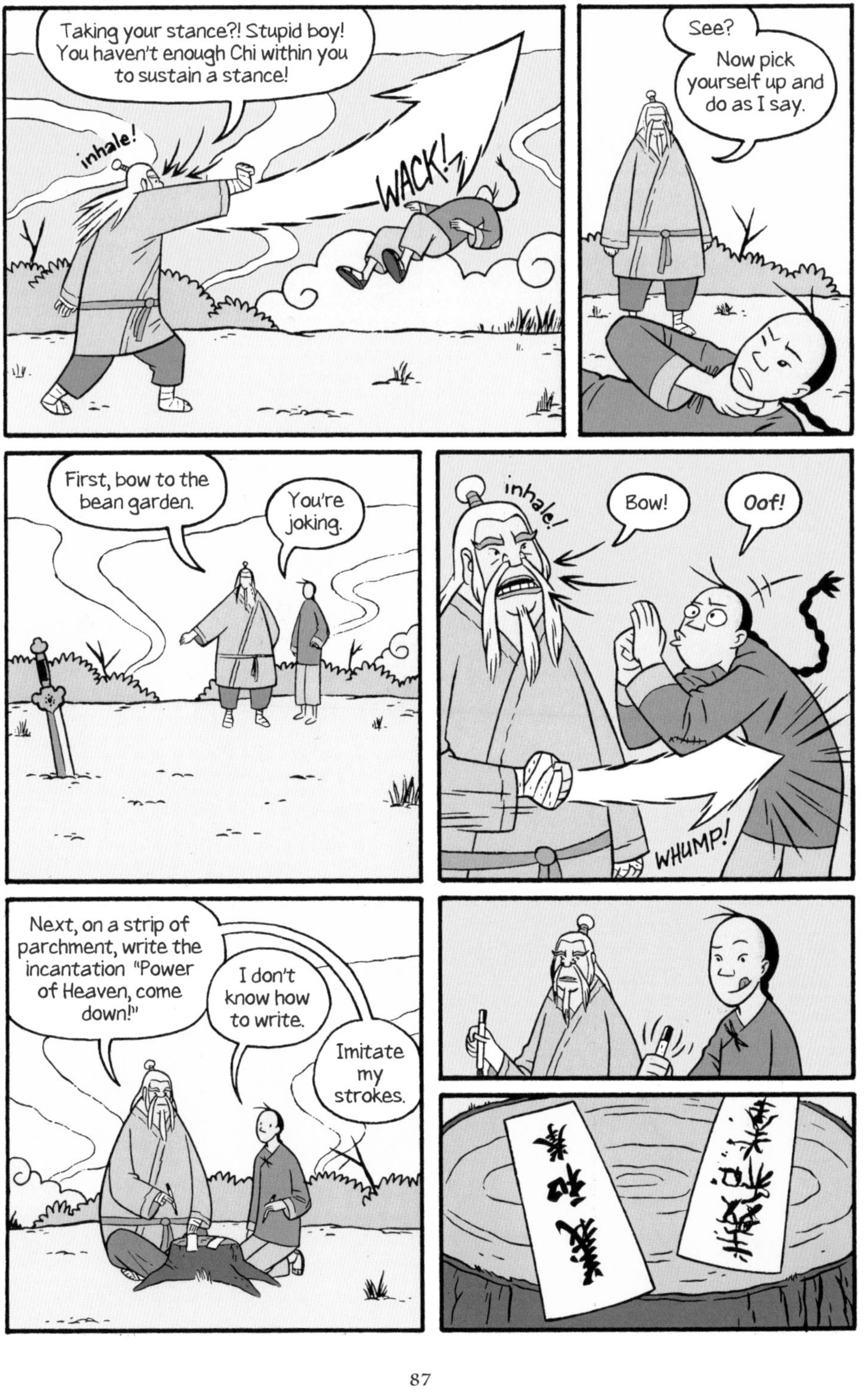
Taking your stance?! Stupid boy! You haven't enough Chi within you to sustain a stance!
inhale!
WACK!
See?
Now pick yourself up and do as I say.
First, bow to the bean garden.
You're joking.
inhale!
Bow!
Oof!
WHUMP!
Next, on a strip of parchment, write the incantation "Power of Heaven, come down!"
I don't know how to write.
Imitate my strokes.

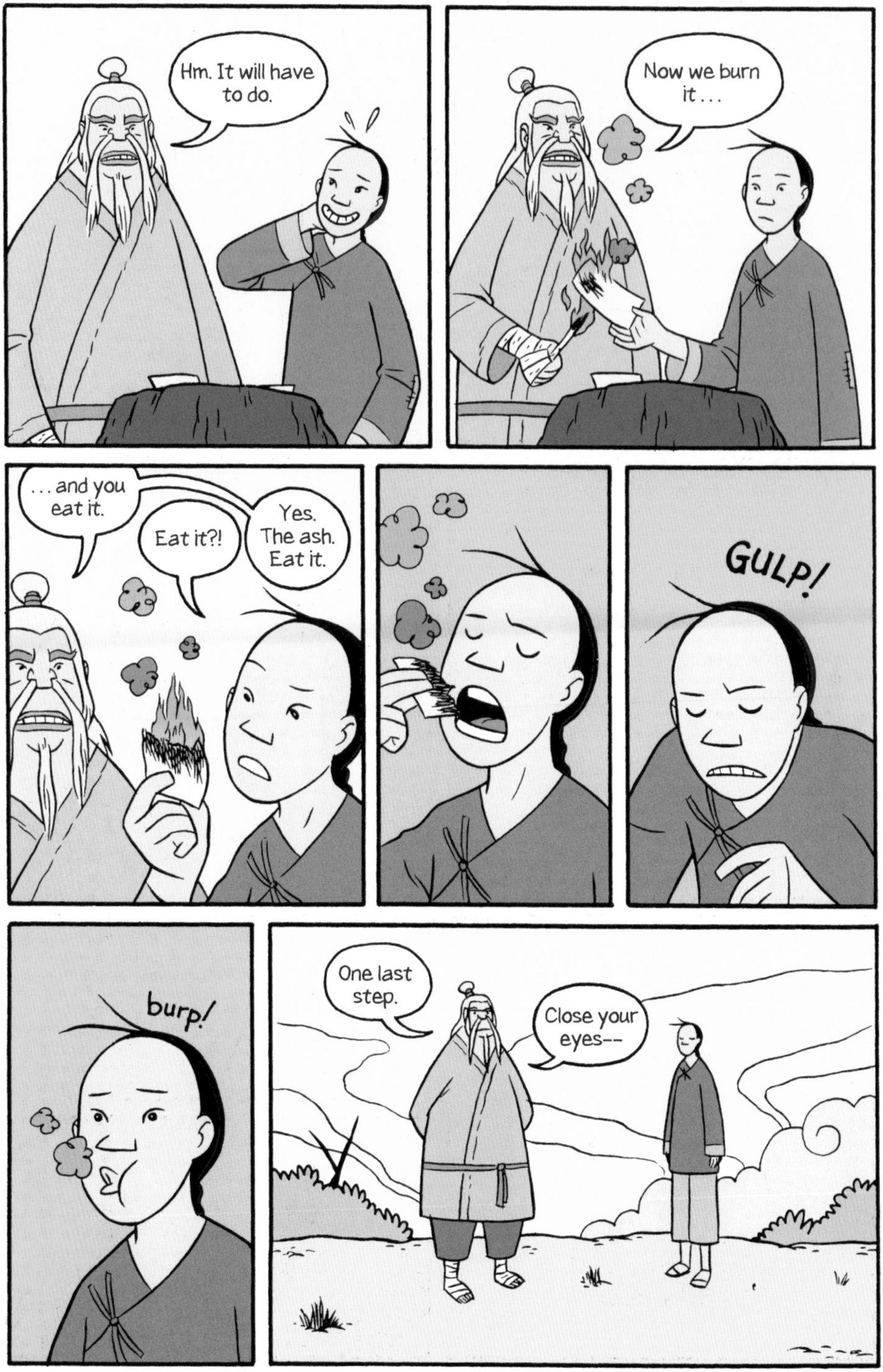
Hm. It will have to do.
Now we burn it . . .
. . . and you eat it.
Eat it?!
Yes. The ash. Eat it.
GULP!
burp!
One last step.
Close your eyes--

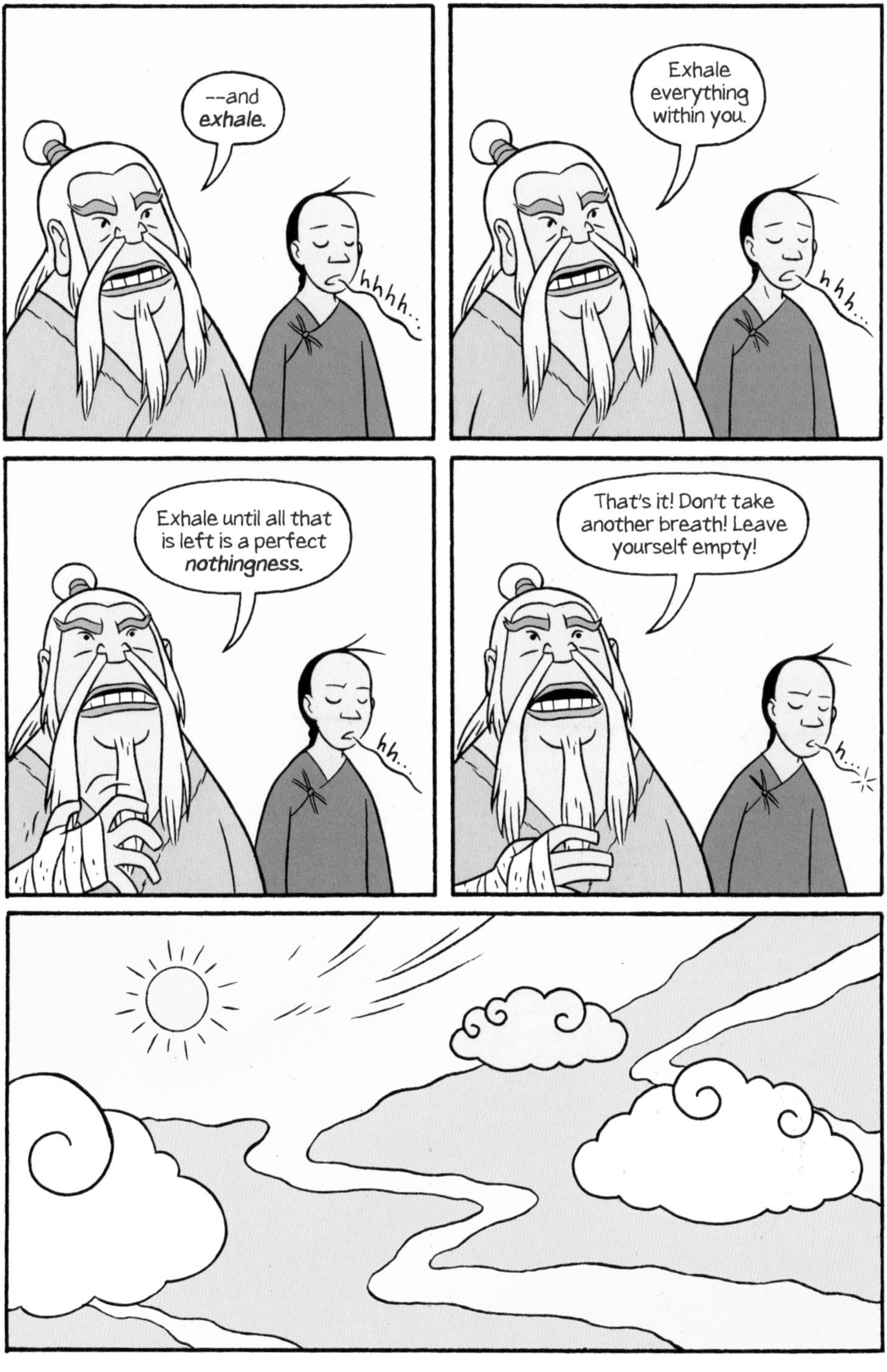
--and *exhale.*
hhhh...
Exhale everything within you.
hhh...
Exhale until all that is left is a perfect *nothingness.*
hh...
That's it! Don't take another breath! Leave yourself empty!
h...

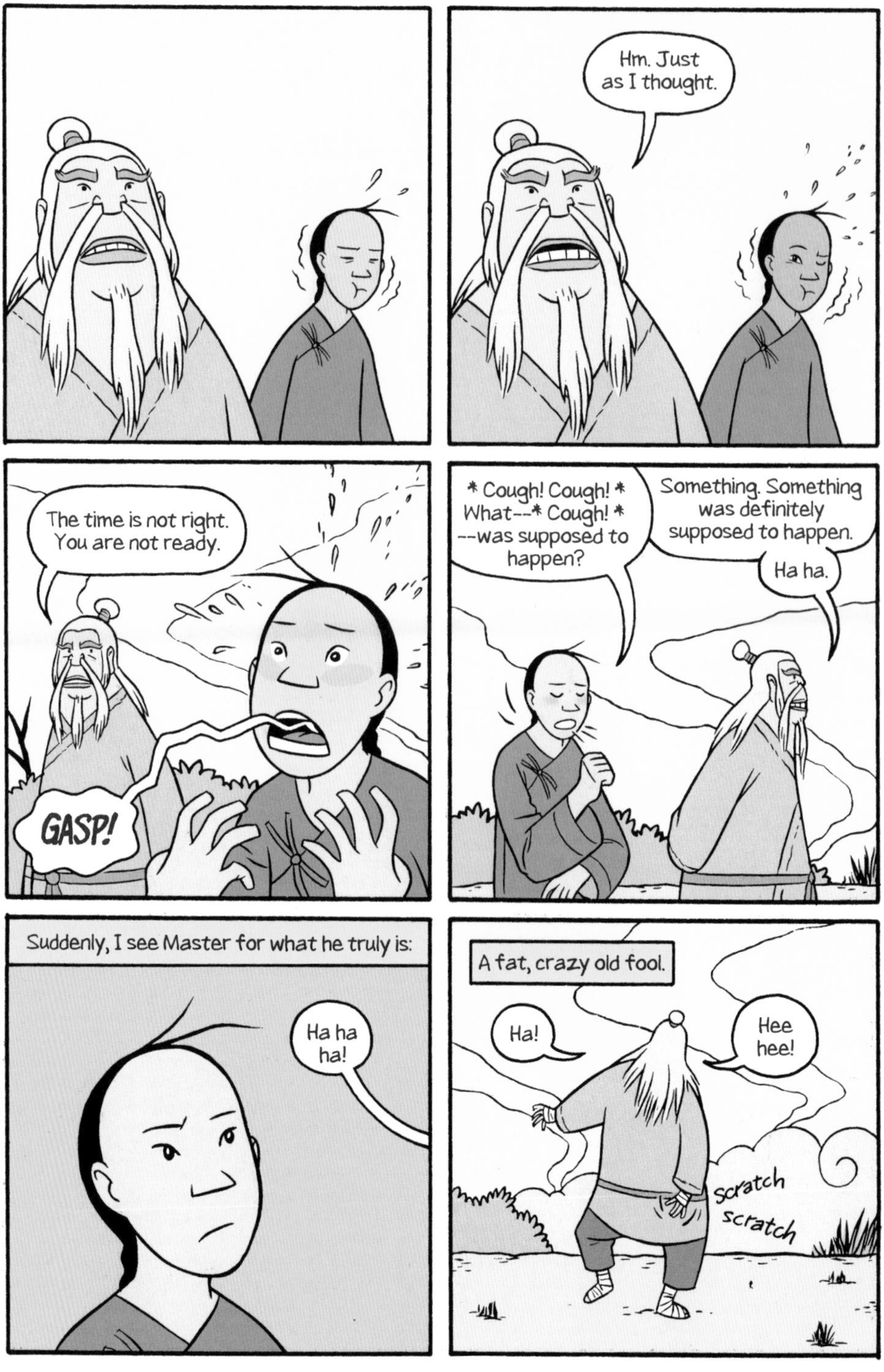
Hm. Just as I thought.
The time is not right. You are not ready.
GASP!
* Cough! Cough! * What--* Cough! * --was supposed to happen?
Something. Something was definitely supposed to happen.
Ha ha.
Suddenly, I see Master for what he truly is:
Ha ha ha!
A fat, crazy old fool.
Ha!
Hee hee!
scratch
scratch

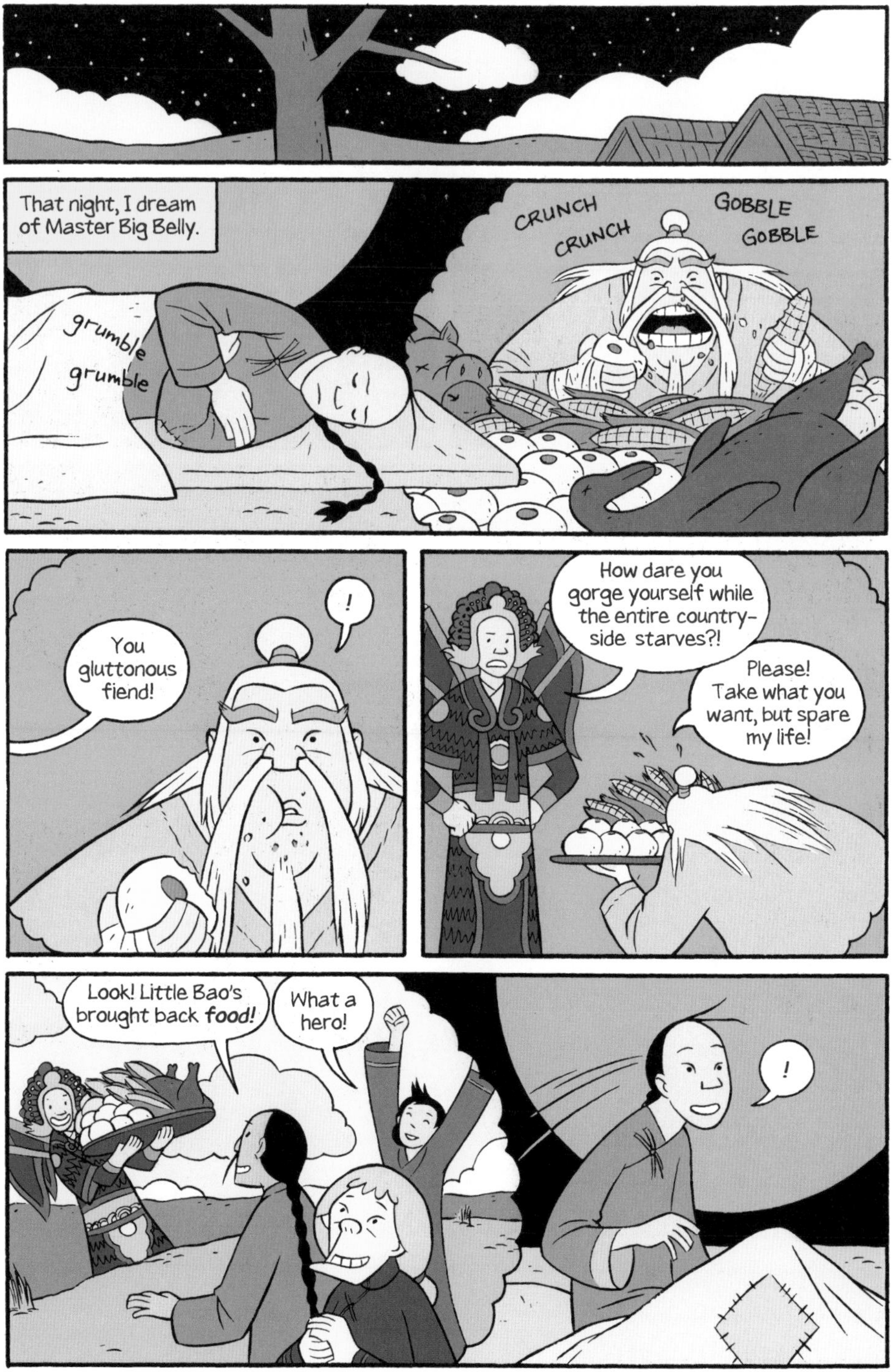
That night, I dream of Master Big Belly.
grumble grumble
CRUNCH
CRUNCH
GOBBLE
GOBBLE
You gluttonous fiend!
!
How dare you gorge yourself while the entire country-side starves?!
Please! Take what you want, but spare my life!
Look! Little Bao's brought back **food**!
What a hero!
!

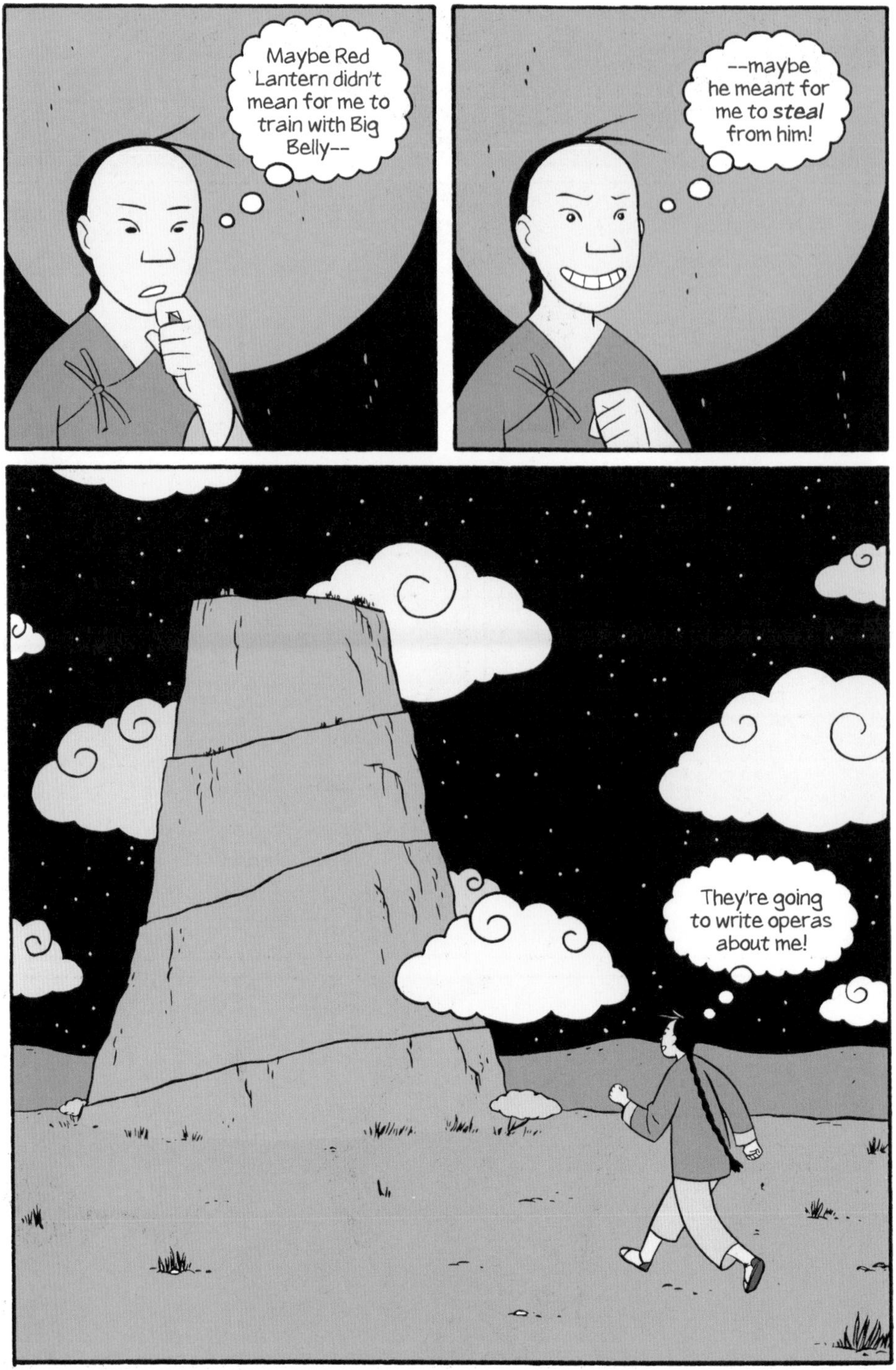
Maybe Red Lantern didn't mean for me to train with Big Belly--
--maybe he meant for me to *steal* from him!
They're going to write operas about me!

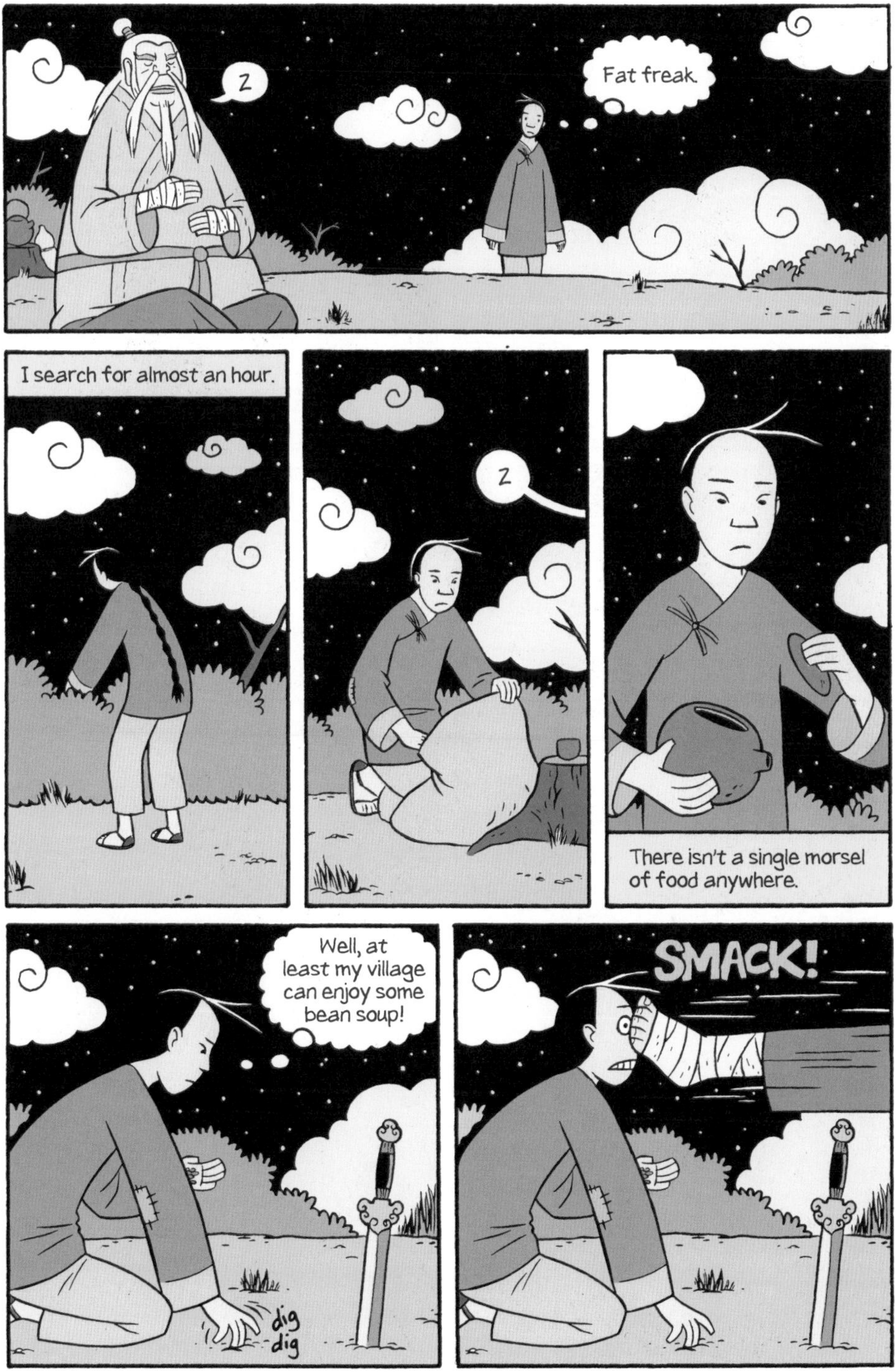
Z
Fat freak.
I search for almost an hour.
Z
There isn't a single morsel of food anywhere.
Well, at least my village can enjoy some bean soup!
dig dig
SMACK!

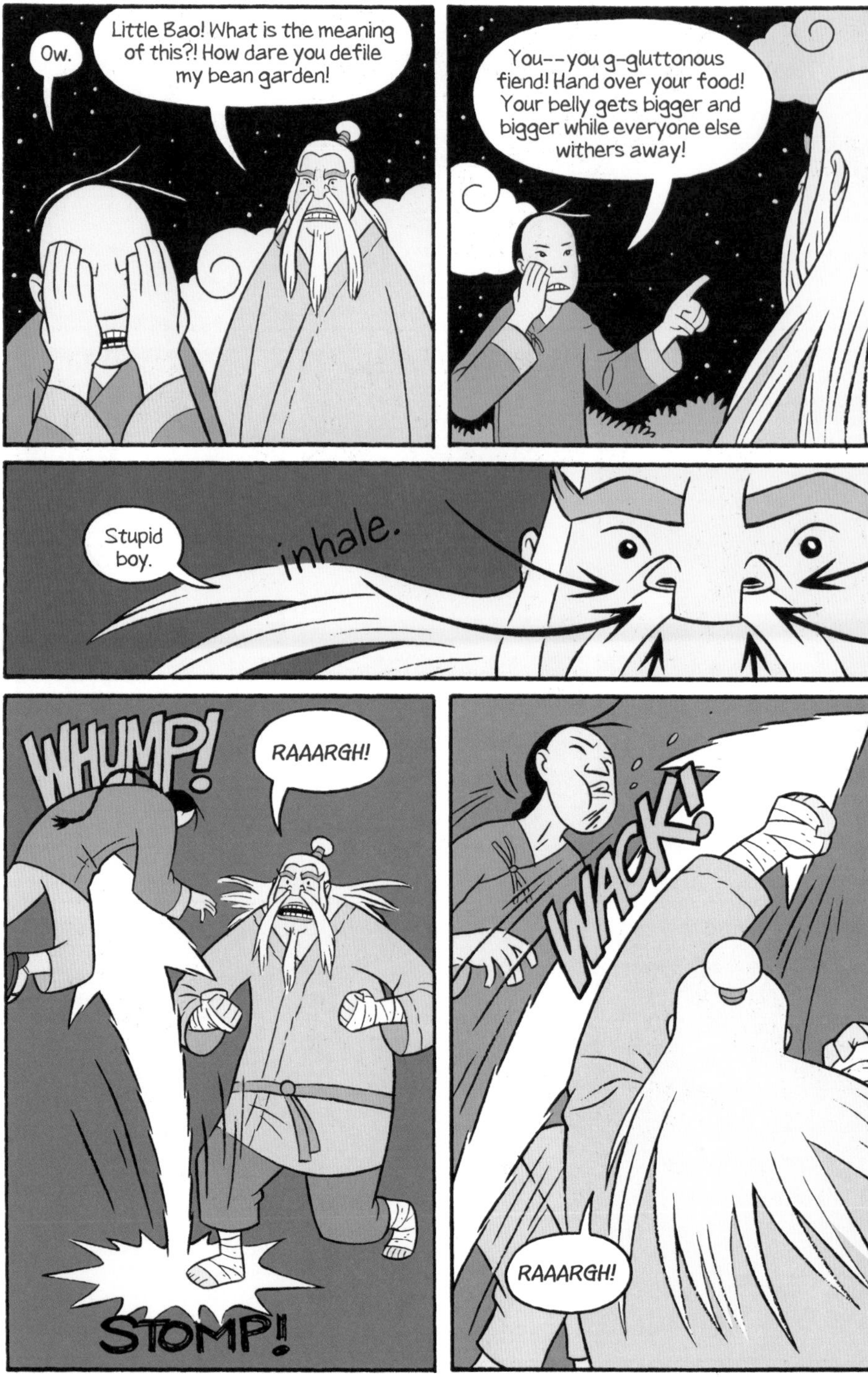
Ow.
Little Bao! What is the meaning of this?! How dare you defile my bean garden!
You--you g-gluttonous fiend! Hand over your food! Your belly gets bigger and bigger while everyone else withers away!
Stupid boy.
inhale.
WHUMP!
RAAARGH!
STOMP!
WACK!
RAAARGH!

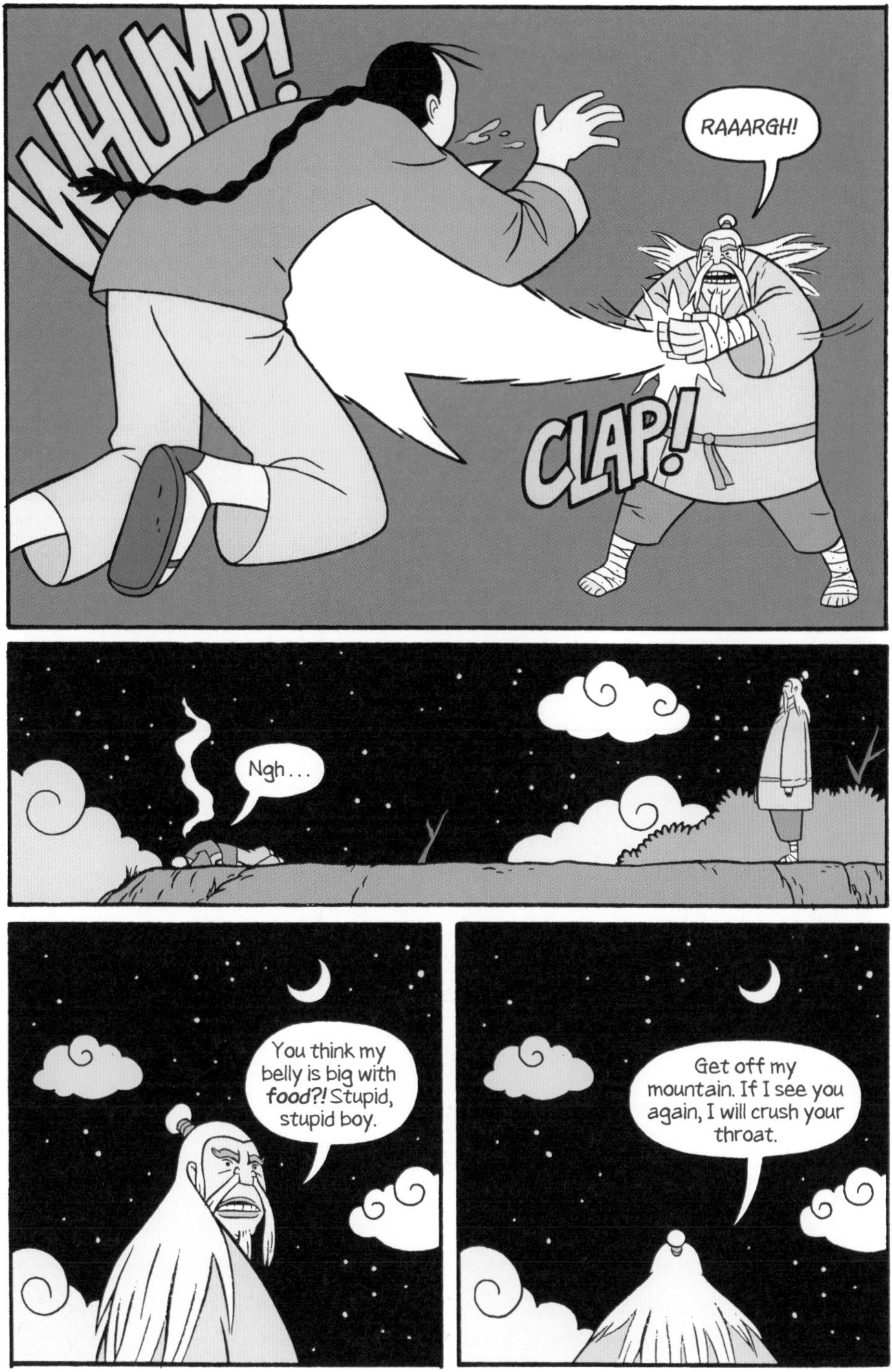
WHUMP!
RAAARGH!
CLAP!
Ngh...
You think my belly is big with *food?!* Stupid, stupid boy.
Get off my mountain. If I see you again, I will crush your throat.

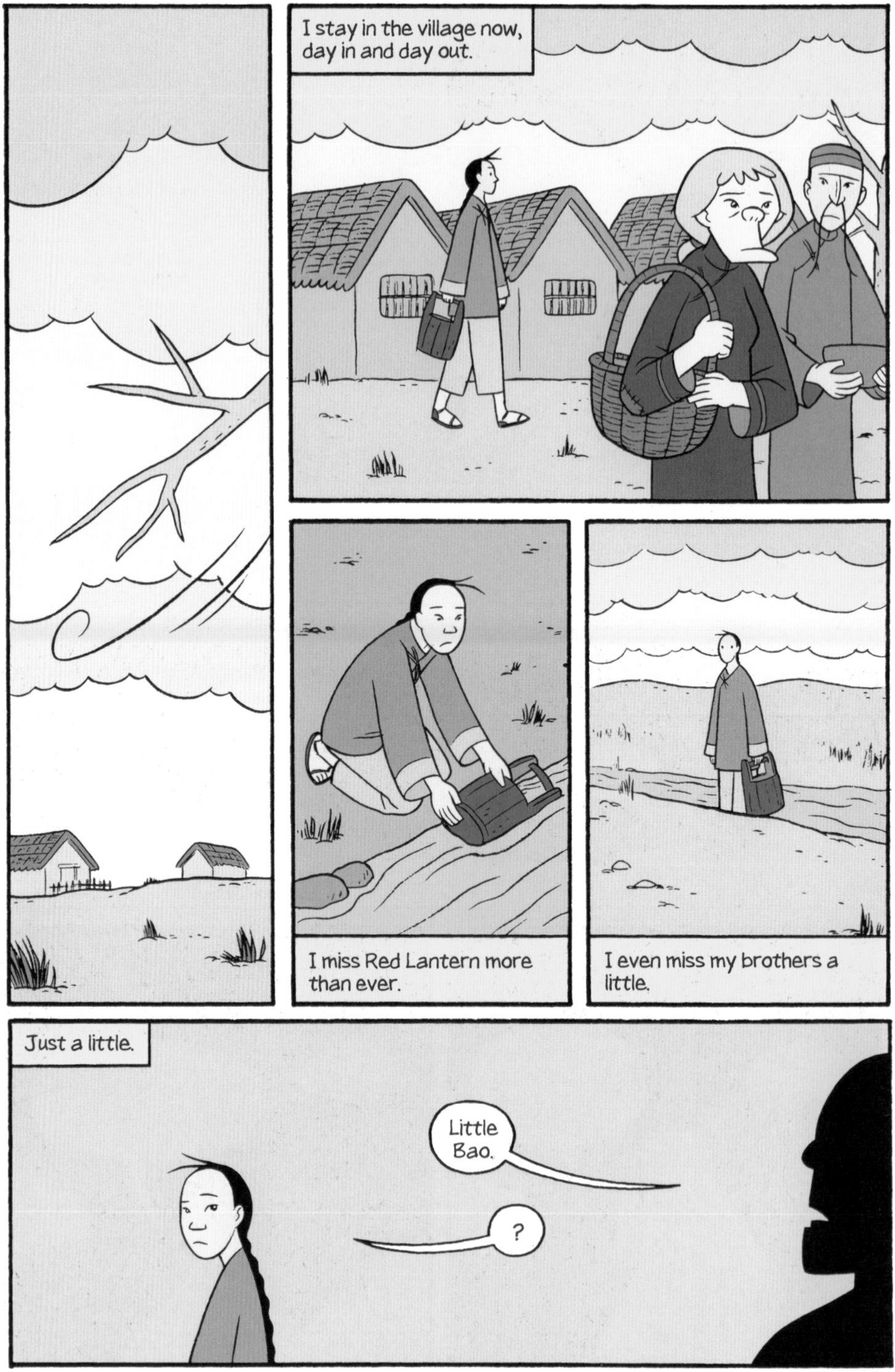
I stay in the village now, day in and day out.
I miss Red Lantern more than ever.
I even miss my brothers a little.
Just a little.
Little Bao.
?

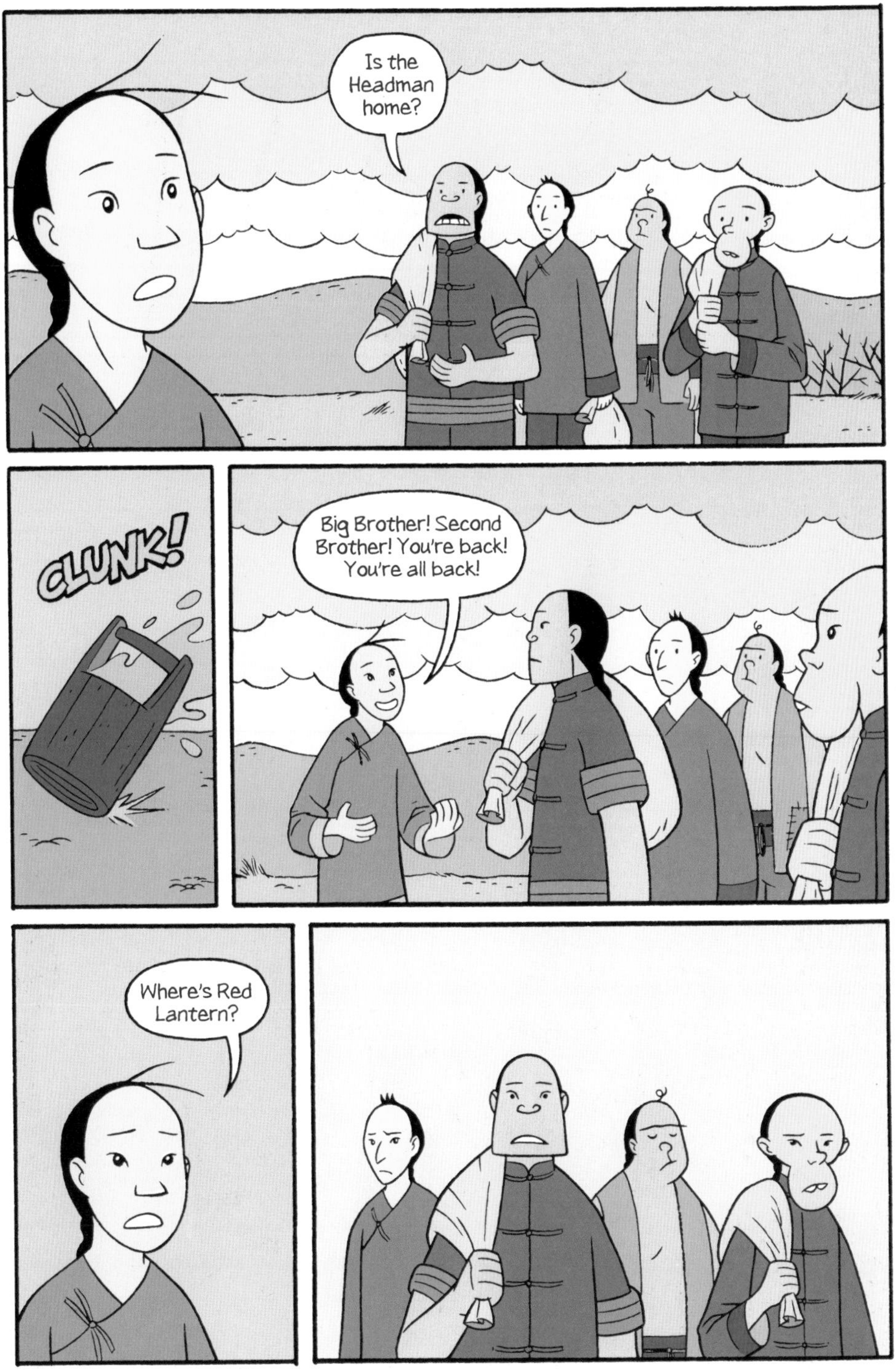
Is the Headman home?
CLUNK!
Big Brother! Second Brother! You're back! You're all back!
Where's Red Lantern?

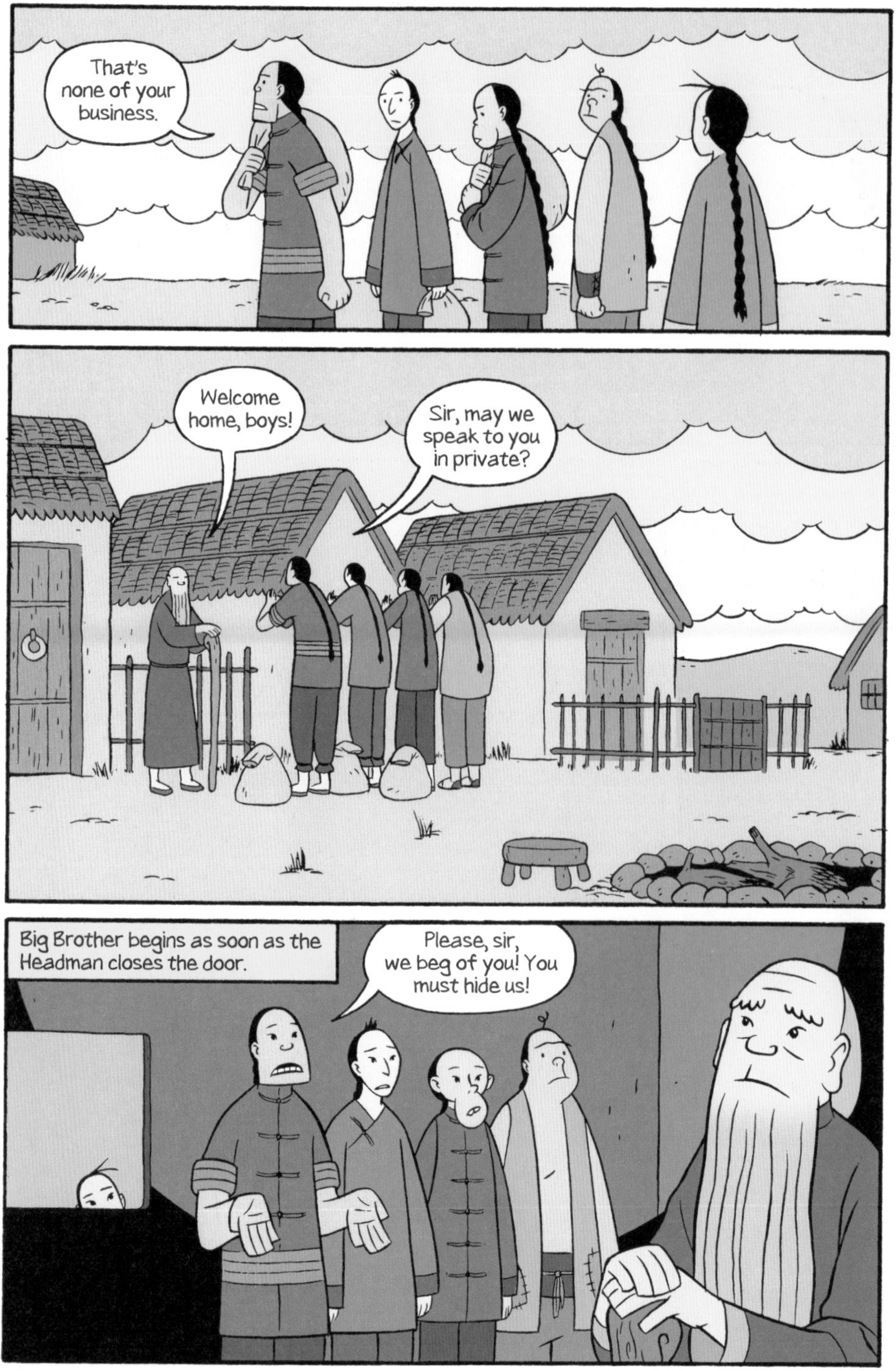
That's none of your business.
Welcome home, boys!
Sir, may we speak to you in private?
Big Brother begins as soon as the Headman closes the door.
Please, sir, we beg of you! You must hide us!

What's this about?

The Imperial troops are roaming the area, searching for Brother-Disciples of the Big Sword Society! If they find us, we'll be arrested and . . .

. . . probably *executed.*

What about Red Lantern? Can't he help you?

It was . . . it was *horrible,* sir.

Big Brother tells his story methodically, like he's rehearsed it over and over in his head.

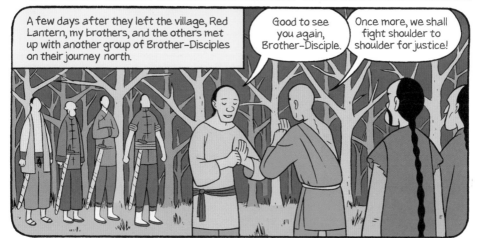

A few days after they left the village, Red Lantern, my brothers, and the others met up with another group of Brother-Disciples on their journey north.

Good to see you again, Brother-Disciple.

Once more, we shall fight shoulder to shoulder for justice!

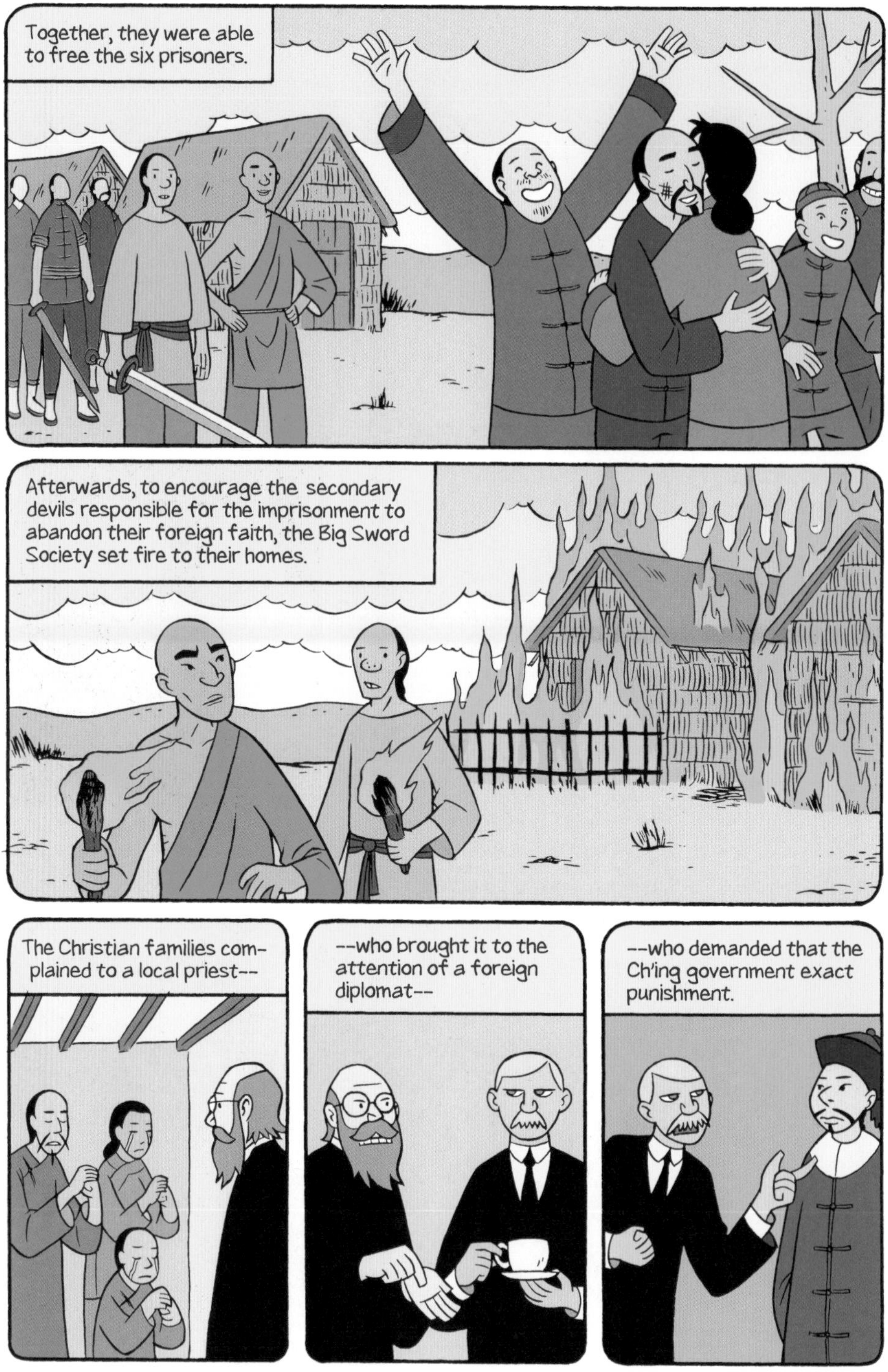

Together, they were able to free the six prisoners.
Afterwards, to encourage the secondary devils responsible for the imprisonment to abandon their foreign faith, the Big Sword Society set fire to their homes.
The Christian families complained to a local priest--
--who brought it to the attention of a foreign diplomat--
--who demanded that the Ch'ing government exact punishment.

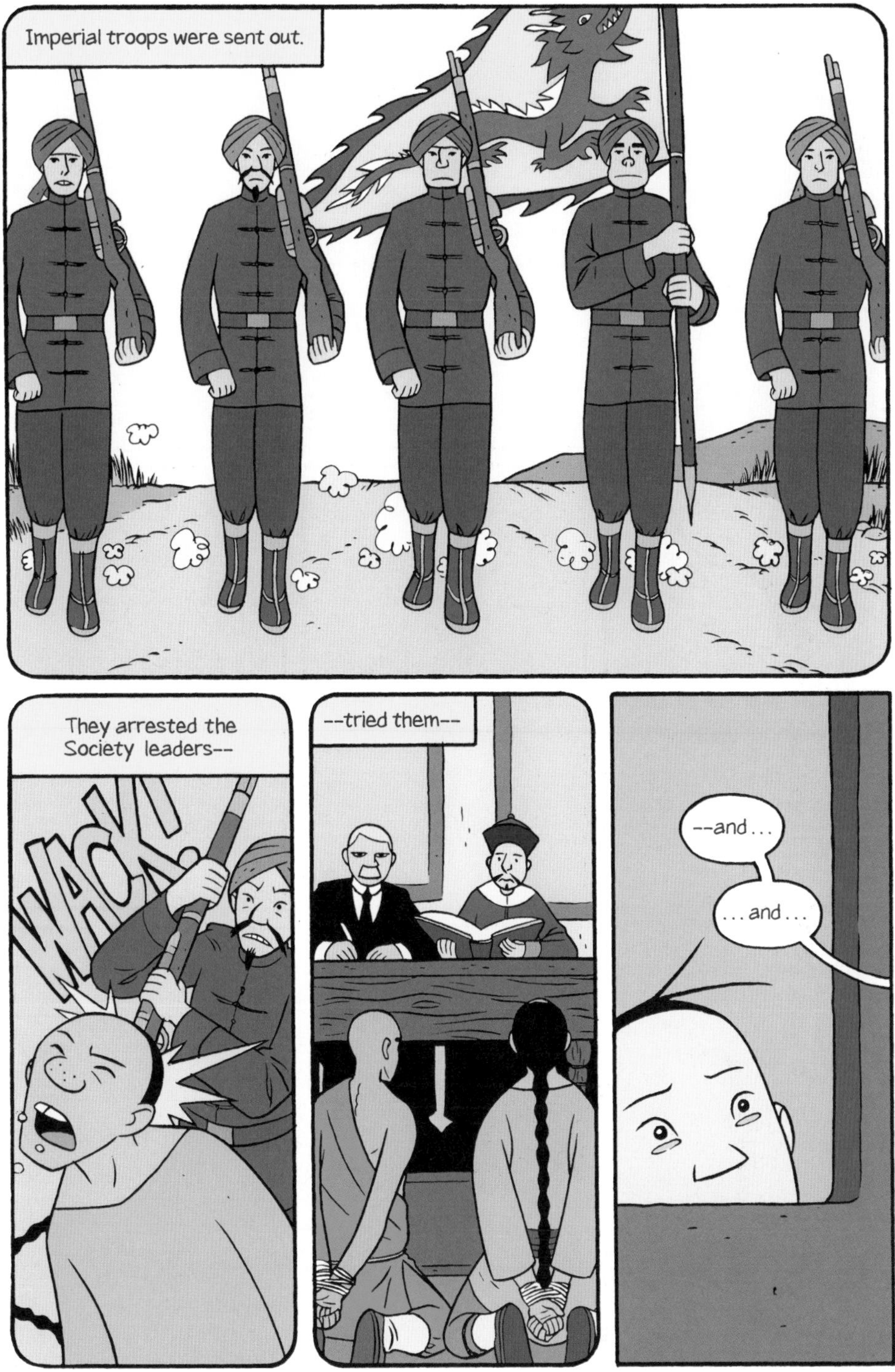
Imperial troops were sent out.
They arrested the Society leaders--
WACK!
--tried them--
--and...
...and...

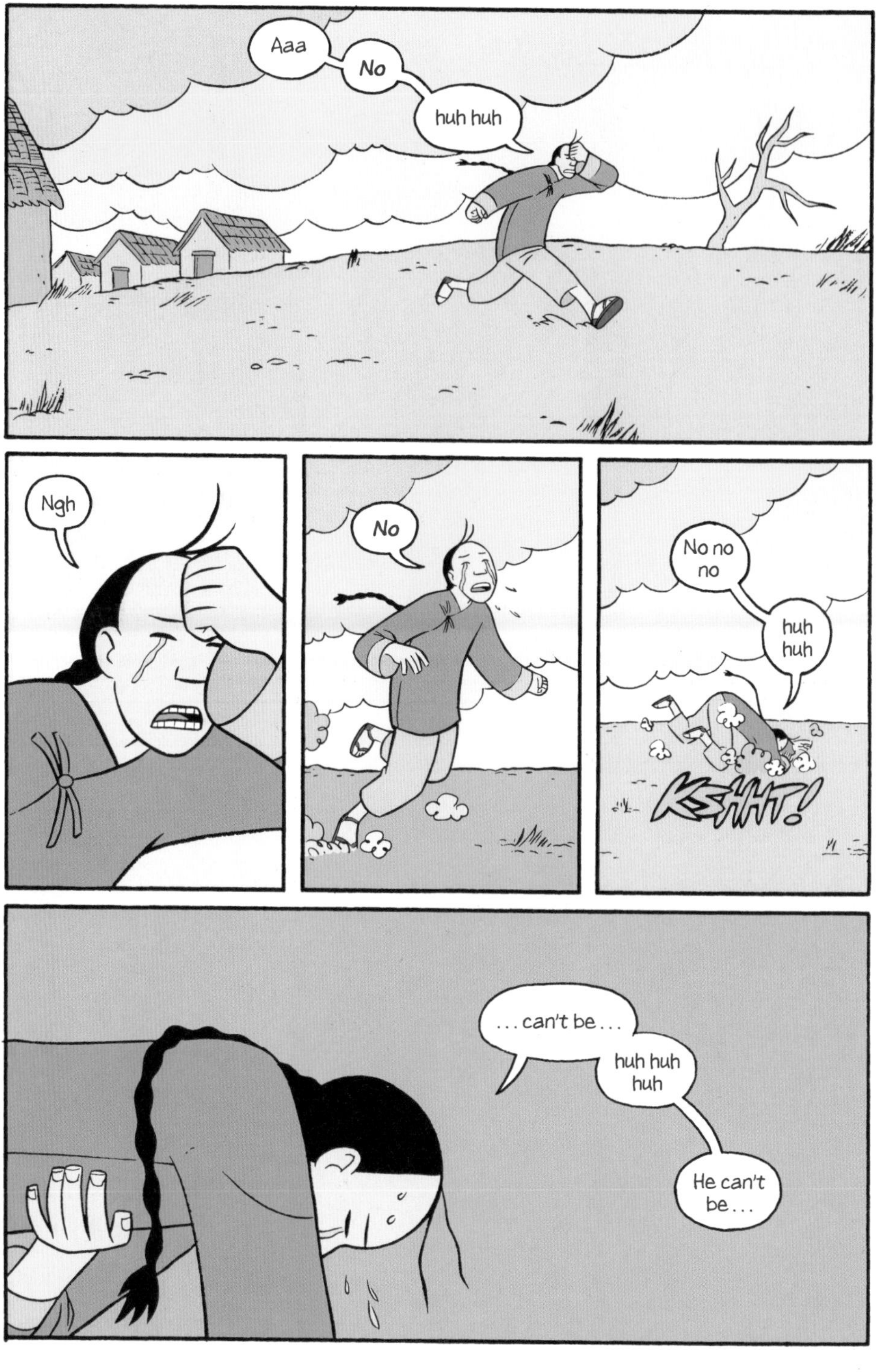
Aaa
No
huh huh
Ngh
No
No no no
huh huh
KSHHT!
. . . can't be . . .
huh huh huh
He can't be . . .

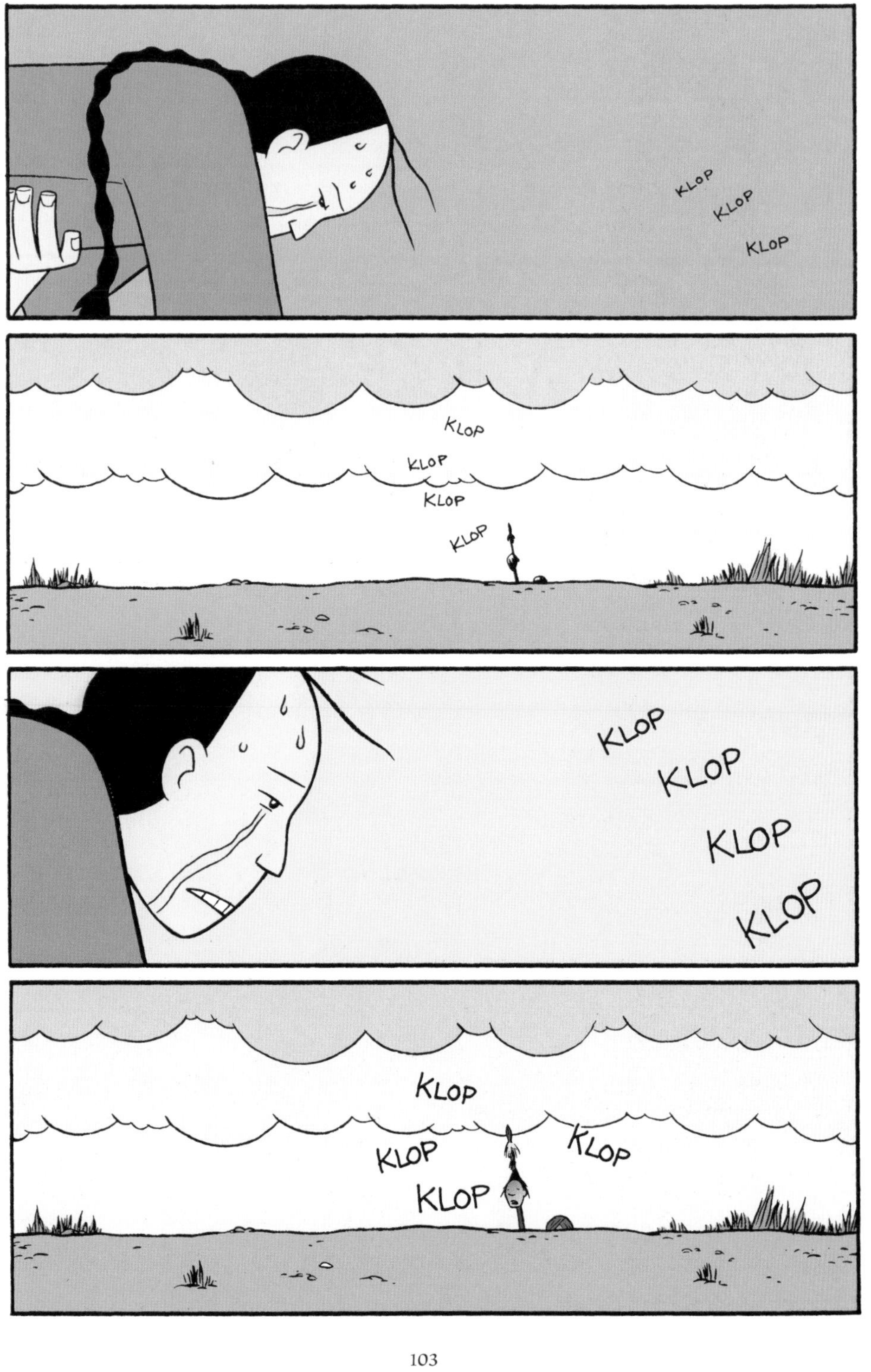
KLOP
KLOP
KLOP
KLOP
KLOP
KLOP
KLOP
KLOP
KLOP
KLOP
KLOP
KLOP
KLOP
KLOP
KLOP

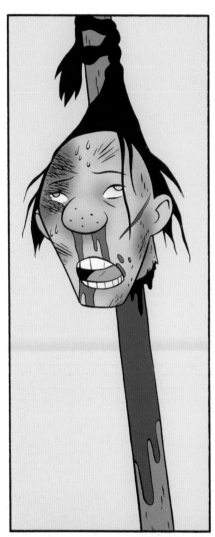

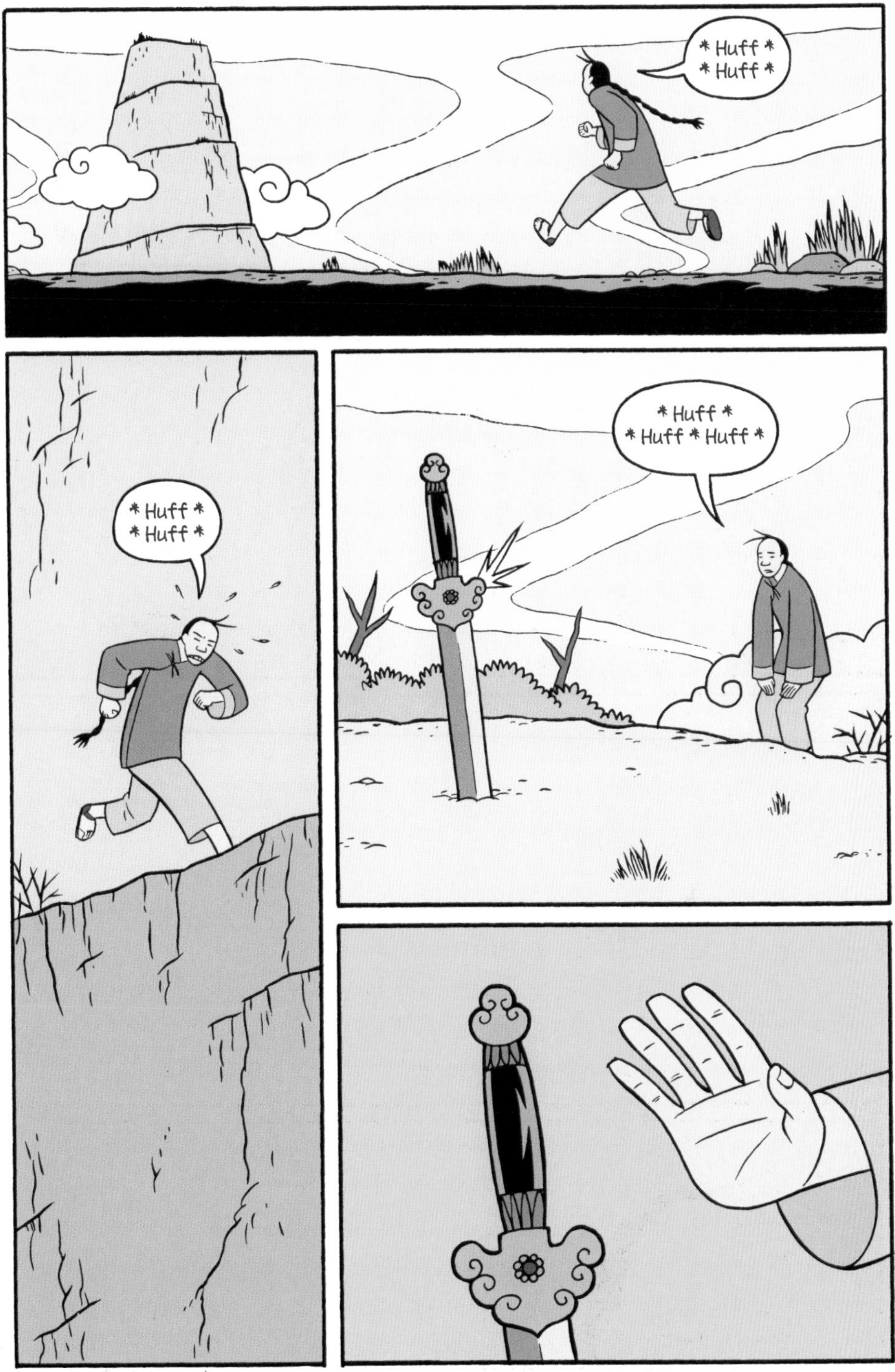
* Huff *
* Huff *
* Huff *
* Huff *
* Huff *
* Huff * Huff *

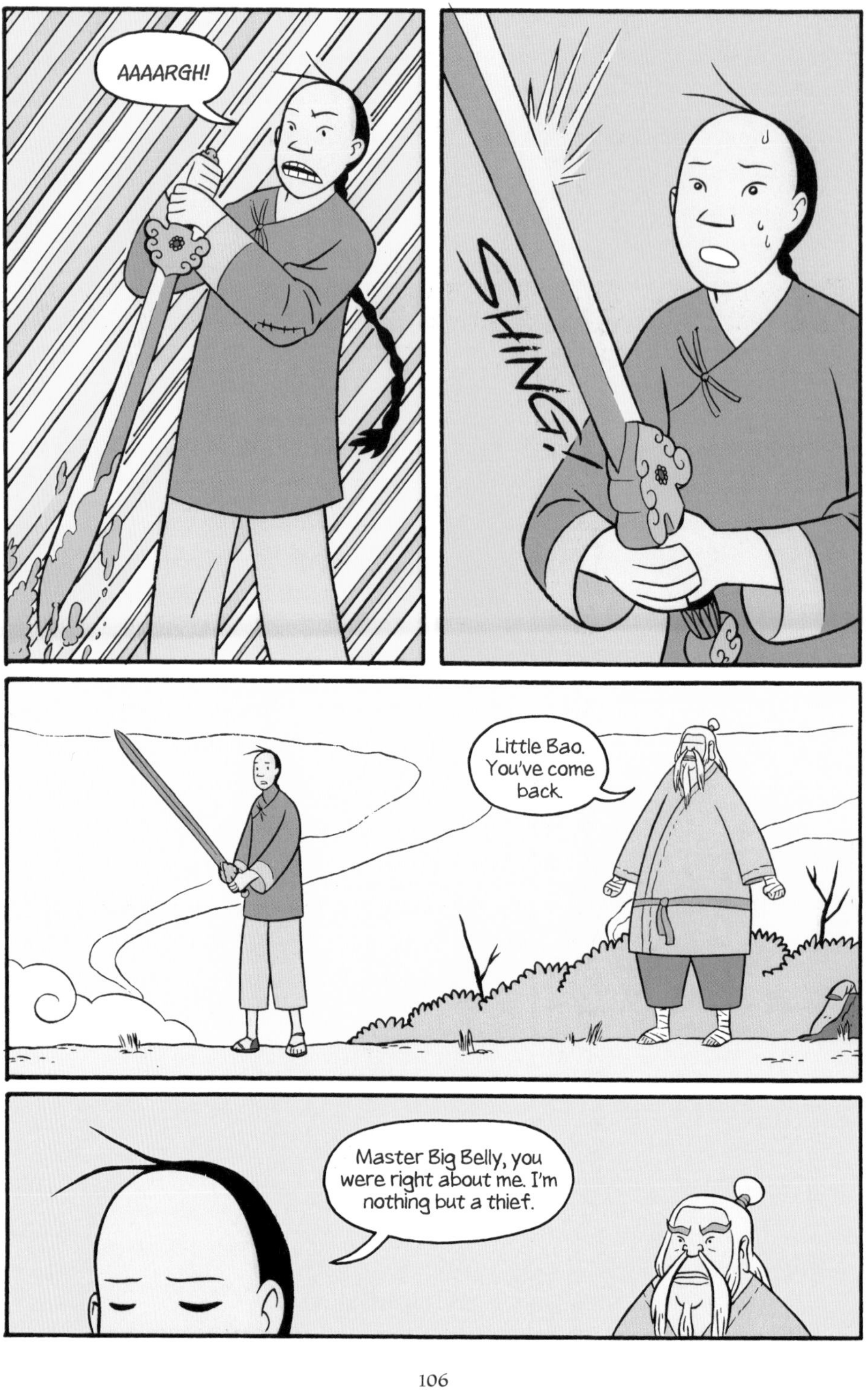
AAAARGH!
SHING!
Little Bao. You've come back.
Master Big Belly, you were right about me. I'm nothing but a thief.

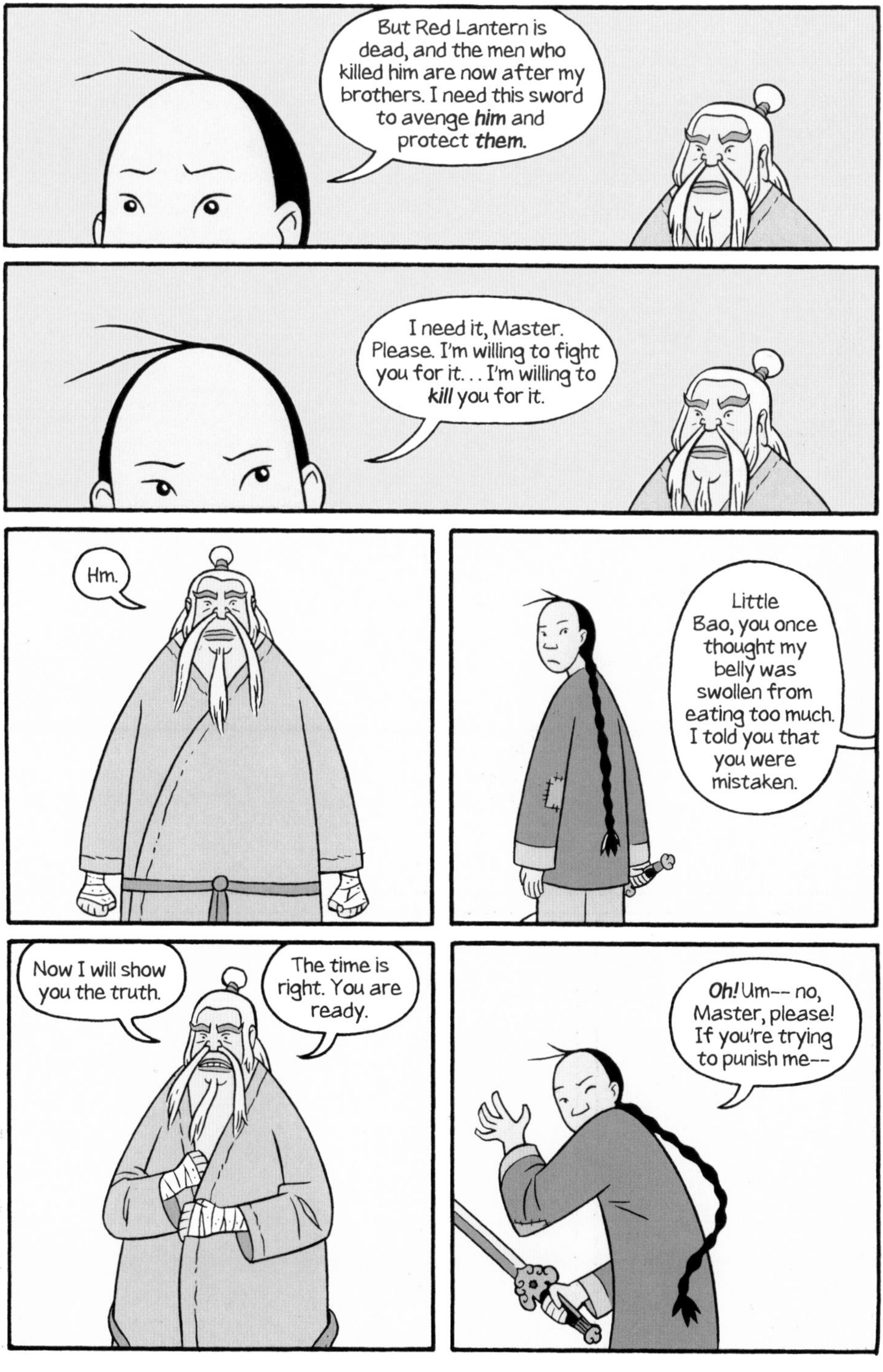

But Red Lantern is dead, and the men who killed him are now after my brothers. I need this sword to avenge *him* and protect *them*.
I need it, Master. Please. I'm willing to fight you for it... I'm willing to *kill* you for it.
Hm.
Little Bao, you once thought my belly was swollen from eating too much. I told you that you were mistaken.
Now I will show you the truth.
The time is right. You are ready.
Oh! Um-- no, Master, please! If you're trying to punish me--

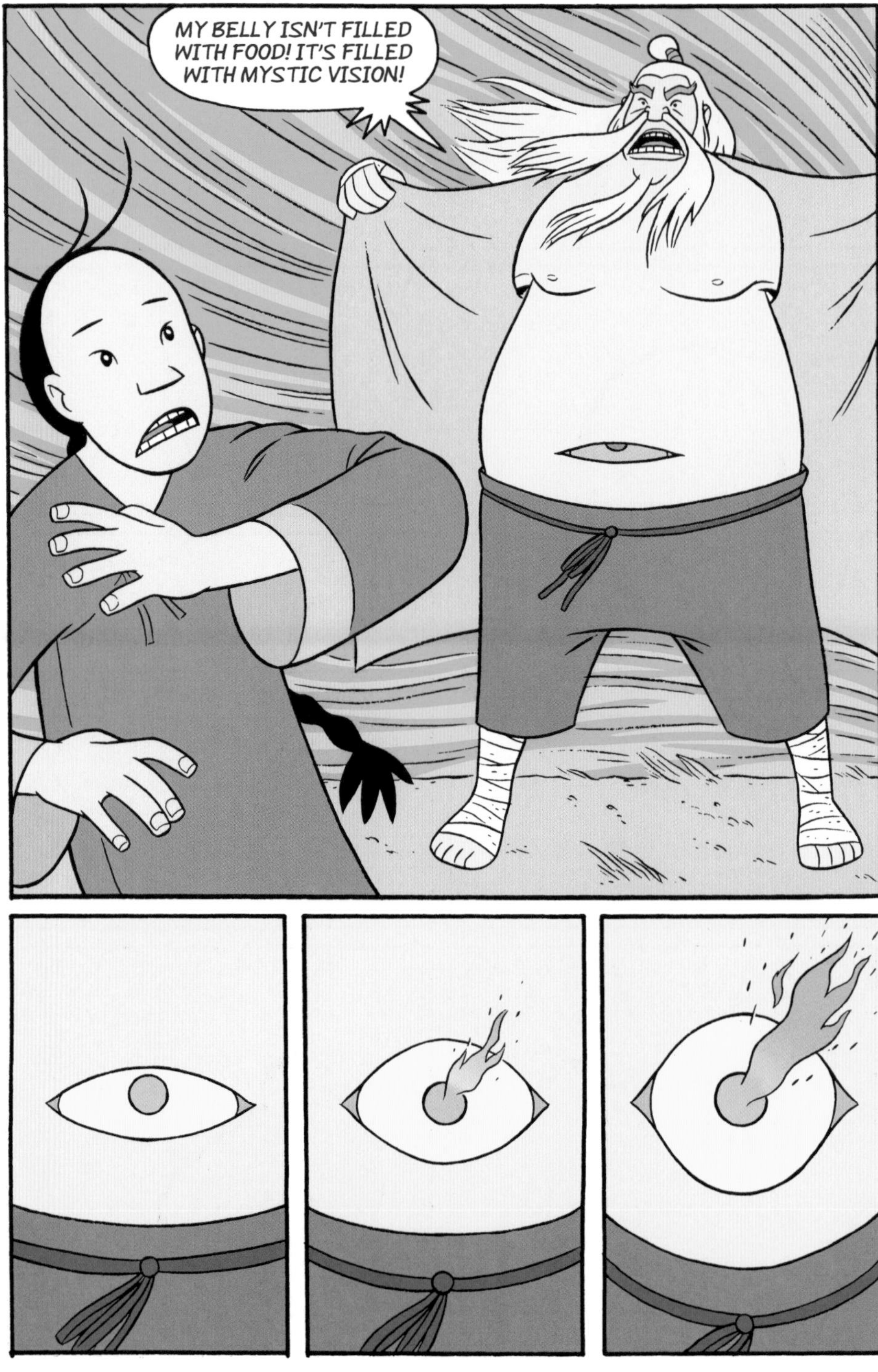
MY BELLY ISN'T FILLED WITH FOOD! IT'S FILLED WITH MYSTIC VISION!

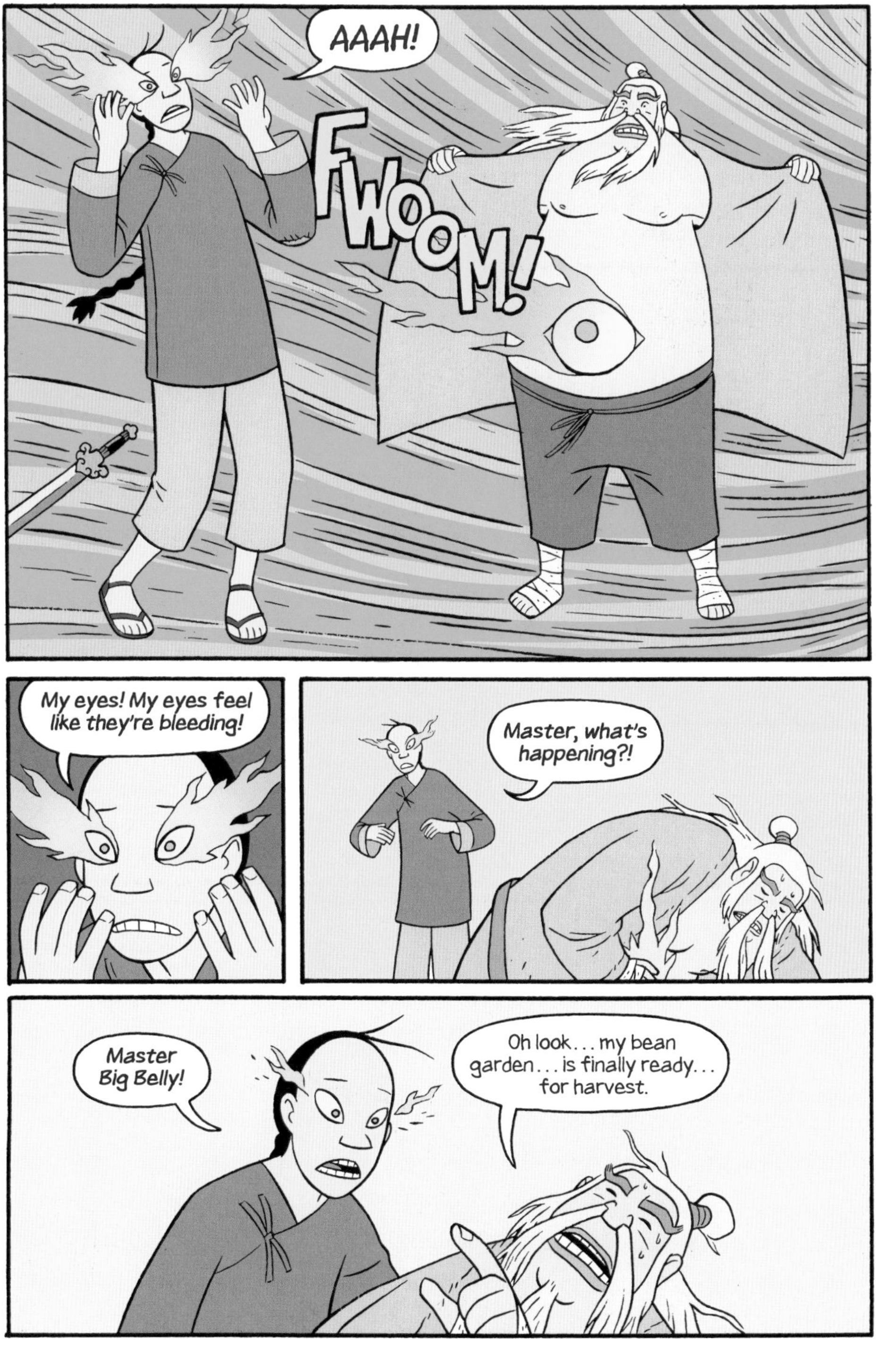
AAAH!
FWOOM!
My eyes! My eyes feel like they're bleeding!
Master, what's happening?!
Master Big Belly!
Oh look... my bean garden... is finally ready... for harvest.

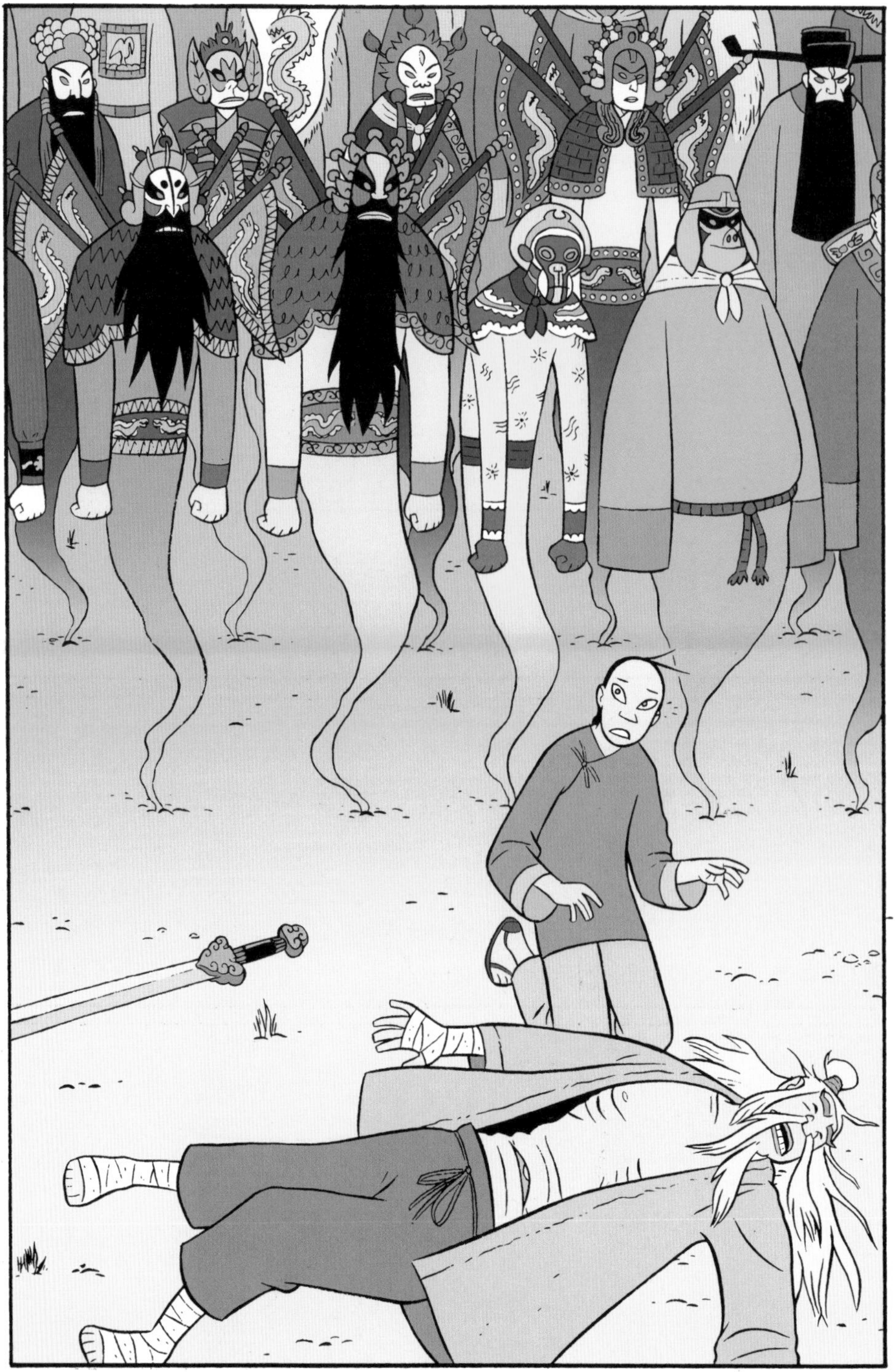

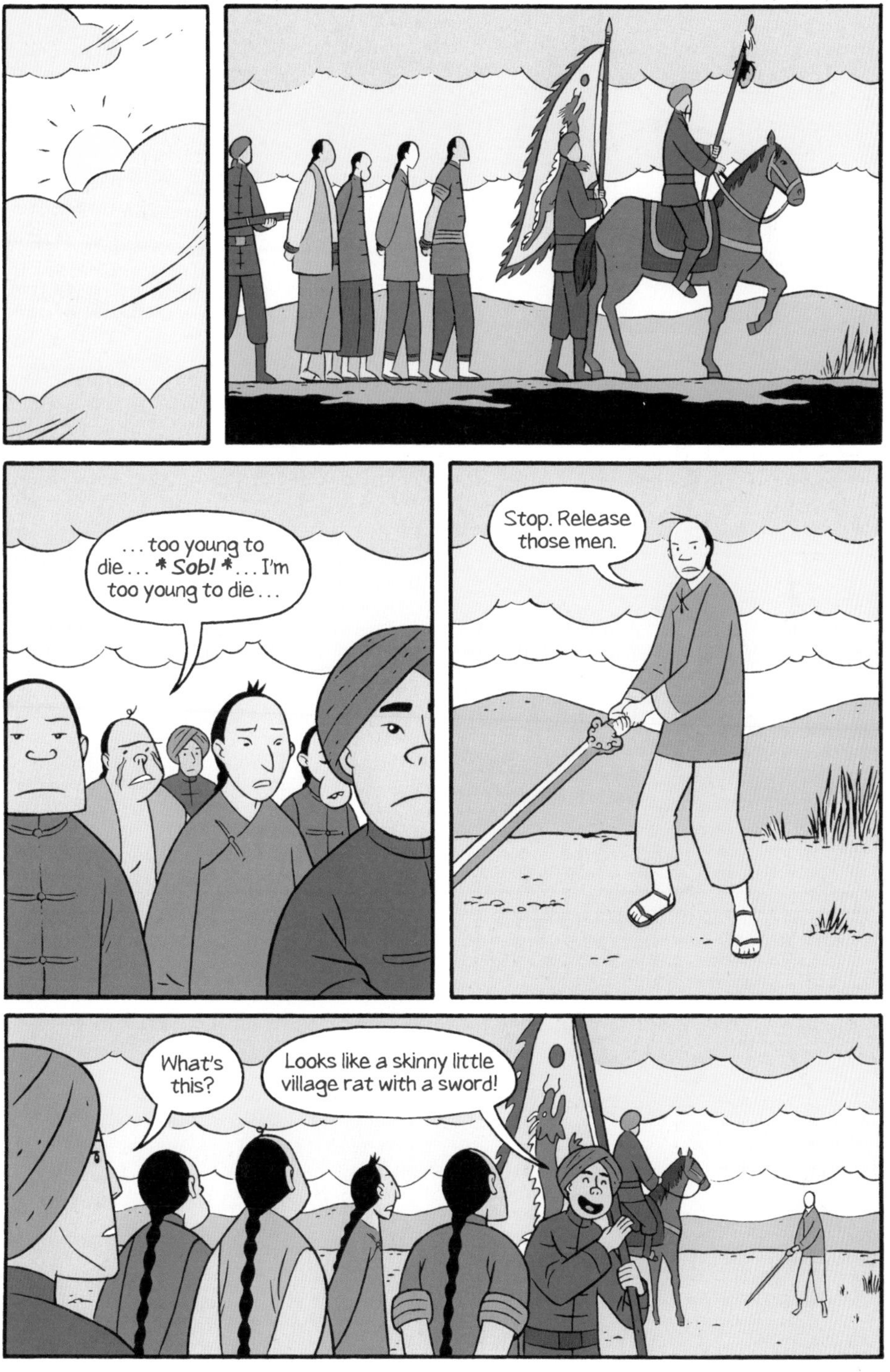

. . . too young to die . . . * Sob! * . . . I'm too young to die . . .
Stop. Release those men.
What's this?
Looks like a skinny little village rat with a sword!

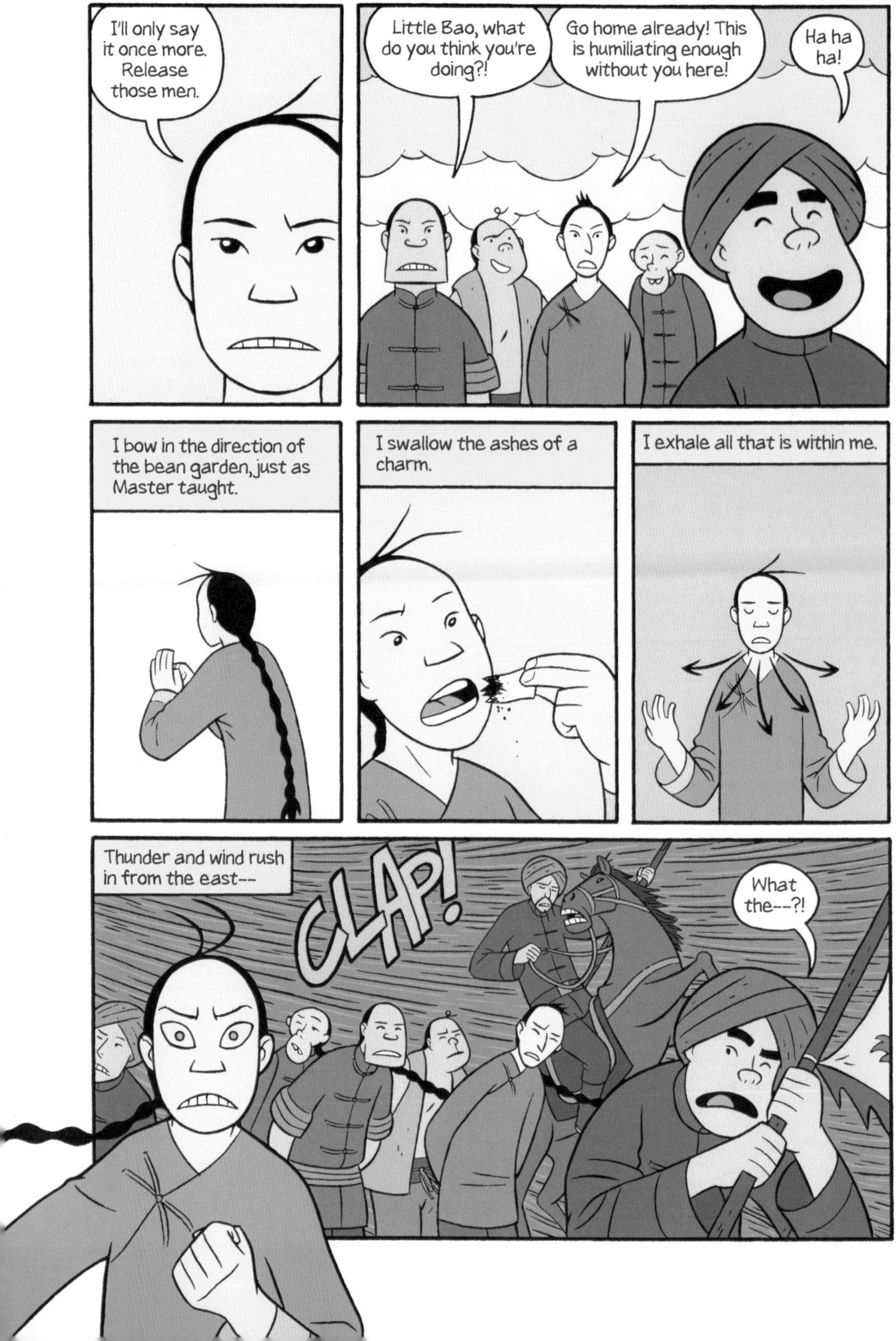
I'll only say it once more. Release those men.
Little Bao, what do you think you're doing?!
Go home already! This is humiliating enough without you here!
Ha ha ha!
I bow in the direction of the bean garden, just as Master taught.
I swallow the ashes of a charm.
I exhale all that is within me.
Thunder and wind rush in from the east--
CLAP!
What the--?!

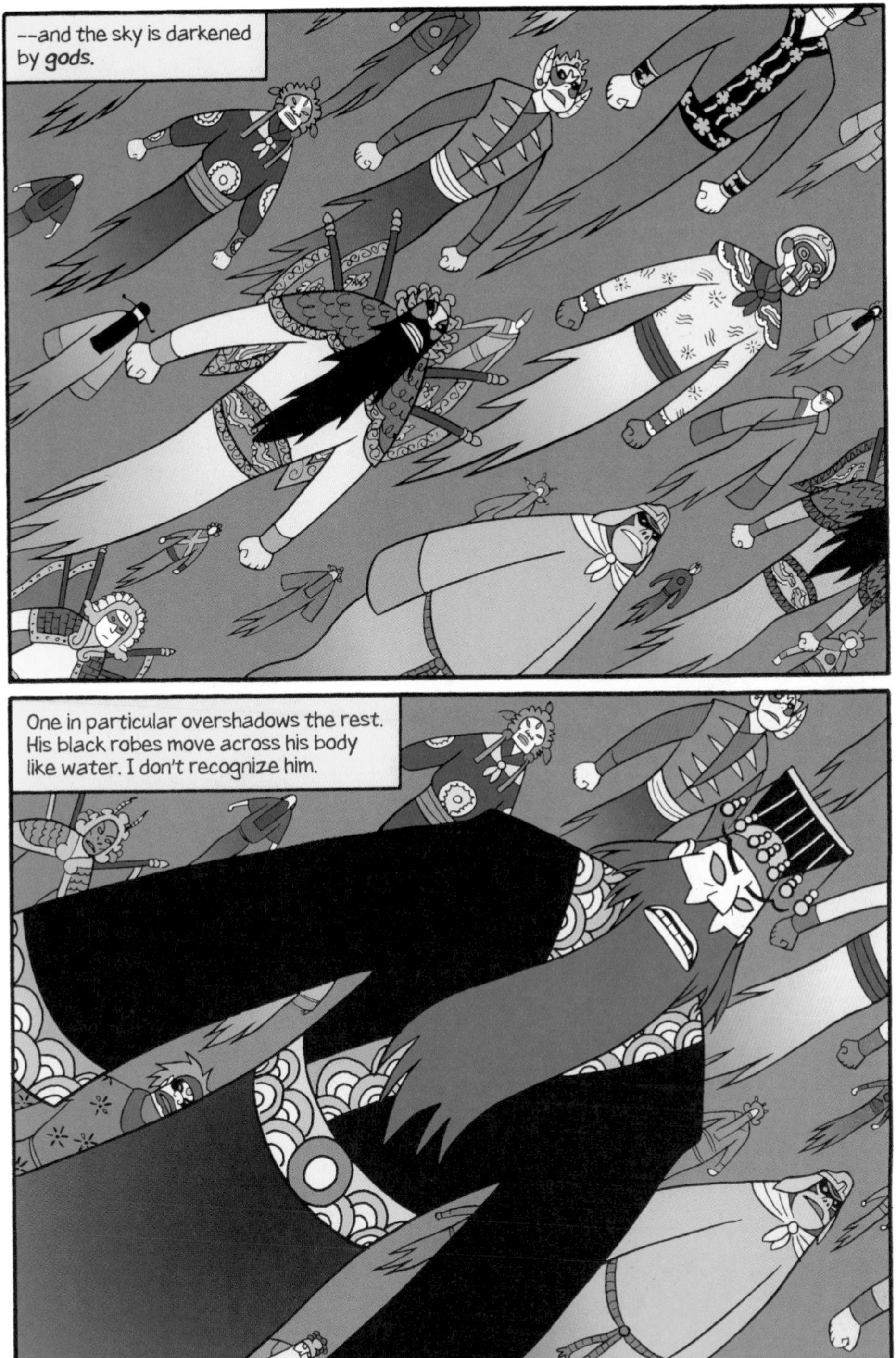
--and the sky is darkened by **gods.**
One in particular overshadows the rest. His black robes move across his body like water. I don't recognize him.

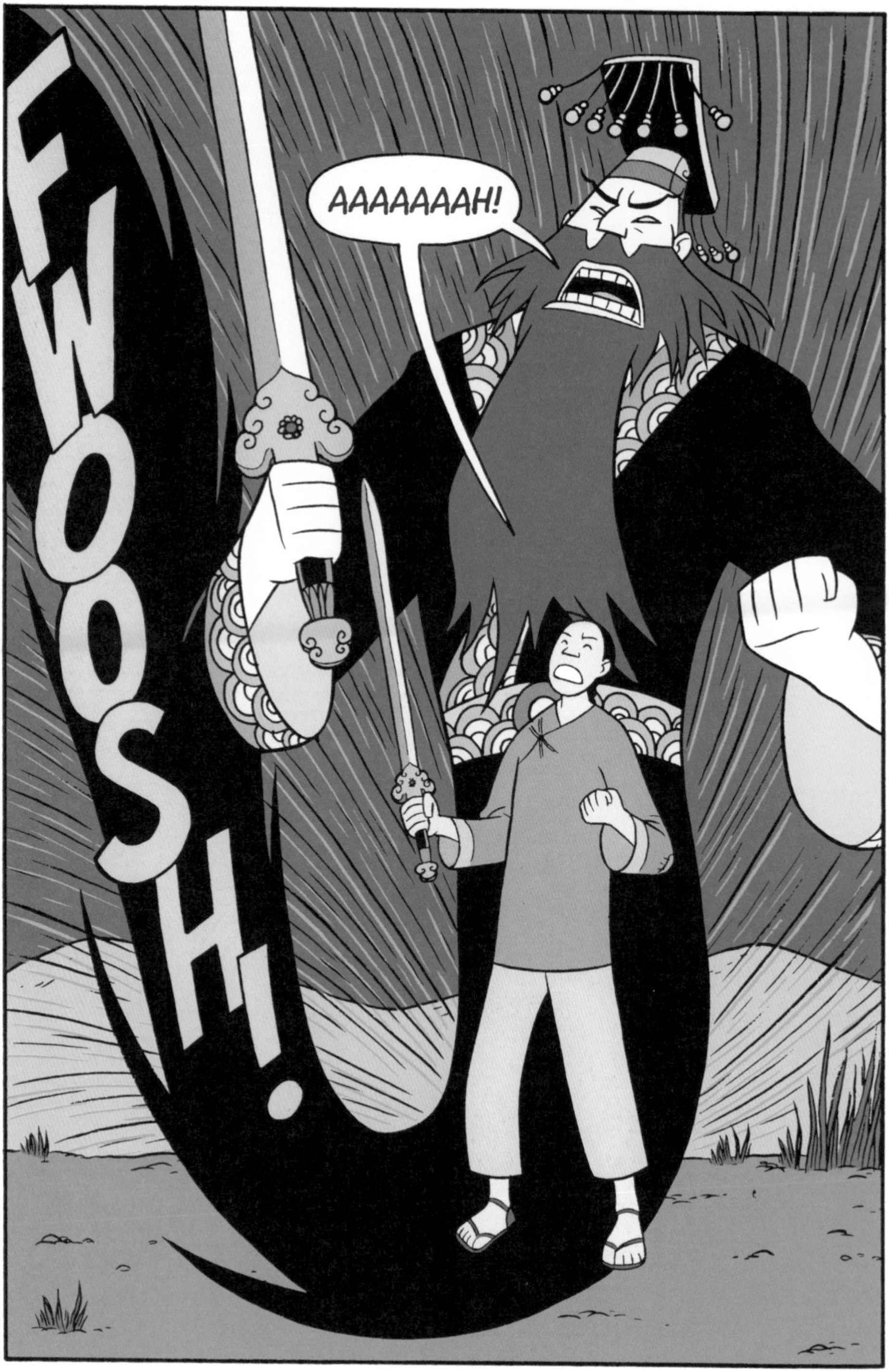
AAAAAAAH!
FWOOSH!

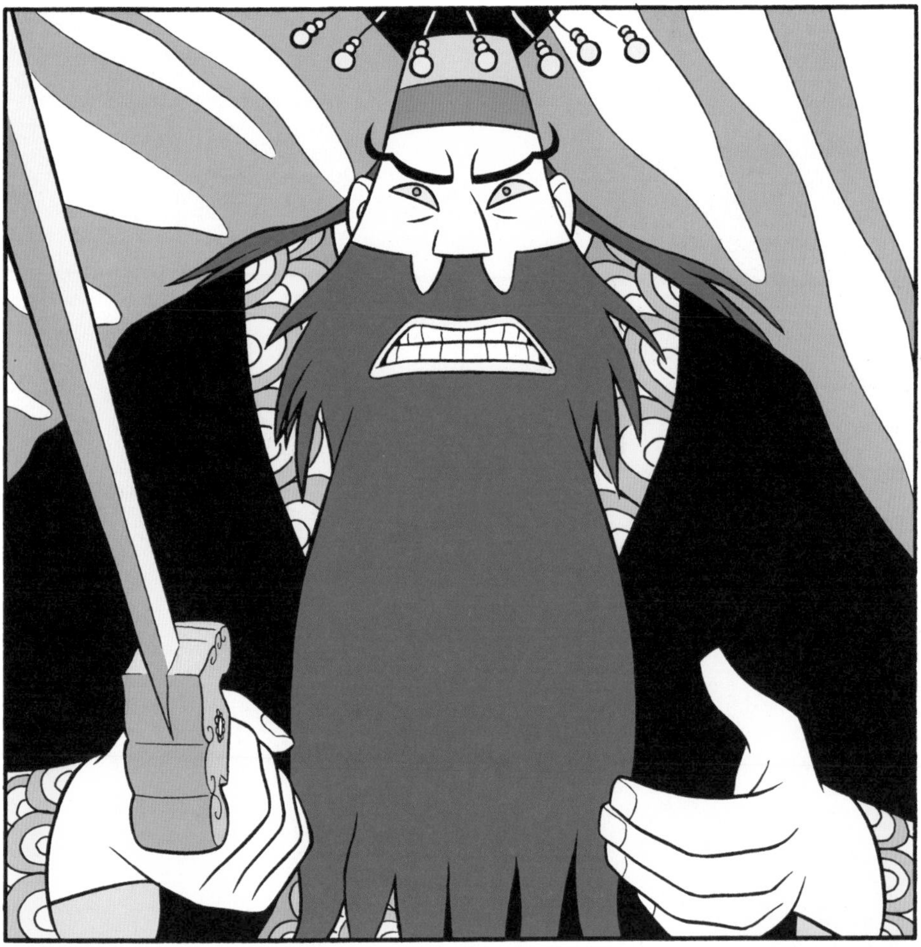

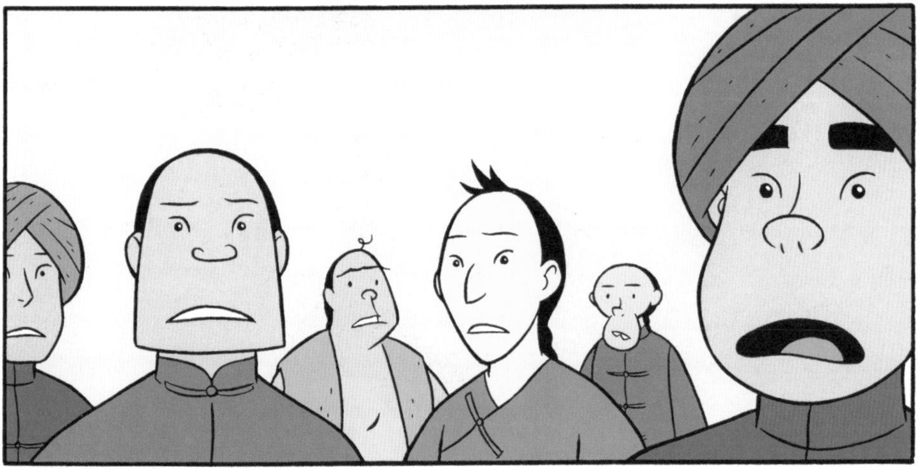

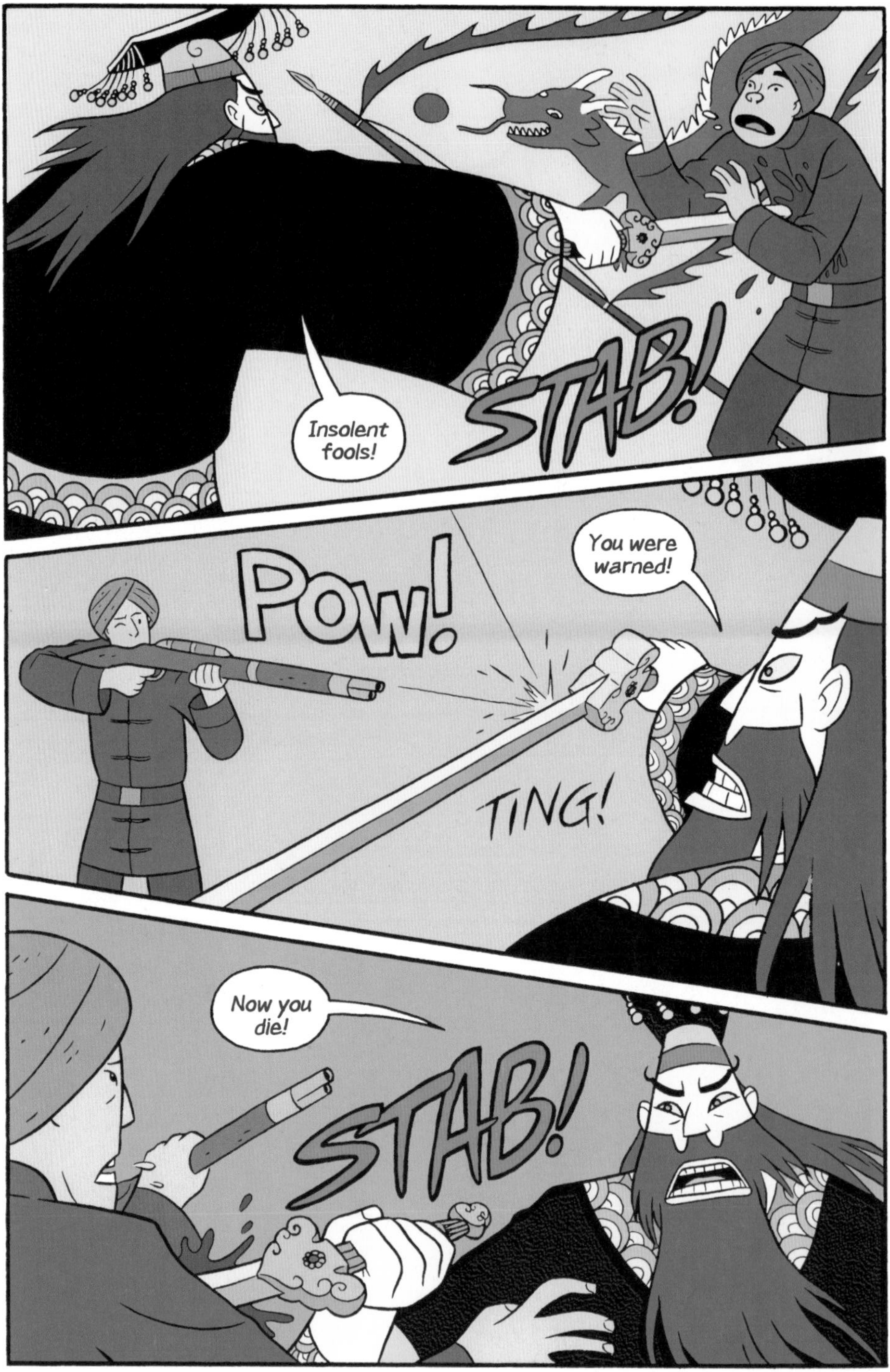
Insolent fools!
STAB!
POW!
You were warned!
TING!
Now you die!
STAB!

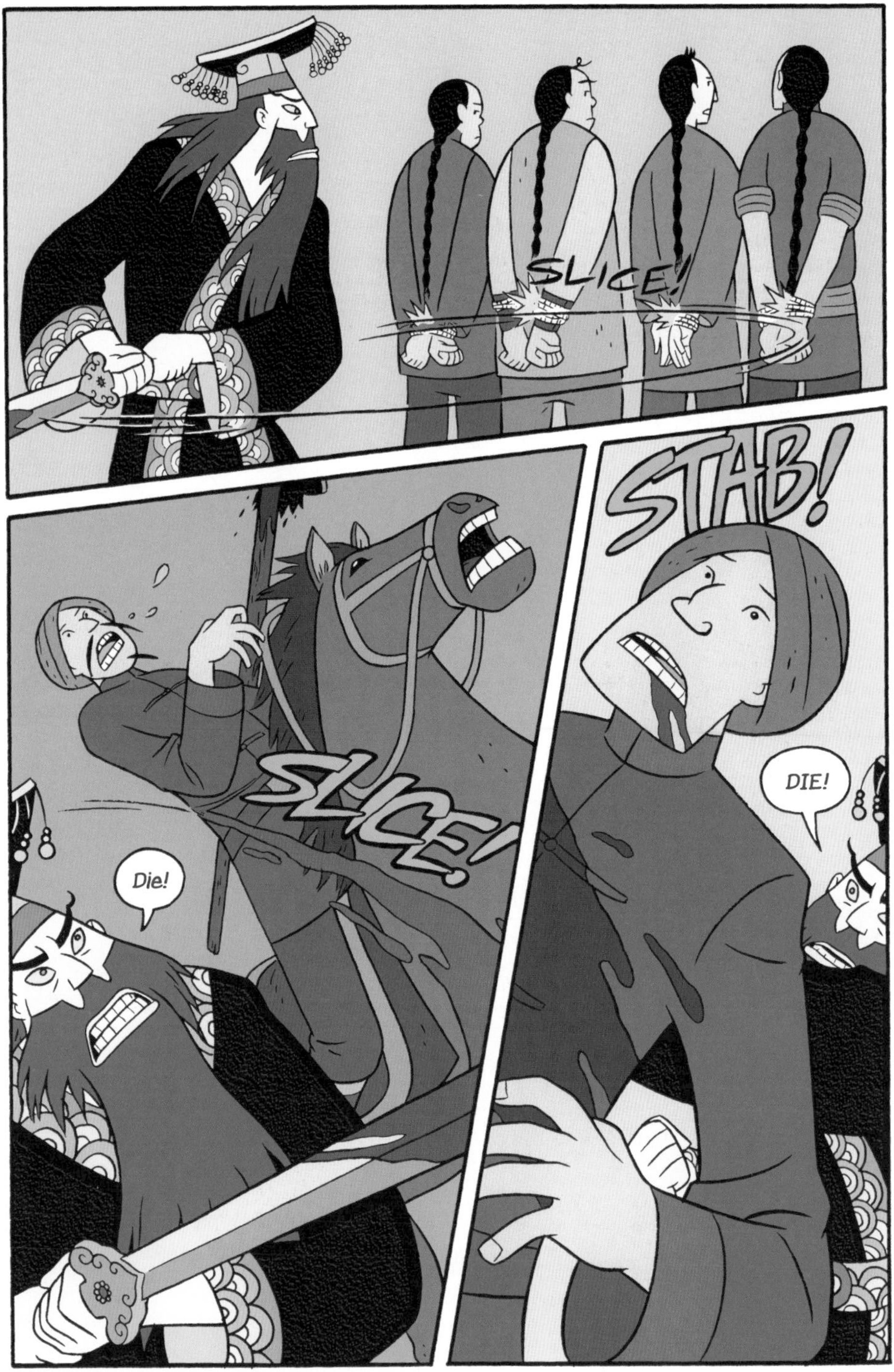
SLICE!
SLICE!
Die!
STAB!
DIE!

SIGH!

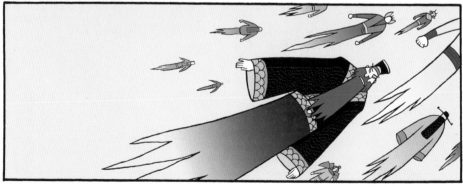

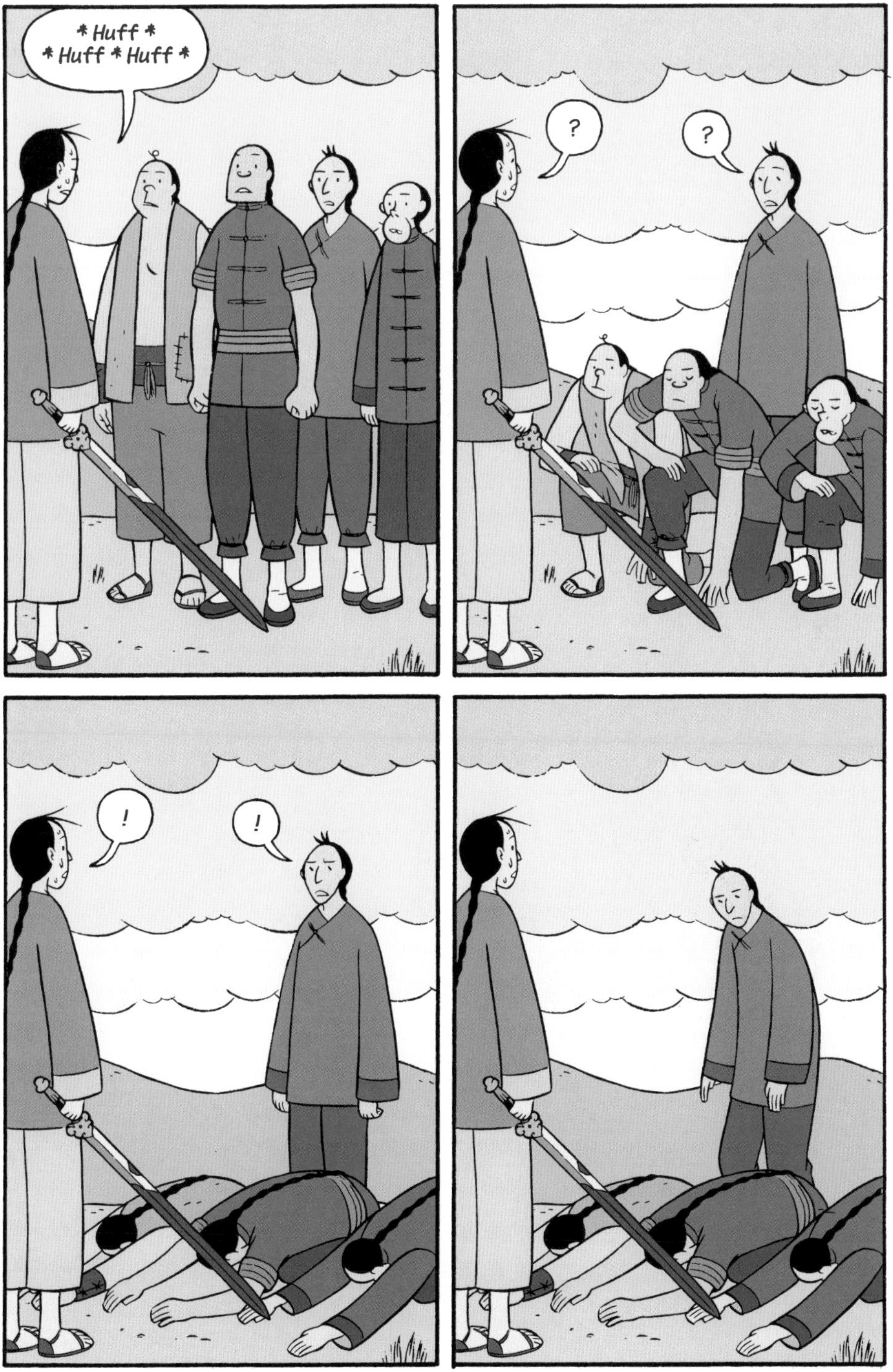
* Huff *
* Huff * Huff *
?
?
!
!

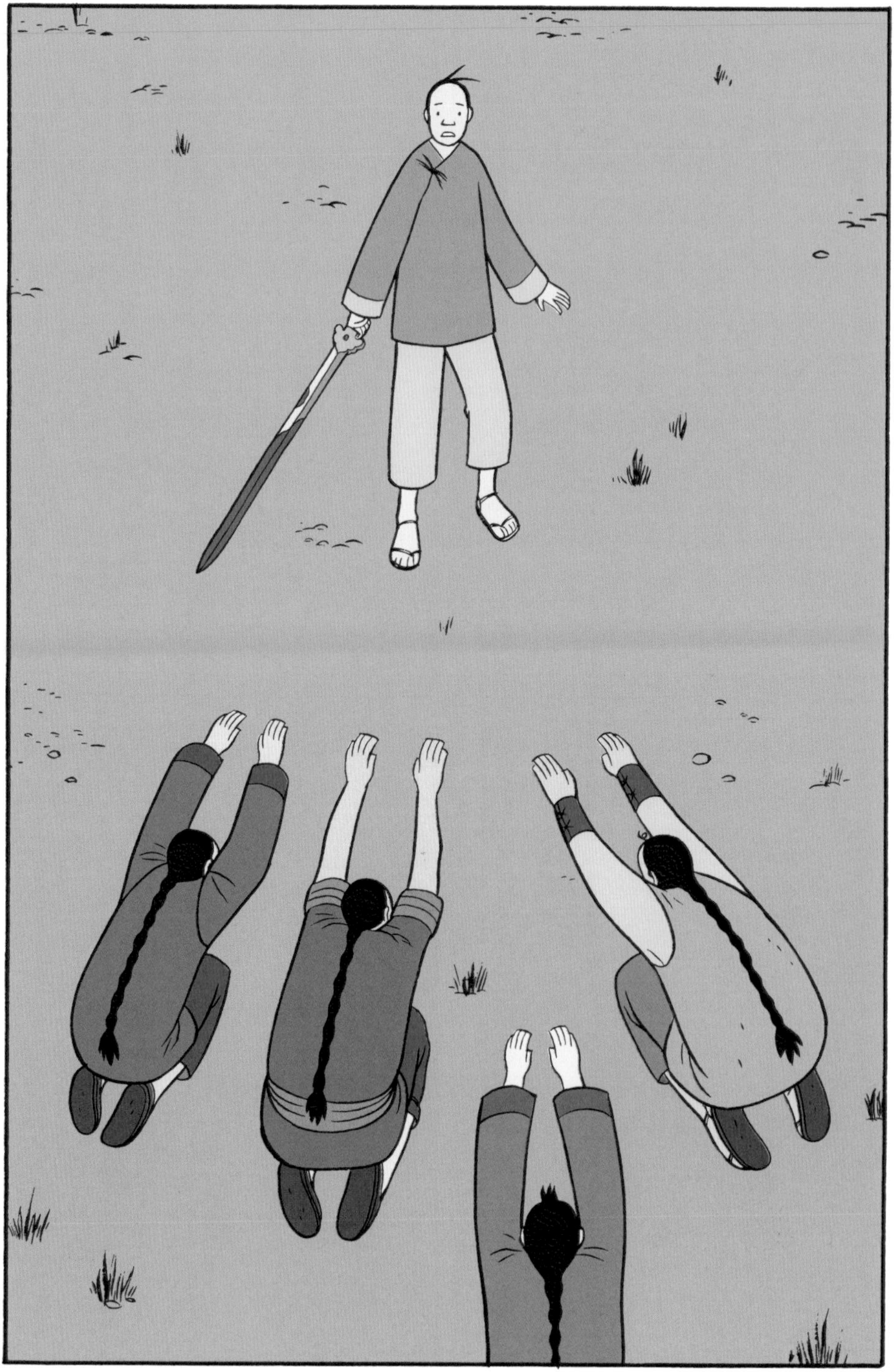

第四章

Northern Shan-tung Province, China
Fall 1899

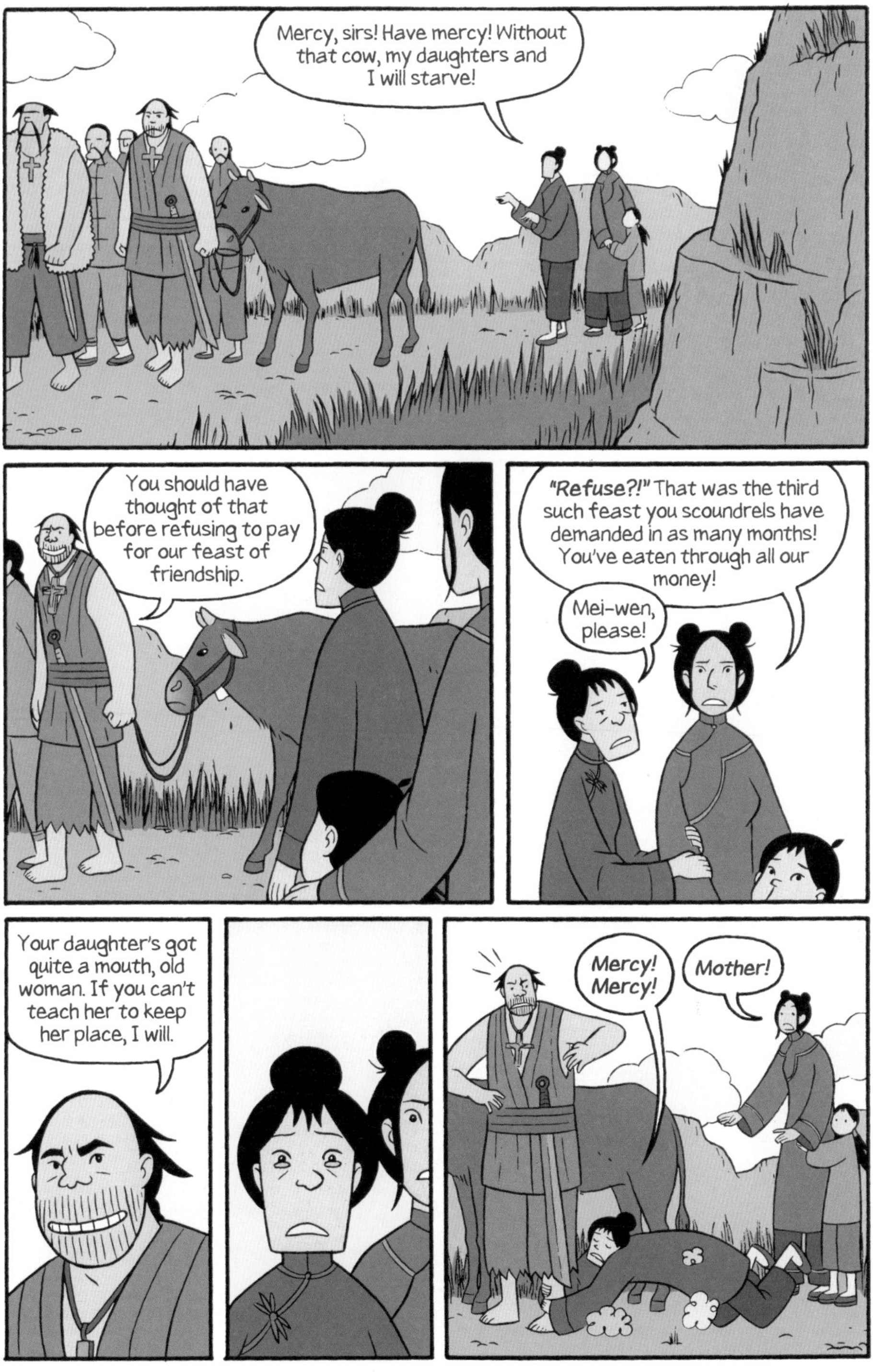
Mercy, sirs! Have mercy! Without that cow, my daughters and I will starve!
You should have thought of that before refusing to pay for our feast of friendship.
"Refuse?!" That was the third such feast you scoundrels have demanded in as many months! You've eaten through all our money!
Mei-wen, please!
Your daughter's got quite a mouth, old woman. If you can't teach her to keep her place, I will.
Mercy! Mercy!
Mother!

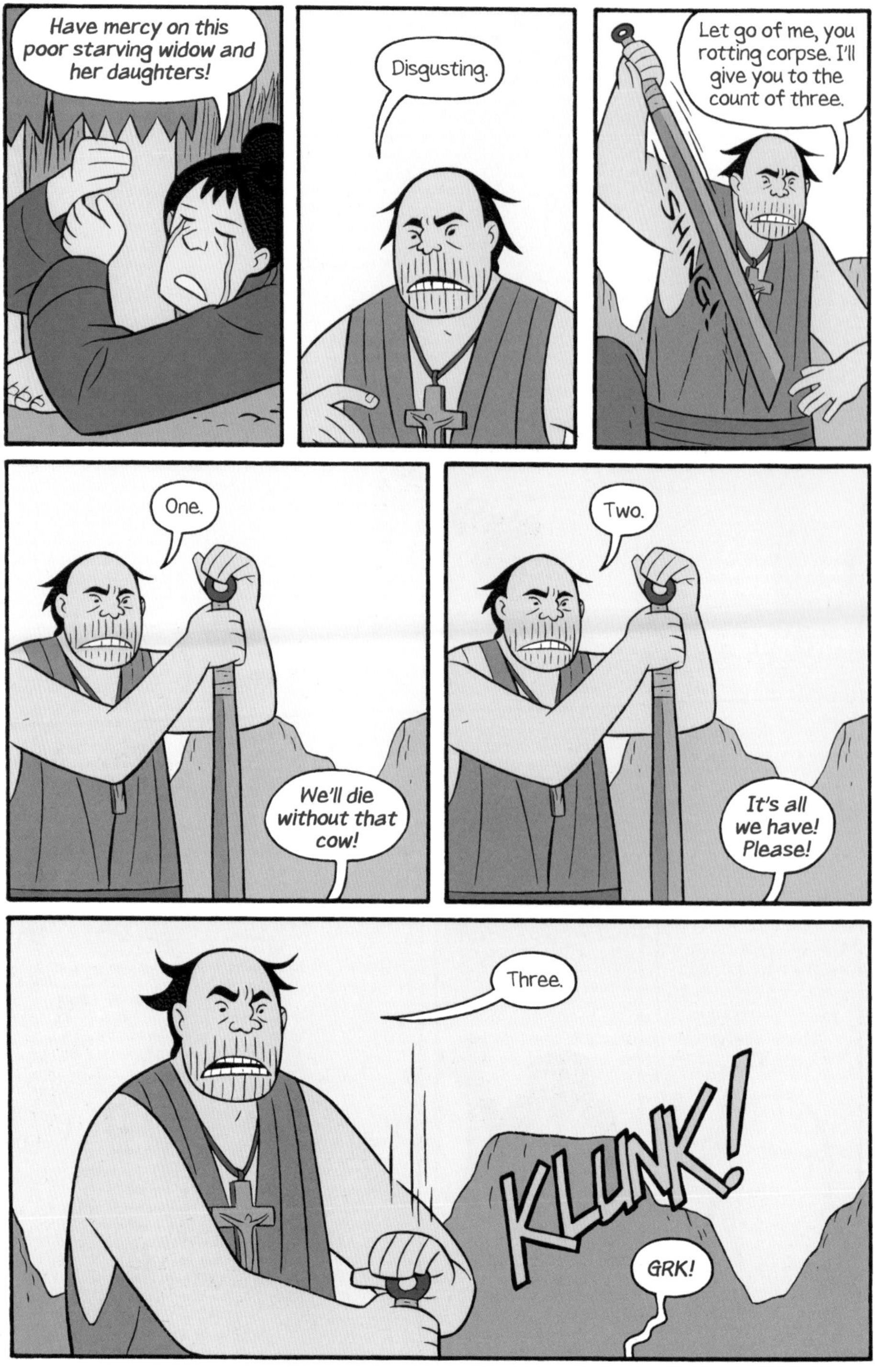
Have mercy on this poor starving widow and her daughters!
Disgusting.
Let go of me, you rotting corpse. I'll give you to the count of three.
SHING!
One.
We'll die without that cow!
Two.
It's all we have! Please!
Three.
KLUNK!
GRK!

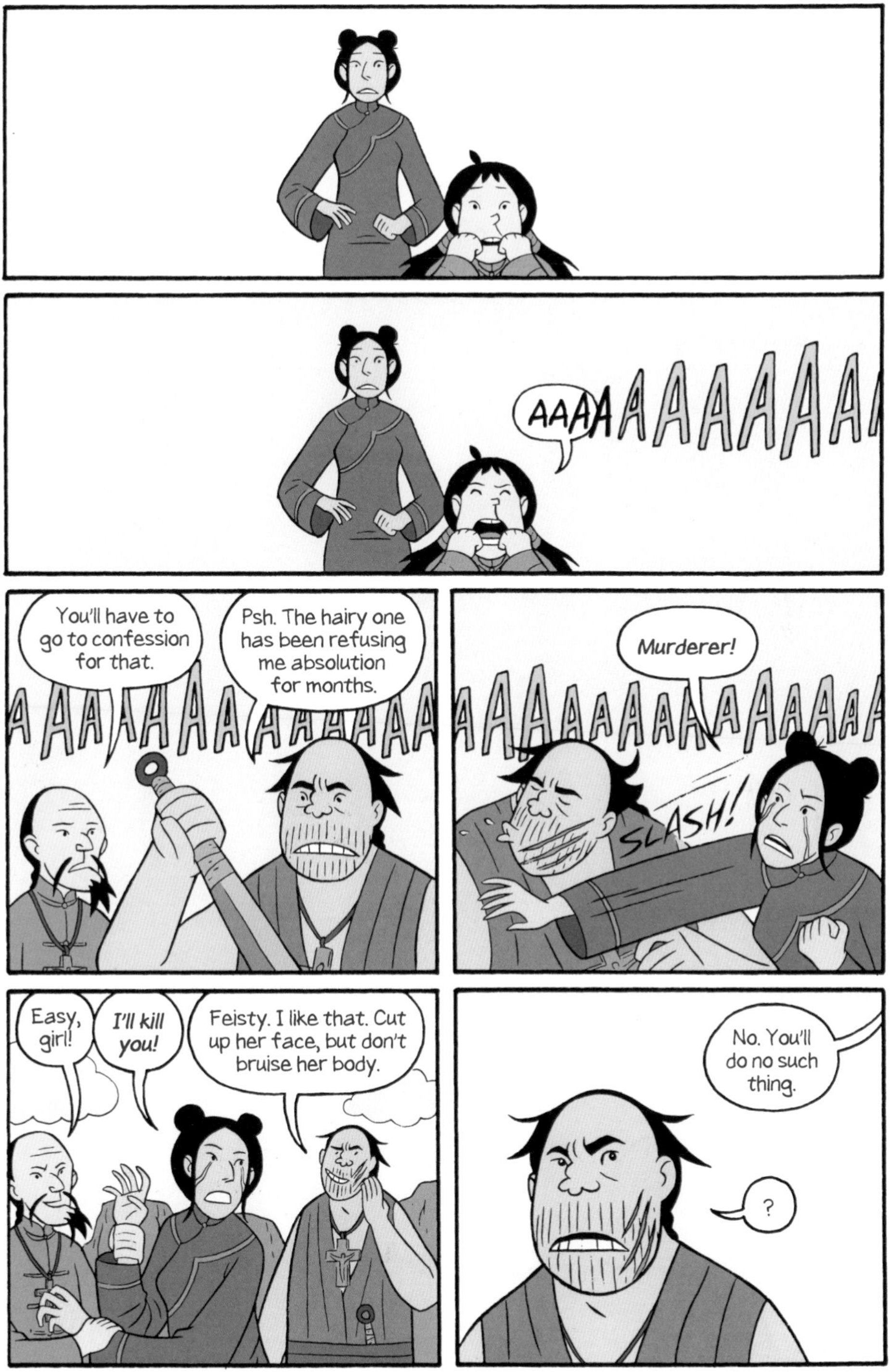
AAAAAAAAAAAAA
You'll have to go to confession for that.
Psh. The hairy one has been refusing me absolution for months.
Murderer!
SLASH!
Easy, girl!
I'll kill you!
Feisty. I like that. Cut up her face, but don't bruise her body.
No. You'll do no such thing.
?

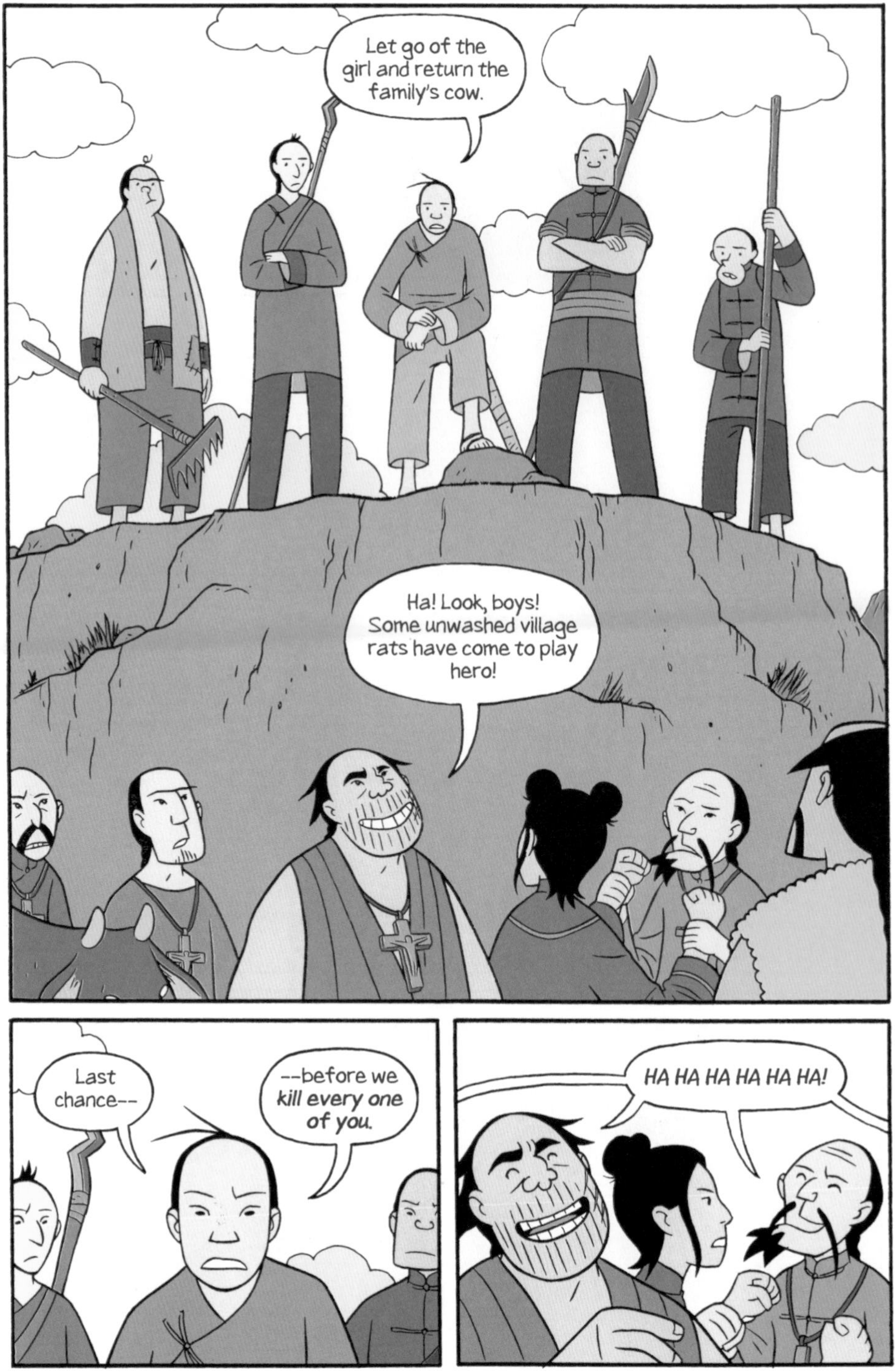
Let go of the girl and return the family's cow.
Ha! Look, boys! Some unwashed village rats have come to play hero!
Last chance--
--before we *kill every one of you.*
HA HA HA HA HA HA!

My brothers and the other boys are fast learners. They mastered the Ritual after practicing it just a couple of times.

Together, we bow toward the bean garden--

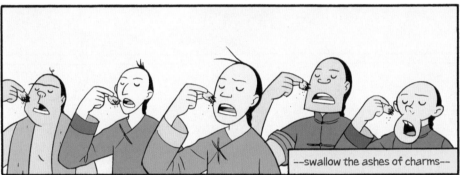

--swallow the ashes of charms--

--and exhale all that is within us.

Thunder and wind rush in from the east--

CLAP!

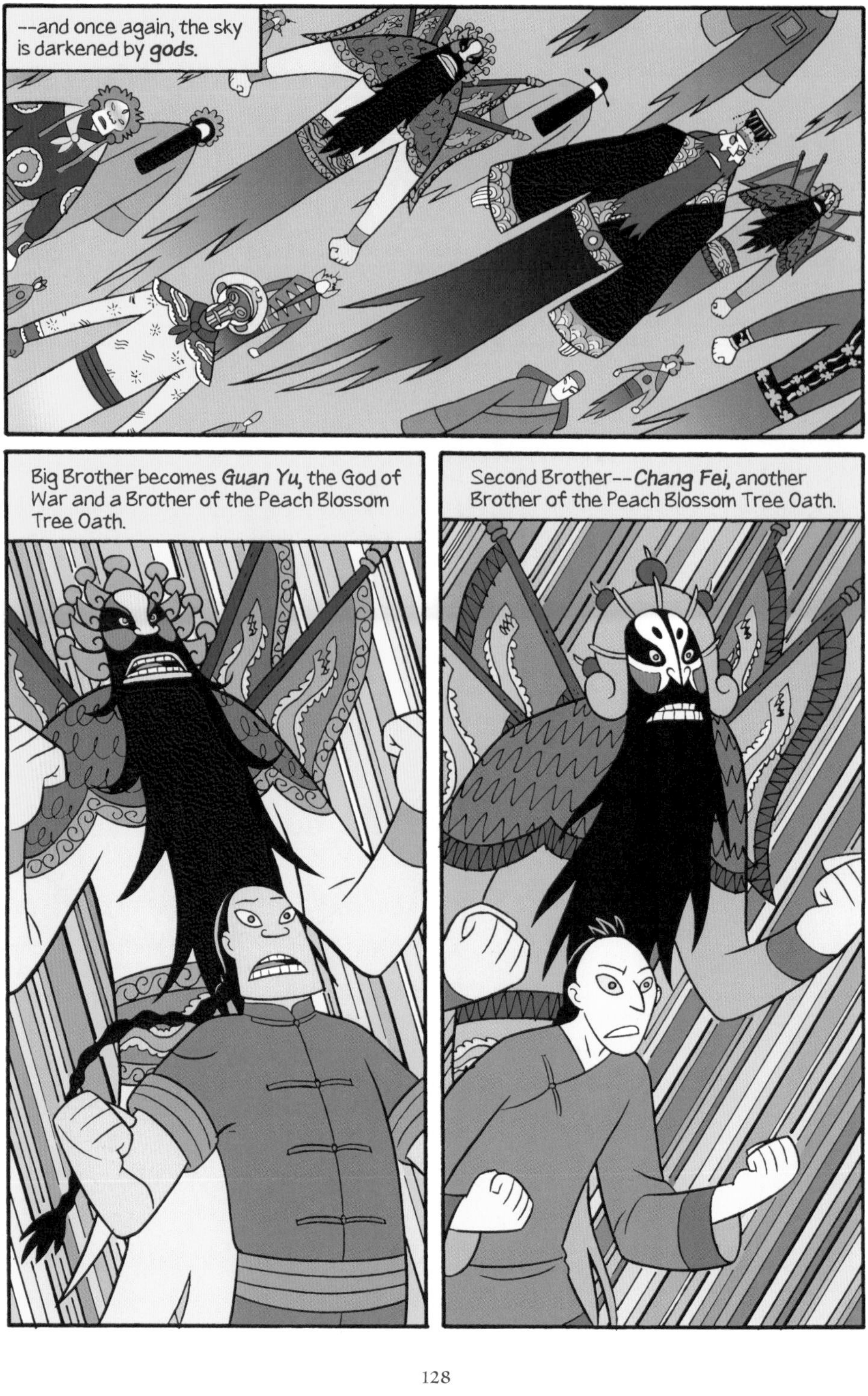
--and once again, the sky is darkened by ***gods***.
Big Brother becomes ***Guan Yu***, the God of War and a Brother of the Peach Blossom Tree Oath.
Second Brother--***Chang Fei***, another Brother of the Peach Blossom Tree Oath.

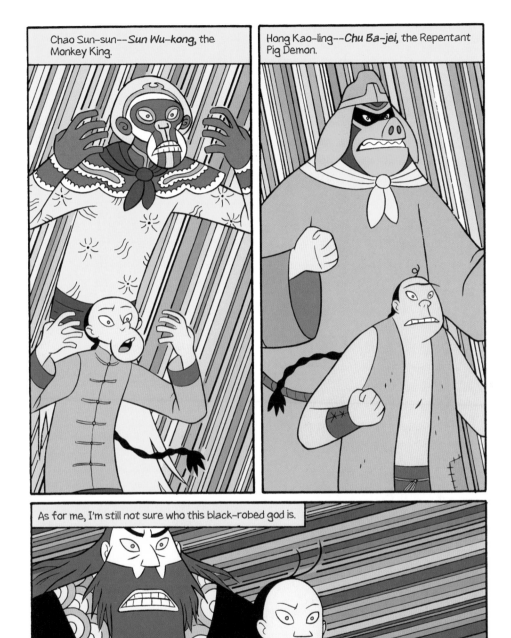

Chao Sun-sun--*Sun Wu-kong,* the Monkey King.

Hong Kao-ling--*Chu Ba-jei,* the Repentant Pig Demon.

As for me, I'm still not sure who this black-robed god is.

For an instant just as I transform, my breath catches in my throat and I feel like I'm about to drown.

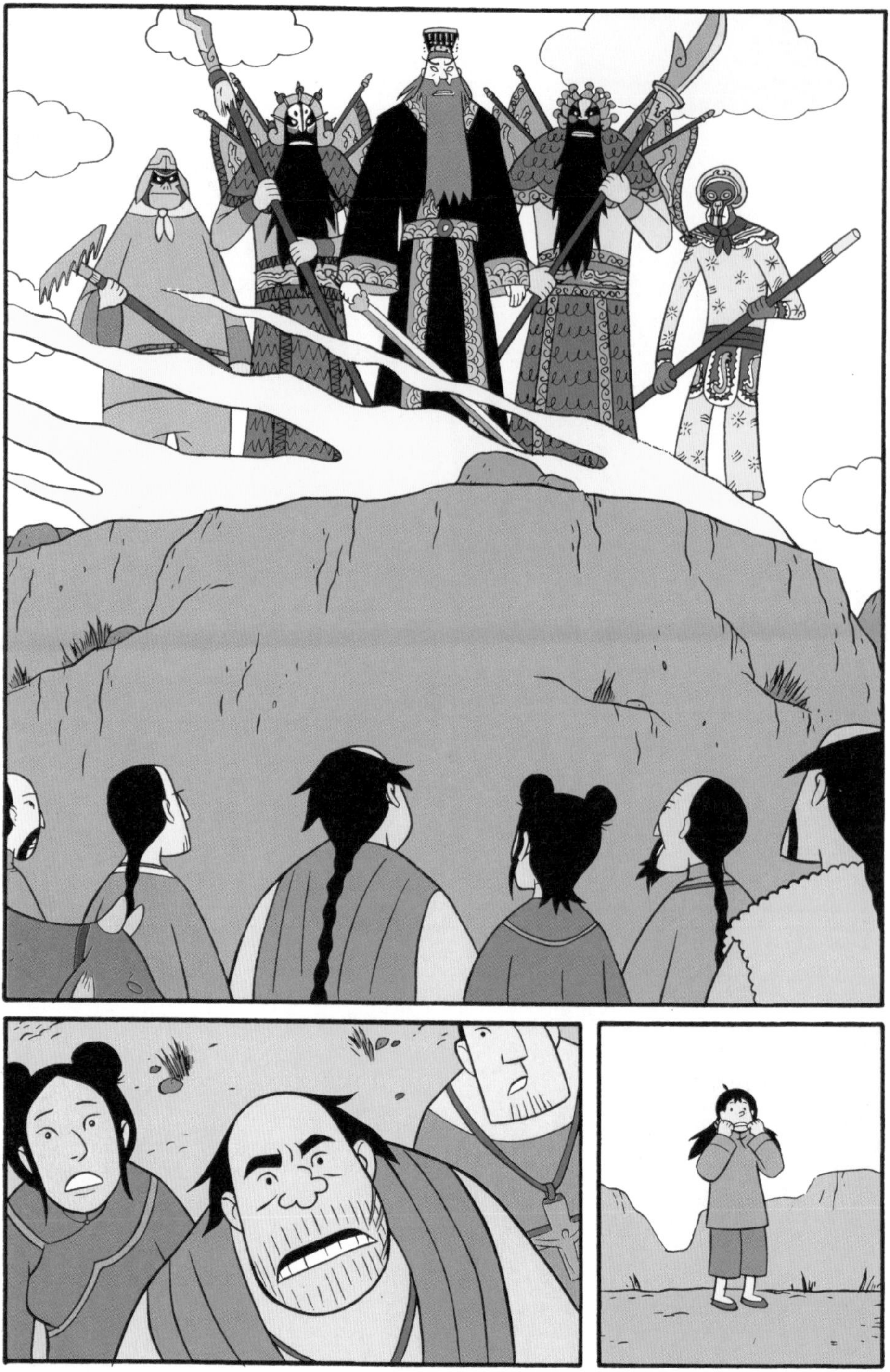

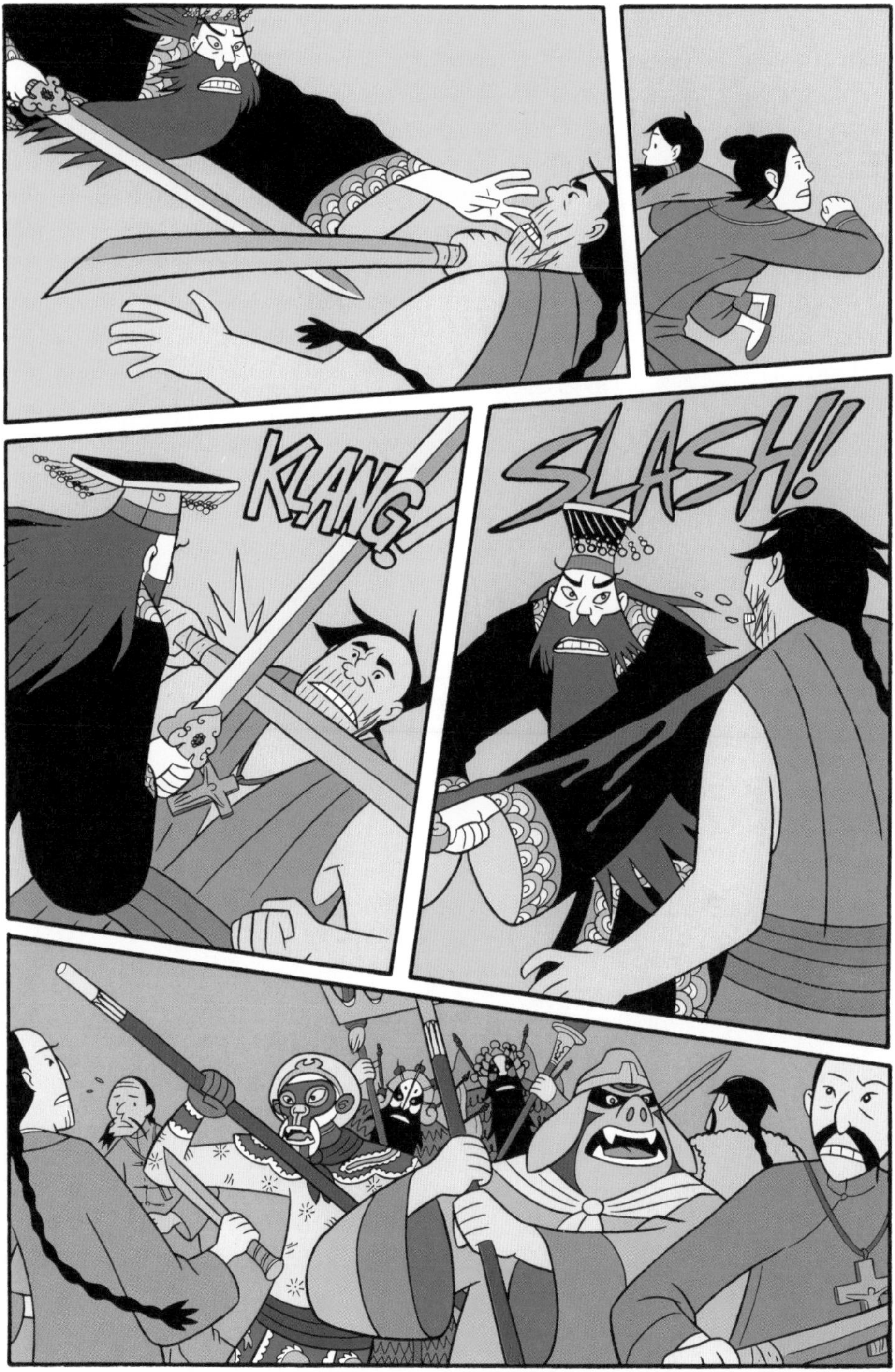
KLANG!
SLASH!

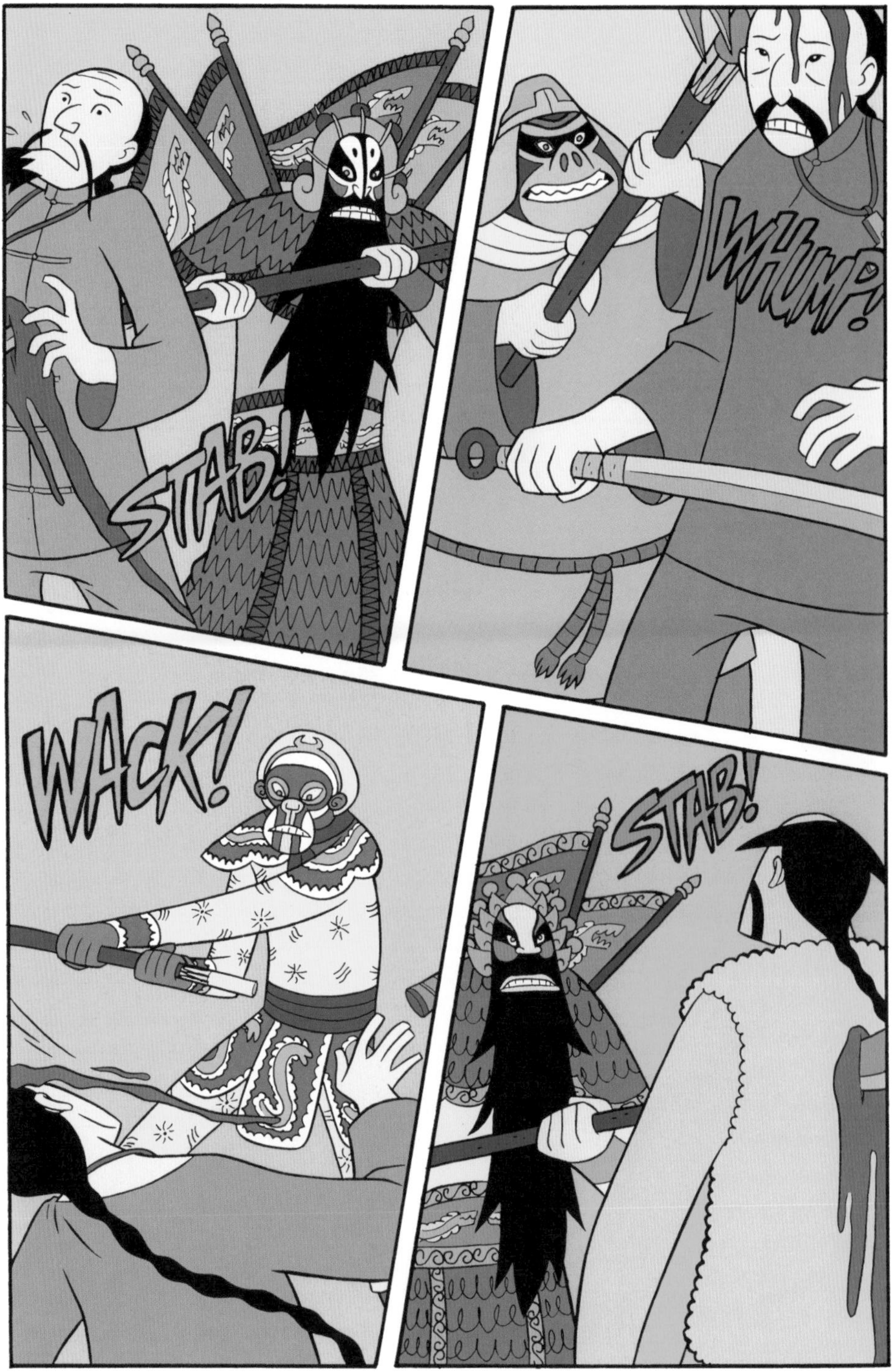
STAB!
WHUMP!
WACK!
STAB!

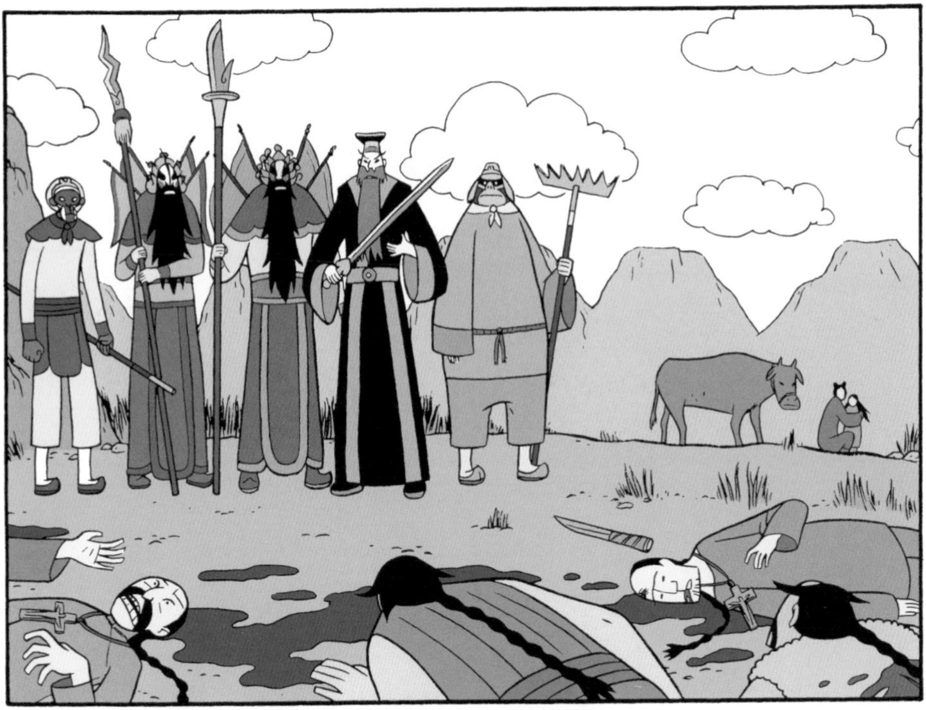

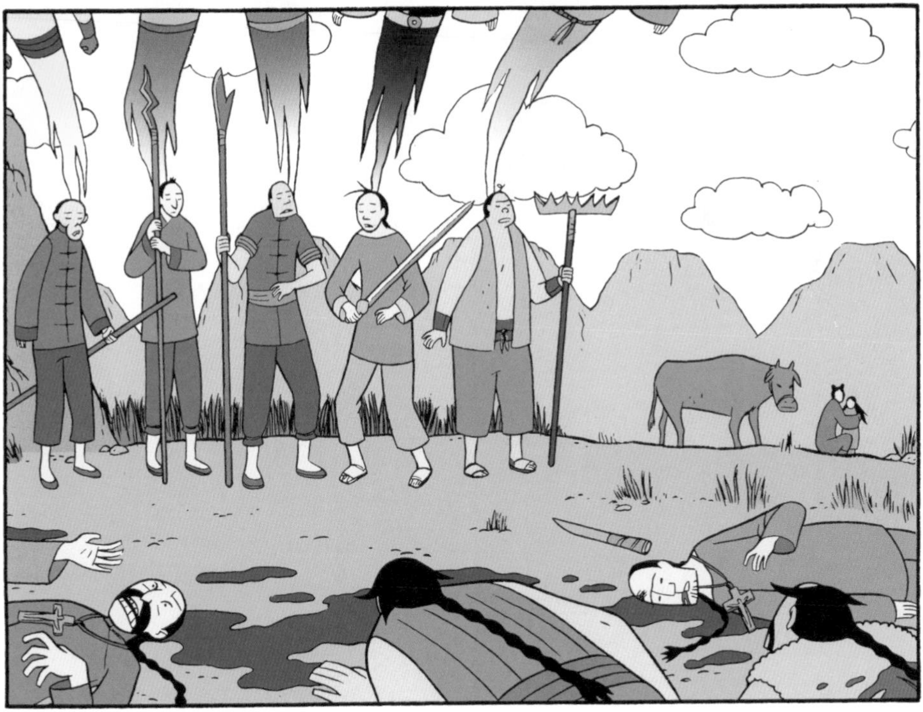

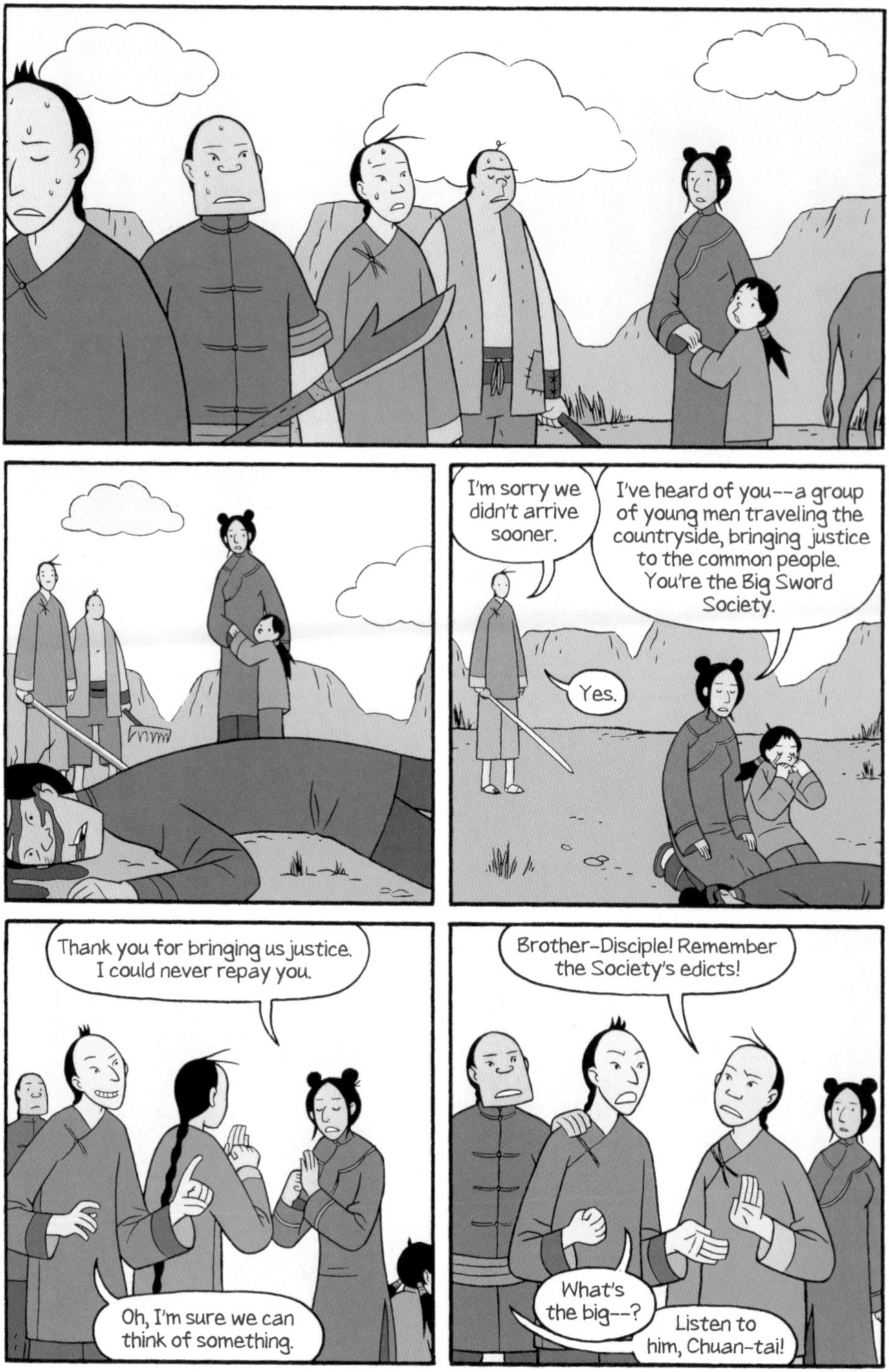
I'm sorry we didn't arrive sooner.
I've heard of you--a group of young men traveling the countryside, bringing justice to the common people. You're the Big Sword Society.
Yes.
Thank you for bringing us justice. I could never repay you.
Oh, I'm sure we can think of something.
Brother-Disciple! Remember the Society's edicts!
What's the big--?
Listen to him, Chuan-tai!

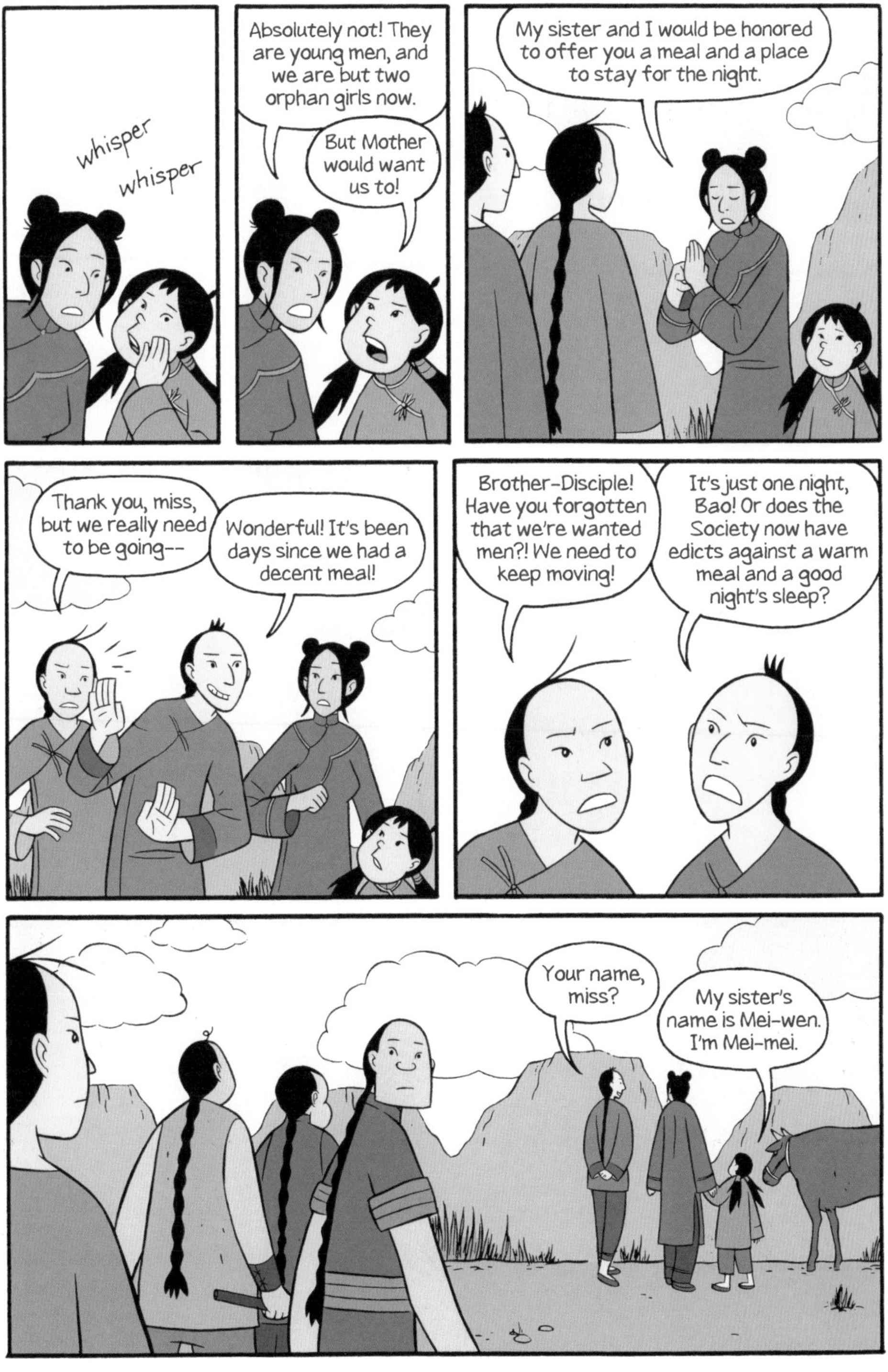
whisper
whisper
Absolutely not! They are young men, and we are but two orphan girls now.
But Mother would want us to!
My sister and I would be honored to offer you a meal and a place to stay for the night.
Thank you, miss, but we really need to be going--
Wonderful! It's been days since we had a decent meal!
Brother-Disciple! Have you forgotten that we're wanted men?! We need to keep moving!
It's just one night, Bao! Or does the Society now have edicts against a warm meal and a good night's sleep?
Your name, miss?
My sister's name is Mei-wen. I'm Mei-mei.

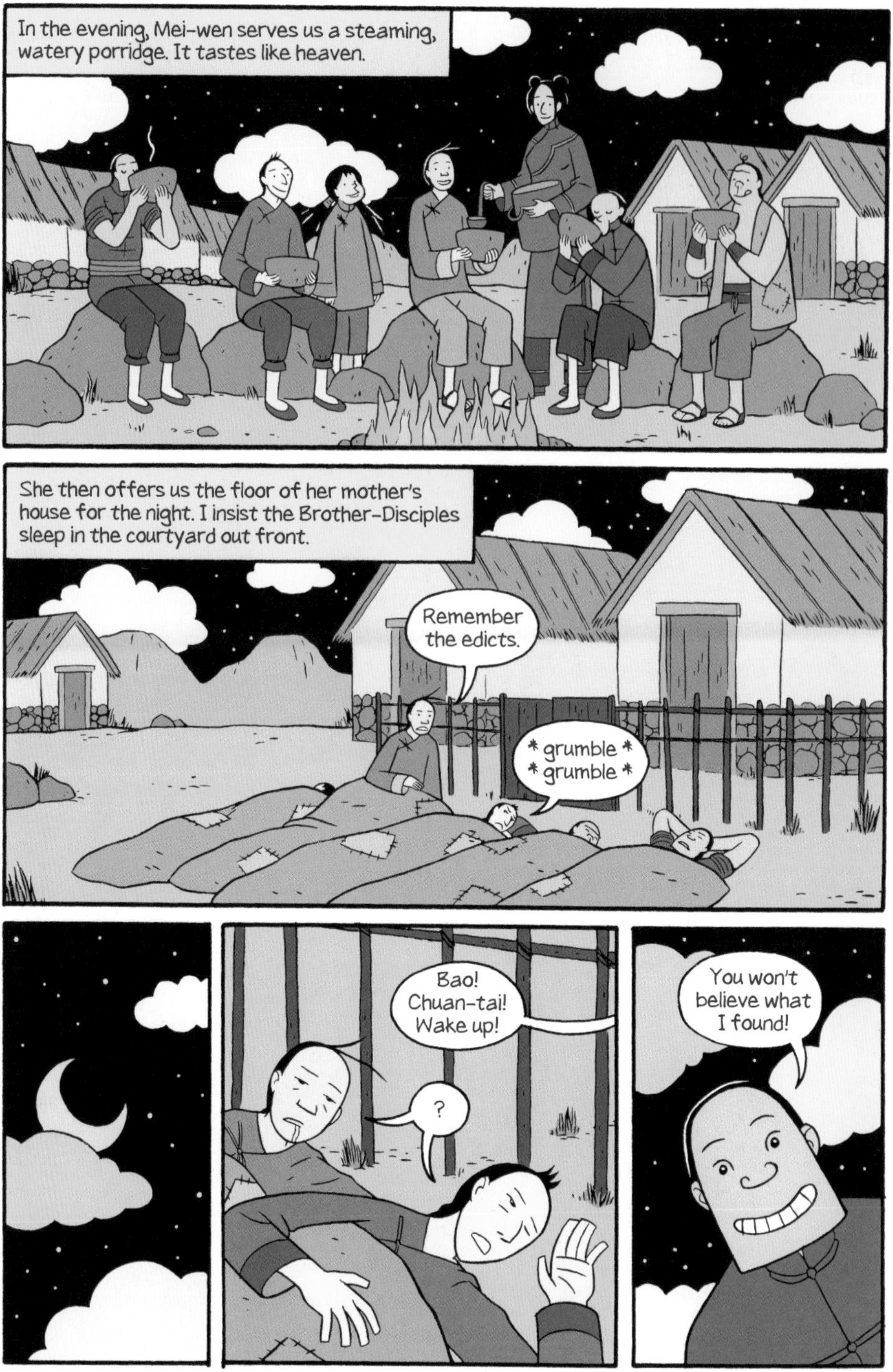
In the evening, Mei-wen serves us a steaming, watery porridge. It tastes like heaven.
She then offers us the floor of her mother's house for the night. I insist the Brother-Disciples sleep in the courtyard out front.
Remember the edicts.
* grumble * * grumble *
Bao! Chuan-tai! Wake up!
?
You won't believe what I found!

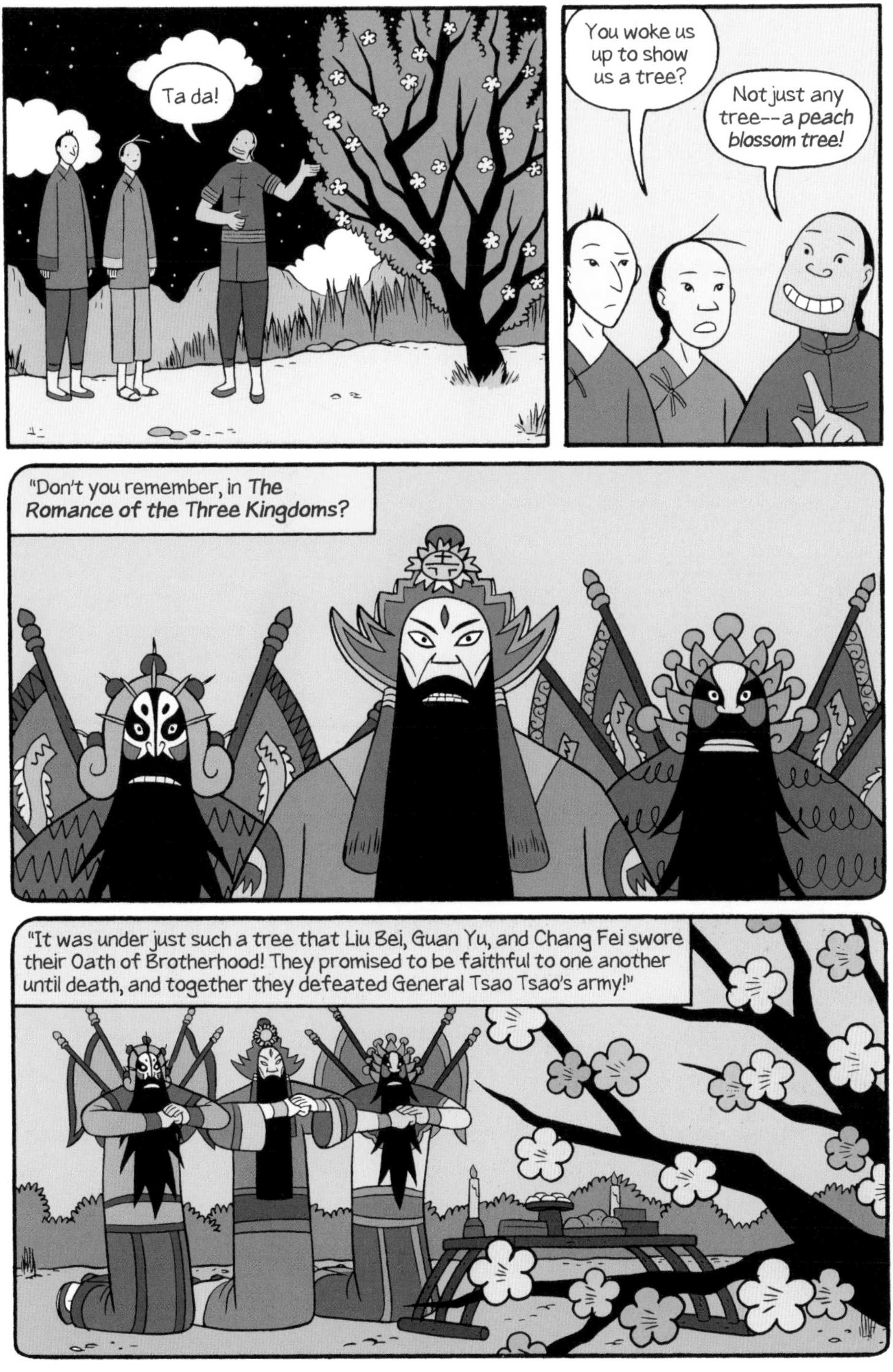
Ta da!
You woke us up to show us a tree?
Not just any tree--a *peach blossom tree!*
"Don't you remember, in *The Romance of the Three Kingdoms*?
"It was under just such a tree that Liu Bei, Guan Yu, and Chang Fei swore their Oath of Brotherhood! They promised to be faithful to one another until death, and together they defeated General Tsao Tsao's army!"

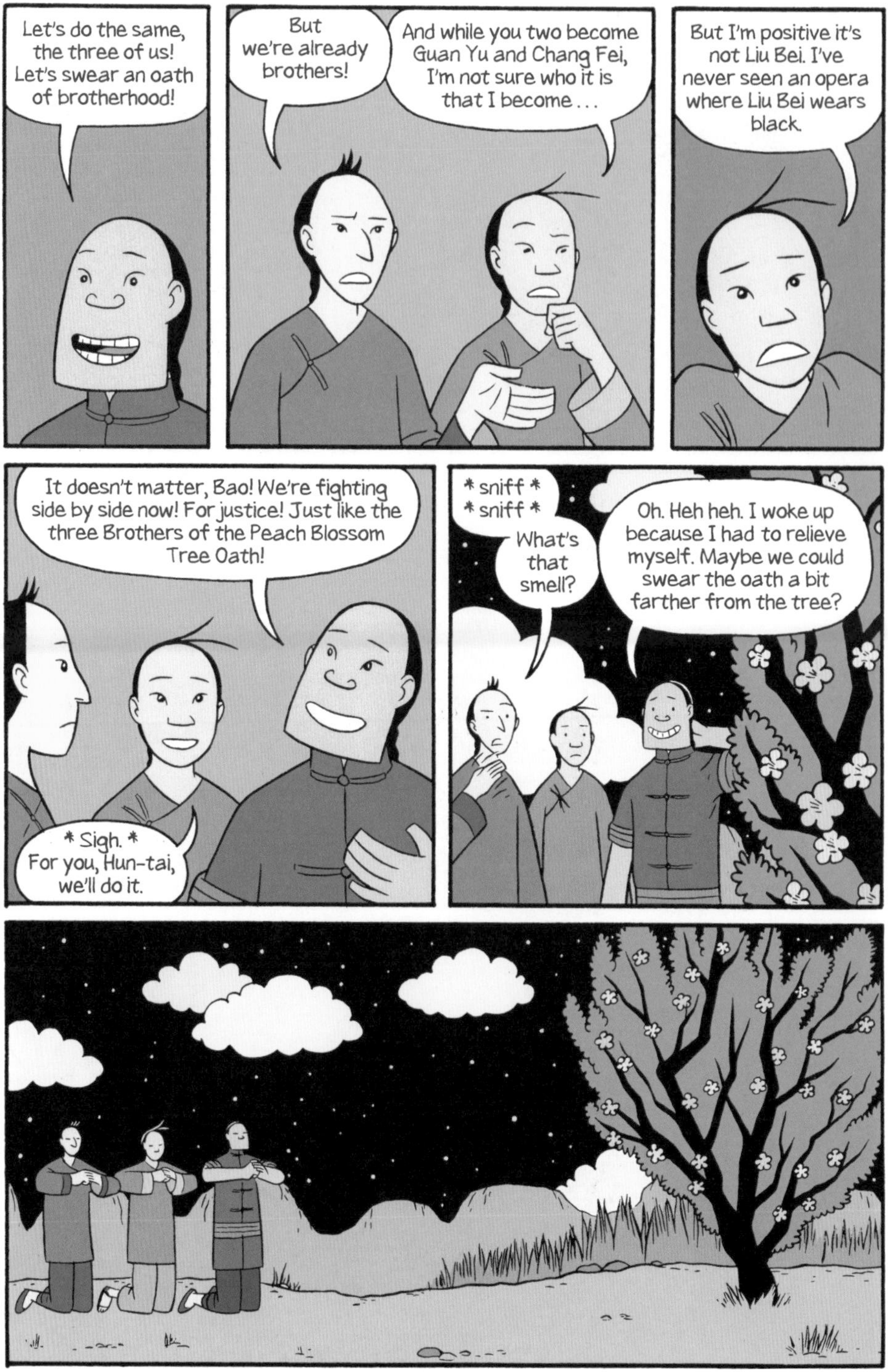
Let's do the same, the three of us! Let's swear an oath of brotherhood!
But we're already brothers!
And while you two become Guan Yu and Chang Fei, I'm not sure who it is that I become . . .
But I'm positive it's not Liu Bei. I've never seen an opera where Liu Bei wears black.
It doesn't matter, Bao! We're fighting side by side now! For justice! Just like the three Brothers of the Peach Blossom Tree Oath!
* Sigh. * For you, Hun-tai, we'll do it.
* sniff *
* sniff *
What's that smell?
Oh. Heh heh. I woke up because I had to relieve myself. Maybe we could swear the oath a bit farther from the tree?

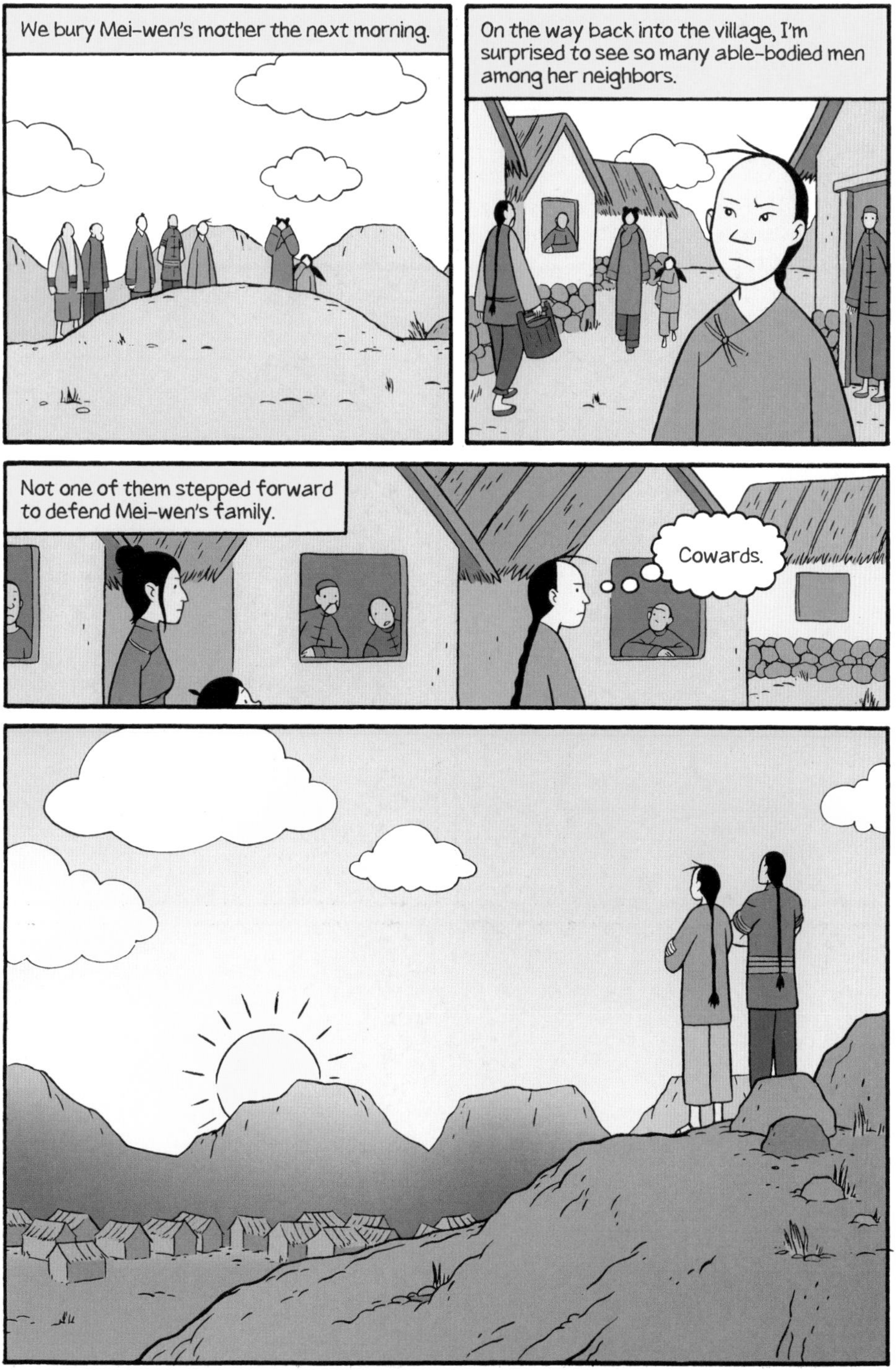
We bury Mei-wen's mother the next morning.
On the way back into the village, I'm surprised to see so many able-bodied men among her neighbors.
Not one of them stepped forward to defend Mei-wen's family.
Cowards.

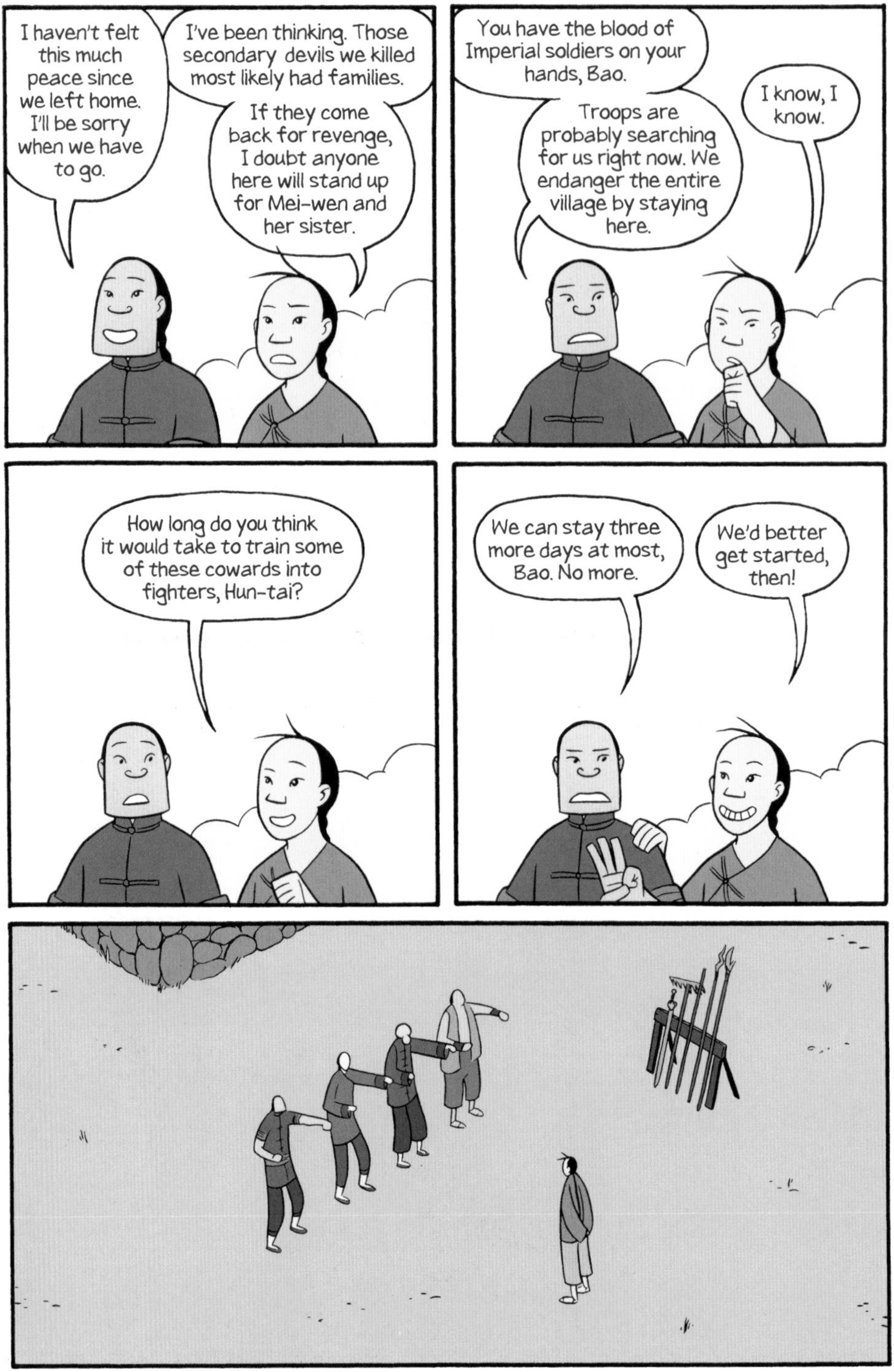

I haven't felt this much peace since we left home. I'll be sorry when we have to go.
I've been thinking. Those secondary devils we killed most likely had families.
If they come back for revenge, I doubt anyone here will stand up for Mei-wen and her sister.
You have the blood of Imperial soldiers on your hands, Bao.
Troops are probably searching for us right now. We endanger the entire village by staying here.
I know, I know.
How long do you think it would take to train some of these cowards into fighters, Hun-tai?
We can stay three more days at most, Bao. No more.
We'd better get started, then!

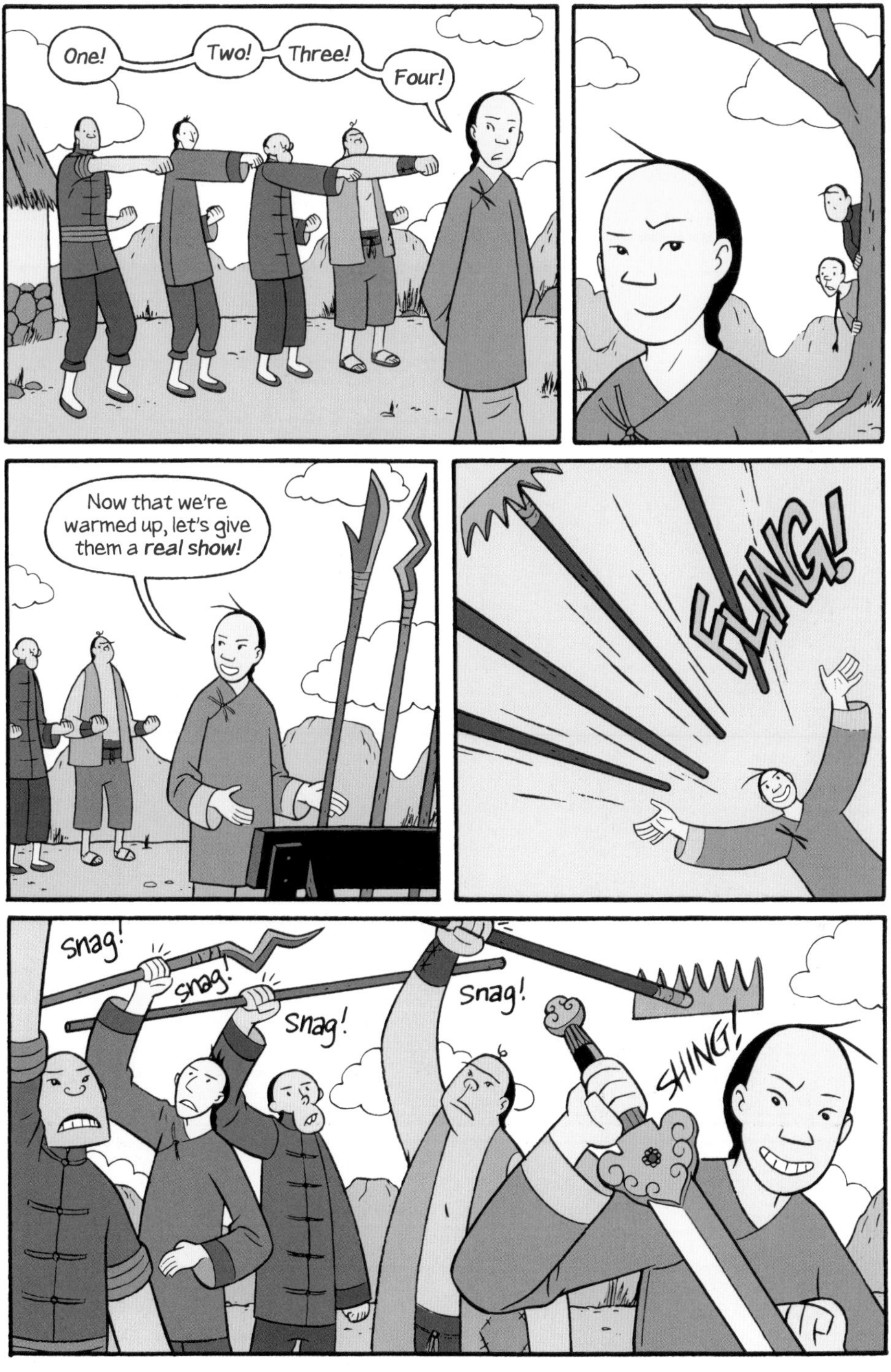
One!
Two!
Three!
Four!
Now that we're warmed up, let's give them a *real show!*
FLING!
snag!
snag!
snag!
snag!
SHING!

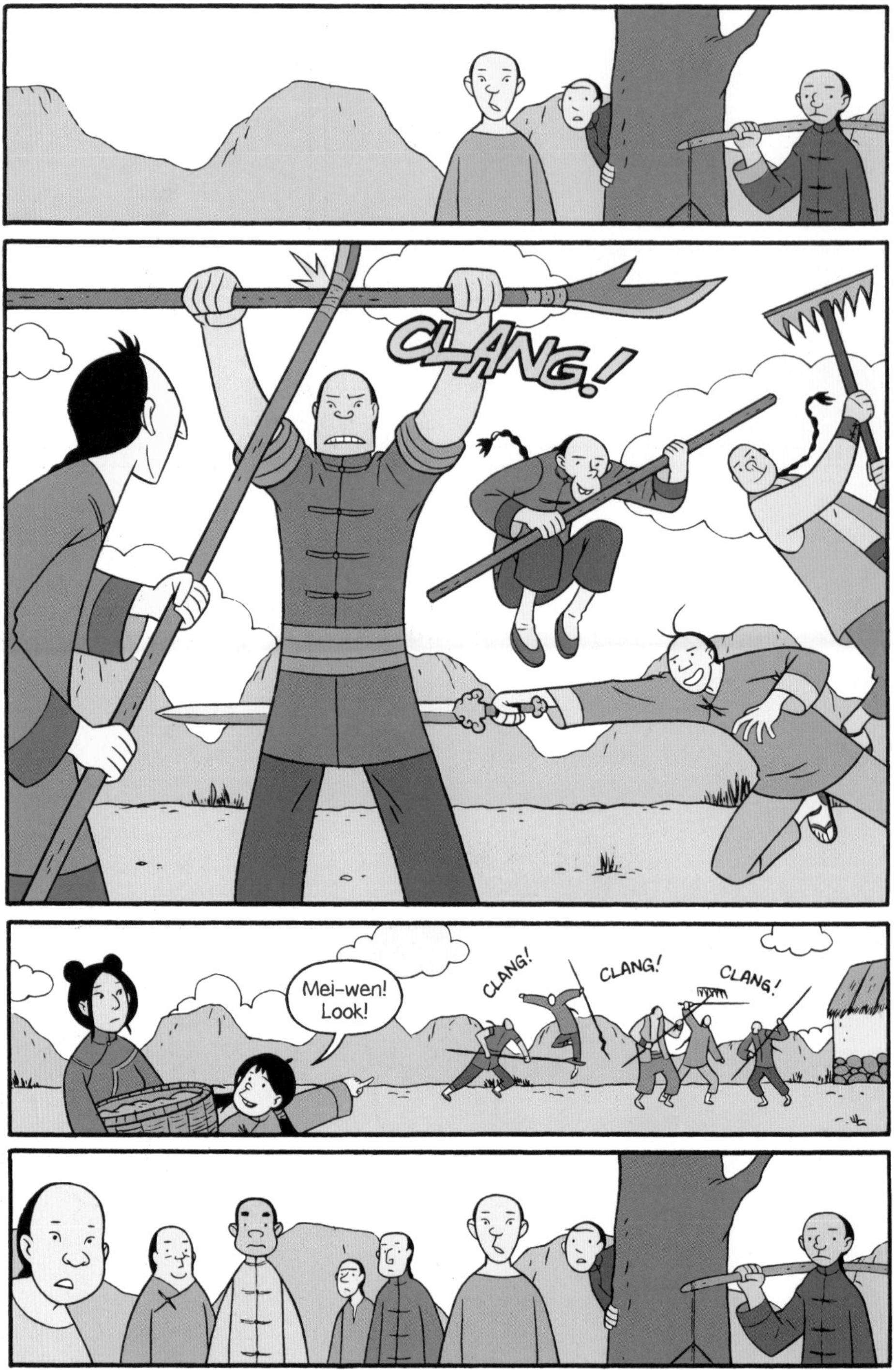
CLANG!
Mei-wen! Look!
CLANG!
CLANG!
CLANG!

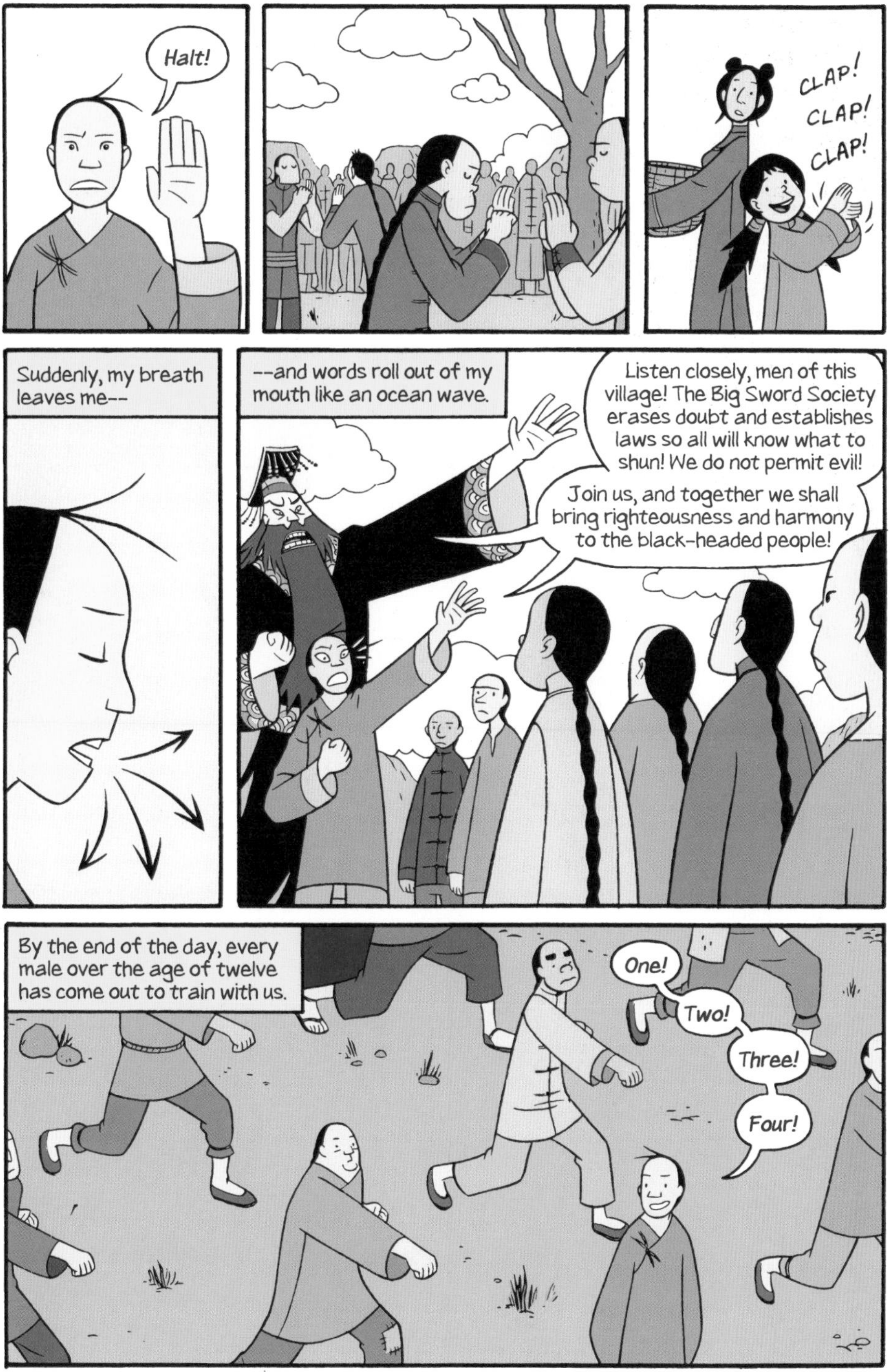
Halt!
CLAP!
CLAP!
CLAP!
Suddenly, my breath leaves me--
--and words roll out of my mouth like an ocean wave.
Listen closely, men of this village! The Big Sword Society erases doubt and establishes laws so all will know what to shun! We do not permit evil!
Join us, and together we shall bring righteousness and harmony to the black-headed people!
By the end of the day, every male over the age of twelve has come out to train with us.
One!
Two!
Three!
Four!

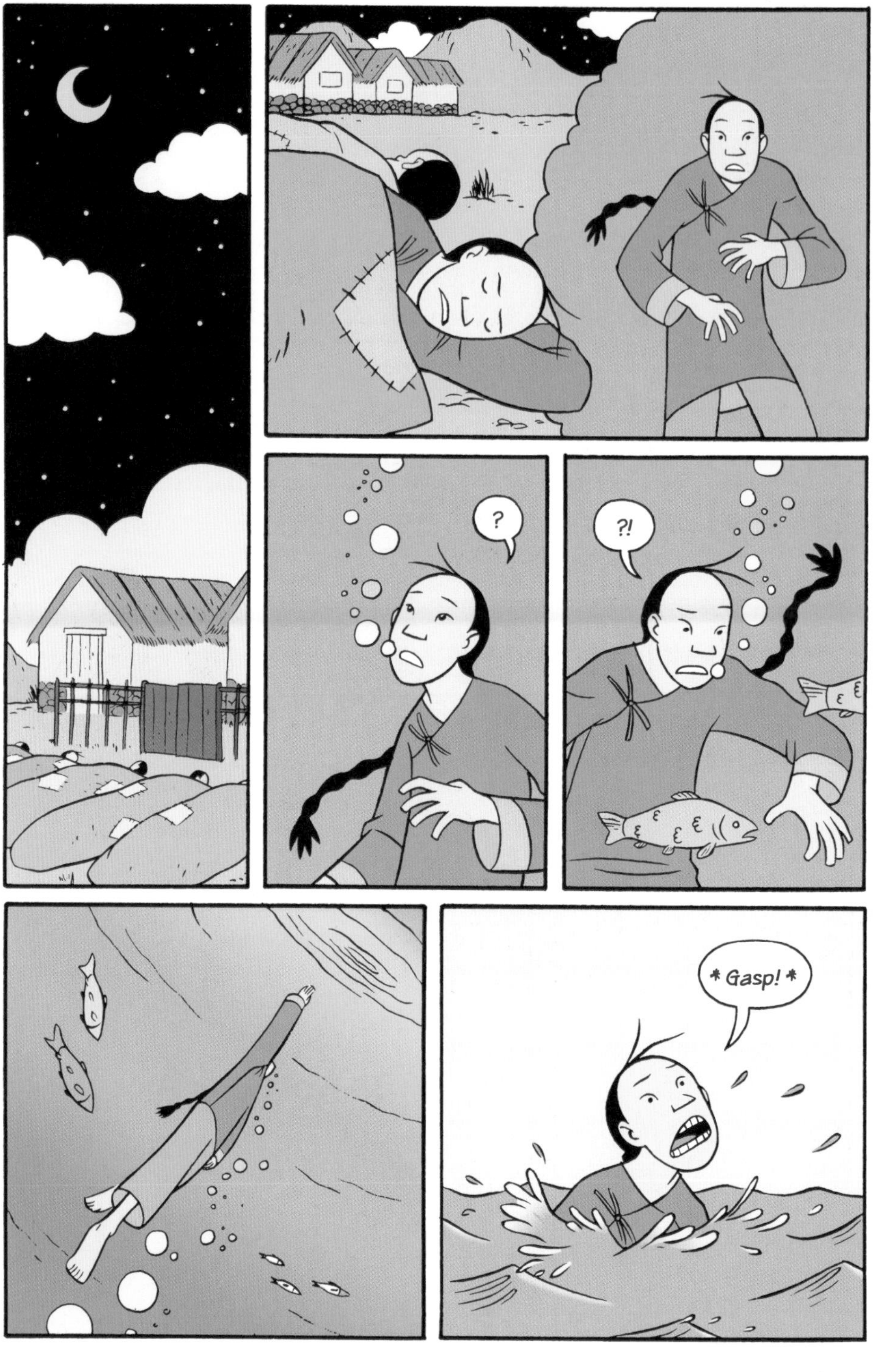
?
?!
Gasp!

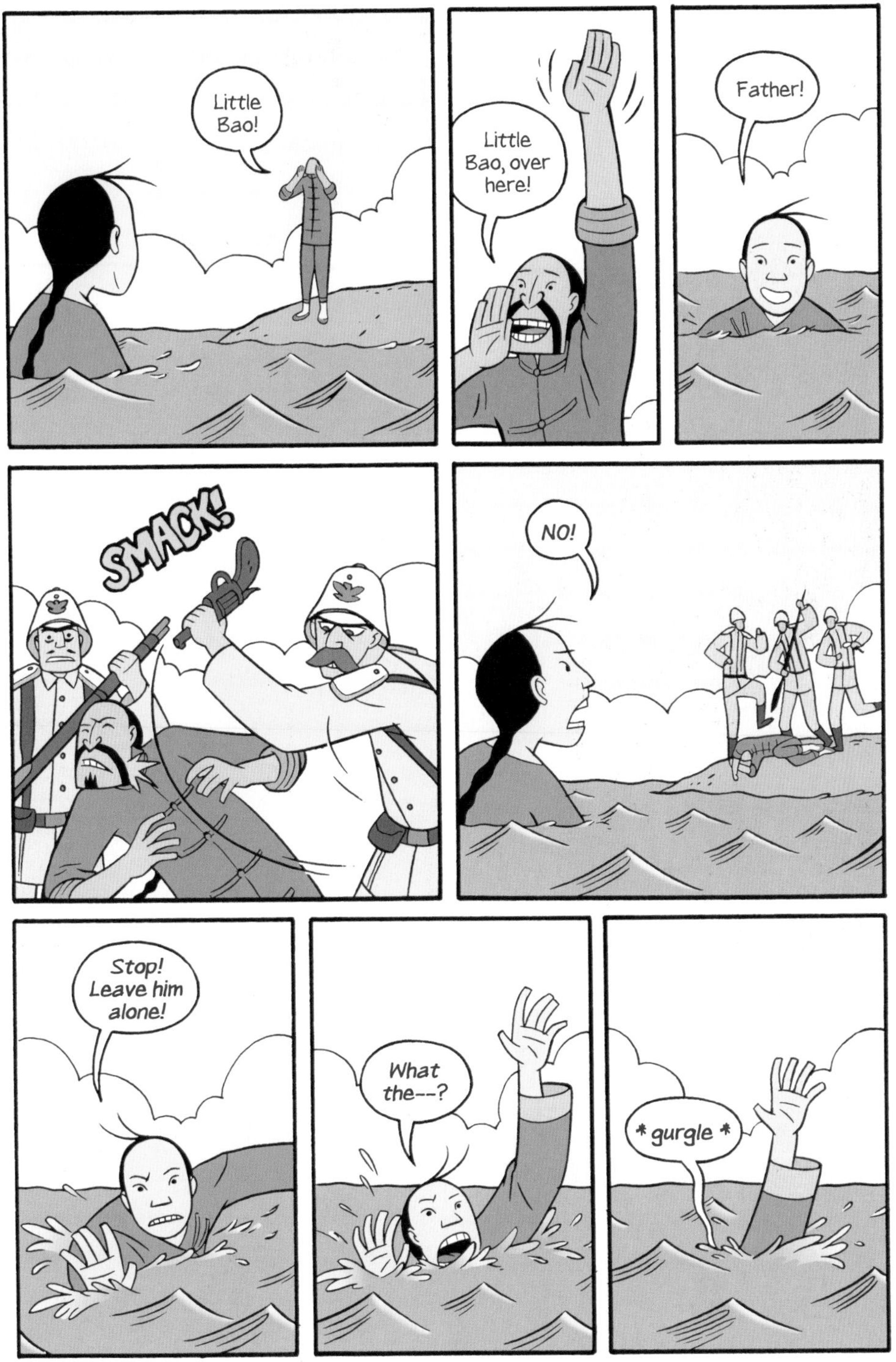
Little Bao!
Little Bao, over here!
Father!
SMACK!
NO!
Stop! Leave him alone!
What the--?
* gurgle *

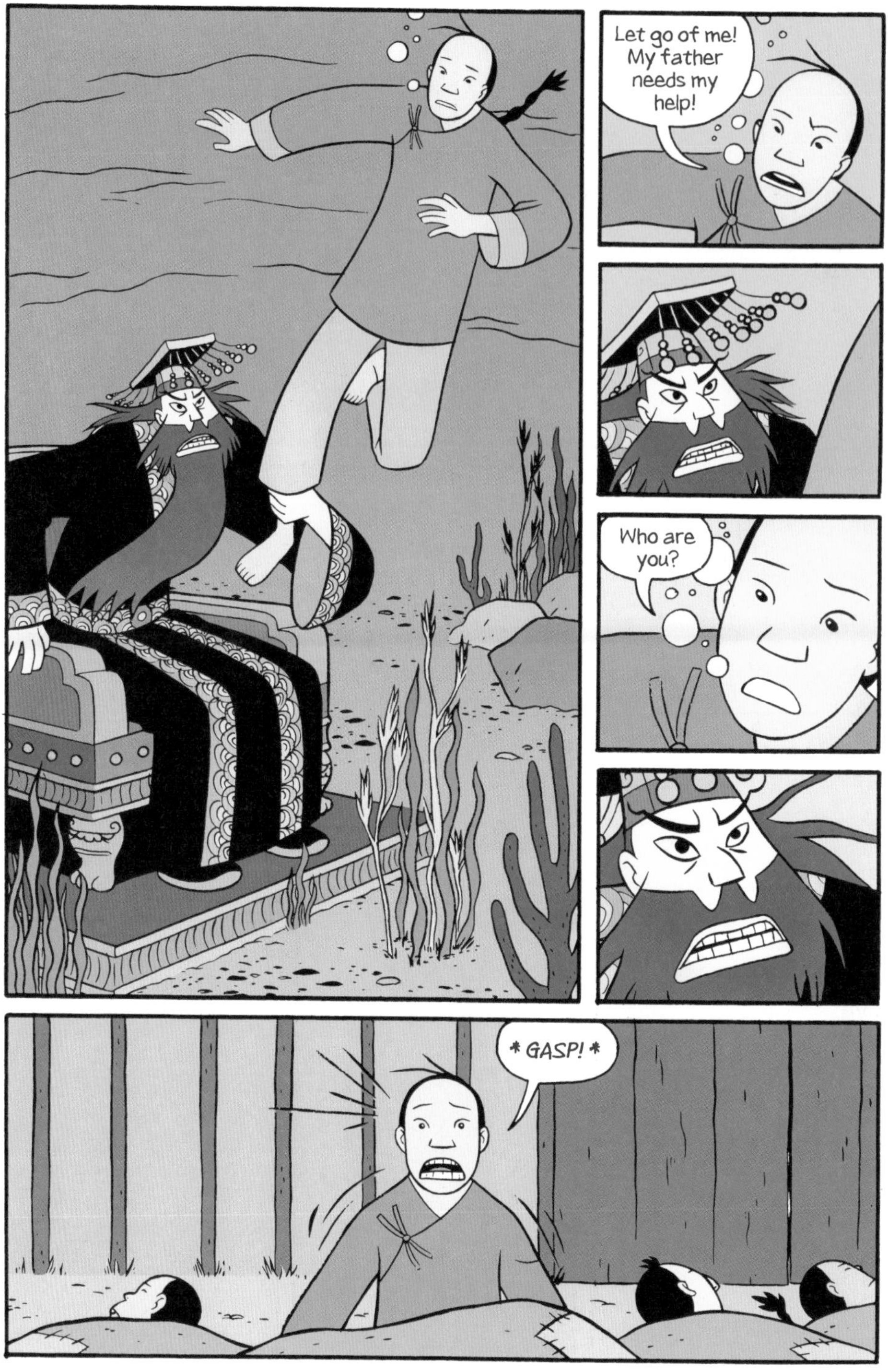
Let go of me! My father needs my help!
Who are you?
* GASP! *

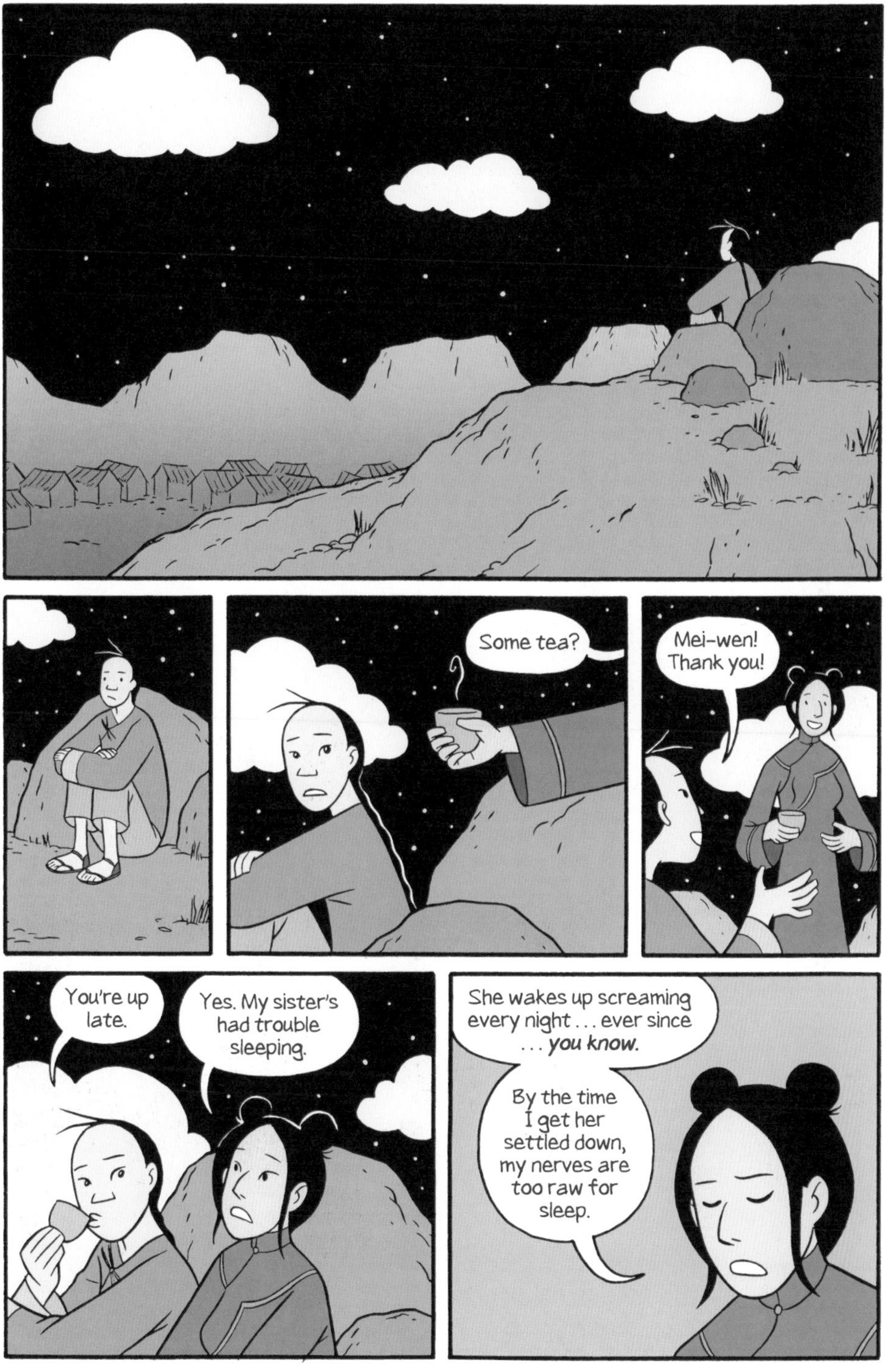
Some tea?
Mei-wen! Thank you!
You're up late.
Yes. My sister's had trouble sleeping.
She wakes up screaming every night . . . ever since . . . *you know.*
By the time I get her settled down, my nerves are too raw for sleep.

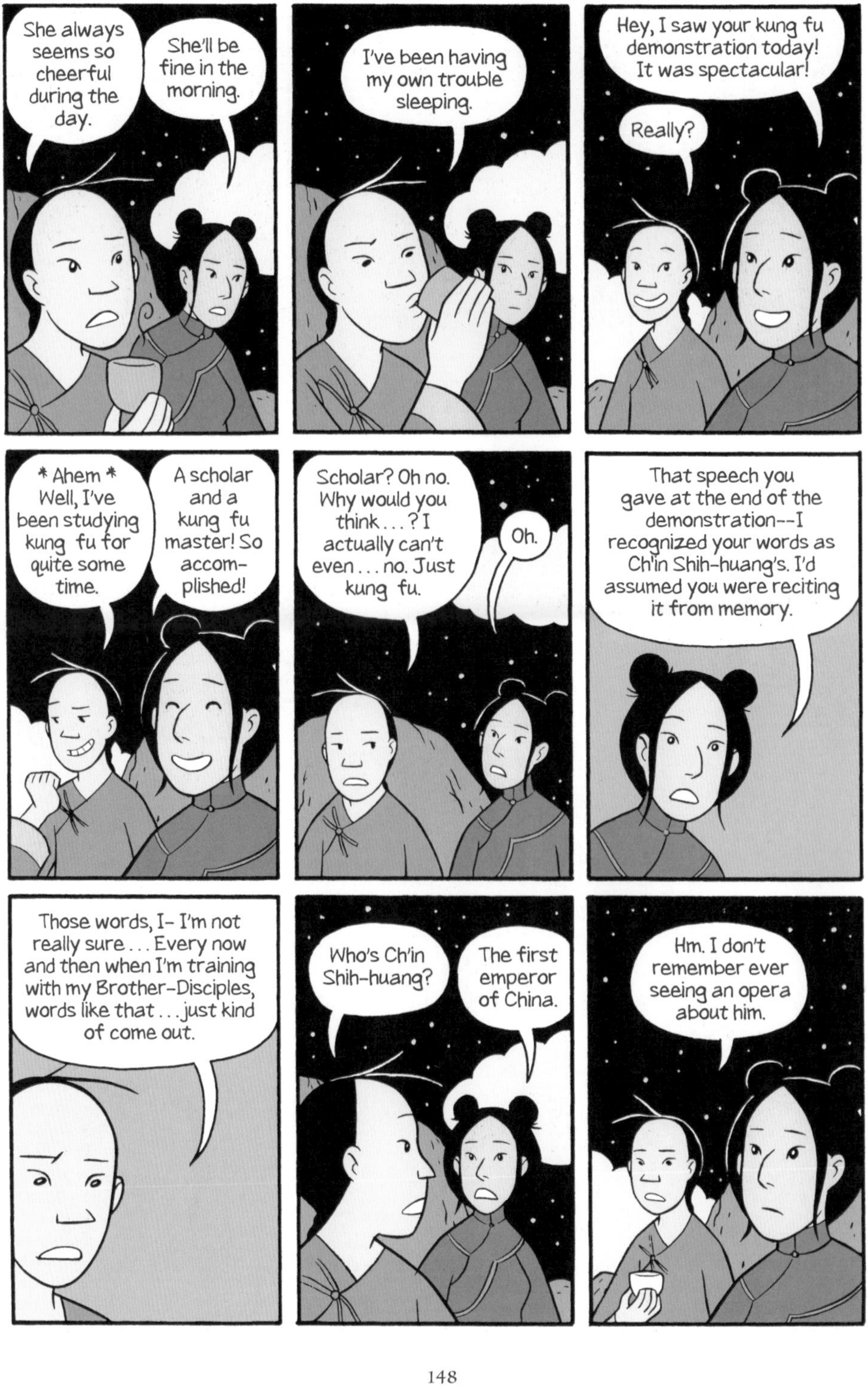
She always seems so cheerful during the day.
She'll be fine in the morning.
I've been having my own trouble sleeping.
Hey, I saw your kung fu demonstration today! It was spectacular!
Really?
* Ahem * Well, I've been studying kung fu for quite some time.
A scholar and a kung fu master! So accom-plished!
Scholar? Oh no. Why would you think...? I actually can't even... no. Just kung fu.
Oh.
That speech you gave at the end of the demonstration--I recognized your words as Ch'in Shih-huang's. I'd assumed you were reciting it from memory.
Those words, I- I'm not really sure... Every now and then when I'm training with my Brother-Disciples, words like that... just kind of come out.
Who's Ch'in Shih-huang?
The first emperor of China.
Hm. I don't remember ever seeing an opera about him.

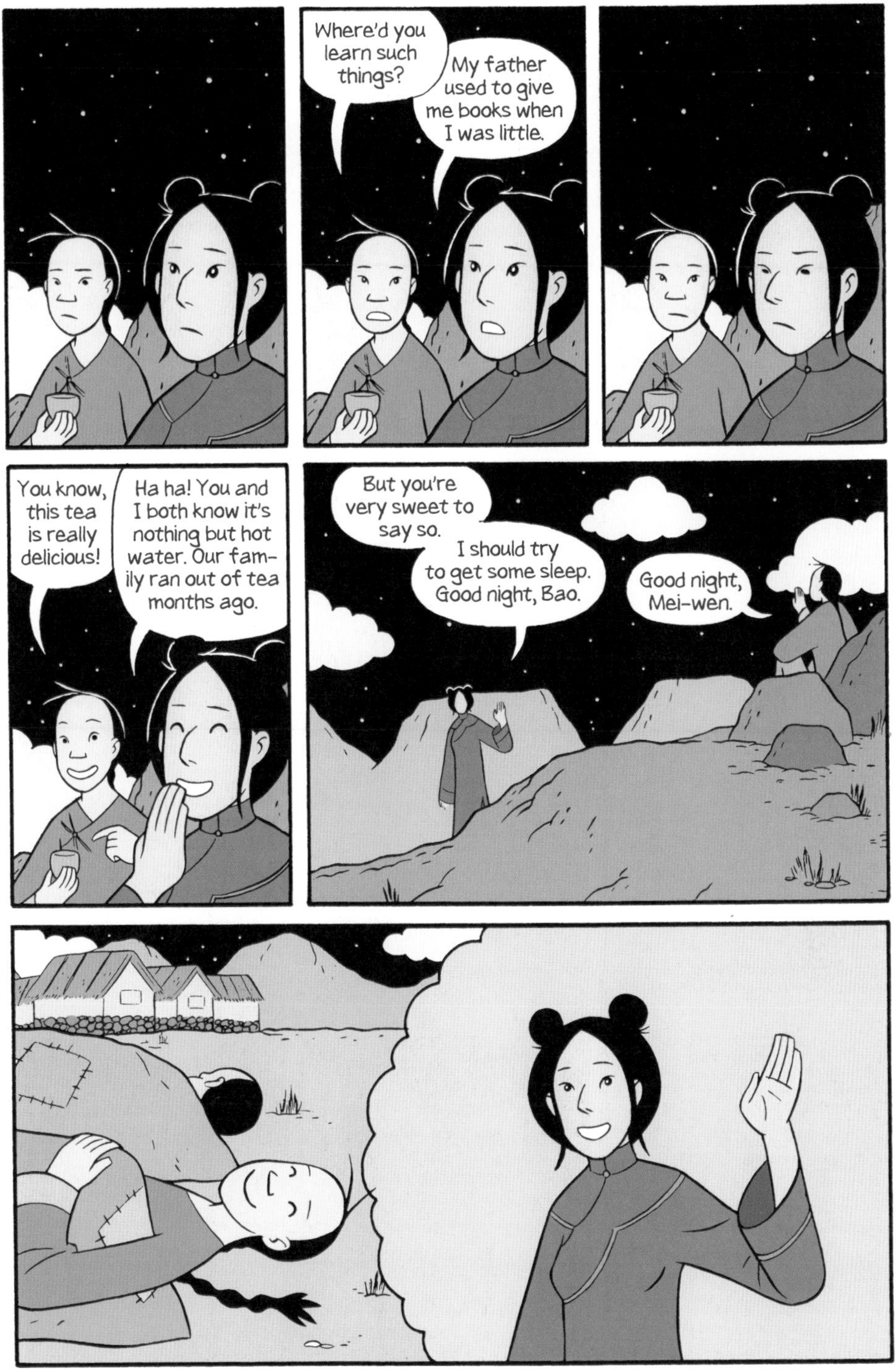
Where'd you learn such things?
My father used to give me books when I was little.
You know, this tea is really delicious!
Ha ha! You and I both know it's nothing but hot water. Our family ran out of tea months ago.
But you're very sweet to say so.
I should try to get some sleep. Good night, Bao.
Good night, Mei-wen.

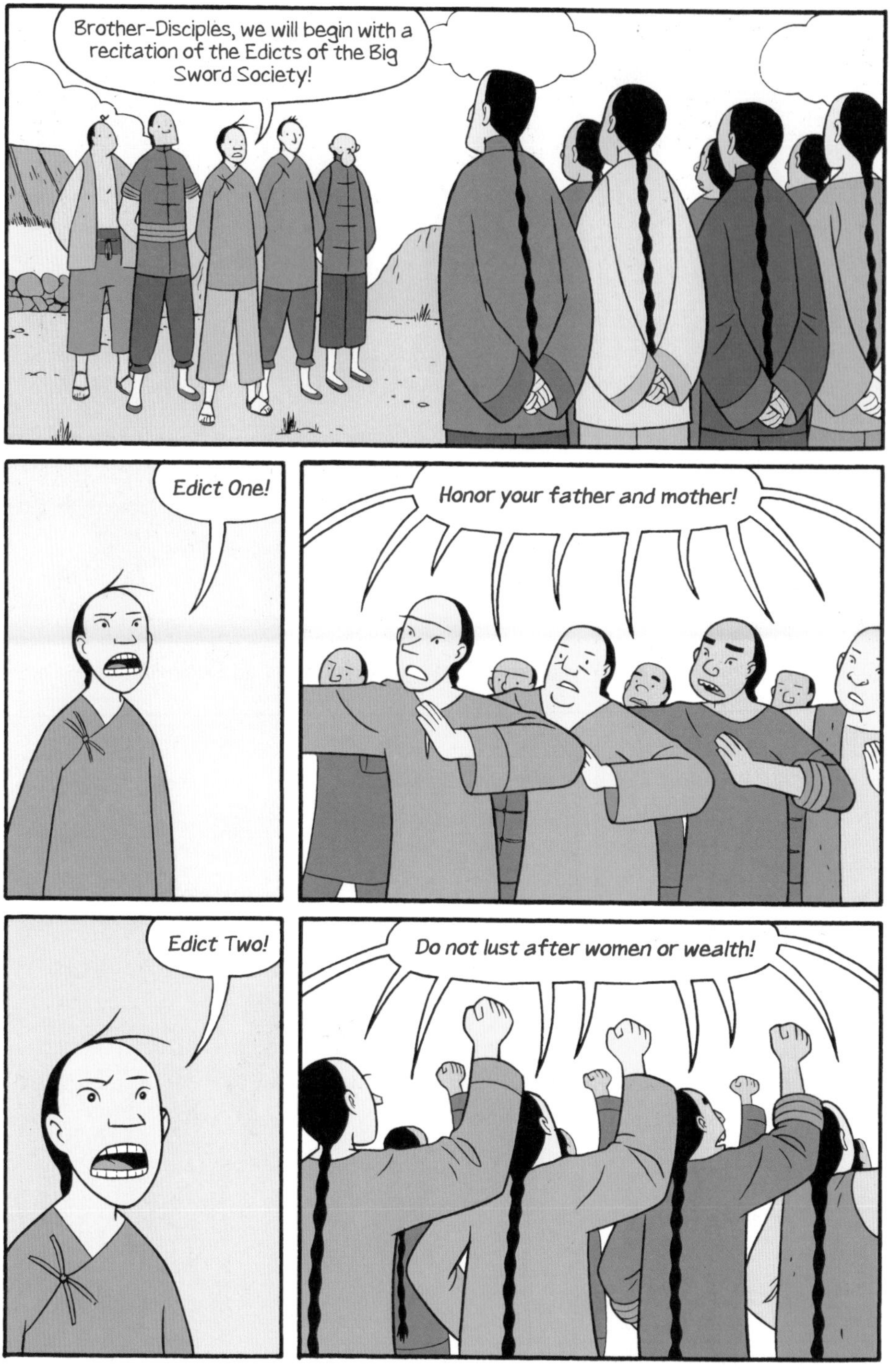
Brother-Disciples, we will begin with a recitation of the Edicts of the Big Sword Society!
Edict One!
Honor your father and mother!
Edict Two!
Do not lust after women or wealth!

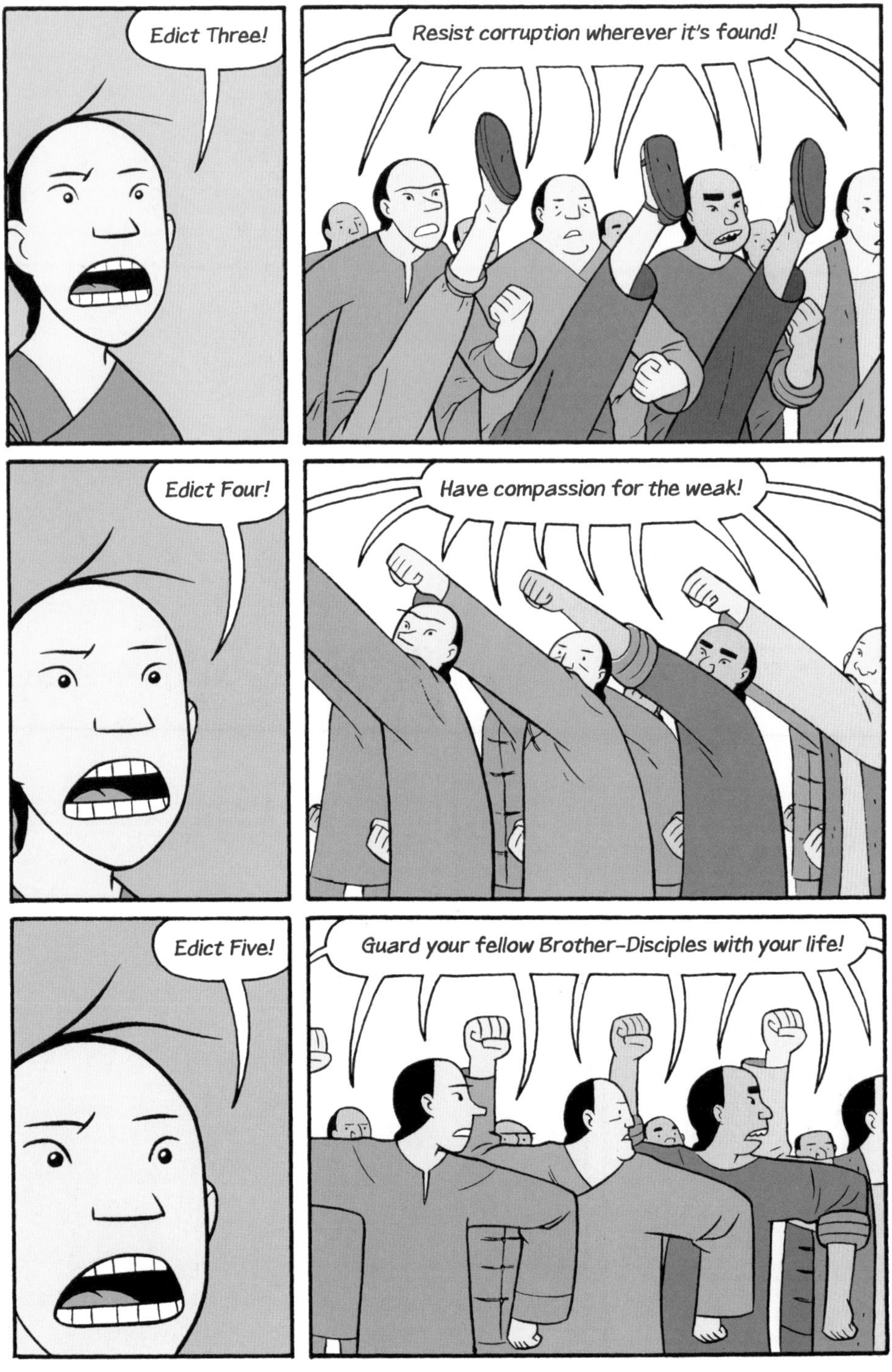
Edict Three!
Resist corruption wherever it's found!
Edict Four!
Have compassion for the weak!
Edict Five!
Guard your fellow Brother-Disciples with your life!

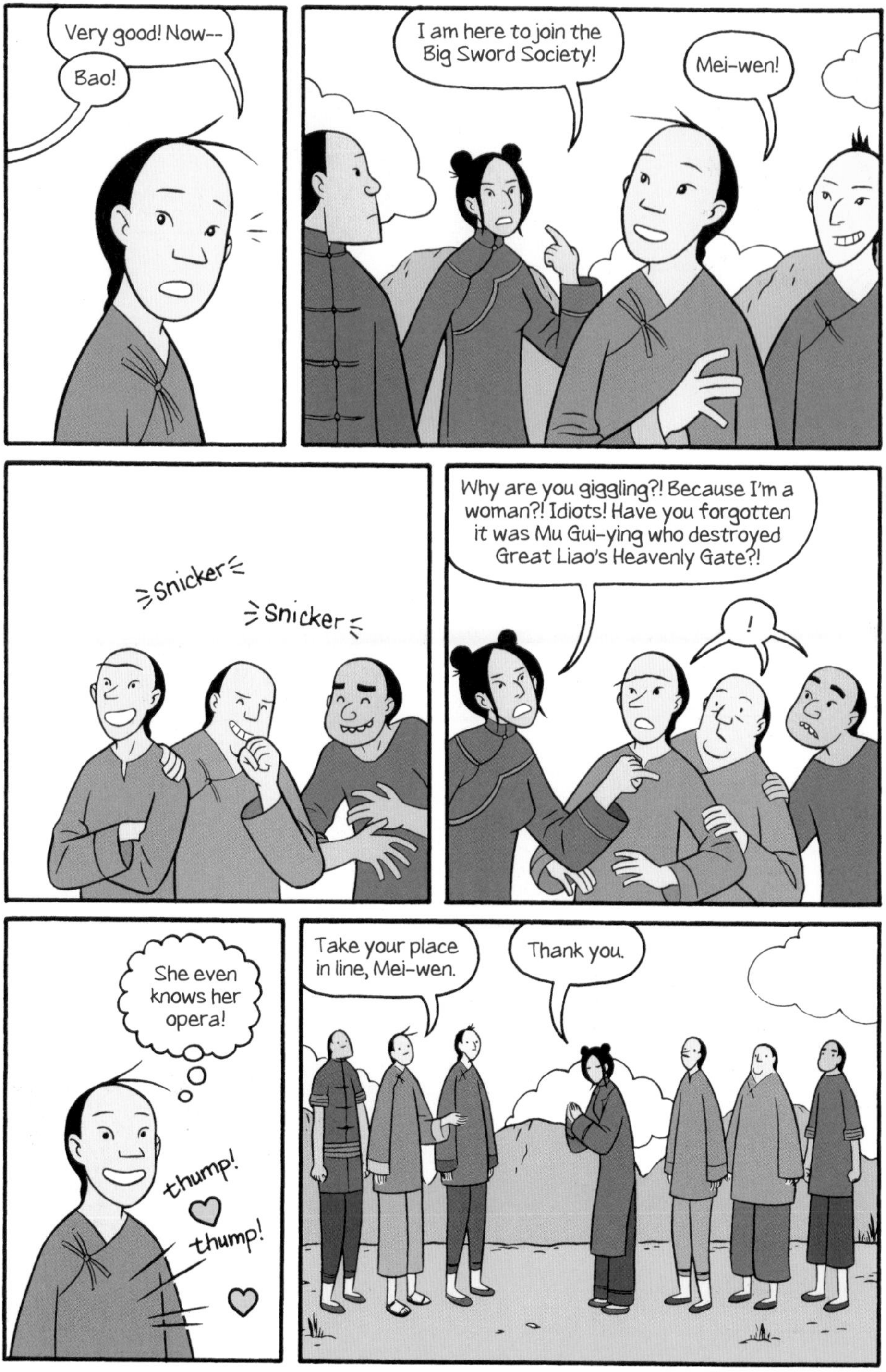
Very good! Now--
Bao!
I am here to join the Big Sword Society!
Mei-wen!
Snicker
Snicker
Why are you giggling?! Because I'm a woman?! Idiots! Have you forgotten it was Mu Gui-ying who destroyed Great Liao's Heavenly Gate?!
!
She even knows her opera!
thump!
thump!
Take your place in line, Mei-wen.
Thank you.

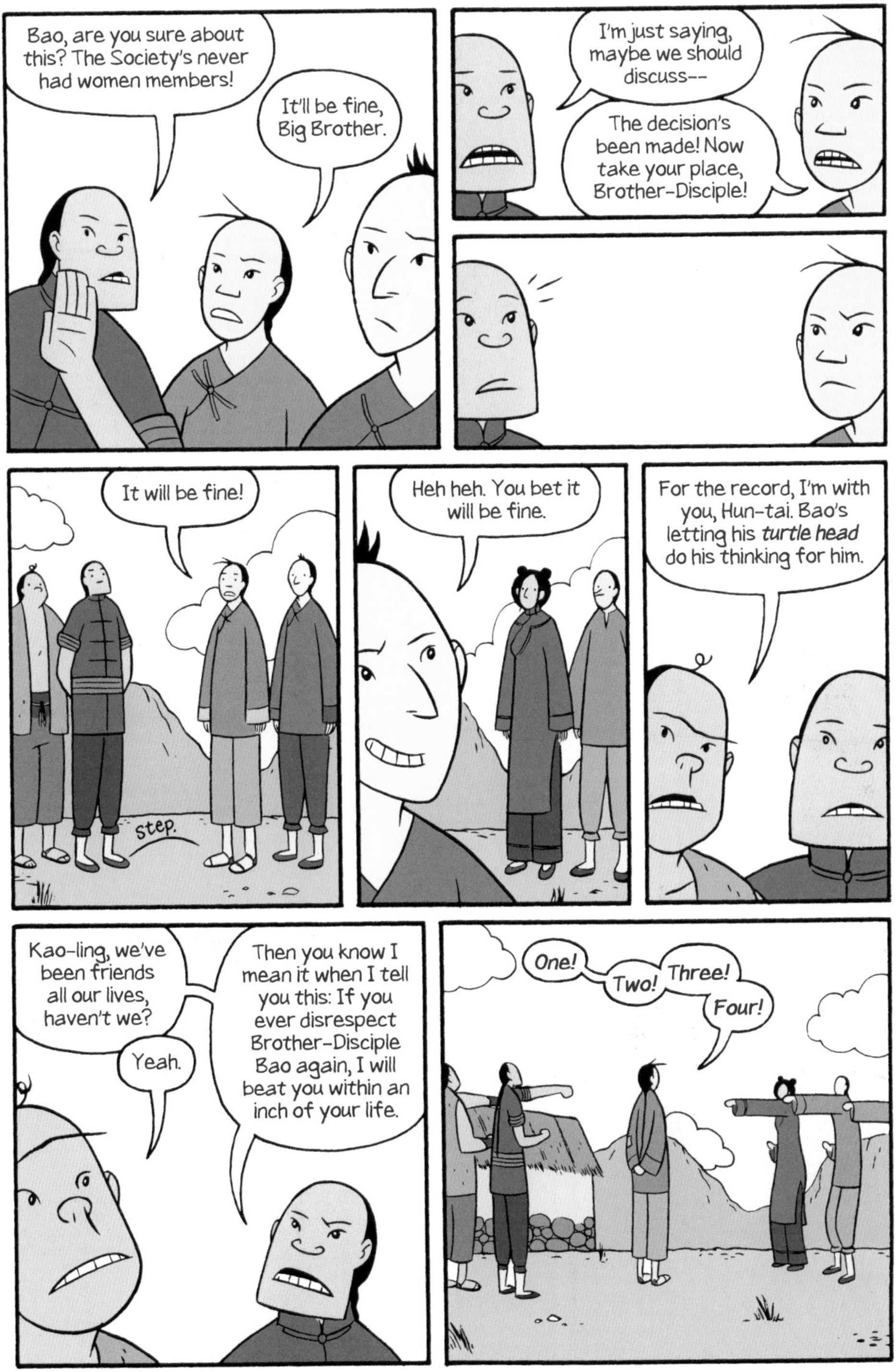
Bao, are you sure about this? The Society's never had women members!
It'll be fine, Big Brother.
I'm just saying, maybe we should discuss--
The decision's been made! Now take your place, Brother-Disciple!
It will be fine!
step.
Heh heh. You bet it will be fine.
For the record, I'm with you, Hun-tai. Bao's letting his *turtle head* do his thinking for him.
Kao-ling, we've been friends all our lives, haven't we?
Yeah.
Then you know I mean it when I tell you this: If you ever disrespect Brother-Disciple Bao again, I will beat you within an inch of your life.
One!
Two!
Three!
Four!

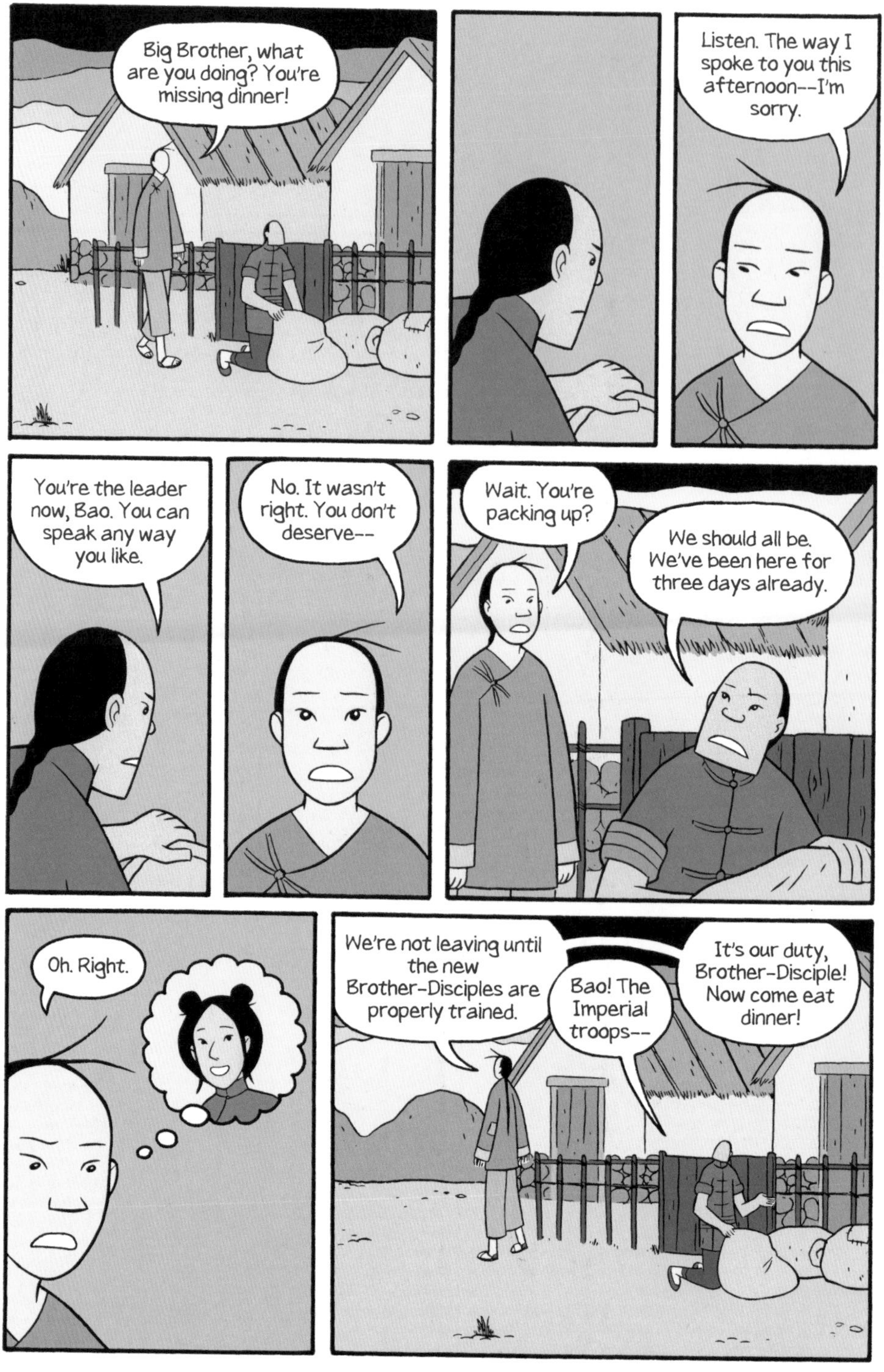
Big Brother, what are you doing? You're missing dinner!
Listen. The way I spoke to you this afternoon--I'm sorry.
You're the leader now, Bao. You can speak any way you like.
No. It wasn't right. You don't deserve--
Wait. You're packing up?
We should all be. We've been here for three days already.
Oh. Right.
We're not leaving until the new Brother-Disciples are properly trained.
Bao! The Imperial troops--
It's our duty, Brother-Disciple! Now come eat dinner!

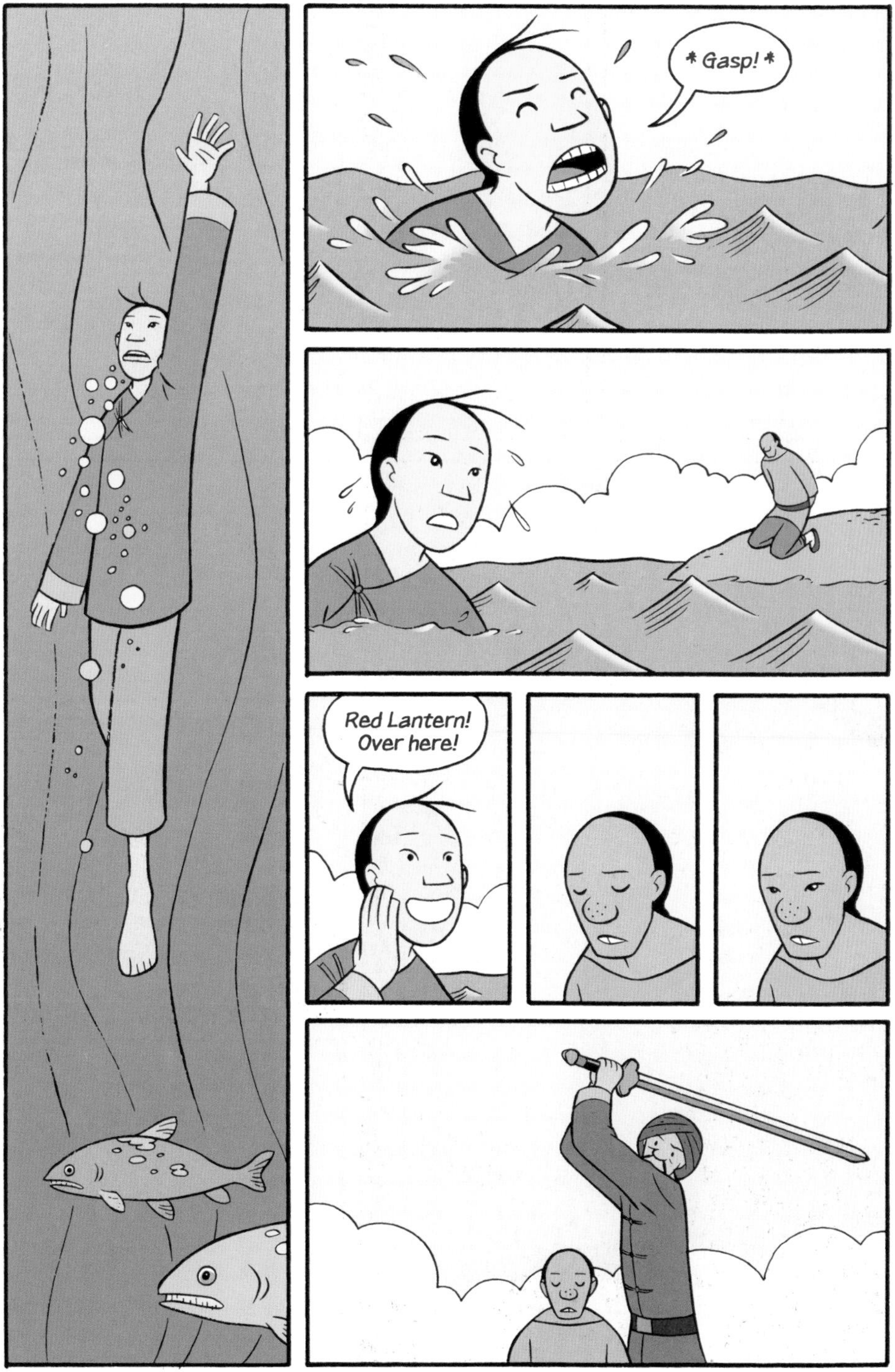
* Gasp! *
Red Lantern! Over here!

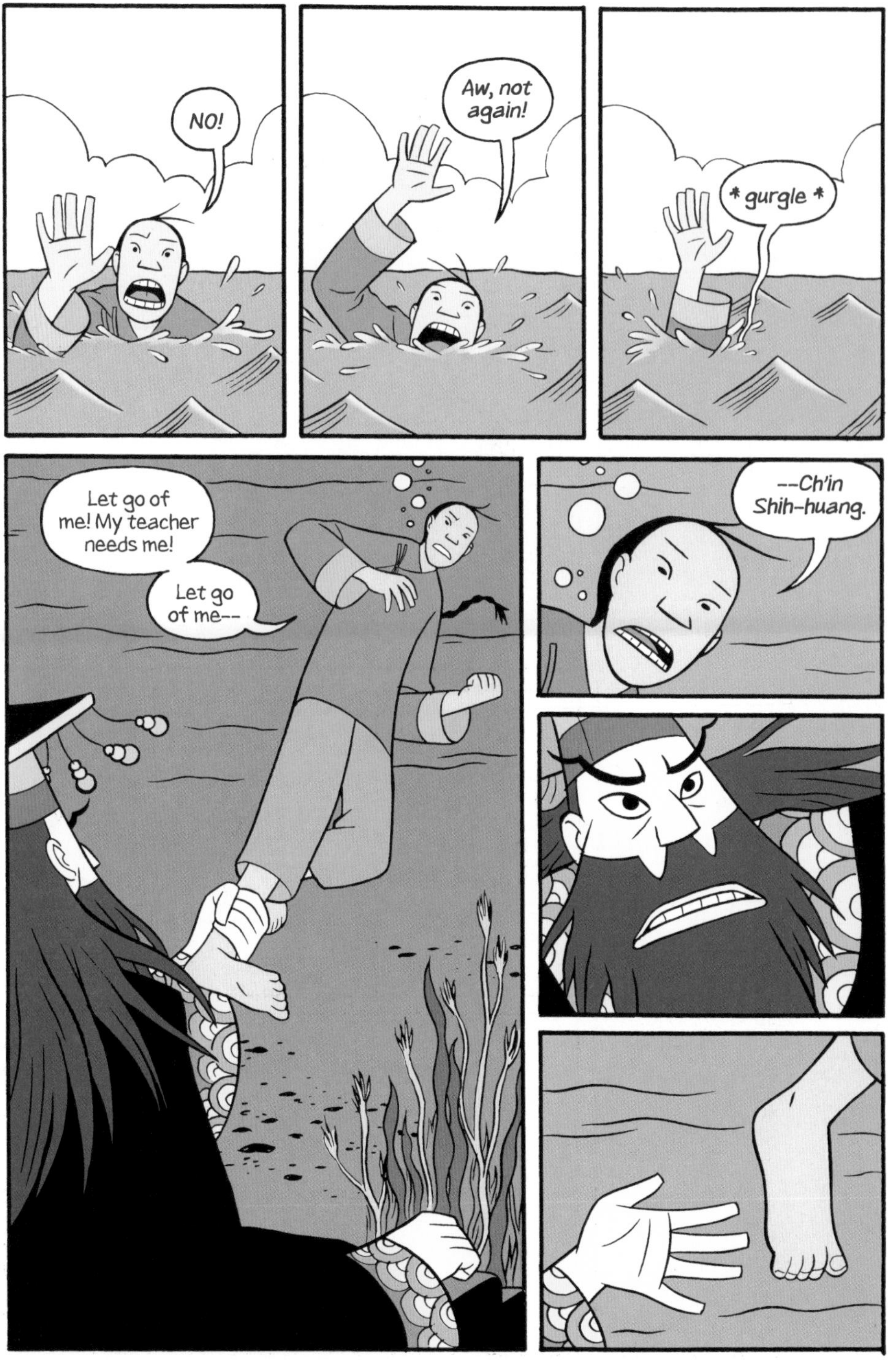
NO!
Aw, not again!
* gurgle *
Let go of me! My teacher needs me!
Let go of me--
--Ch'in Shih-huang.

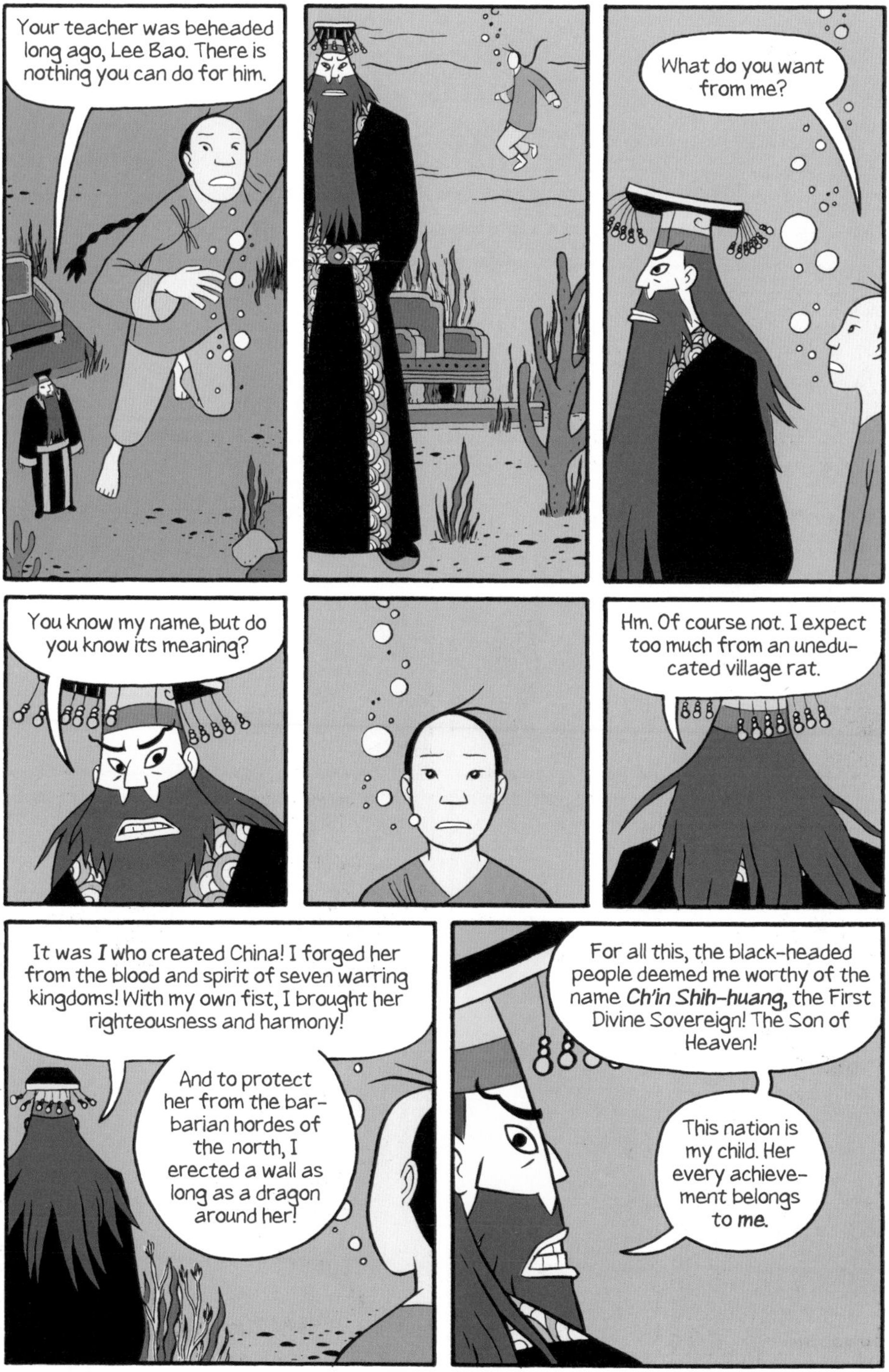

Your teacher was beheaded long ago, Lee Bao. There is nothing you can do for him.
What do you want from me?
You know my name, but do you know its meaning?
Hm. Of course not. I expect too much from an uneducated village rat.
It was *I* who created China! I forged her from the blood and spirit of seven warring kingdoms! With my own fist, I brought her righteousness and harmony!
And to protect her from the barbarian hordes of the north, I erected a wall as long as a dragon around her!
For all this, the black-headed people deemed me worthy of the name ***Ch'in Shih-huang,*** the First Divine Sovereign! The Son of Heaven!
This nation is my child. Her every achievement belongs to ***me.***

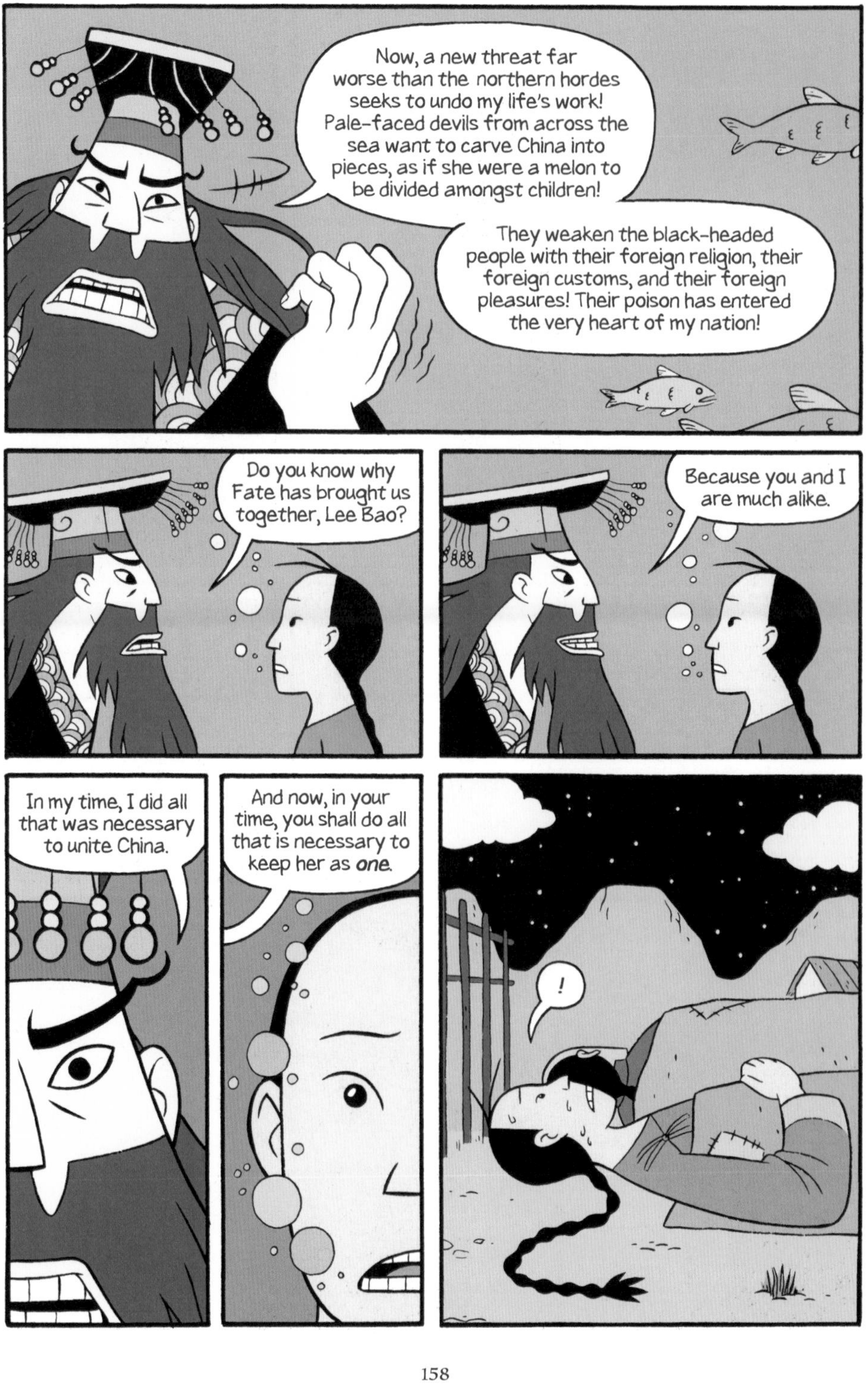
Now, a new threat far worse than the northern hordes seeks to undo my life's work! Pale-faced devils from across the sea want to carve China into pieces, as if she were a melon to be divided amongst children!
They weaken the black-headed people with their foreign religion, their foreign customs, and their foreign pleasures! Their poison has entered the very heart of my nation!
Do you know why Fate has brought us together, Lee Bao?
Because you and I are much alike.
In my time, I did all that was necessary to unite China.
And now, in your time, you shall do all that is necessary to keep her as *one*.
!

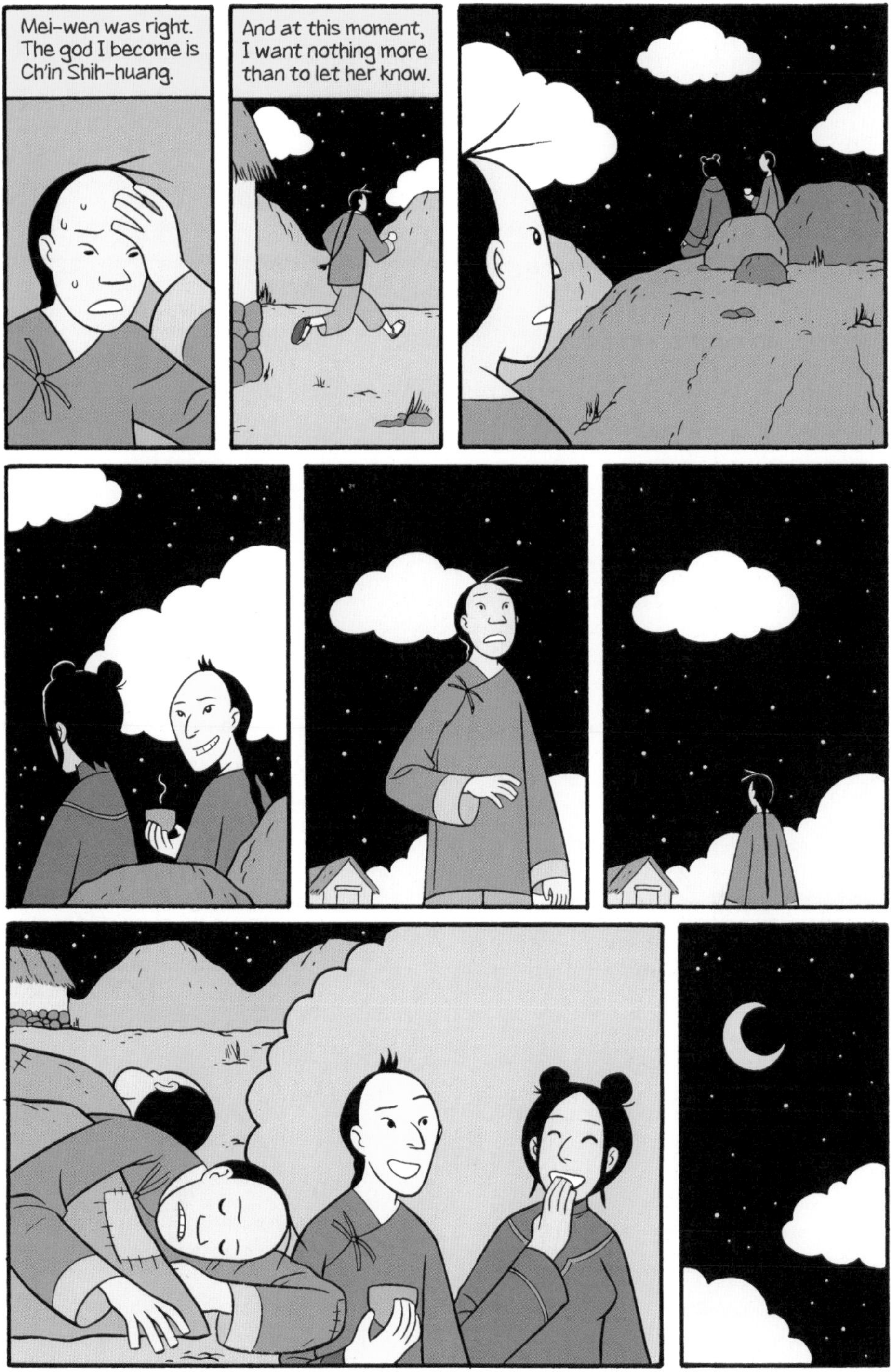
Mei-wen was right. The god I become is Ch'in Shih-huang.
And at this moment, I want nothing more than to let her know.

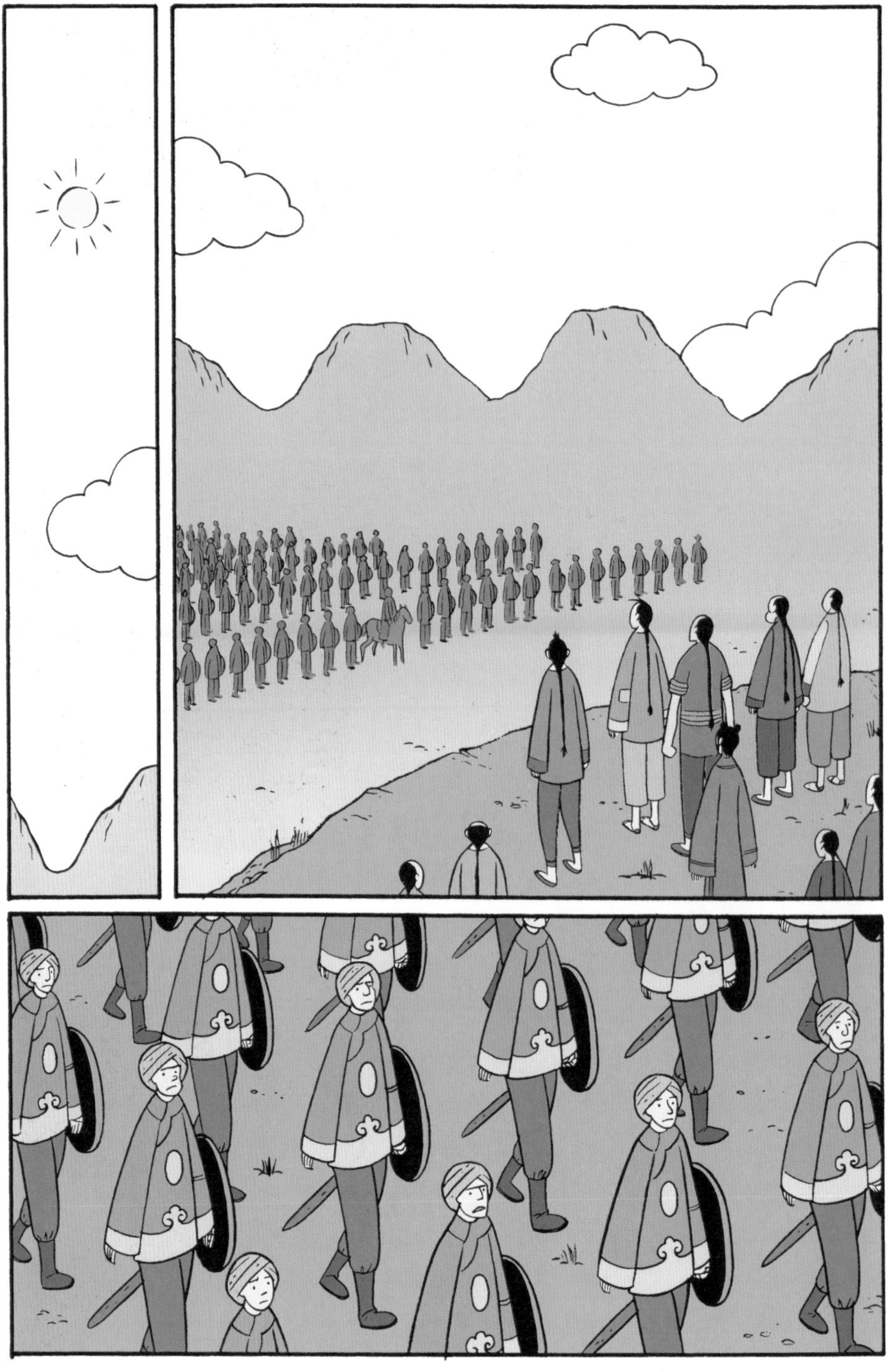

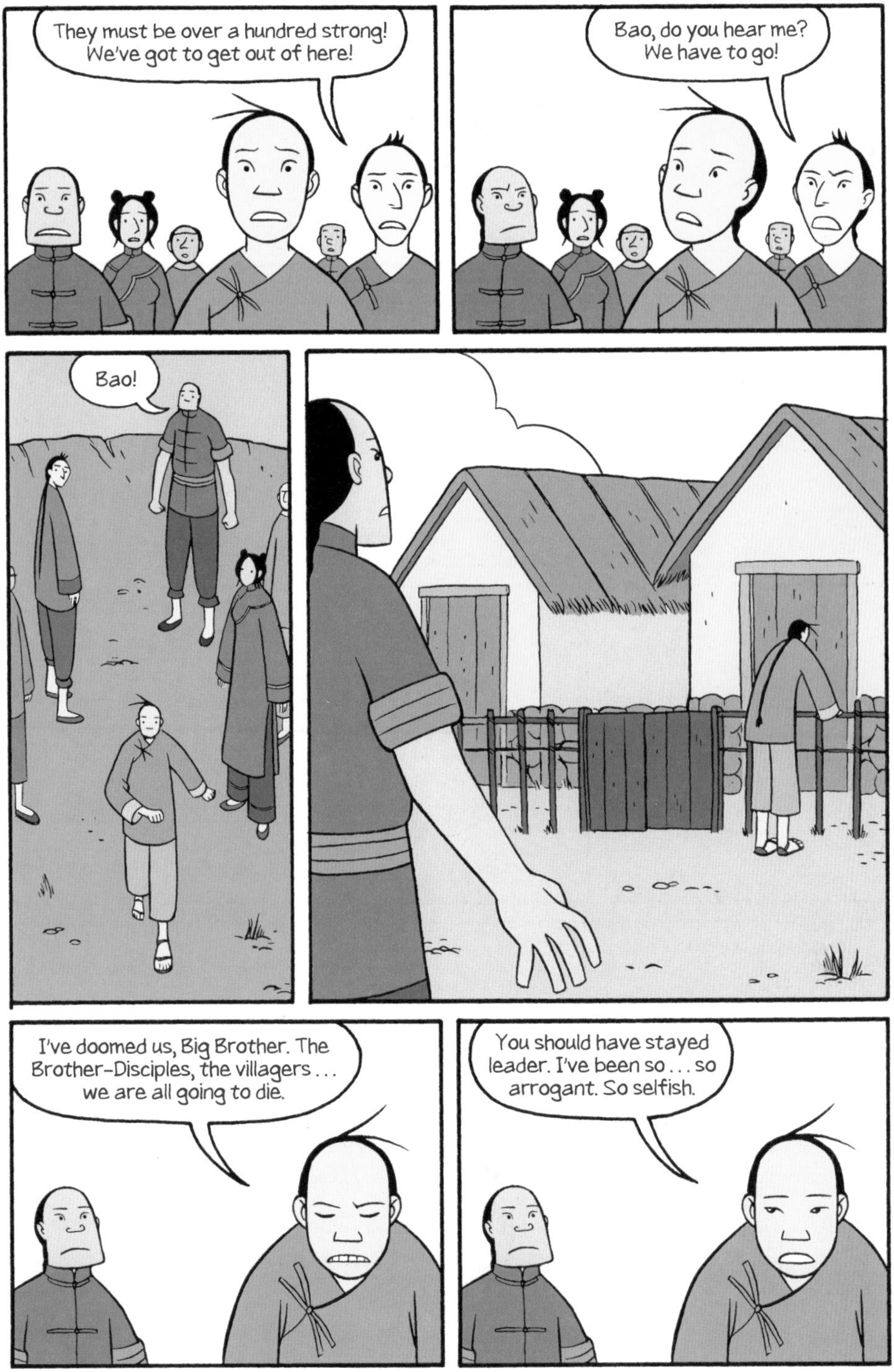
They must be over a hundred strong! We've got to get out of here!
Bao, do you hear me? We have to go!
Bao!
I've doomed us, Big Brother. The Brother-Disciples, the villagers . . . we are all going to die.
You should have stayed leader. I've been so . . . so arrogant. So selfish.

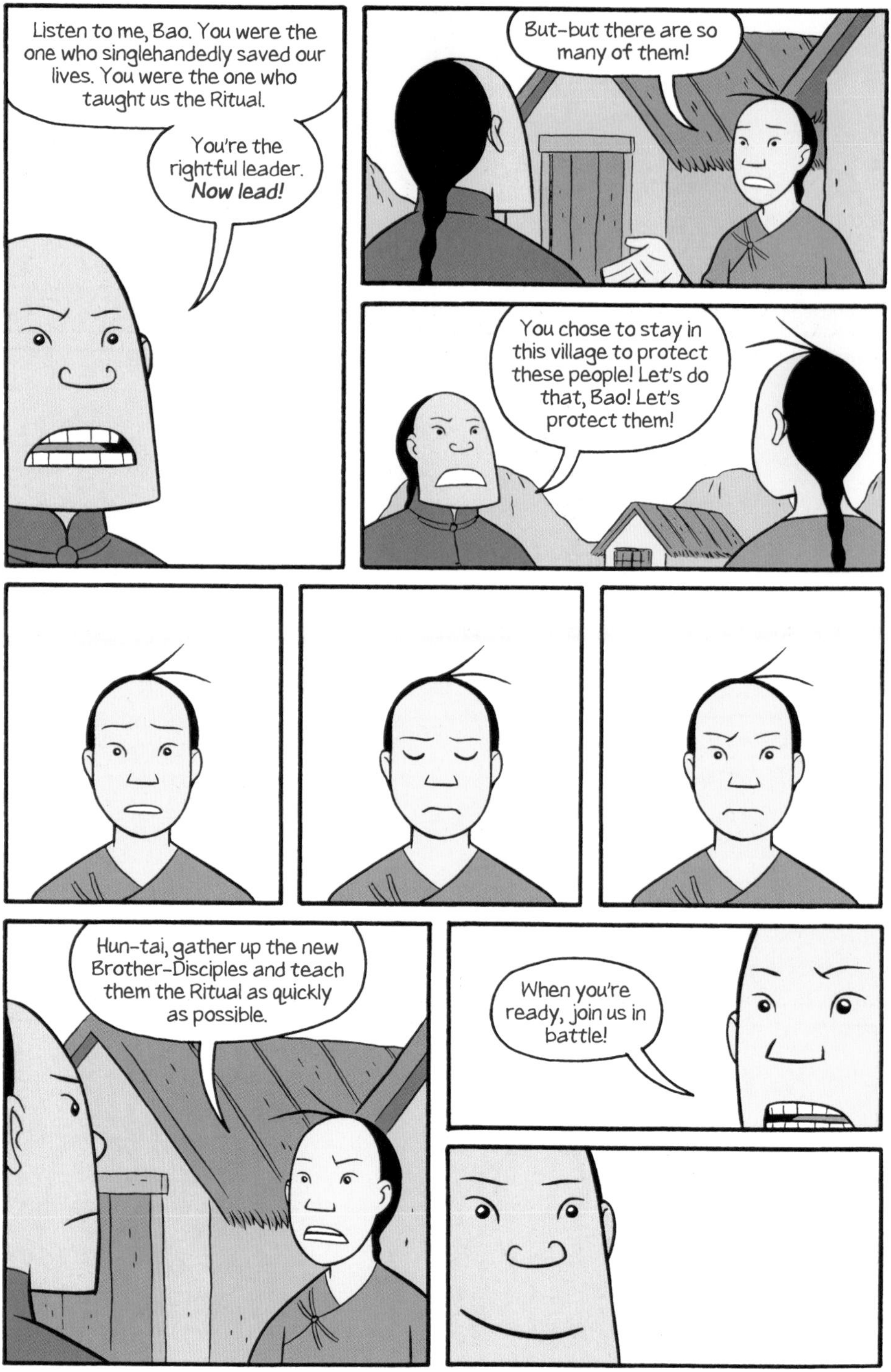
Listen to me, Bao. You were the one who singlehandedly saved our lives. You were the one who taught us the Ritual.
You're the rightful leader. **Now lead!**
But-but there are so many of them!
You chose to stay in this village to protect these people! Let's do that, Bao! Let's protect them!
Hun-tai, gather up the new Brother-Disciples and teach them the Ritual as quickly as possible.
When you're ready, join us in battle!

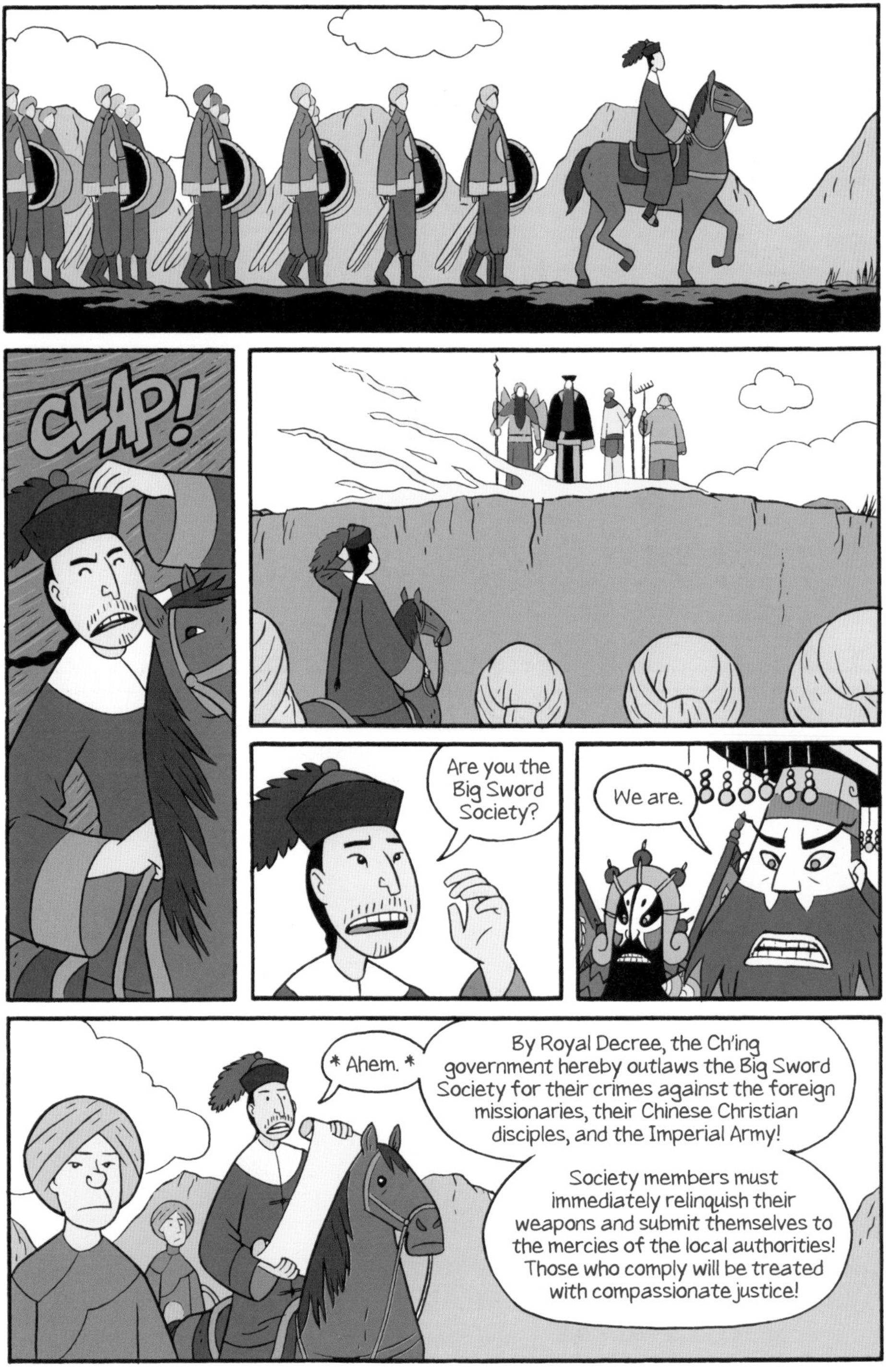
CLAP!
Are you the Big Sword Society?
We are.
* Ahem. *
By Royal Decree, the Ch'ing government hereby outlaws the Big Sword Society for their crimes against the foreign missionaries, their Chinese Christian disciples, and the Imperial Army!
Society members must immediately relinquish their weapons and submit themselves to the mercies of the local authorities! Those who comply will be treated with compassionate justice!

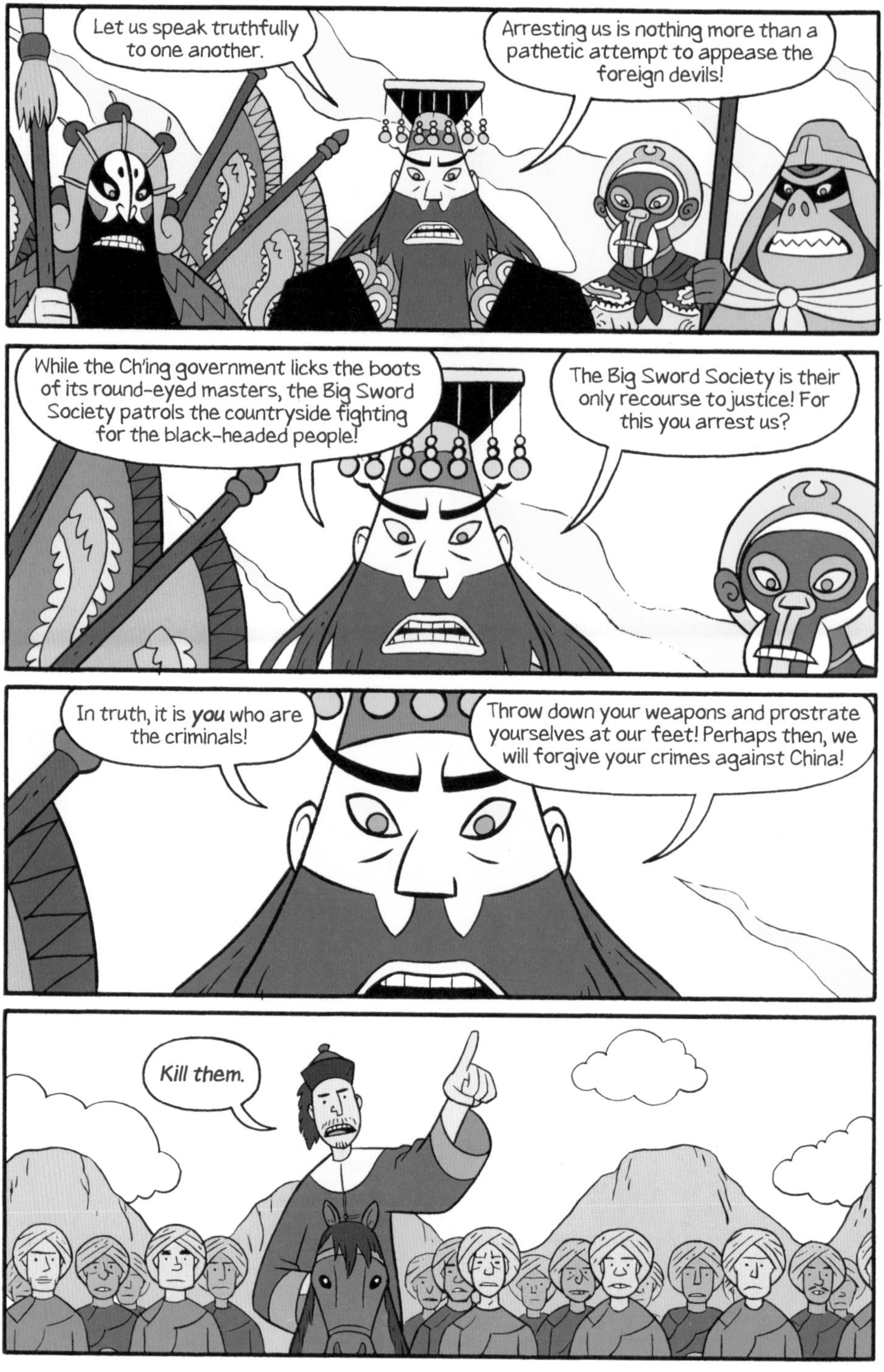
Let us speak truthfully to one another.
Arresting us is nothing more than a pathetic attempt to appease the foreign devils!
While the Ch'ing government licks the boots of its round-eyed masters, the Big Sword Society patrols the countryside fighting for the black-headed people!
The Big Sword Society is their only recourse to justice! For this you arrest us?
In truth, it is *you* who are the criminals!
Throw down your weapons and prostrate yourselves at our feet! Perhaps then, we will forgive your crimes against China!
Kill them.

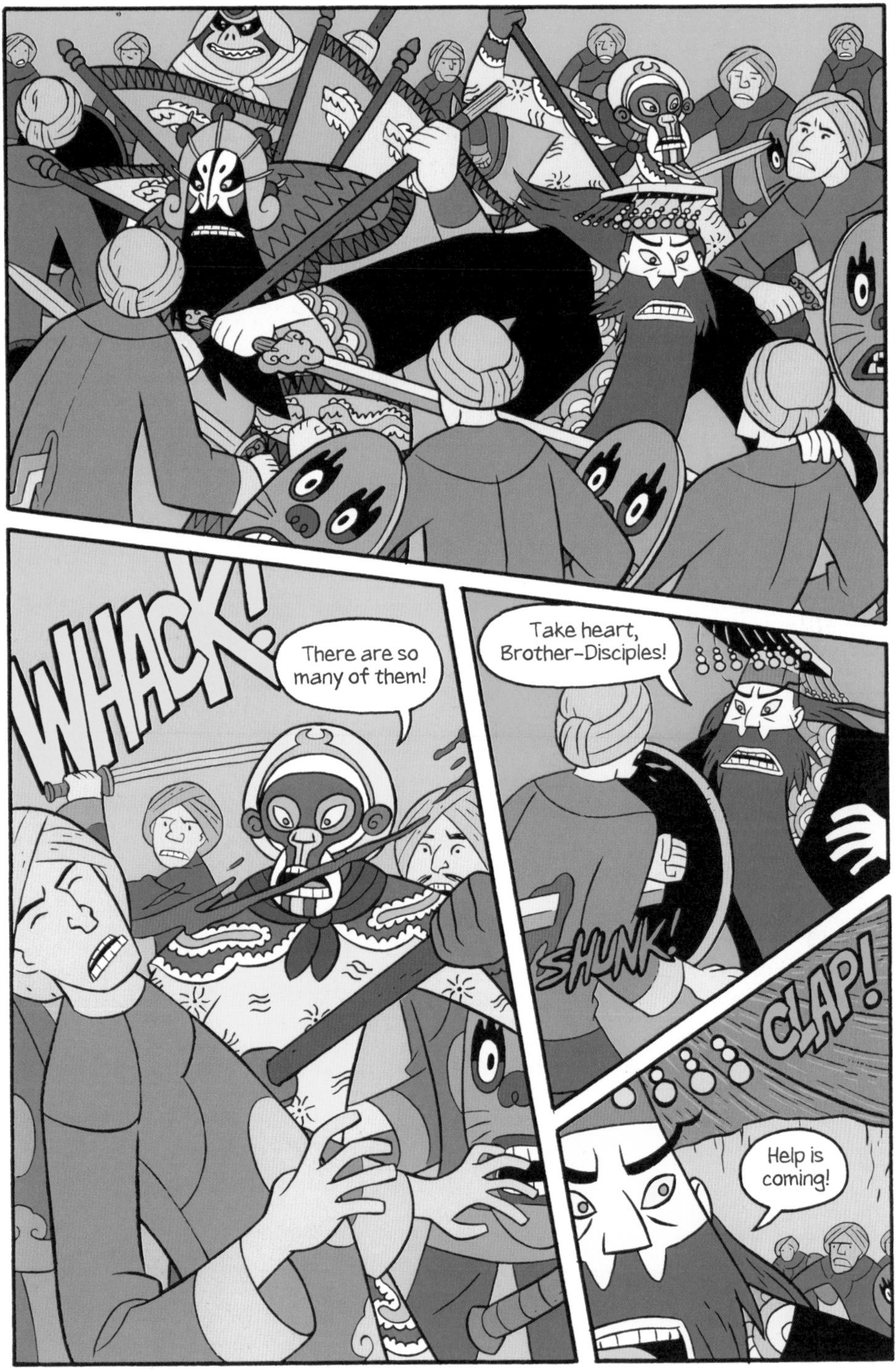
WHACK!
There are so many of them!
Take heart, Brother-Disciples!
SHUNK!
CLAP!
Help is coming!

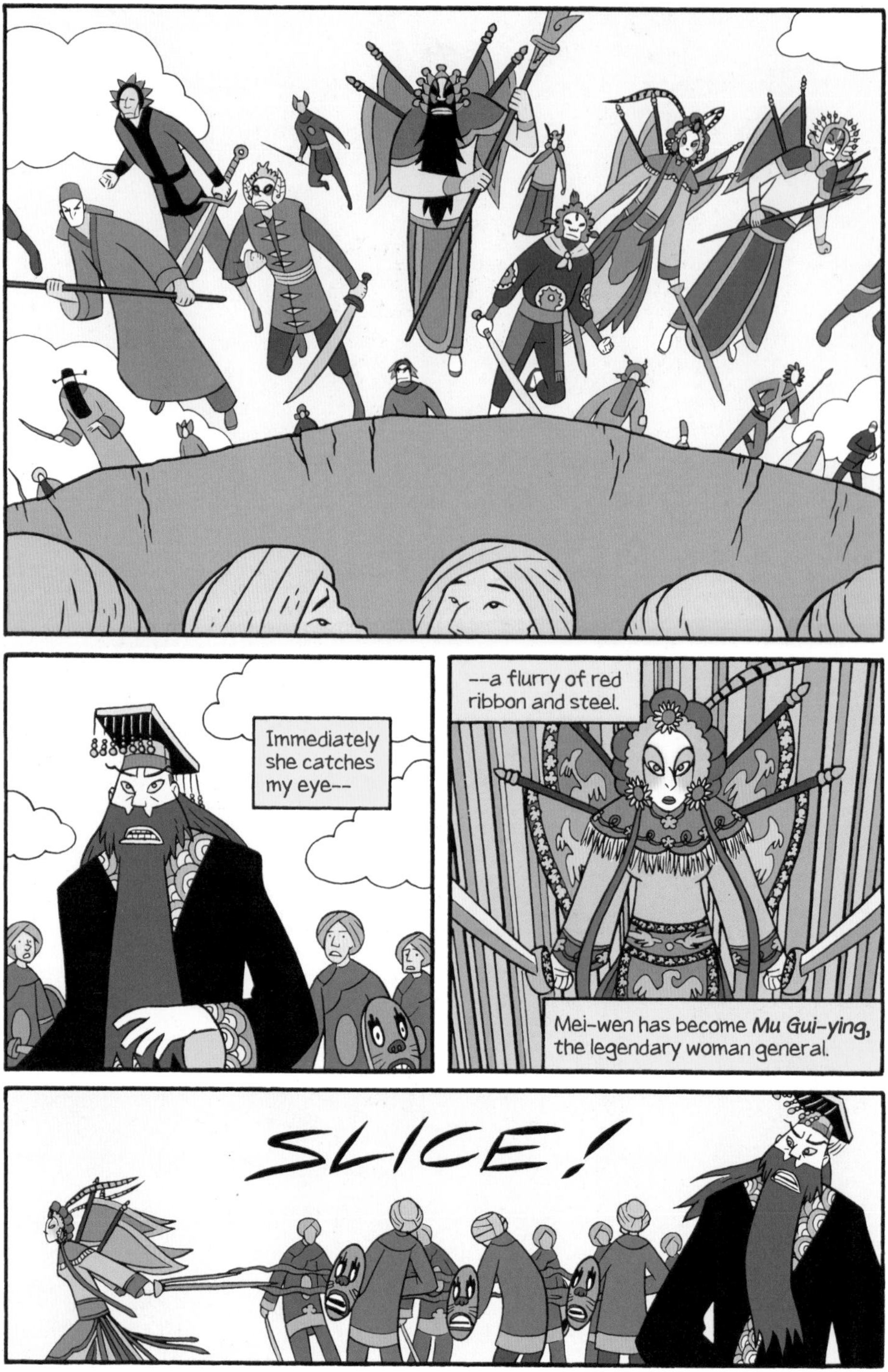
Immediately she catches my eye--
--a flurry of red ribbon and steel.
Mei-wen has become *Mu Gui-ying*, the legendary woman general.
SLICE!

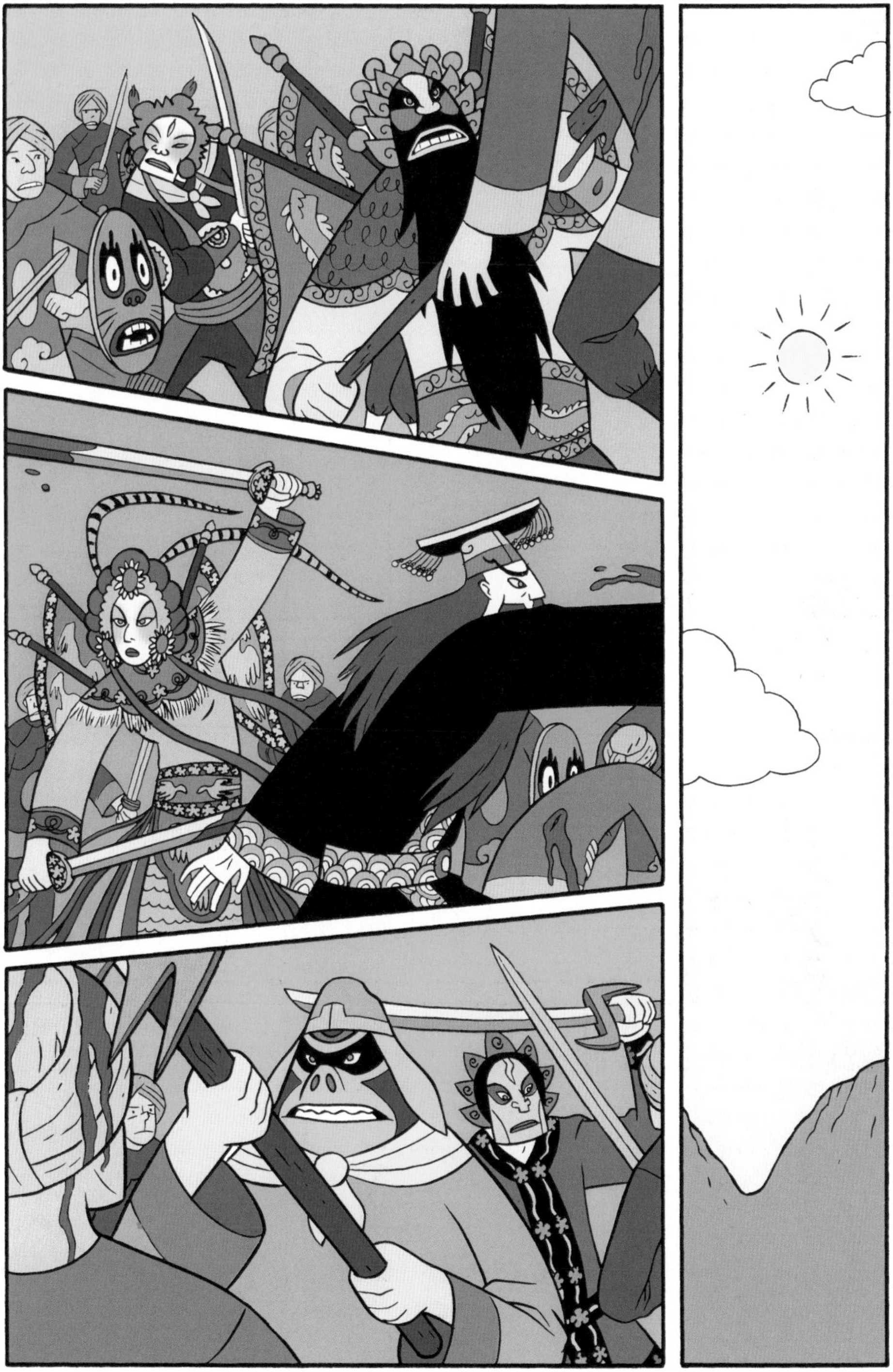

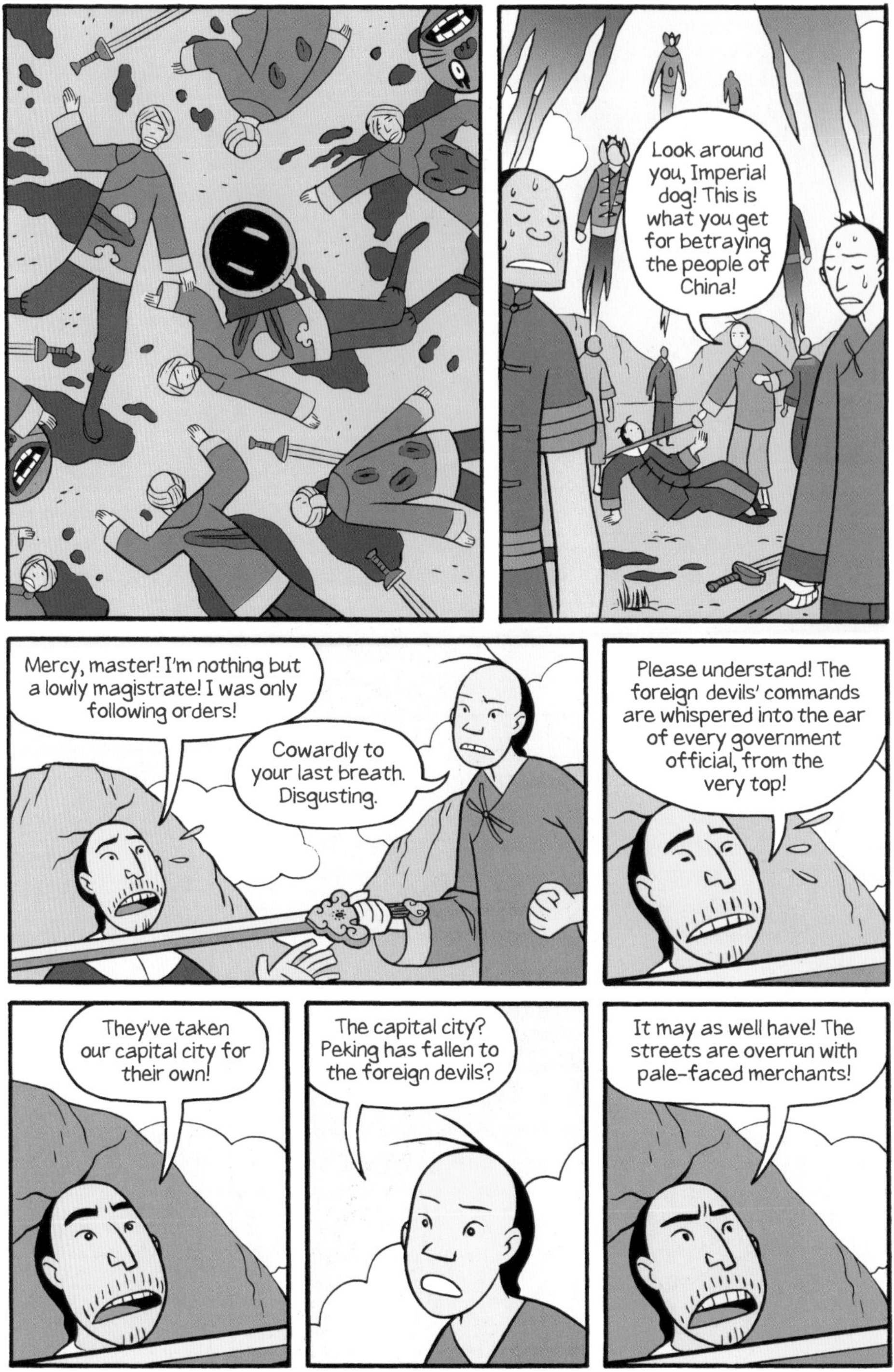
Look around you, Imperial dog! This is what you get for betraying the people of China!
Mercy, master! I'm nothing but a lowly magistrate! I was only following orders!
Cowardly to your last breath. Disgusting.
Please understand! The foreign devils' commands are whispered into the ear of every government official, from the very top!
They've taken our capital city for their own!
The capital city? Peking has fallen to the foreign devils?
It may as well have! The streets are overrun with pale-faced merchants!

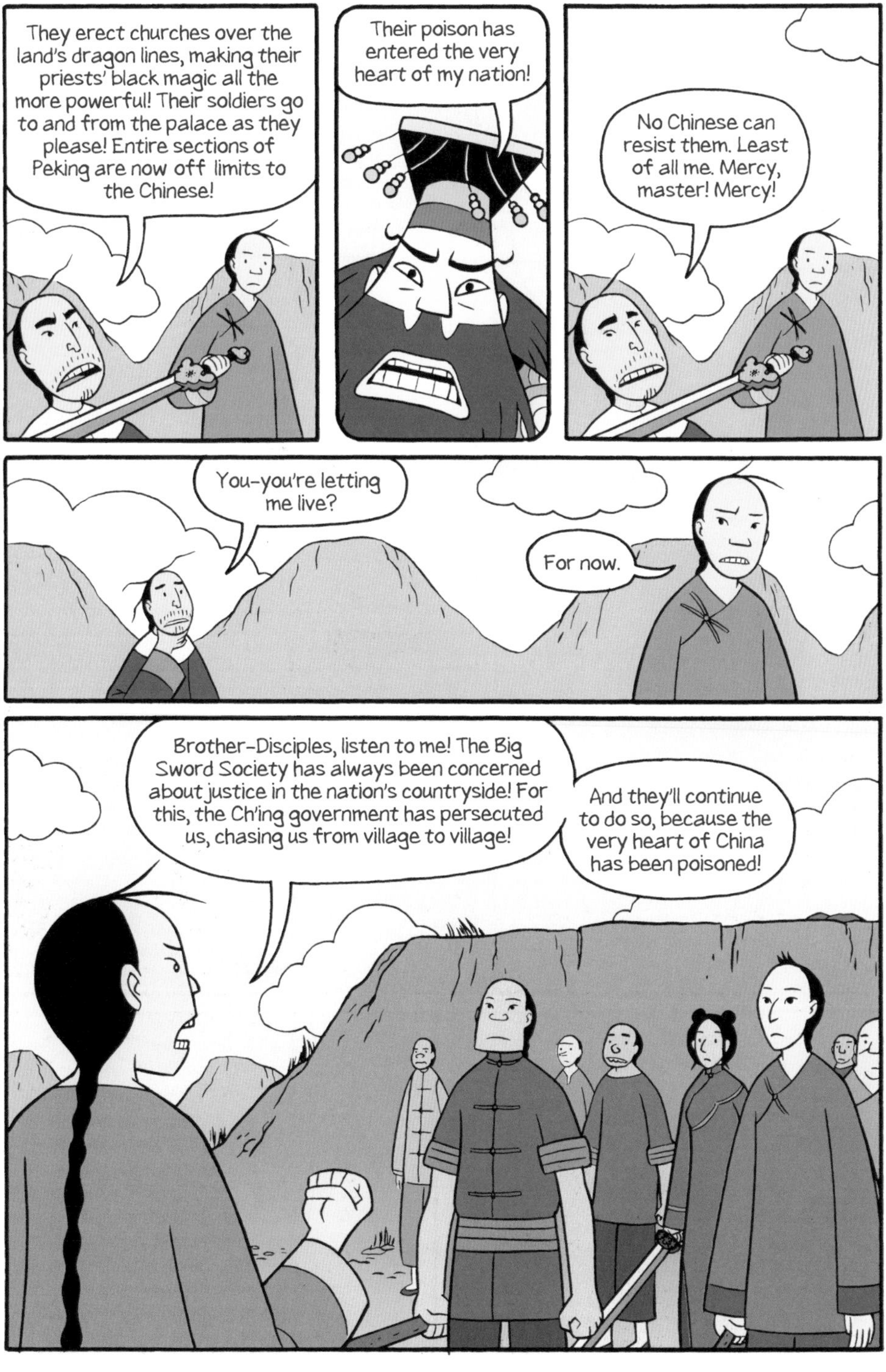
They erect churches over the land's dragon lines, making their priests' black magic all the more powerful! Their soldiers go to and from the palace as they please! Entire sections of Peking are now off limits to the Chinese!
Their poison has entered the very heart of my nation!
No Chinese can resist them. Least of all me. Mercy, master! Mercy!
You-you're letting me live?
For now.
Brother-Disciples, listen to me! The Big Sword Society has always been concerned about justice in the nation's countryside! For this, the Ch'ing government has persecuted us, chasing us from village to village!
And they'll continue to do so, because the very heart of China has been poisoned!

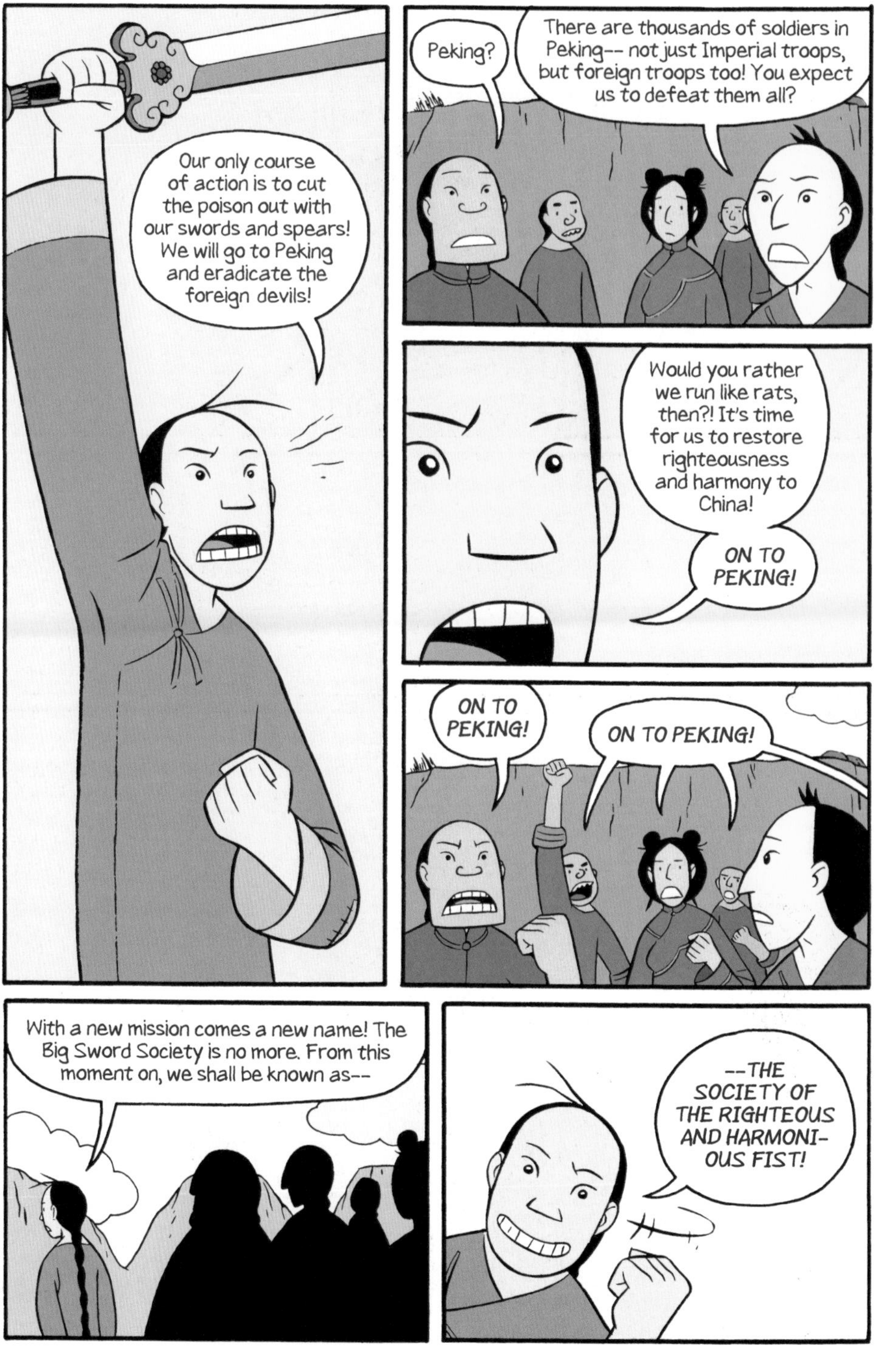
Our only course of action is to cut the poison out with our swords and spears! We will go to Peking and eradicate the foreign devils!
Peking?
There are thousands of soldiers in Peking-- not just Imperial troops, but foreign troops too! You expect us to defeat them all?
Would you rather we run like rats, then?! It's time for us to restore righteousness and harmony to China!
ON TO PEKING!
ON TO PEKING!
ON TO PEKING!
With a new mission comes a new name! The Big Sword Society is no more. From this moment on, we shall be known as--
--THE SOCIETY OF THE RIGHTEOUS AND HARMONIOUS FIST!

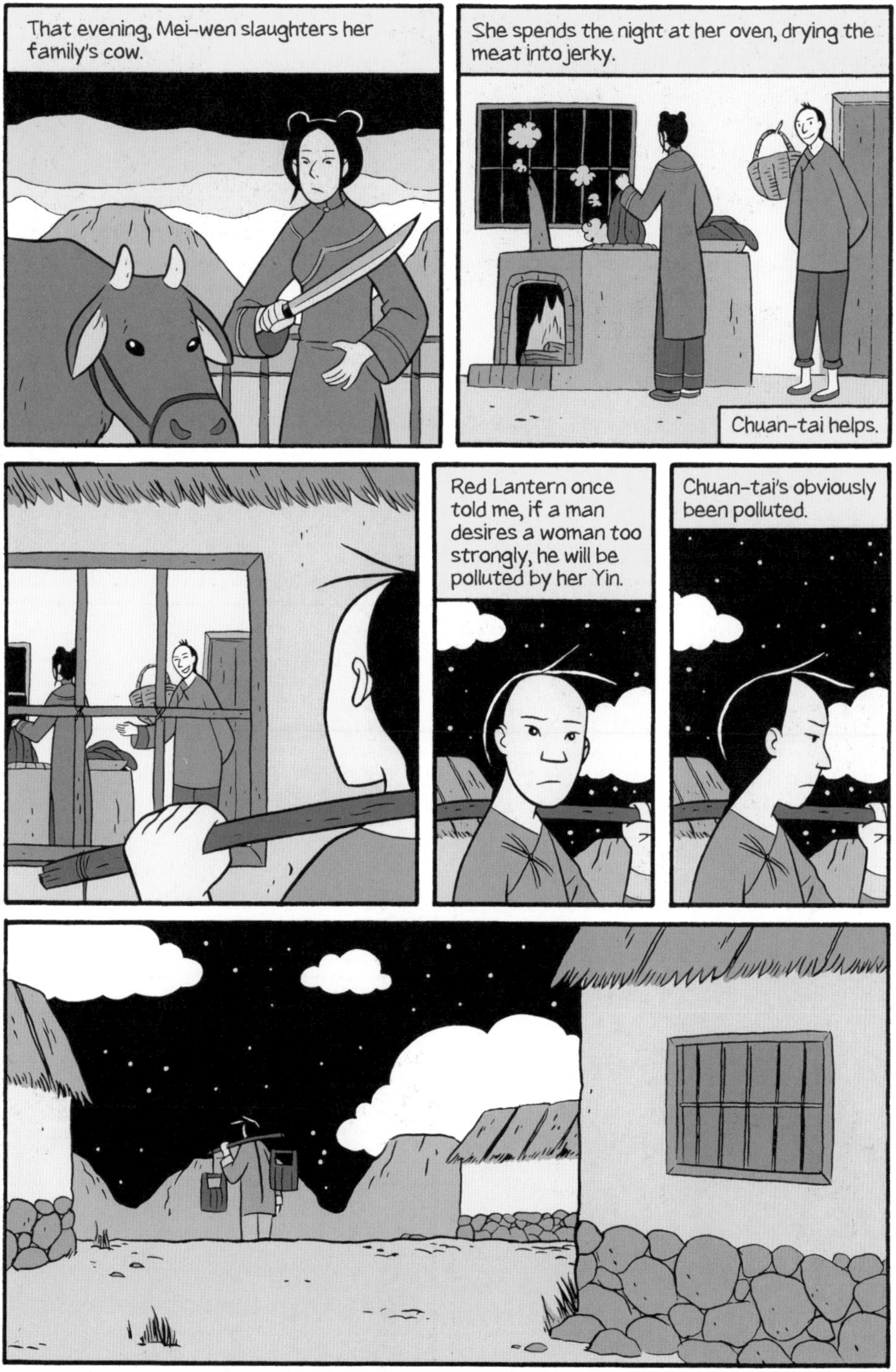
That evening, Mei-wen slaughters her family's cow.
She spends the night at her oven, drying the meat into jerky.
Chuan-tai helps.
Red Lantern once told me, if a man desires a woman too strongly, he will be polluted by her Yin.
Chuan-tai's obviously been polluted.

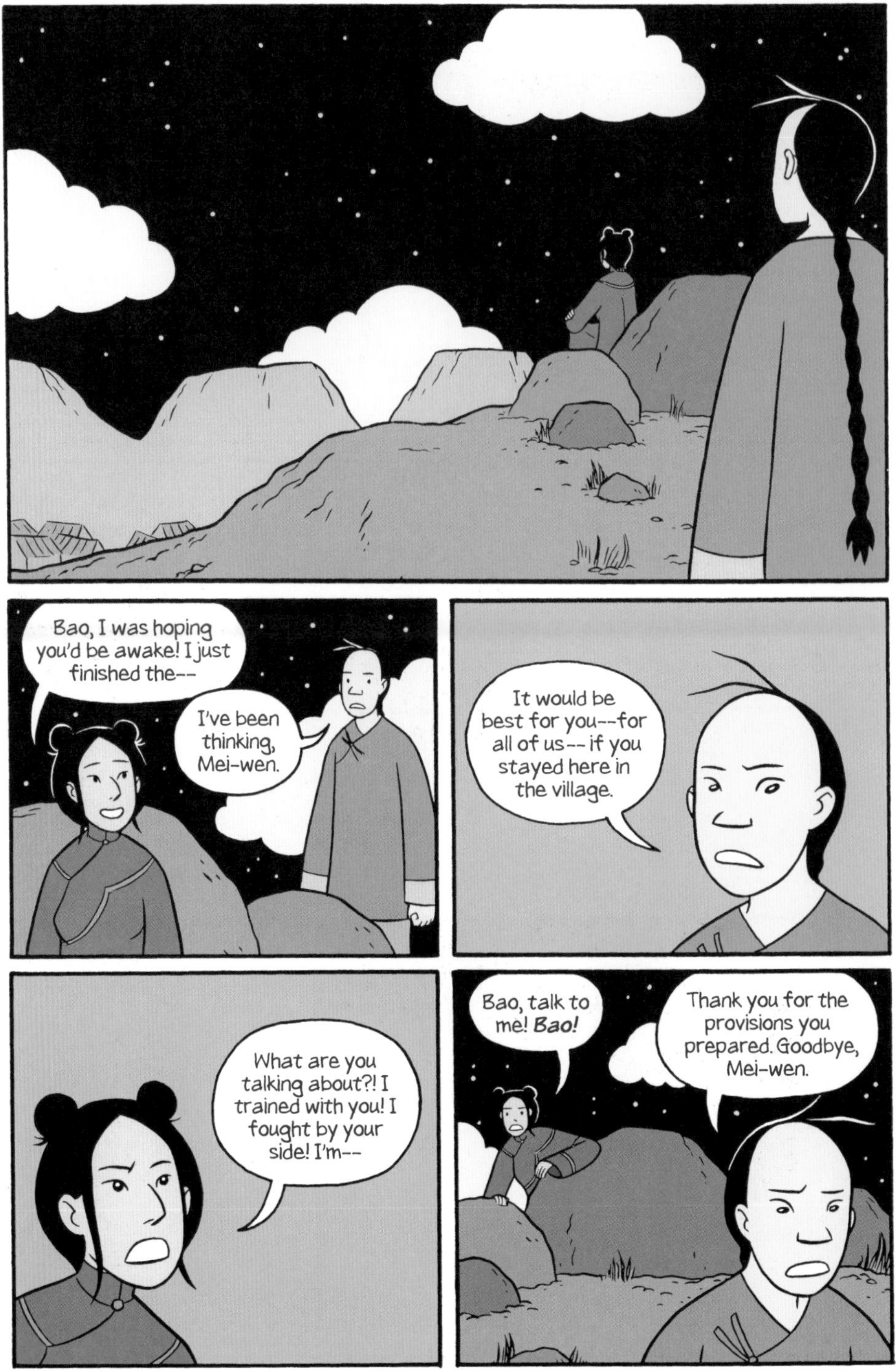
Bao, I was hoping you'd be awake! I just finished the--
I've been thinking, Mei-wen.
It would be best for you--for all of us-- if you stayed here in the village.
What are you talking about?! I trained with you! I fought by your side! I'm--
Bao, talk to me! *Bao!*
Thank you for the provisions you prepared. Goodbye, Mei-wen.

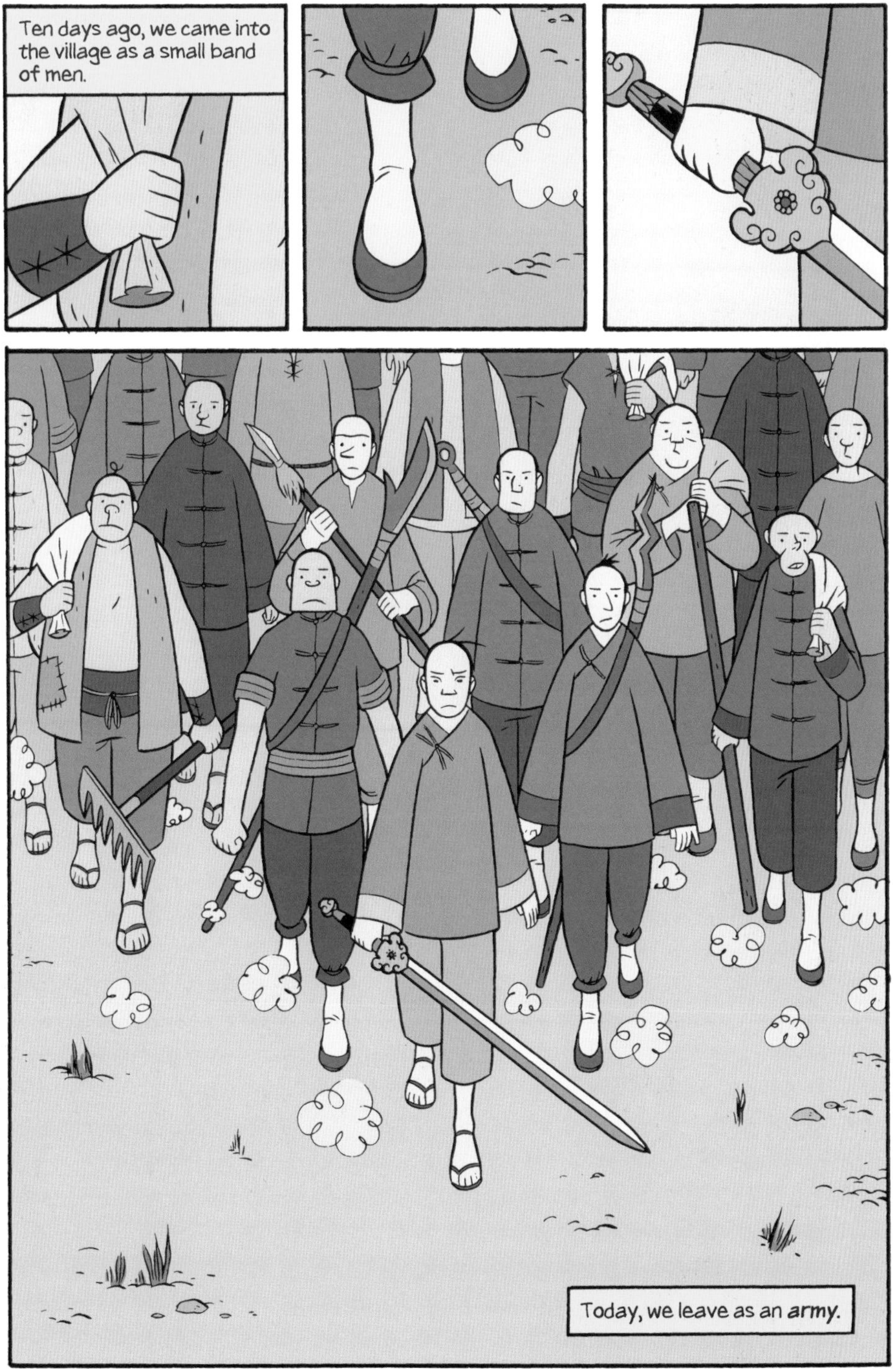
Ten days ago, we came into the village as a small band of men.
Today, we leave as an army.

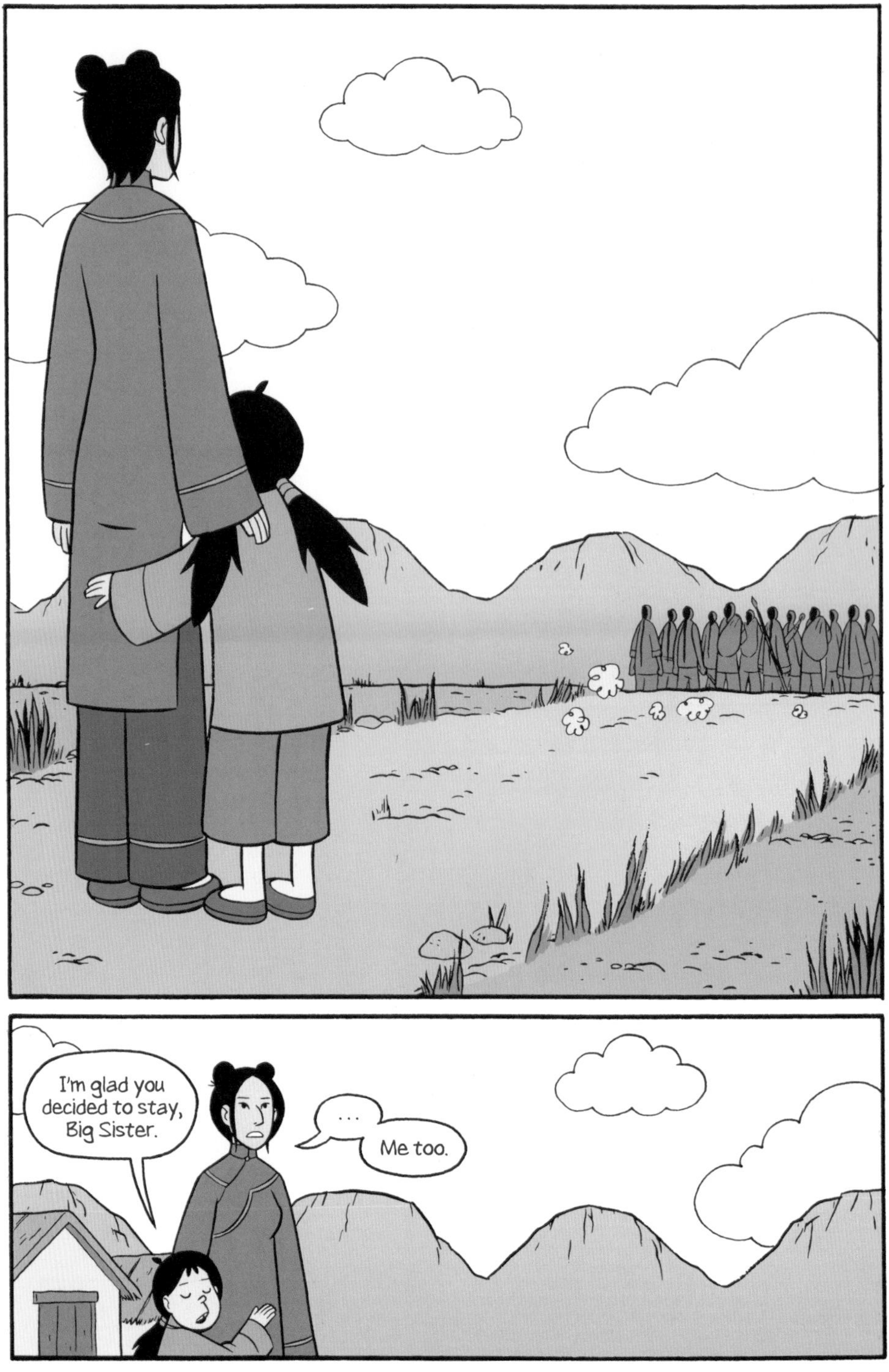
I'm glad you decided to stay, Big Sister.
...
Me too.

第五章

Southern Hebei Province, China
Spring 1900

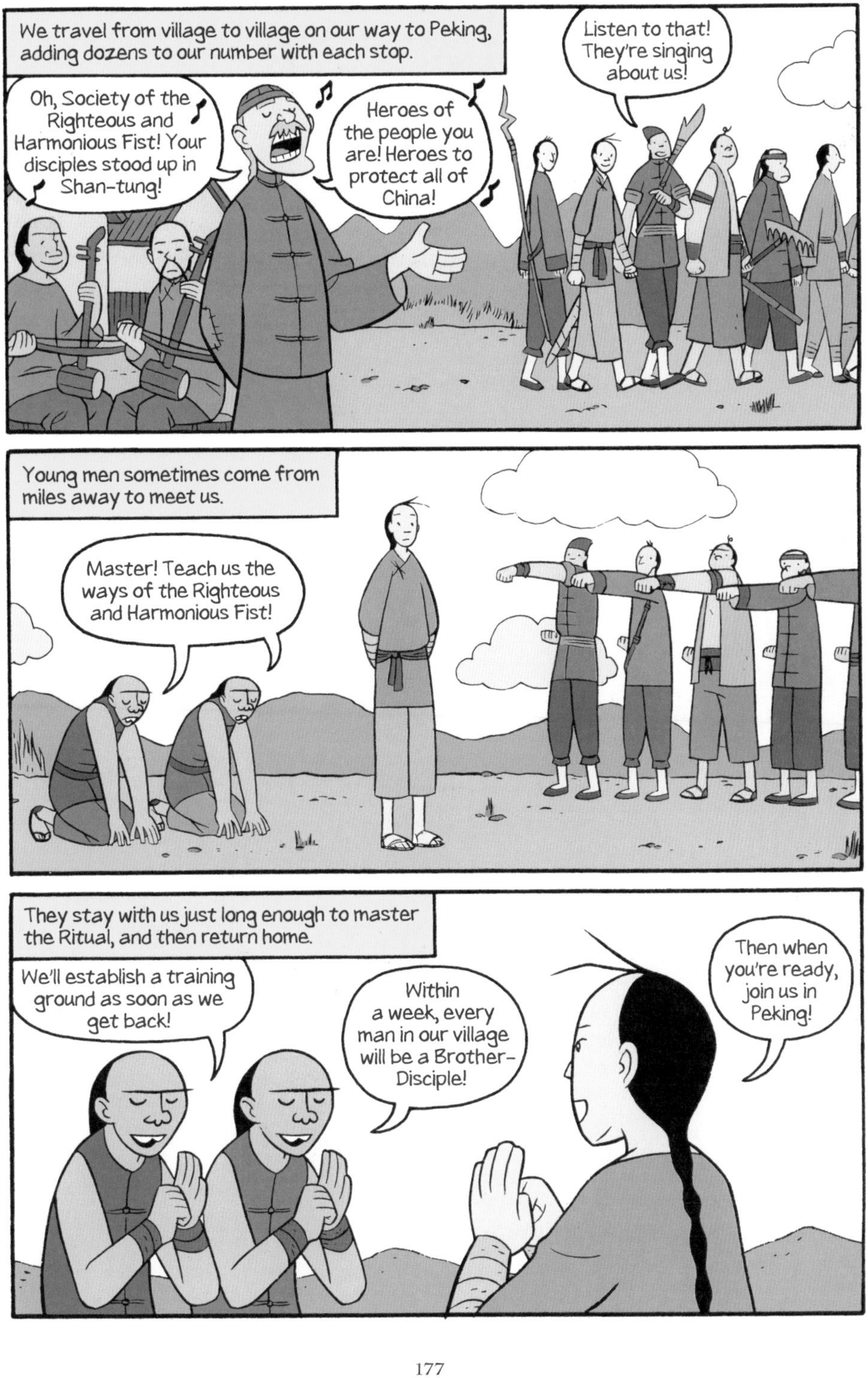
We travel from village to village on our way to Peking, adding dozens to our number with each stop.
Oh, Society of the Righteous and Harmonious Fist! Your disciples stood up in Shan-tung!
Heroes of the people you are! Heroes to protect all of China!
Listen to that! They're singing about us!
Young men sometimes come from miles away to meet us.
Master! Teach us the ways of the Righteous and Harmonious Fist!
They stay with us just long enough to master the Ritual, and then return home.
We'll establish a training ground as soon as we get back!
Within a week, every man in our village will be a Brother-Disciple!
Then when you're ready, join us in Peking!

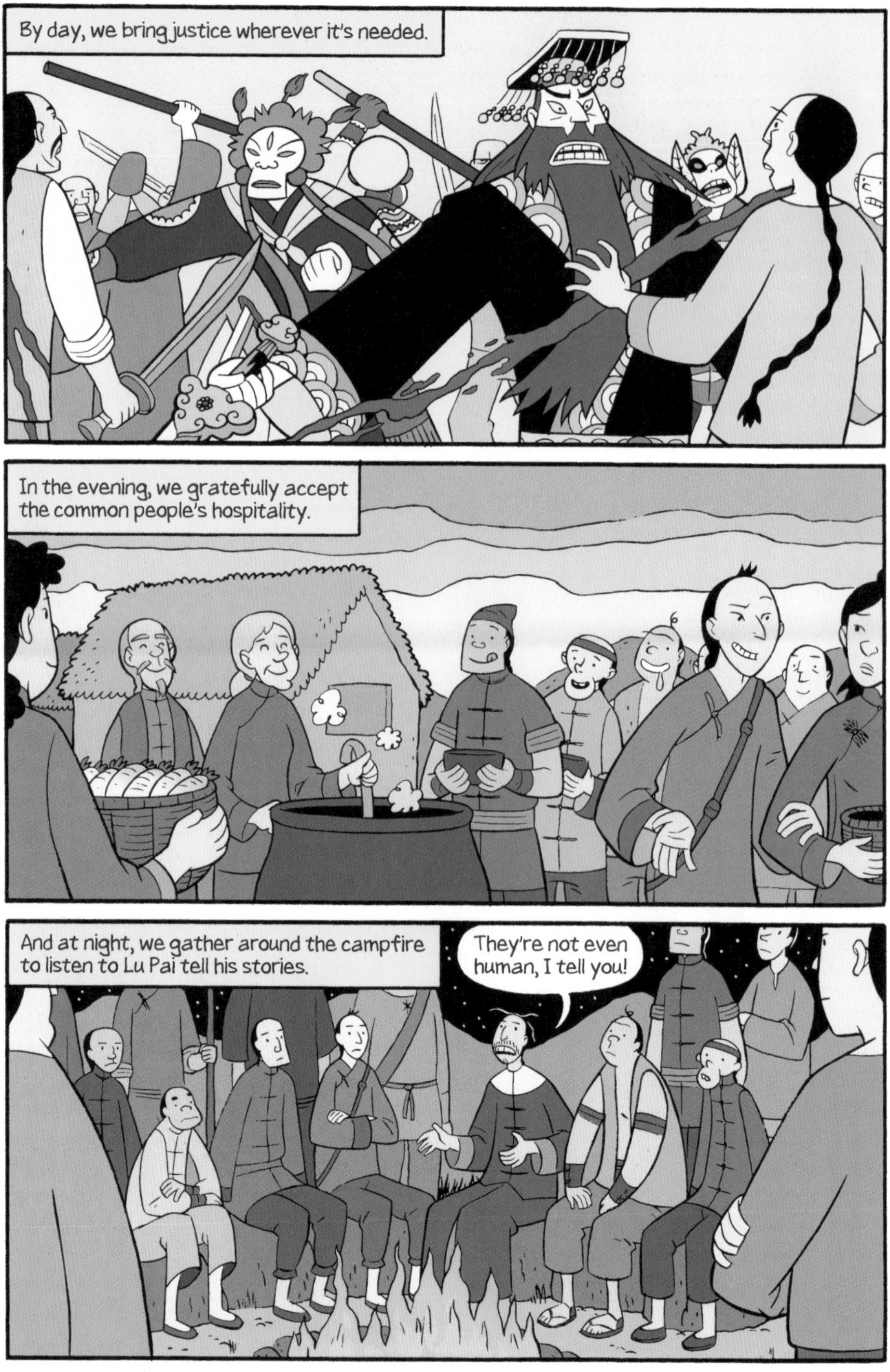
By day, we bring justice wherever it's needed.
In the evening, we gratefully accept the common people's hospitality.
And at night, we gather around the campfire to listen to Lu Pai tell his stories.
They're not even human, I tell you!

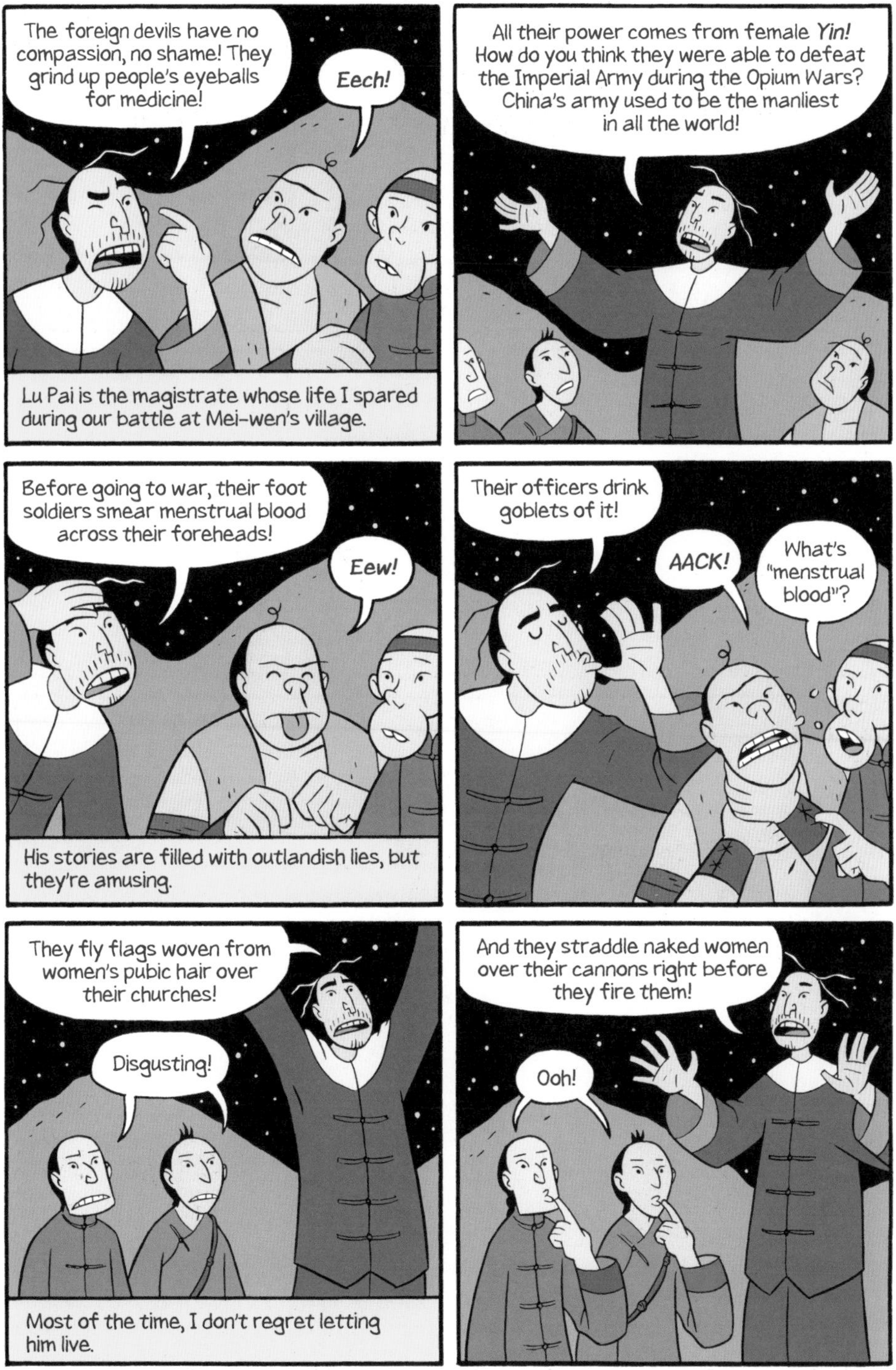
The foreign devils have no compassion, no shame! They grind up people's eyeballs for medicine!
Eech!
Lu Pai is the magistrate whose life I spared during our battle at Mei-wen's village.
All their power comes from female *Yin!* How do you think they were able to defeat the Imperial Army during the Opium Wars? China's army used to be the manliest in all the world!
Before going to war, their foot soldiers smear menstrual blood across their foreheads!
Eew!
His stories are filled with outlandish lies, but they're amusing.
Their officers drink goblets of it!
AACK!
What's "menstrual blood"?
They fly flags woven from women's pubic hair over their churches!
Disgusting!
Most of the time, I don't regret letting him live.
And they straddle naked women over their cannons right before they fire them!
Ooh!

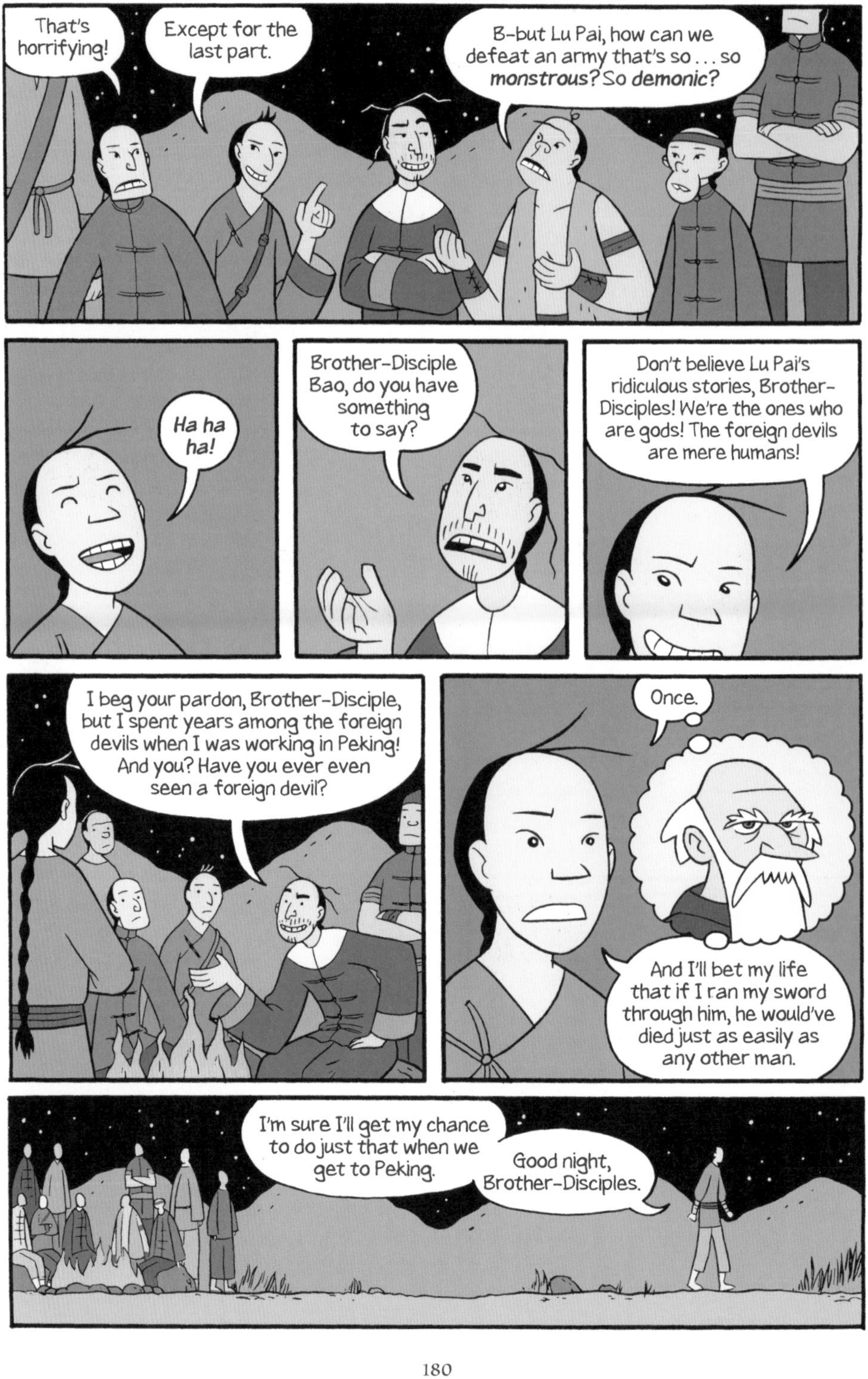
That's horrifying!
Except for the last part.
B-but Lu Pai, how can we defeat an army that's so . . . so *monstrous*? So *demonic*?
Ha ha ha!
Brother-Disciple Bao, do you have something to say?
Don't believe Lu Pai's ridiculous stories, Brother-Disciples! We're the ones who are gods! The foreign devils are mere humans!
I beg your pardon, Brother-Disciple, but I spent years among the foreign devils when I was working in Peking! And you? Have you ever even seen a foreign devil?
Once.
And I'll bet my life that if I ran my sword through him, he would've died just as easily as any other man.
I'm sure I'll get my chance to do just that when we get to Peking.
Good night, Brother-Disciples.

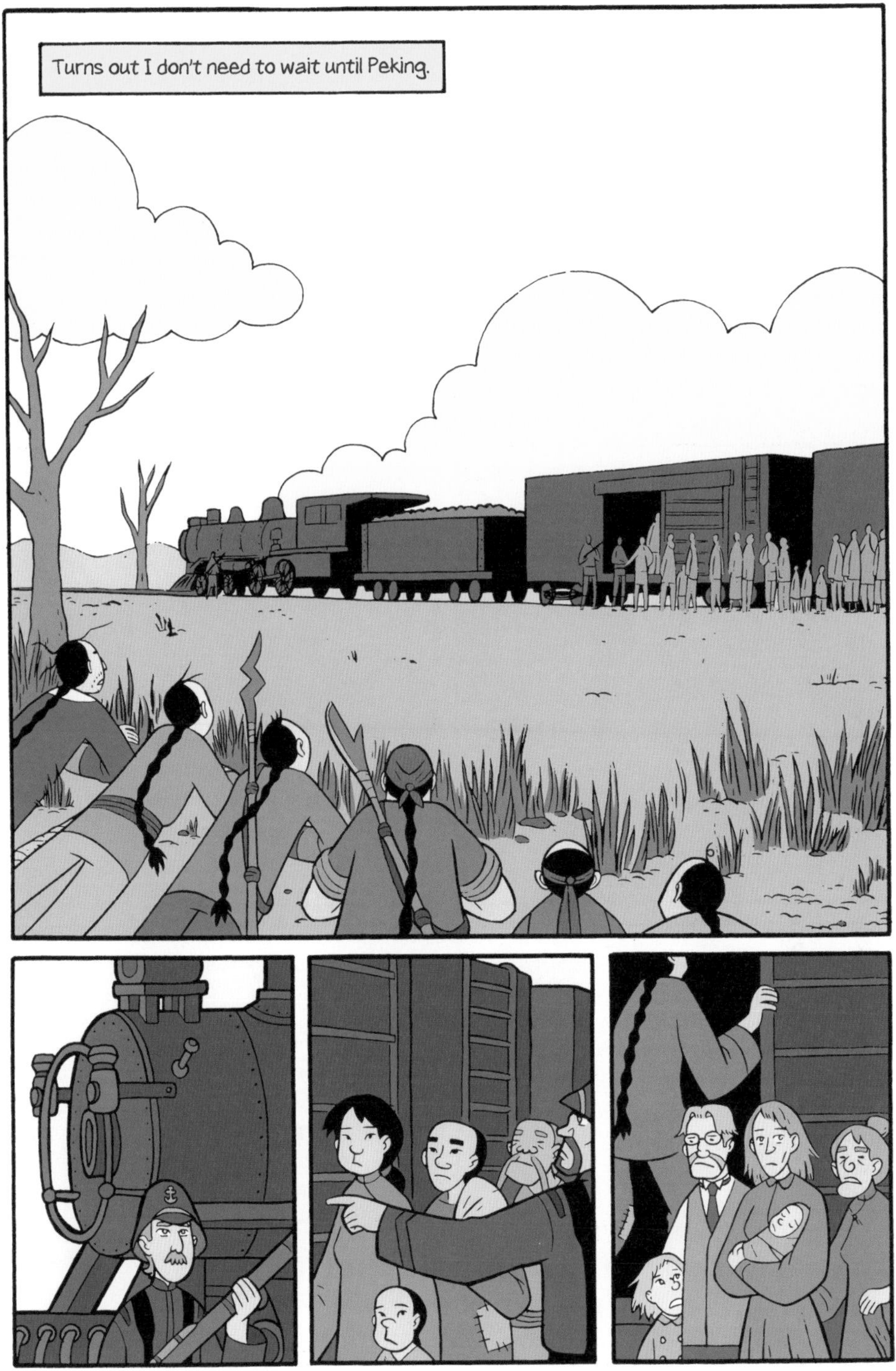
Turns out I don't need to wait until Peking.

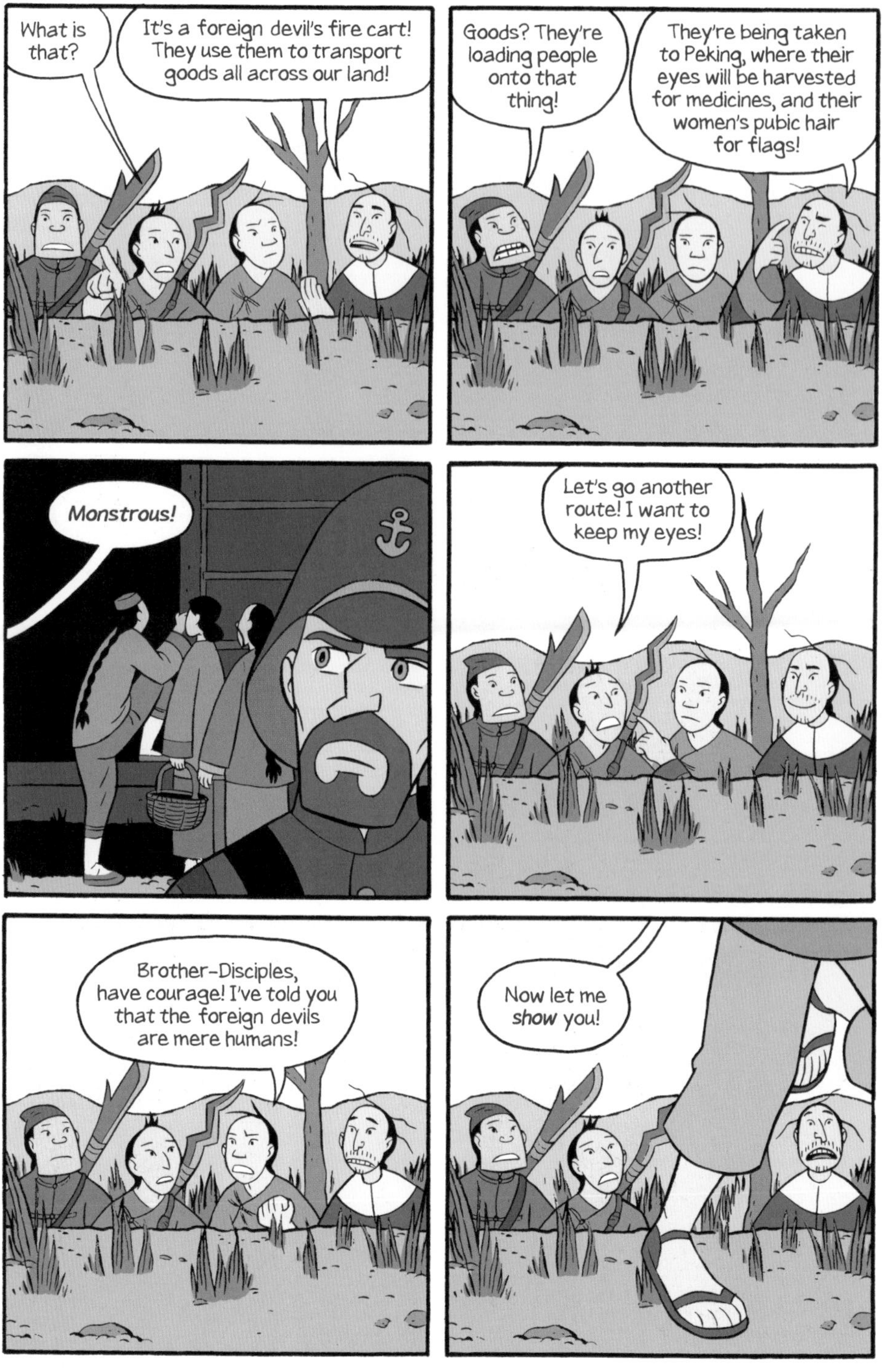
What is that?
It's a foreign devil's fire cart! They use them to transport goods all across our land!
Goods? They're loading people onto that thing!
They're being taken to Peking, where their eyes will be harvested for medicines, and their women's pubic hair for flags!
Monstrous!
Let's go another route! I want to keep my eyes!
Brother-Disciples, have courage! I've told you that the foreign devils are mere humans!
Now let me *show* you!

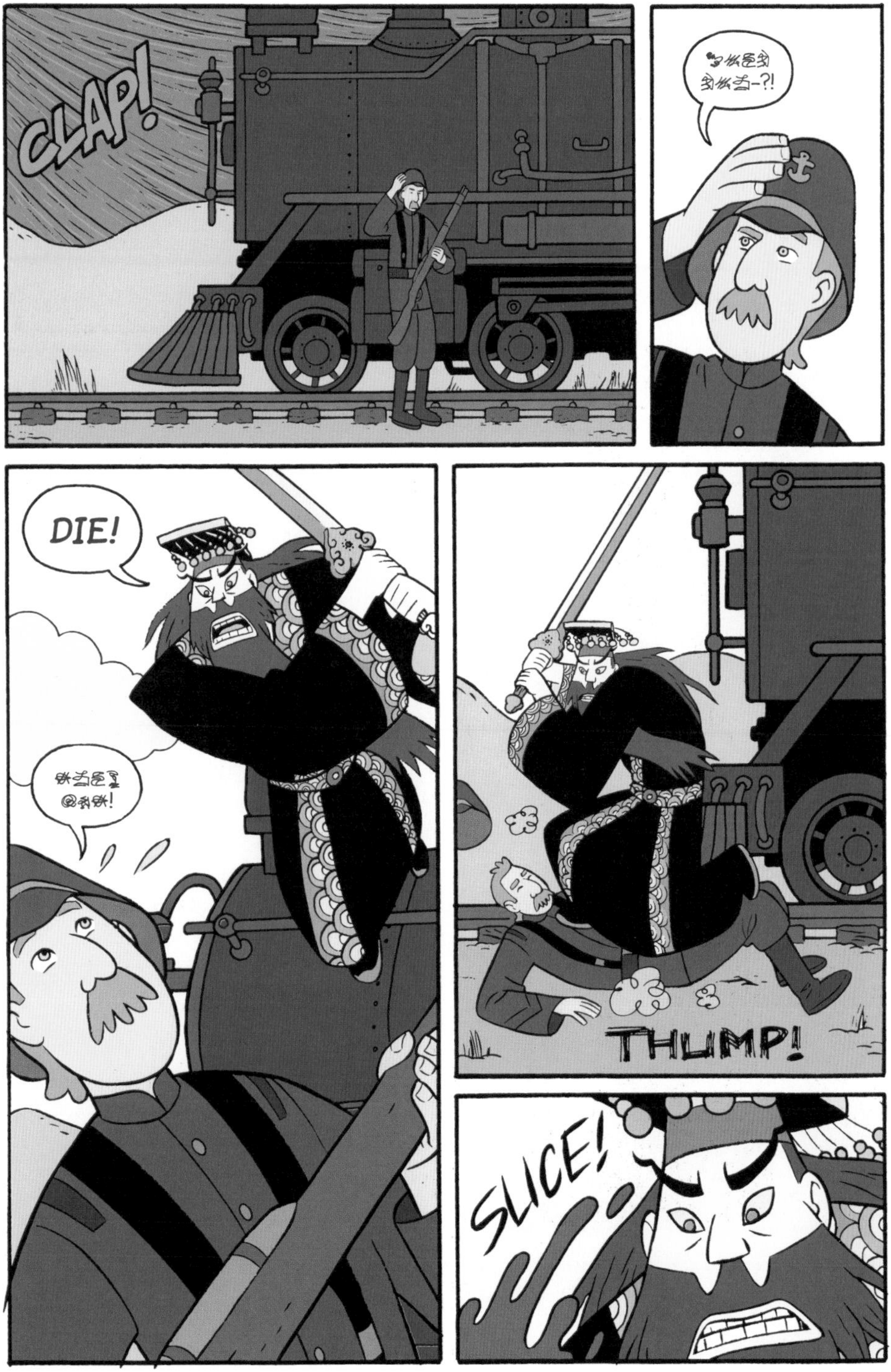
CLAP!
DIE!
THUMP!
SLICE!

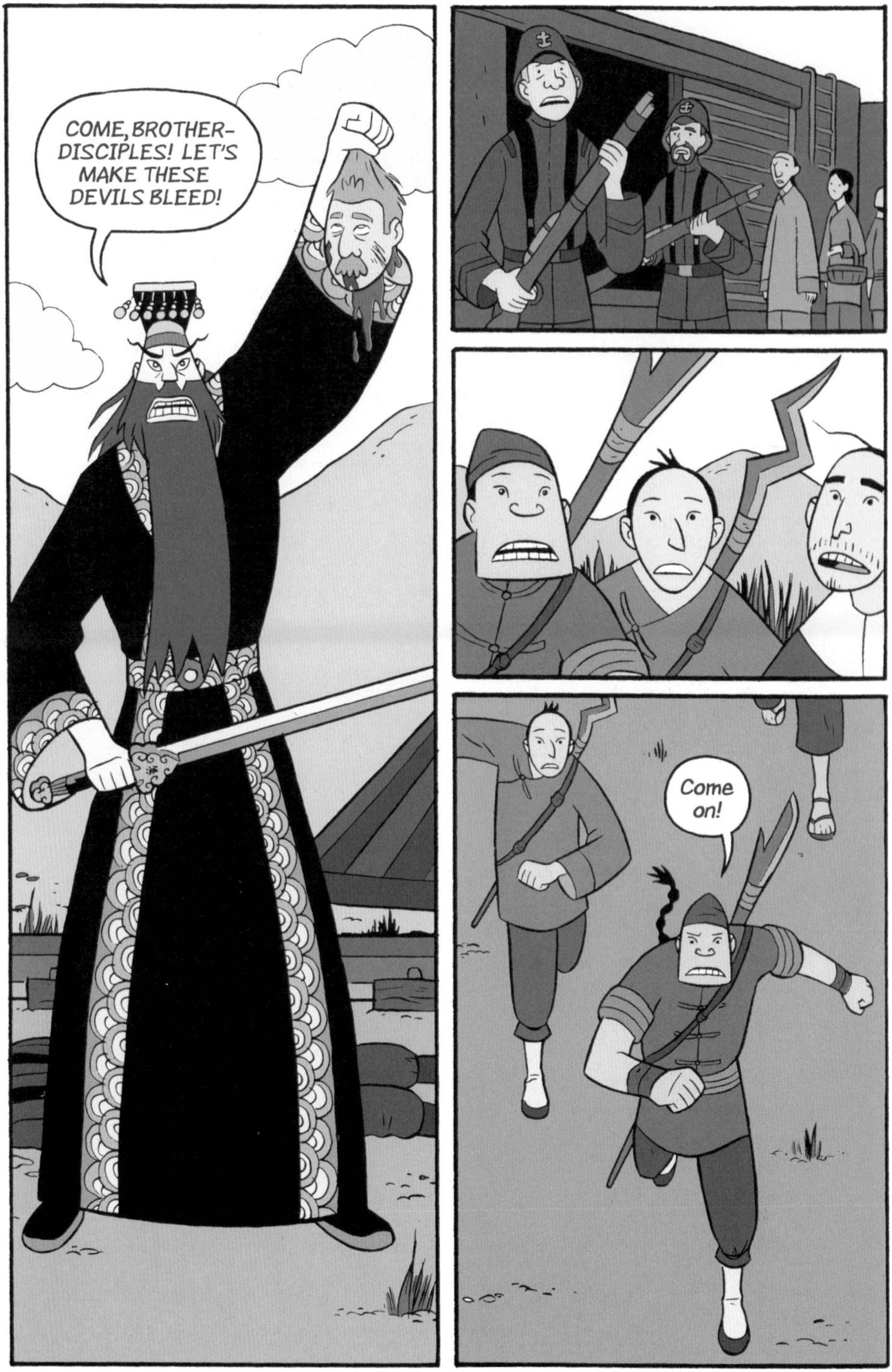
COME, BROTHER-DISCIPLES! LET'S MAKE THESE DEVILS BLEED!
Come on!

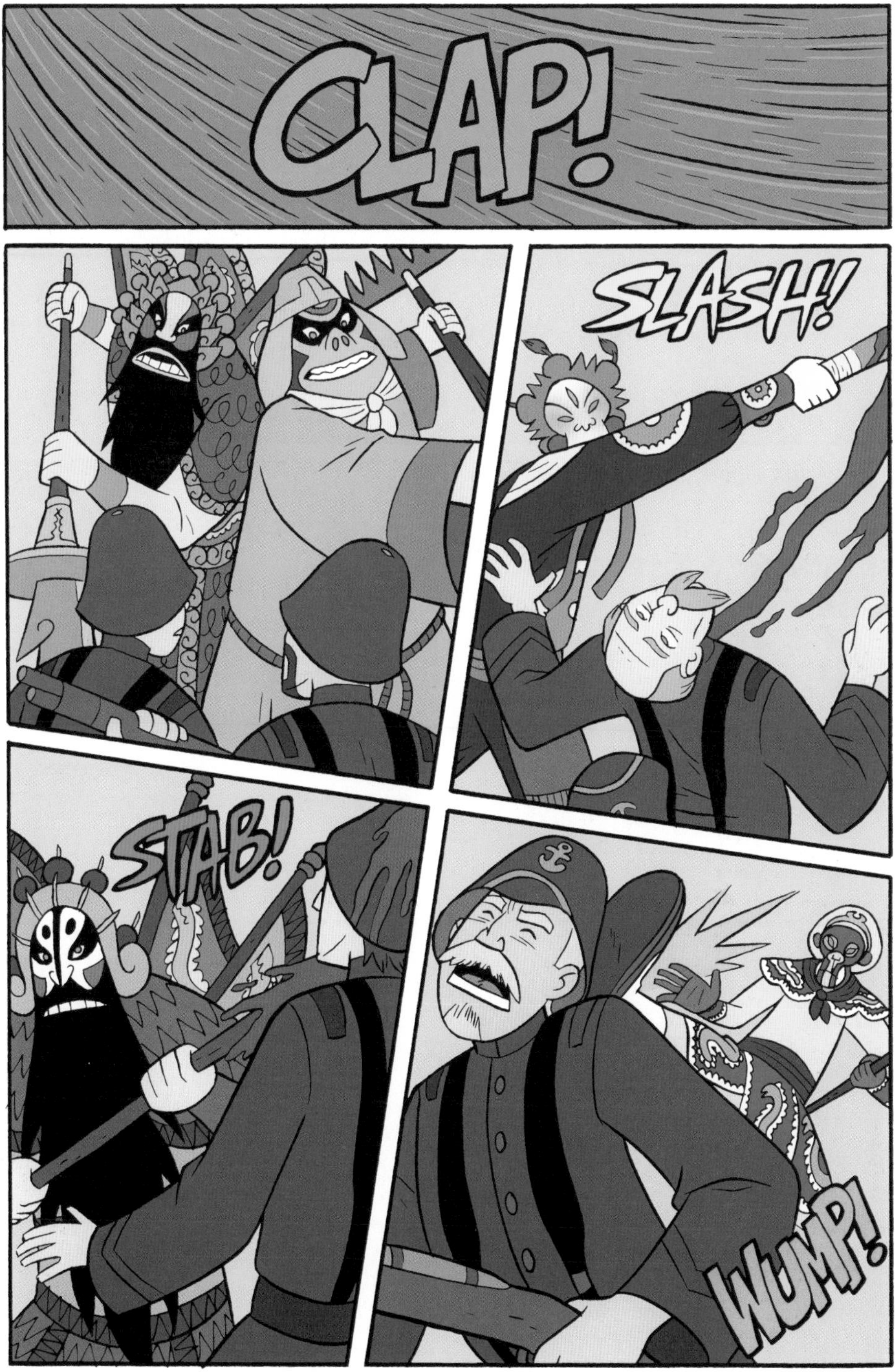
CLAP!
SLASH!
STAB!
WUMP!

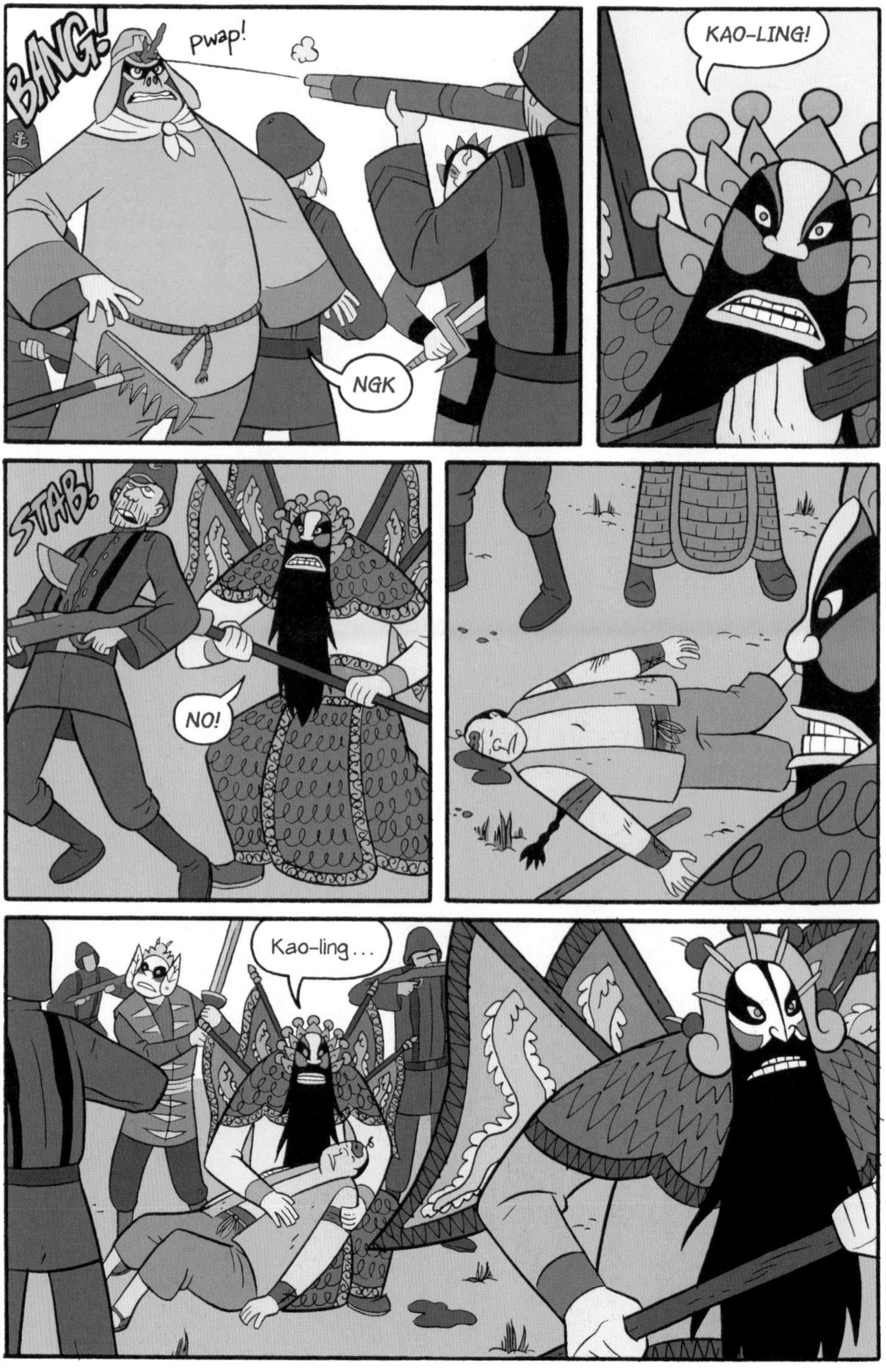
BANG!
Pwap!
NGK
KAO-LING!
STAB!
NO!
Kao-ling...

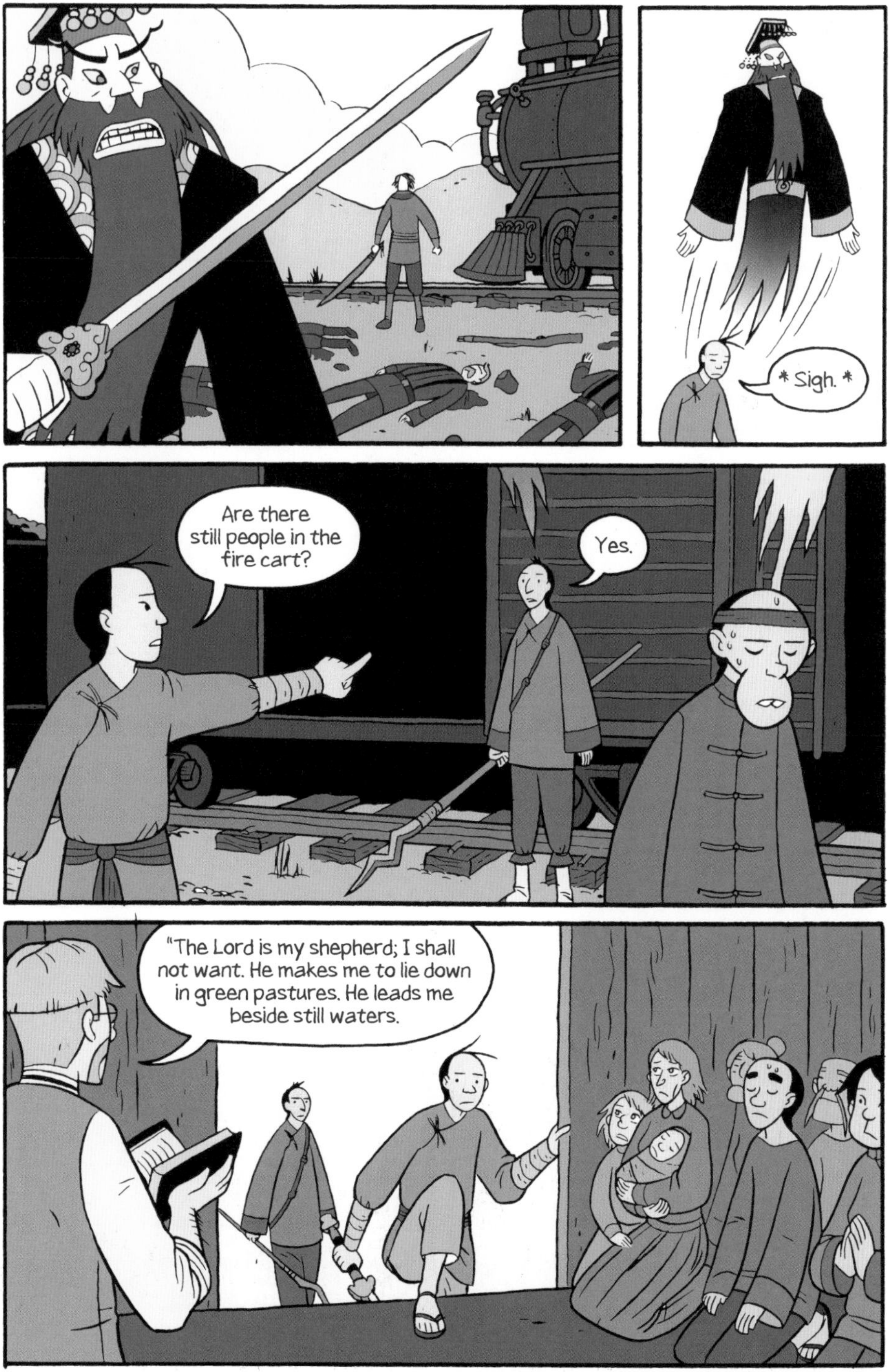
* Sigh. *
Are there still people in the fire cart?
Yes.
"The Lord is my shepherd; I shall not want. He makes me to lie down in green pastures. He leads me beside still waters.

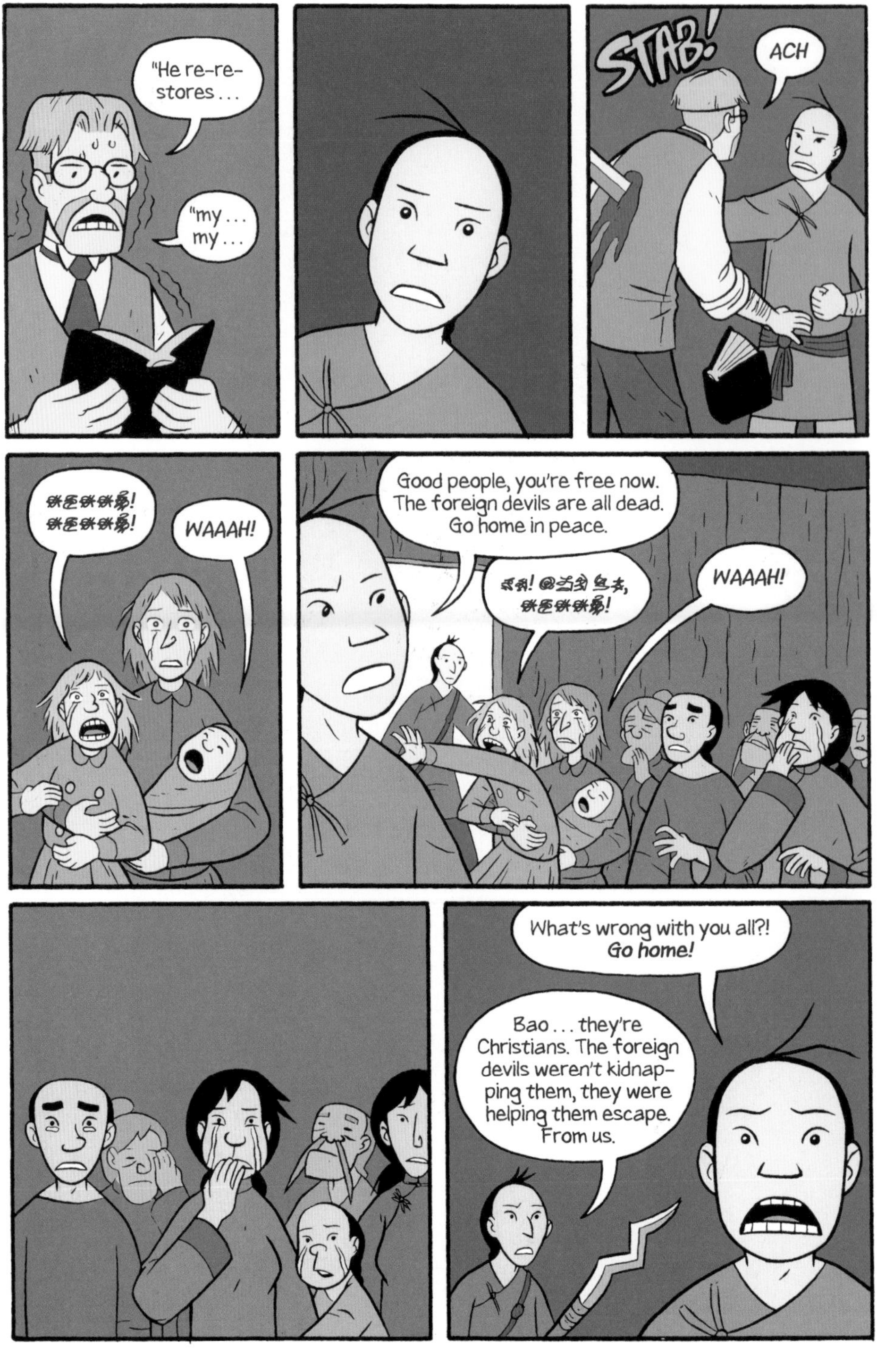
"He re-re-
stores . . .
"my . . .
my . . .
STAB!
ACH
WAAAH!
Good people, you're free now.
The foreign devils are all dead.
Go home in peace.
WAAAH!
What's wrong with you all?!
Go home!
Bao . . . they're Christians. The foreign devils weren't kidnapping them, they were helping them escape. From us.

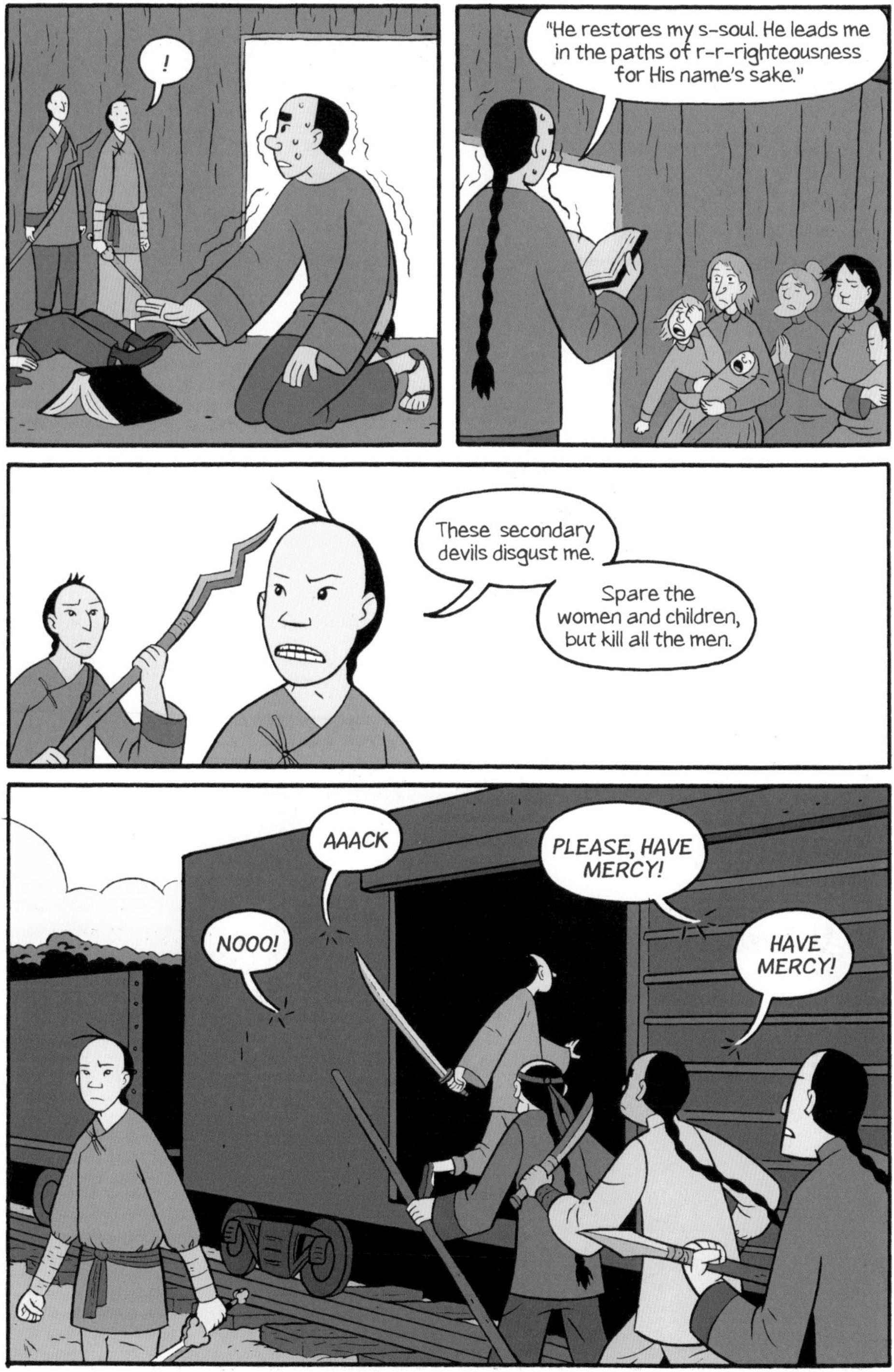
!
"He restores my s-soul. He leads me in the paths of r-r-righteousness for His name's sake."
These secondary devils disgust me.
Spare the women and children, but kill all the men.
AAACK
PLEASE, HAVE MERCY!
NOOO!
HAVE MERCY!

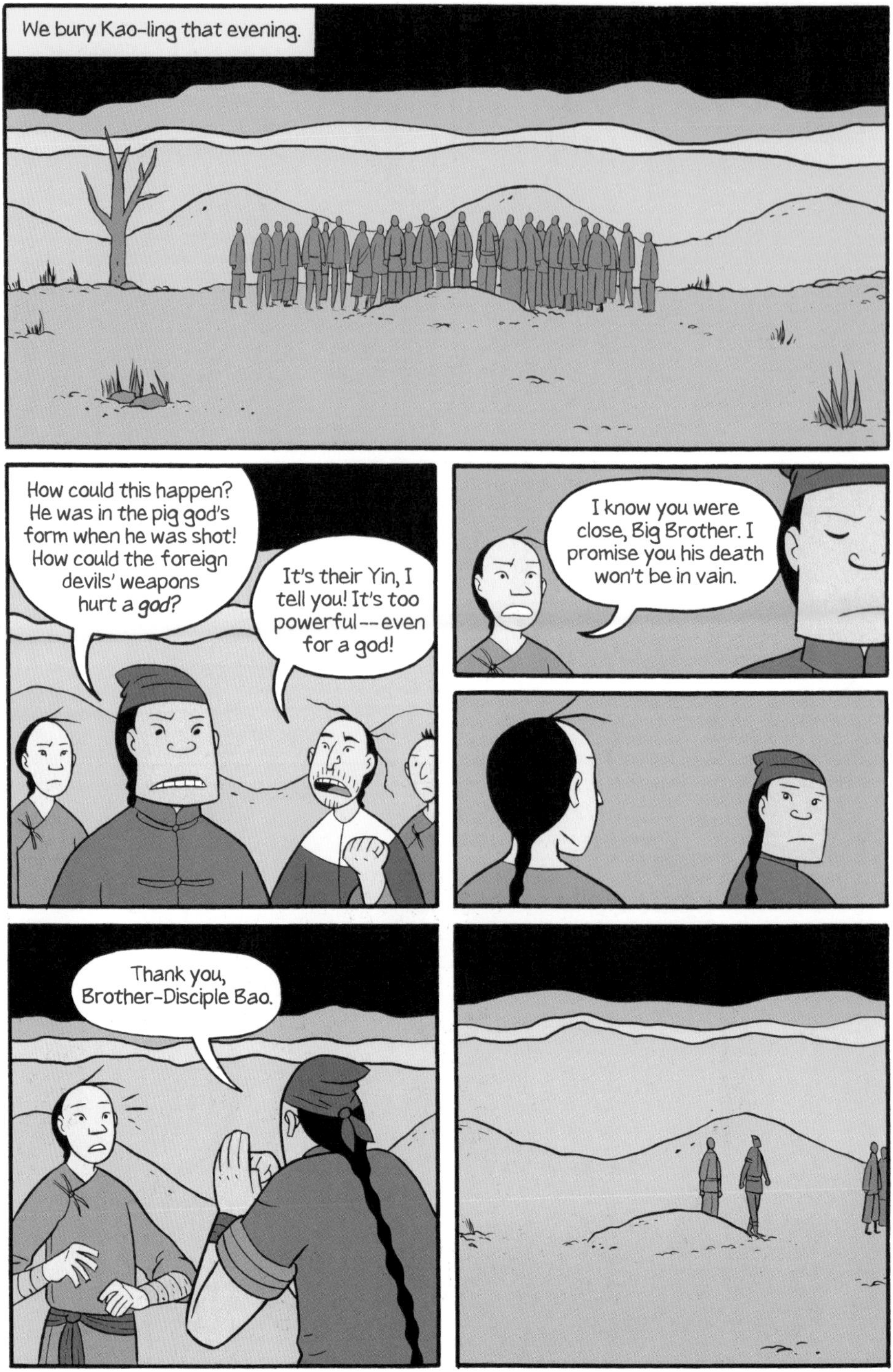
We bury Kao-ling that evening.
How could this happen? He was in the pig god's form when he was shot! How could the foreign devils' weapons hurt a *god*?
It's their Yin, I tell you! It's too powerful--even for a god!
I know you were close, Big Brother. I promise you his death won't be in vain.
Thank you, Brother-Disciple Bao.

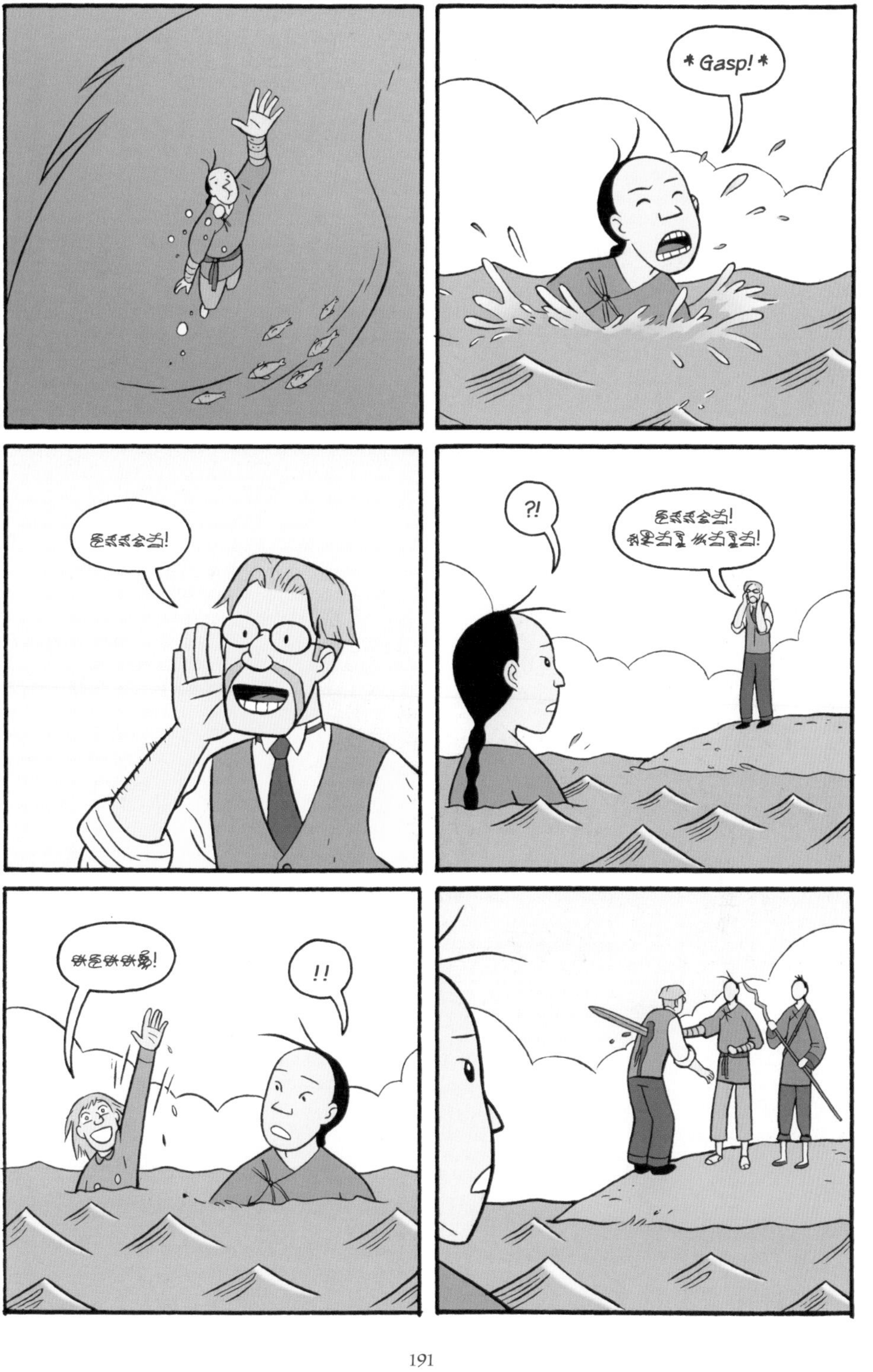
* Gasp! *
?!
!!

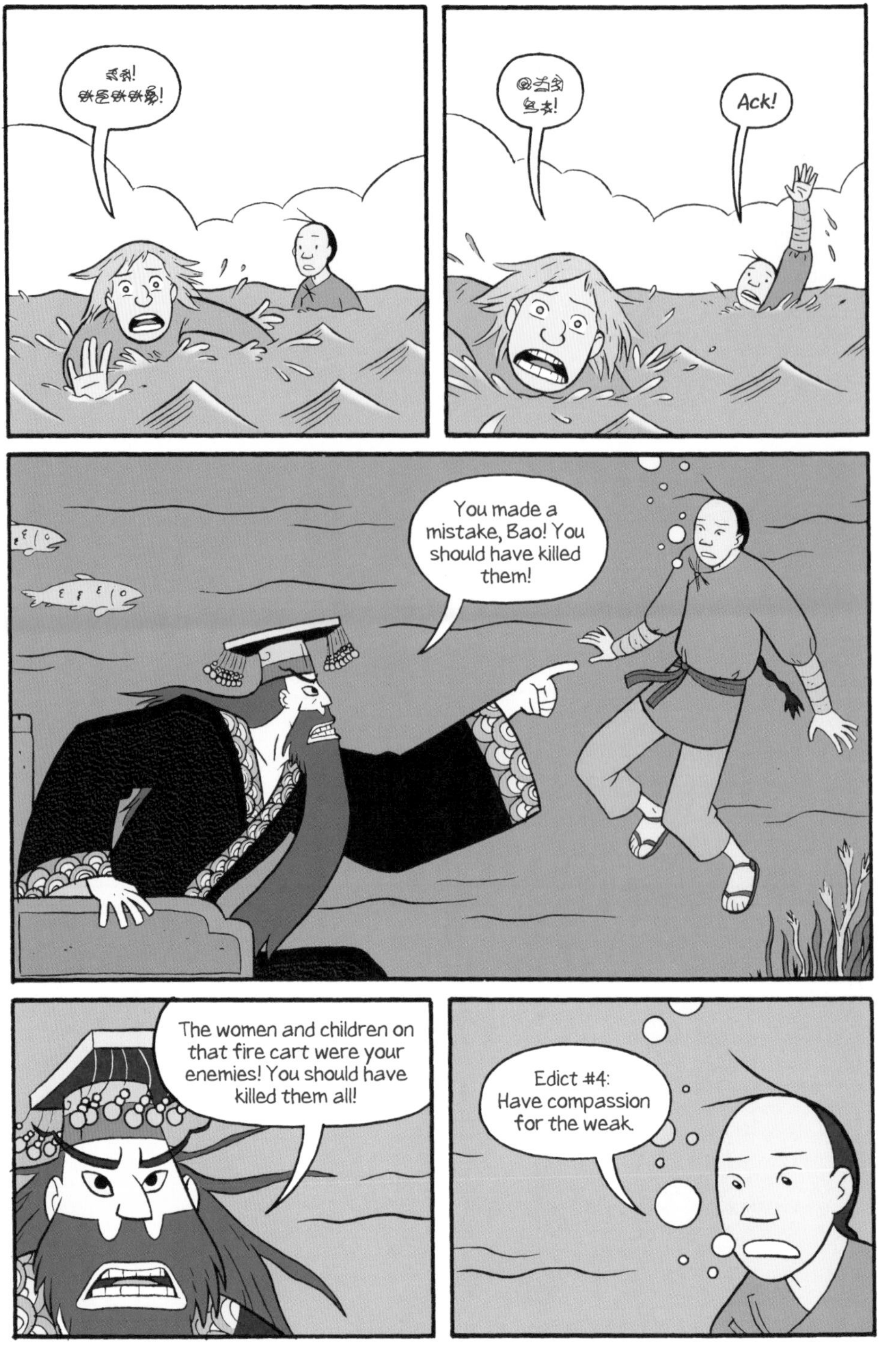
Ack!
You made a mistake, Bao! You should have killed them!
The women and children on that fire cart were your enemies! You should have killed them all!
Edict #4: Have compassion for the weak.

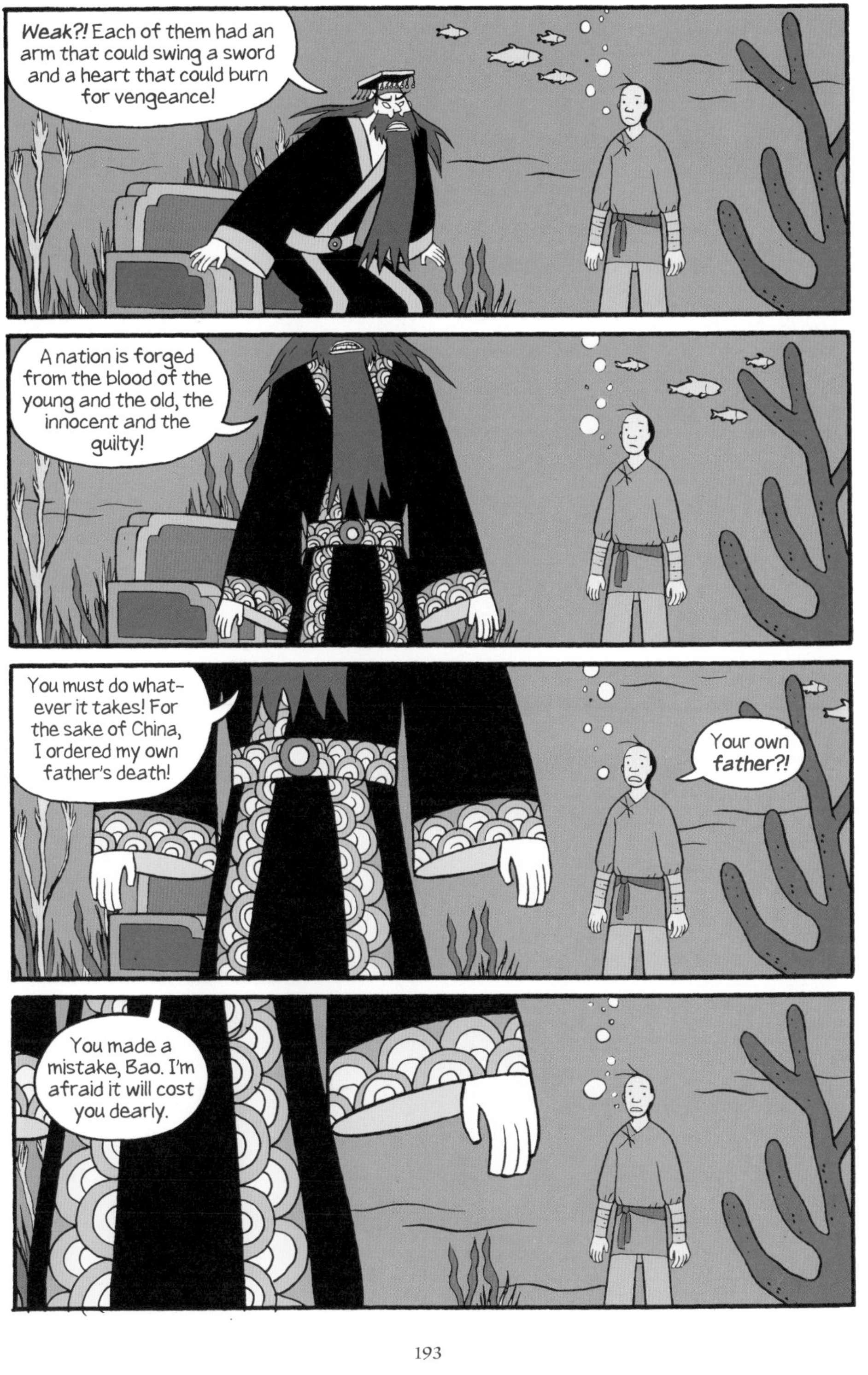
Weak?! Each of them had an arm that could swing a sword and a heart that could burn for vengeance!
A nation is forged from the blood of the young and the old, the innocent and the guilty!
You must do whatever it takes! For the sake of China, I ordered my own father's death!
Your own father?!
You made a mistake, Bao. I'm afraid it will cost you dearly.

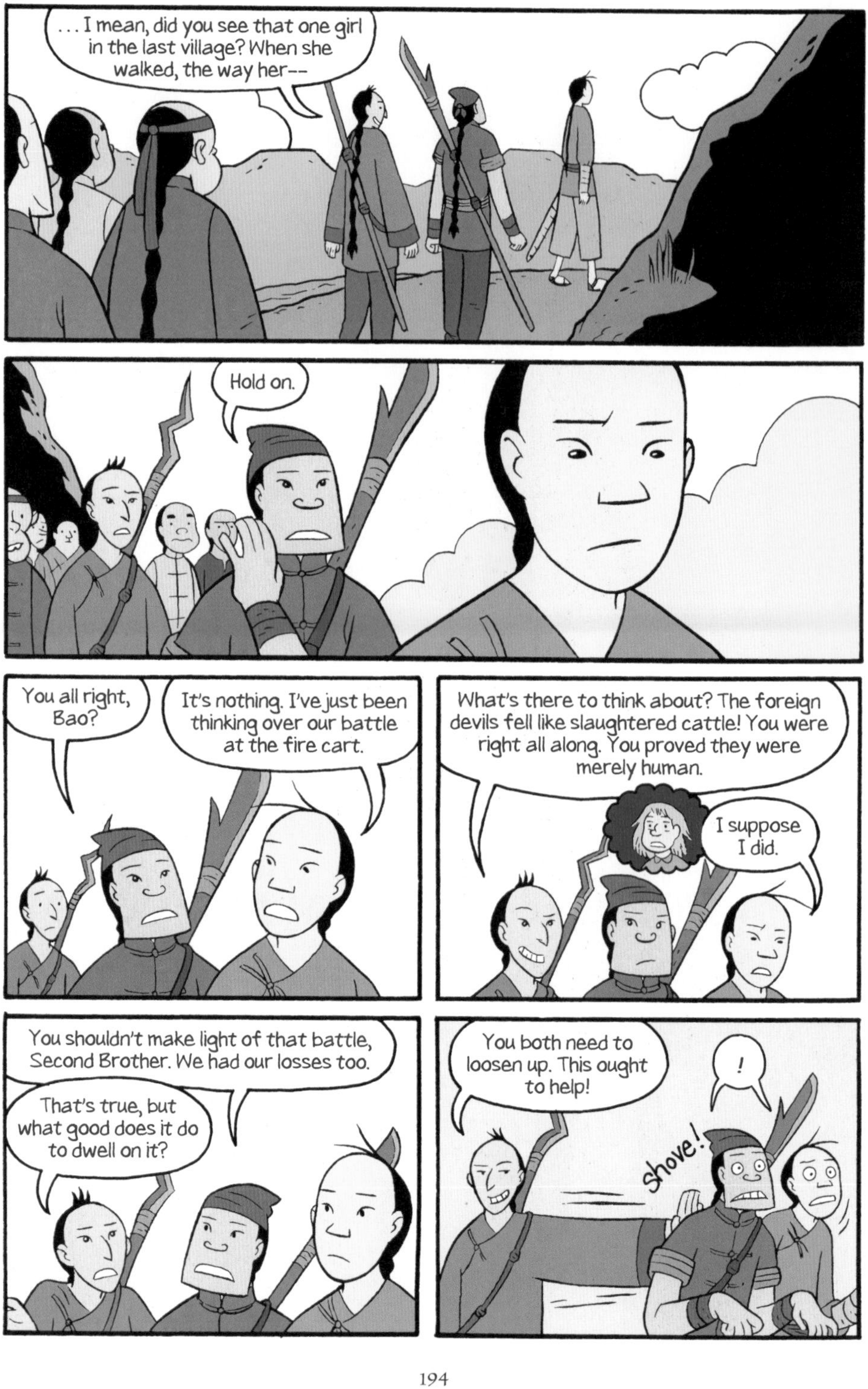

. . . I mean, did you see that one girl in the last village? When she walked, the way her--
Hold on.
You all right, Bao?
It's nothing. I've just been thinking over our battle at the fire cart.
What's there to think about? The foreign devils fell like slaughtered cattle! You were right all along. You proved they were merely human.
I suppose I did.
You shouldn't make light of that battle, Second Brother. We had our losses too.
That's true, but what good does it do to dwell on it?
You both need to loosen up. This ought to help!
!
Shove!

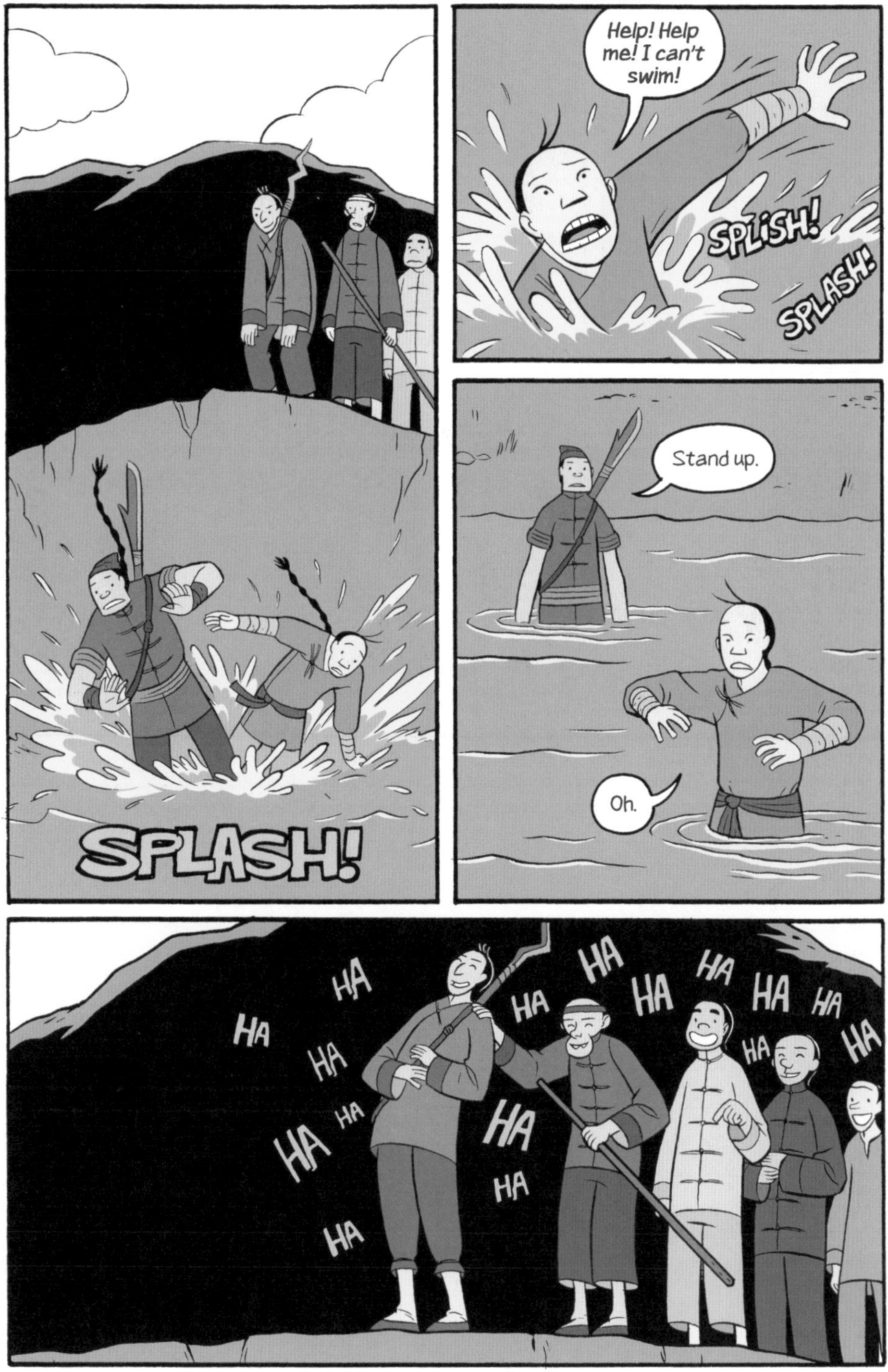
Help! Help me! I can't swim!
SPLISH!
SPLASH!
SPLASH!
Stand up.
Oh.
HA
HA
HA
HA
HA
HA
HA
HA
HA
HA
HA
HA
HA
HA
HA
HA
HA
HA

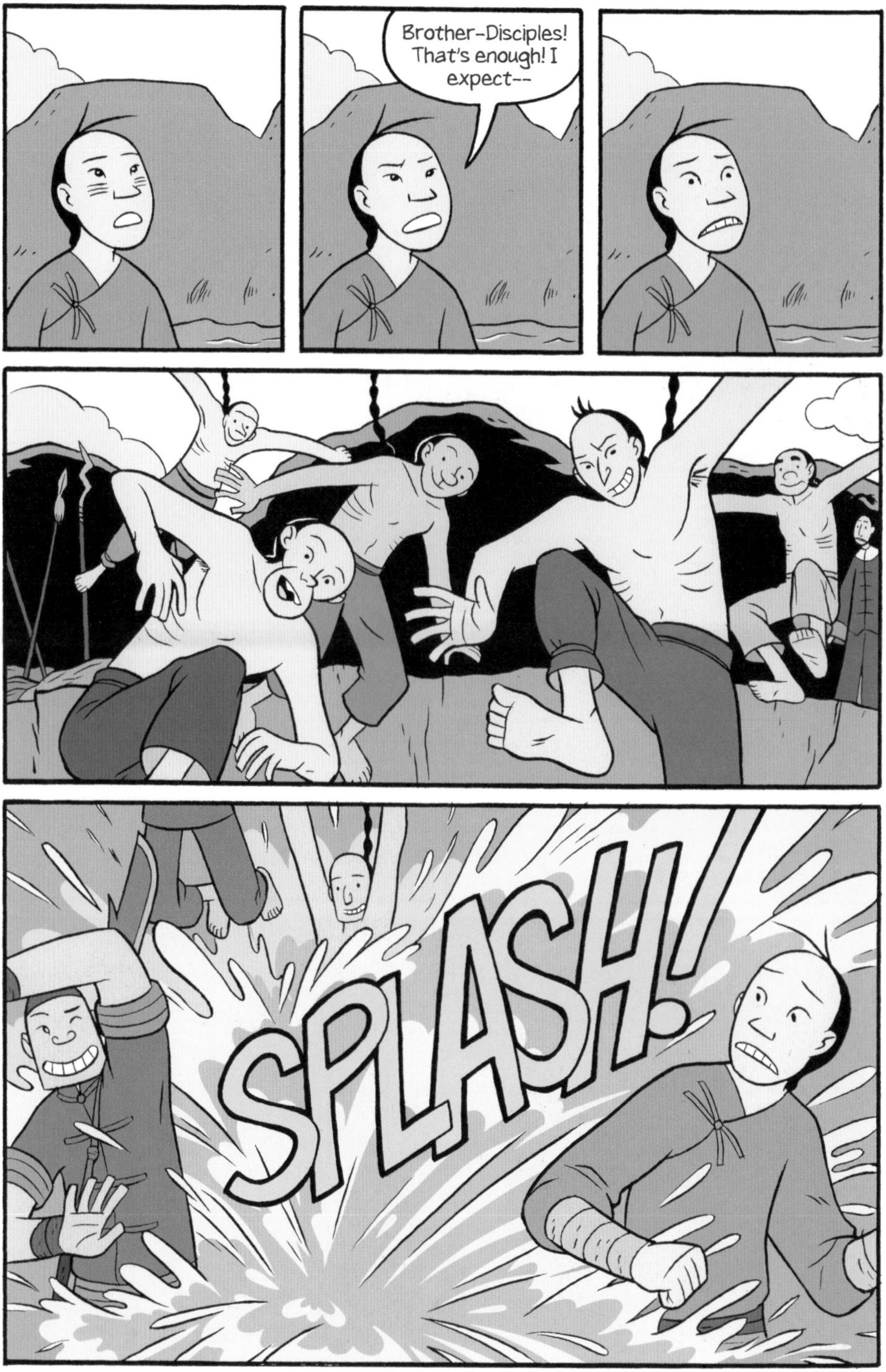
Brother-Disciples! That's enough! I expect--
SPLASH!

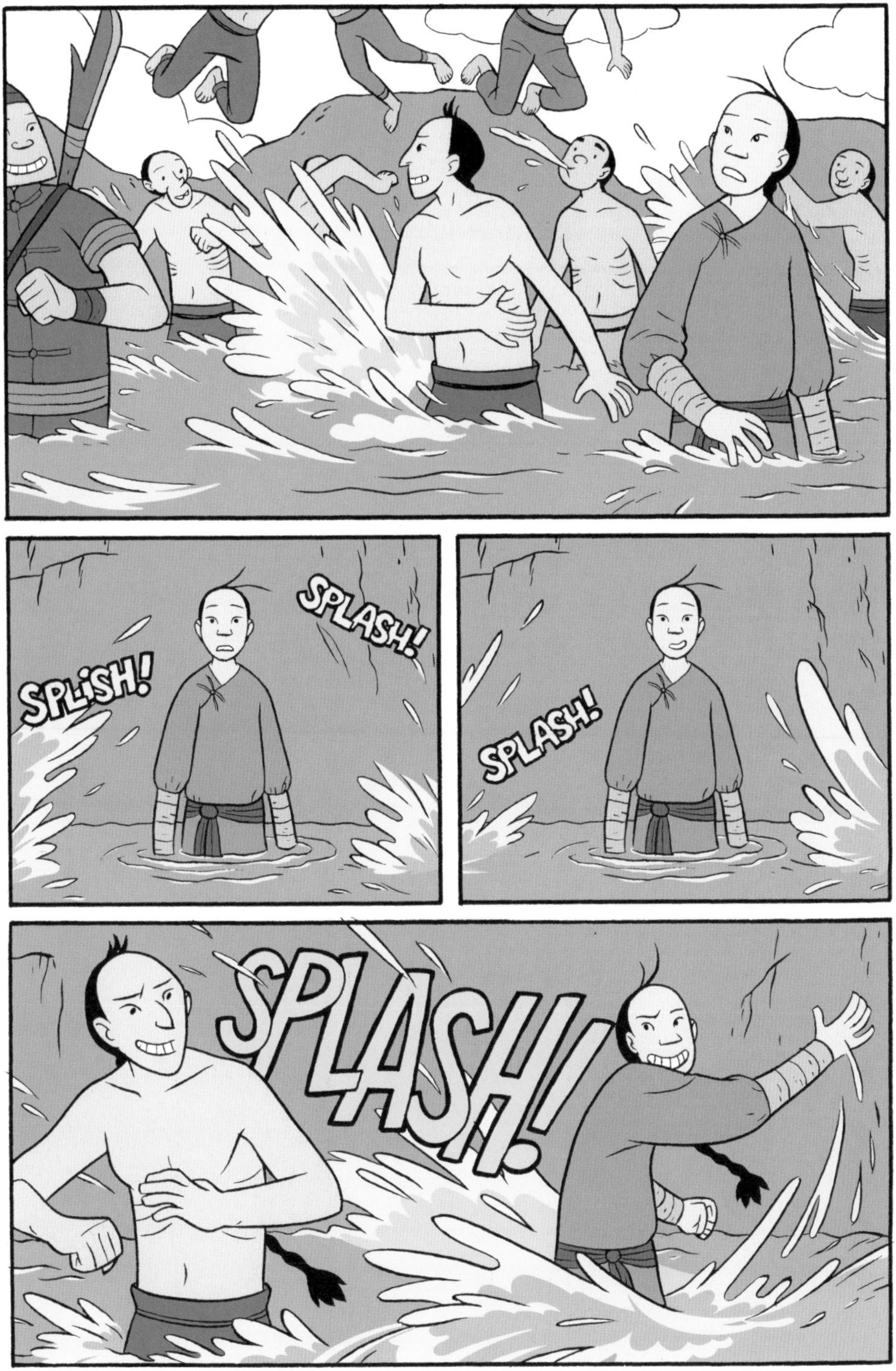
SPLISH!
SPLASH!
SPLASH!
SPLASH!

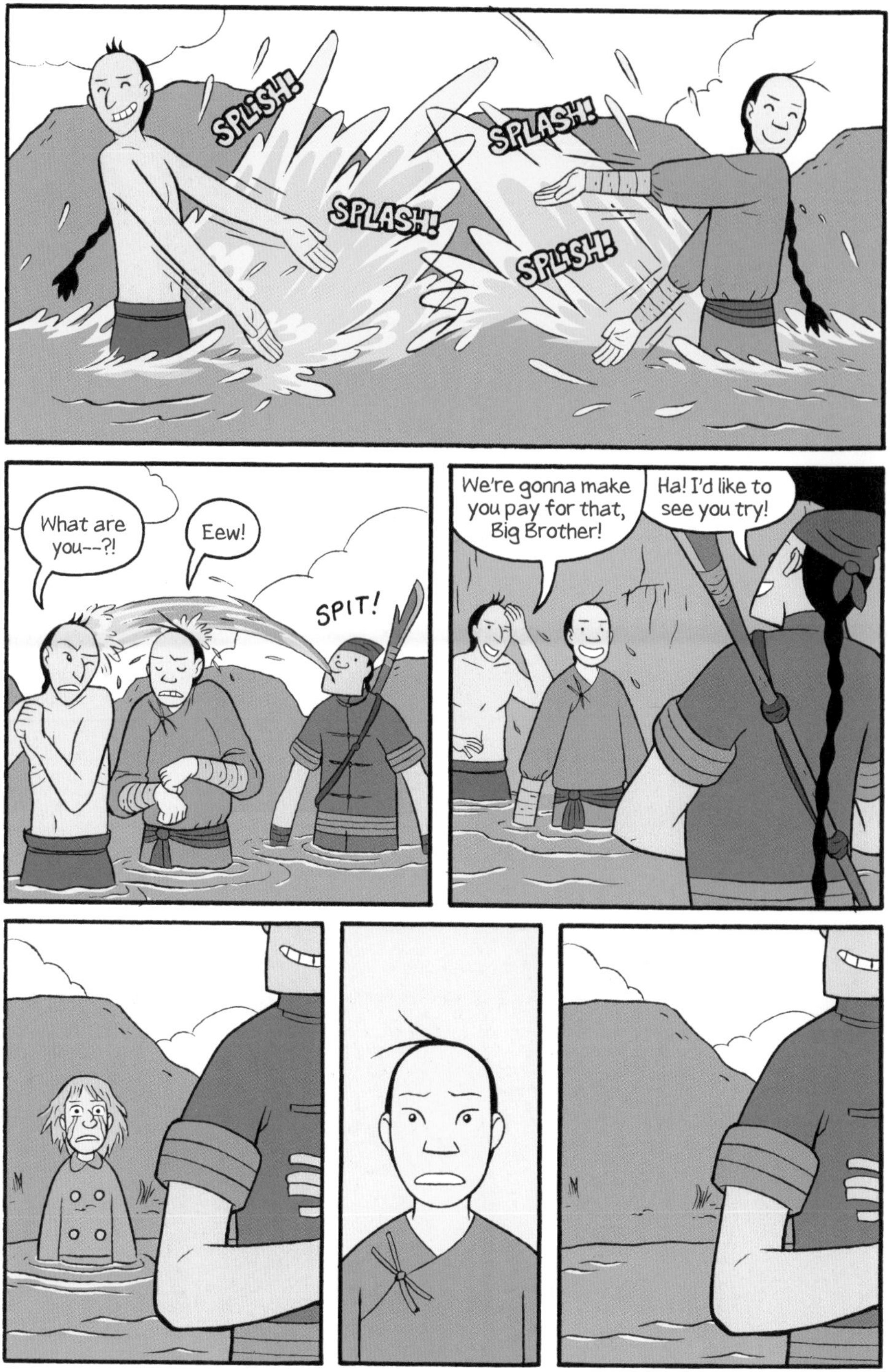
SPLISH!
SPLASH!
SPLASH!
SPLISH!
What are you--?!
Eew!
SPIT!
We're gonna make you pay for that, Big Brother!
Ha! I'd like to see you try!

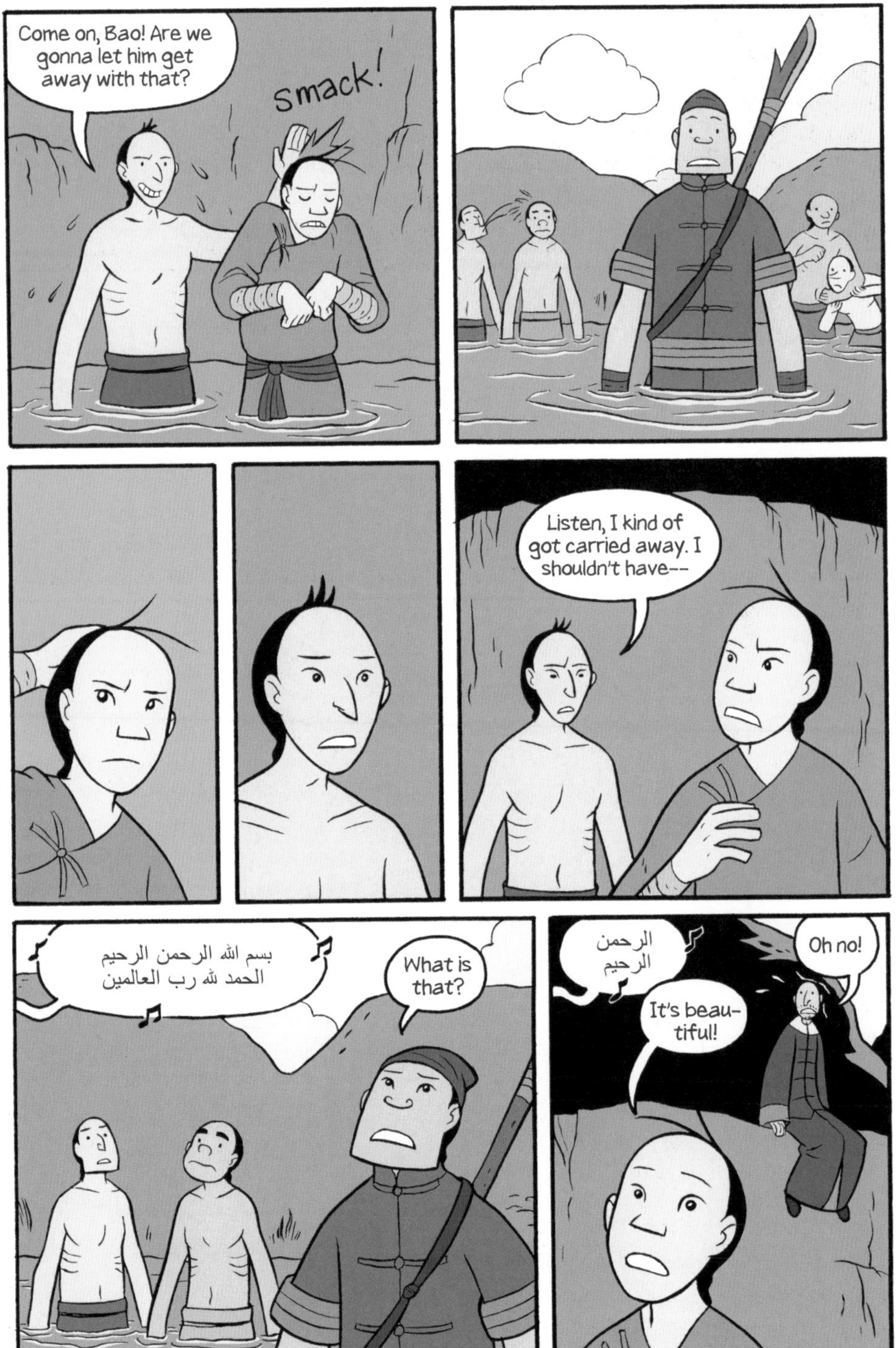
Come on, Bao! Are we gonna let him get away with that?
Smack!
Listen, I kind of got carried away. I shouldn't have--
بسم الله الرحمن الرحيم
الحمد لله رب العالمين
What is that?
الرحمن
الرحيم
Oh no!
It's beau-tiful!

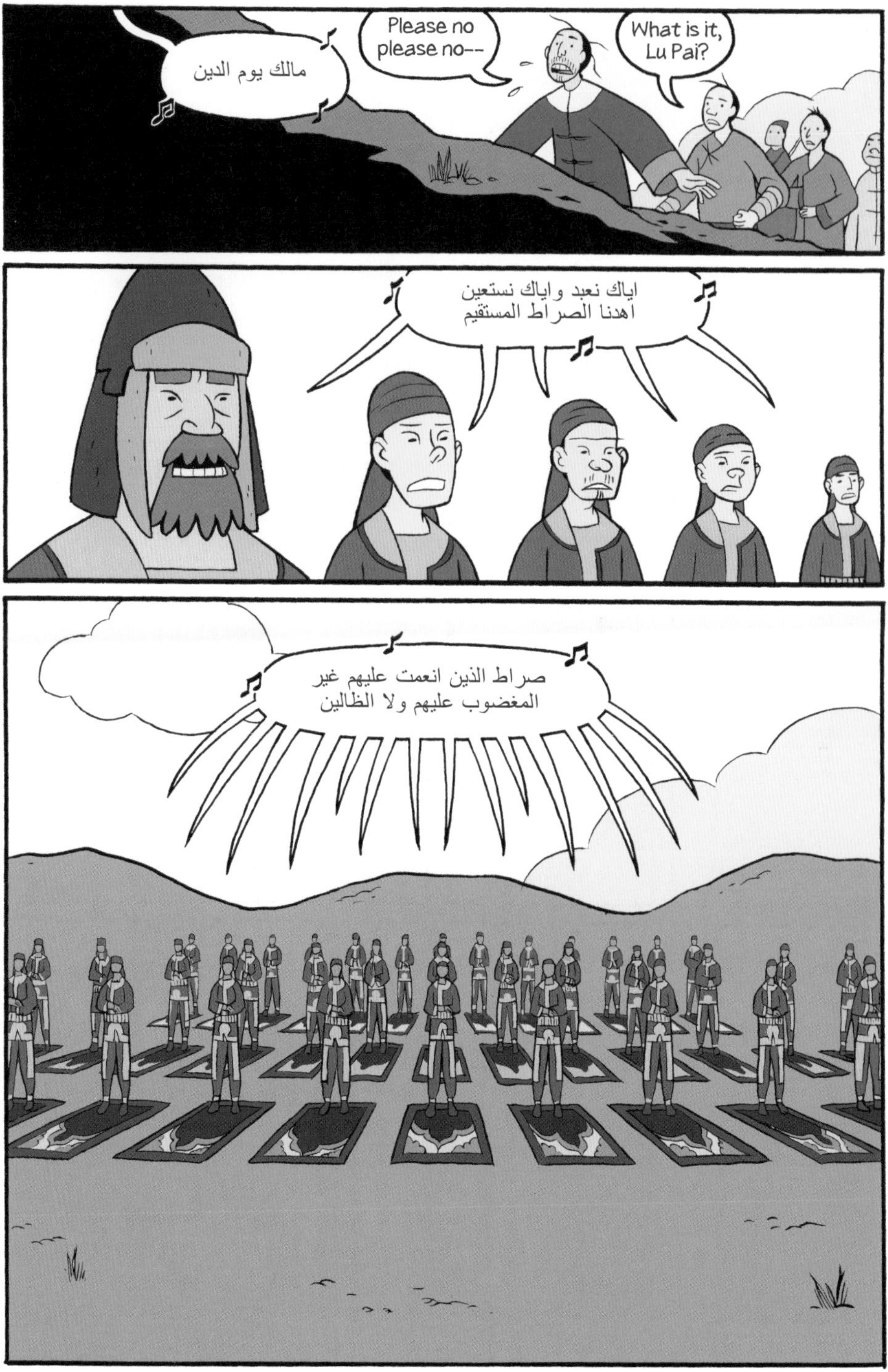
مالك يوم الدين
Please no please no--
What is it, Lu Pai?
اياك نعبد و اياك نستعين
اهدنا الصراط المستقيم
صراط الذين انعمت عليهم غير
المغضوب عليهم ولا الظالين

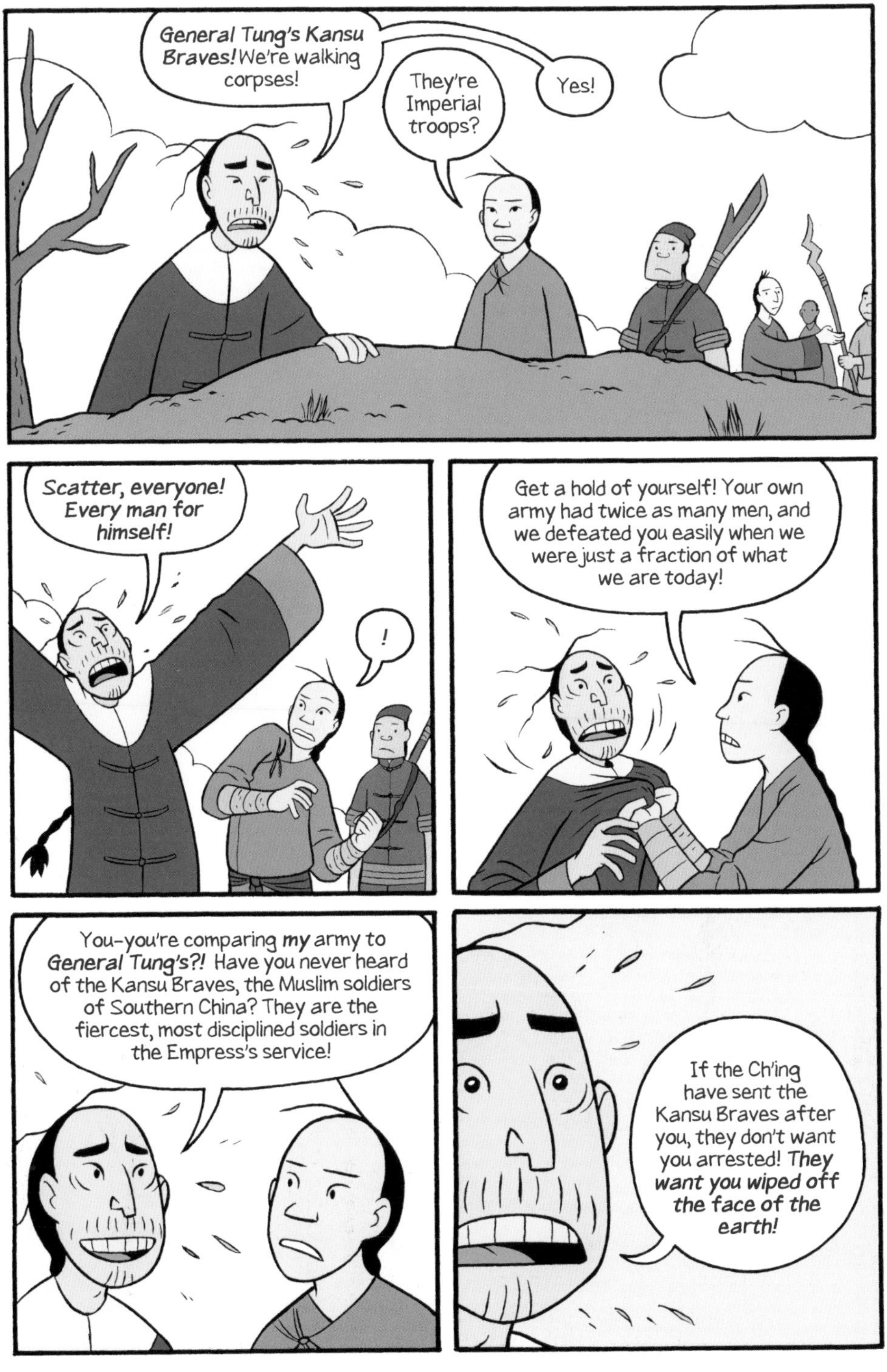

General Tung's Kansu Braves! We're walking corpses!
They're Imperial troops?
Yes!
Scatter, everyone! Every man for himself!
!
Get a hold of yourself! Your own army had twice as many men, and we defeated you easily when we were just a fraction of what we are today!
You-you're comparing **my** army to *General Tung's?!* Have you never heard of the Kansu Braves, the Muslim soldiers of Southern China? They are the fiercest, most disciplined soldiers in the Empress's service!
If the Ch'ing have sent the Kansu Braves after you, they don't want you arrested! **They want you wiped off the face of the earth!**

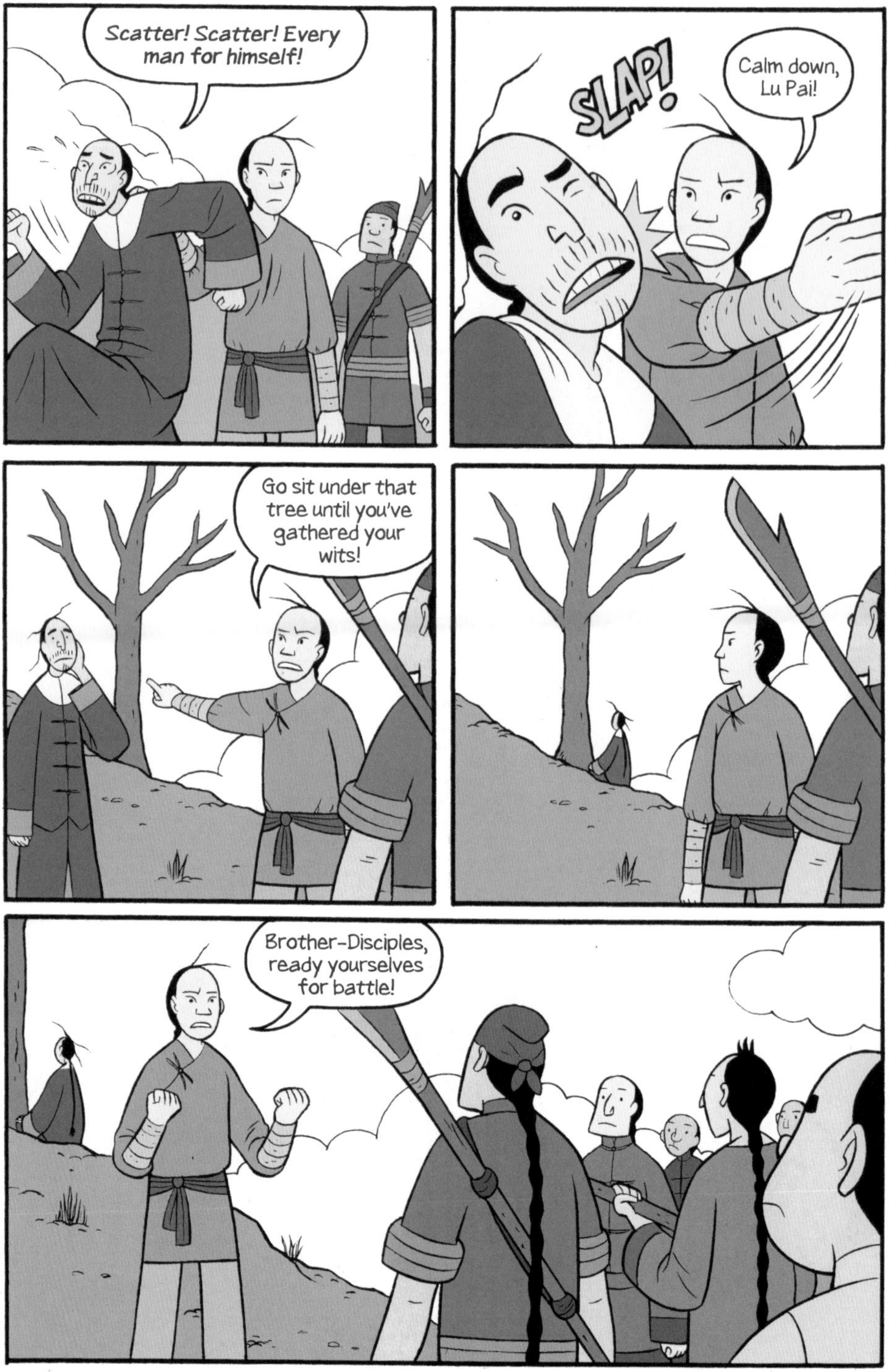
Scatter! Scatter! Every man for himself!
SLAP!
Calm down, Lu Pai!
Go sit under that tree until you've gathered your wits!
Brother-Disciples, ready yourselves for battle!

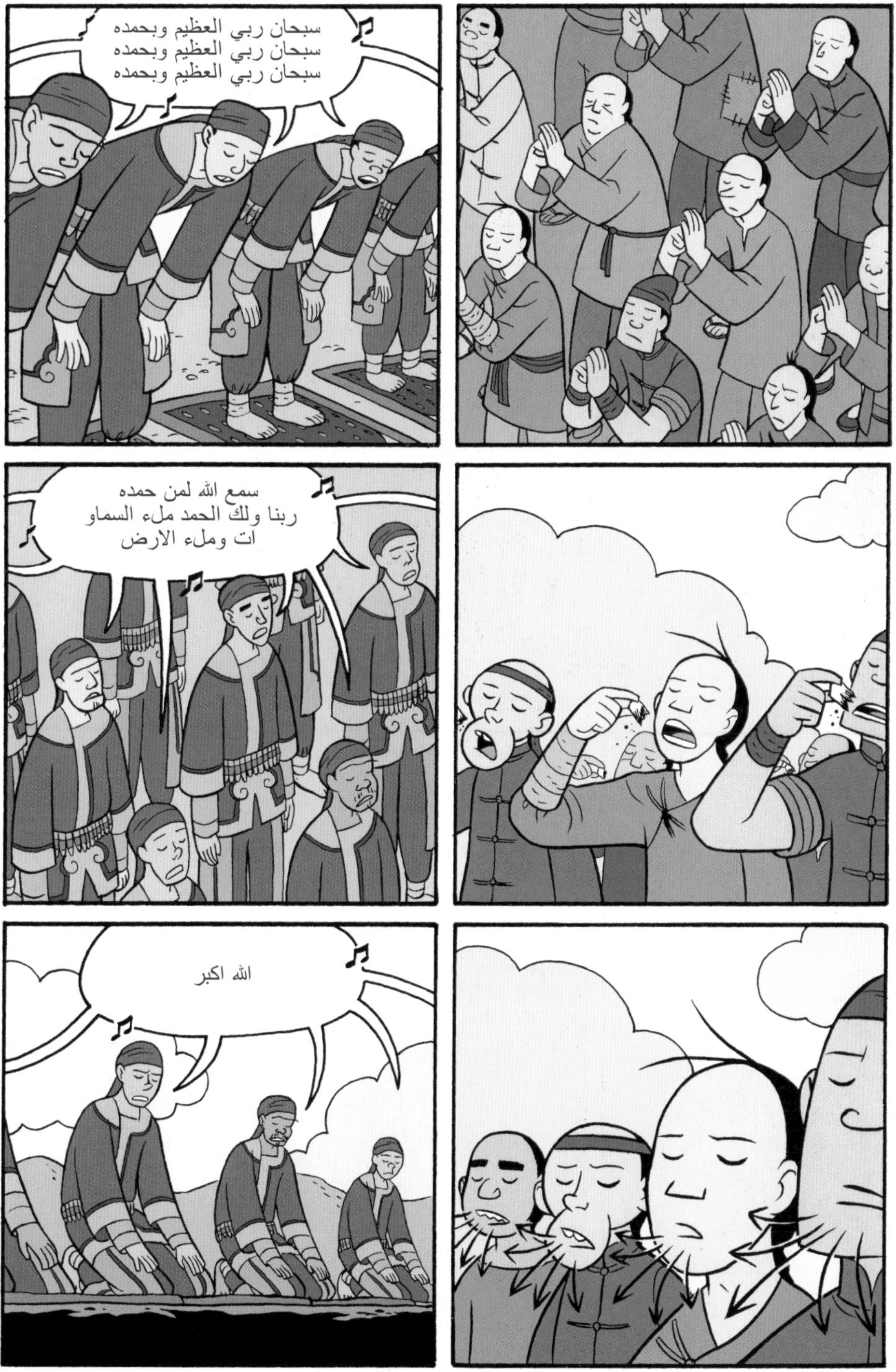
سبحان ربي العظيم وبحمده
سبحان ربي العظيم وبحمده
سبحان ربي العظيم وبحمده
سمع الله لمن حمده
ربنا ولك الحمد ملء السماو
ات وملء الارض
الله اكبر

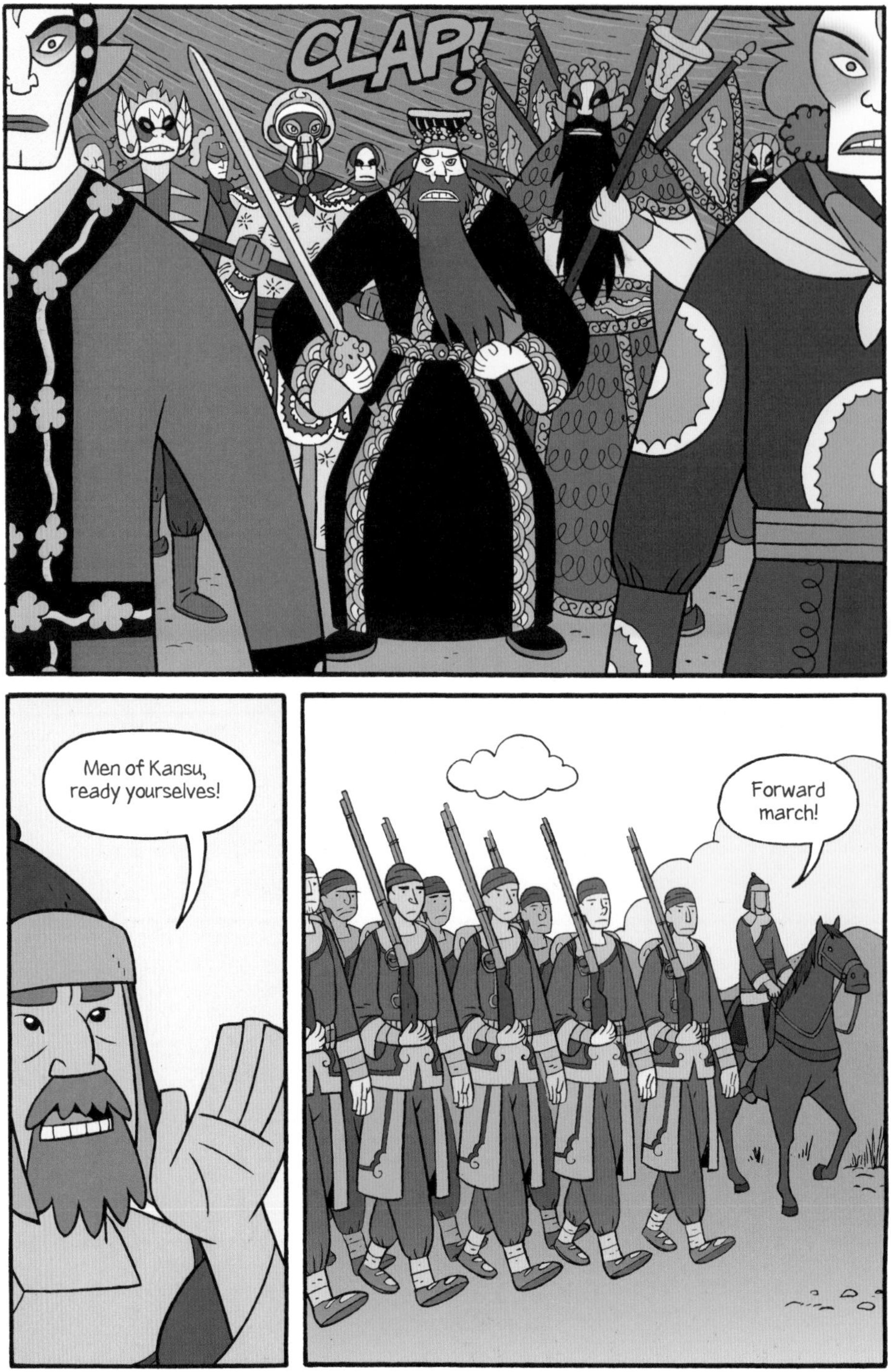
CLAP!
Men of Kansu, ready yourselves!
Forward march!

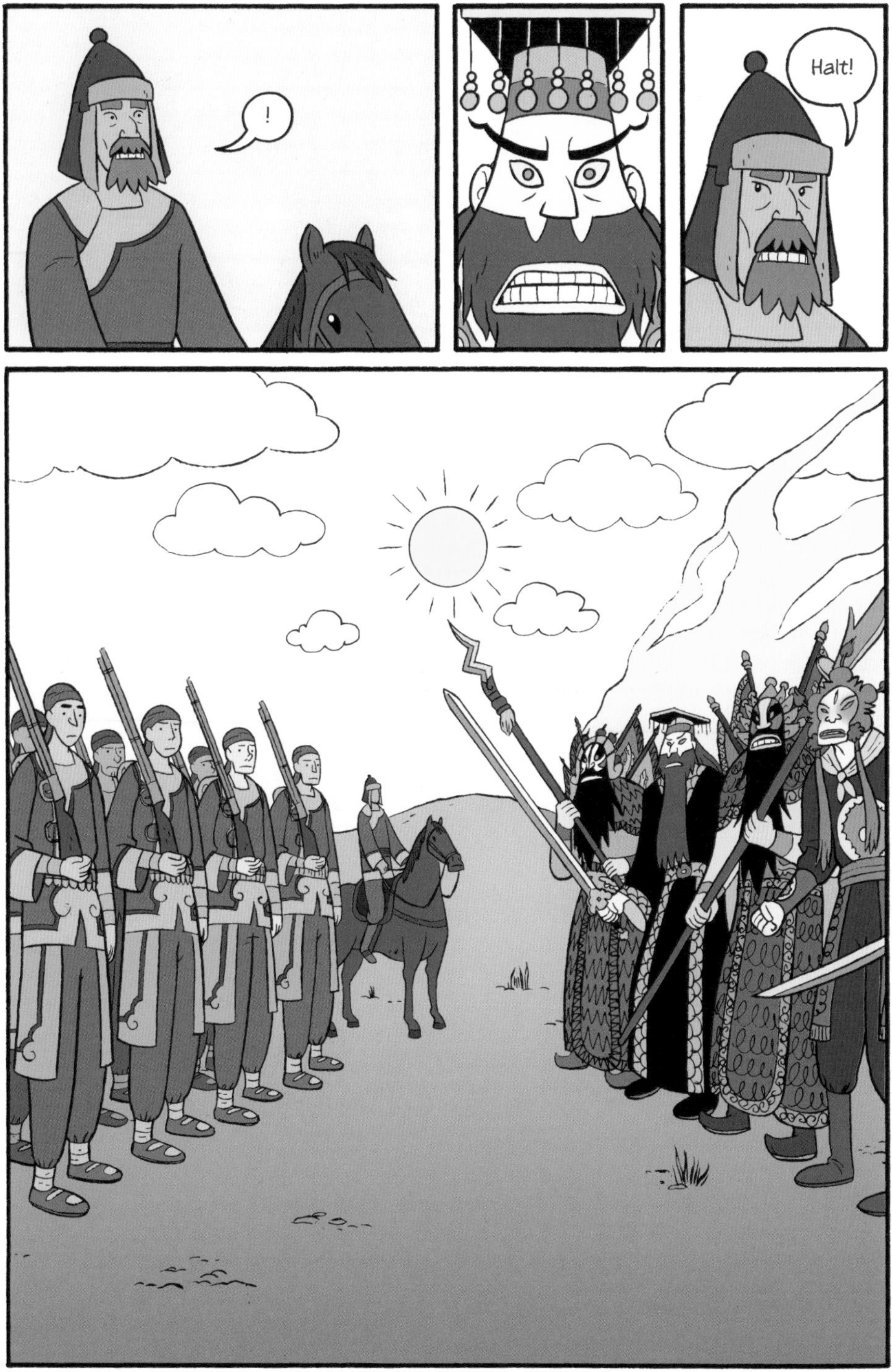
!
Halt!

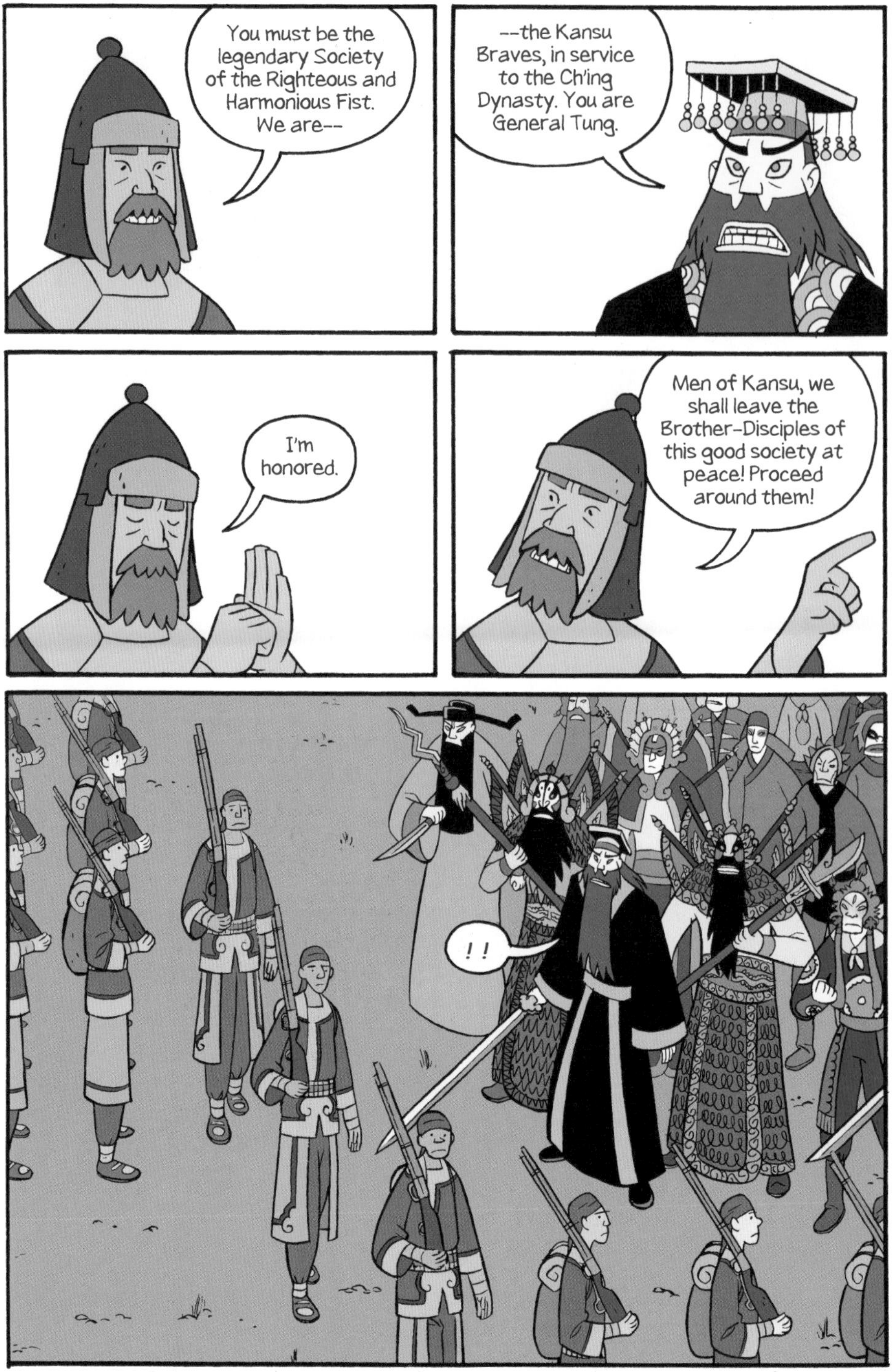
You must be the legendary Society of the Righteous and Harmonious Fist. We are--
--the Kansu Braves, in service to the Ch'ing Dynasty. You are General Tung.
I'm honored.
Men of Kansu, we shall leave the Brother-Disciples of this good society at peace! Proceed around them!
!!

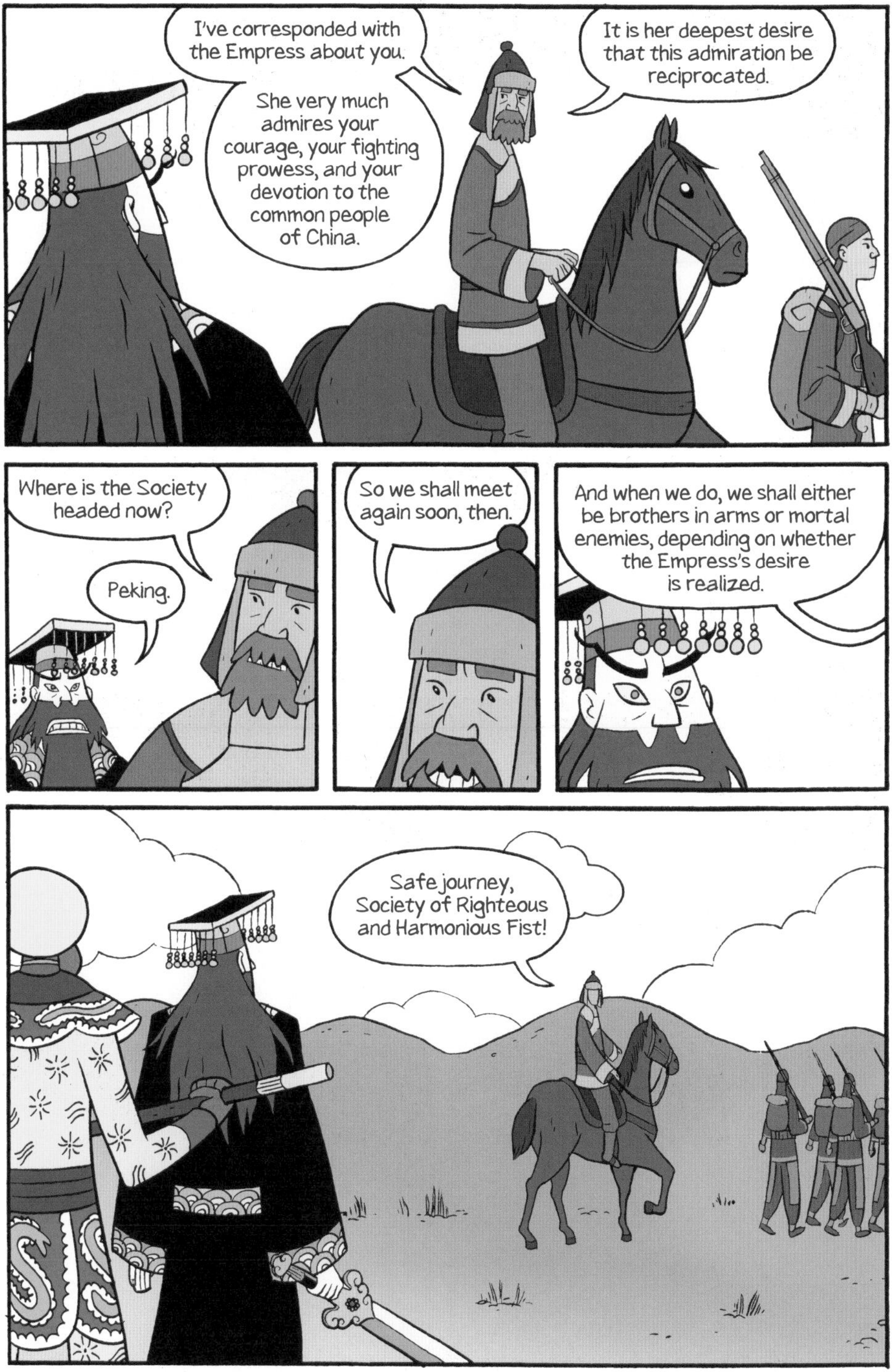
I've corresponded with the Empress about you.
She very much admires your courage, your fighting prowess, and your devotion to the common people of China.
It is her deepest desire that this admiration be reciprocated.
Where is the Society headed now?
Peking.
So we shall meet again soon, then.
And when we do, we shall either be brothers in arms or mortal enemies, depending on whether the Empress's desire is realized.
Safe journey, Society of Righteous and Harmonious Fist!

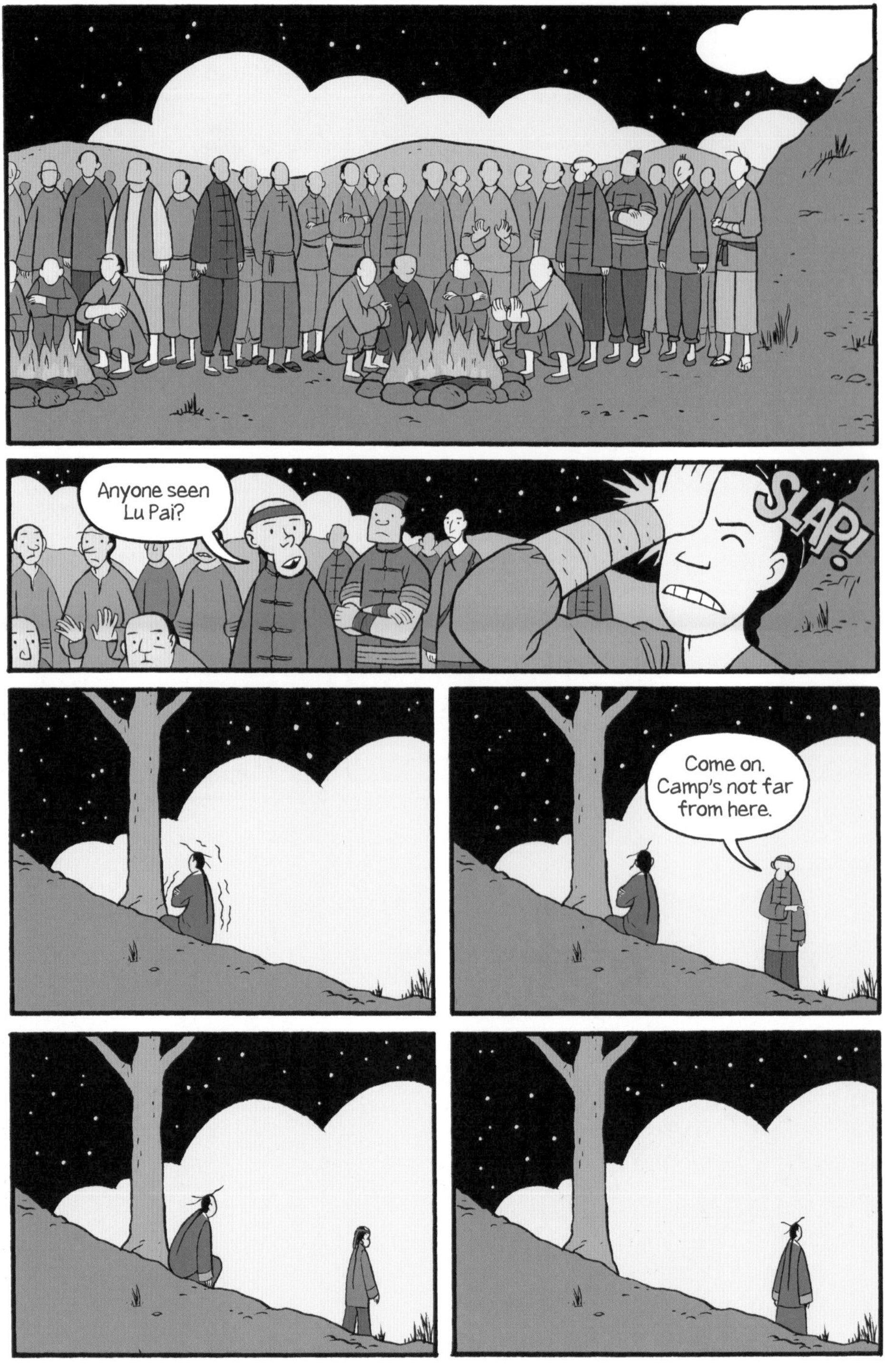
Anyone seen Lu Pai?
SLAP!
Come on. Camp's not far from here.

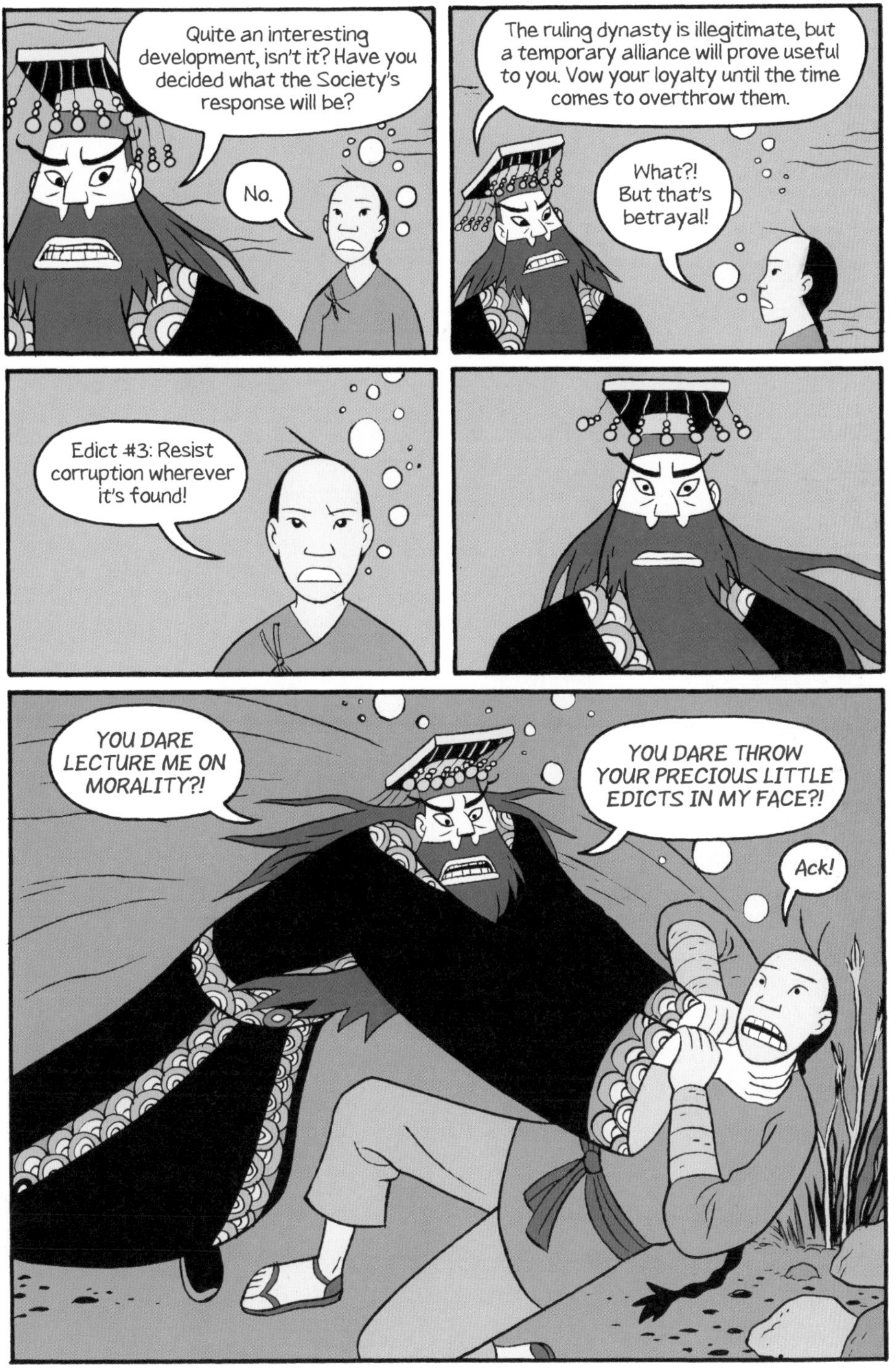
Quite an interesting development, isn't it? Have you decided what the Society's response will be?
No.
The ruling dynasty is illegitimate, but a temporary alliance will prove useful to you. Vow your loyalty until the time comes to overthrow them.
What?! But that's betrayal!
Edict #3: Resist corruption wherever it's found!
YOU DARE LECTURE ME ON MORALITY?!
YOU DARE THROW YOUR PRECIOUS LITTLE EDICTS IN MY FACE?!
Ack!

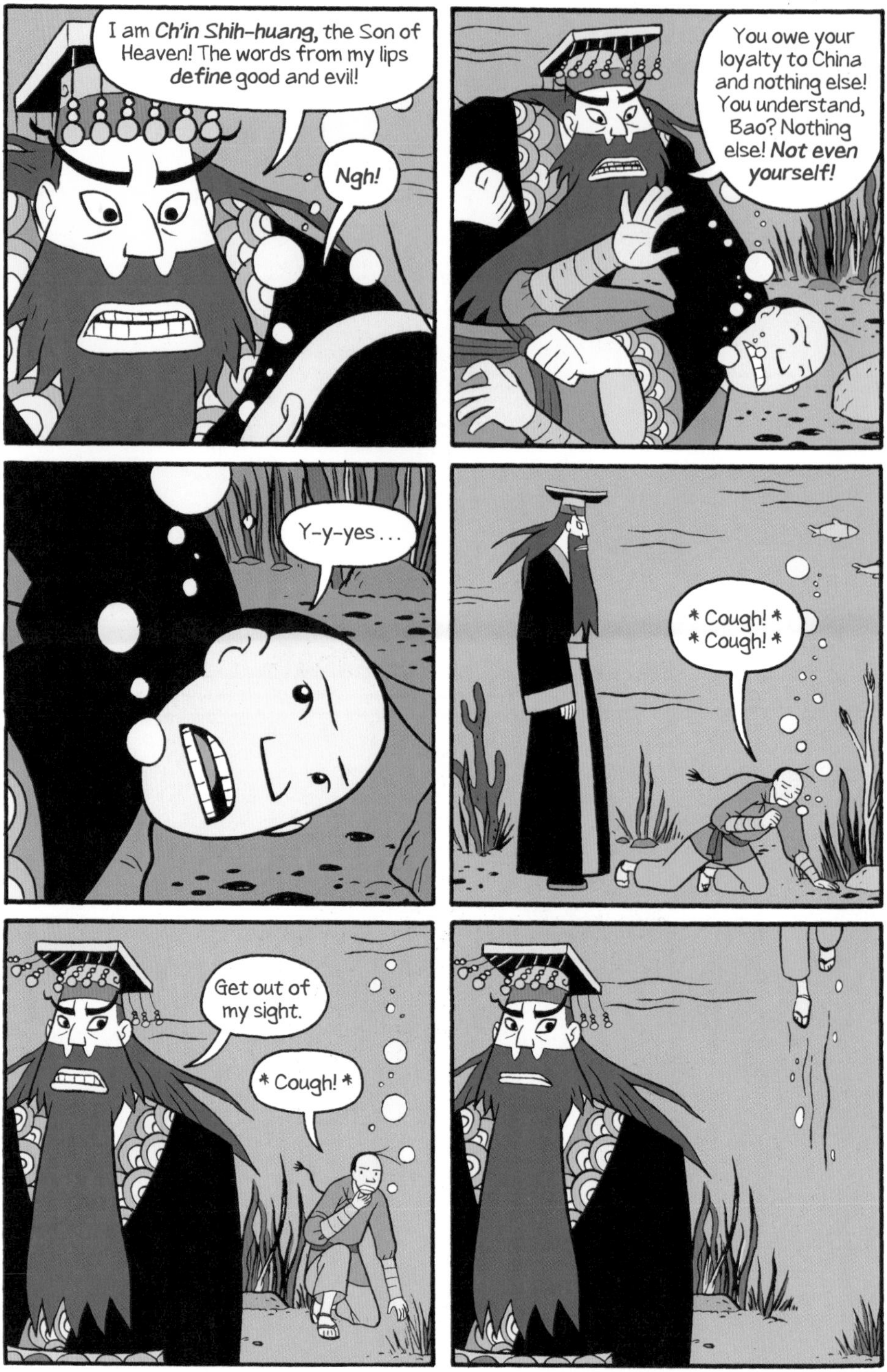
I am *Ch'in Shih-huang,* the Son of Heaven! The words from my lips *define* good and evil!
Ngh!
You owe your loyalty to China and nothing else! You understand, Bao? Nothing else! ***Not even yourself!***
Y-y-yes . . .
* Cough! * * Cough! *
Get out of my sight.
* Cough! *

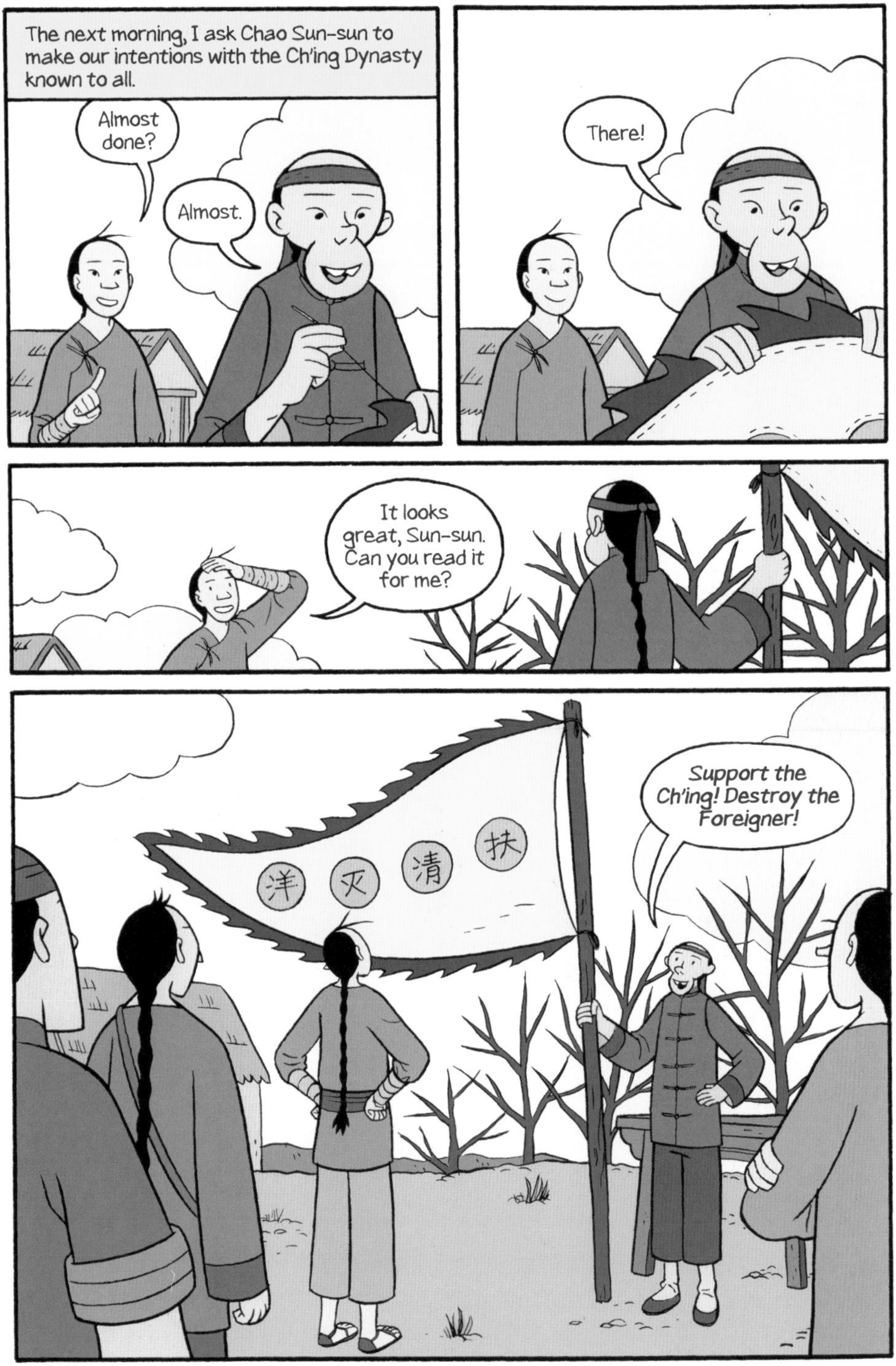
The next morning, I ask Chao Sun-sun to make our intentions with the Ch'ing Dynasty known to all.
Almost done?
Almost.
There!
It looks great, Sun-sun. Can you read it for me?
扶
清
灭
洋
Support the Ch'ing! Destroy the Foreigner!

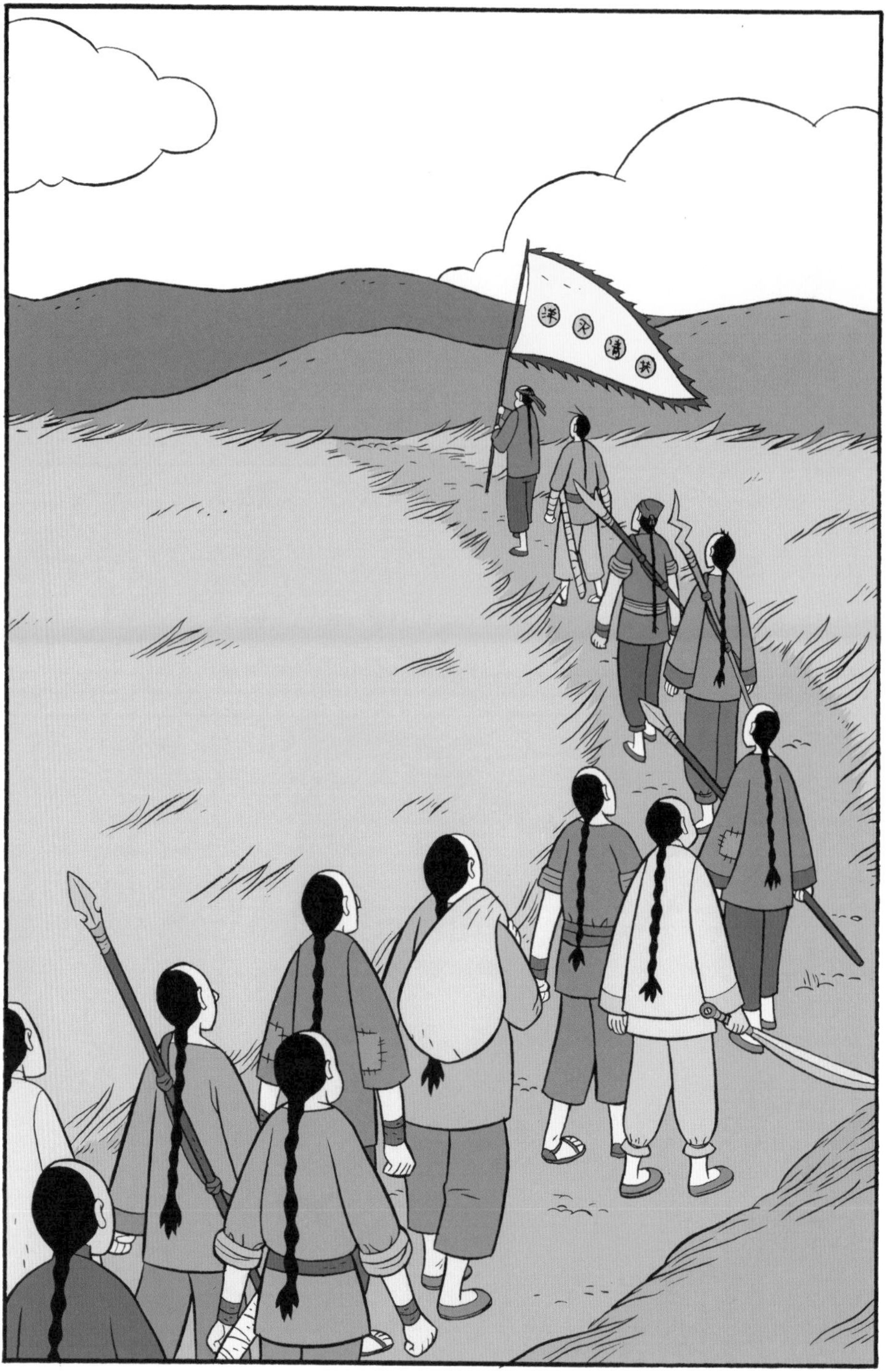
扶清灭洋

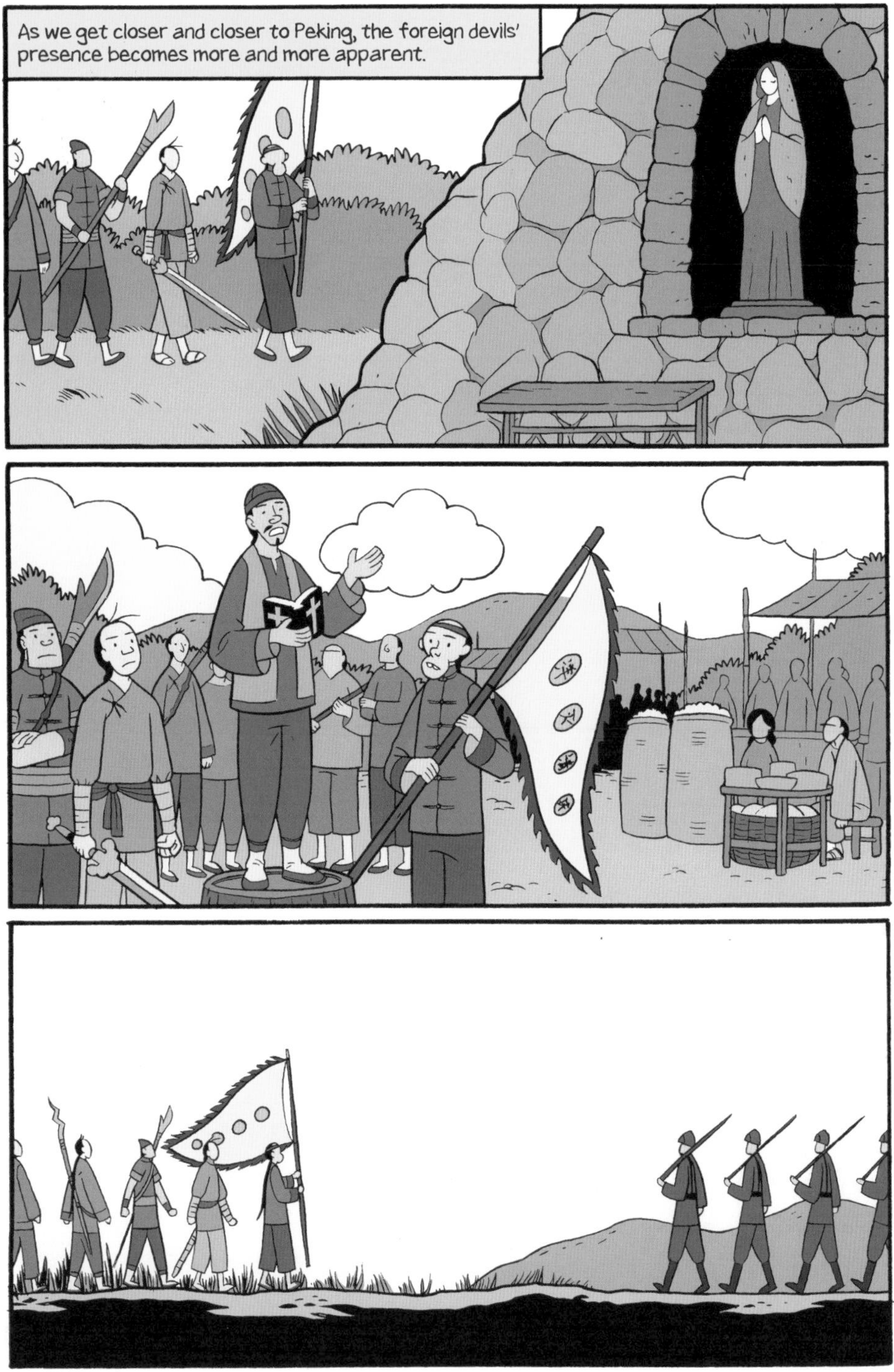
As we get closer and closer to Peking, the foreign devils' presence becomes more and more apparent.

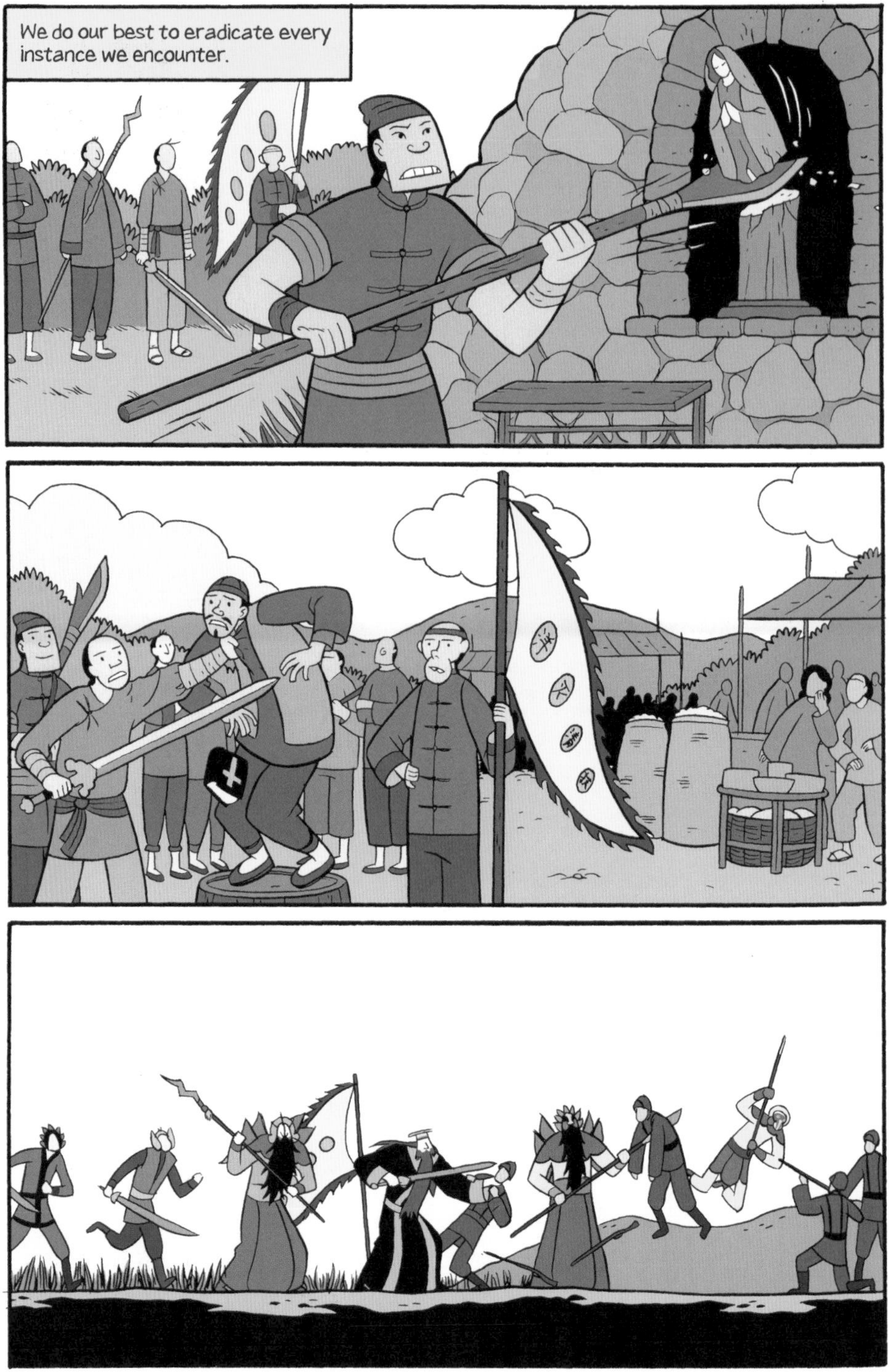
We do our best to eradicate every instance we encounter.

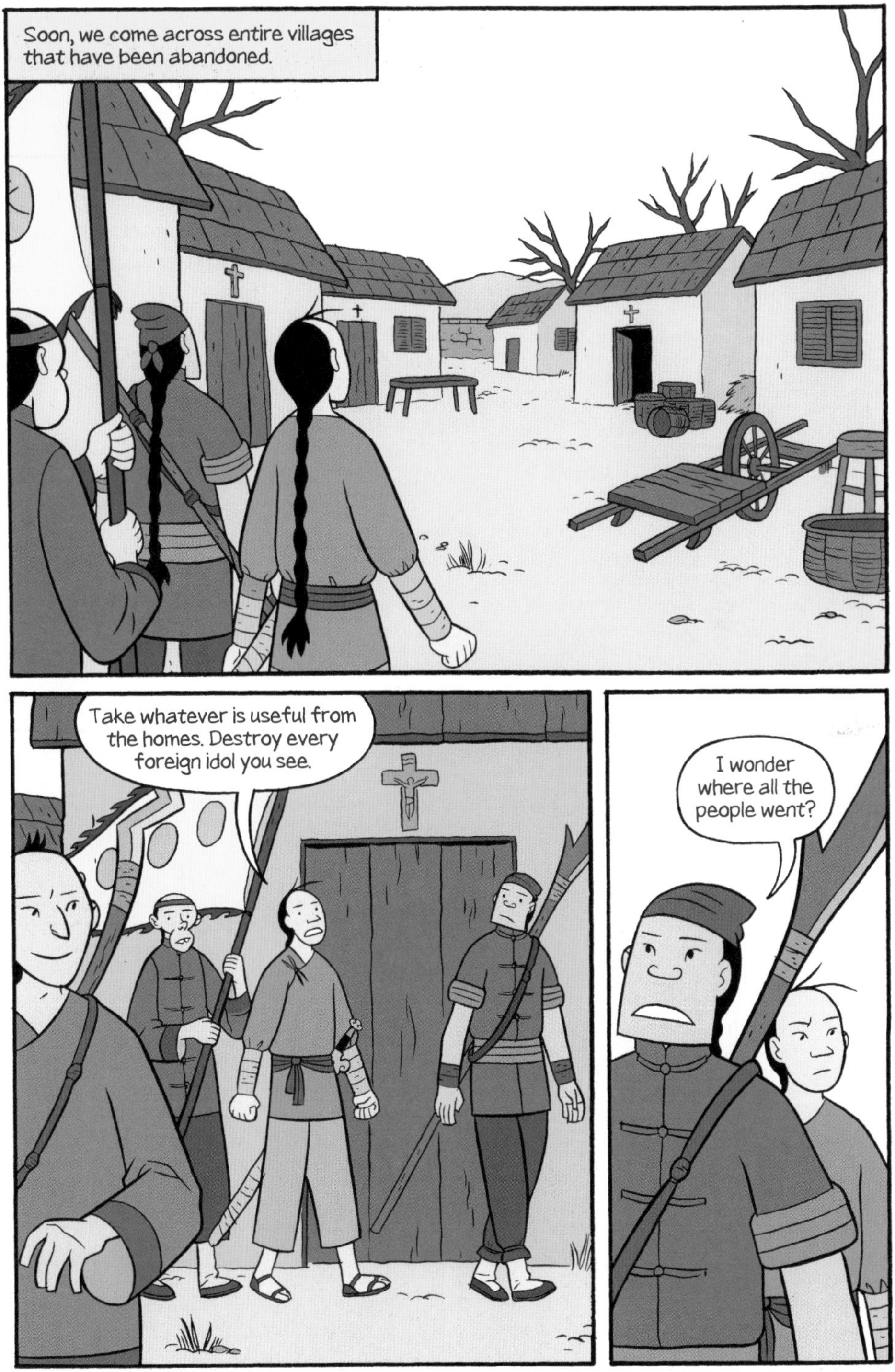
Soon, we come across entire villages that have been abandoned.
Take whatever is useful from the homes. Destroy every foreign idol you see.
I wonder where all the people went?

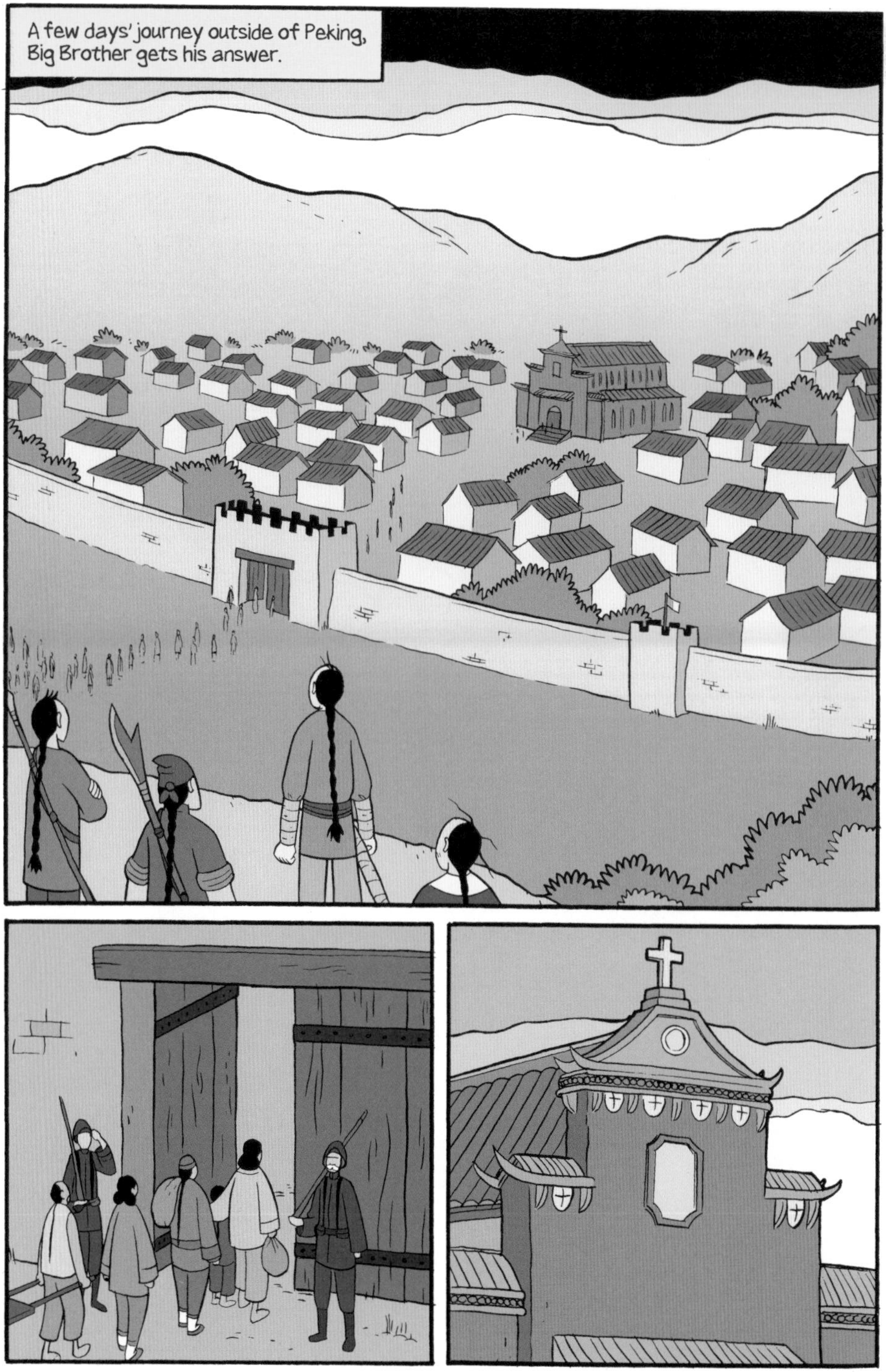
A few days' journey outside of Peking, Big Brother gets his answer.

It's some sort of Christian stronghold.

A stronghold of Yin!

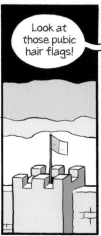

Look at those pubic hair flags!

Oh, heavens! I feel my strength being sapped from me as I speak!

I'll go find a tree to sit under.

Tell the Brother-Disciples to rest well tonight. We attack at dawn.

SSSSSSSSS

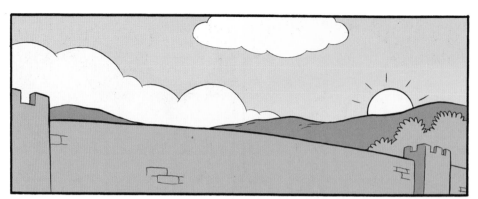

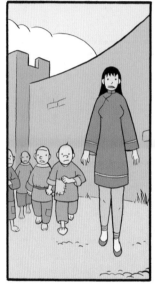

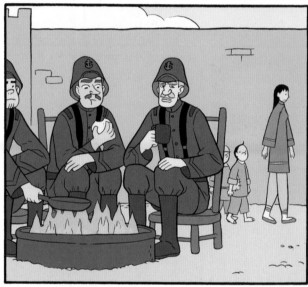

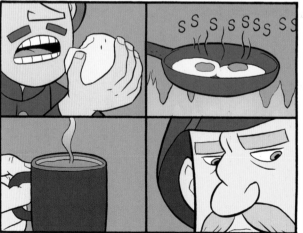

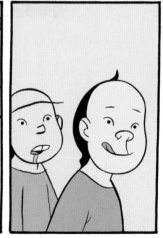

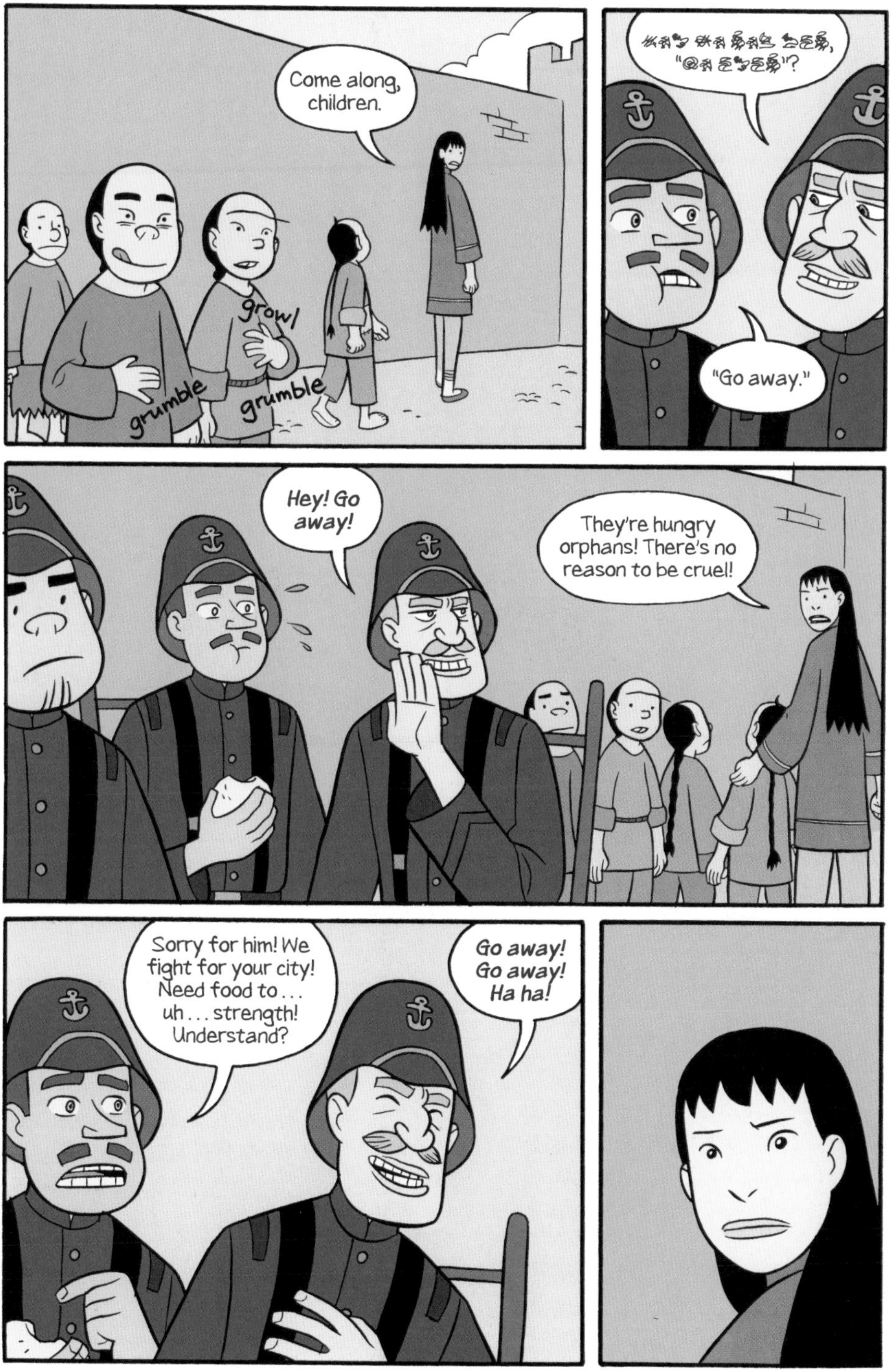
Come along, children.
growl
grumble
grumble
"Go away."
Hey! Go away!
They're hungry orphans! There's no reason to be cruel!
Sorry for him! We fight for your city! Need food to . . . uh . . . strength! Understand?
Go away! Go away! Ha ha!

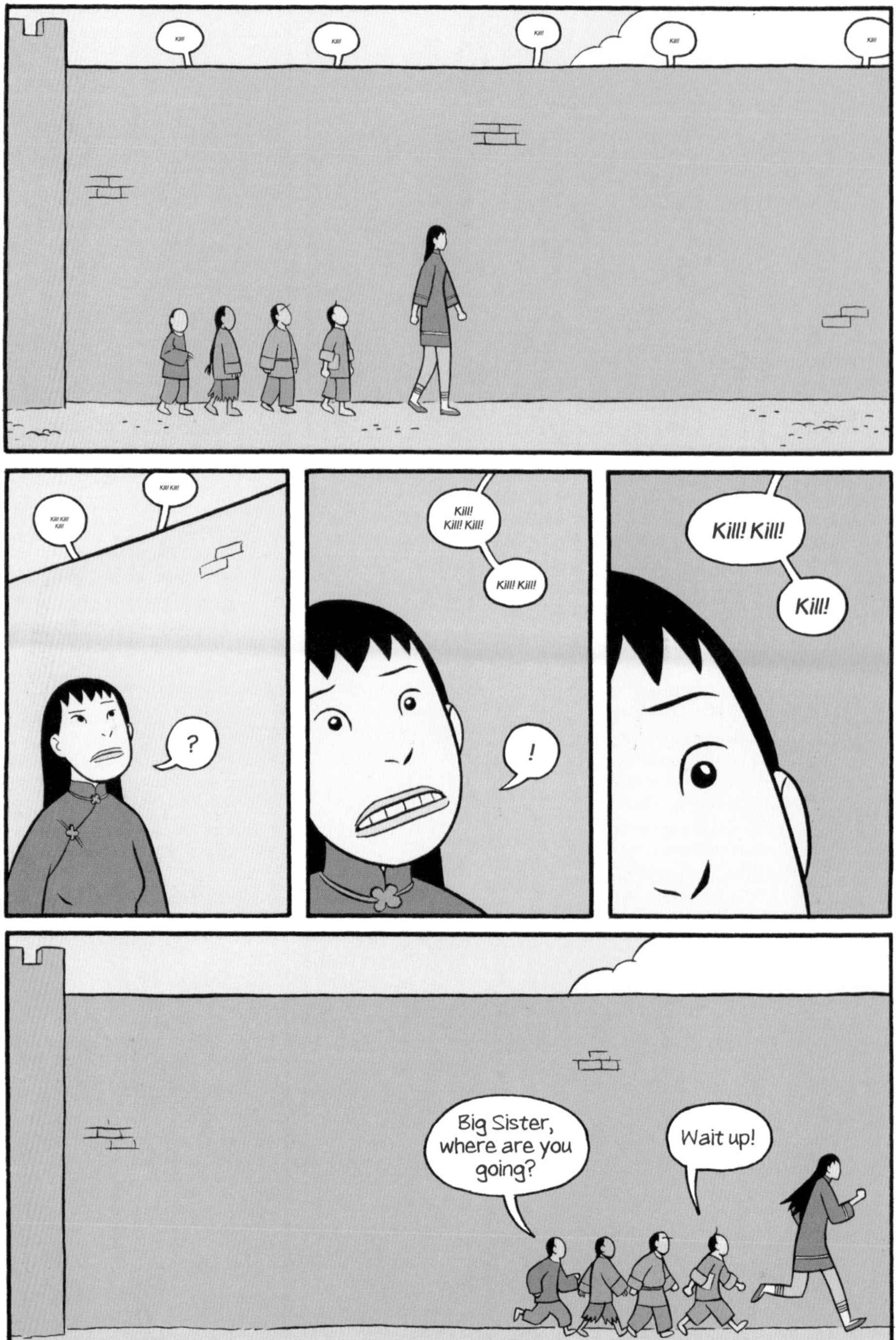
Kill!
Kill!
Kill!
Kill!
Kill!
Kill! Kill!
Kill! Kill! Kill!
?
Kill! Kill! Kill!
Kill! Kill!
!
Kill! Kill!
Kill!
Big Sister, where are you going?
Wait up!

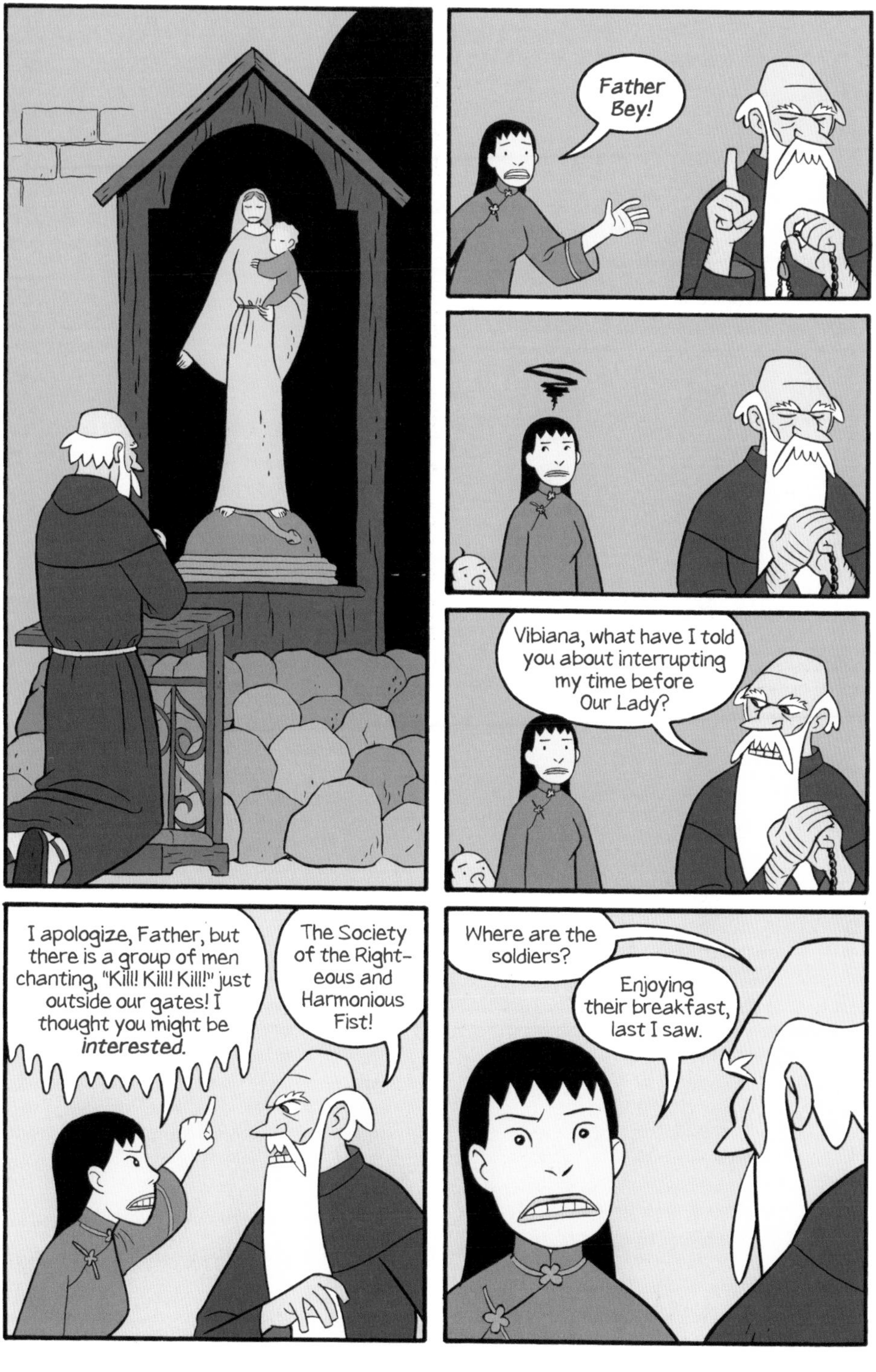
Father Bey!
Vibiana, what have I told you about interrupting my time before Our Lady?
I apologize, Father, but there is a group of men chanting, "Kill! Kill! Kill!" just outside our gates! I thought you might be *interested*.
The Society of the Right-eous and Harmonious Fist!
Where are the soldiers?
Enjoying their breakfast, last I saw.

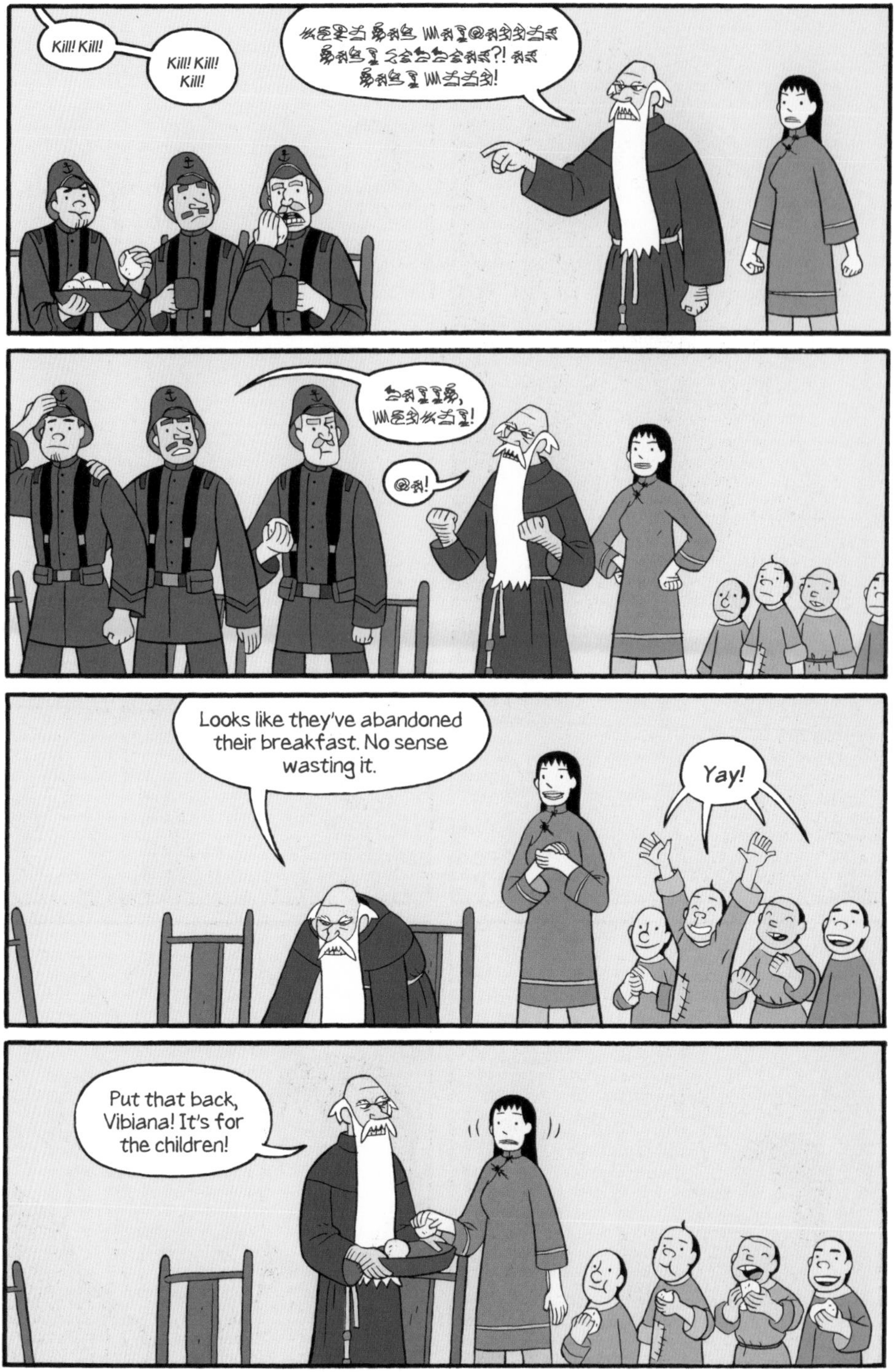
Kill! Kill!
Kill! Kill! Kill!
Looks like they've abandoned their breakfast. No sense wasting it.
Yay!
Put that back, Vibiana! It's for the children!

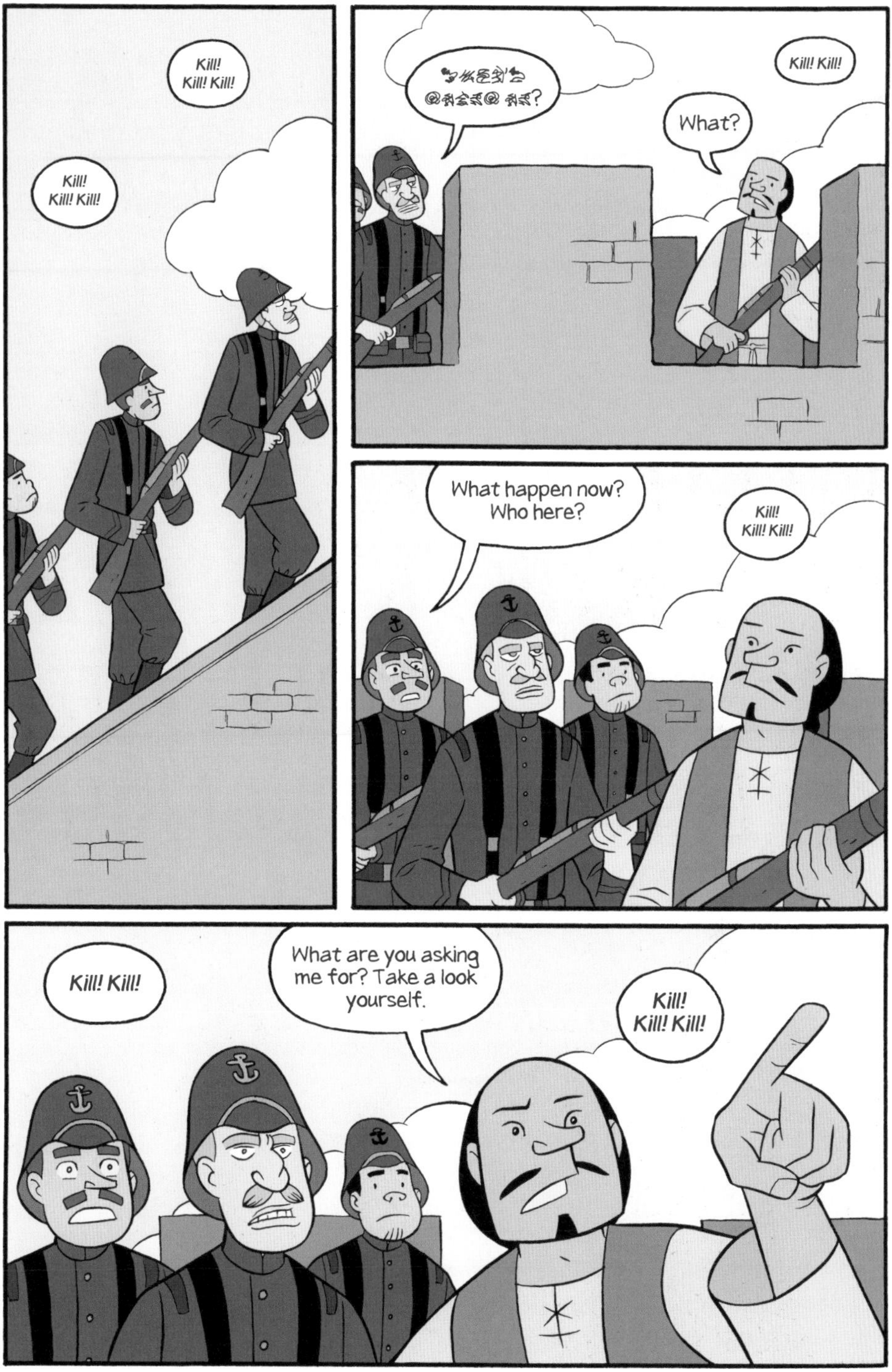
Kill!
Kill! Kill!
Kill!
Kill! Kill!
Kill! Kill!
What?
What happen now?
Who here?
Kill!
Kill! Kill!
Kill! Kill!
What are you asking me for? Take a look yourself.
Kill!
Kill! Kill!

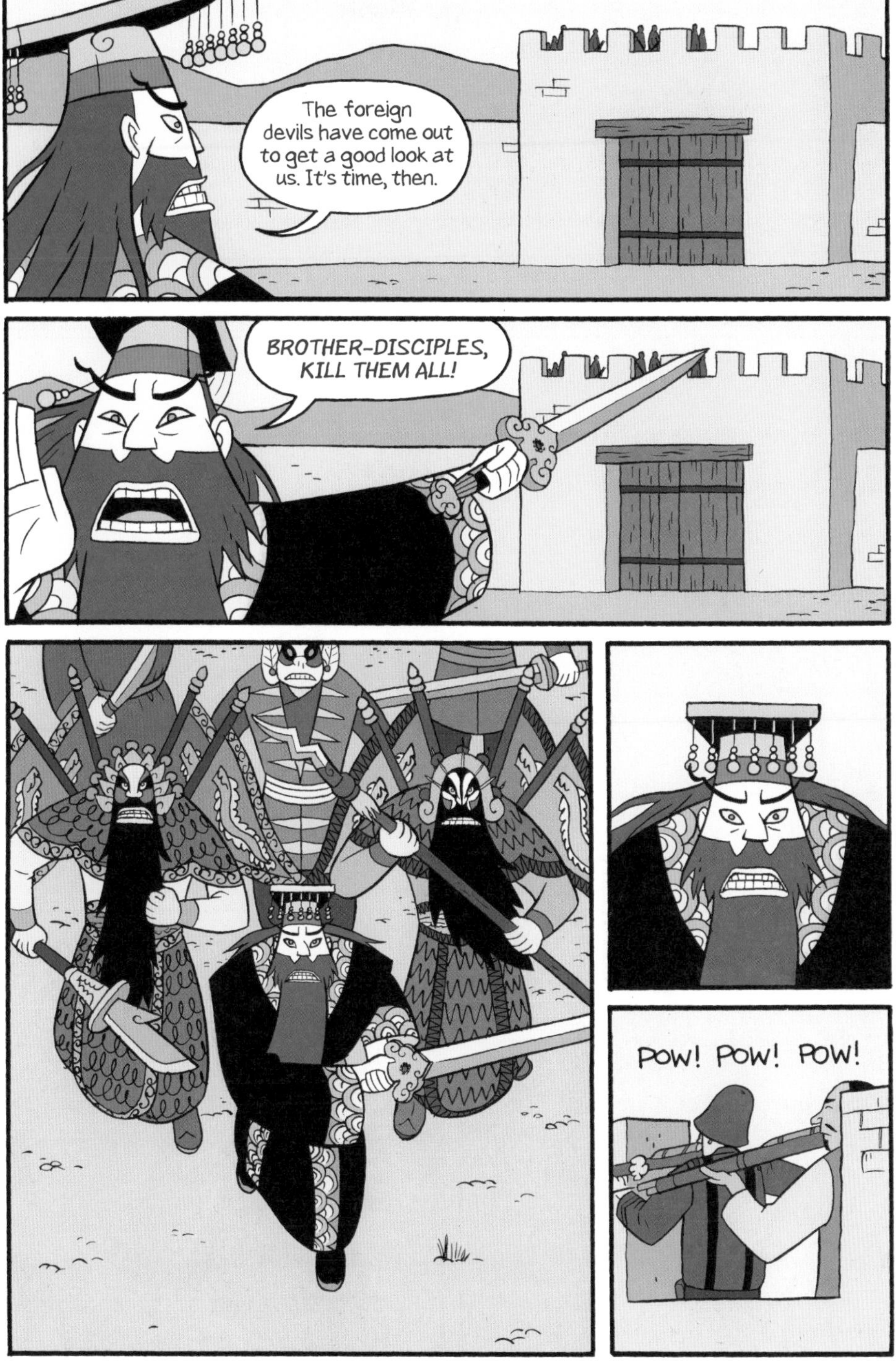
The foreign devils have come out to get a good look at us. It's time, then.
BROTHER-DISCIPLES, KILL THEM ALL!
POW! POW! POW!

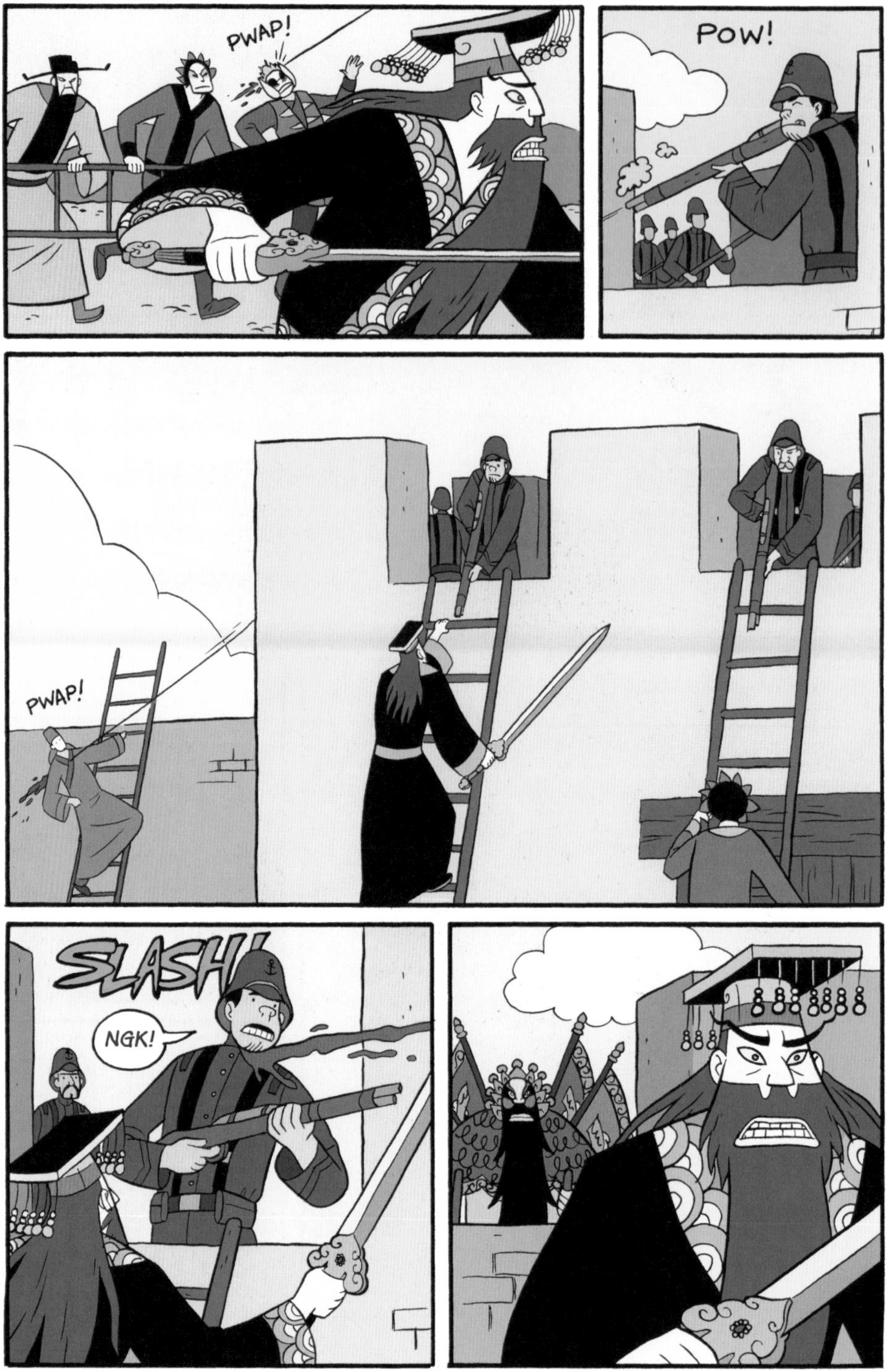
PWAP!
POW!
PWAP!
SLASH!
NGK!

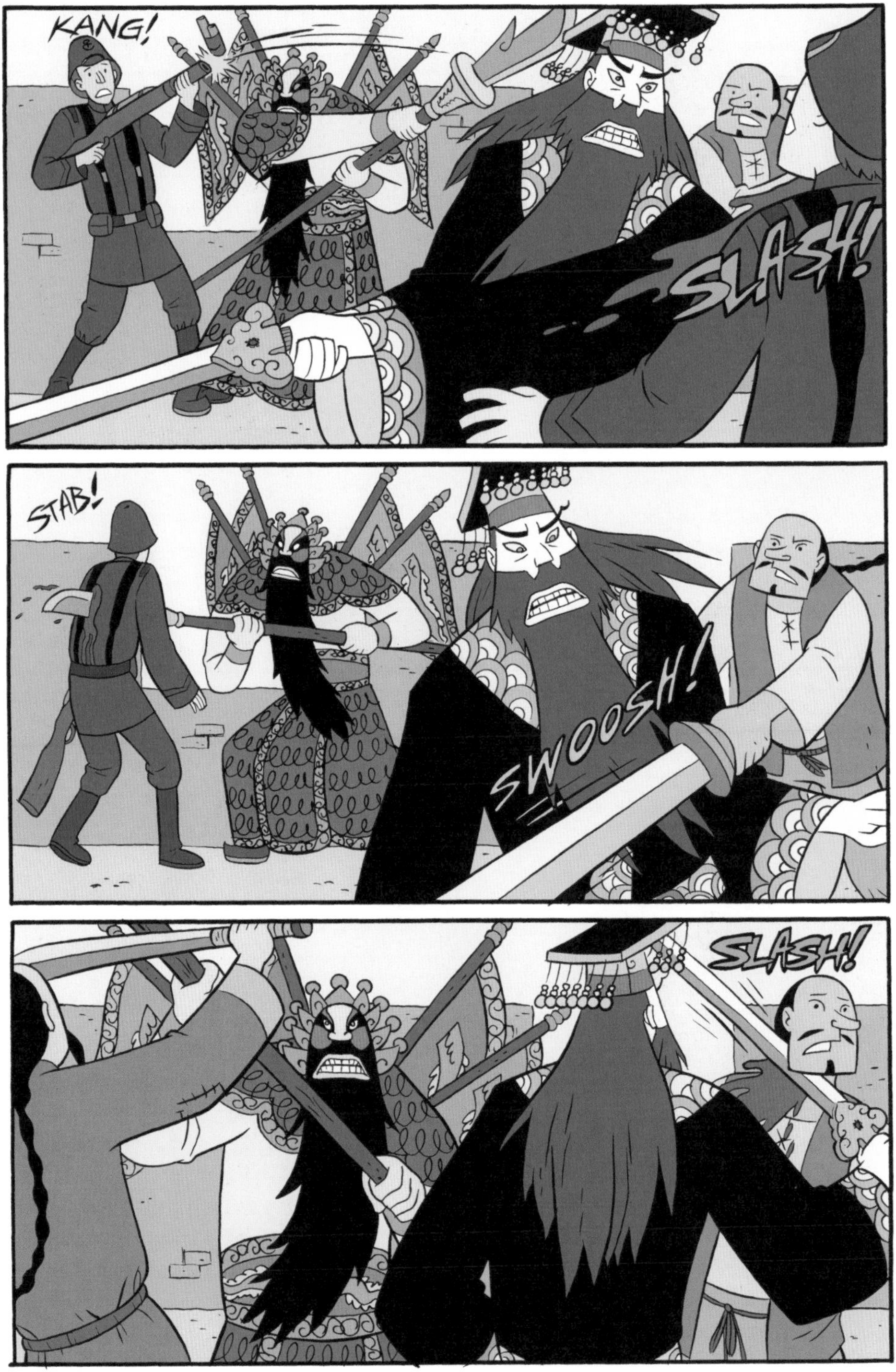
KANG!
SLASH!
STAB!
SWOOSH!
SLASH!

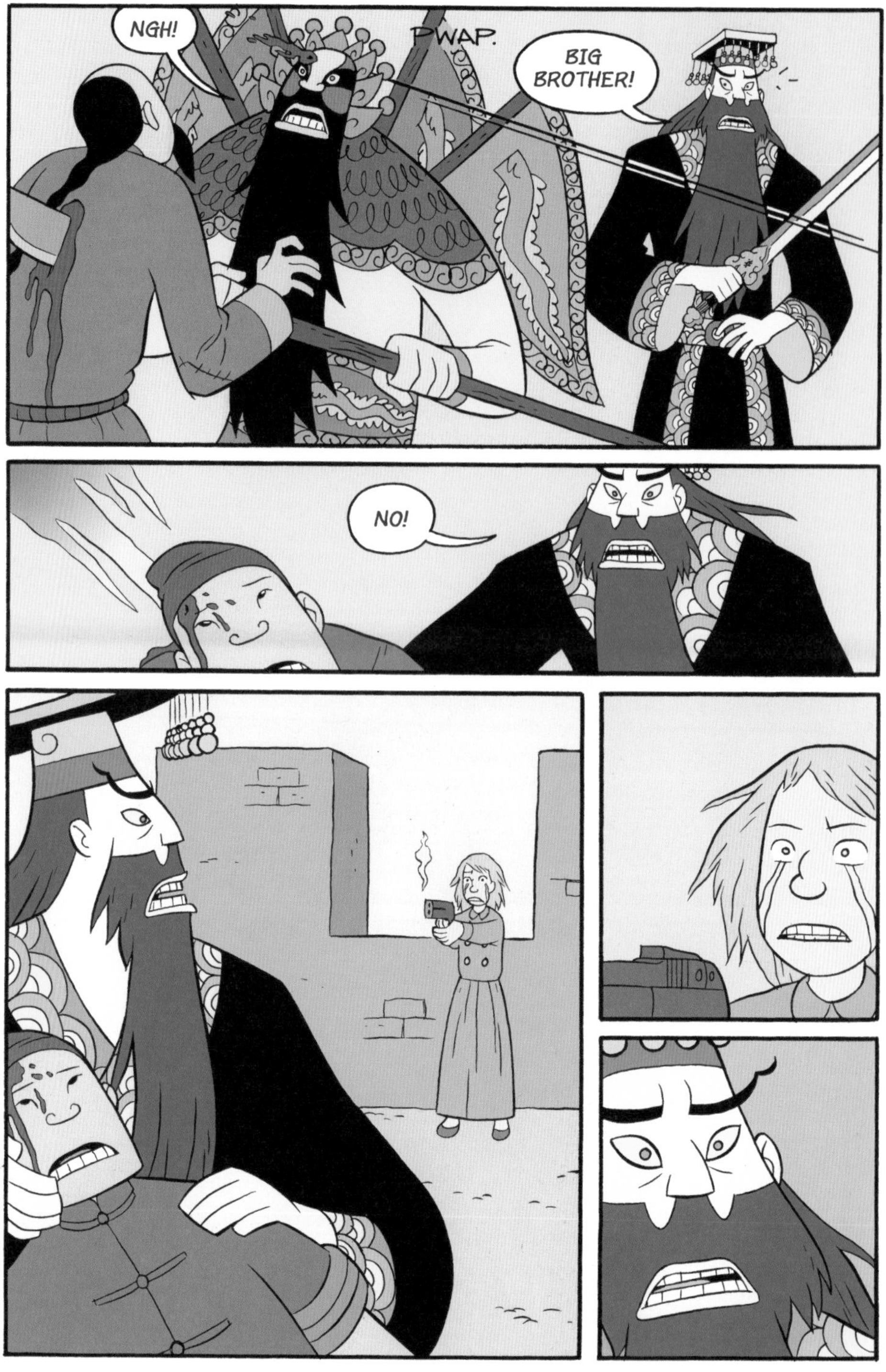
NGH!
PWAP.
BIG BROTHER!
NO!

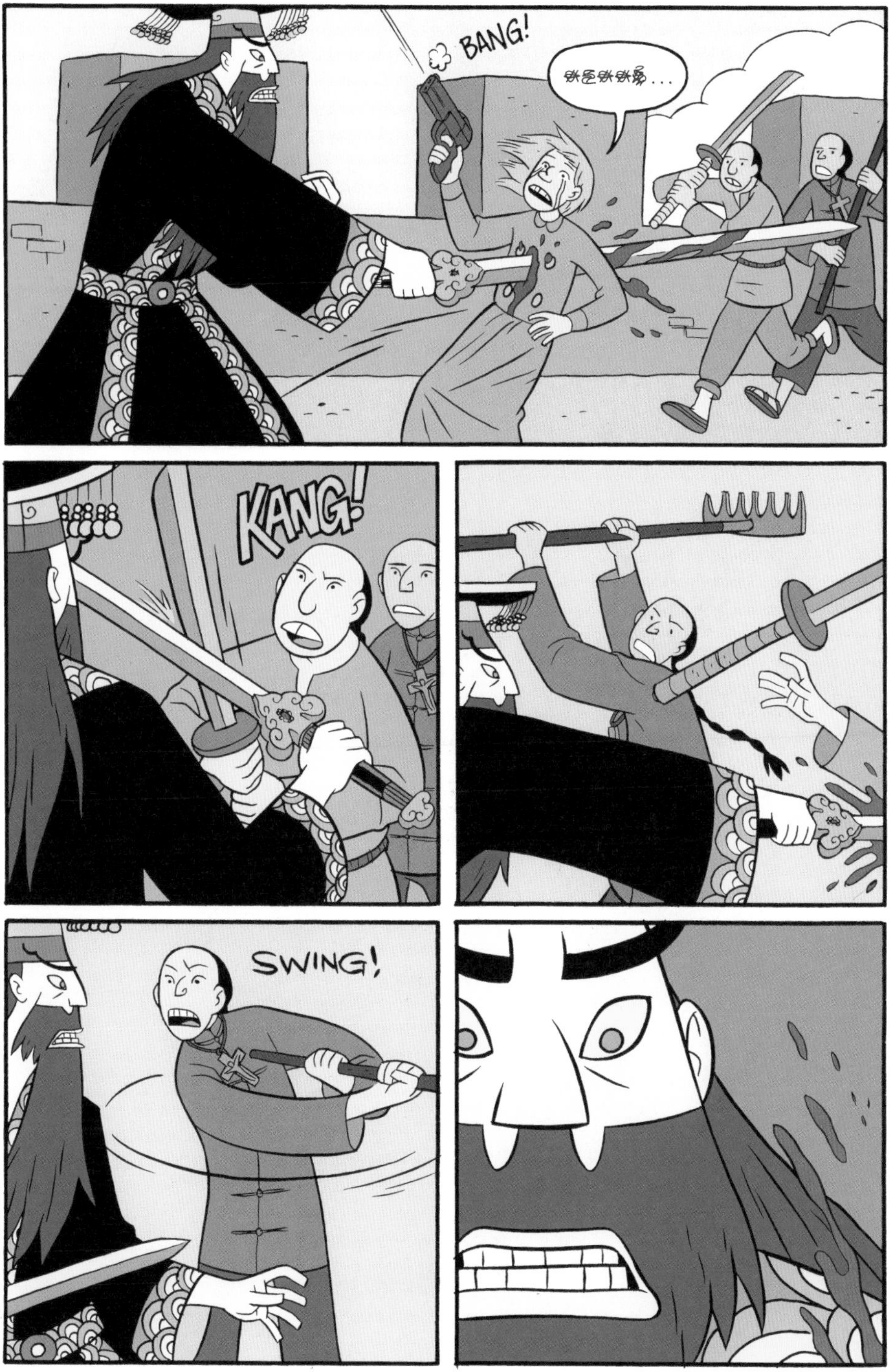
BANG!
KANG!
SWING!

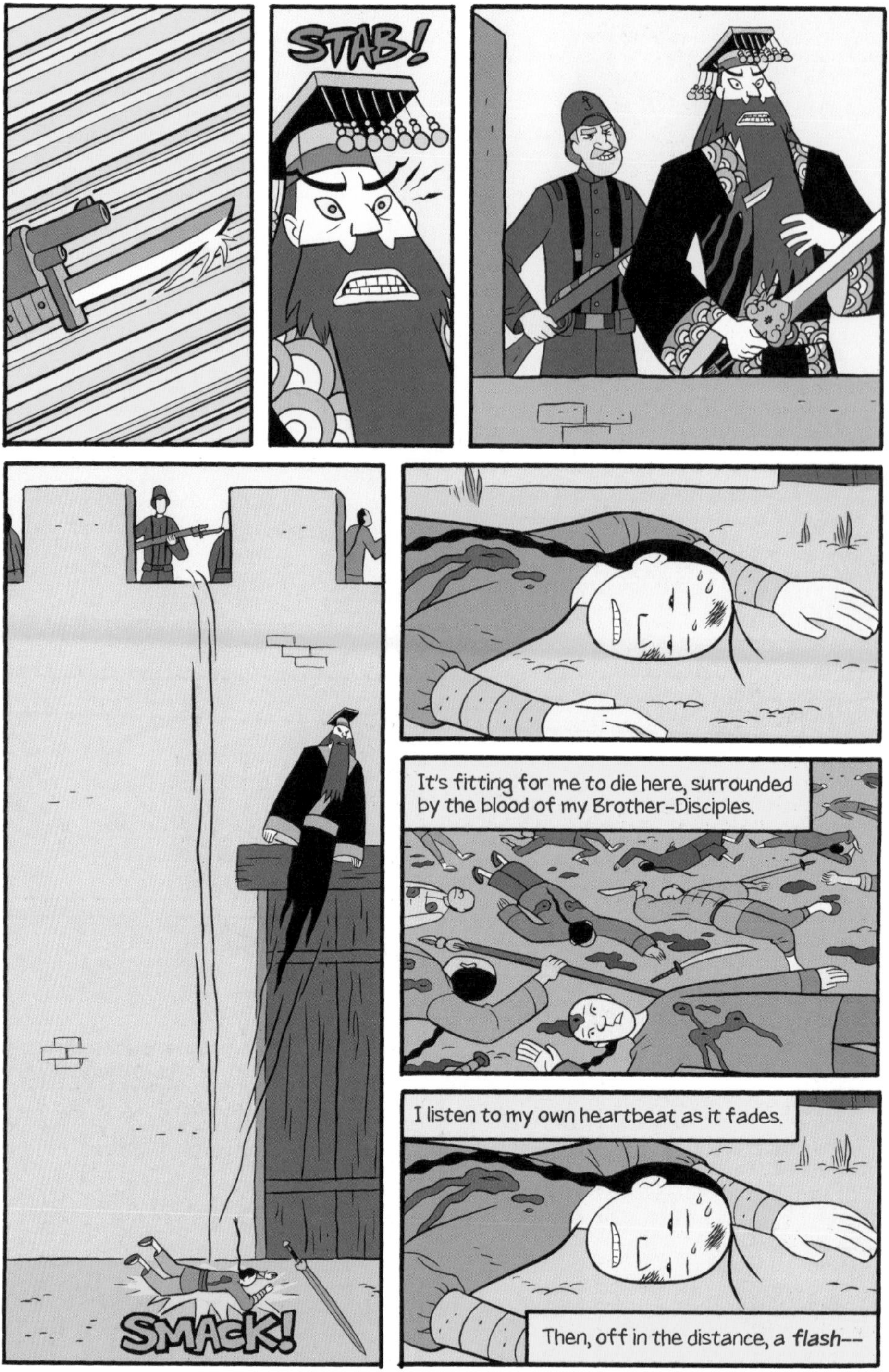
STAB!
SMACK!
It's fitting for me to die here, surrounded by the blood of my Brother-Disciples.
I listen to my own heartbeat as it fades.
Then, off in the distance, a *flash*--

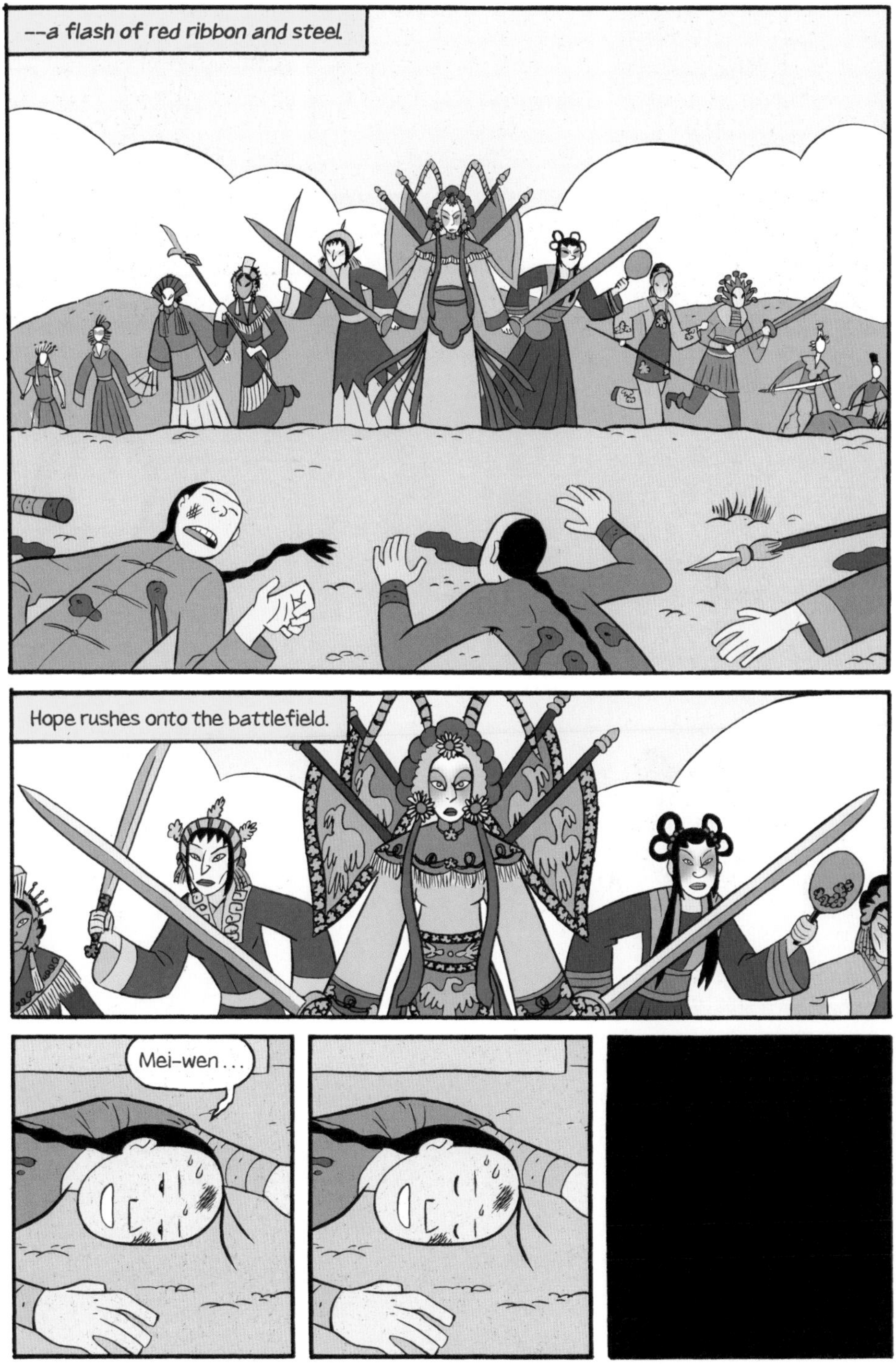
--a flash of red ribbon and steel.
Hope rushes onto the battlefield.
Mei-wen...

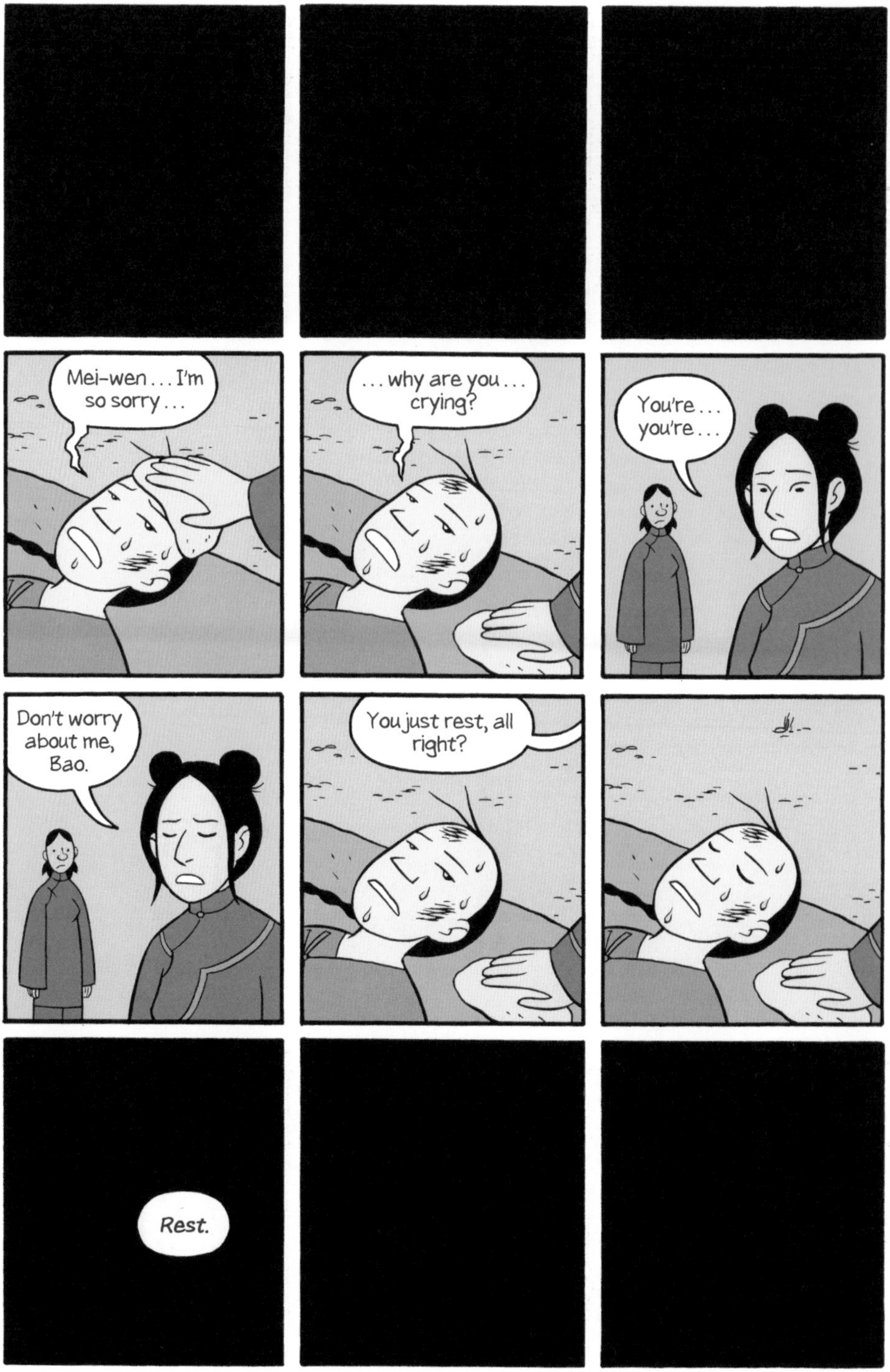

Mei-wen . . . I'm so sorry . . .
. . . why are you . . . crying?
You're . . . you're . . .
Don't worry about me, Bao.
You just rest, all right?
Rest.

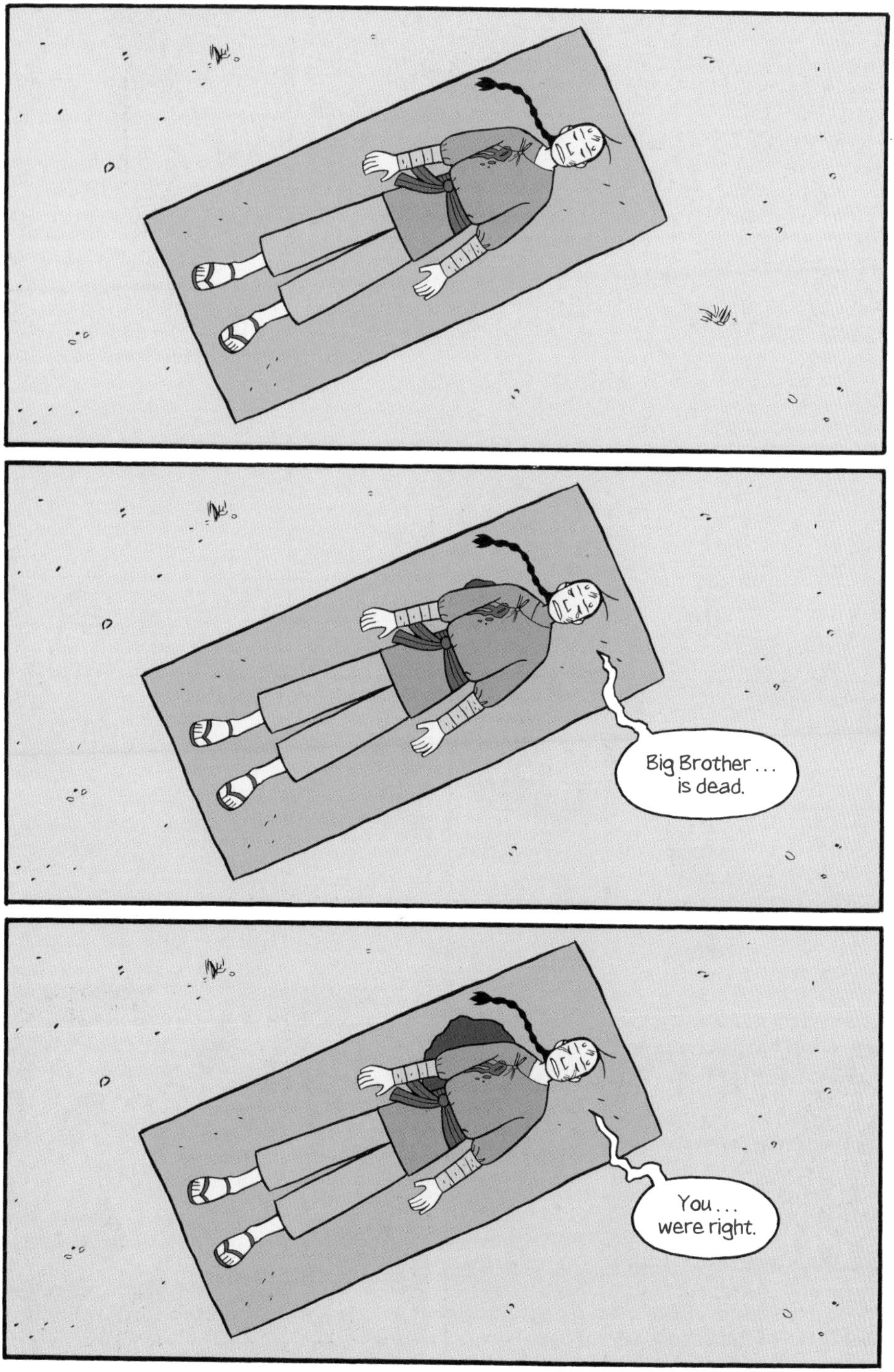
Big Brother . . . is dead.
You . . . were right.

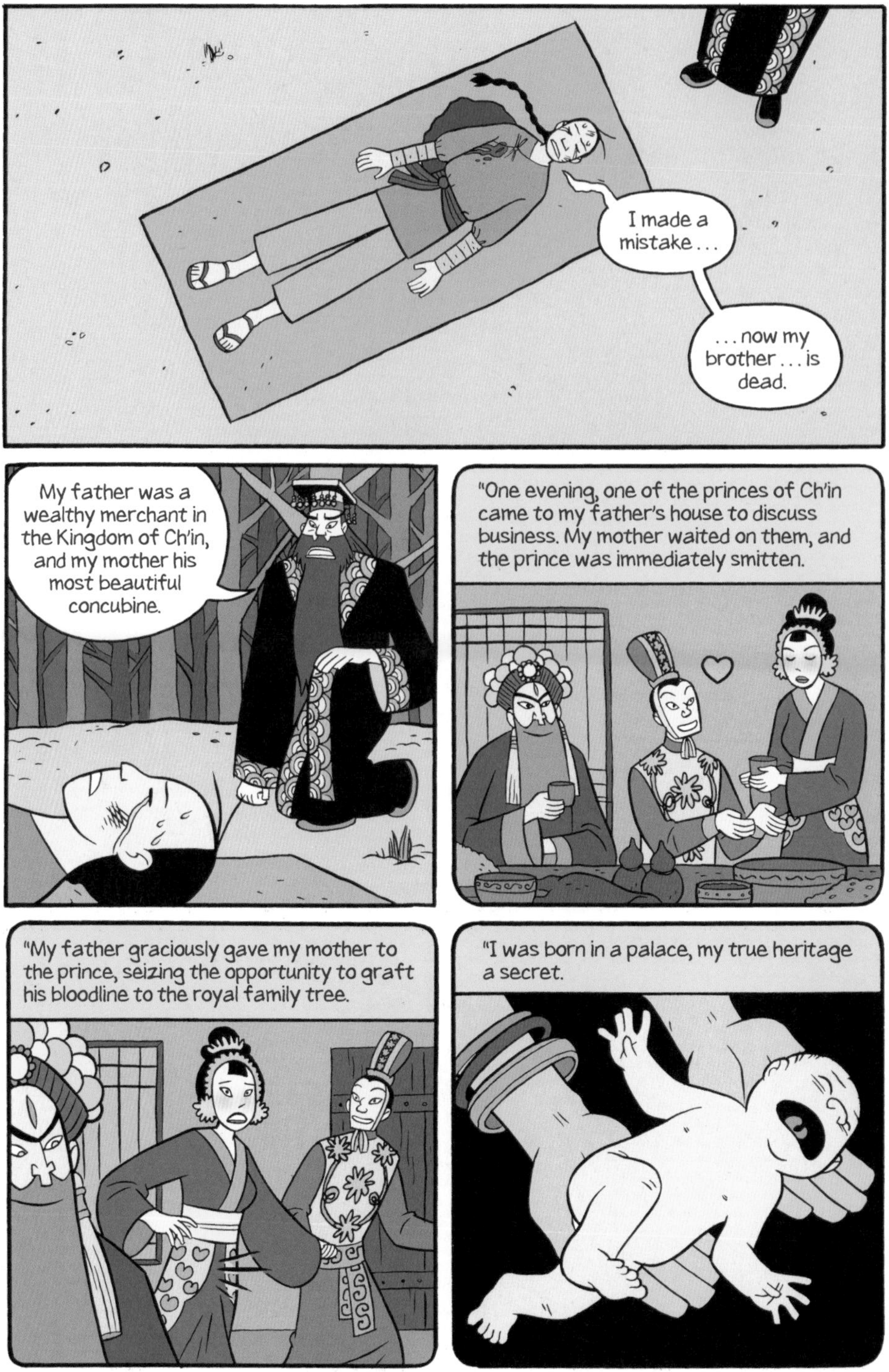

I made a mistake...
...now my brother...is dead.
My father was a wealthy merchant in the Kingdom of Ch'in, and my mother his most beautiful concubine.
"One evening, one of the princes of Ch'in came to my father's house to discuss business. My mother waited on them, and the prince was immediately smitten.
"My father graciously gave my mother to the prince, seizing the opportunity to graft his bloodline to the royal family tree.
"I was born in a palace, my true heritage a secret.

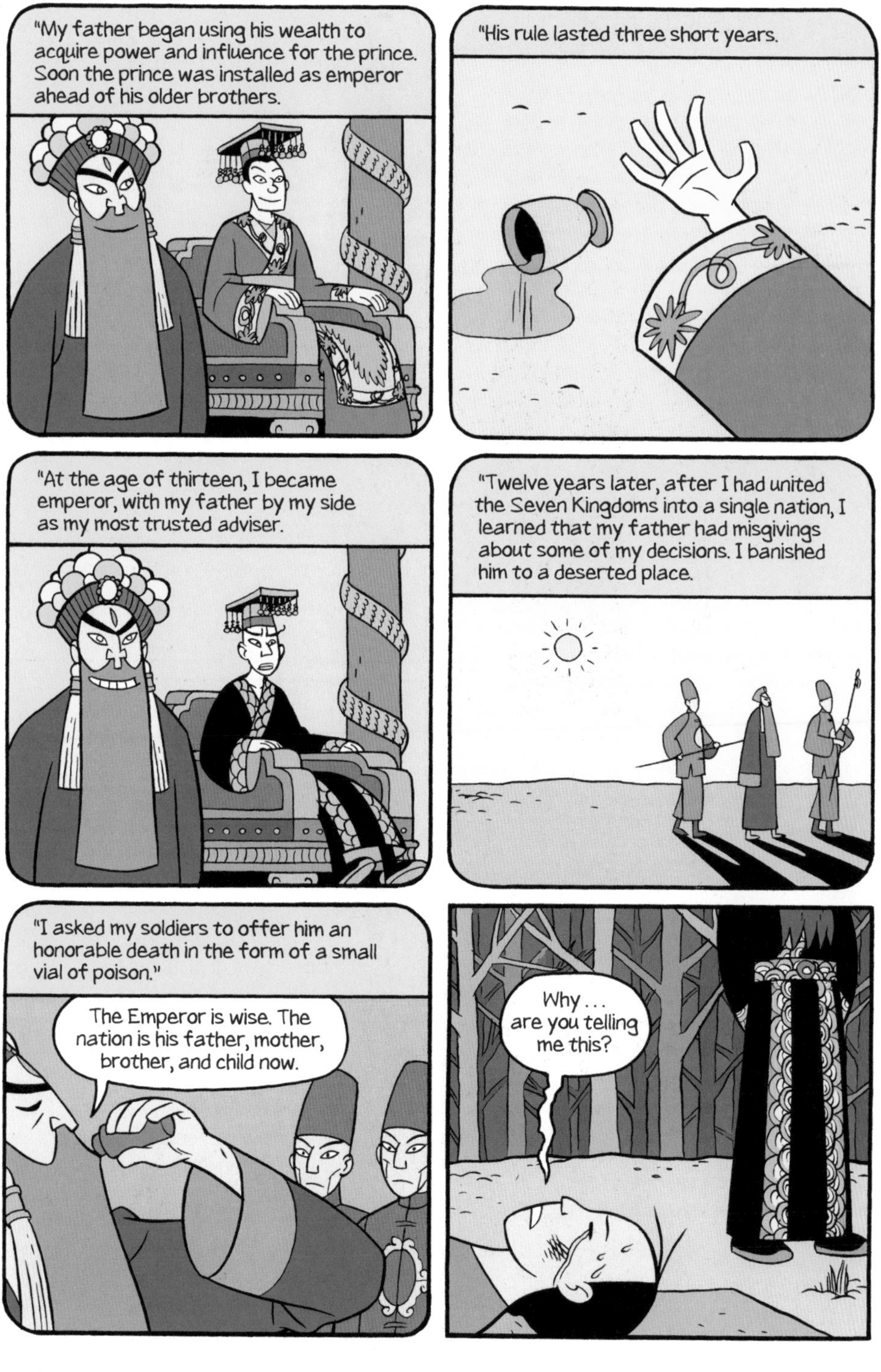
"My father began using his wealth to acquire power and influence for the prince. Soon the prince was installed as emperor ahead of his older brothers.
"His rule lasted three short years.
"At the age of thirteen, I became emperor, with my father by my side as my most trusted adviser.
"Twelve years later, after I had united the Seven Kingdoms into a single nation, I learned that my father had misgivings about some of my decisions. I banished him to a deserted place.
"I asked my soldiers to offer him an honorable death in the form of a small vial of poison."
The Emperor is wise. The nation is his father, mother, brother, and child now.
Why... are you telling me this?

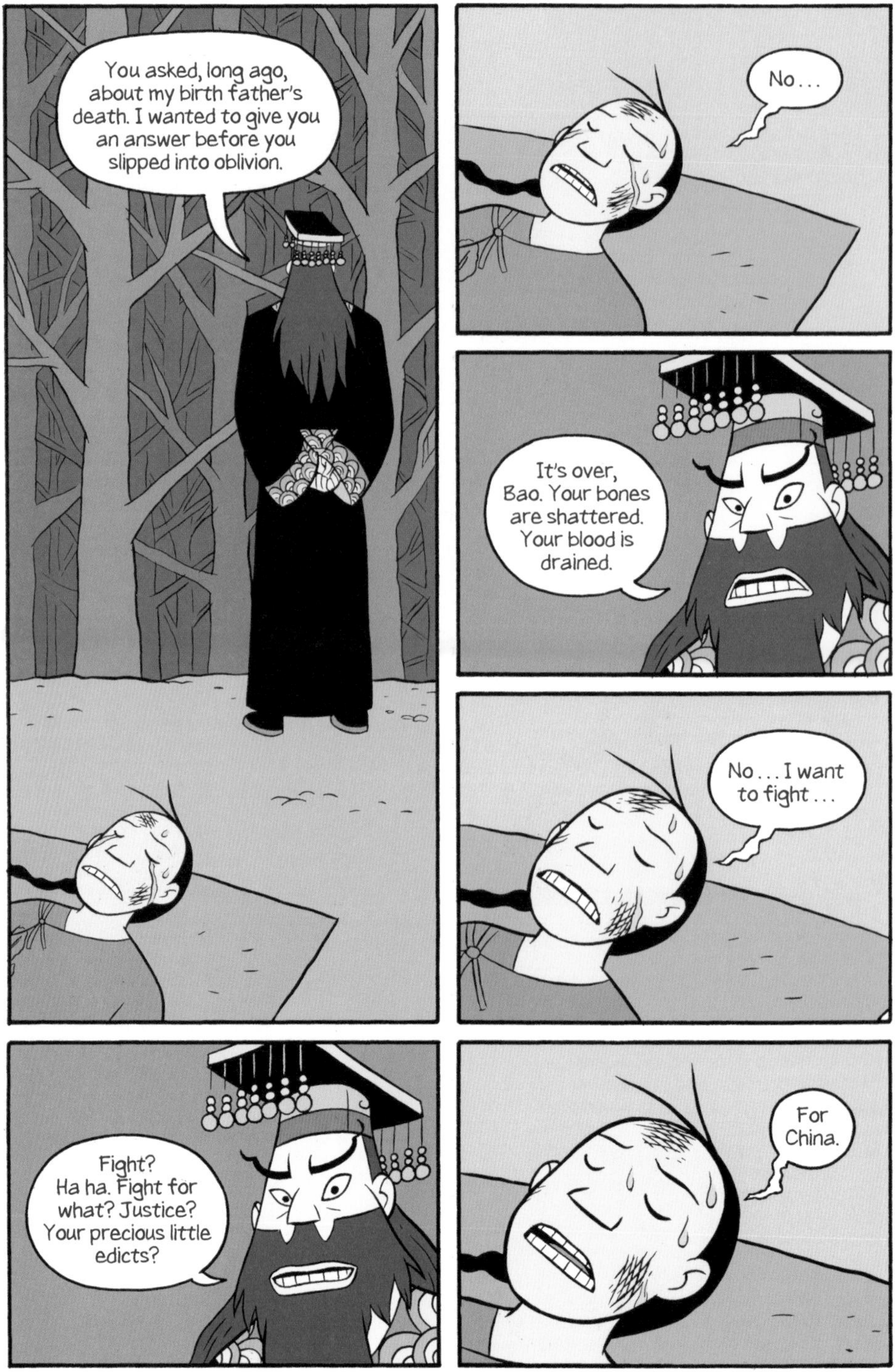
You asked, long ago, about my birth father's death. I wanted to give you an answer before you slipped into oblivion.
No...
It's over, Bao. Your bones are shattered. Your blood is drained.
No...I want to fight...
Fight? Ha ha. Fight for what? Justice? Your precious little edicts?
For China.

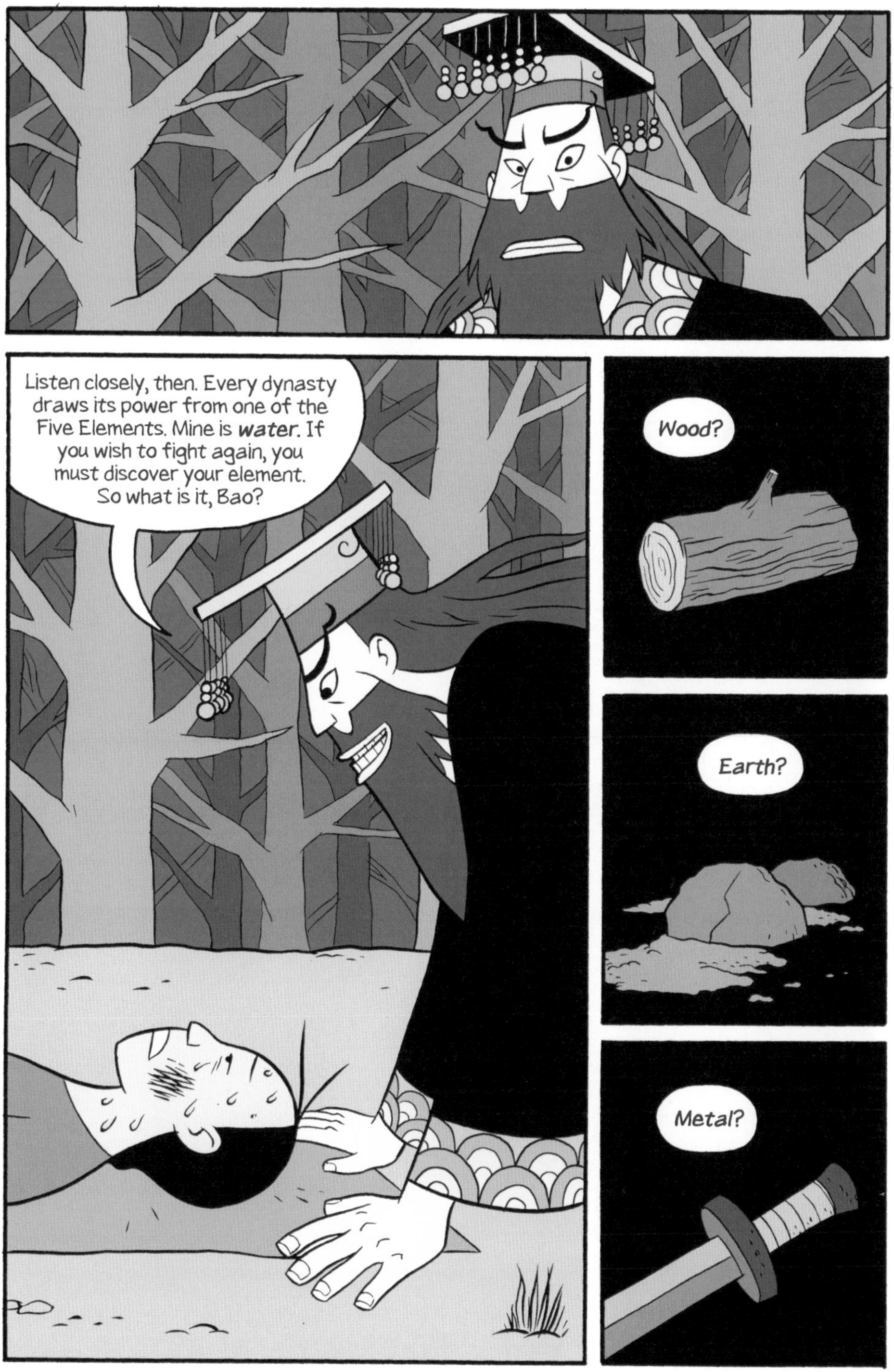
Listen closely, then. Every dynasty draws its power from one of the Five Elements. Mine is ***water***. If you wish to fight again, you must discover your element. So what is it, Bao?
Wood?
Earth?
Metal?

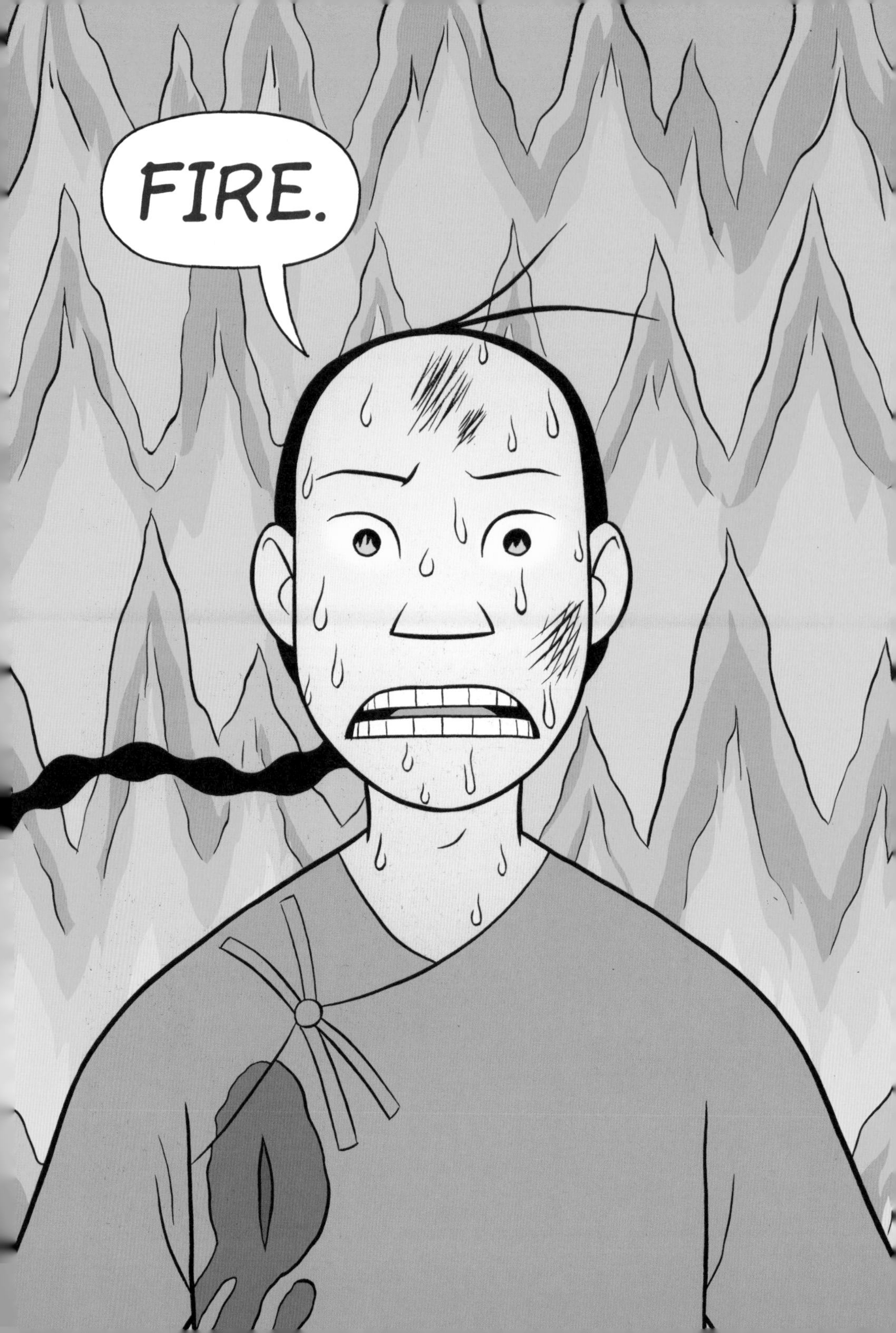
FIRE.

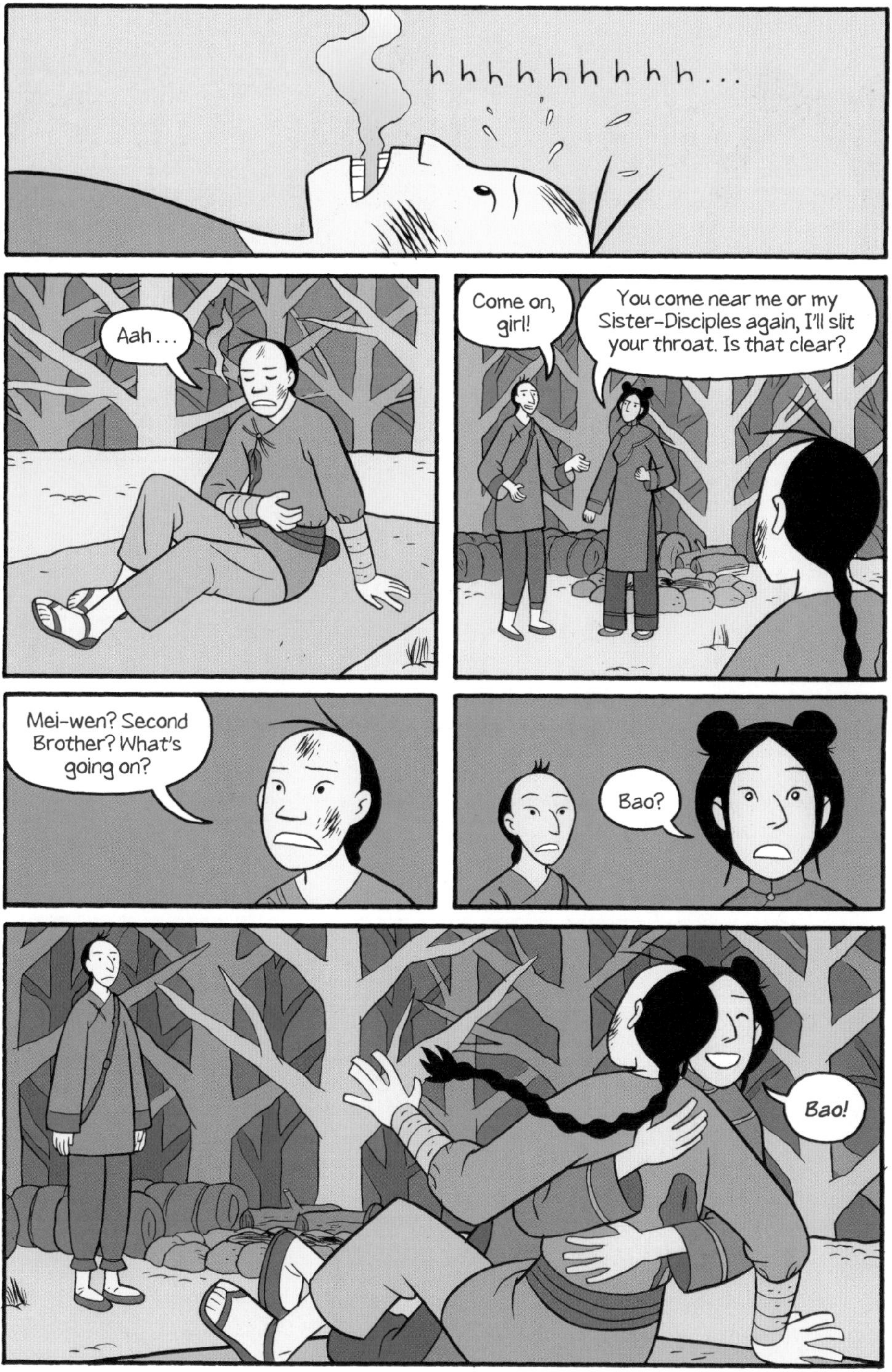
hhhhhhhhh...
Aah...
Come on, girl!
You come near me or my Sister-Disciples again, I'll slit your throat. Is that clear?
Mei-wen? Second Brother? What's going on?
Bao?
Bao!

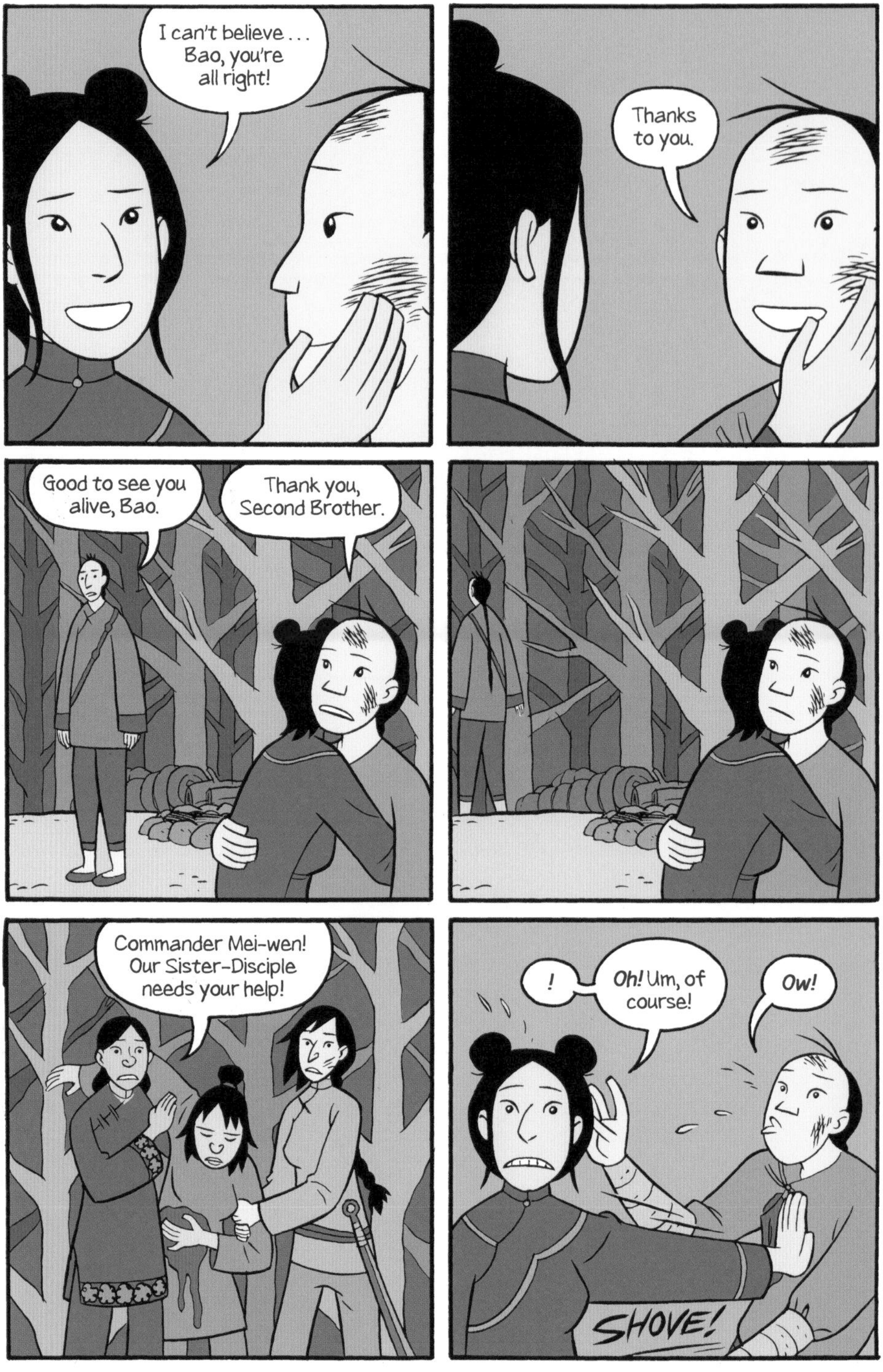
I can't believe . . .
Bao, you're
all right!
Thanks
to you.
Good to see you
alive, Bao.
Thank you,
Second Brother.
Commander Mei-wen!
Our Sister-Disciple
needs your help!
!
Oh! Um, of
course!
Ow!
SHOVE!

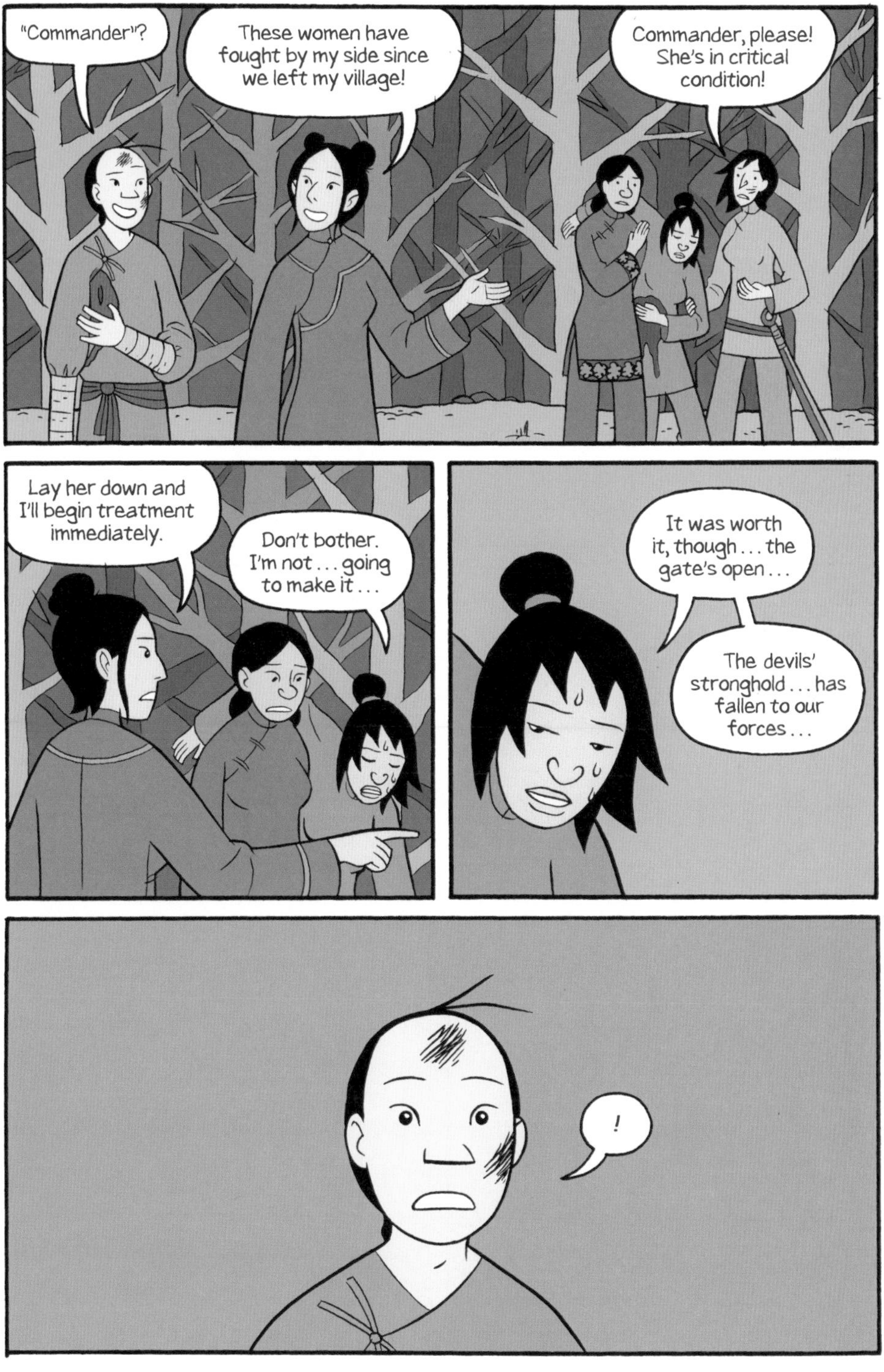
"Commander"?
These women have fought by my side since we left my village!
Commander, please! She's in critical condition!
Lay her down and I'll begin treatment immediately.
Don't bother. I'm not . . . going to make it . . .
It was worth it, though . . . the gate's open . . .
The devils' stronghold . . . has fallen to our forces . . .
!

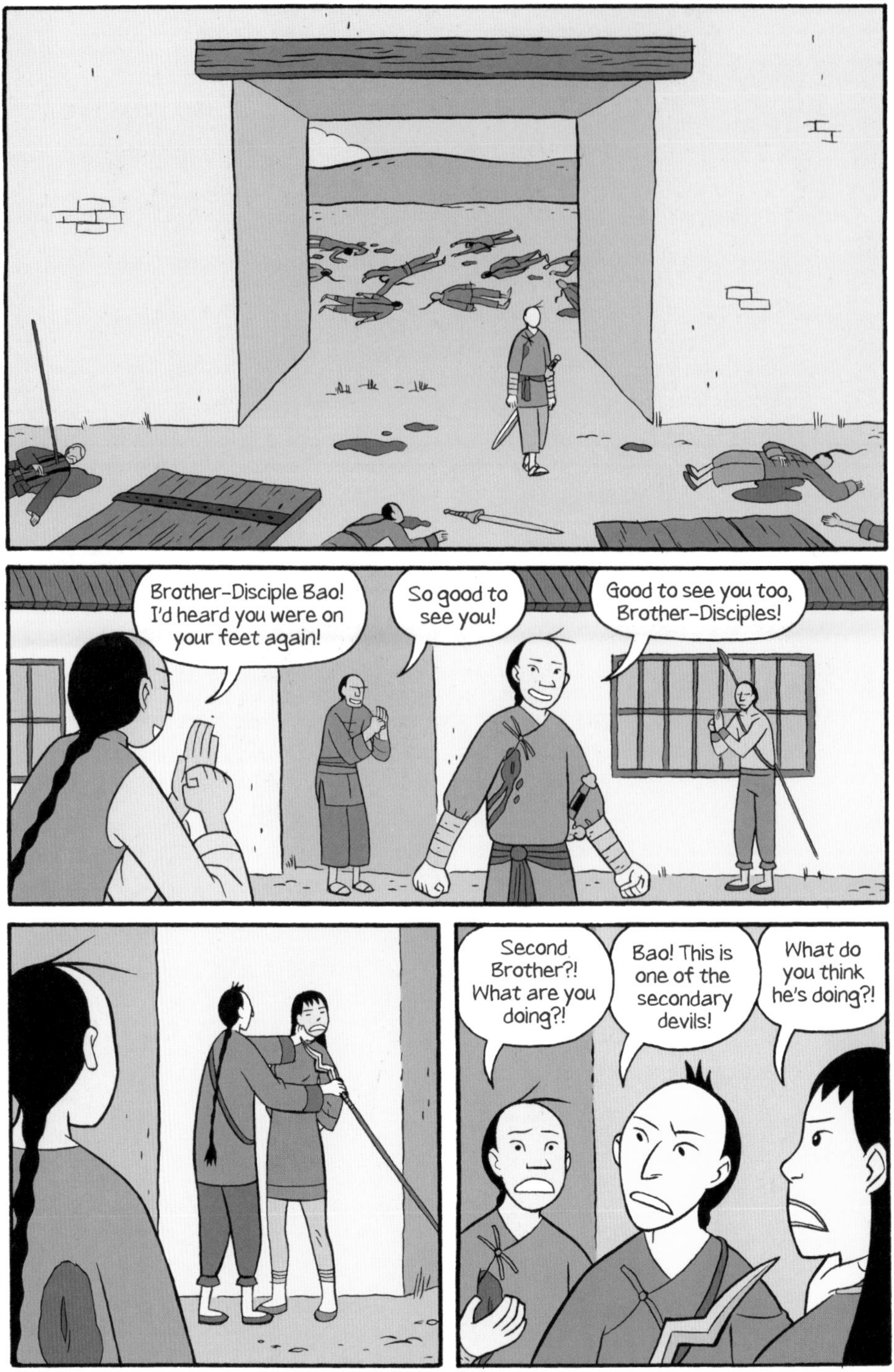
Brother-Disciple Bao! I'd heard you were on your feet again!
So good to see you!
Good to see you too, Brother-Disciples!
Second Brother?! What are you doing?!
Bao! This is one of the secondary devils!
What do you think he's doing?!

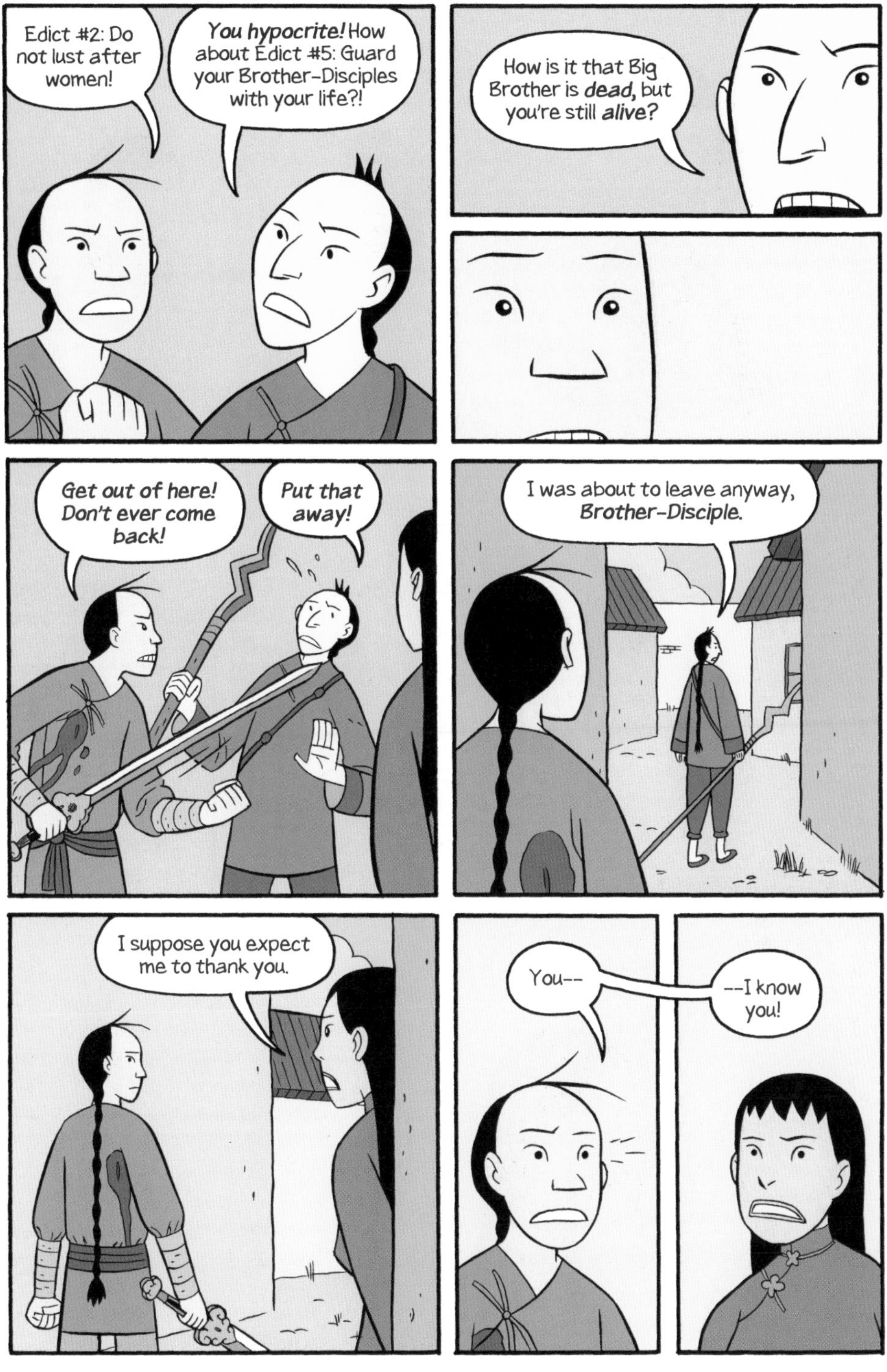
Edict #2: Do not lust after women!
You hypocrite! How about Edict #5: Guard your Brother-Disciples with your life?!
How is it that Big Brother is *dead,* but you're still *alive?*
Get out of here! Don't ever come back!
Put that away!
I was about to leave anyway, *Brother-Disciple.*
I suppose you expect me to thank you.
You--
--I know you!

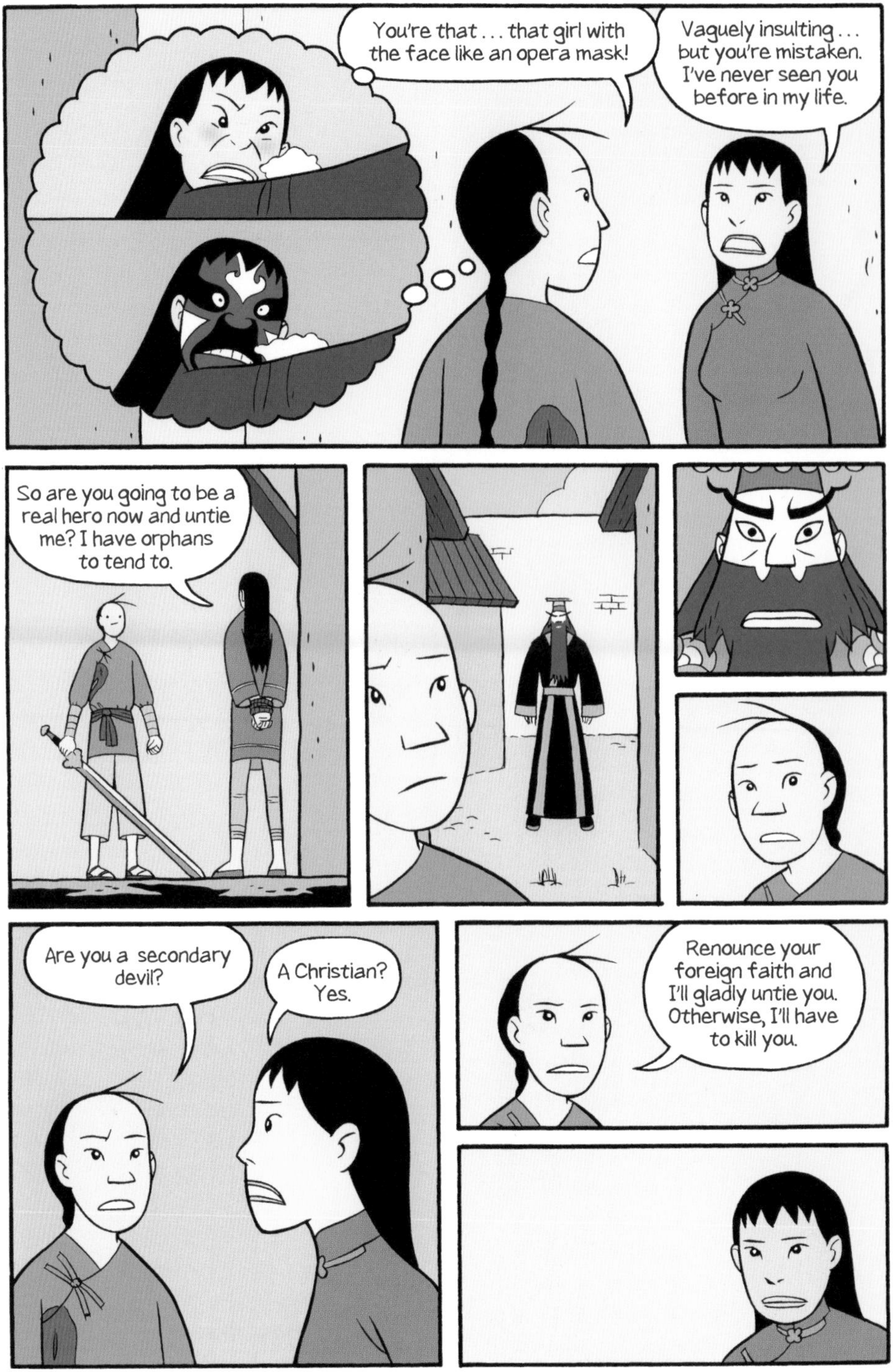
You're that . . . that girl with the face like an opera mask!
Vaguely insulting . . . but you're mistaken. I've never seen you before in my life.
So are you going to be a real hero now and untie me? I have orphans to tend to.
Are you a secondary devil?
A Christian? Yes.
Renounce your foreign faith and I'll gladly untie you. Otherwise, I'll have to kill you.

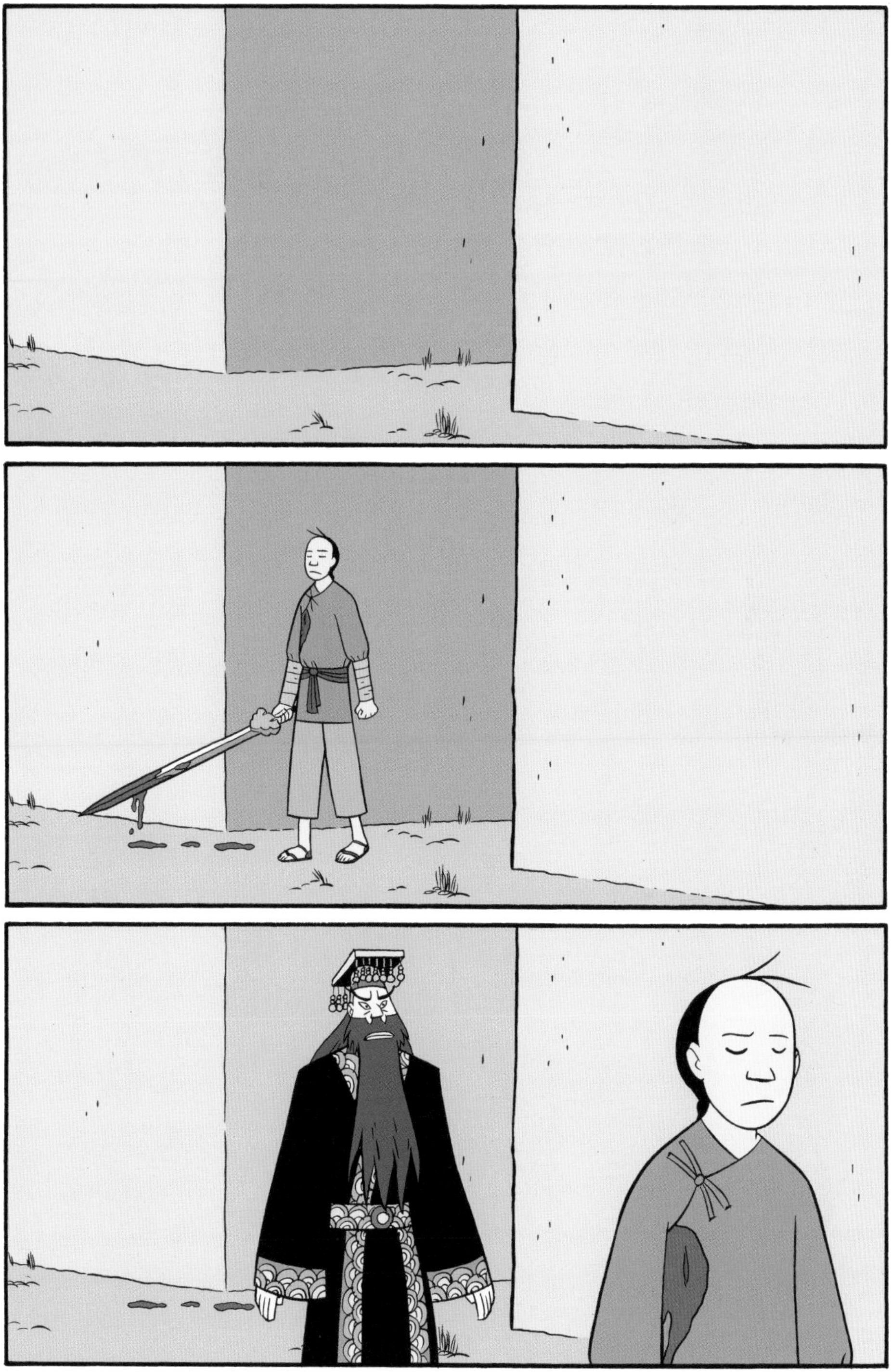

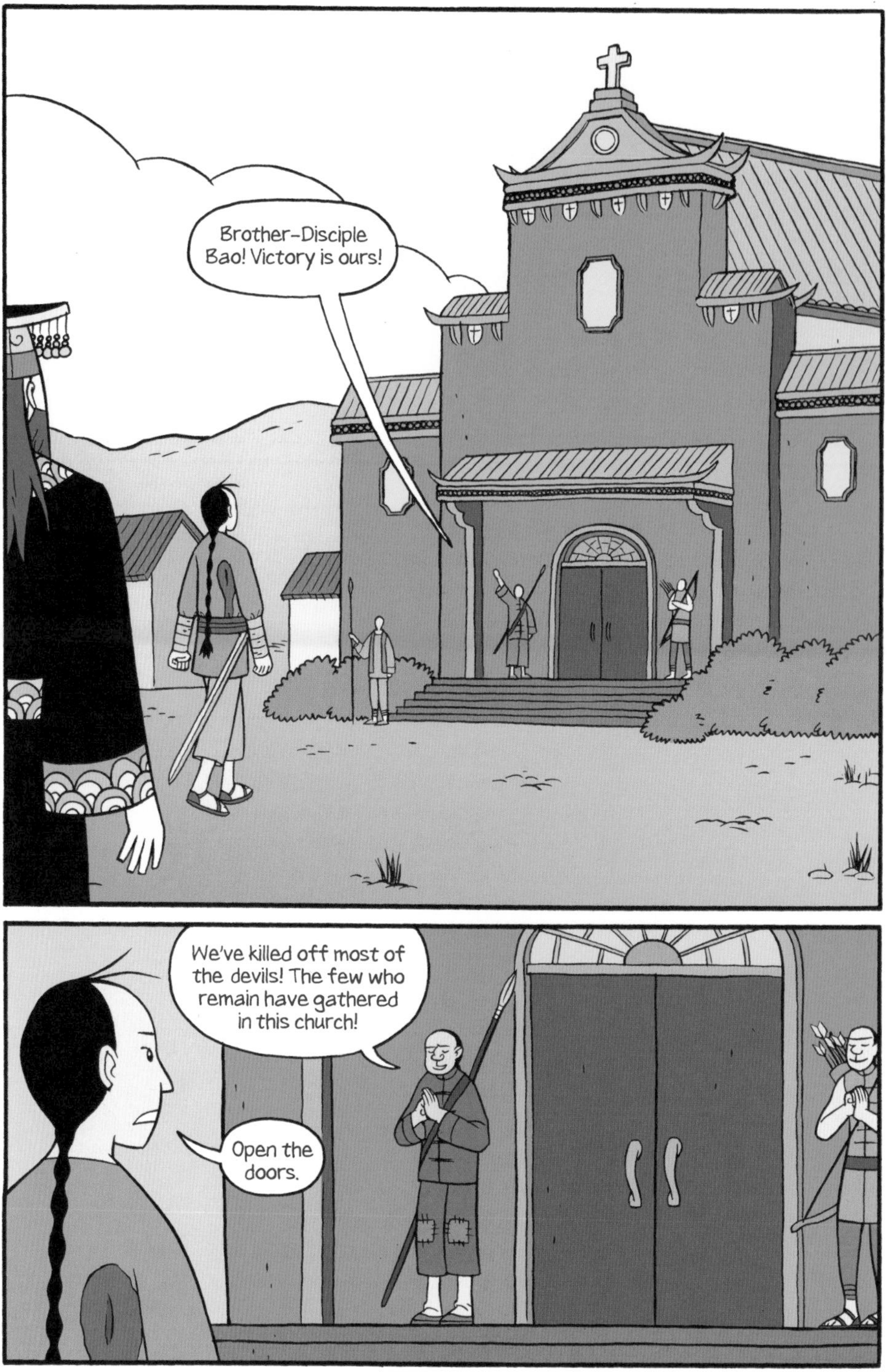
Brother-Disciple Bao! Victory is ours!
We've killed off most of the devils! The few who remain have gathered in this church!
Open the doors.

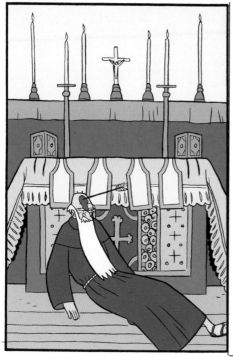

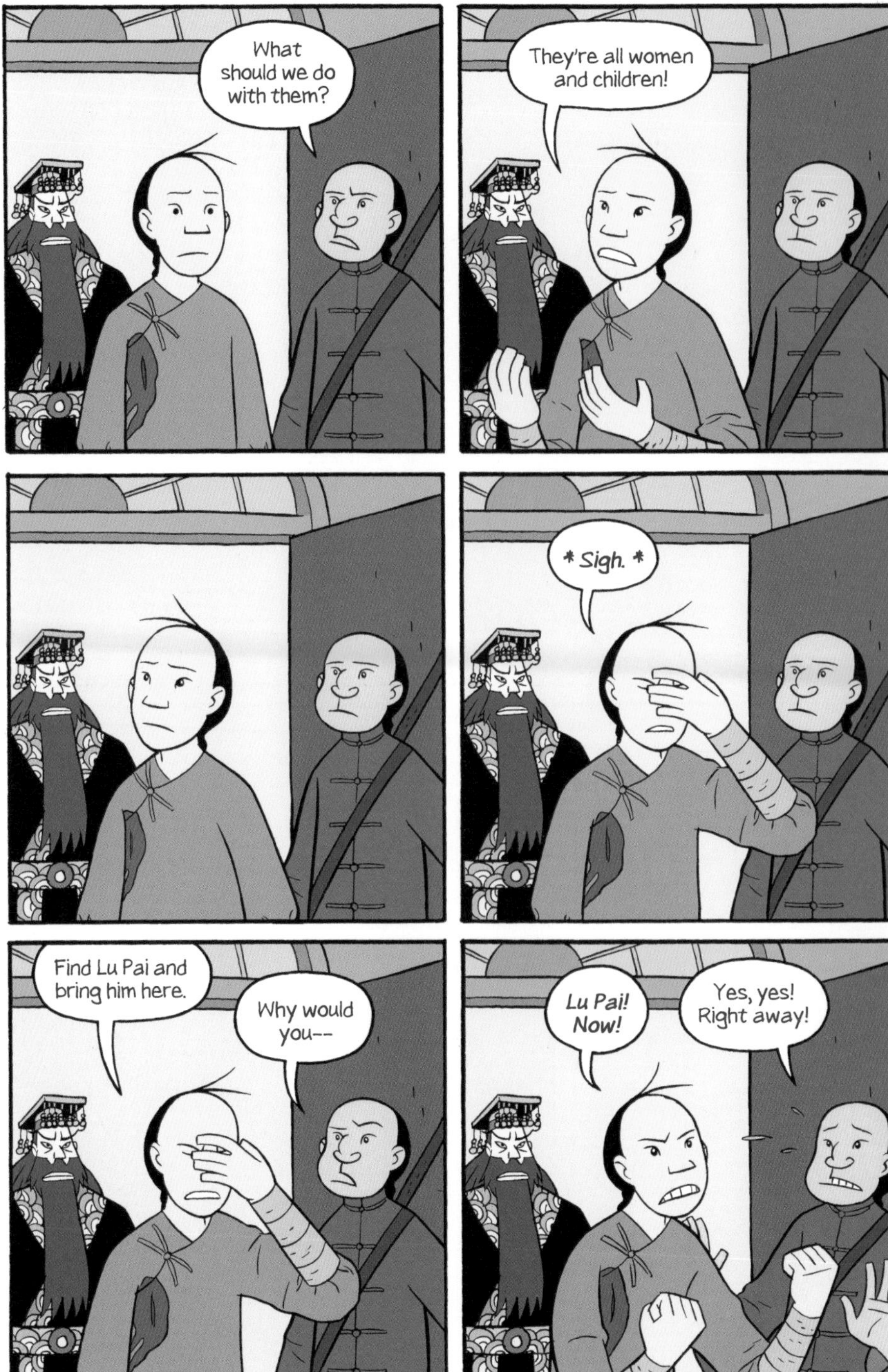
What should we do with them?
They're all women and children!
* Sigh. *
Find Lu Pai and bring him here.
Why would you--
Lu Pai! Now!
Yes, yes! Right away!

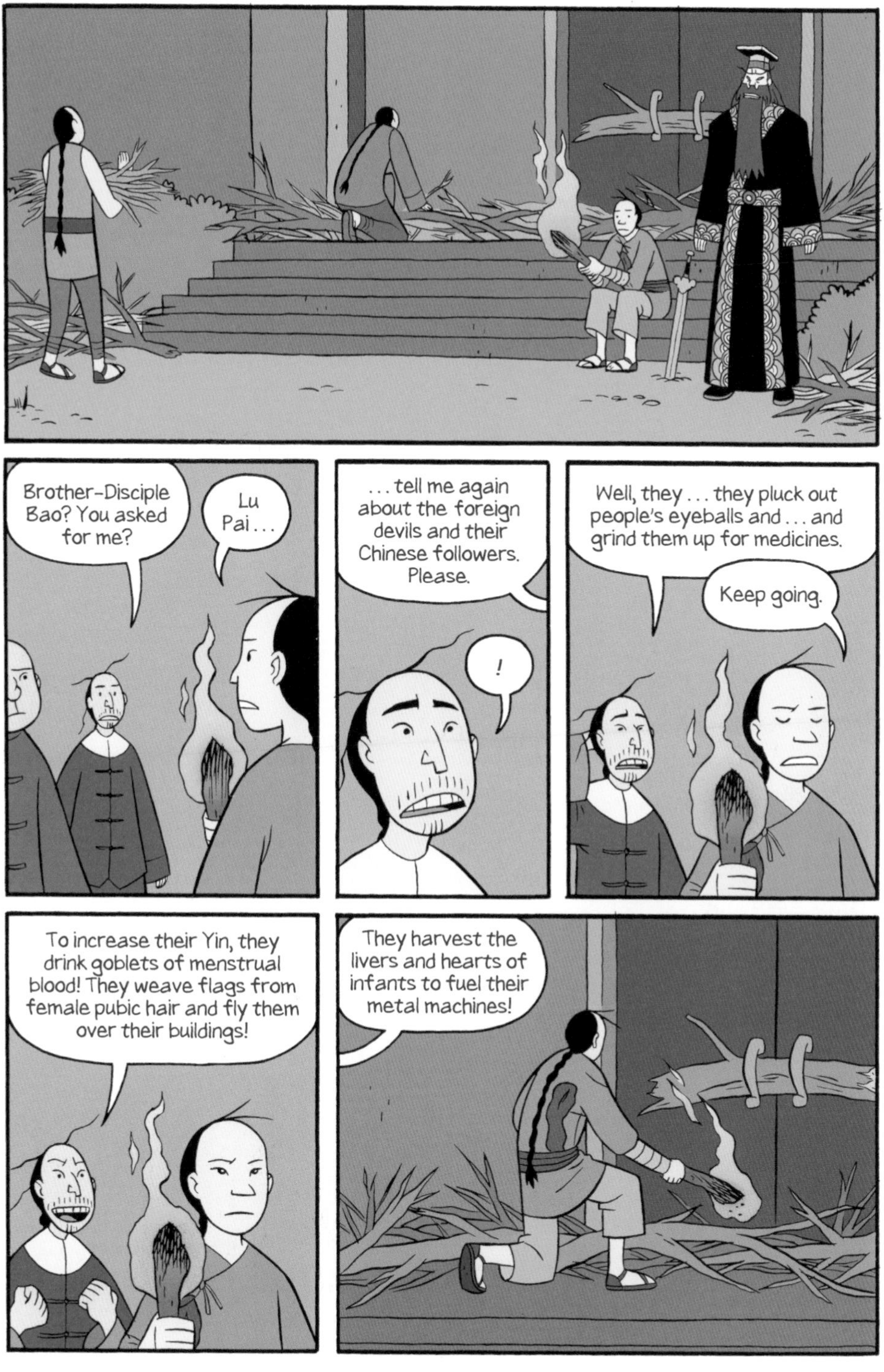
Brother-Disciple Bao? You asked for me?
Lu Pai...
...tell me again about the foreign devils and their Chinese followers. Please.
!
Well, they... they pluck out people's eyeballs and... and grind them up for medicines.
Keep going.
To increase their Yin, they drink goblets of menstrual blood! They weave flags from female pubic hair and fly them over their buildings!
They harvest the livers and hearts of infants to fuel their metal machines!

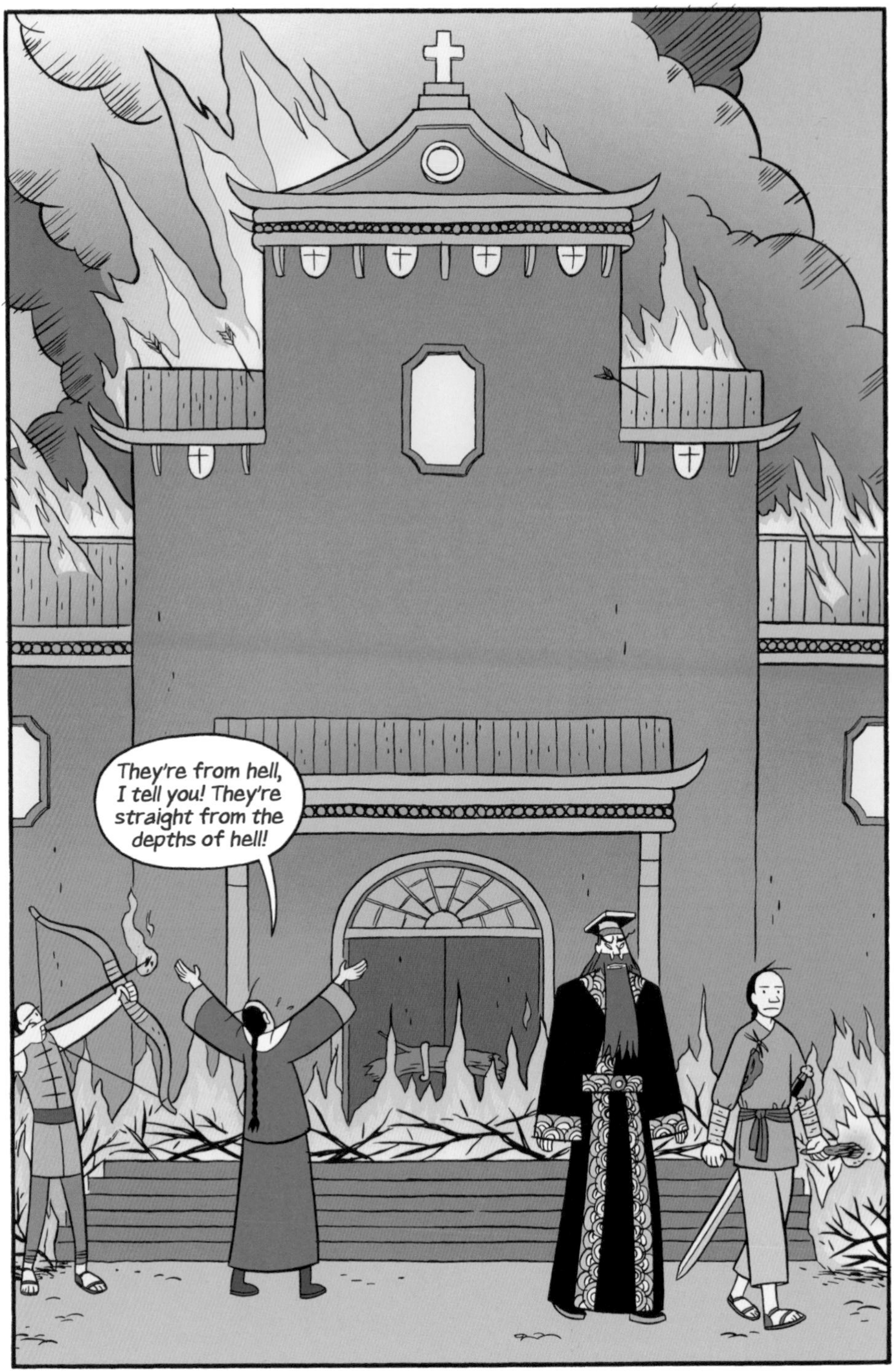
They're from hell, I tell you! They're straight from the depths of hell!

第六章

Peking, China

Summer 1900

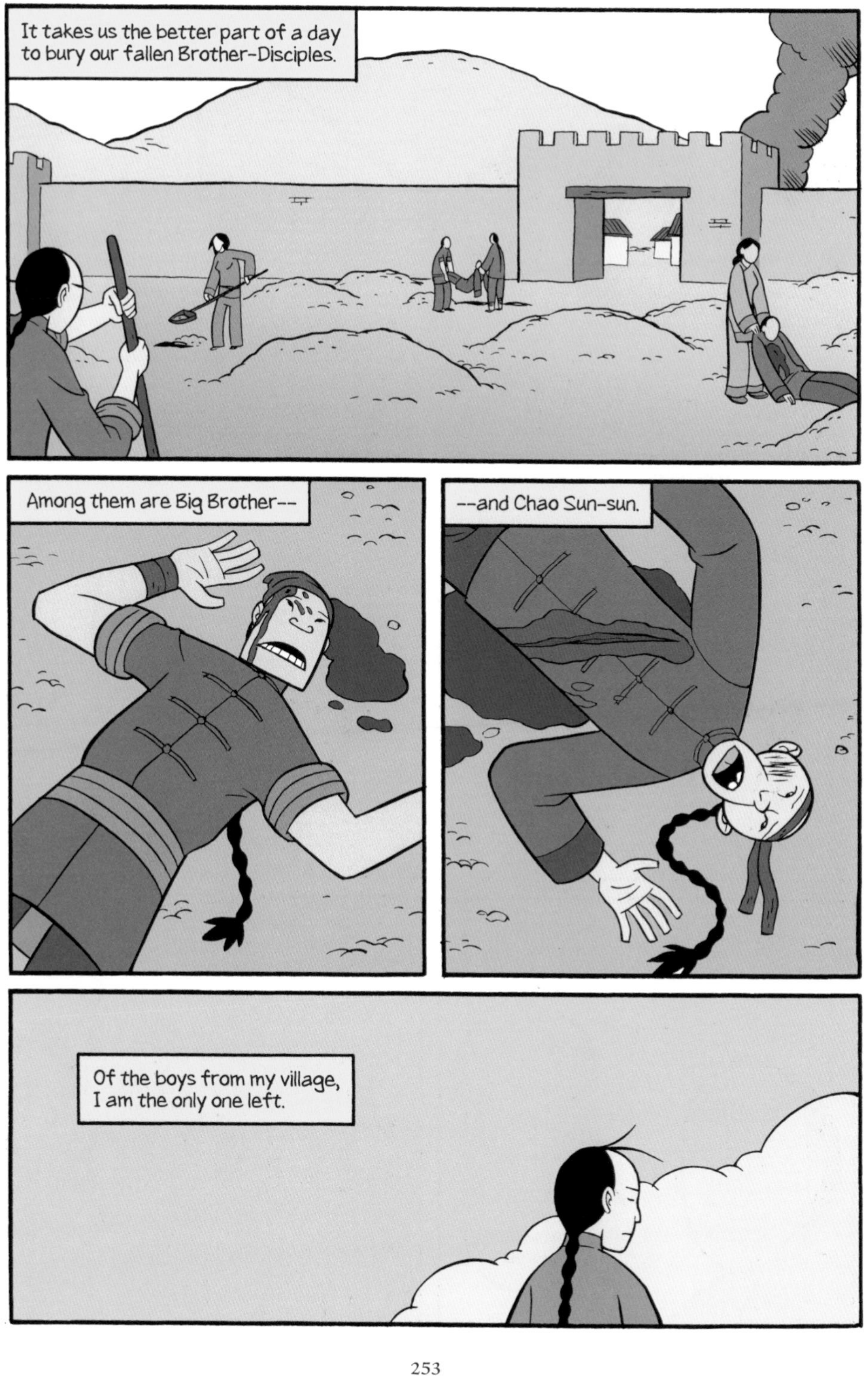
It takes us the better part of a day to bury our fallen Brother-Disciples.
Among them are Big Brother--
--and Chao Sun-sun.
Of the boys from my village, I am the only one left.

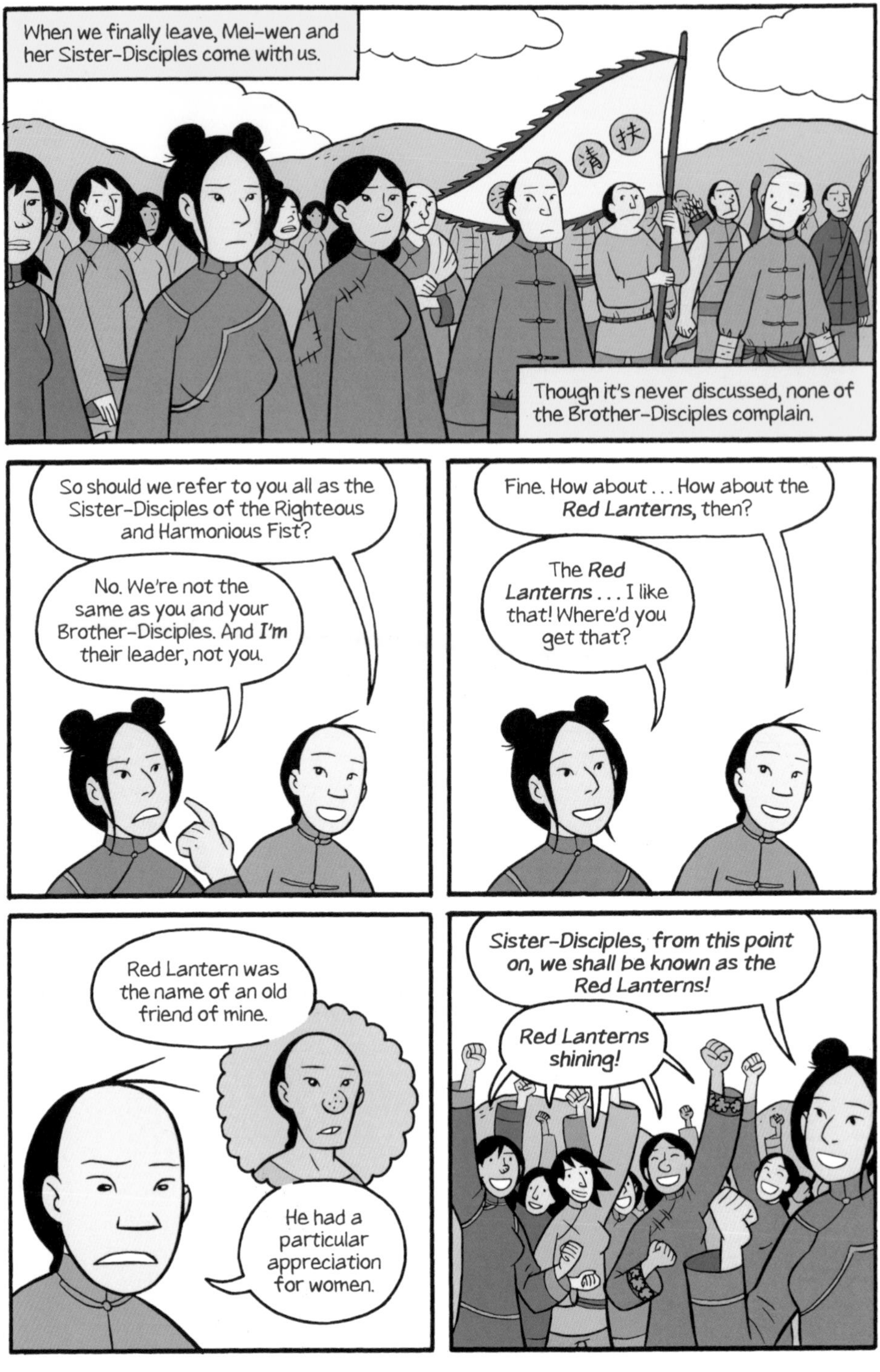

When we finally leave, Mei-wen and her Sister-Disciples come with us.
Though it's never discussed, none of the Brother-Disciples complain.
So should we refer to you all as the Sister-Disciples of the Righteous and Harmonious Fist?
No. We're not the same as you and your Brother-Disciples. And *I'm* their leader, not you.
Fine. How about . . . How about the *Red Lanterns,* then?
The *Red Lanterns* . . . I like that! Where'd you get that?
Red Lantern was the name of an old friend of mine.
He had a particular appreciation for women.
Sister-Disciples, from this point on, we shall be known as the Red Lanterns!
Red Lanterns shining!

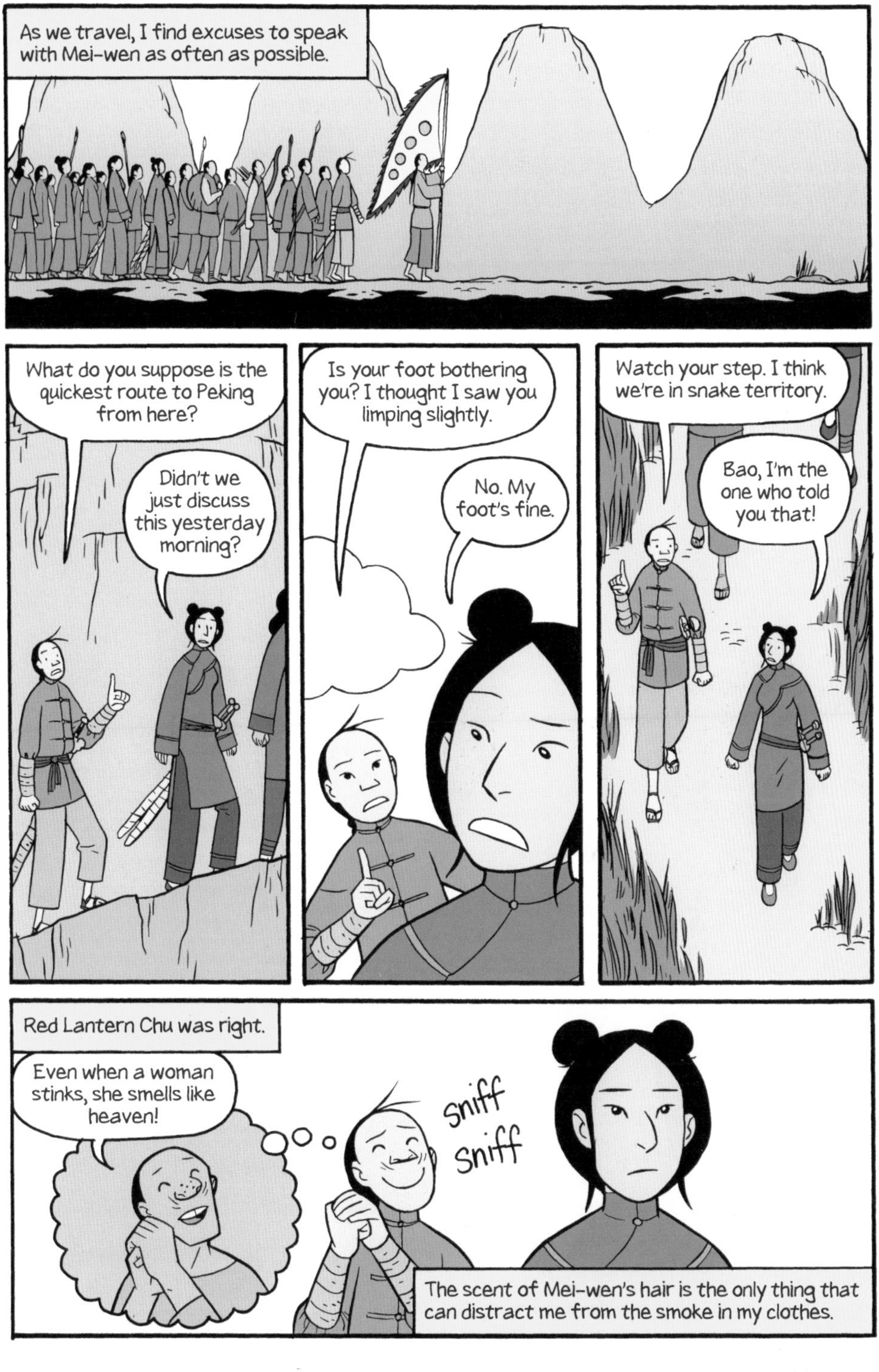

As we travel, I find excuses to speak with Mei-wen as often as possible.
What do you suppose is the quickest route to Peking from here?
Didn't we just discuss this yesterday morning?
Is your foot bothering you? I thought I saw you limping slightly.
No. My foot's fine.
Watch your step. I think we're in snake territory.
Bao, I'm the one who told you that!
Red Lantern Chu was right.
Even when a woman stinks, she smells like heaven!
Sniff Sniff
The scent of Mei-wen's hair is the only thing that can distract me from the smoke in my clothes.

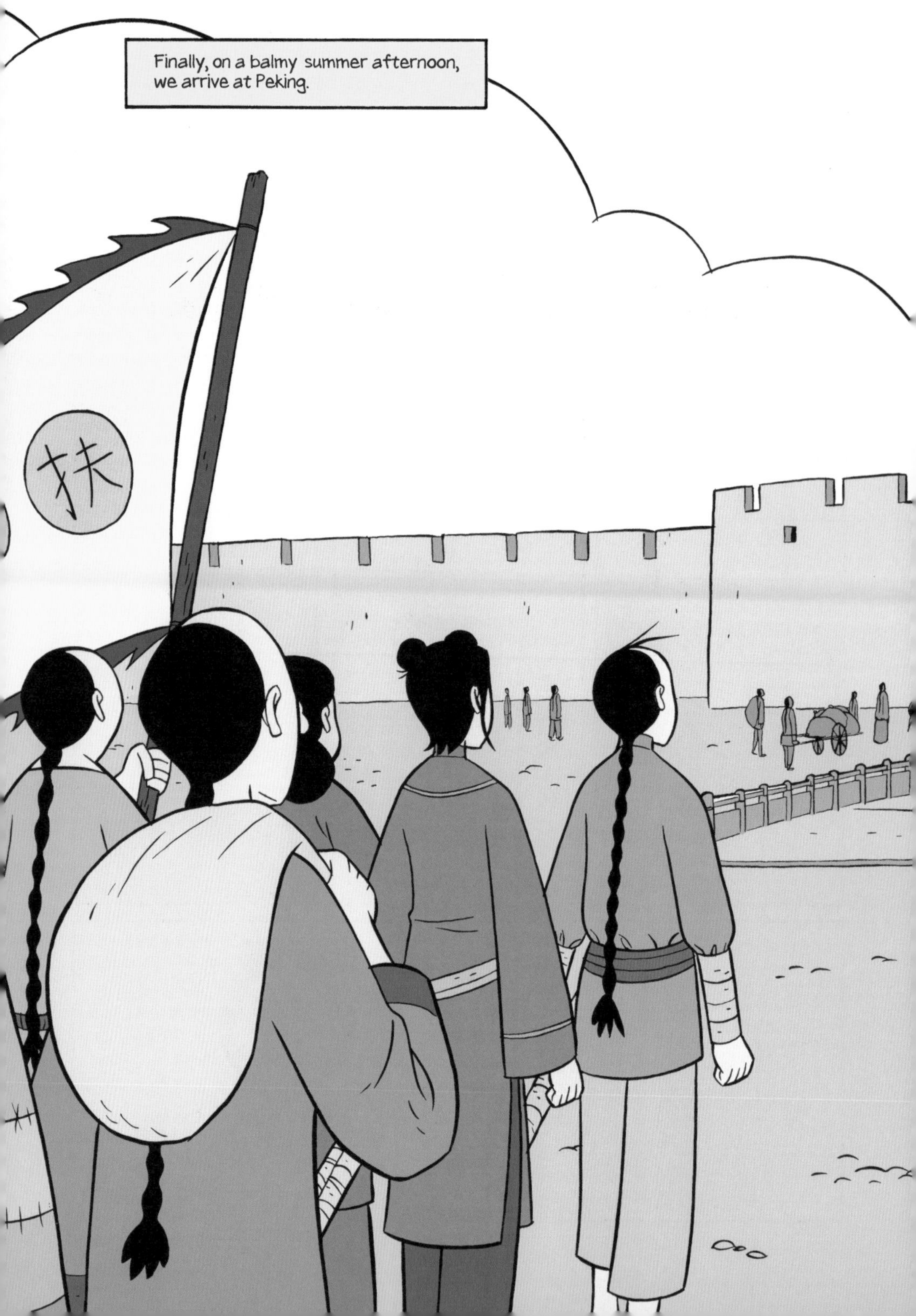
Finally, on a balmy summer afternoon, we arrive at Peking.
扶

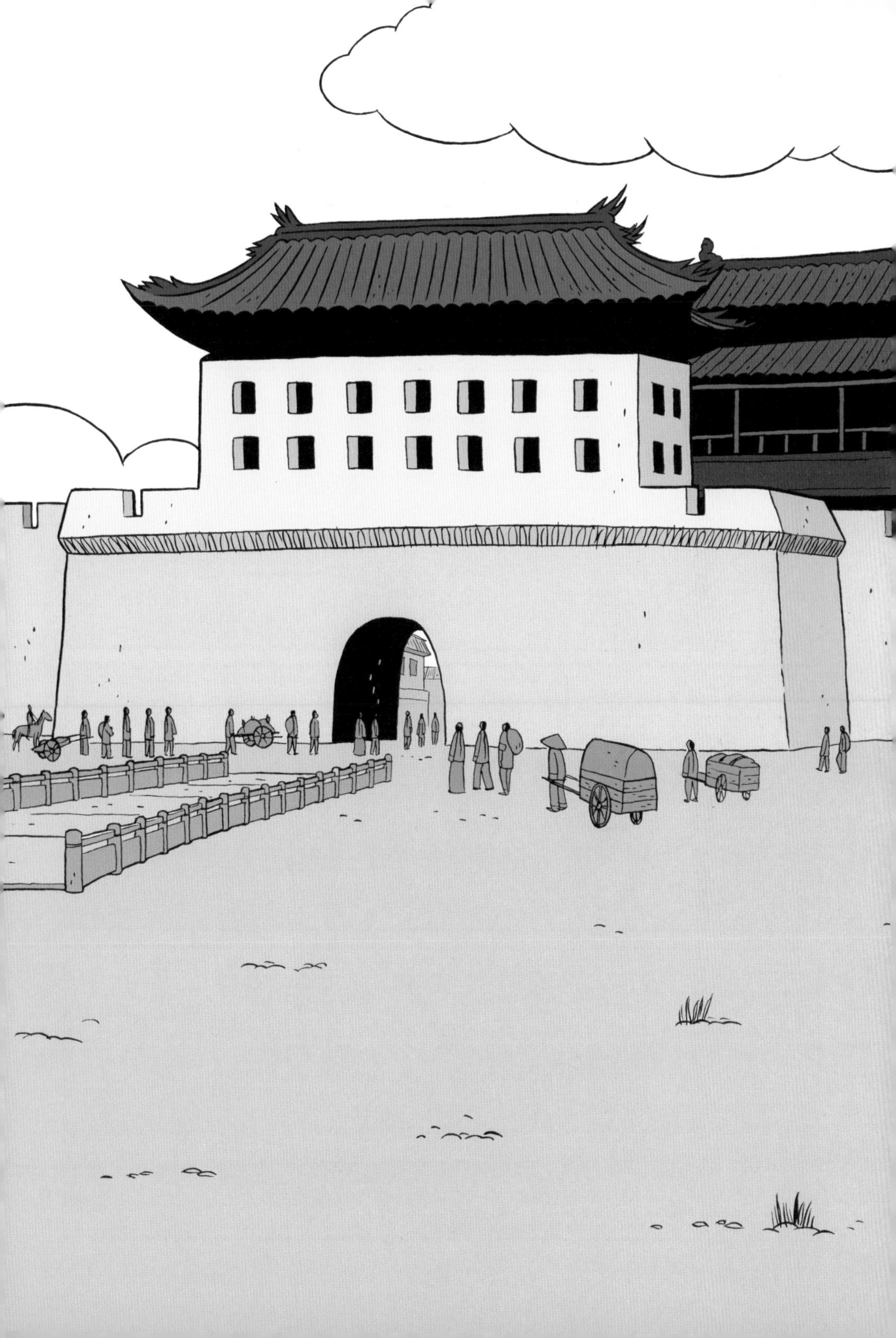

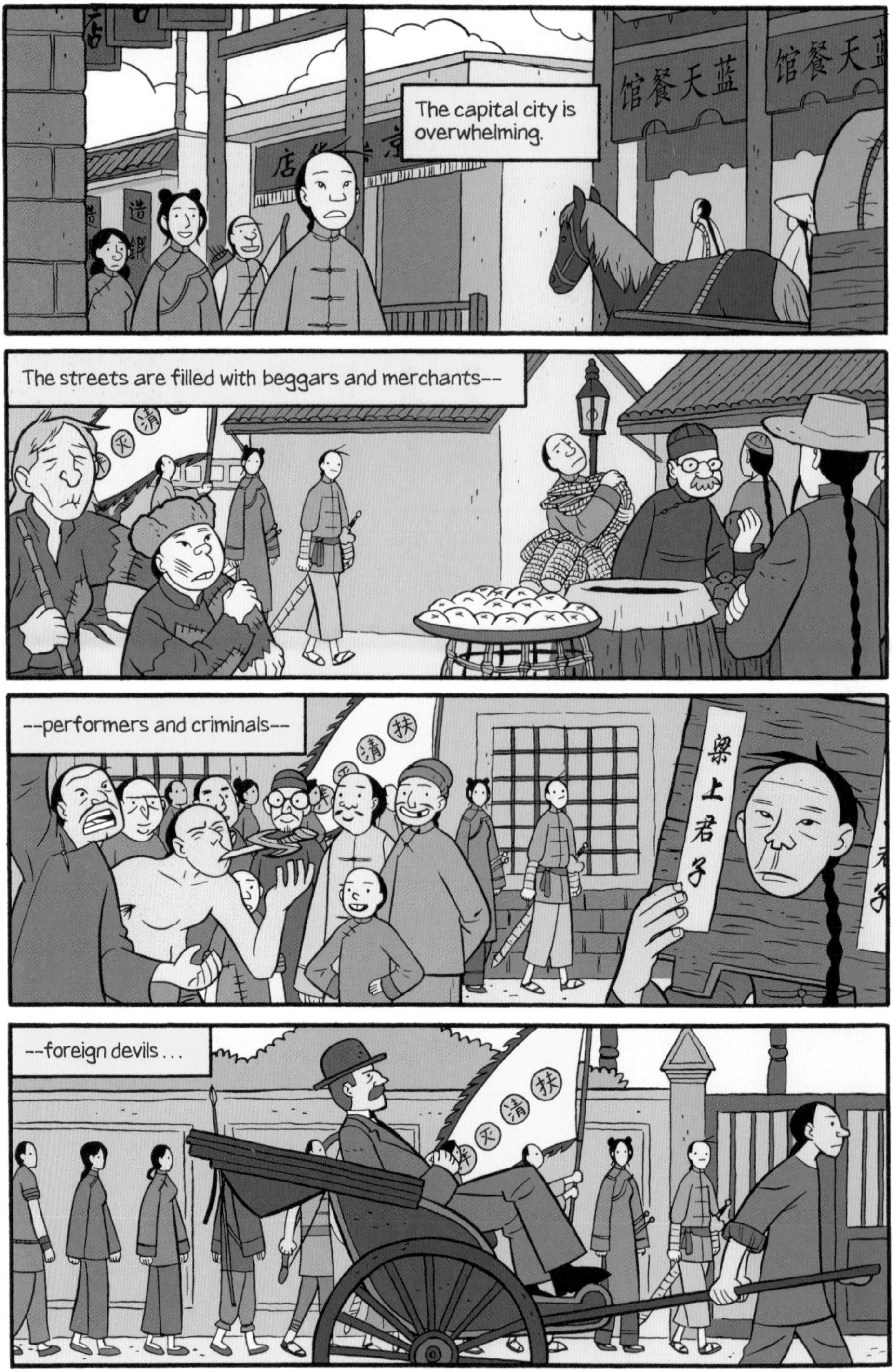
蓝天餐馆
The capital city is overwhelming.
The streets are filled with beggars and merchants--
--performers and criminals--
梁上君子
--foreign devils . . .

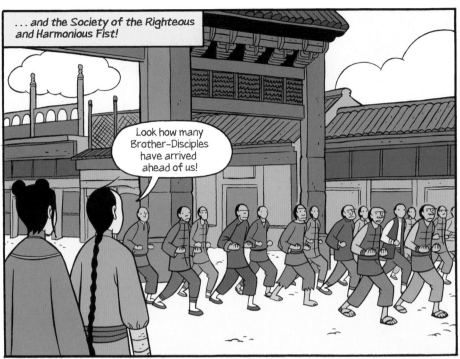

... and the *Society of the Righteous and Harmonious Fist!*

Look how many Brother-Disciples have arrived ahead of us!

I don't recognize any of them!

It's as if every man in the entire countryside has joined us!

Ow!

WAP!

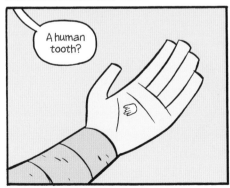

A human tooth?

Bing Wong-bing!

Little Bao!

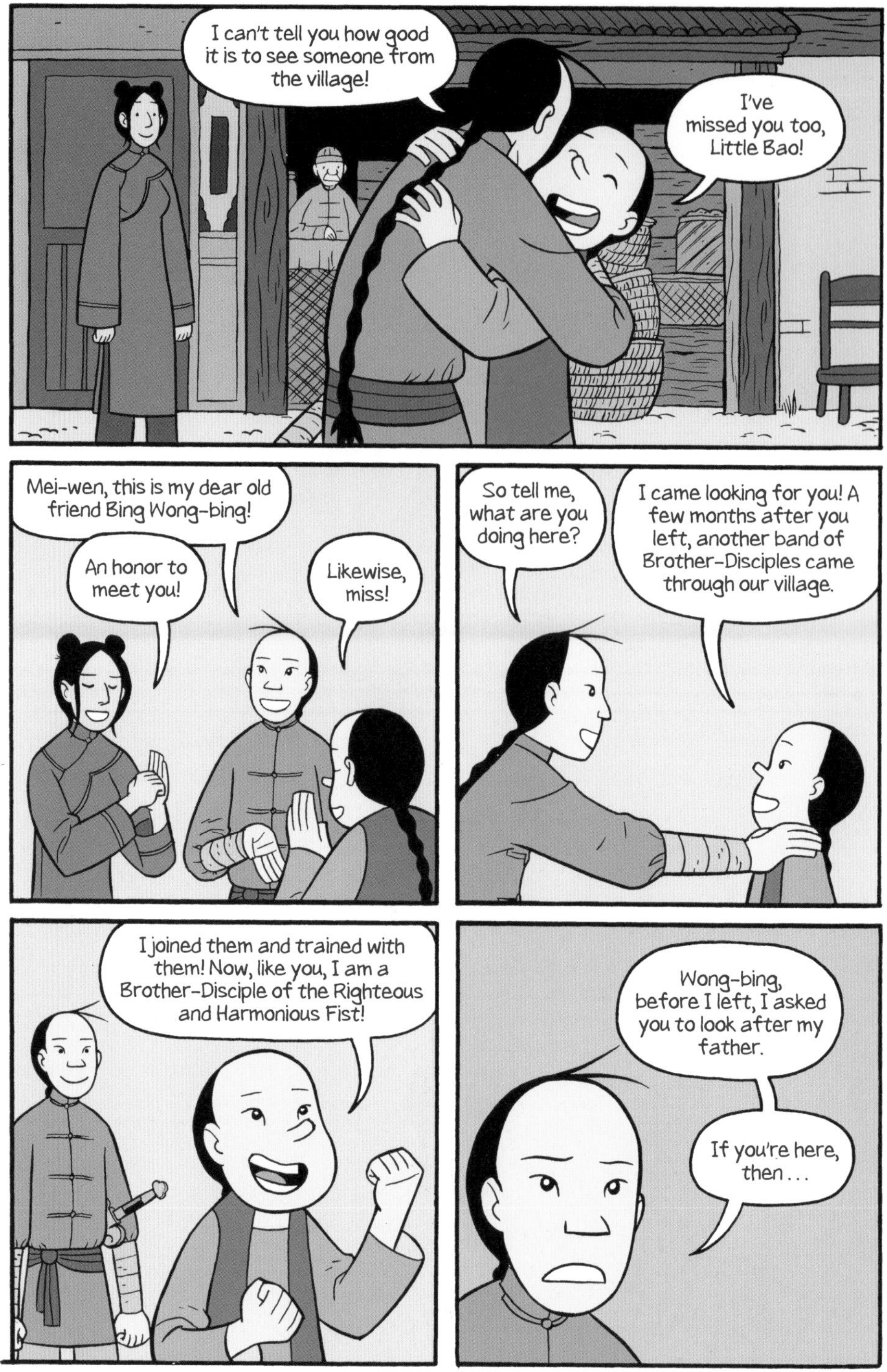
I can't tell you how good it is to see someone from the village!
I've missed you too, Little Bao!
Mei-wen, this is my dear old friend Bing Wong-bing!
An honor to meet you!
Likewise, miss!
So tell me, what are you doing here?
I came looking for you! A few months after you left, another band of Brother-Disciples came through our village.
I joined them and trained with them! Now, like you, I am a Brother-Disciple of the Righteous and Harmonious Fist!
Wong-bing, before I left, I asked you to look after my father.
If you're here, then...

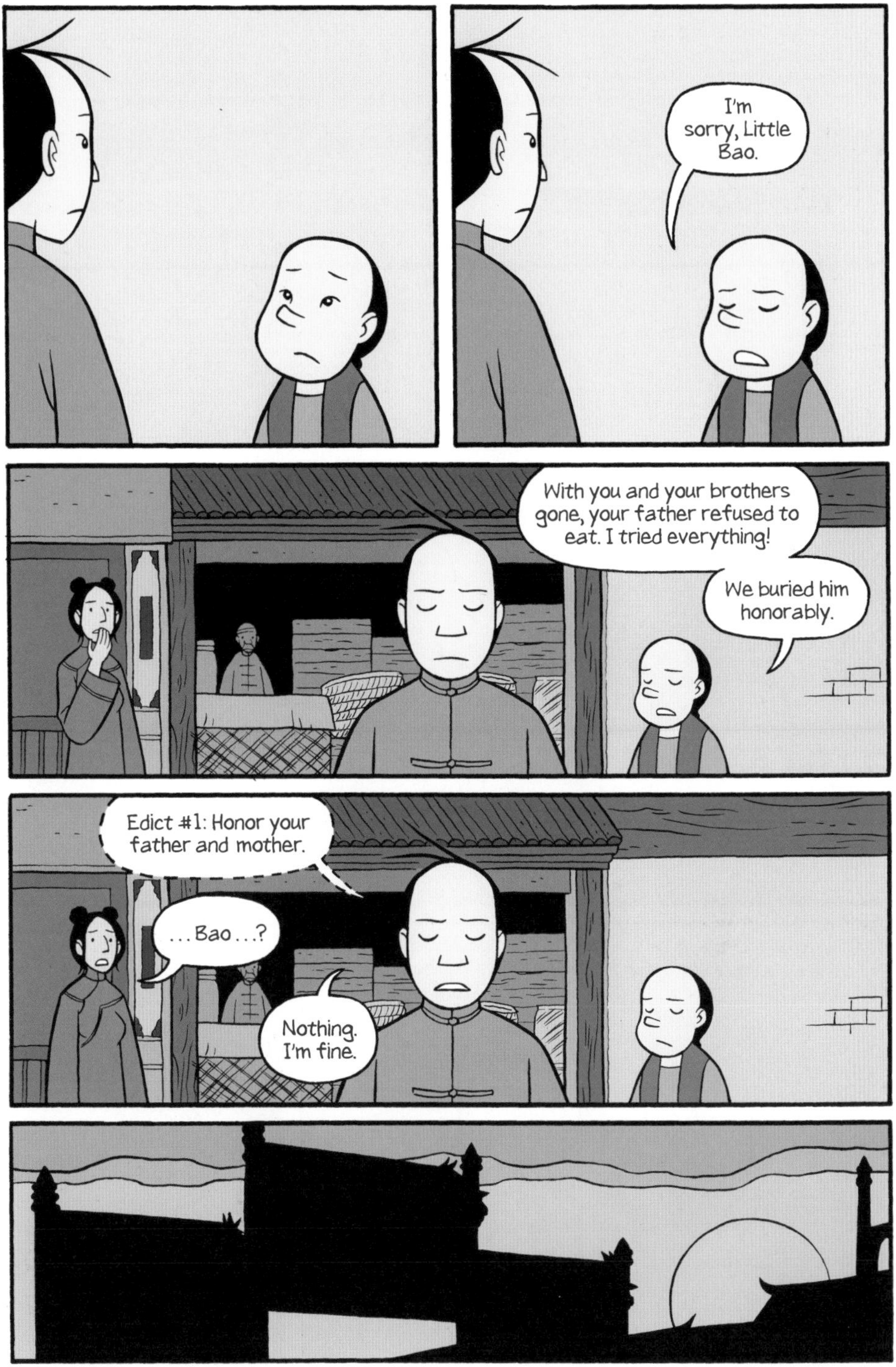
I'm sorry, Little Bao.
With you and your brothers gone, your father refused to eat. I tried everything!
We buried him honorably.
Edict #1: Honor your father and mother.
...Bao...?
Nothing. I'm fine.

That night, Lu Pai introduces us to an acquaintance of his.

Prince Tuan is a very, very important man! You are all very, very lucky he's agreed to put us up for the night!

Bow lower, Brother-Disciples! Lower!

Please! No need for such formalities! As I told the Brother-Disciples who arrived before you--

--it is my honor to serve the Society of the Right-eous and Harmonious Fist, *SAVIORS OF CHINA!*

Prince Tuan quarters the Brother-Disciples in the east wing of his home and the Red Lanterns in the west wing.

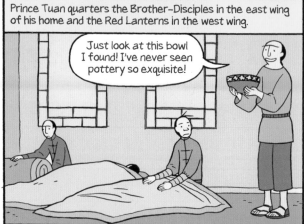

Just look at this bowl I found! I've never seen pottery so exquisite!

Imagine eating hot noodle soup out of this! Mm! Such luxury!

Put that down! That's no bowl! That's a bedpan!

!

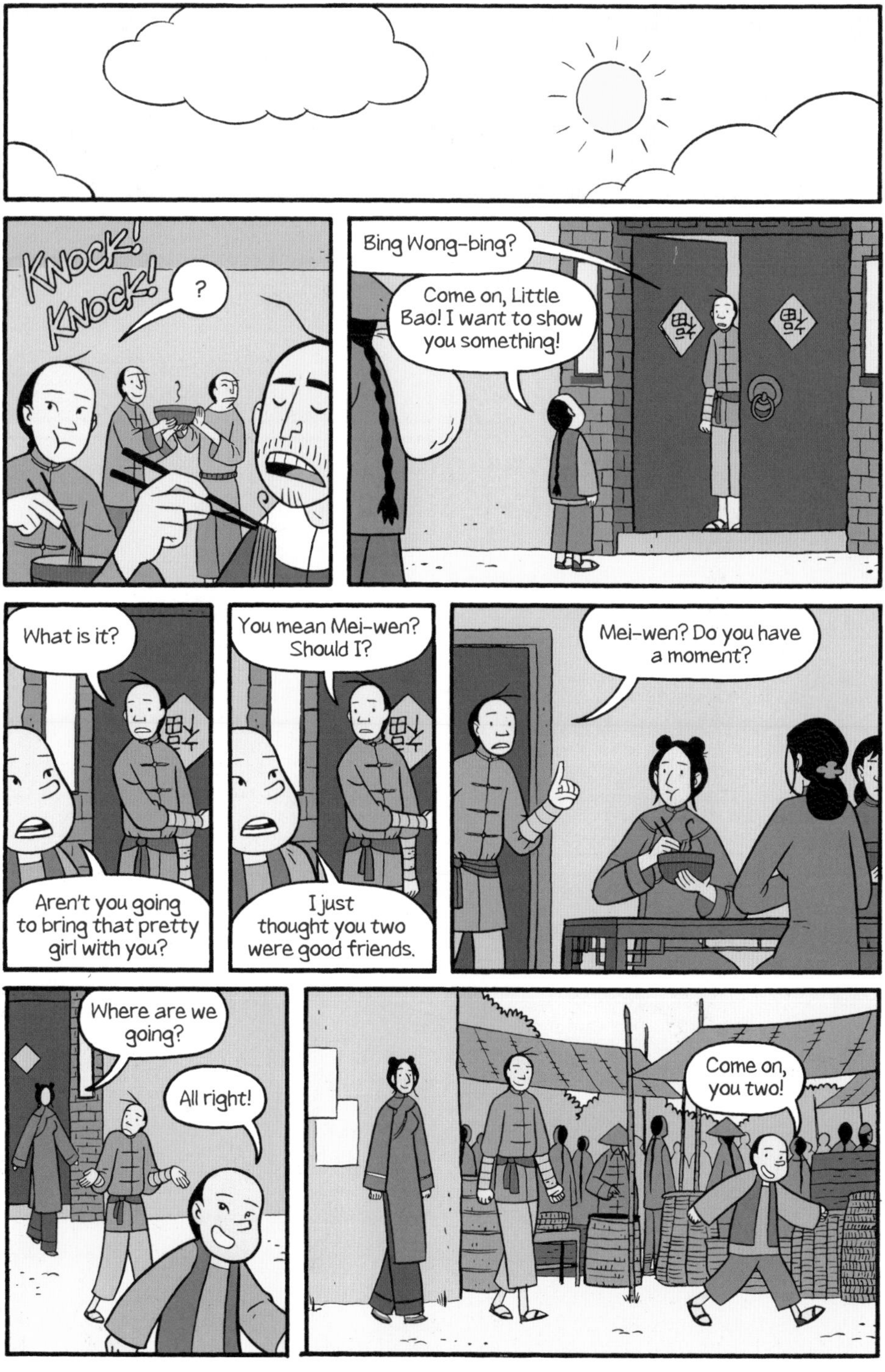
KNOCK! KNOCK!
?
Bing Wong-bing?
Come on, Little Bao! I want to show you something!
What is it?
Aren't you going to bring that pretty girl with you?
You mean Mei-wen? Should I?
I just thought you two were good friends.
Mei-wen? Do you have a moment?
Where are we going?
All right!
Come on, you two!

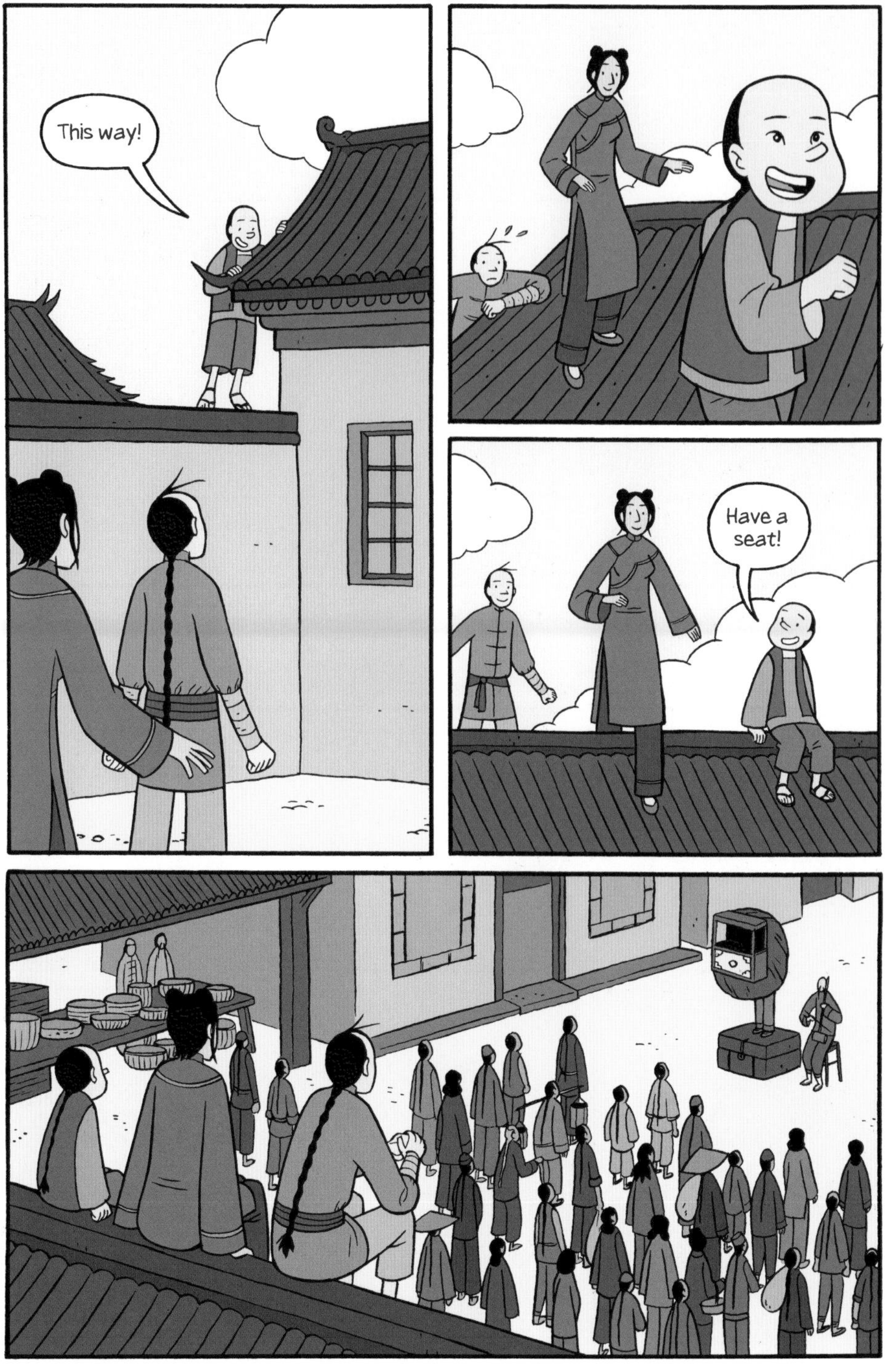
This way!
Have a seat!

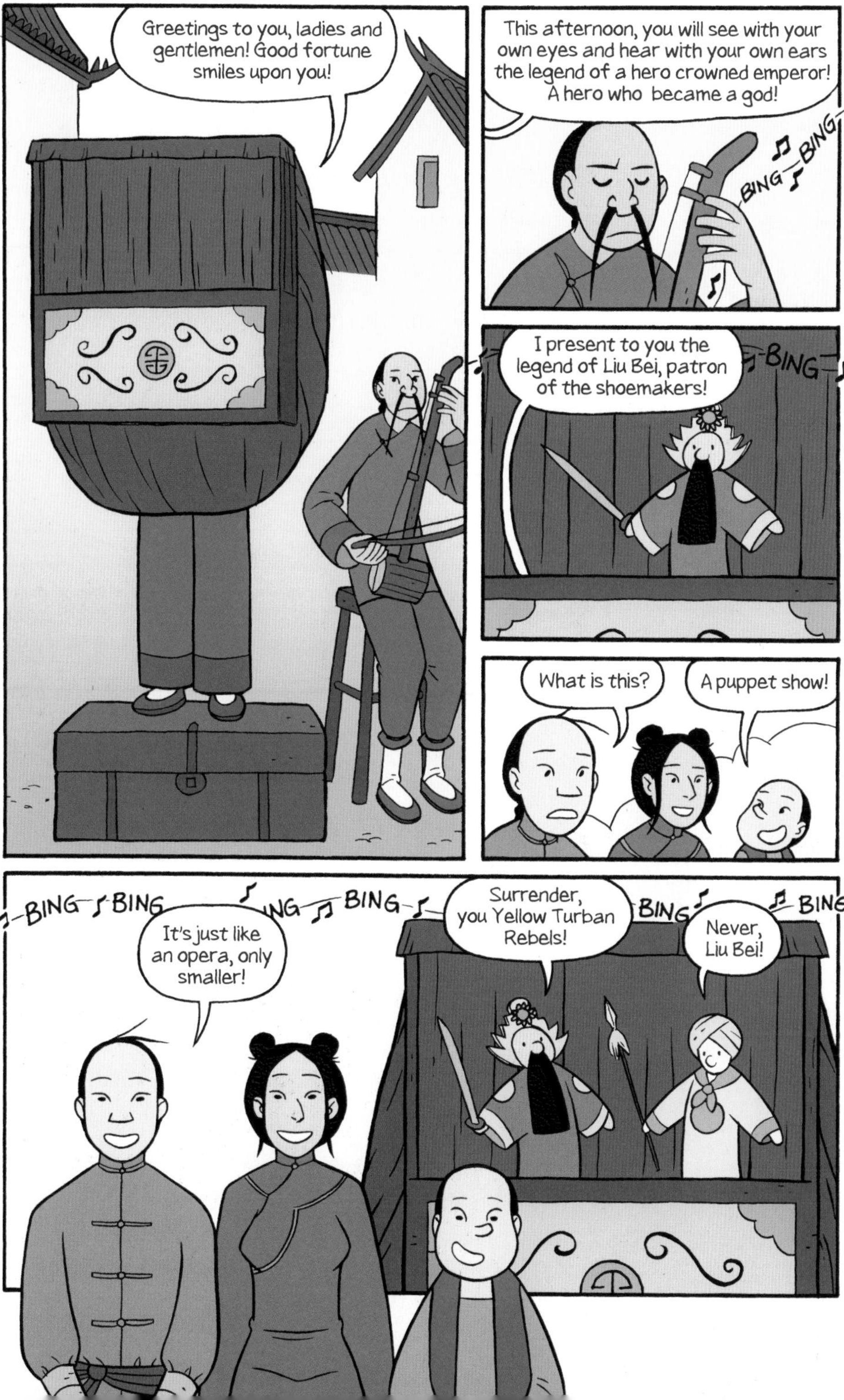
Greetings to you, ladies and gentlemen! Good fortune smiles upon you!
This afternoon, you will see with your own eyes and hear with your own ears the legend of a hero crowned emperor! A hero who became a god!
BING BING
I present to you the legend of Liu Bei, patron of the shoemakers!
BING
What is this?
A puppet show!
BING BING
It's just like an opera, only smaller!
NG BING
Surrender, you Yellow Turban Rebels!
BING
Never, Liu Bei!
BING

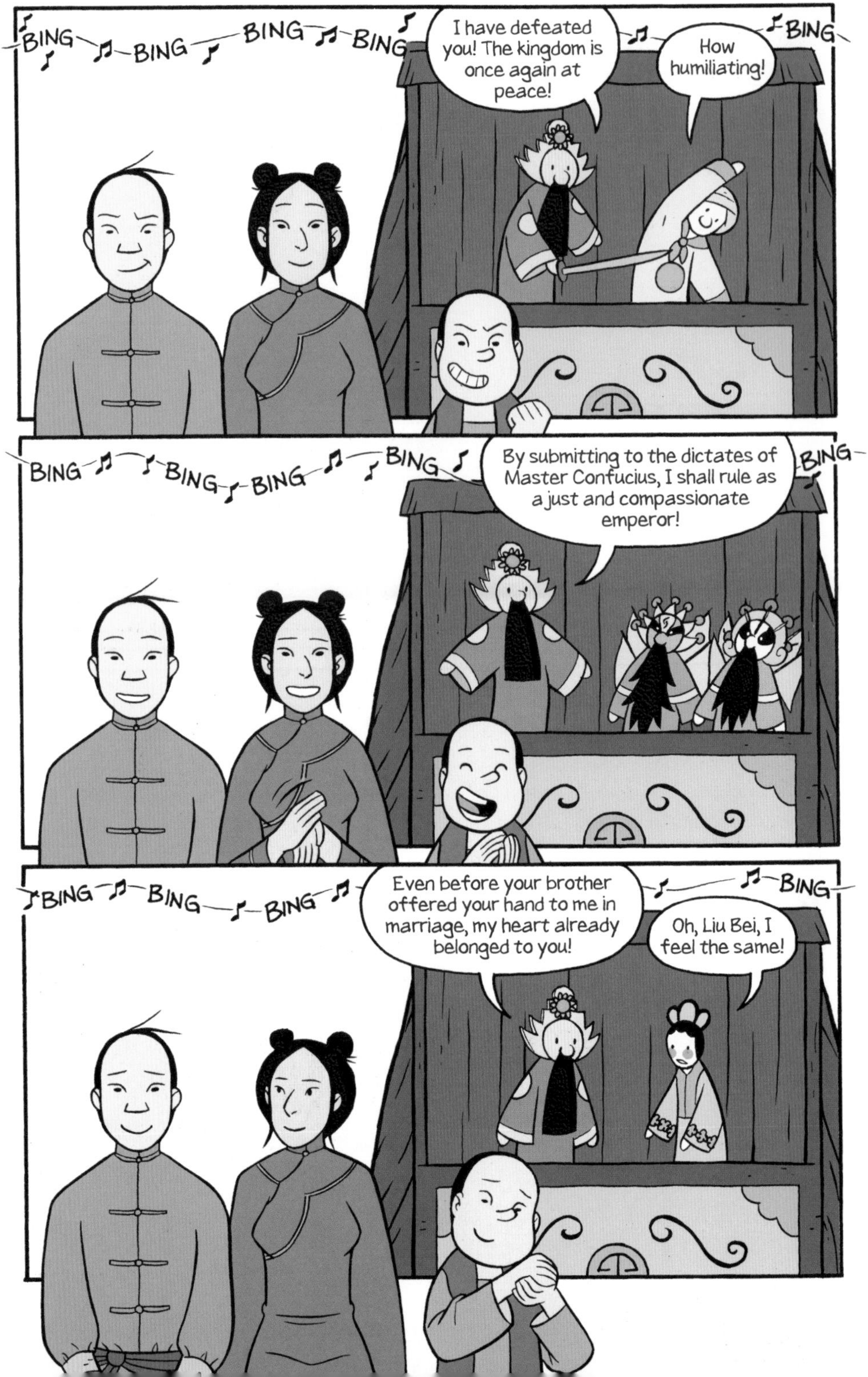
BING BING BING BING
I have defeated you! The kingdom is once again at peace!
How humiliating!
BING
BING BING BING BING
By submitting to the dictates of Master Confucius, I shall rule as a just and compassionate emperor!
BING
BING BING BING
Even before your brother offered your hand to me in marriage, my heart already belonged to you!
Oh, Liu Bei, I feel the same!
BING

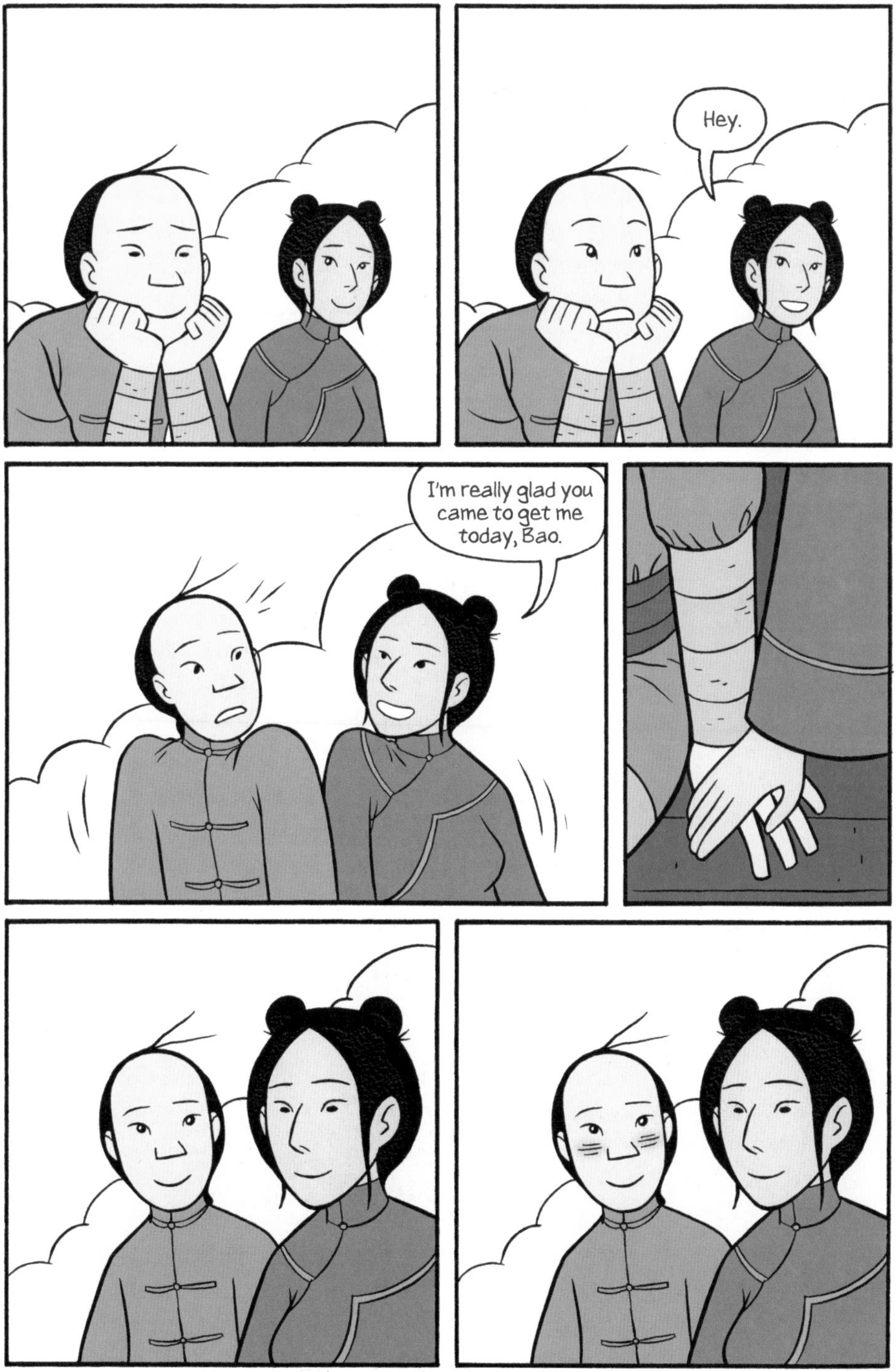
Hey.
I'm really glad you came to get me today, Bao.

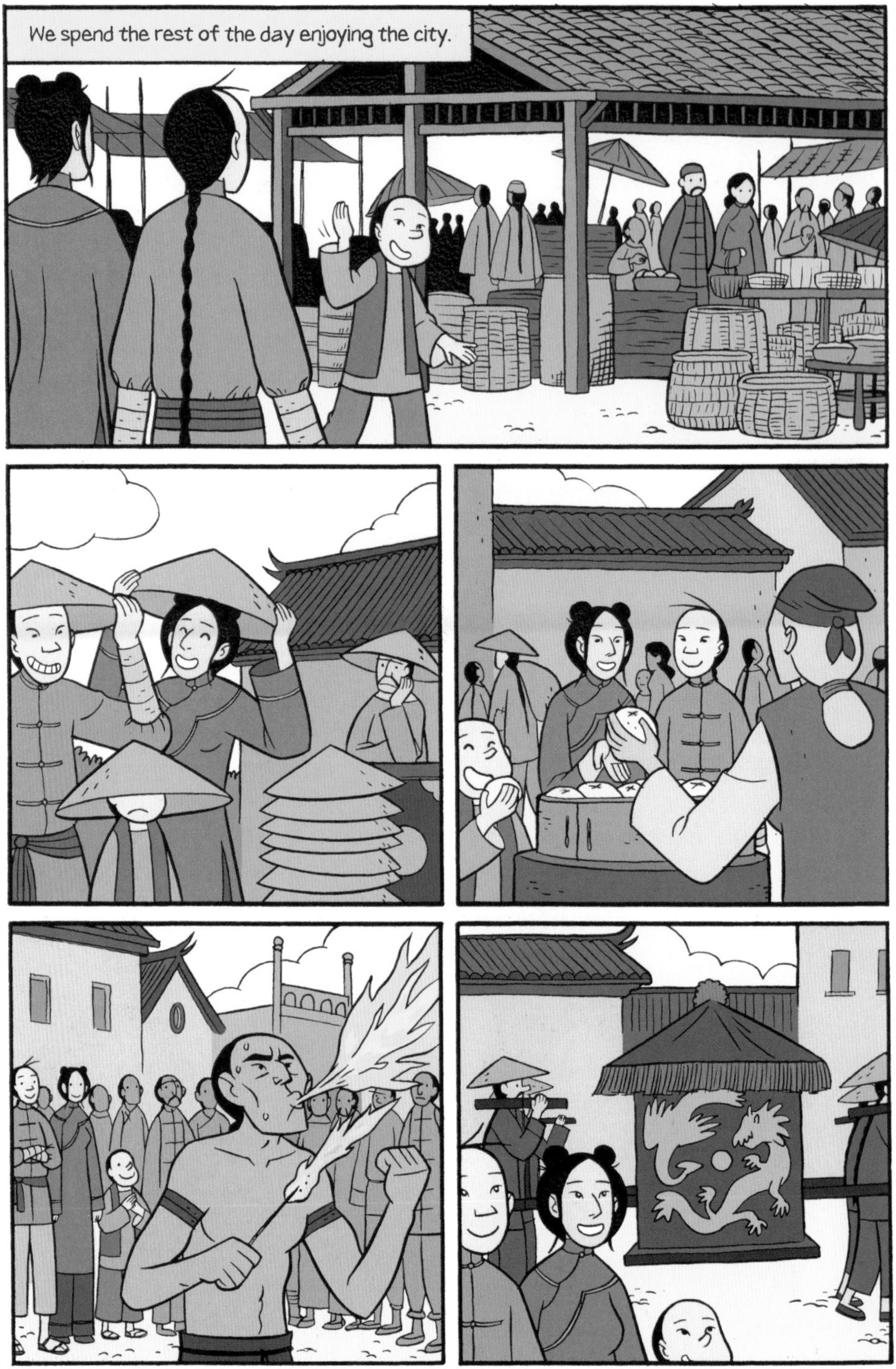
We spend the rest of the day enjoying the city.

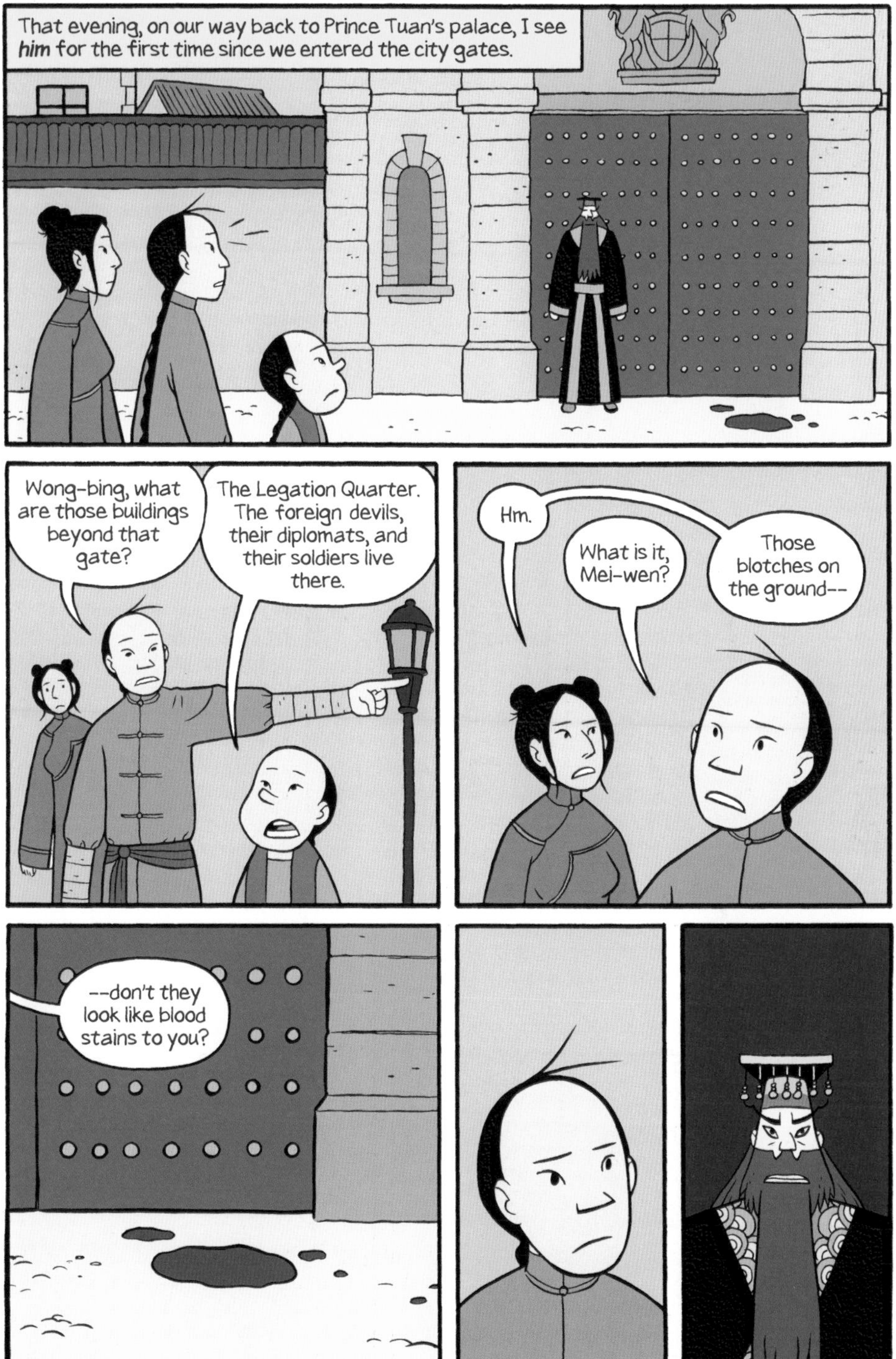
That evening, on our way back to Prince Tuan's palace, I see **him** for the first time since we entered the city gates.
Wong-bing, what are those buildings beyond that gate?
The Legation Quarter. The foreign devils, their diplomats, and their soldiers live there.
Hm.
What is it, Mei-wen?
Those blotches on the ground--
--don't they look like blood stains to you?

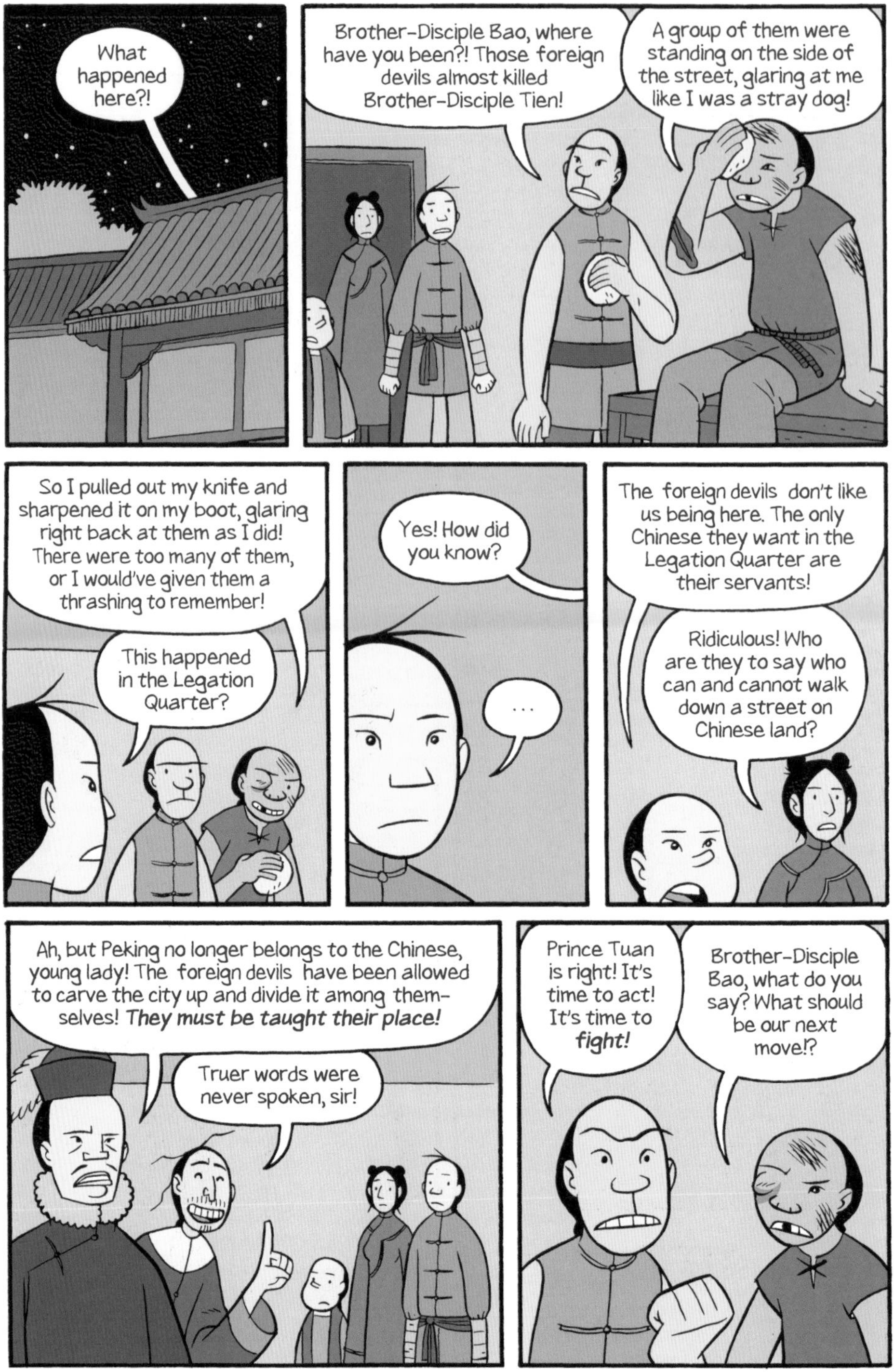
What happened here?!
Brother-Disciple Bao, where have you been?! Those foreign devils almost killed Brother-Disciple Tien!
A group of them were standing on the side of the street, glaring at me like I was a stray dog!
So I pulled out my knife and sharpened it on my boot, glaring right back at them as I did! There were too many of them, or I would've given them a thrashing to remember!
This happened in the Legation Quarter?
Yes! How did you know?
...
The foreign devils don't like us being here. The only Chinese they want in the Legation Quarter are their servants!
Ridiculous! Who are they to say who can and cannot walk down a street on Chinese land?
Ah, but Peking no longer belongs to the Chinese, young lady! The foreign devils have been allowed to carve the city up and divide it among them-selves! *They must be taught their place!*
Truer words were never spoken, sir!
Prince Tuan is right! It's time to act! It's time to ***fight!***
Brother-Disciple Bao, what do you say? What should be our next move!?

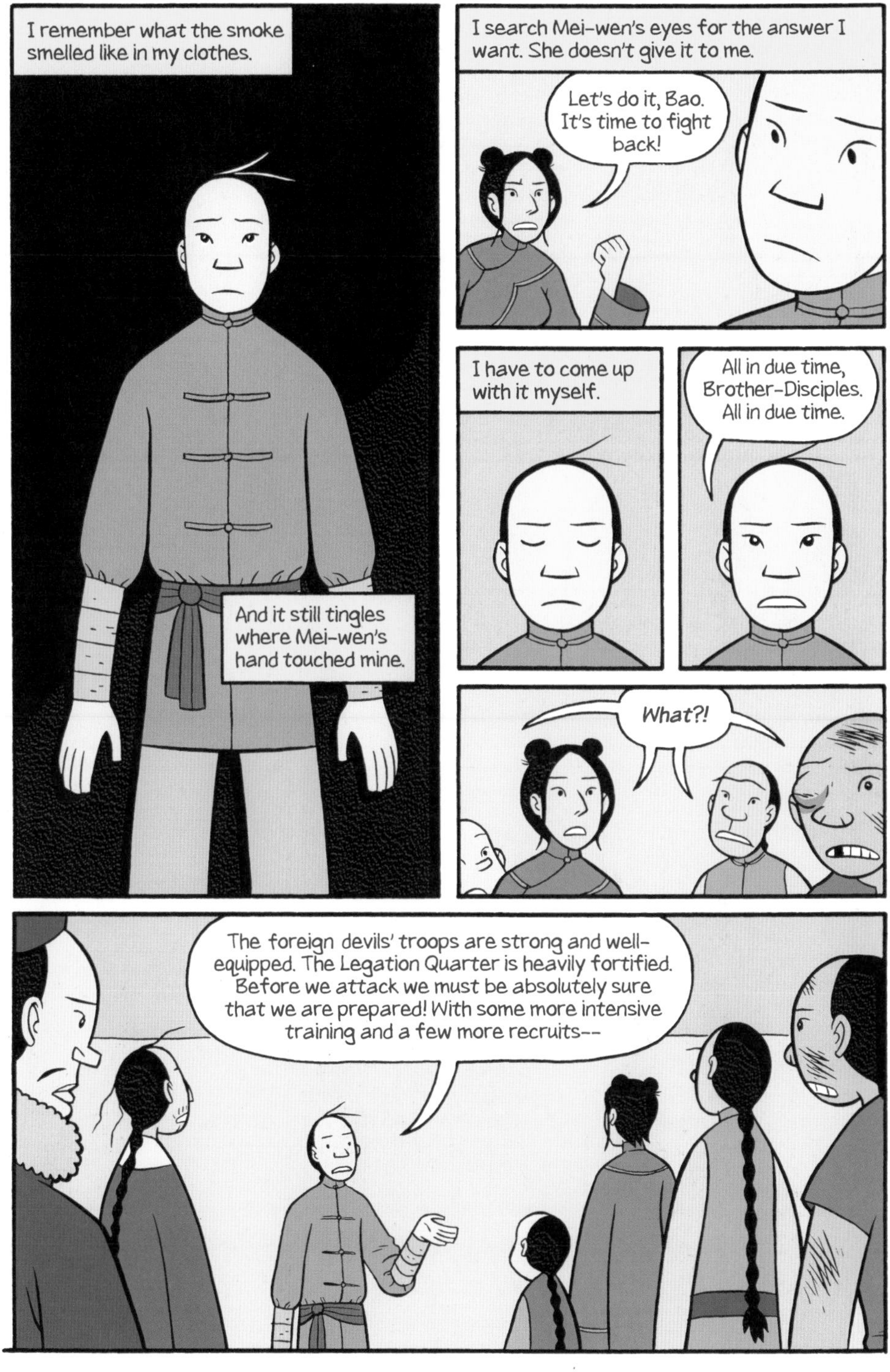
I remember what the smoke smelled like in my clothes.
And it still tingles where Mei-wen's hand touched mine.
I search Mei-wen's eyes for the answer I want. She doesn't give it to me.
Let's do it, Bao. It's time to fight back!
I have to come up with it myself.
All in due time, Brother-Disciples. All in due time.
What?!
The foreign devils' troops are strong and well-equipped. The Legation Quarter is heavily fortified. Before we attack we must be absolutely sure that we are prepared! With some more intensive training and a few more recruits--

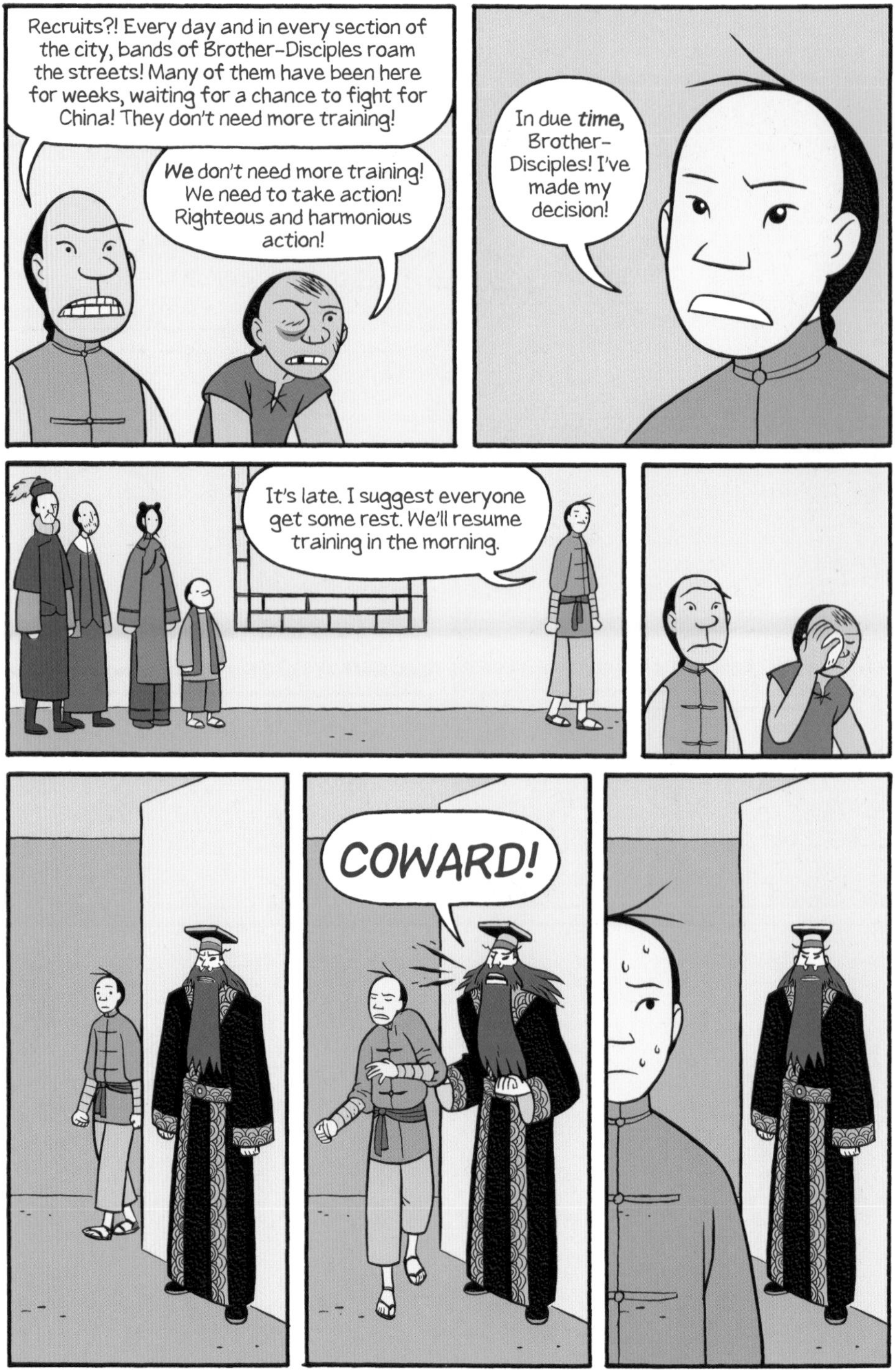
Recruits?! Every day and in every section of the city, bands of Brother-Disciples roam the streets! Many of them have been here for weeks, waiting for a chance to fight for China! They don't need more training!
We don't need more training! We need to take action! Righteous and harmonious action!
In due time, Brother-Disciples! I've made my decision!
It's late. I suggest everyone get some rest. We'll resume training in the morning.
COWARD!

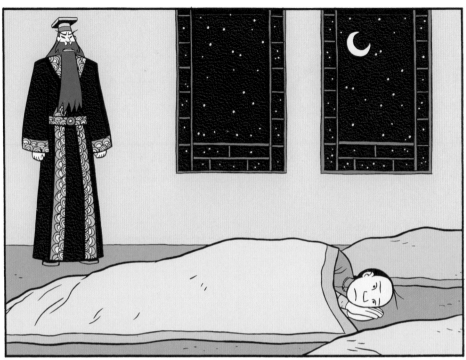

I know he's there.

I'm determined not to look at him.

But I still feel him.

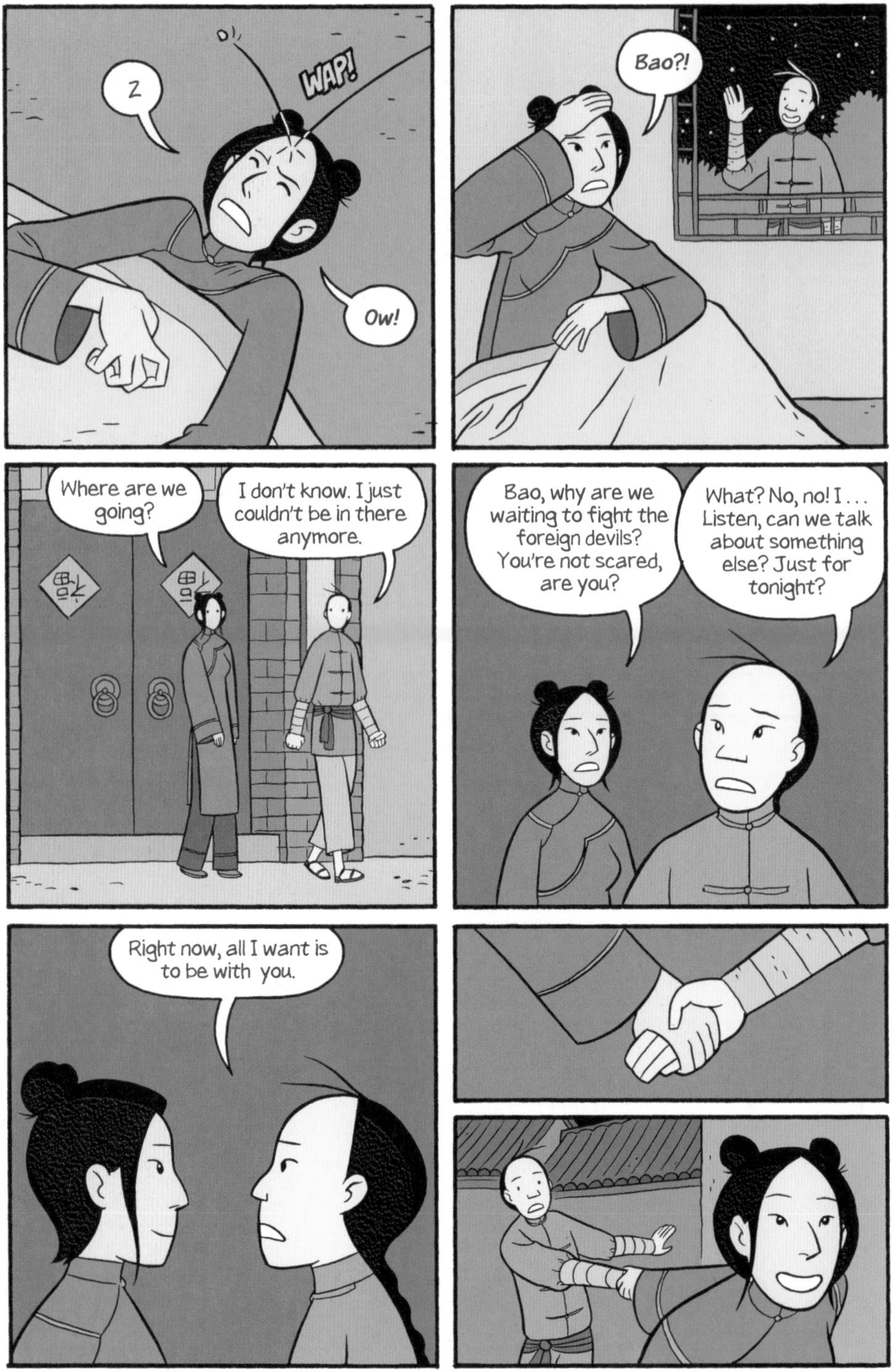
Z
WAP!
Ow!
Bao?!
Where are we going?
I don't know. I just couldn't be in there anymore.
Bao, why are we waiting to fight the foreign devils? You're not scared, are you?
What? No, no! I . . . Listen, can we talk about something else? Just for tonight?
Right now, all I want is to be with you.

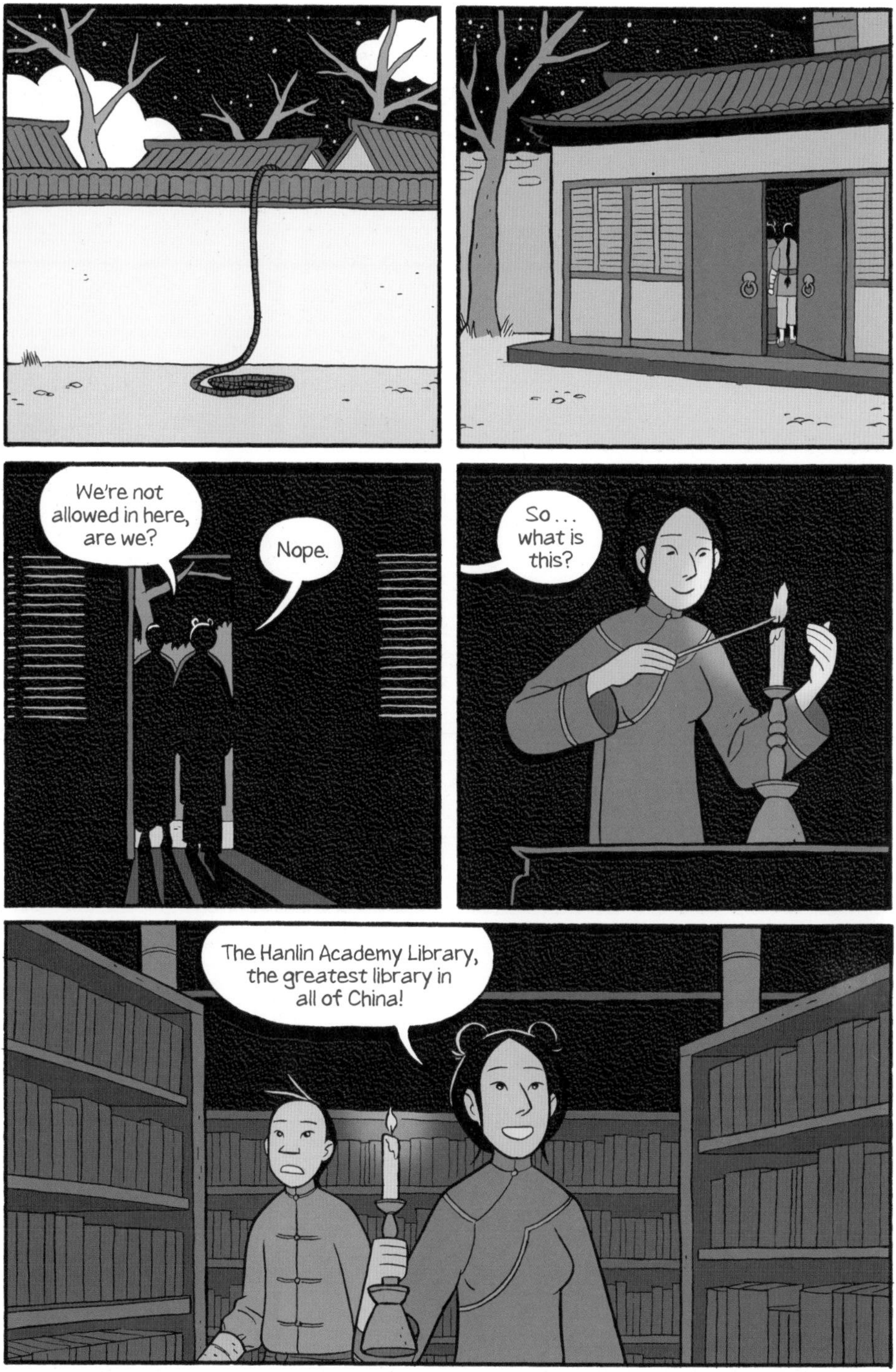
We're not allowed in here, are we?
Nope.
So... what is this?
The Hanlin Academy Library, the greatest library in all of China!

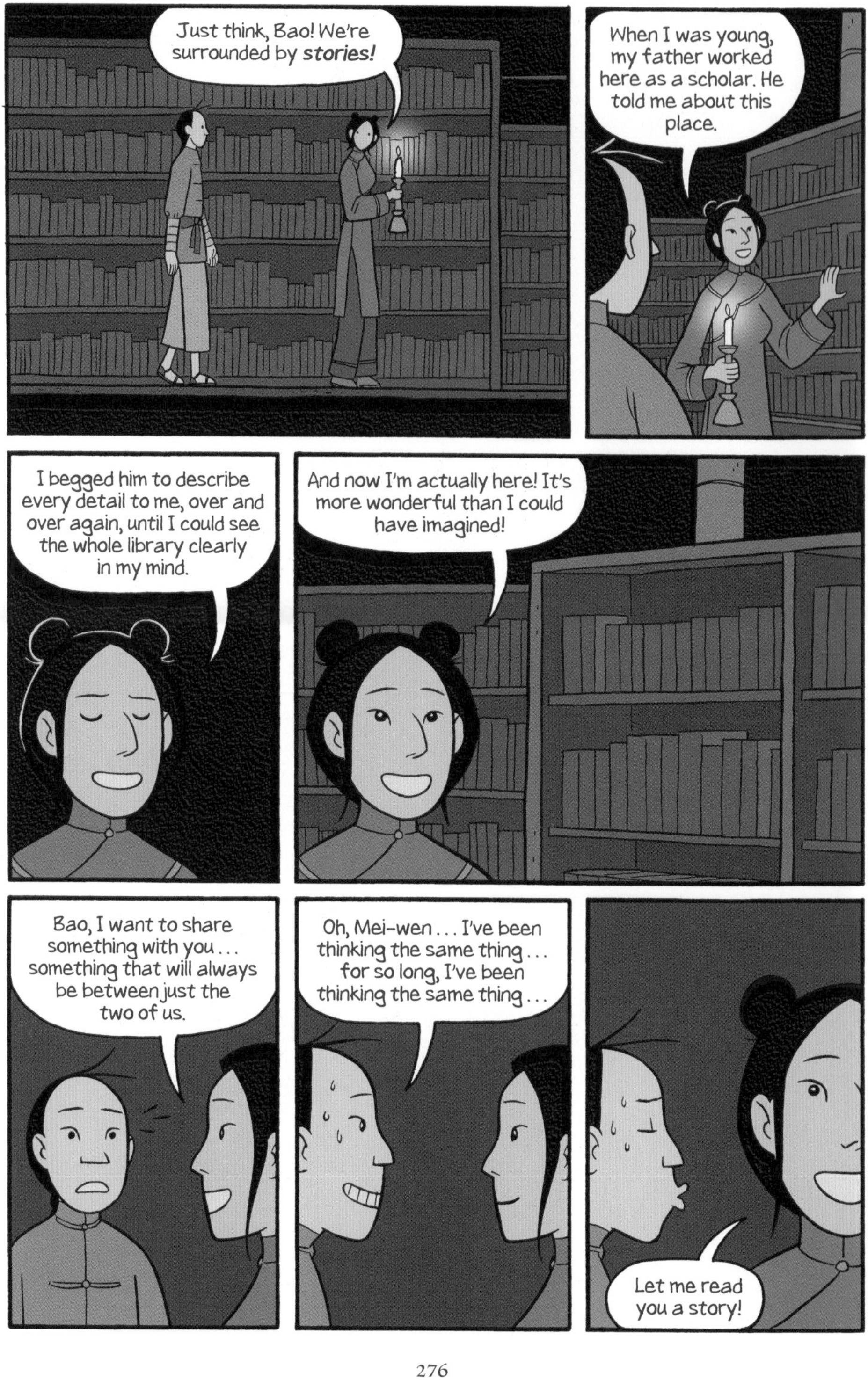
Just think, Bao! We're surrounded by **stories!**
When I was young, my father worked here as a scholar. He told me about this place.
I begged him to describe every detail to me, over and over again, until I could see the whole library clearly in my mind.
And now I'm actually here! It's more wonderful than I could have imagined!
Bao, I want to share something with you... something that will always be between just the two of us.
Oh, Mei-wen... I've been thinking the same thing... for so long, I've been thinking the same thing...
Let me read you a story!

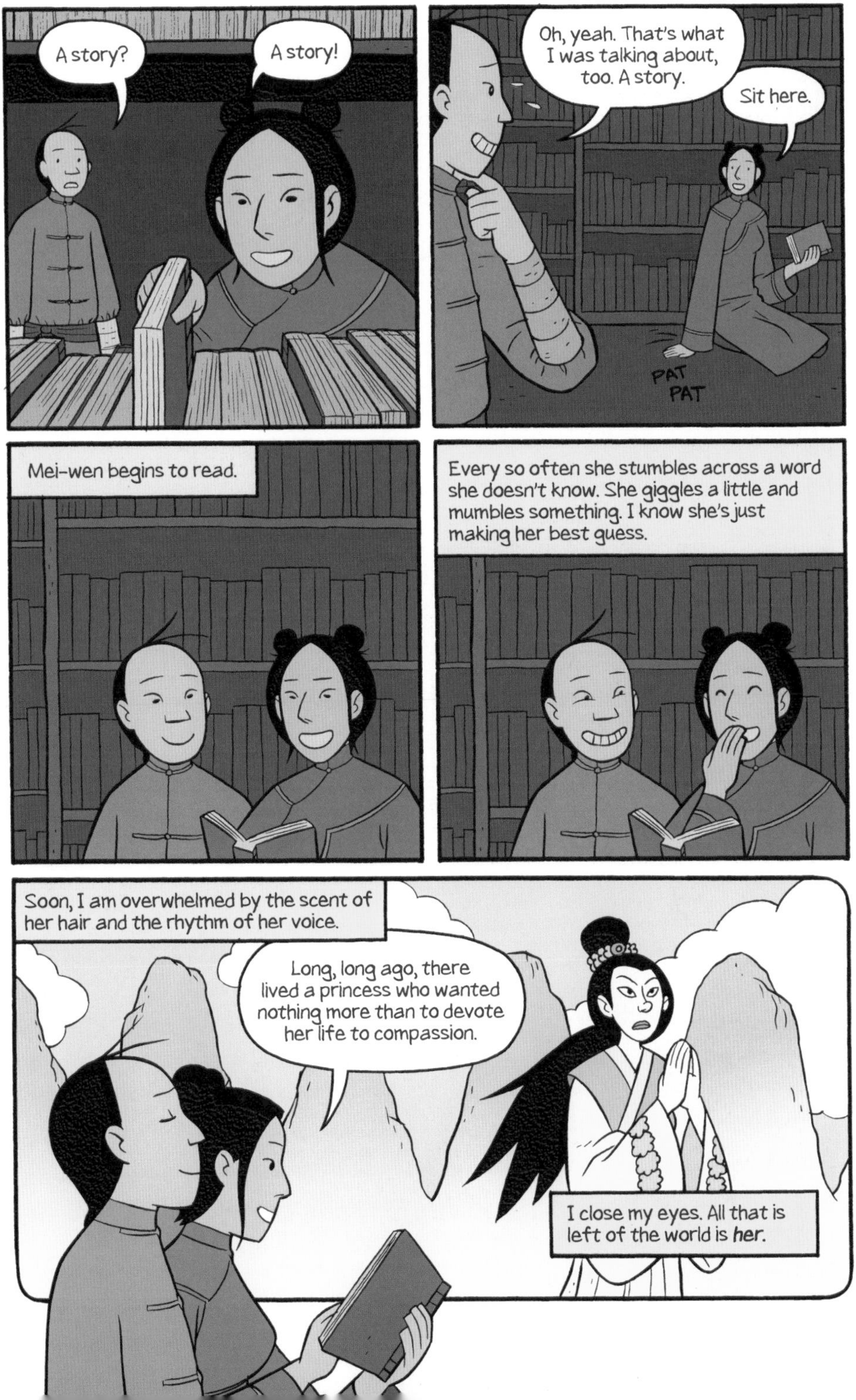
A story?
A story!
Oh, yeah. That's what I was talking about, too. A story.
Sit here.
PAT PAT
Mei-wen begins to read.
Every so often she stumbles across a word she doesn't know. She giggles a little and mumbles something. I know she's just making her best guess.
Soon, I am overwhelmed by the scent of her hair and the rhythm of her voice.
Long, long ago, there lived a princess who wanted nothing more than to devote her life to compassion.
I close my eyes. All that is left of the world is *her*.

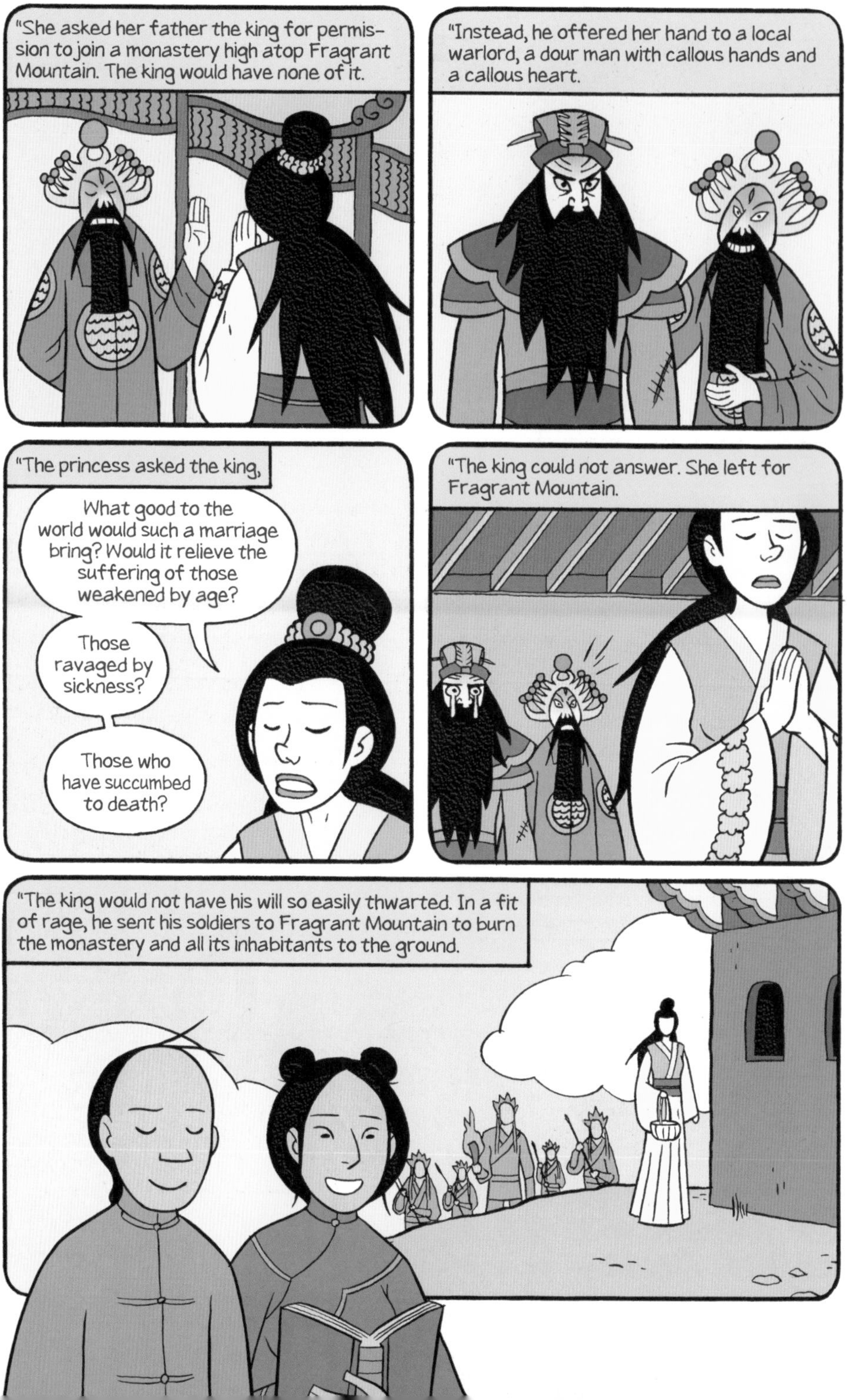

"She asked her father the king for permission to join a monastery high atop Fragrant Mountain. The king would have none of it.
"Instead, he offered her hand to a local warlord, a dour man with callous hands and a callous heart.
"The princess asked the king,
What good to the world would such a marriage bring? Would it relieve the suffering of those weakened by age?
Those ravaged by sickness?
Those who have succumbed to death?
"The king could not answer. She left for Fragrant Mountain.
"The king would not have his will so easily thwarted. In a fit of rage, he sent his soldiers to Fragrant Mountain to burn the monastery and all its inhabitants to the ground.

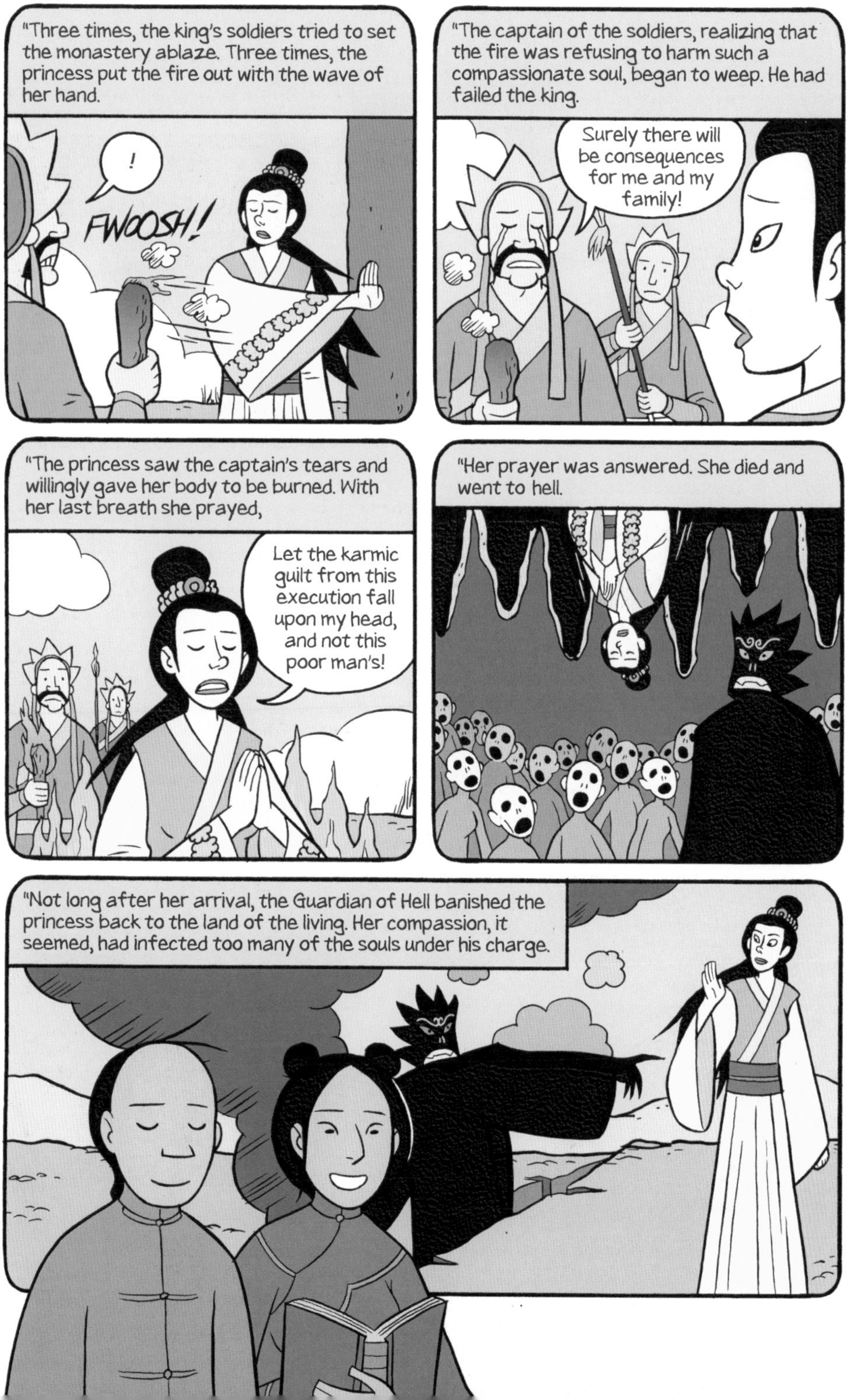
"Three times, the king's soldiers tried to set the monastery ablaze. Three times, the princess put the fire out with the wave of her hand.
!
FWOOSH!
"The captain of the soldiers, realizing that the fire was refusing to harm such a compassionate soul, began to weep. He had failed the king.
Surely there will be consequences for me and my family!
"The princess saw the captain's tears and willingly gave her body to be burned. With her last breath she prayed,
Let the karmic guilt from this execution fall upon my head, and not this poor man's!
"Her prayer was answered. She died and went to hell.
"Not long after her arrival, the Guardian of Hell banished the princess back to the land of the living. Her compassion, it seemed, had infected too many of the souls under his charge.

"She returned to Fragrant Mountain and took her place at the monastery.

"Years later, the king had grown old and weak. He suffered terribly from jaundice, and only a medicine made from the eyes and hands of a righteous person could relieve his pain.

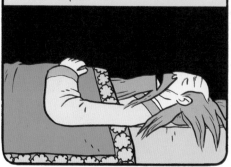

"News of the king's condition made its way to the princess. She went to the palace and offered her father what he needed.

"The king made a full recovery. When he learned the true identity of his benefactor, he made his way up to Fragrant Mountain to beg his daughter's forgiveness.

The king established a temple in his daughter's honor. The daughter became *Guan Yin,* the Goddess of Compassion -- the goddess with one thousand eyes to look for suffering and one thousand hands to relieve it.

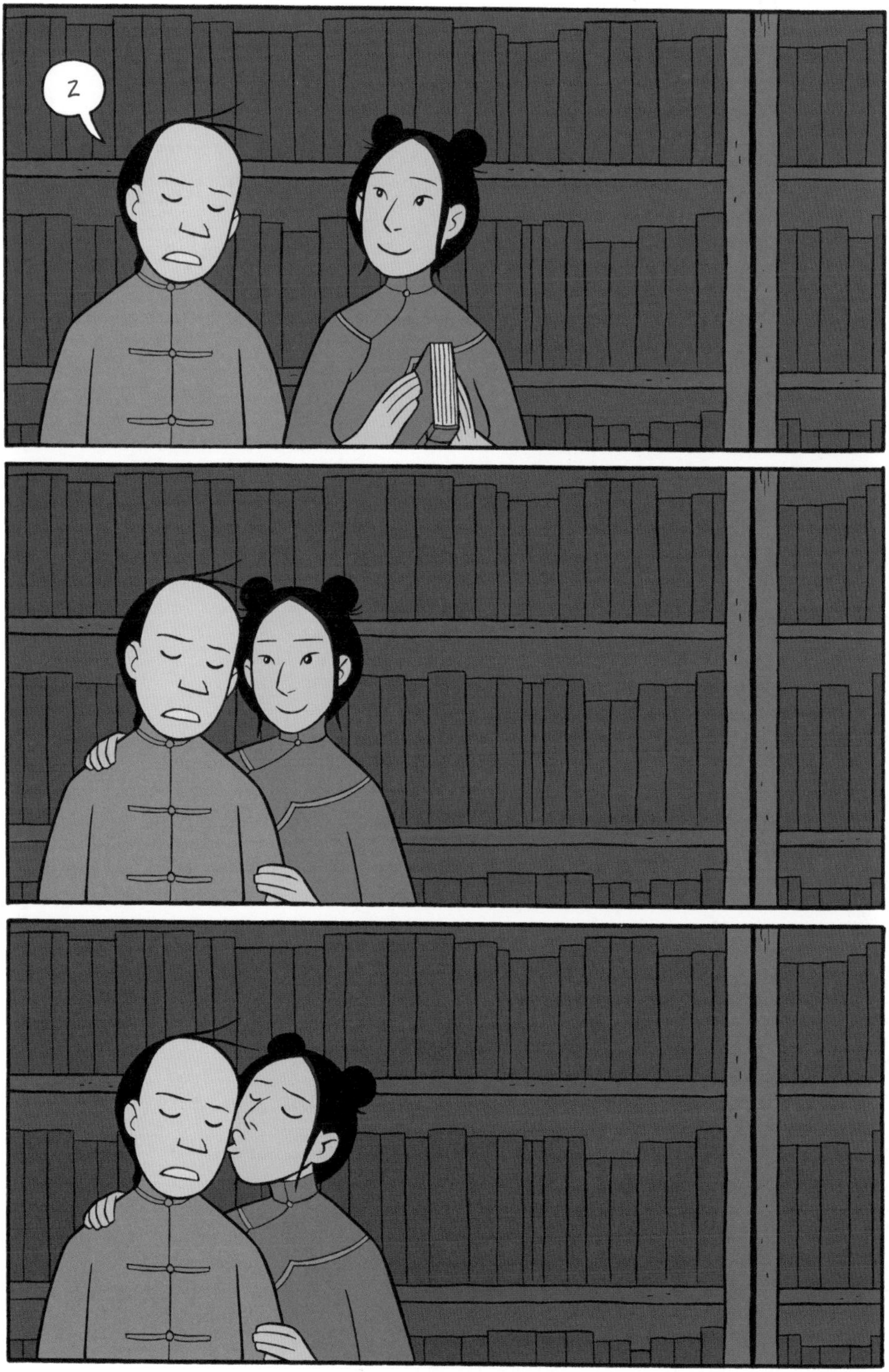
Z

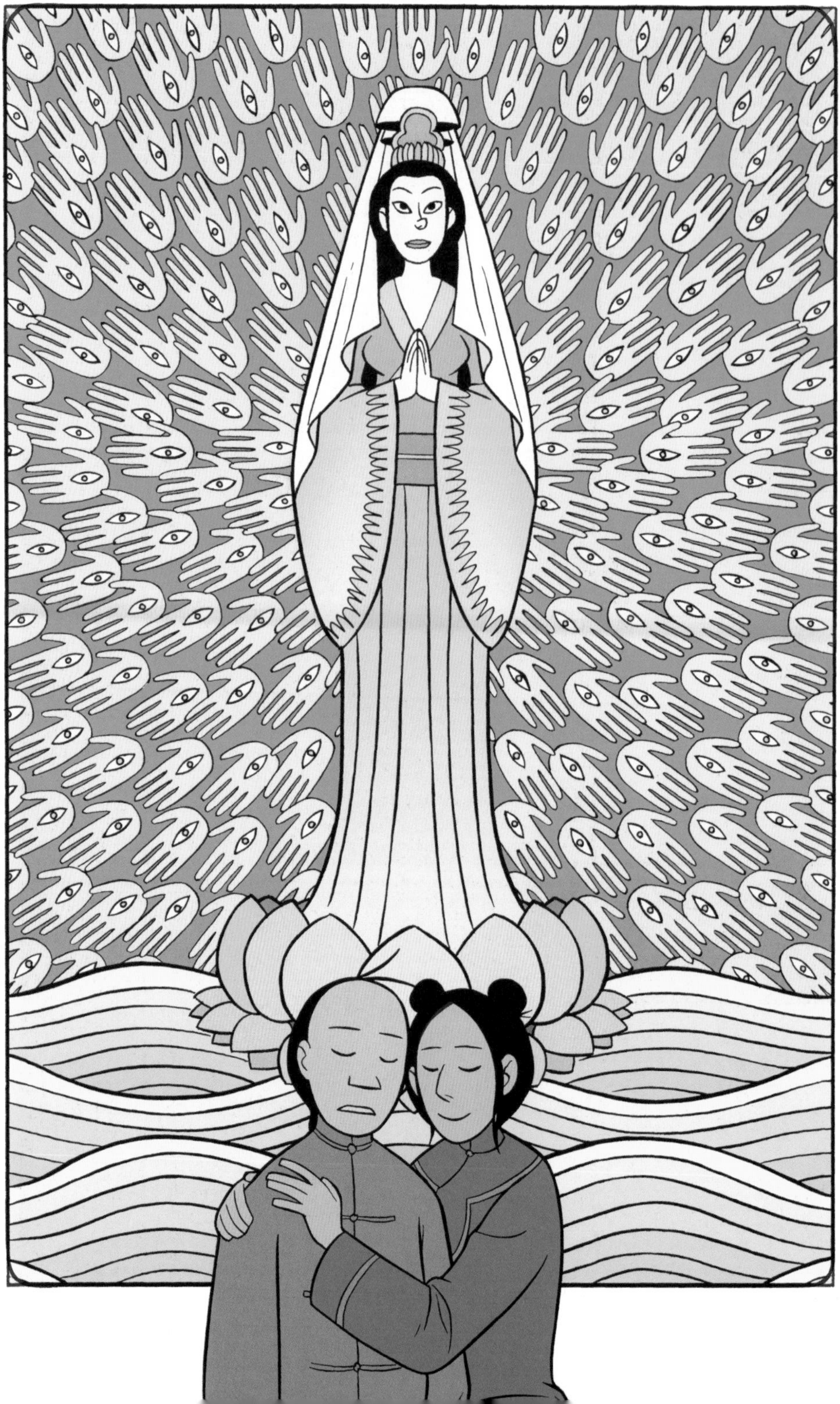

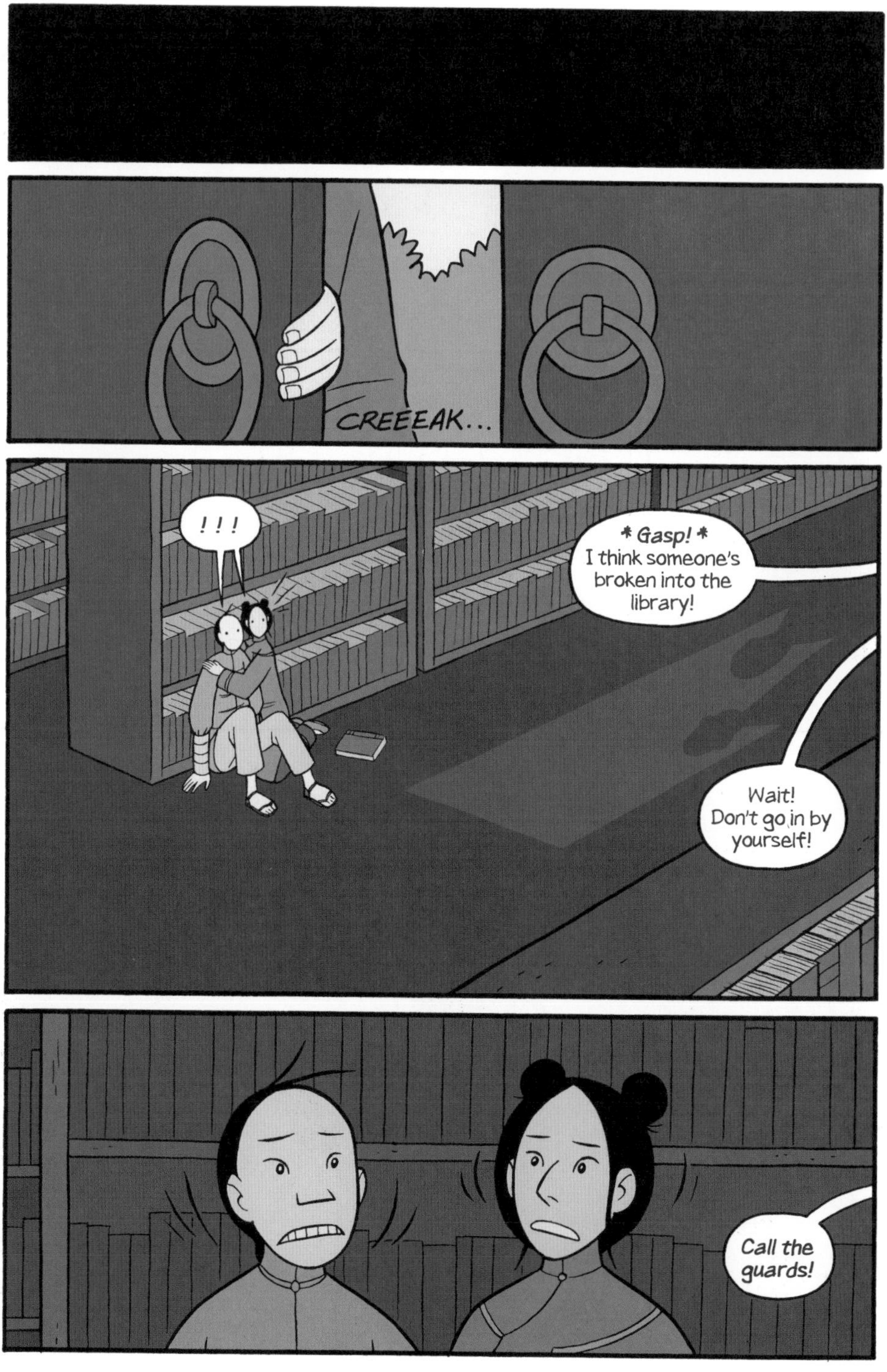

CREEEAK...
!!!
* Gasp! * I think someone's broken into the library!
Wait! Don't go in by yourself!
Call the guards!

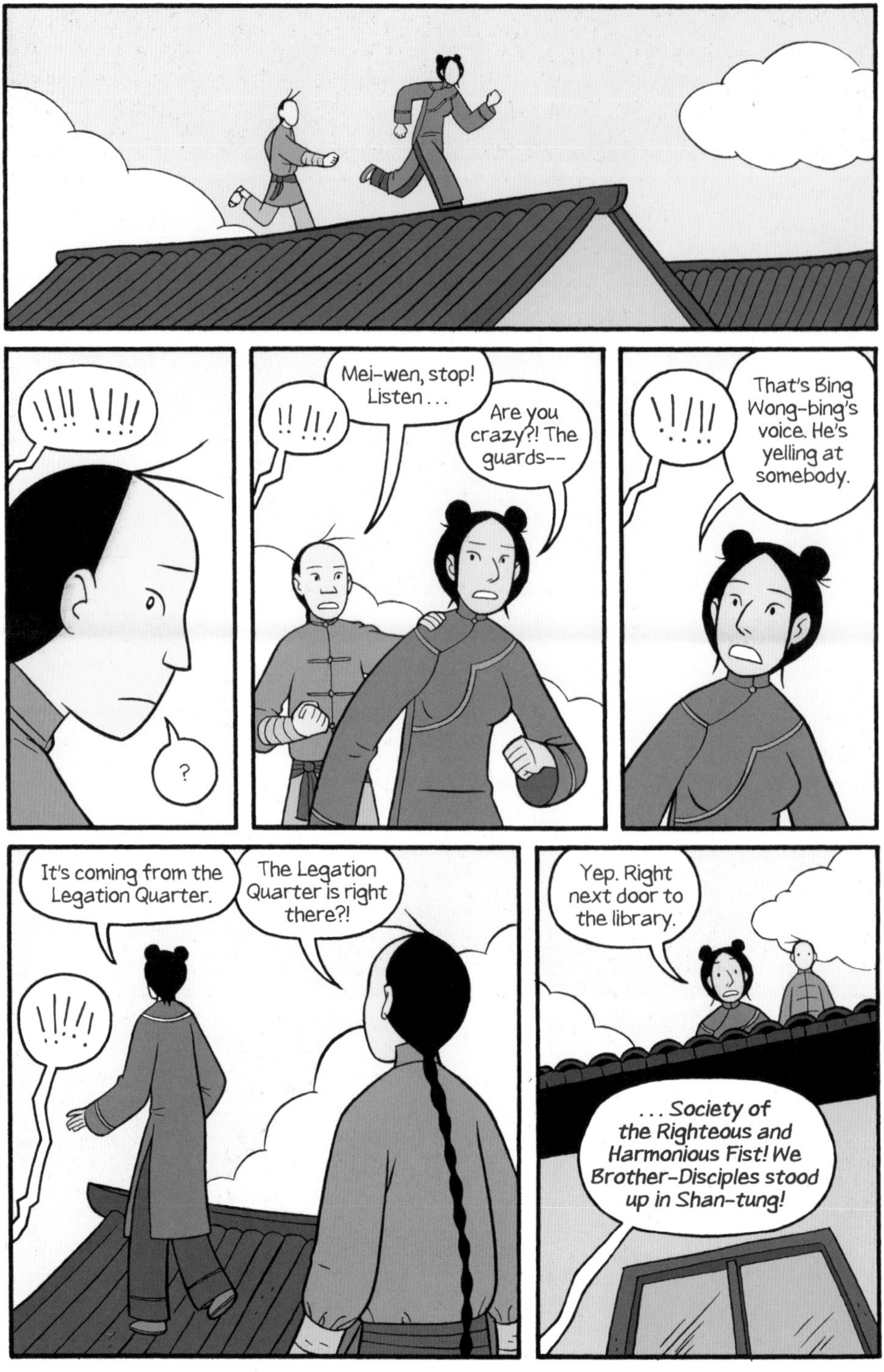

!!!! !!!!
?
!! !!!
Mei-wen, stop! Listen . . .
Are you crazy?! The guards--
!!!!
That's Bing Wong-bing's voice. He's yelling at somebody.
It's coming from the Legation Quarter.
The Legation Quarter is right there?!
!!!!
Yep. Right next door to the library.
. . . Society of the Righteous and Harmonious Fist! We Brother-Disciples stood up in Shan-tung!

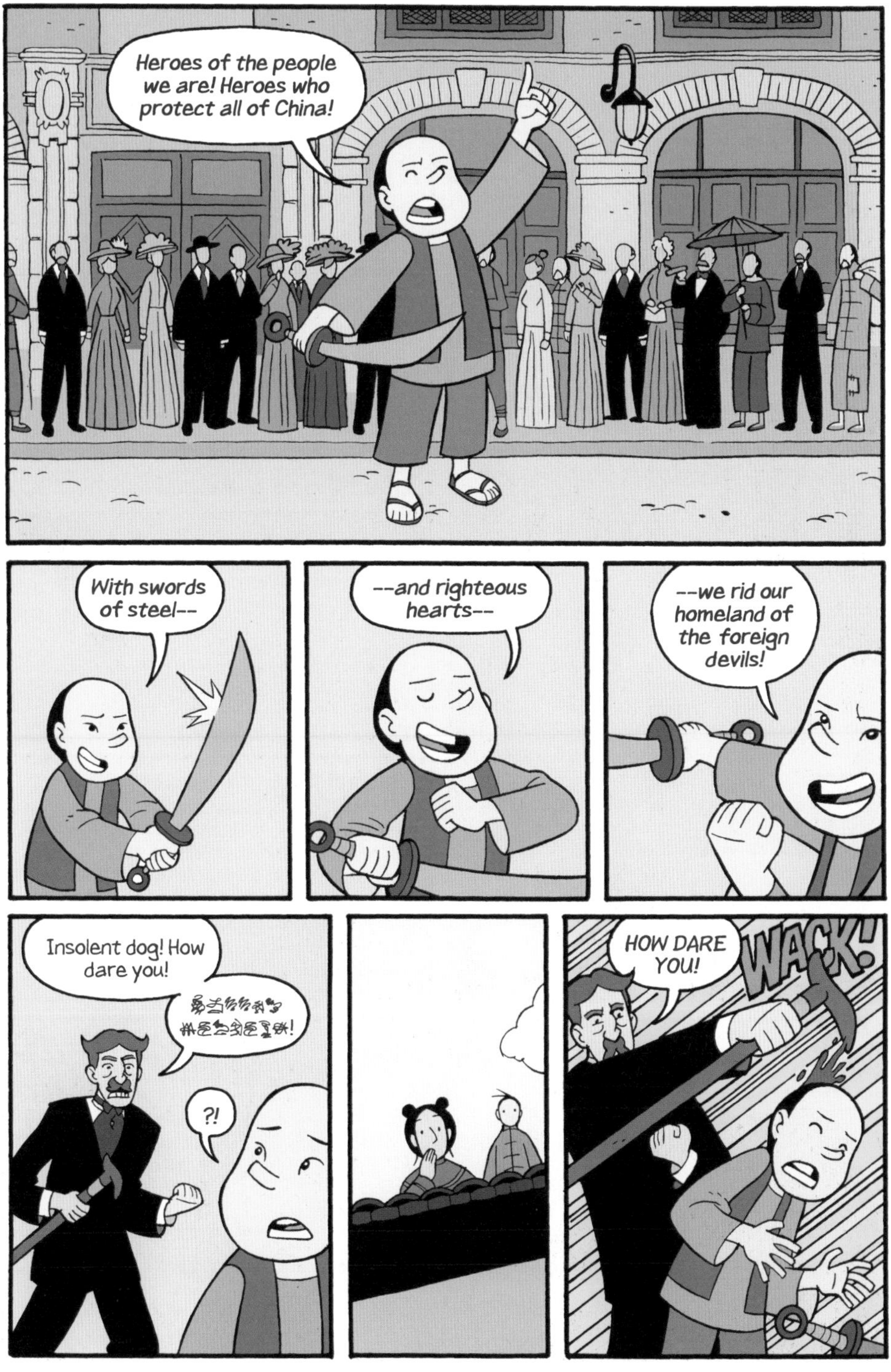
Heroes of the people we are! Heroes who protect all of China!
With swords of steel--
--and righteous hearts--
--we rid our homeland of the foreign devils!
Insolent dog! How dare you!
?!
HOW DARE YOU!
WACK!

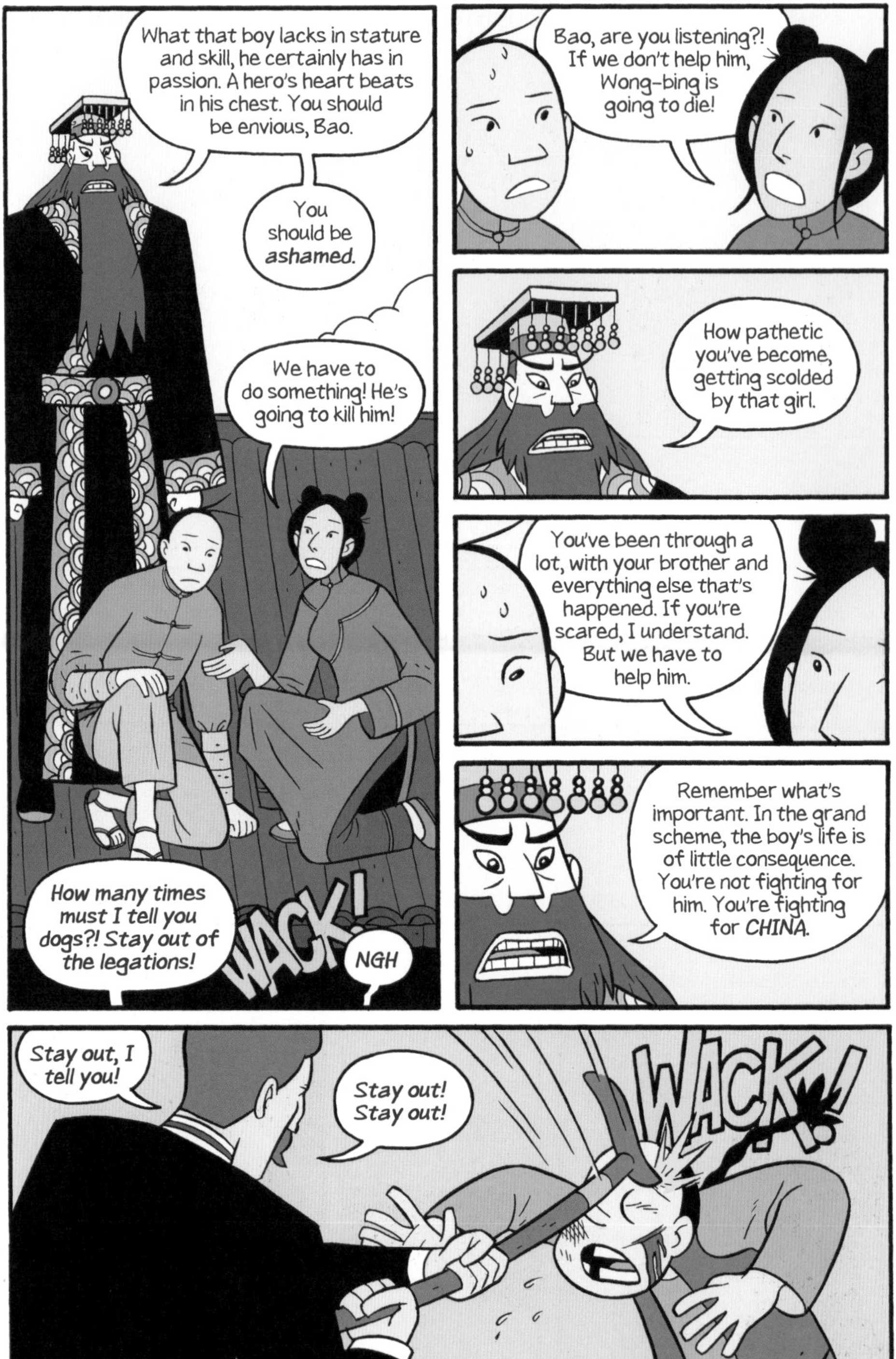

What that boy lacks in stature and skill, he certainly has in passion. A hero's heart beats in his chest. You should be envious, Bao.
You should be *ashamed.*
We have to do something! He's going to kill him!
How many times must I tell you dogs?! Stay out of the legations!
WACK!
NGH
Bao, are you listening?! If we don't help him, Wong-bing is going to die!
How pathetic you've become, getting scolded by that girl.
You've been through a lot, with your brother and everything else that's happened. If you're scared, I understand. But we have to help him.
Remember what's important. In the grand scheme, the boy's life is of little consequence. You're not fighting for him. You're fighting for *CHINA*.
Stay out, I tell you!
Stay out! Stay out!
WACK!

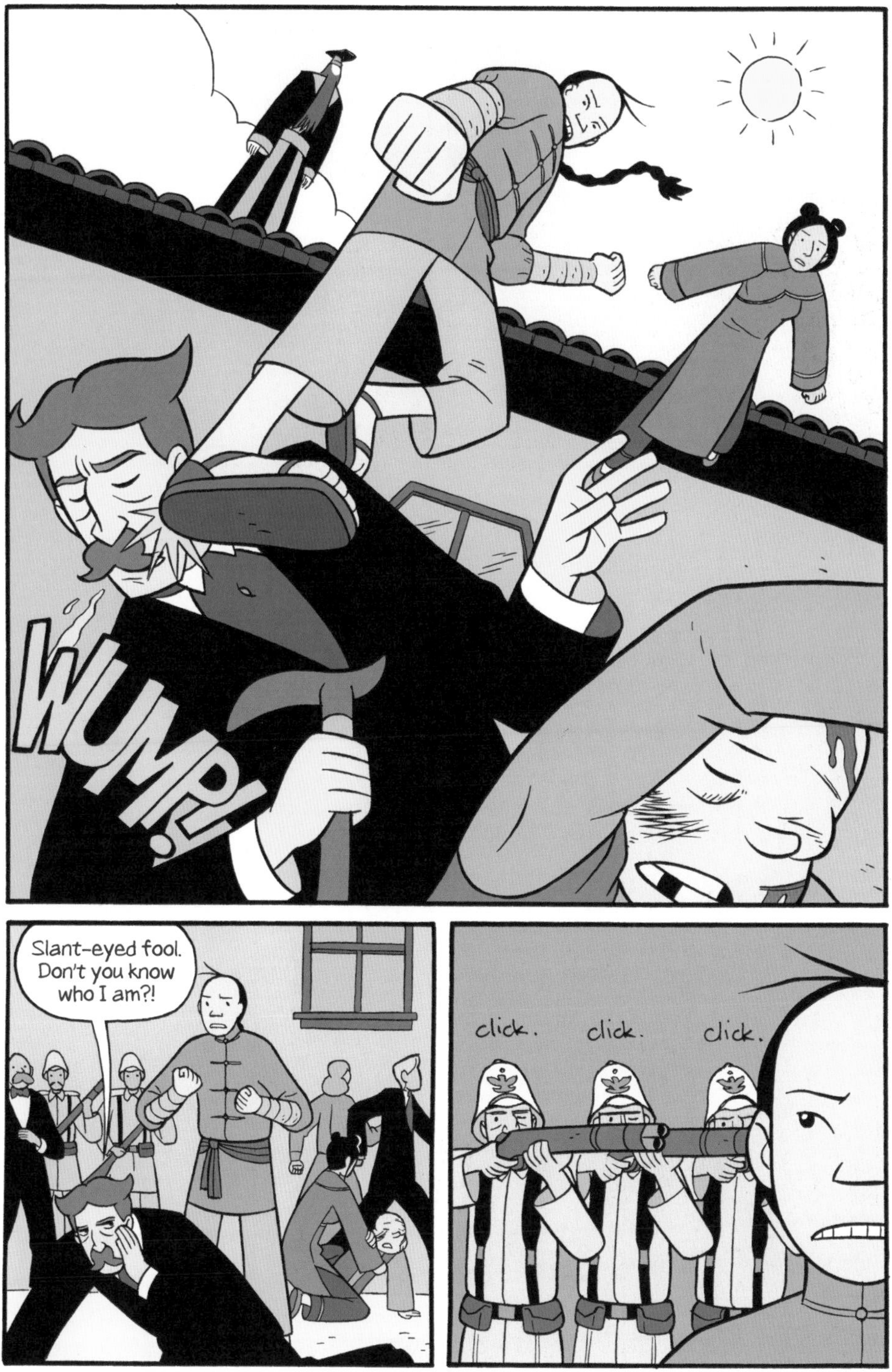
WUMP!
Slant-eyed fool. Don't you know who I am?!
click. click. click.

I am *Baron von Ketteler*, Germany's official minister to Peking.

I have a dozen Chinese in my home, each cleaner and better-fed than you. They shine my shoes and serve me tea each morning.

You have just put your dirty, miserable foot against my cheek. You'll die for that, but I won't be the one to kill you. I wouldn't want to risk sullying my suit with your blood. I'll have your own empress do that, right after she kisses my boots and begs for my country's forgiveness.

Mei-wen and I have no swords, no ashes of charms, no time for the Ritual.

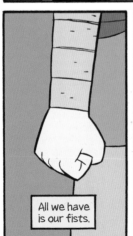

All we have is our fists.

They will have to do.

Is there a problem here?

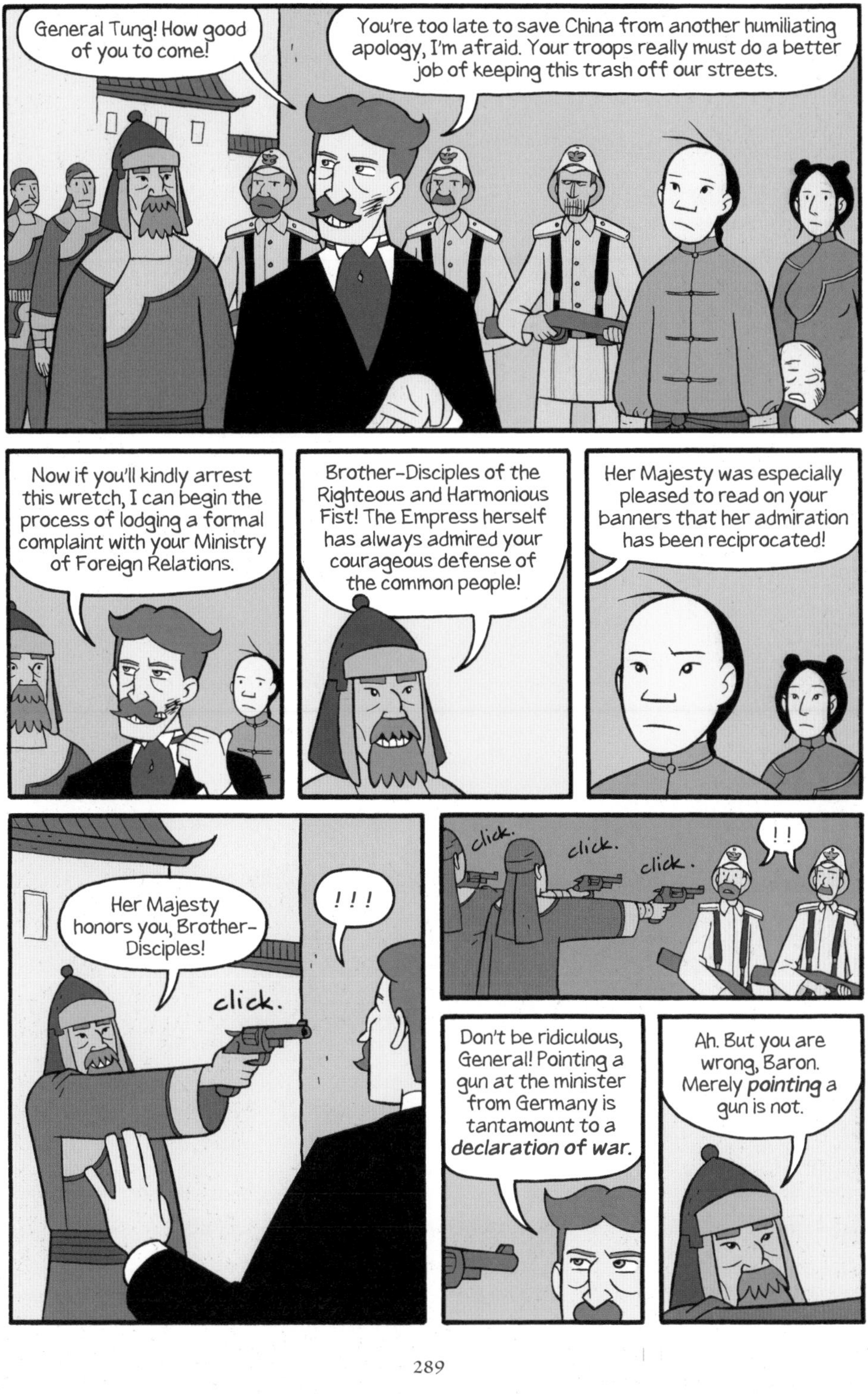
General Tung! How good of you to come!
You're too late to save China from another humiliating apology, I'm afraid. Your troops really must do a better job of keeping this trash off our streets.
Now if you'll kindly arrest this wretch, I can begin the process of lodging a formal complaint with your Ministry of Foreign Relations.
Brother-Disciples of the Righteous and Harmonious Fist! The Empress herself has always admired your courageous defense of the common people!
Her Majesty was especially pleased to read on your banners that her admiration has been reciprocated!
Her Majesty honors you, Brother-Disciples!
!!!
click.
click.
click.
click.
!!
Don't be ridiculous, General! Pointing a gun at the minister from Germany is tantamount to a *declaration of war*.
Ah. But you are wrong, Baron. Merely *pointing* a gun is not.

And just like that--

--the war begins.

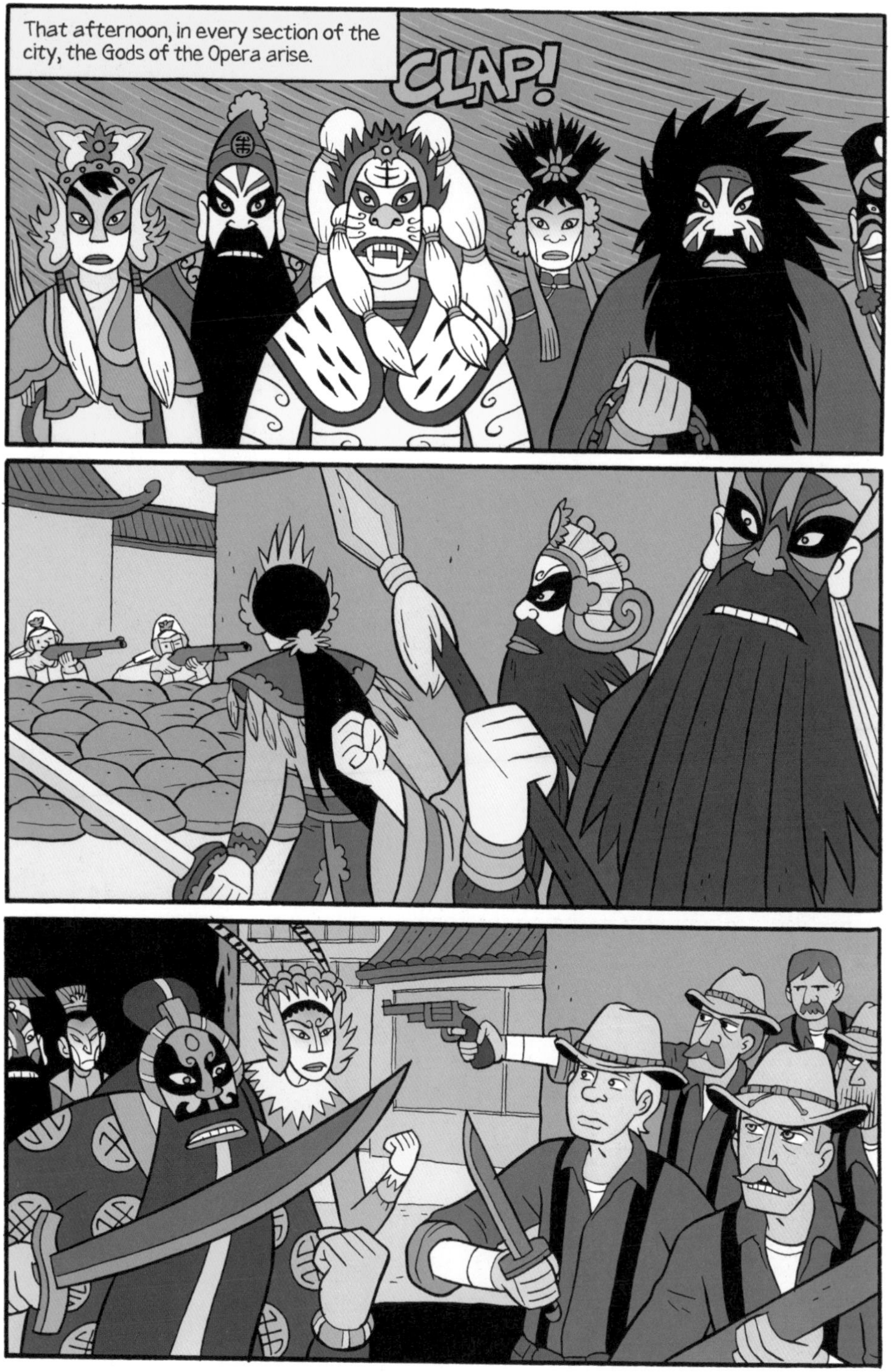
That afternoon, in every section of the city, the Gods of the Opera arise.
CLAP!

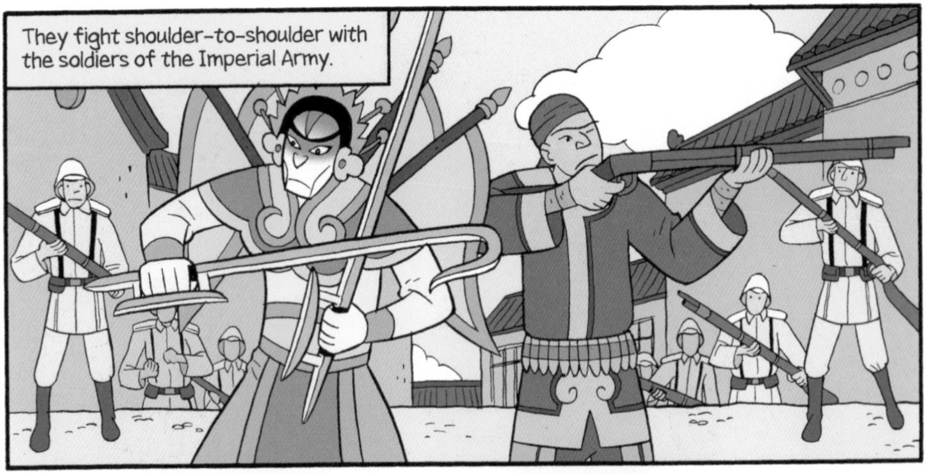
They fight shoulder-to-shoulder with the soldiers of the Imperial Army.

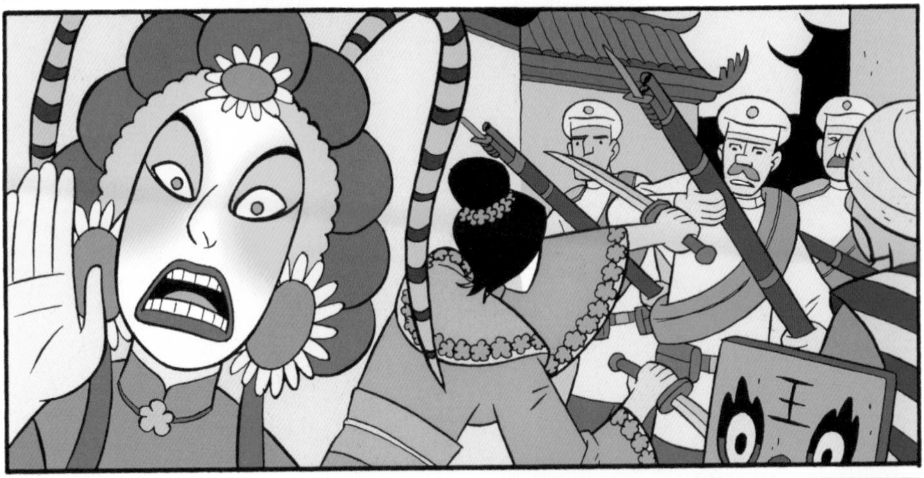

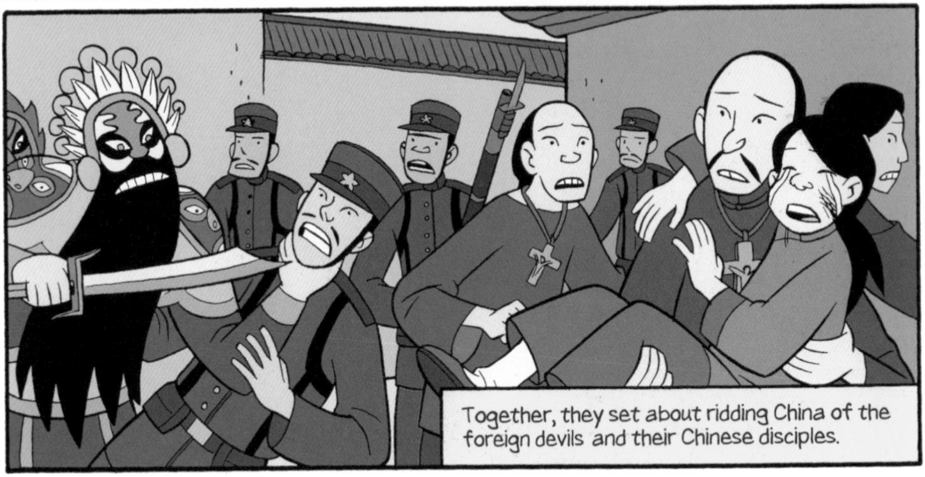
Together, they set about ridding China of the foreign devils and their Chinese disciples.

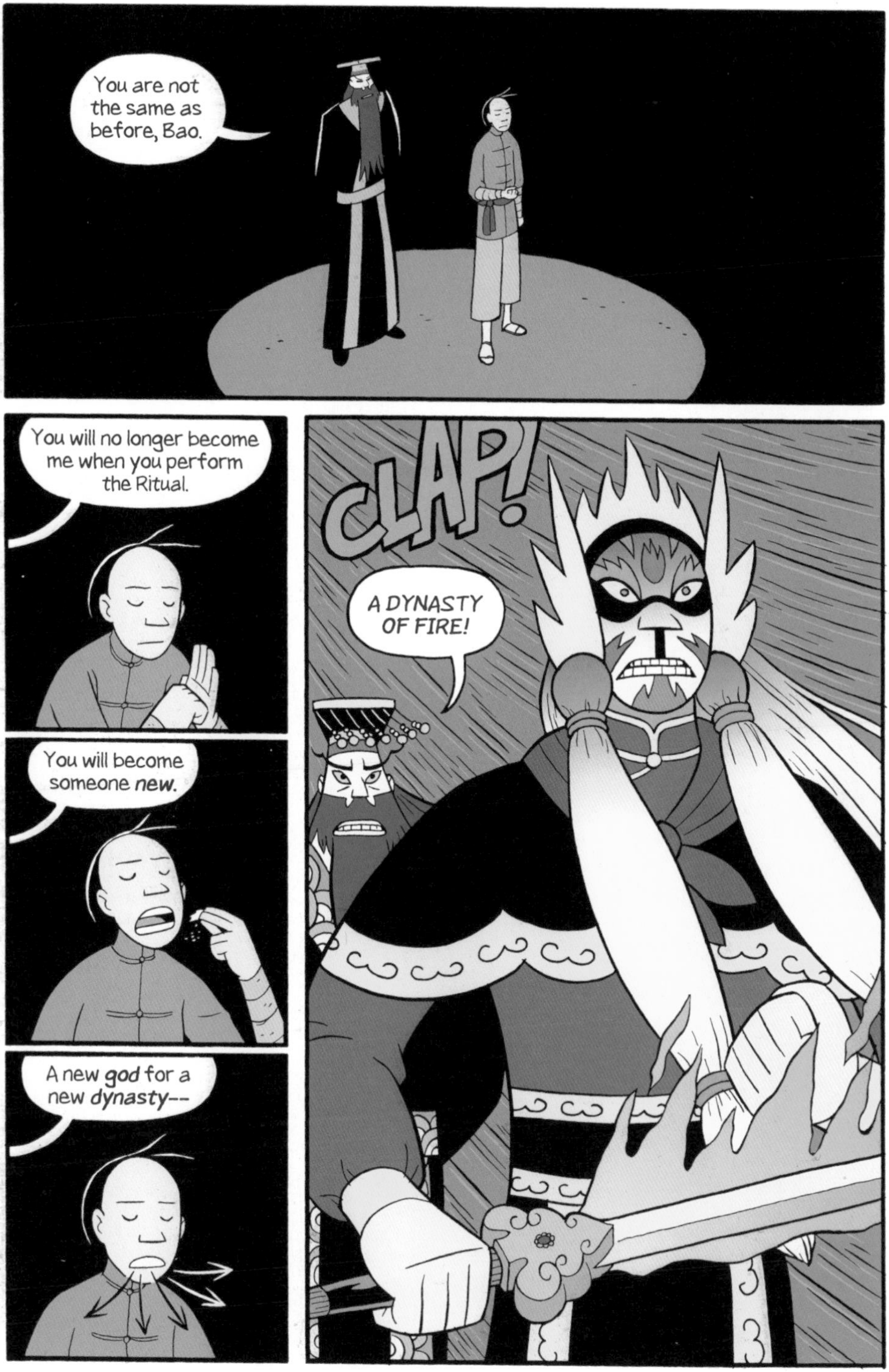
You are not the same as before, Bao.
You will no longer become me when you perform the Ritual.
You will become someone *new*.
A new *god* for a new *dynasty*--
CLAP!
A DYNASTY OF FIRE!

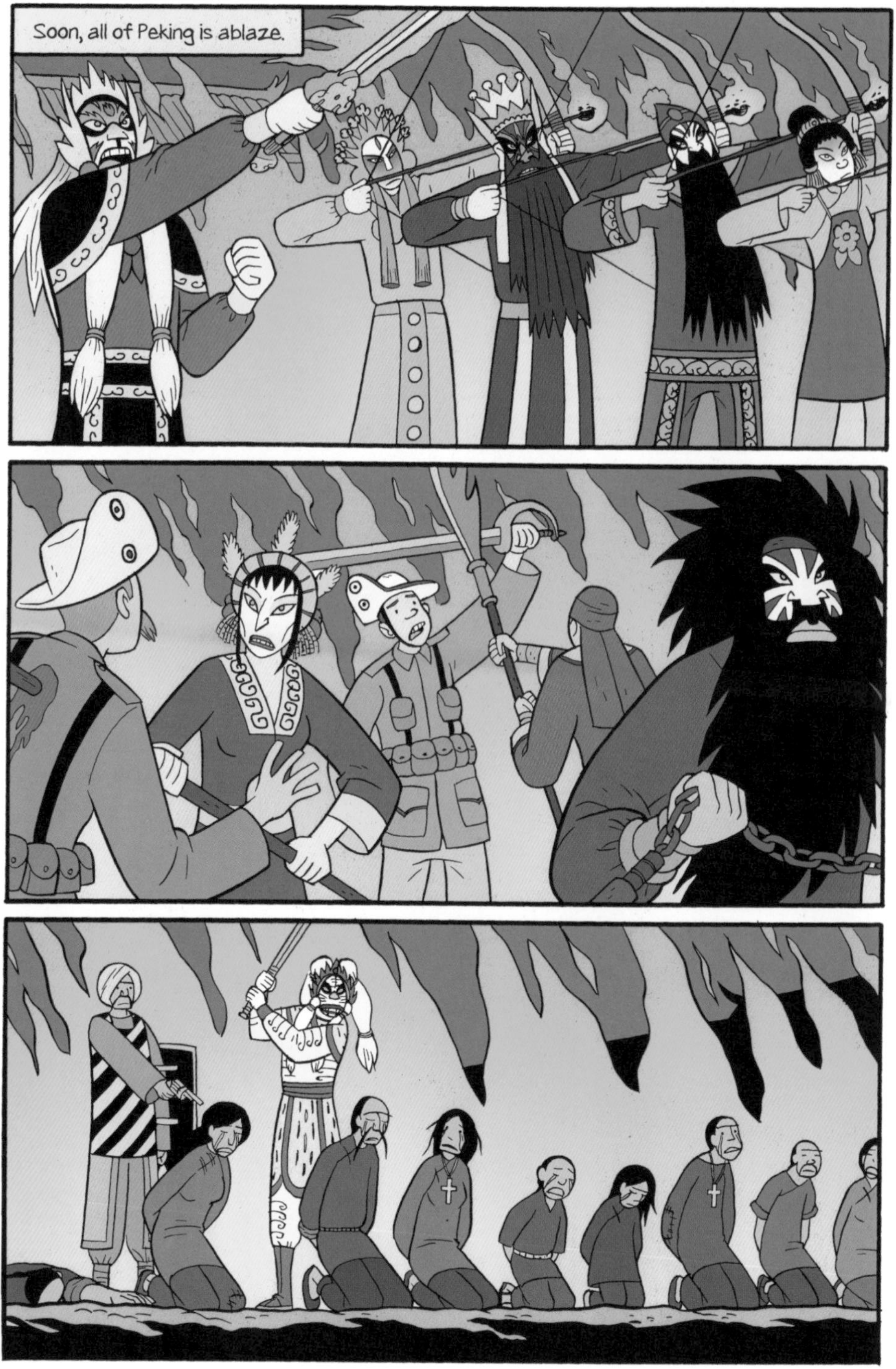
Soon, all of Peking is ablaze.

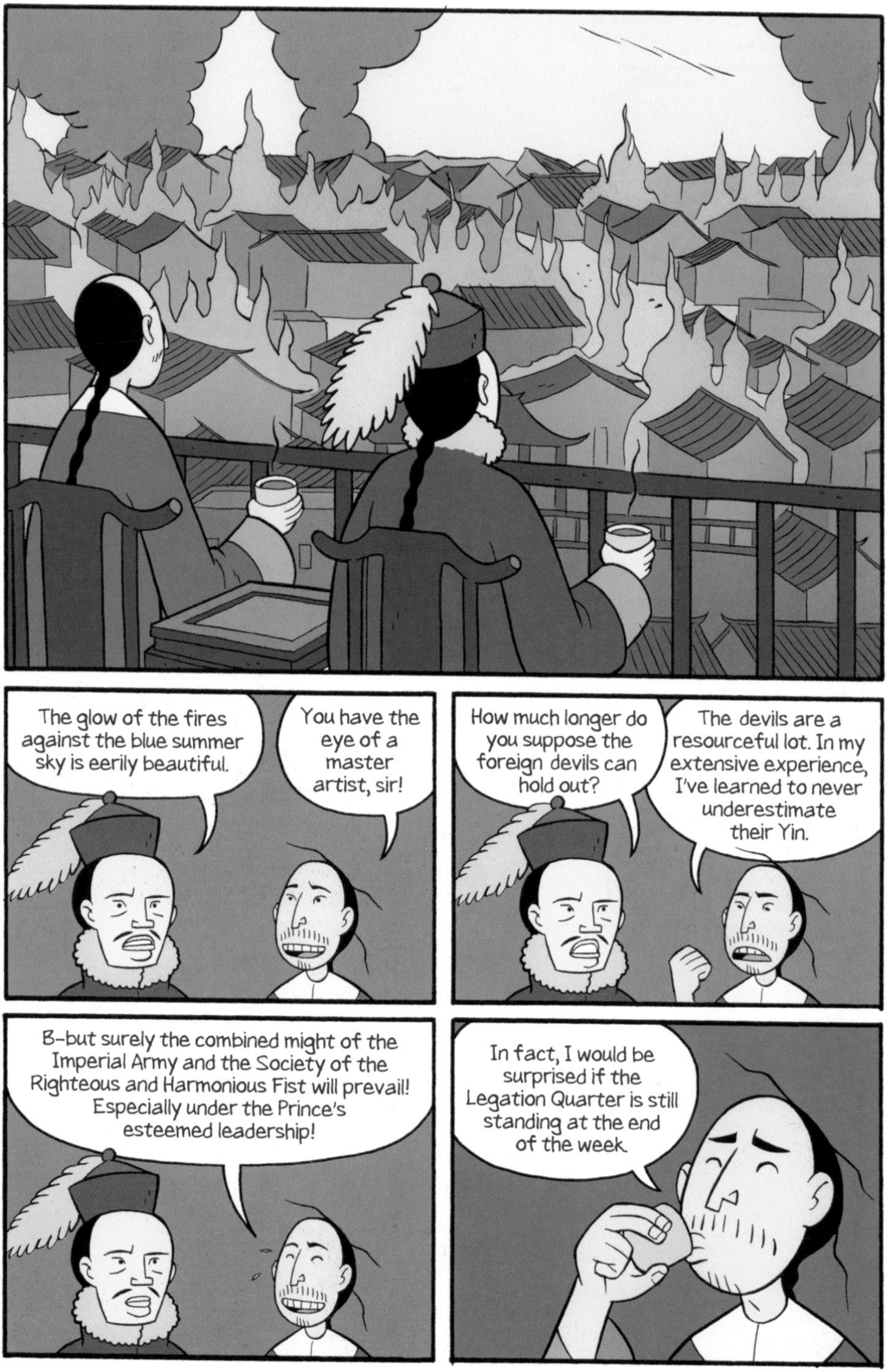
The glow of the fires against the blue summer sky is eerily beautiful.
You have the eye of a master artist, sir!
How much longer do you suppose the foreign devils can hold out?
The devils are a resourceful lot. In my extensive experience, I've learned to never underestimate their Yin.
B-but surely the combined might of the Imperial Army and the Society of the Righteous and Harmonious Fist will prevail! Especially under the Prince's esteemed leadership!
In fact, I would be surprised if the Legation Quarter is still standing at the end of the week.

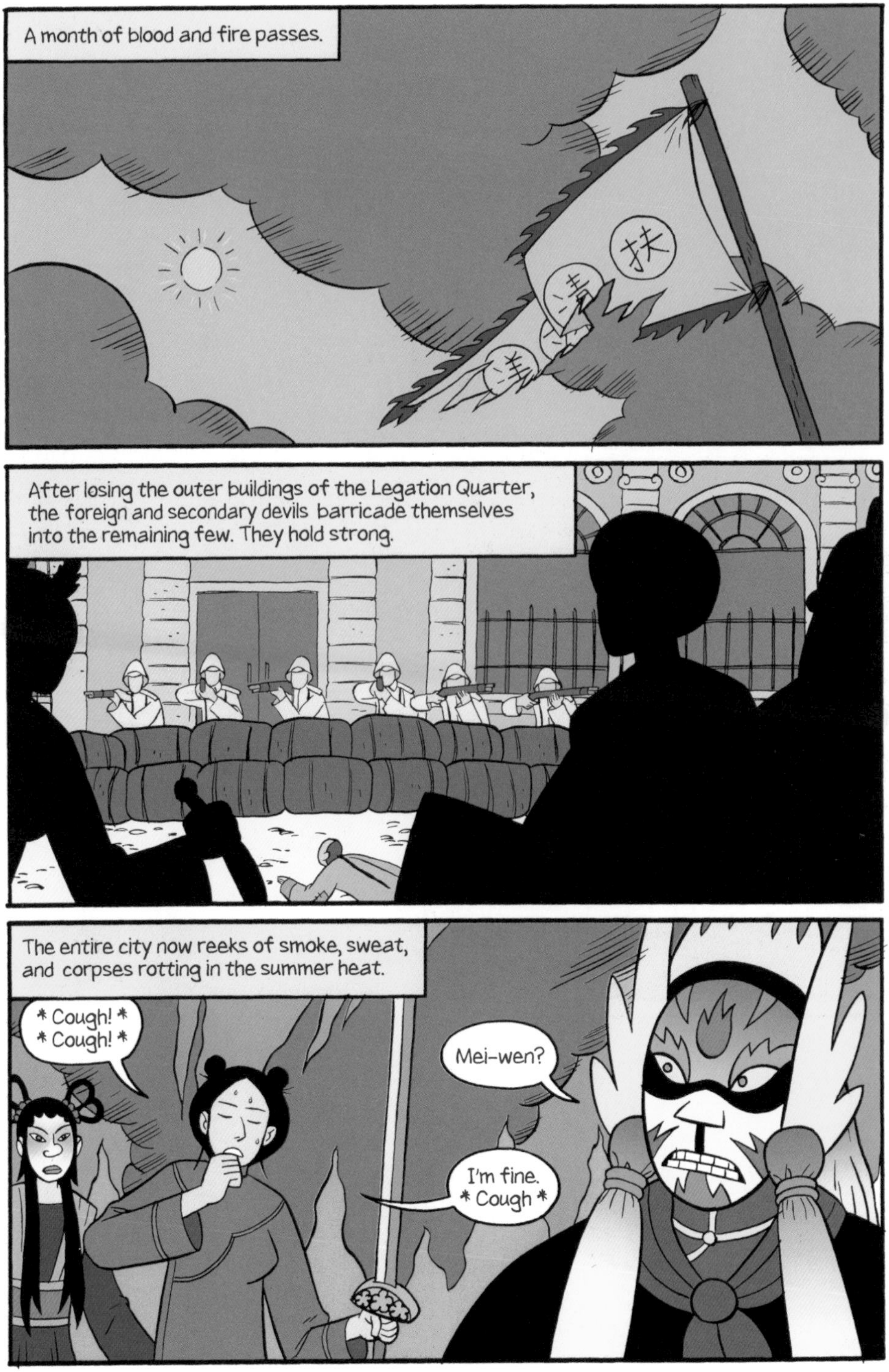
A month of blood and fire passes.
扶
After losing the outer buildings of the Legation Quarter, the foreign and secondary devils barricade themselves into the remaining few. They hold strong.
The entire city now reeks of smoke, sweat, and corpses rotting in the summer heat.
* Cough! * * Cough! *
Mei-wen?
I'm fine. * Cough *

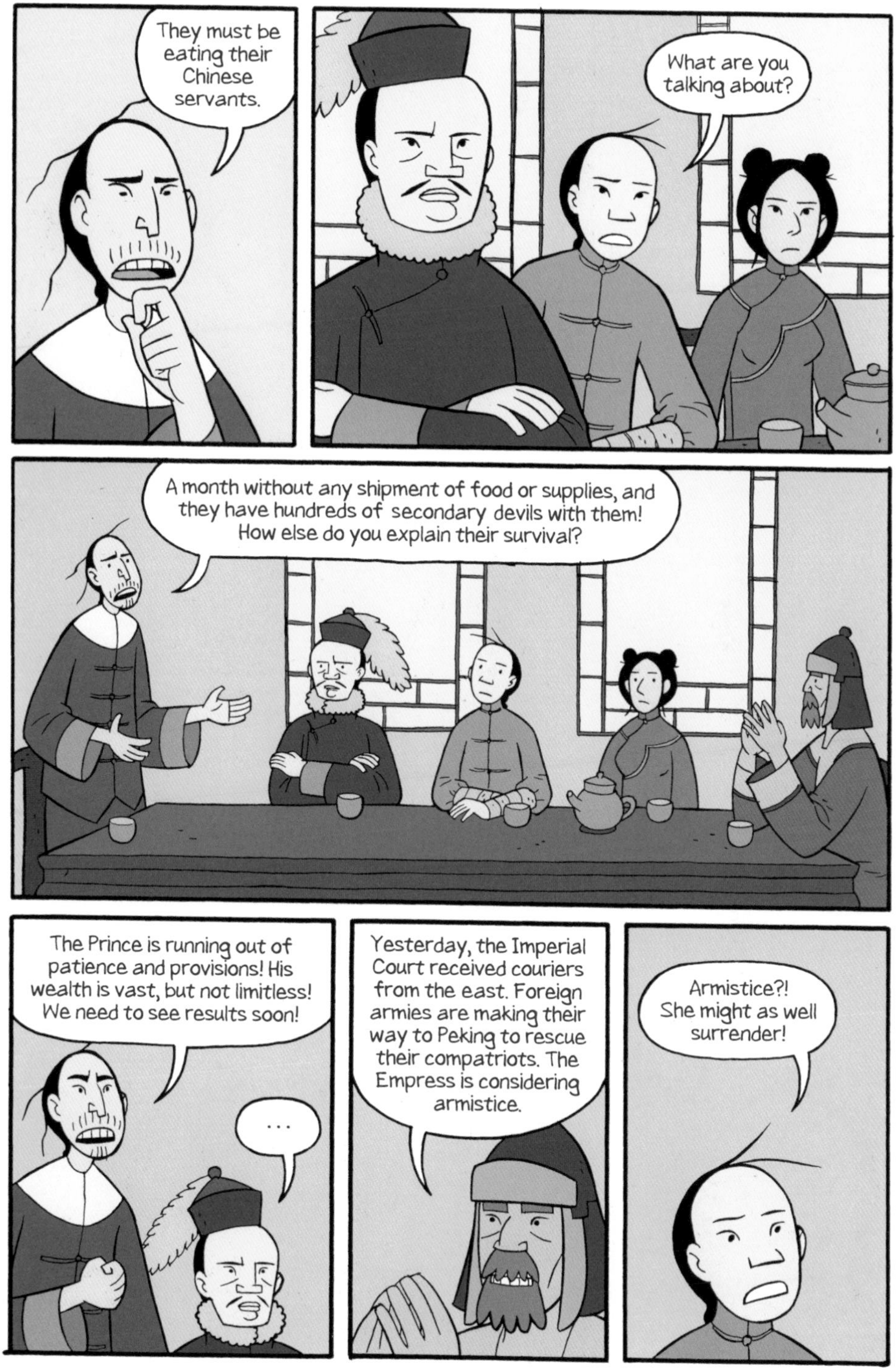
They must be eating their Chinese servants.
What are you talking about?
A month without any shipment of food or supplies, and they have hundreds of secondary devils with them! How else do you explain their survival?
The Prince is running out of patience and provisions! His wealth is vast, but not limitless! We need to see results soon!
...
Yesterday, the Imperial Court received couriers from the east. Foreign armies are making their way to Peking to rescue their compatriots. The Empress is considering armistice.
Armistice?! She might as well surrender!

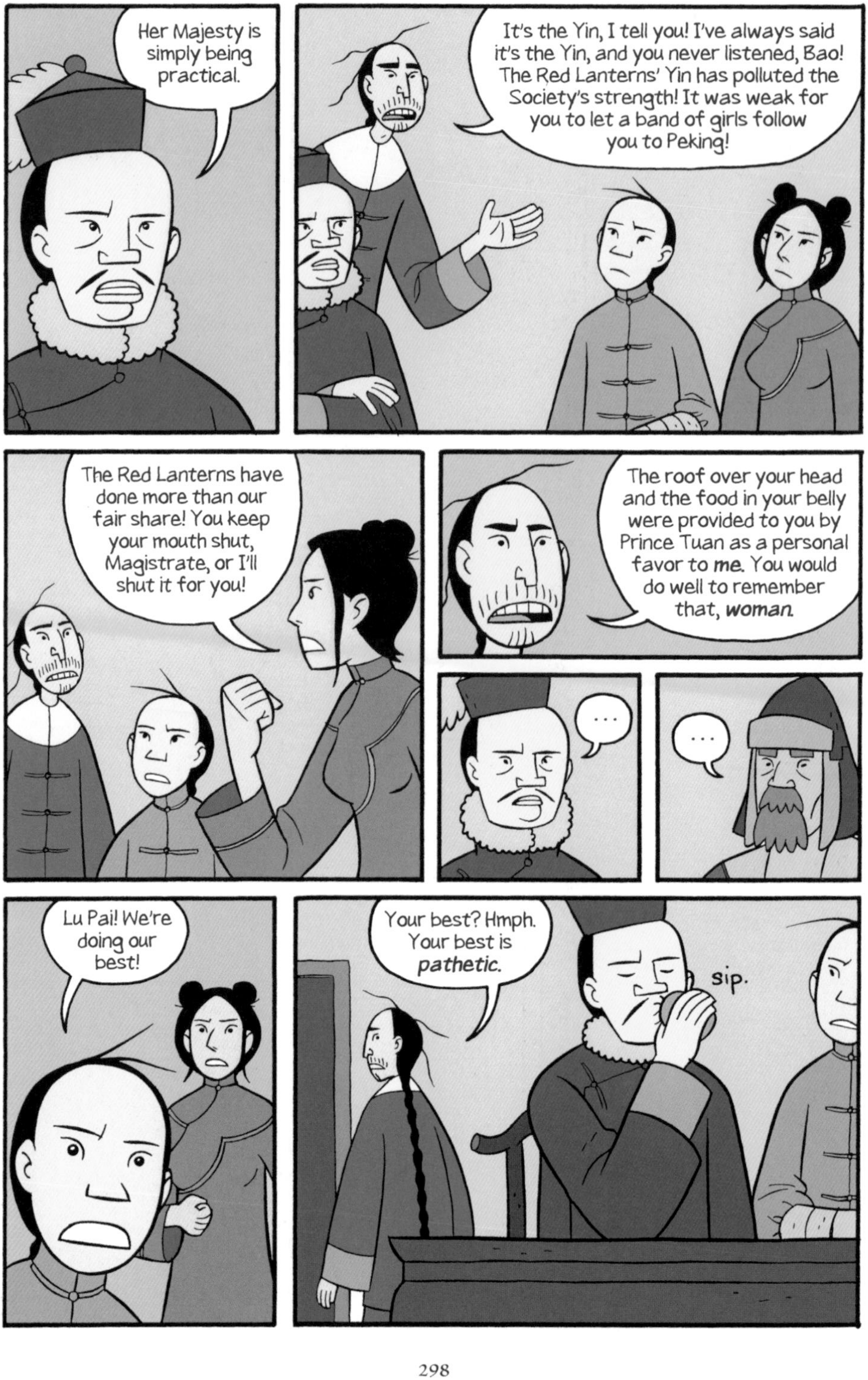
Her Majesty is simply being practical.
It's the Yin, I tell you! I've always said it's the Yin, and you never listened, Bao! The Red Lanterns' Yin has polluted the Society's strength! It was weak for you to let a band of girls follow you to Peking!
The Red Lanterns have done more than our fair share! You keep your mouth shut, Magistrate, or I'll shut it for you!
The roof over your head and the food in your belly were provided to you by Prince Tuan as a personal favor to **me**. You would do well to remember that, ***woman***.
...
...
Lu Pai! We're doing our best!
Your best? Hmph. Your best is ***pathetic***.
sip.

Mei-wen has turned Prince Tuan's courtyard into a makeshift infirmary.

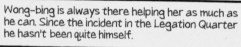

Wong-bing is always there helping her as much as he can. Since the incident in the Legation Quarter he hasn't been quite himself.

water?

You don't agree with that imbecile, do you?

Lu Pai? No. Of course not.

You haven't been out on the battlefield in a while, Mei-wen. The Red Lanterns seem directionless without you.

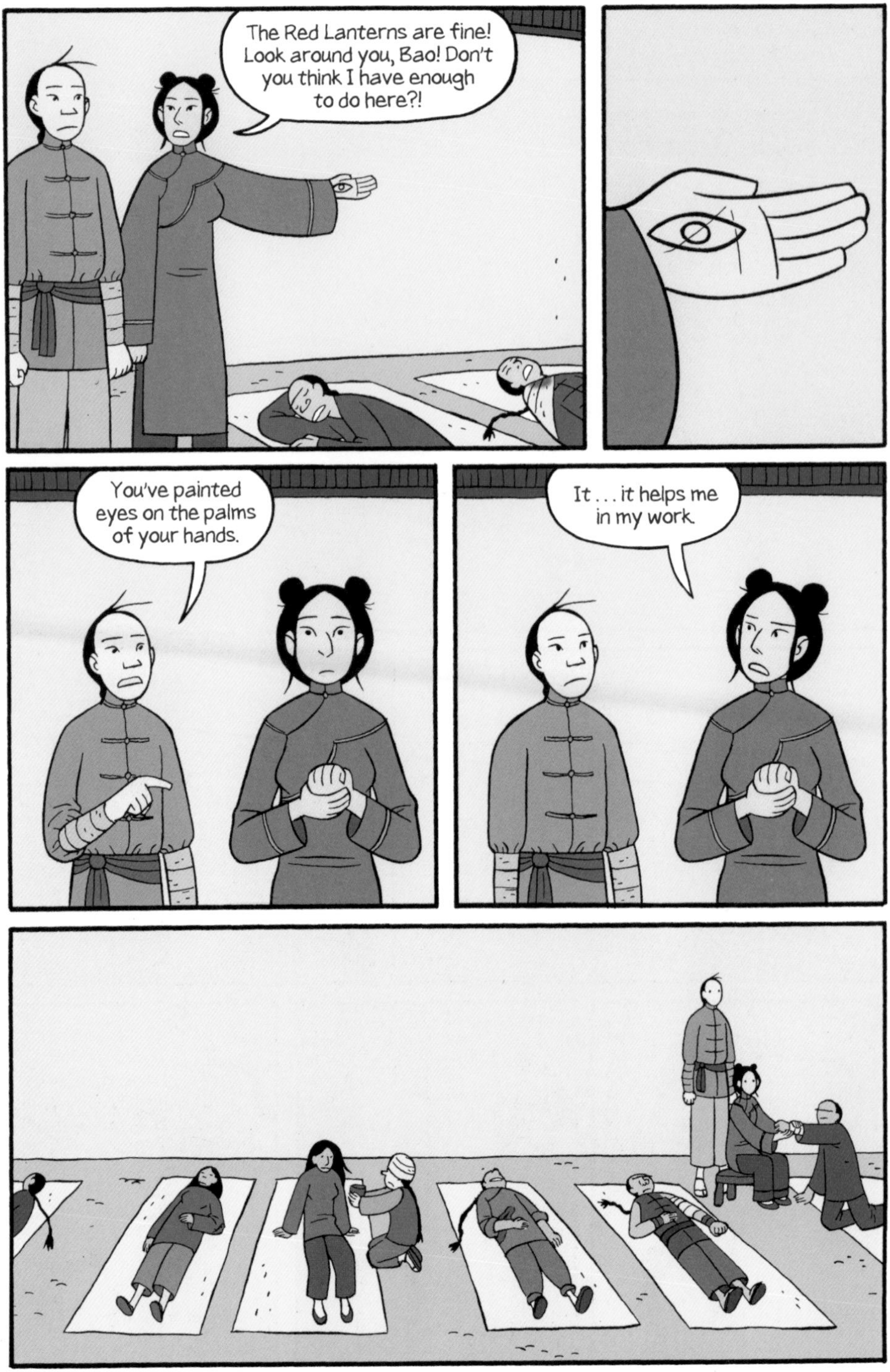
The Red Lanterns are fine! Look around you, Bao! Don't you think I have enough to do here?!
You've painted eyes on the palms of your hands.
It . . . it helps me in my work.

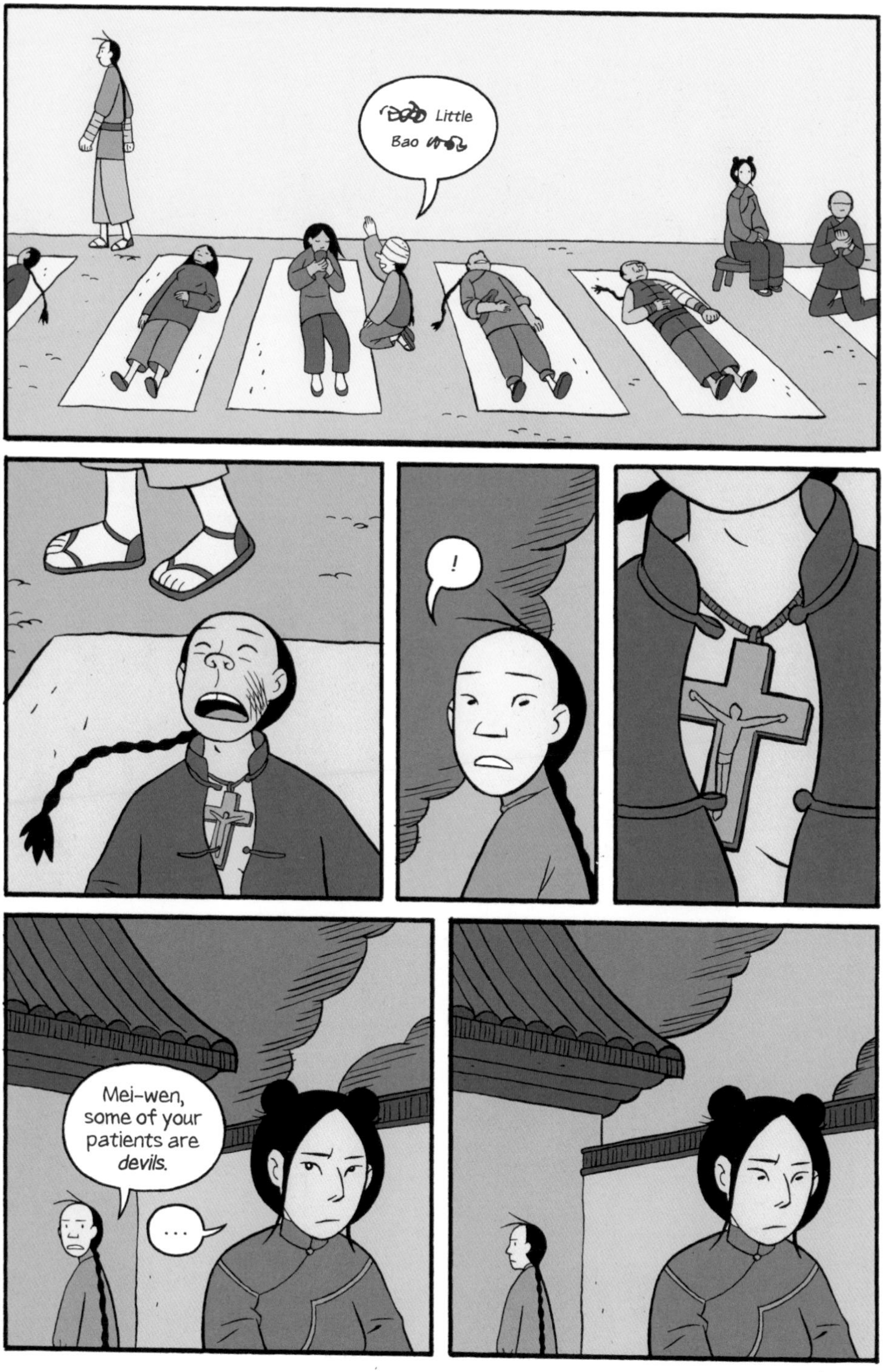
Little Bao
!
Mei-wen, some of your patients are *devils.*
. . .

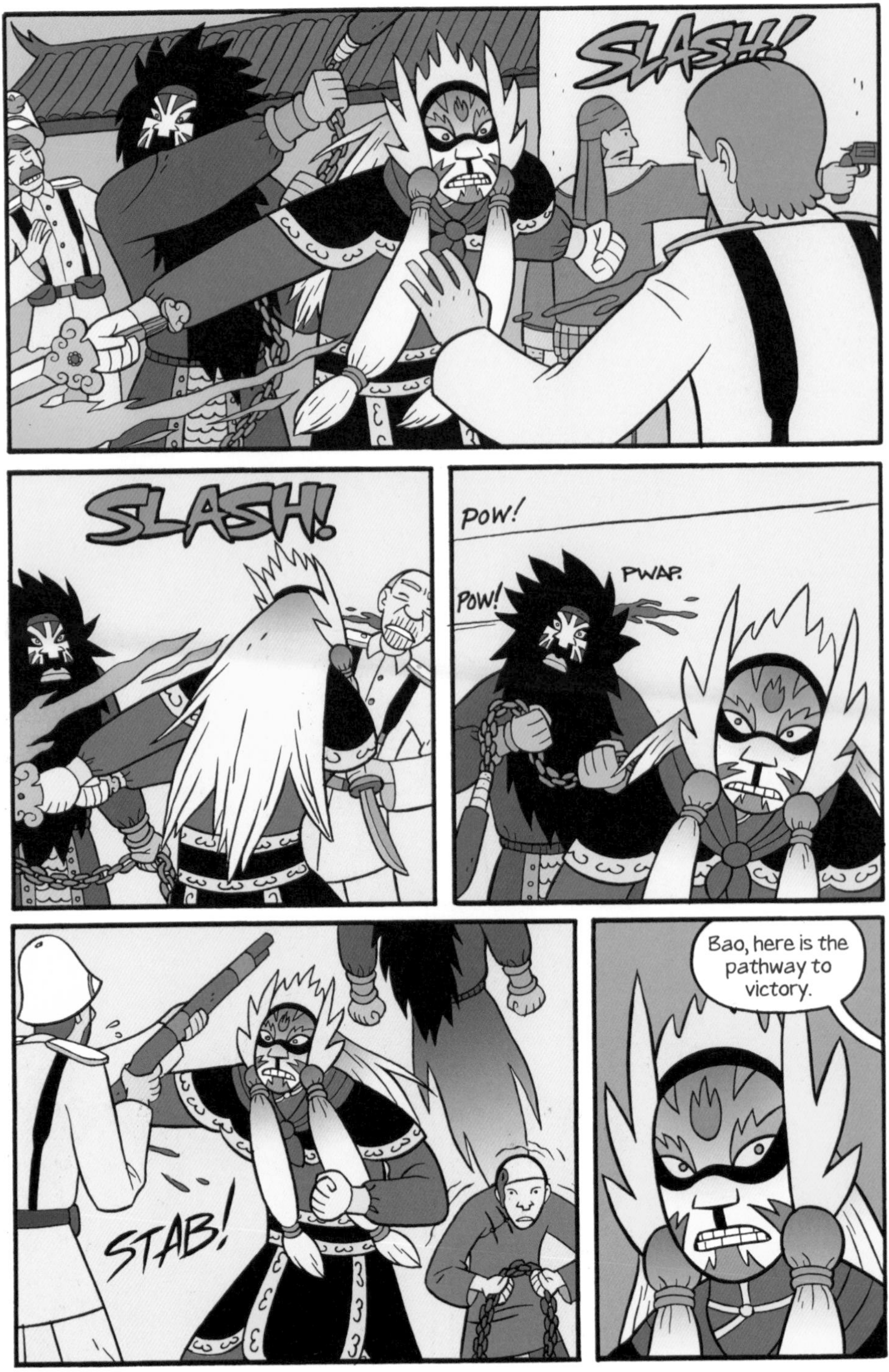
SLASH!
SLASH!
POW!
POW!
PWAP.
STAB!
Bao, here is the pathway to victory.

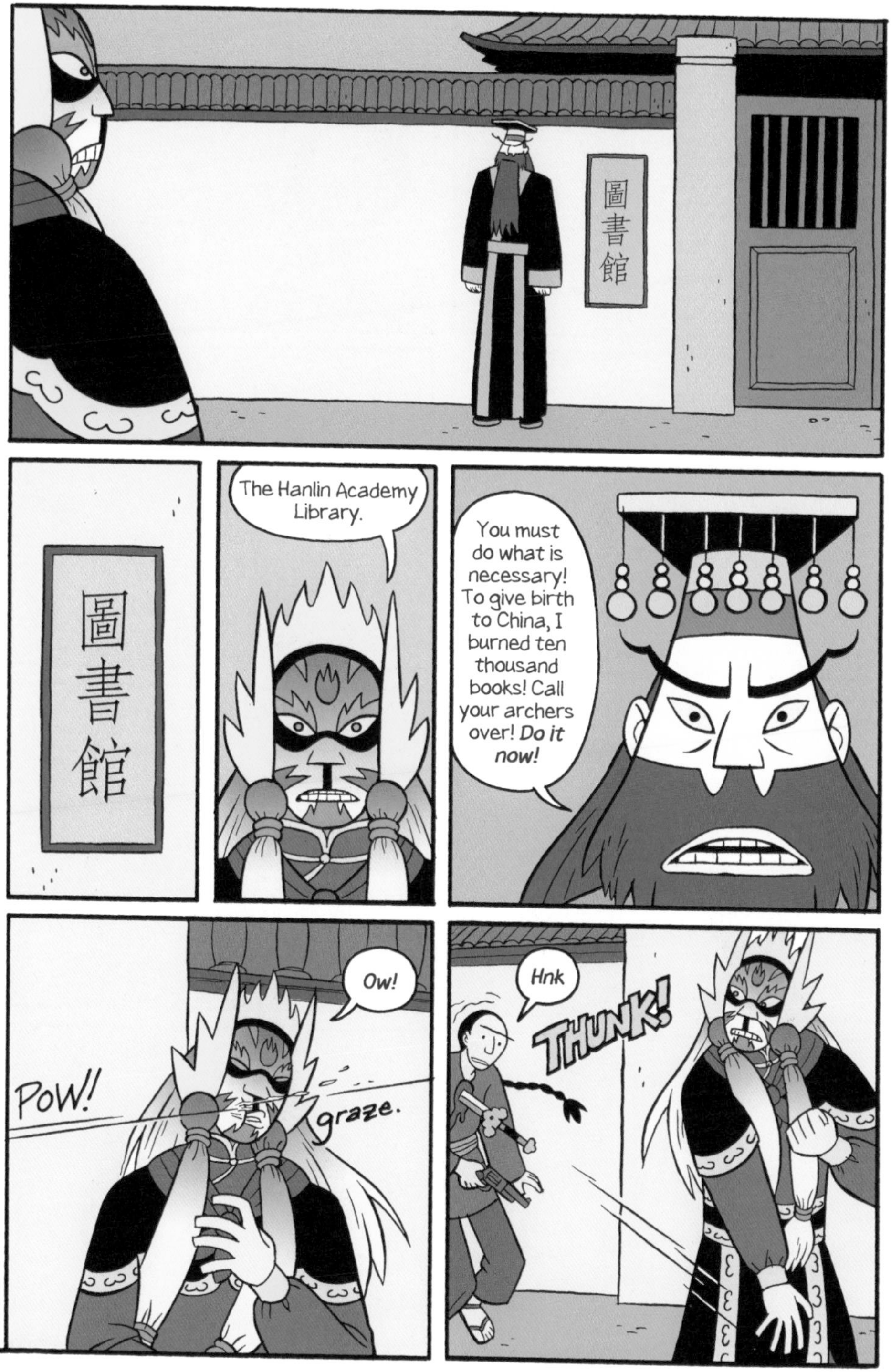
圖書館
圖書館
The Hanlin Academy Library.
You must do what is necessary! To give birth to China, I burned ten thousand books! Call your archers over! *Do it now!*
Ow!
POW!
graze.
Hnk
THUNK!

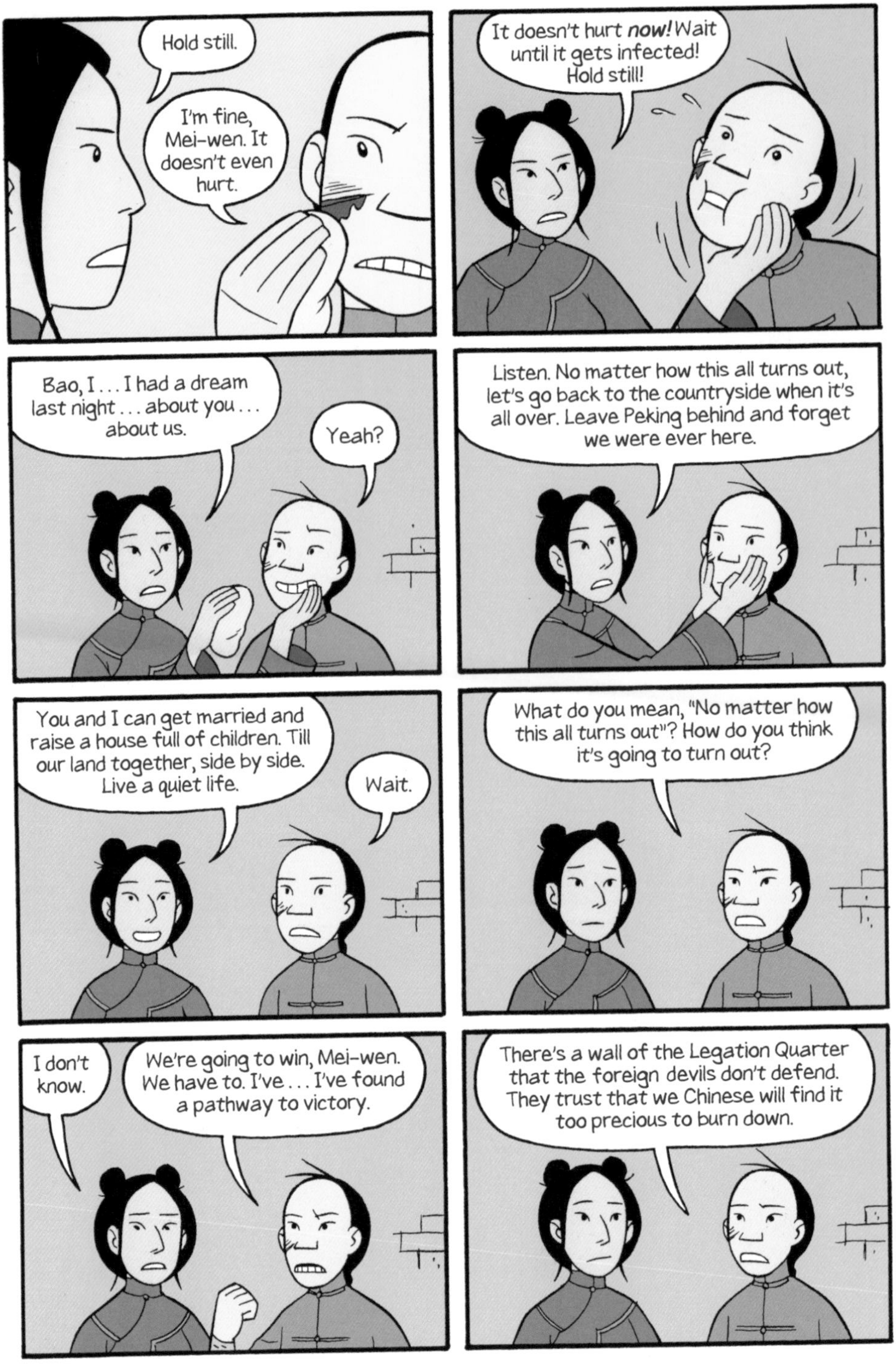

Hold still.
I'm fine, Mei-wen. It doesn't even hurt.
It doesn't hurt now! Wait until it gets infected! Hold still!
Bao, I . . . I had a dream last night . . . about you . . . about us.
Yeah?
Listen. No matter how this all turns out, let's go back to the countryside when it's all over. Leave Peking behind and forget we were ever here.
You and I can get married and raise a house full of children. Till our land together, side by side. Live a quiet life.
Wait.
What do you mean, "No matter how this all turns out"? How do you think it's going to turn out?
I don't know.
We're going to win, Mei-wen. We have to. I've . . . I've found a pathway to victory.
There's a wall of the Legation Quarter that the foreign devils don't defend. They trust that we Chinese will find it too precious to burn down.

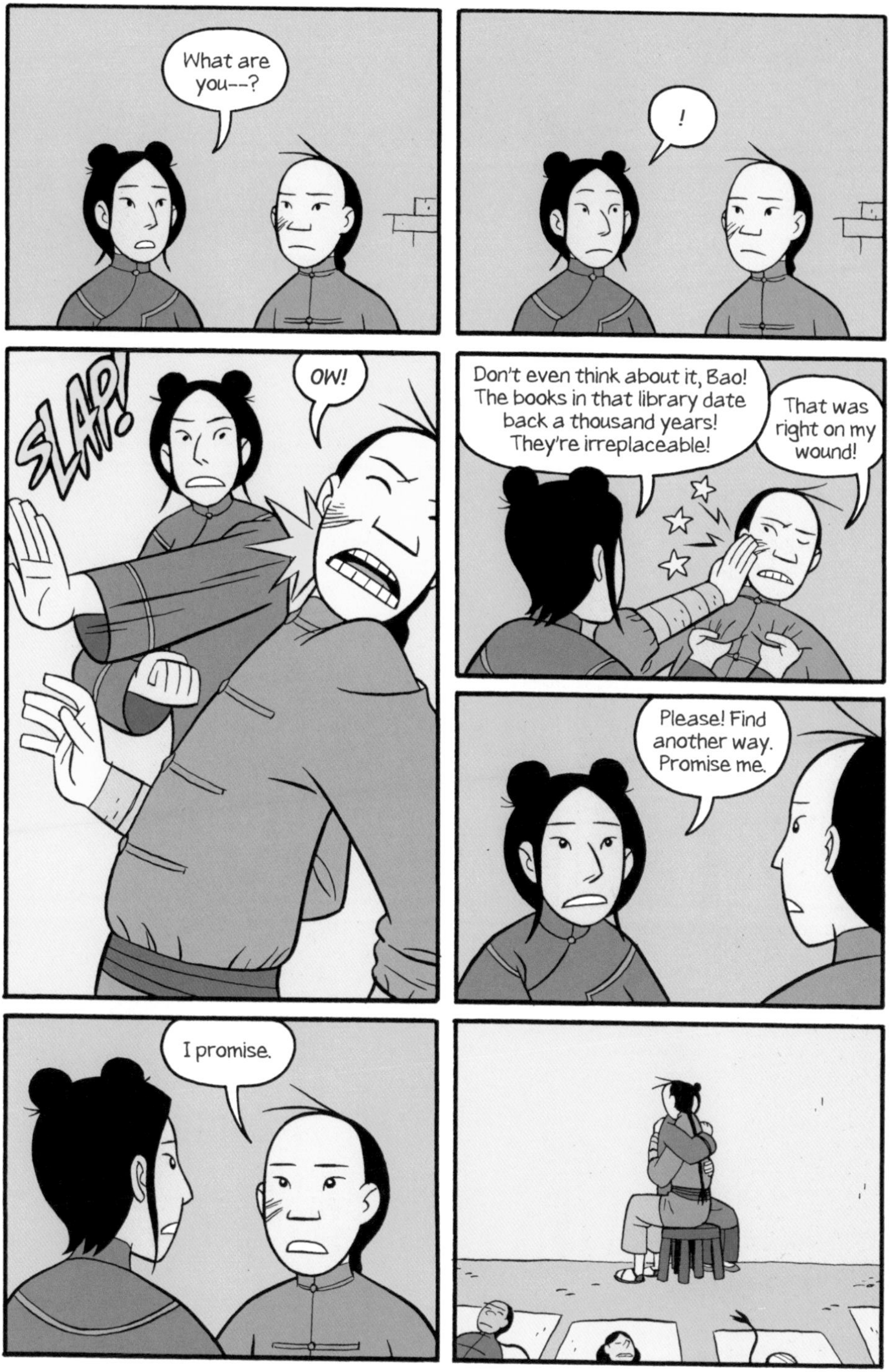
What are you--?
!
SLAP!
OW!
Don't even think about it, Bao! The books in that library date back a thousand years! They're irreplaceable!
That was right on my wound!
Please! Find another way. Promise me.
I promise.

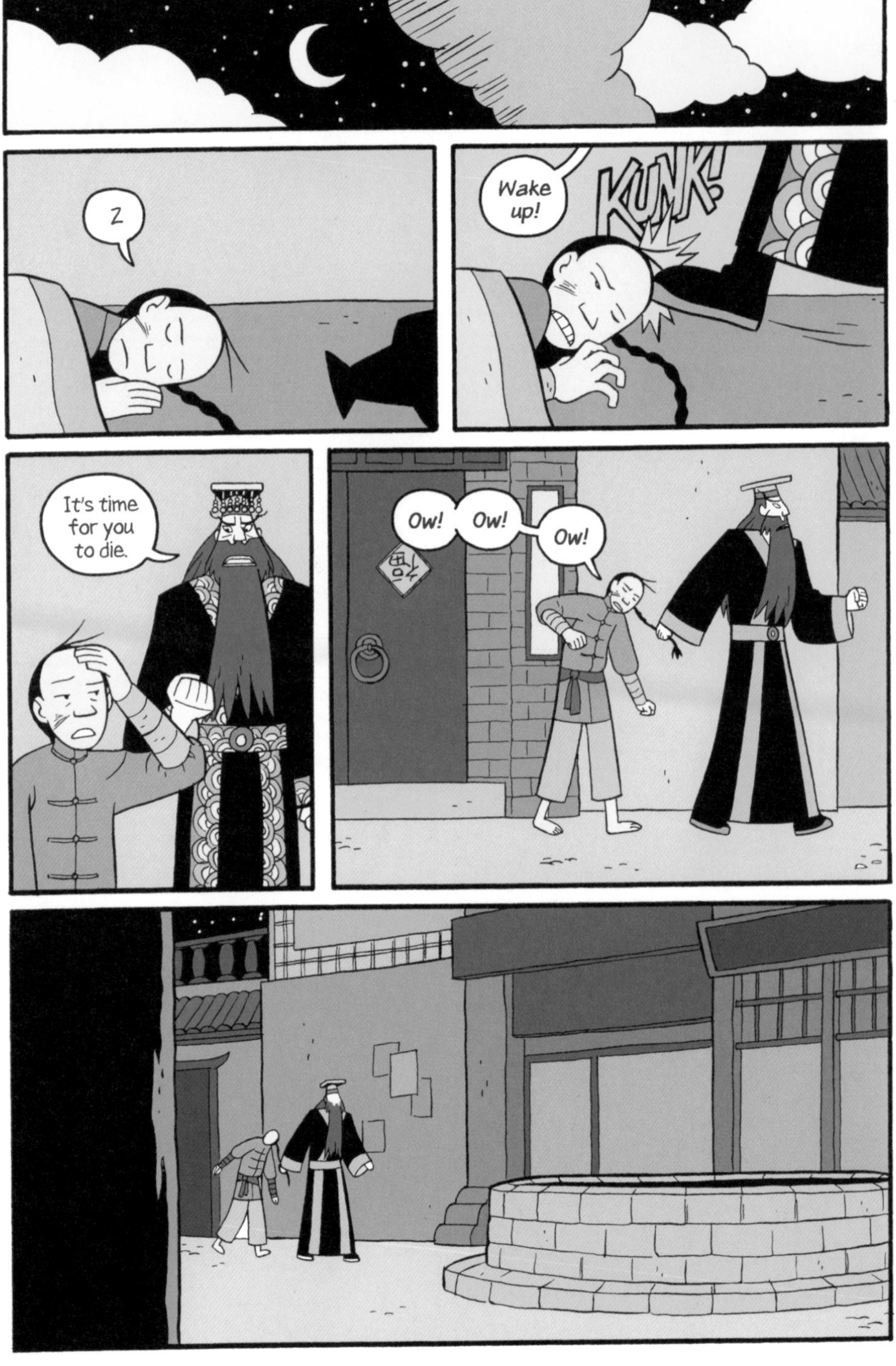
Z
Wake up!
KUNK!
It's time for you to die.
Ow!
Ow!
Ow!

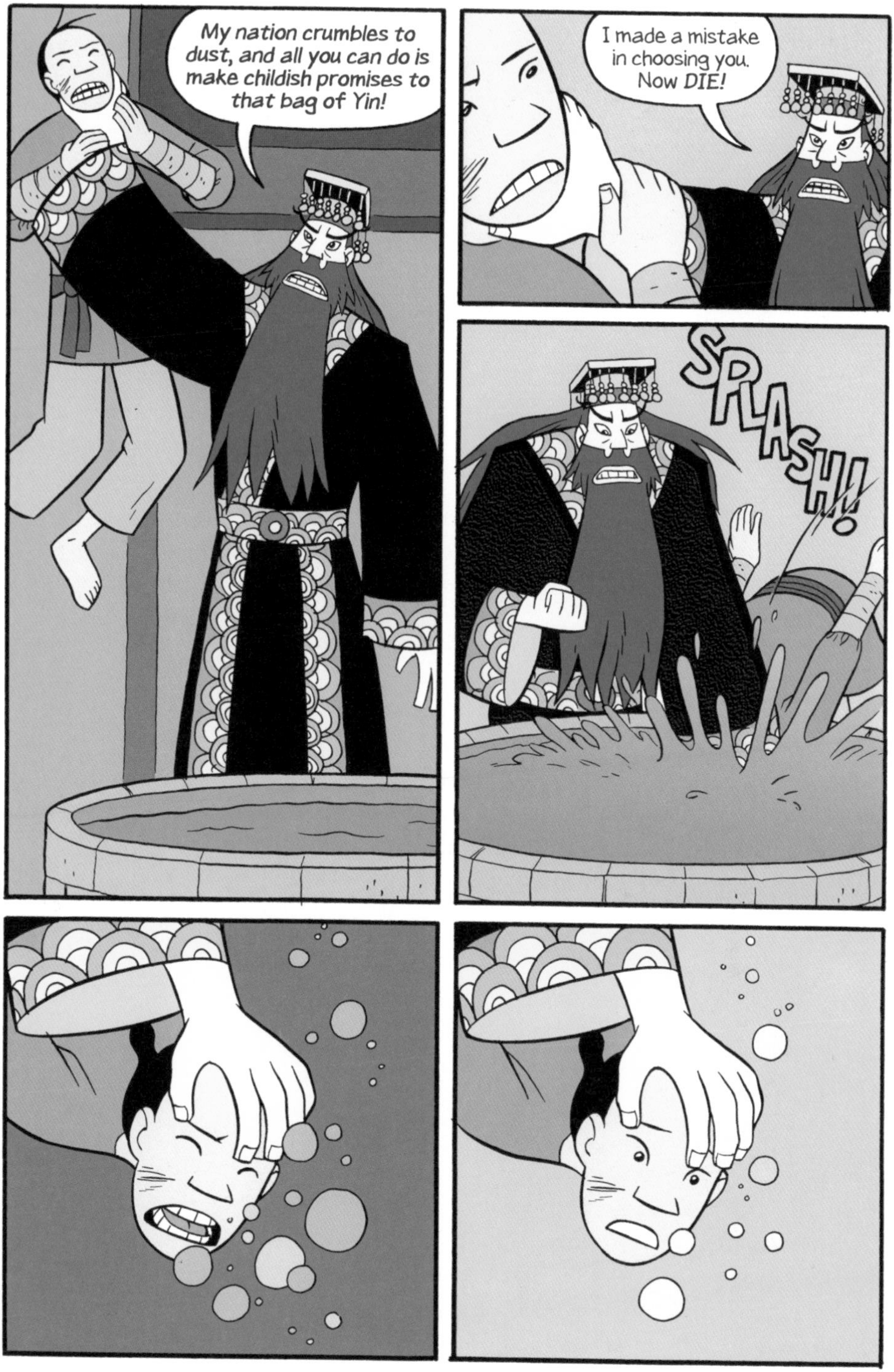
My nation crumbles to dust, and all you can do is make childish promises to that bag of Yin!
I made a mistake in choosing you. Now DIE!
SPLASH!

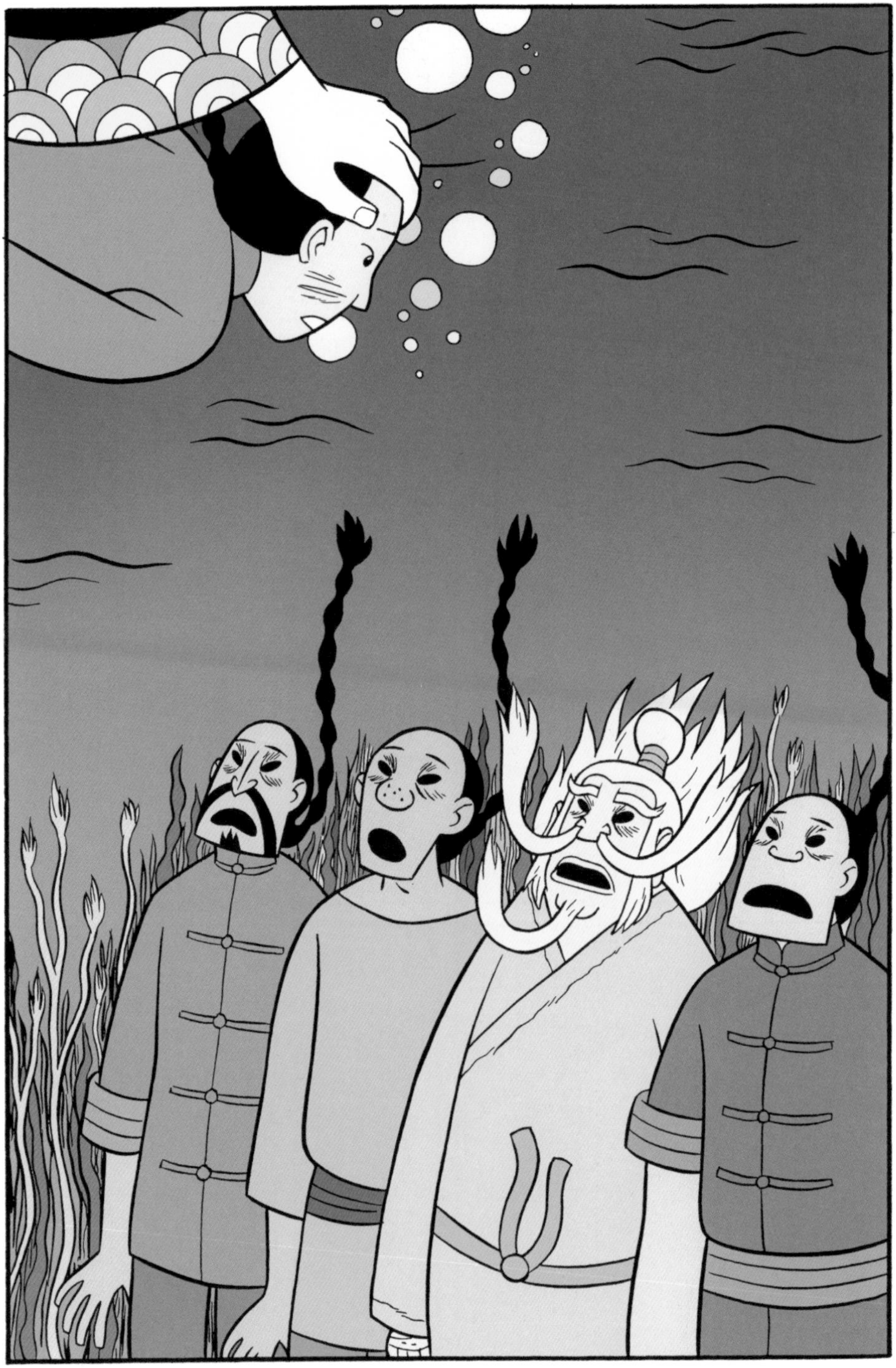

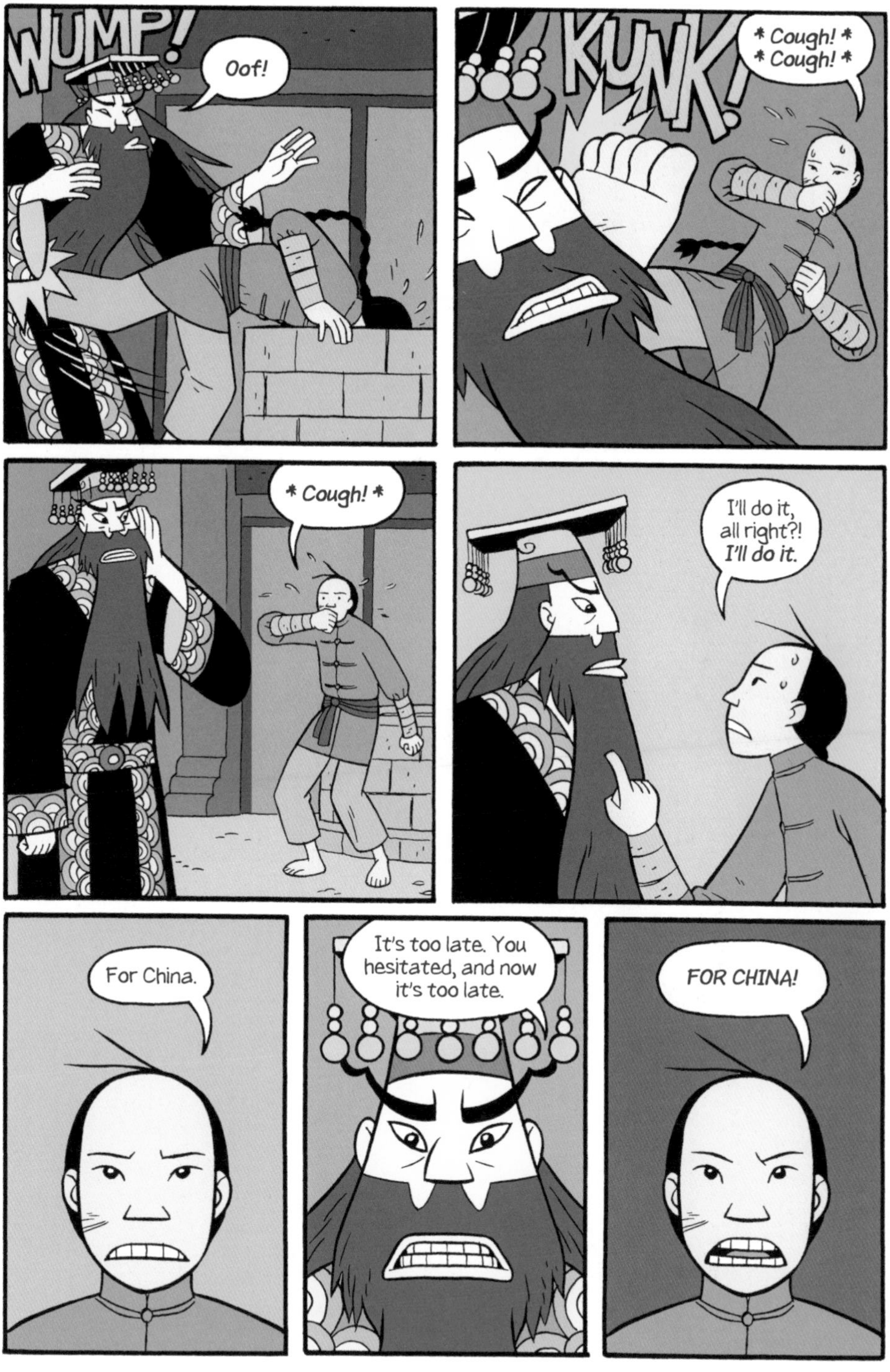
WUMP!
Oof!
KUNK!
* Cough! *
* Cough! *
* Cough! *
I'll do it,
all right?!
I'll do it.
For China.
It's too late. You hesitated, and now it's too late.
FOR CHINA!

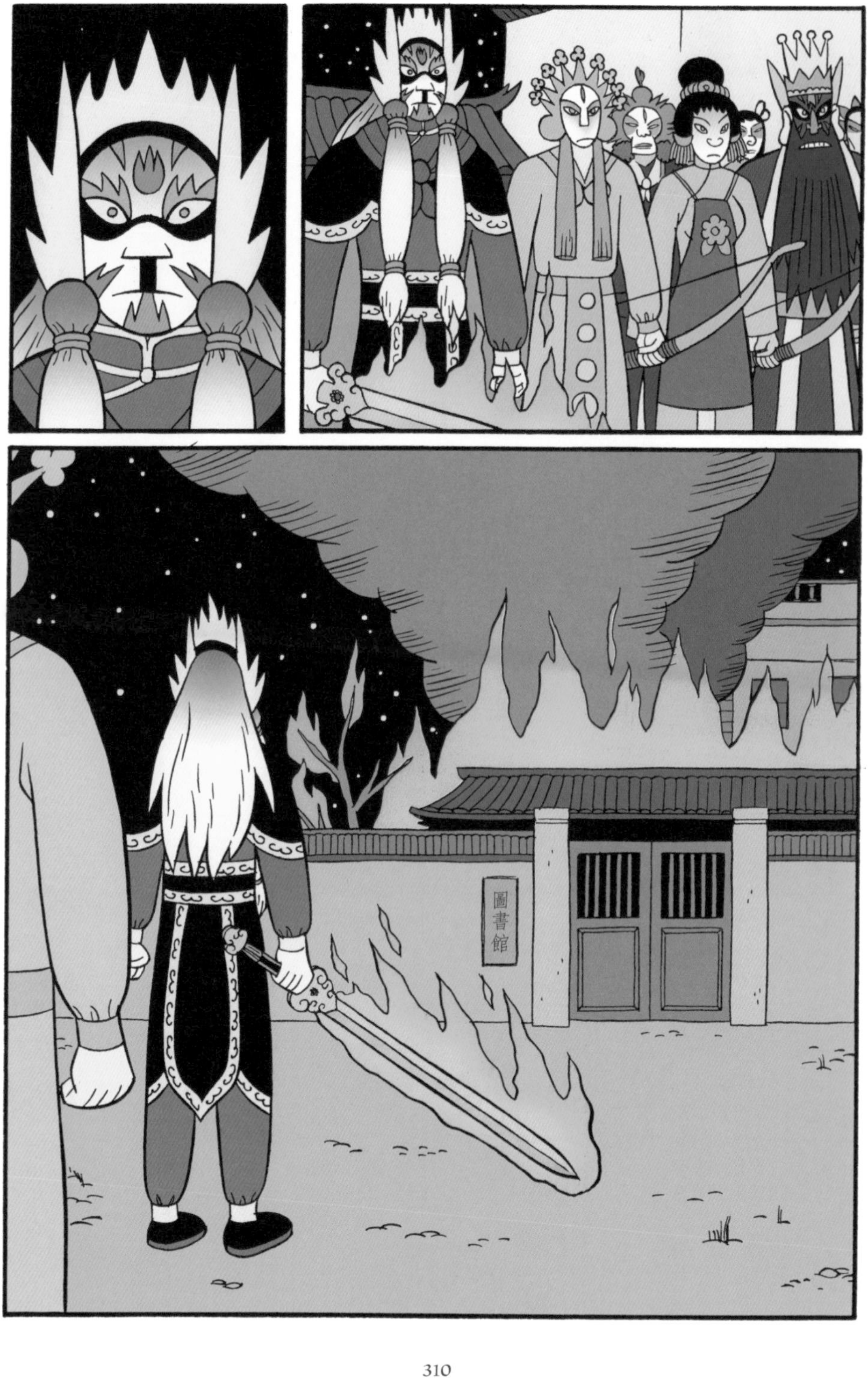
圖書館

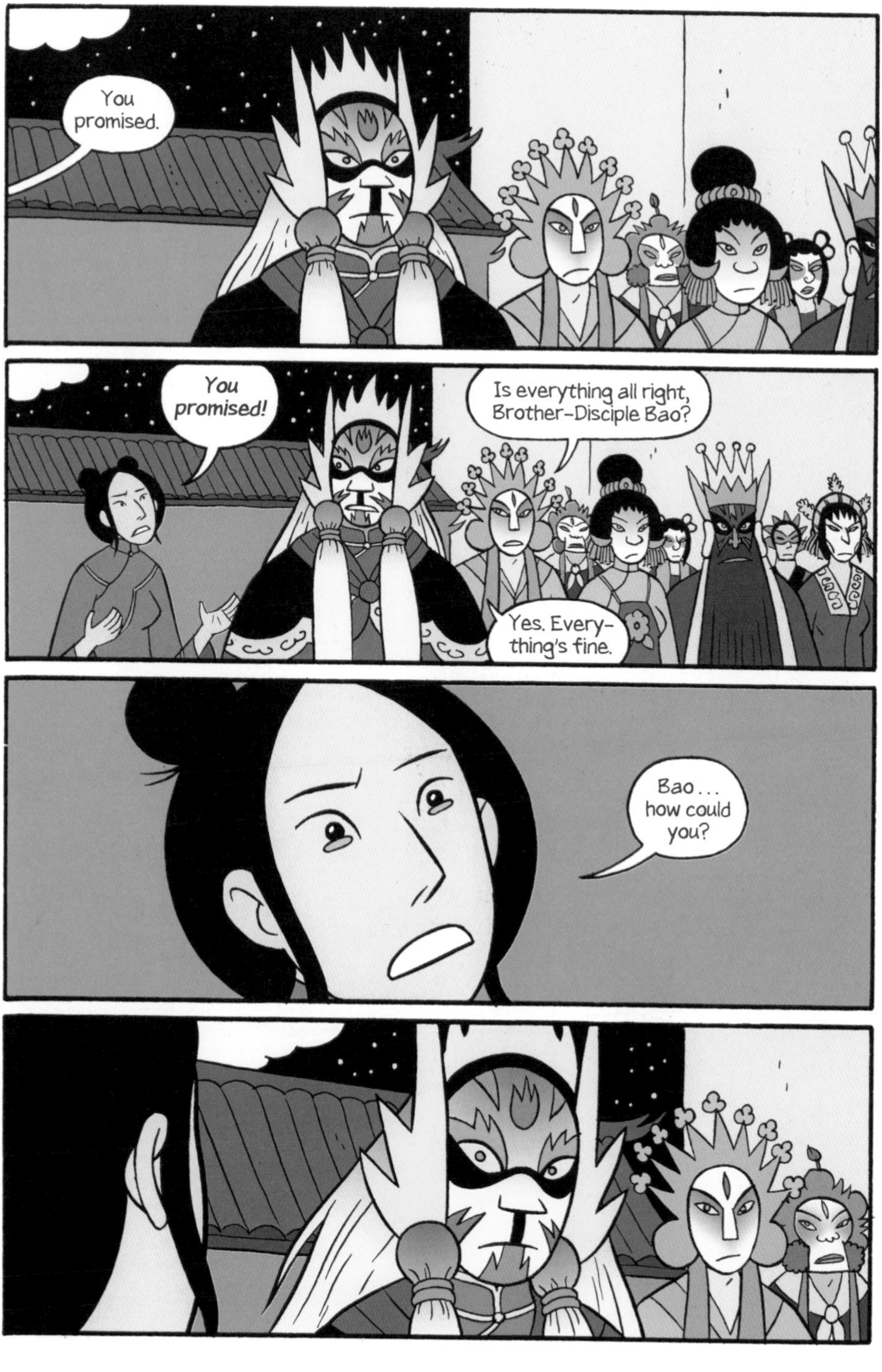
You promised.
You promised!
Is everything all right, Brother-Disciple Bao?
Yes. Everything's fine.
Bao... how could you?

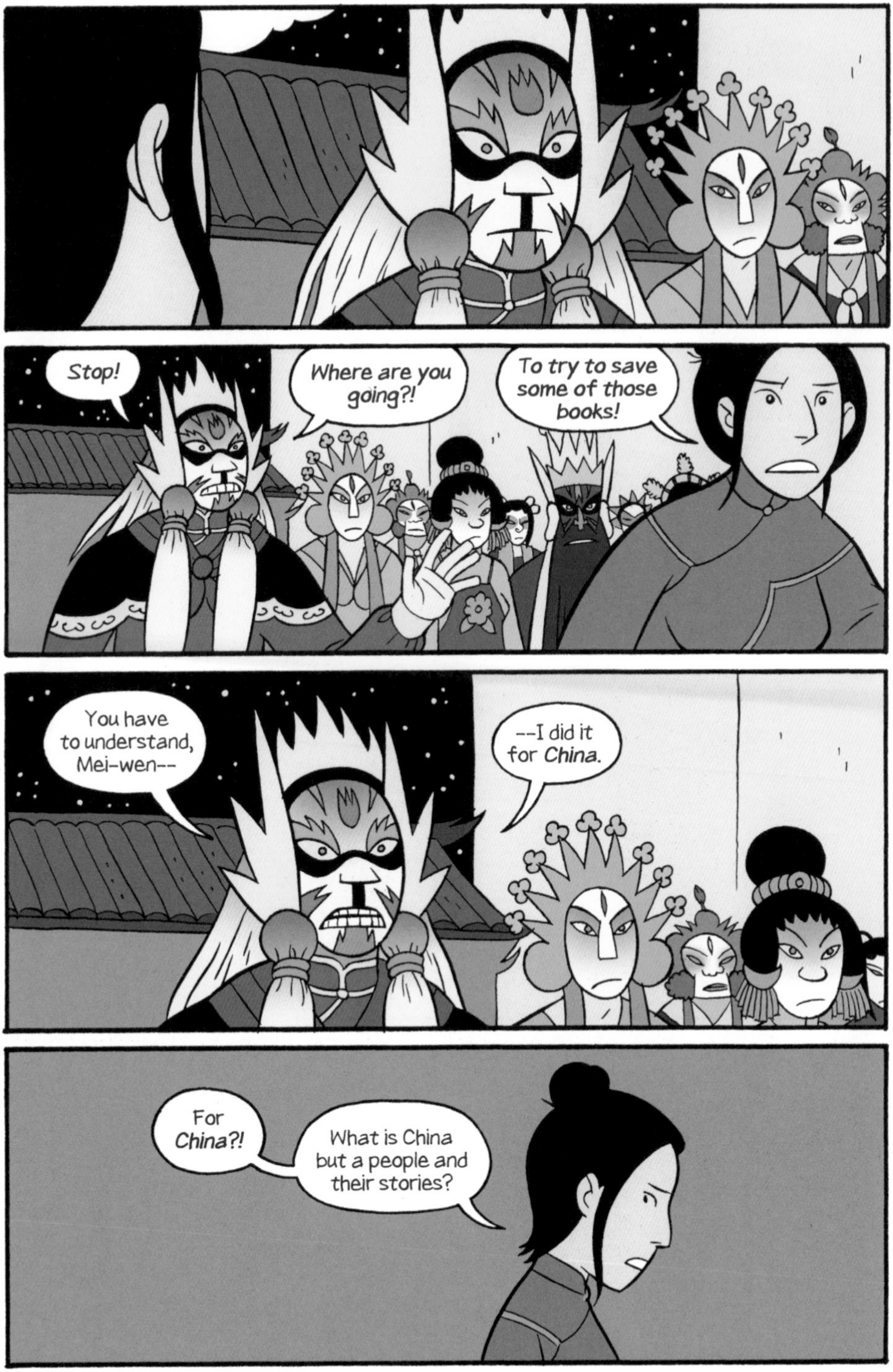

Stop!
Where are you going?!
To try to save some of those books!
You have to understand, Mei-wen--
--I did it for China.
For China?!
What is China but a people and their stories?

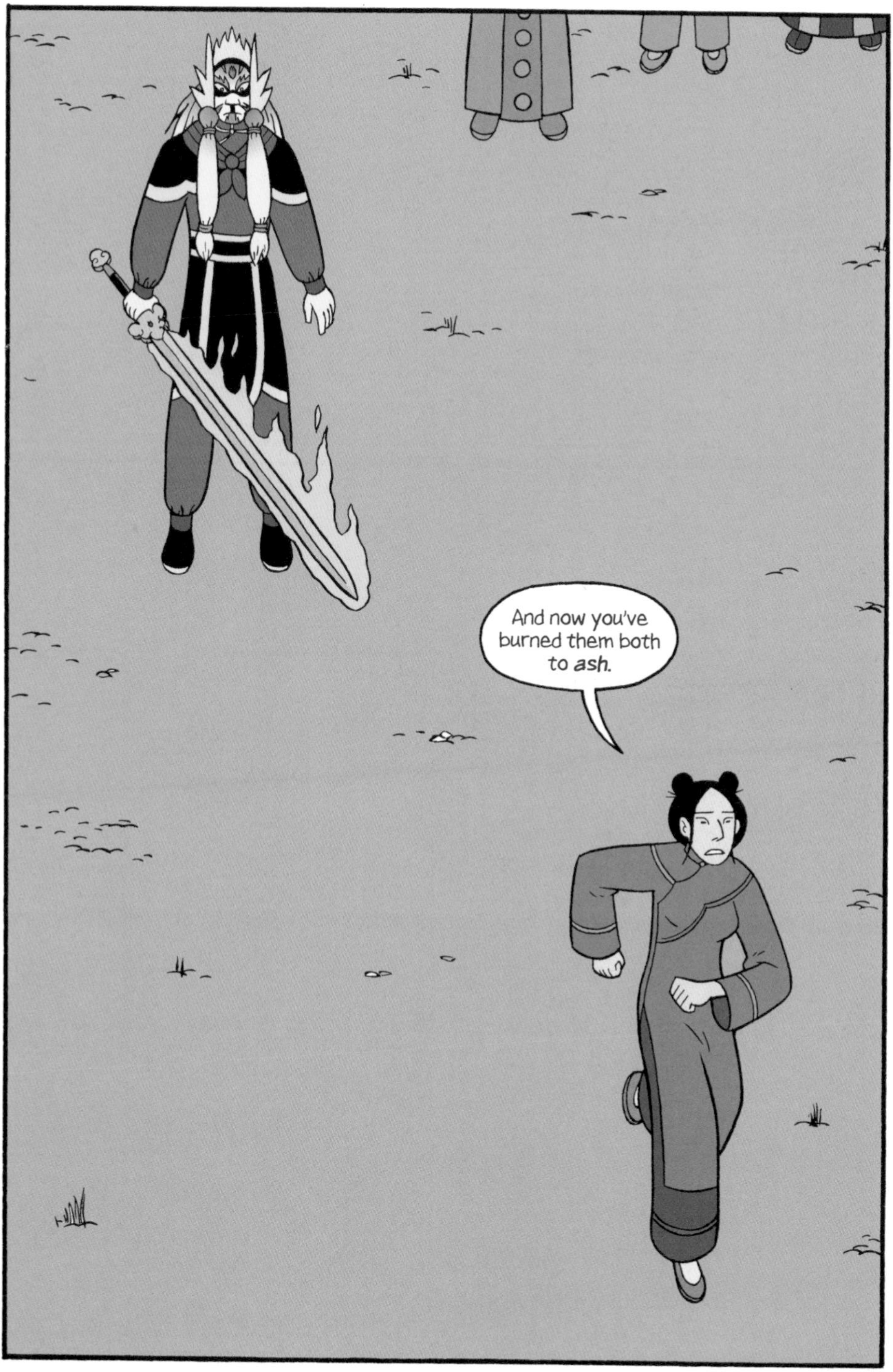
And now you've burned them both to *ash*.

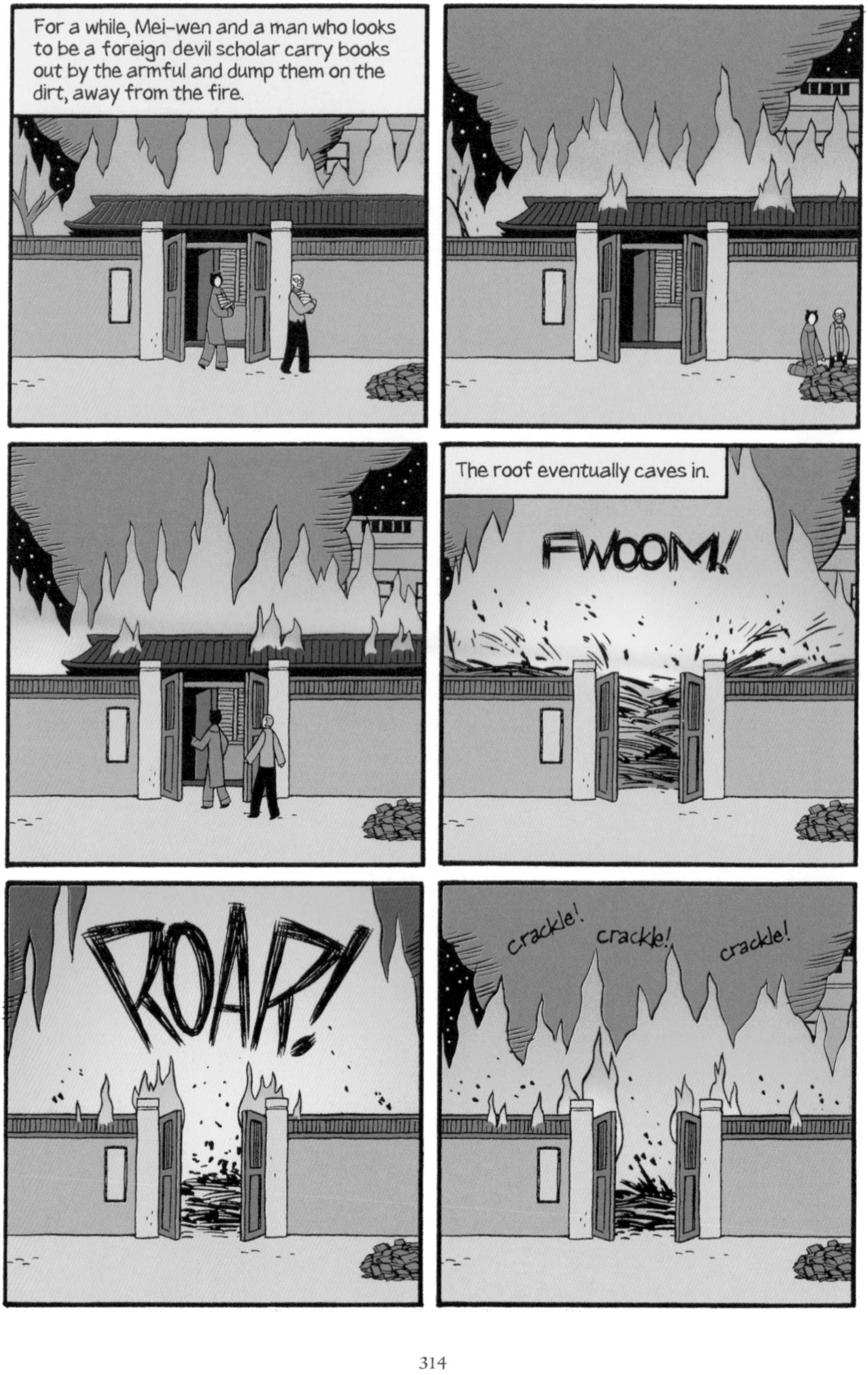
For a while, Mei-wen and a man who looks to be a foreign devil scholar carry books out by the armful and dump them on the dirt, away from the fire.
The roof eventually caves in.
FWOOM!
ROAR!
crackle!
crackle!
crackle!

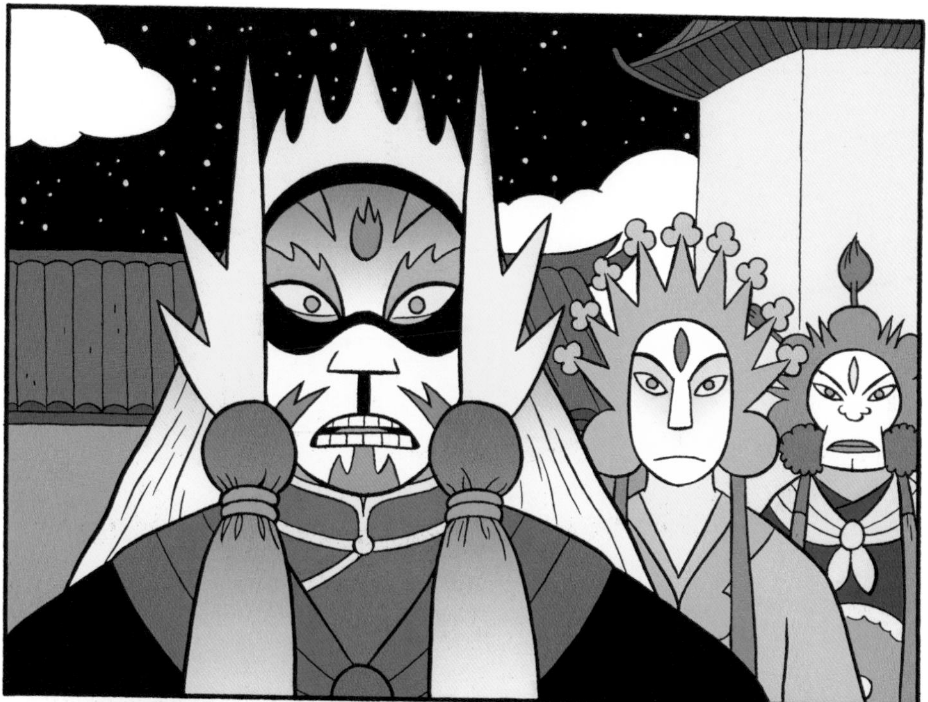

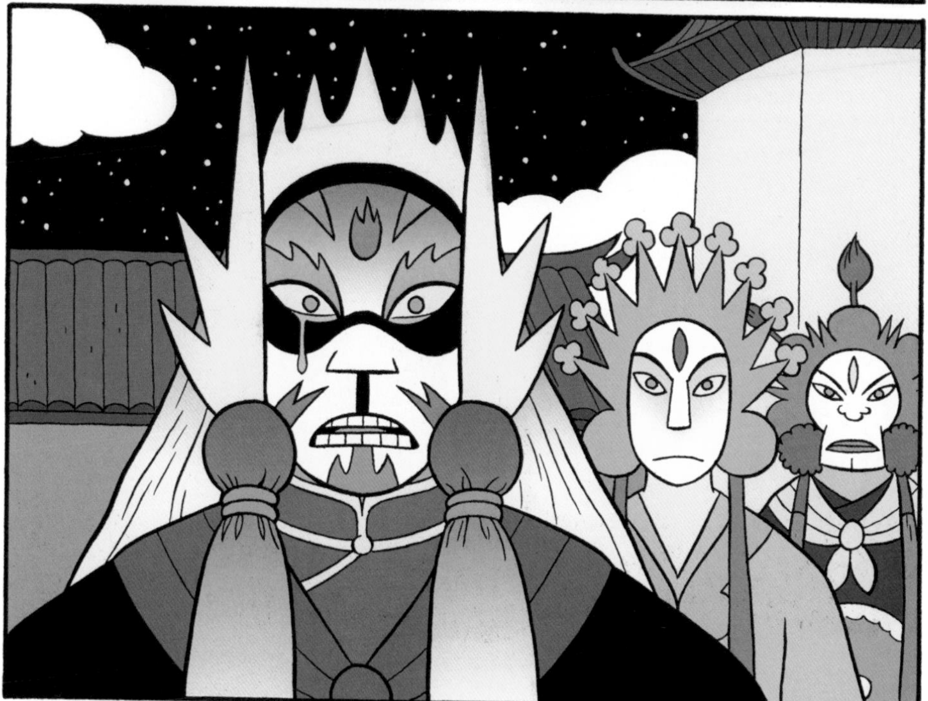

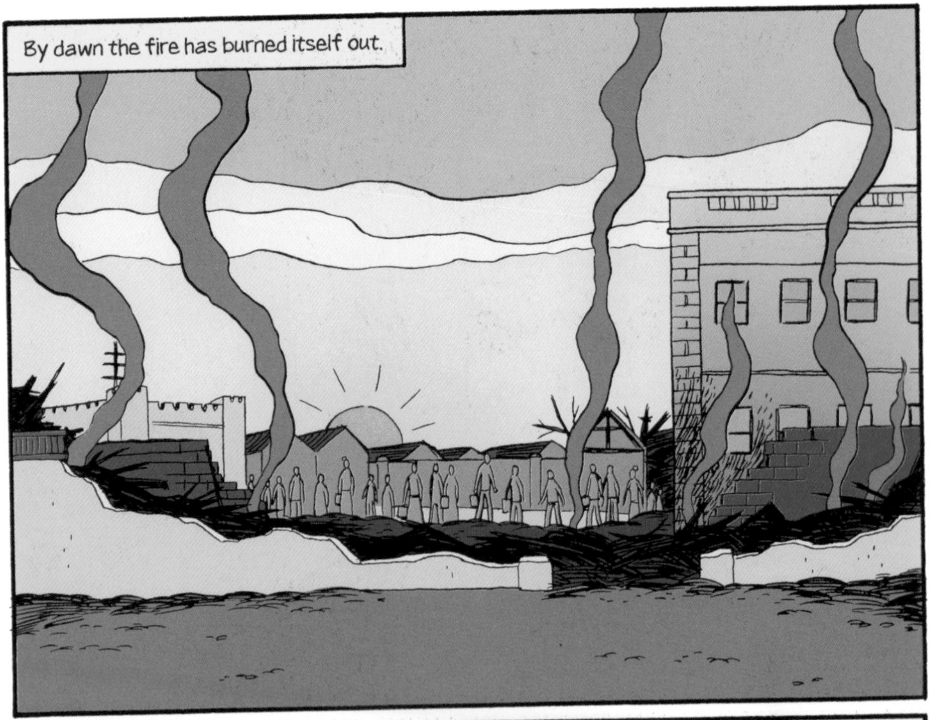
By dawn the fire has burned itself out.

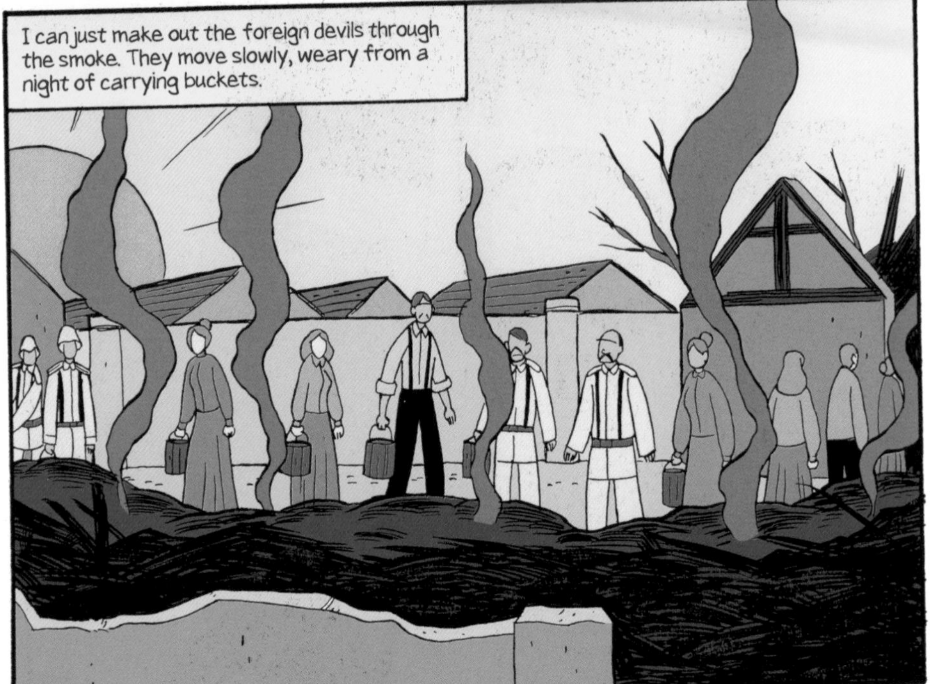
I can just make out the foreign devils through the smoke. They move slowly, weary from a night of carrying buckets.

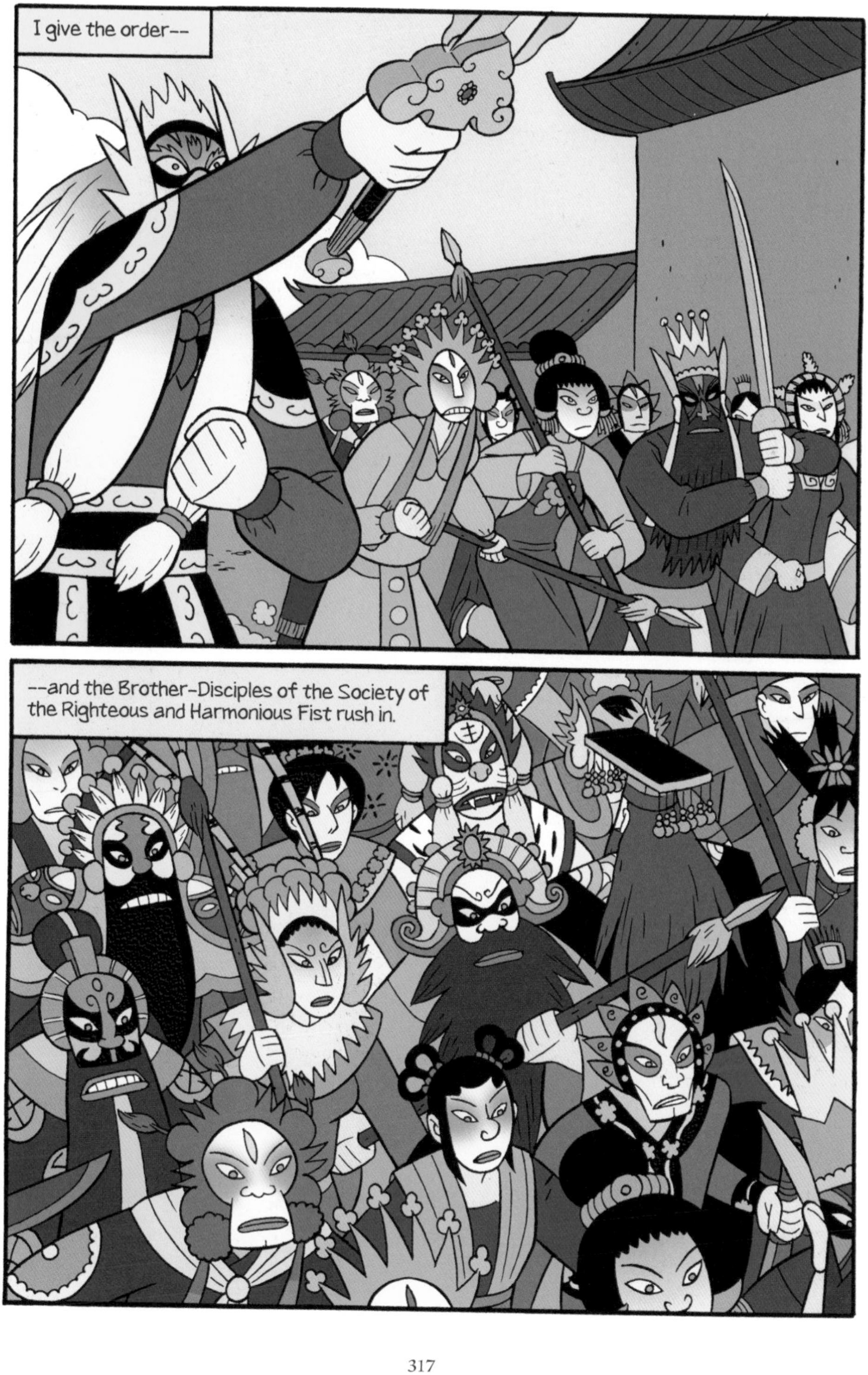
I give the order--
--and the Brother-Disciples of the Society of the Righteous and Harmonious Fist rush in.

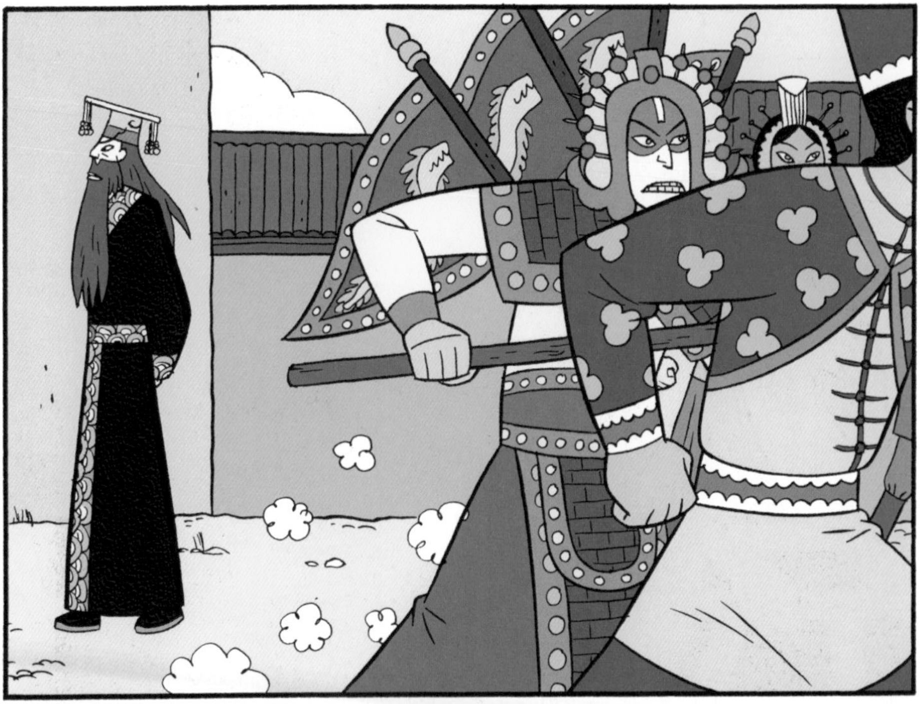

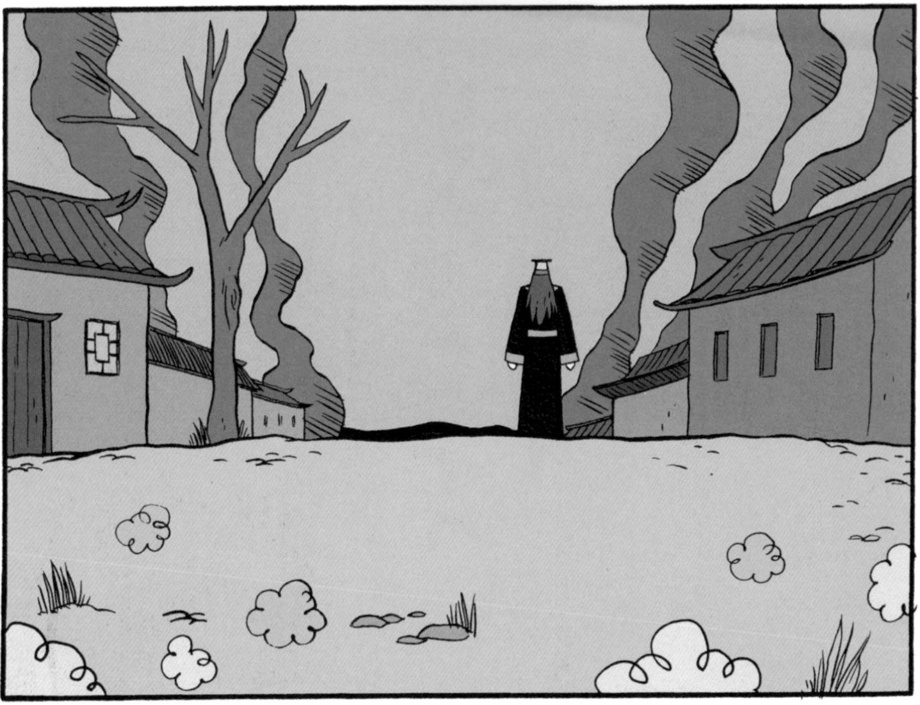

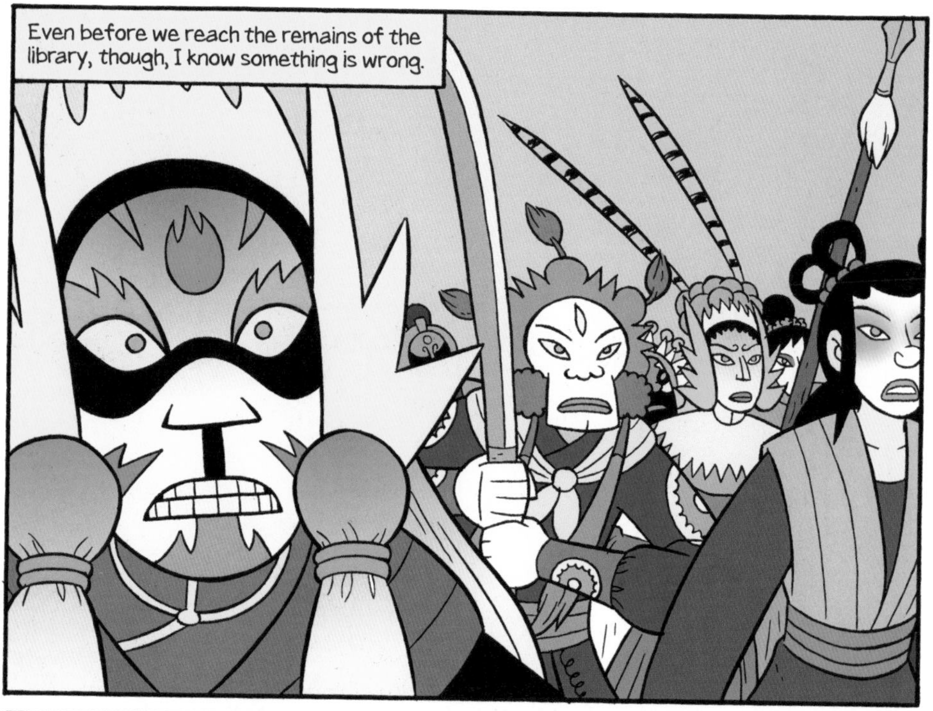
Even before we reach the remains of the library, though, I know something is wrong.

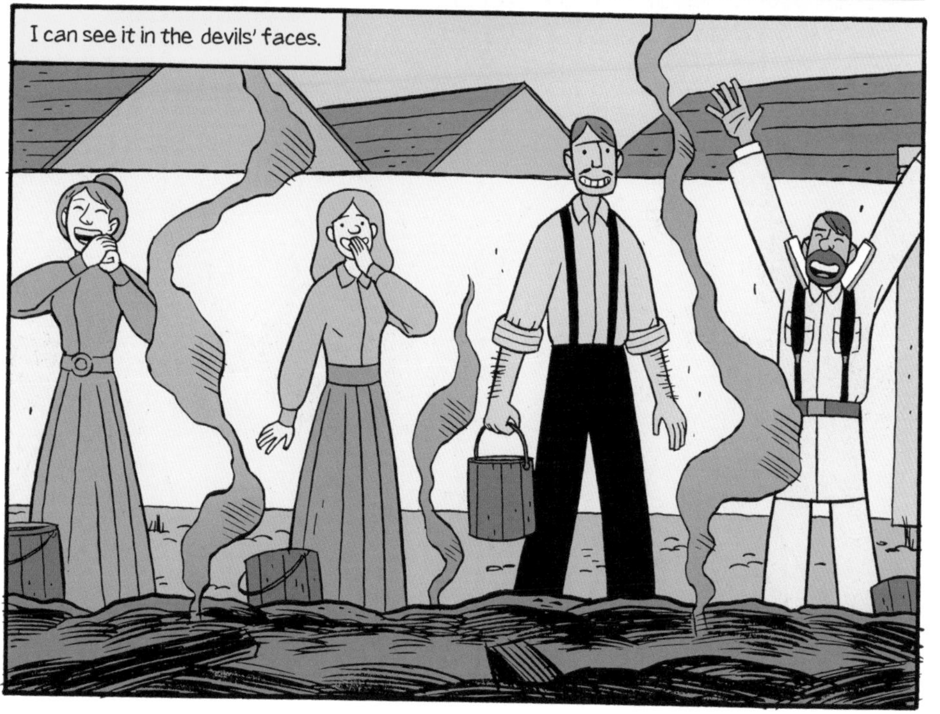
I can see it in the devils' faces.

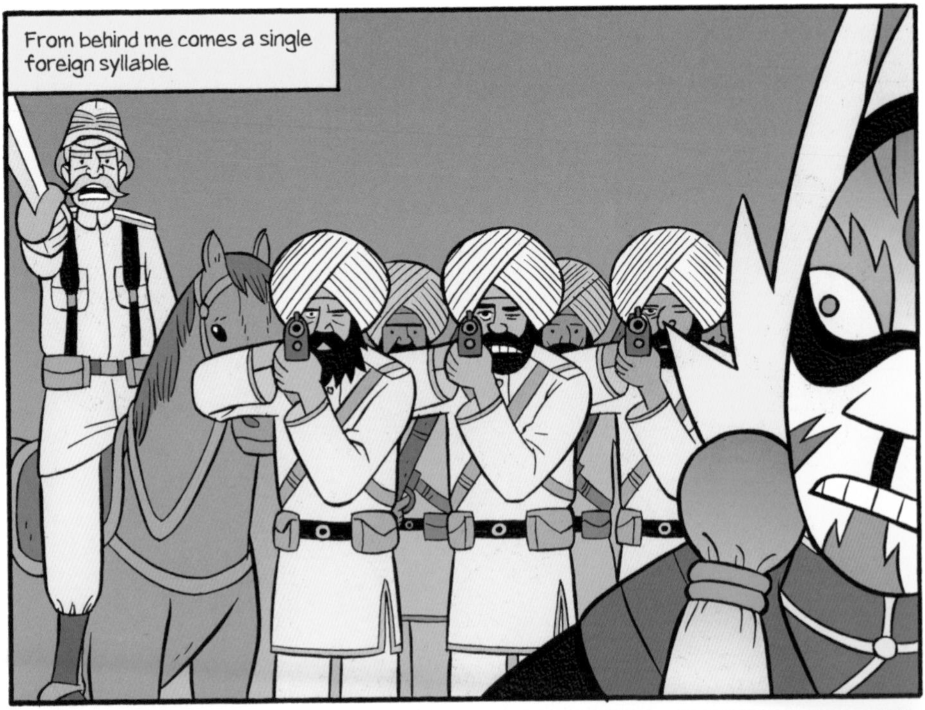
From behind me comes a single foreign syllable.

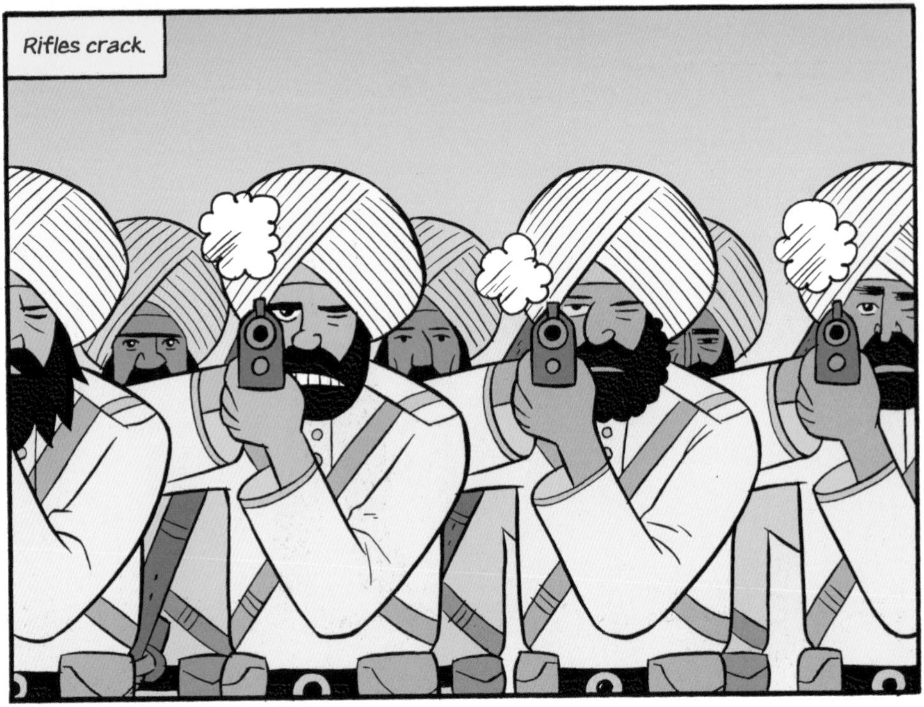
Rifles crack.

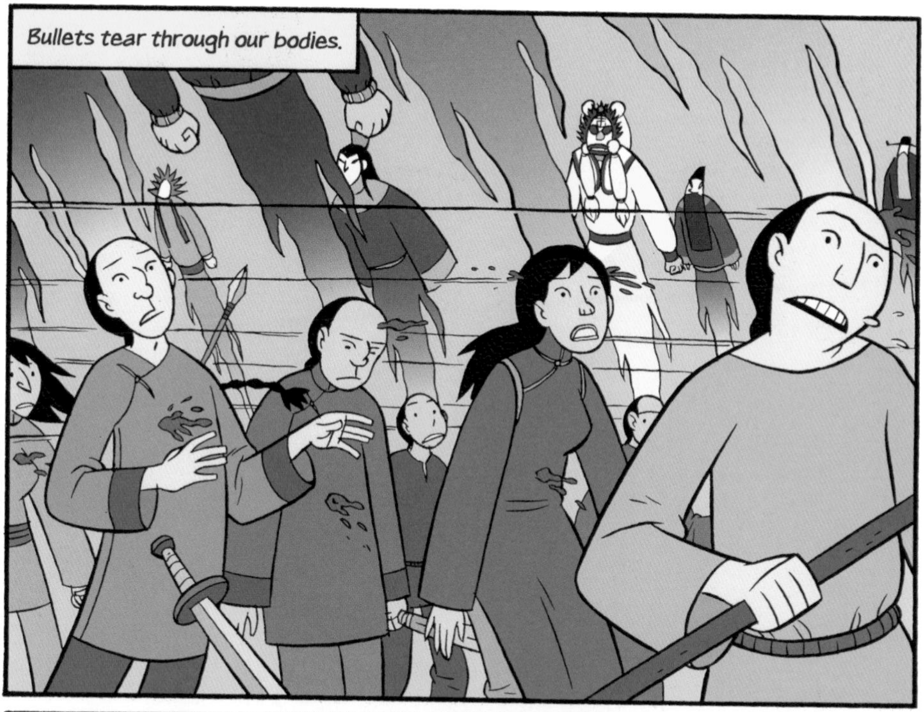
Bullets tear through our bodies.

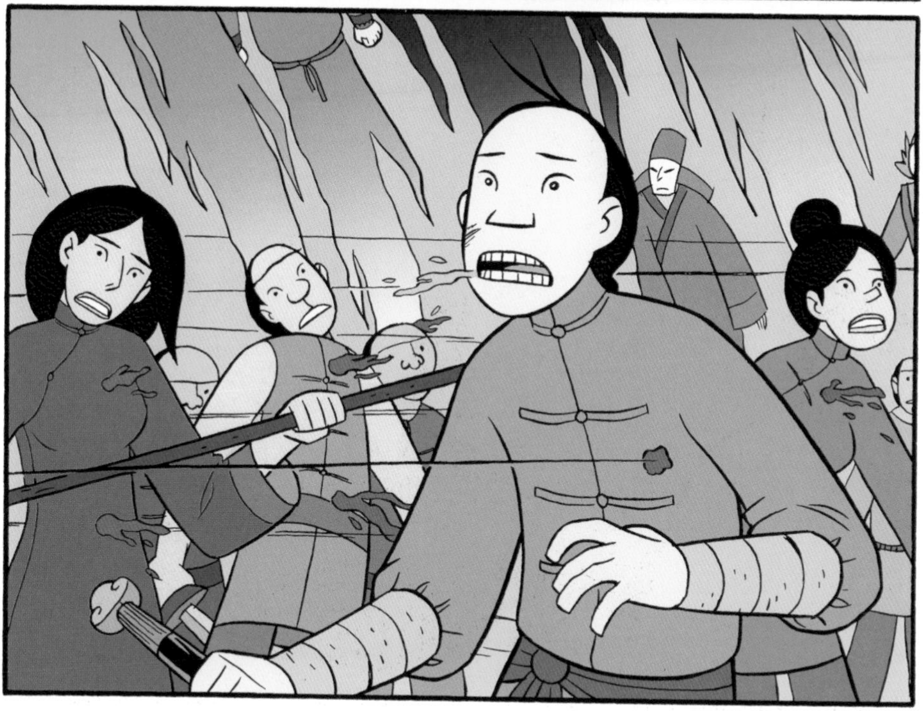

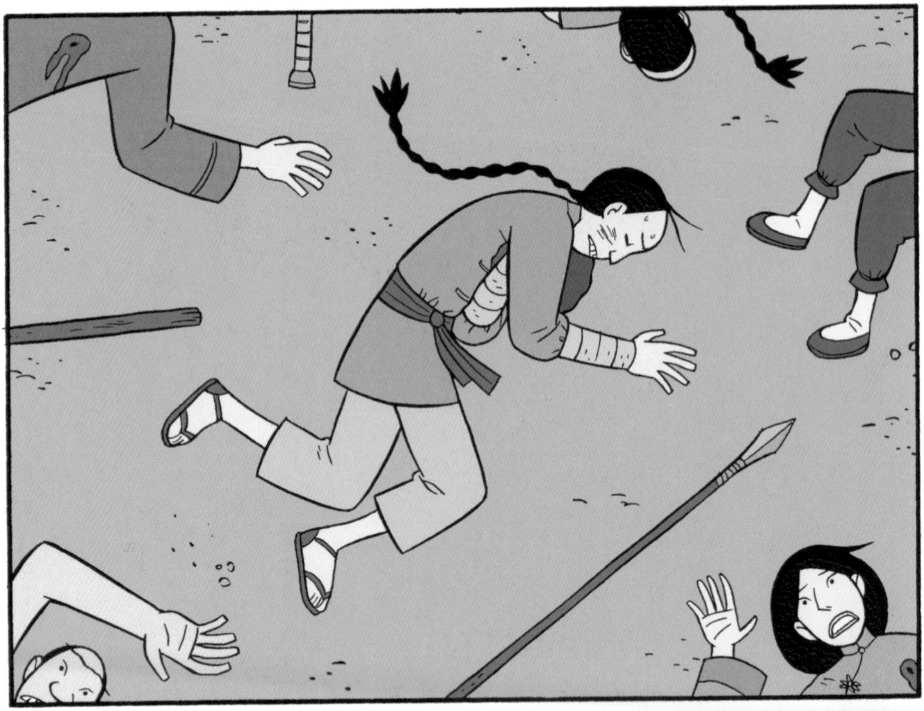
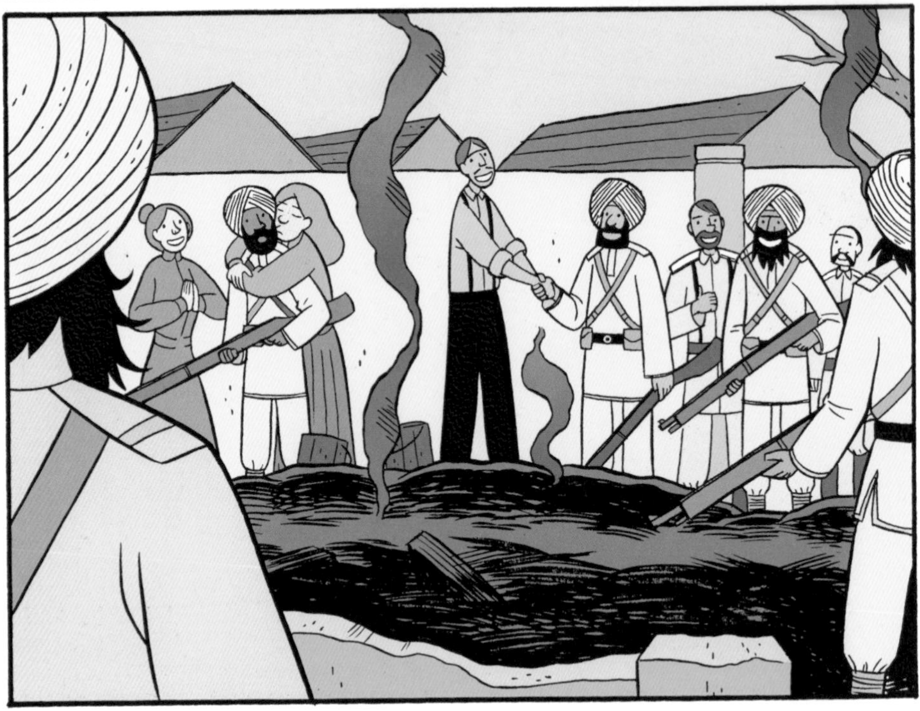

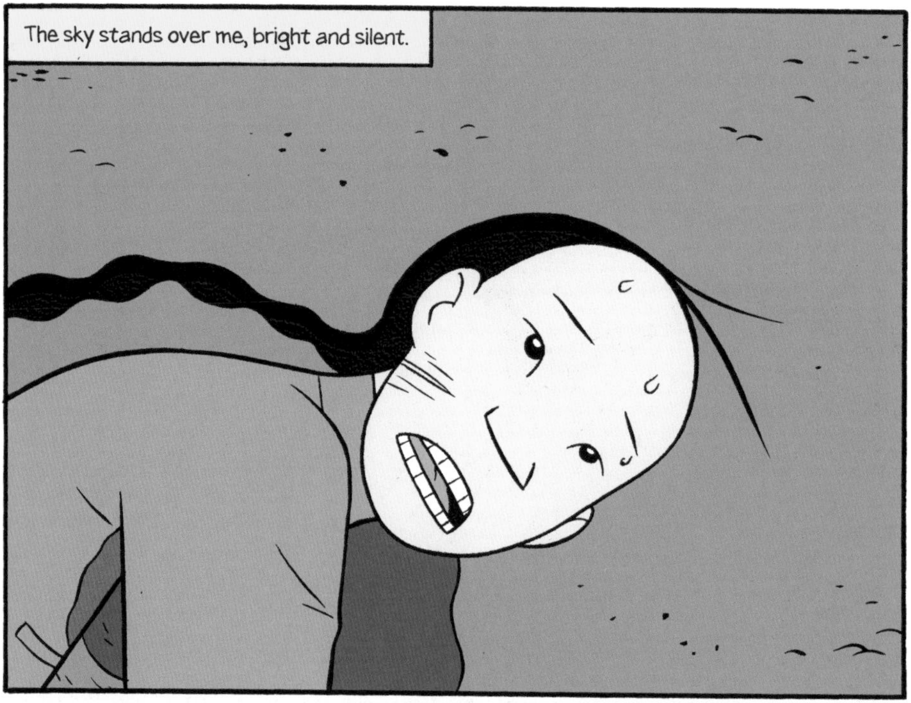
The sky stands over me, bright and silent.

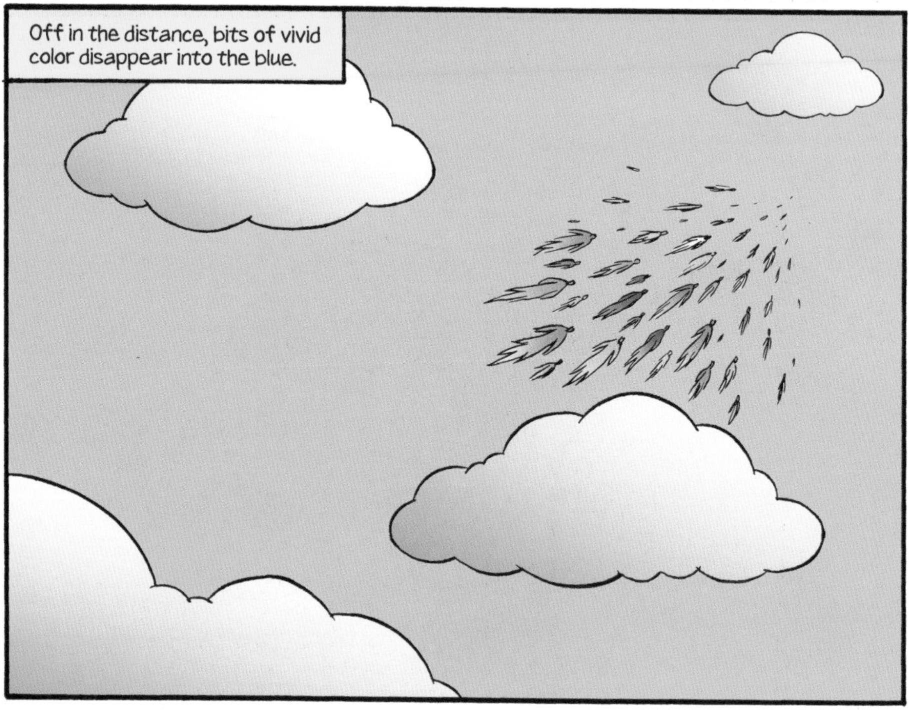
Off in the distance, bits of vivid color disappear into the blue.

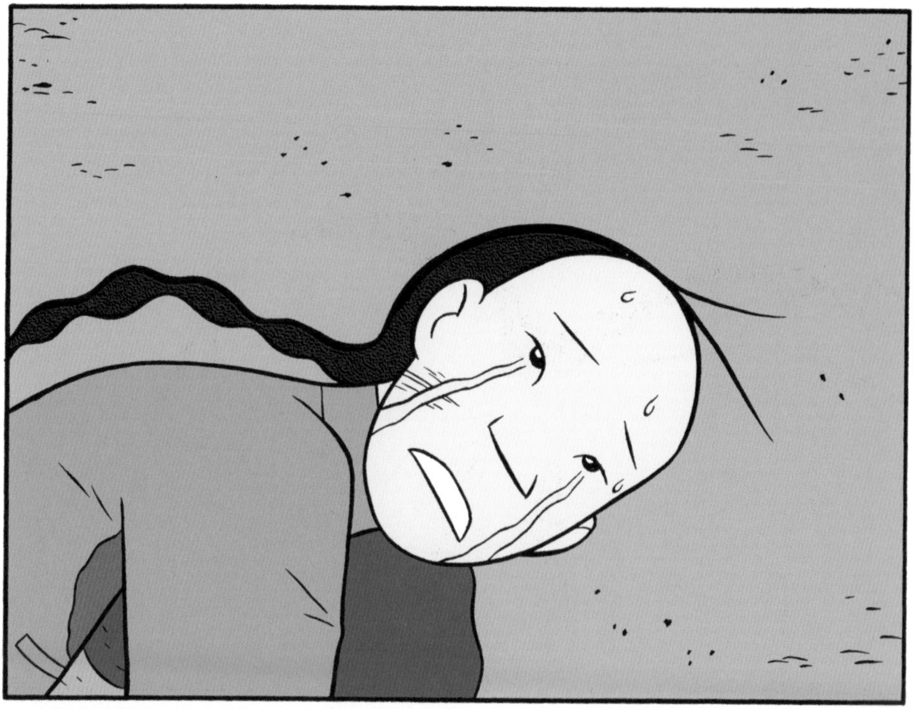

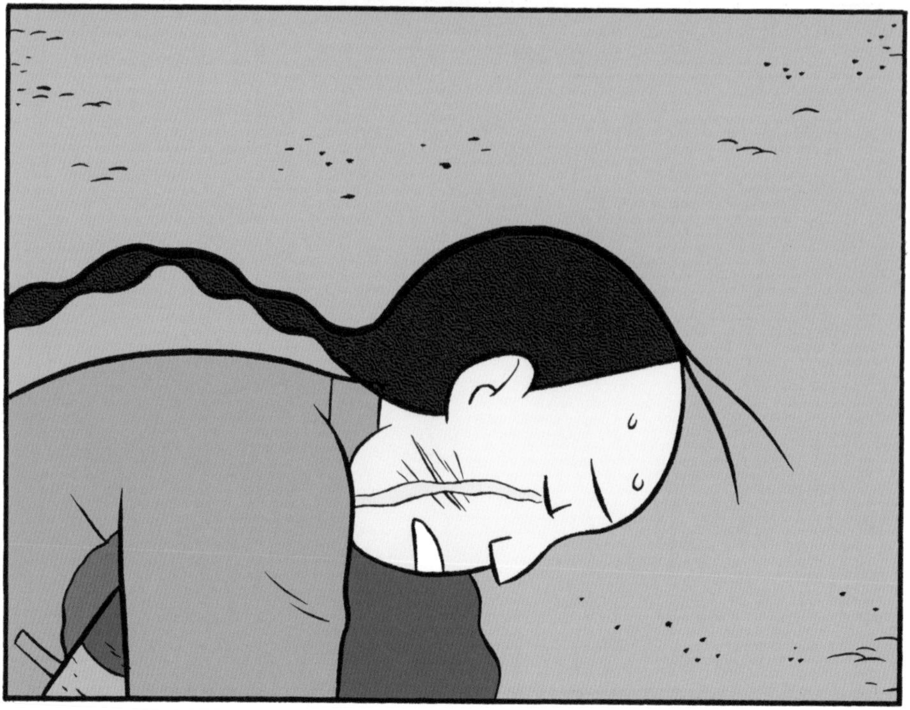

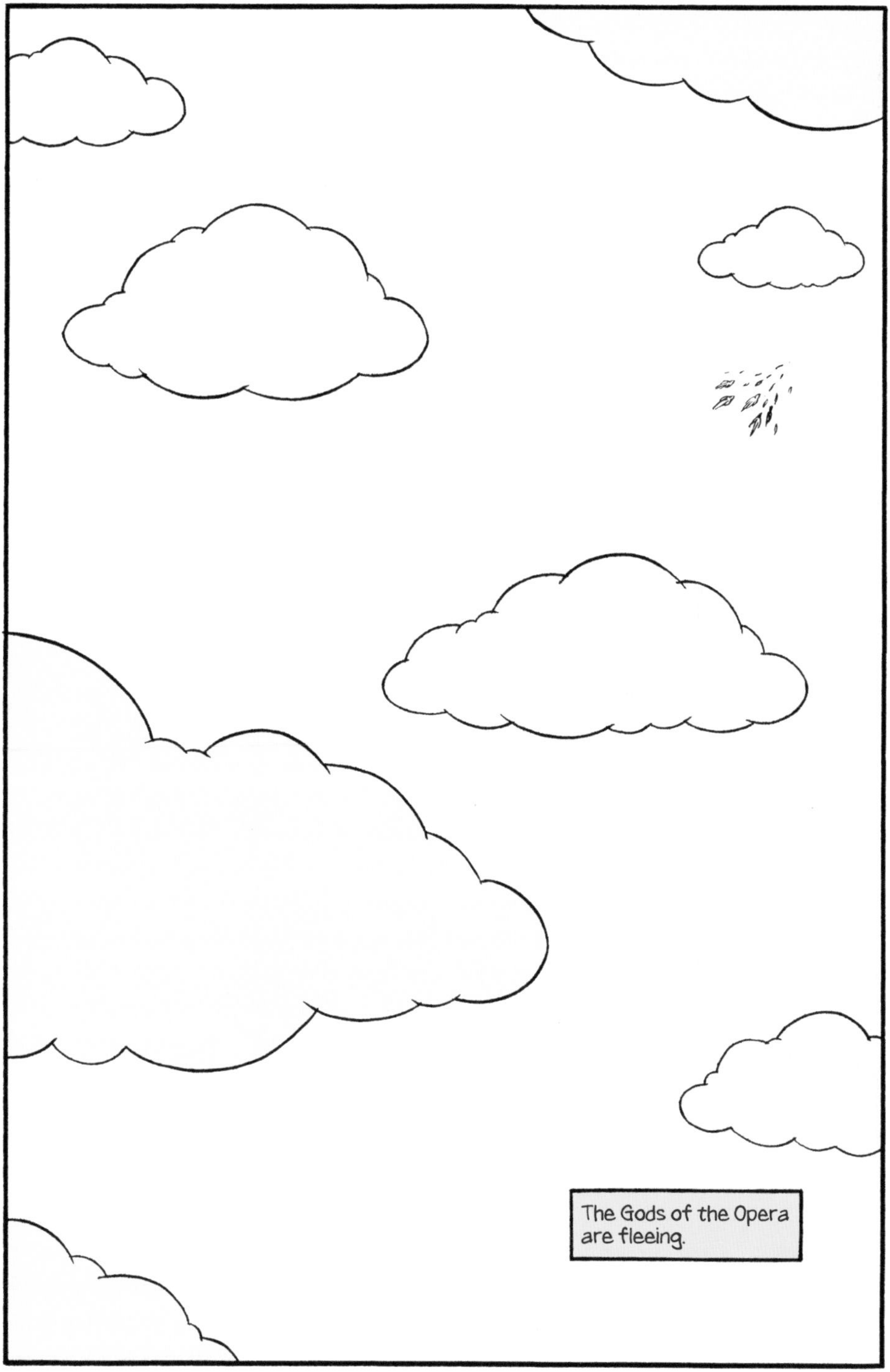
The Gods of the Opera are fleeing.

FURTHER READING

THE ORIGINS OF THE BOXER UPRISING by Joseph Esherick, University of California Press, 1988

THE BOXER REBELLION: THE DRAMATIC STORY OF CHINA'S WAR ON FOREIGNERS THAT SHOOK THE WORLD IN THE SUMMER OF 1900 by Diana Preston, Berkley Books, 2001

HISTORY IN THREE KEYS: THE BOXERS AS EVENT, EXPERIENCE, AND MYTH by Paul A. Cohen, Columbia University Press, 1998

ENCOUNTERS WITH CHINA: MERCHANTS, MISSIONARIES AND MANDARINS by Trea Wiltshire, Weatherhill, 1999

CHINA ILLUSTRATED: WESTERN VIEWS OF THE MIDDLE KINGDOM by Arthur Hacker, Tuttle Publishing, 2004

THE BOXER REBELLION (MEN-AT-ARMS) by Lynn Bodin and Chris Warner, Osprey Publishing, 1979

PEKING 1900: THE BOXER REBELLION (PRAEGER ILLUSTRATED MILITARY HISTORY) by Peter Harrington, Praeger Publishers, 2005

CHINESE OPERA by Jessica Tan Gudnason, Abbeville Press, 2001

CHINESE OPERA: IMAGES AND STORIES by Siu Wang-Ngai and Peter Lovrick, University of Washington Press, 1997

THANK YOU

Theresa Kim Yang
Ellen Yang
Henry Yang
Jon Yang
Kolbe Yang
Gianna Yang
Suzanna Yang
Elianna Yang
Lark Pien
Mark Siegel
Calista Brill
Gina Gagliano
Colleen AF Venable
Derek Kirk Kim
Jason Shiga
Jesse Hamm
Thien Pham
Lynn Tang Lee
Hank Lee
Shauna Olson Hong
Albert Olson Hong
Fr. Edward Malatesta
Fr. Joseph Kim
Fr. Robert Bonfils
The Jesuit Archives in Vanves